RAIN OF SHADOWS AND ENDINGS

THE LEGACY SERIES

BOOK ONE

MELISSA K. ROEHRICH

Make sure
you get
back up—

MR

Rain of Shadows and Endings- 1st Ed.

Cover Design: Covers by Jules (www.coversbyjules.crd.co)

ISBN:

978-1-960923-06-6 (Hardcover)

978-1-960923-05-9 (Paperback)

❀ Created with Vellum

A COUPLE THINGS & CONTENT WARNINGS

Before we dive into what is to come, I need to cover a few things. The Legacy Series takes place in the same universe as the Lady of Darkness series, but this is an entirely new world with brand new characters. You do NOT need to read the Darkness series to understand The Legacy Series. This series can be read separately. Theon and Tessa's story will have its own conclusion by the end; however, you will come across spoilers for the Darkness series along the way, even if you don't recognize them as spoilers at the time.

Now that we've covered that, this series is a different vibe from Darkness. I cannot stress enough that Tessa is not Scarlett and Theon is not Sorin. Do not go into this expecting a similar story. Am I still going to rip your heart out? Yep. Are you probably going to HATE some characters for a while? I can almost guarantee it. The world is more advanced. The Legacy rule, and the Fae are there to serve. The themes and writing are darker. Both Tessa and Theon have major trauma. As always, trust the process, but more importantly, remember this is fiction. In no way am I condoning the actions and behaviors in this book. If dark romance is not for you, that's ok! Please don't go into this, and then pretend you were blindsided. This is me telling you.

The book contains heavy themes of severe depression, anxiety, threats of sexual abuse/assault (not between the FMC/MMC), and physical abuse, both on page and memories (not between the FMC/MMC). You can find a complete list of content warnings on my website at www.melissakroehrich.com/trigger-warnings. Many are the same as Darkness, but there are some new ones to be aware of.

Finally, family and friends, I adore you. I love that you want to support me, but this book is very possibly not for you. Please don't force yourself to read it. I promise I would much rather you live in blissful ignorance than have to discuss some of the things in this book the next time I see you. Papa, please don't read this book.

If, after all that, you're still in, grab the wine! In true fashion, there will be Chaos. Welcome to Devram.

XO- Melissa

PLAYLIST

I adore when books come with playlists that follow along with the story. You feel everything more. It immerses you more. It brings everything to life. If you find this to be true for you too, here you go! Enjoy!

If you don't have Spotify, the full Playlist can also be found on my website: https://www.melissakroehrich.com under Book Extras!

For Sara Abel, Tracey Goodson, and Brittney Irvin, who have been feral for this book from the very beginning.

LEGACY SERIES REFERENCE GUIDE

I know. There's a lot to remember and keep straight as you dive into Devram.
So here's a little reference guide to help you out!
See the next page for a Kingdom Breakdown.

OUR MAIN PLAYERS

Tessalyn Ausra:
Tes-uh-lin Ah-sruh
Fae, Source of the Arius Heir,
A little (or a lot) wild and impulsive

Theon St. Orcas:
Thee-on Sānt Or-kus
Legacy, Heir to the Arius Kingdom,
probably not what you're expecting

Luka Mors:
Loo-kuh Morz
Legacy, Theon's best friend and
advisor

Axel St. Orcas:
Ax-ul Sānt Or-kus
Legacy, Second-in-Line for the Arius
Kingdom, Theon's brother

OTHERS OF NOTE

Dex: Dex
Fae, Tessa's best friend

Oralia: Or-āl-eeuh
Fae, Tessa's Friend

Corbin: Kor-bin
Fae, Tessa's friend, involved with
Lange

Lange: Lāng
Fae, Tessa's friend, involved with
Corbin

Brecken: Brek-in
Fae, Tessa's friend

Katya: Kat-ya
Fae, Tessa's friend

Tristyn Blackheart:
Tris-tin Blak-hārt
Mortal

Penelope: Pen-el-ō-pee
Fae, personal servant of Theon & Axel

Cressida St. Orcas:
Cres-ee-duh Sānt Or-kus
Legacy, Theon & Axel's mother

Eviana: Eve-ee-on-uh
Fae, Source of the Arius Lord

Felicity Davers: Fel-i-sit-ee Dav-ers
Legacy, Theon's prospective Match

LEGACY SERIES REFERENCE GUIDE

THE KINGDOMS

ACHAZ KINGDOM

- Ruling Lord: Rordan Jove (Ror-dan Jō-vā)
- Heir: Dagian Jove (Dāj-ee-un Jō-vā)
- Heir's Source: Sasha (Sah-shuh)
- Responsibilities: upholding Devram's laws and accords, ruling the realm
- Loyal Lesser Bloodlines: Zinta and Sirana

ARIUS KINGDOM

- Ruling Lord: Valter St. Orcas (Vall-tār Sānt Or-kus)
- Heir: Theon St. Orcas. (Thee-on Sānt Or-kus)
- Heir's Source: Tessa (Tes-uh)
- Responsibilities: ???
- Loyal Lesser Bloodlines: None

SERAFINA KINGDOM

- Ruling Lady: Maya Isleen (My-uh Iz-lēn)
- Heir: Lealla Isleen (Lee-all-uh Iz-lēn)
- Heir's Source: Maxson (Max-sun)
- Responsibilities: artists and architects
- Loyal Lesser Bloodlines: Anahita and Nith

FALEIN KINGDOM

- Ruling Lady: Raye Farhan (Rā Far-han)
- Heir: Prudence Farhan (Prū-dens Far-han)
- Heir's Source: Dade (Dād)
- Responsibilities: scholars and healers
- Loyal Lesser Bloodlines: Reselda and Pax

ANALA KINGDOM

- Ruling Lady: Kyra Aithne (Kī-ruh Āth-nee)
- Heir: Tana Aithne (Tan-uh Āth-nee)
- Heir's Source: Gatlan (Gat-lan)
- Responsibilities: food and agriculture
- Loyal Lesser Bloodlines: Silas and Rai

CELESTE KINGDOM

- Ruling Lady: Luna Candra (Lū-nuh Can-druh)
- Heir: Mahina Candra (Muh-he-nuh Can-druh)
- Heir's Source: Jasper (Jas-per)
- Responsibilities: running the Selection
- Loyal Lesser Bloodlines: Sefarina and Gracil

LEGACY SERIES REFERENCE GUIDE

THE GODS

THE FIRSTS

Achaz (Ā-kaz)
God of light and beginnings

Serafina (Sār-uh-fee-nuh)
Goddess of dreams and stars

Anala (Uh-nall-uh)
Goddess of sun, day, and fire

Arius (Ar-ee-us)
God of death and endings

Falein (Fā-leen)
Goddess of wisdom/cleverness

Celeste (Sel-est)
Goddess of moon and sky

THE LESSERS

Zinta (Zēn-tuh)
Goddess of magic and sorcery

Sirana (Seer-an-uh)
Goddess of love and fertility

Sargon (Sar-gon)
God of war and courage

Pax (Pax)
God of peace and serenity

Silas (Sī-lus)
God of earth and land

Rai (Rā)
God of seasons

Nith (Neeth)
God of creativity

Anahita (On-uh-hee-tuh)
God of sea, water, and ice

Reselda (Rez-el-duh)
Goddess healing

Sefarina (Sef-uh-ree-nuh)
Goddess of winds and air

Gracil (Grah-sil)
God of empathy

DEVRAM

Orinthia

Fae Estate

Raghnall
Mountains

Fae Esta

ANALA
KINGDOM

FALEIN
KINGDOM

Caelan River

Dolion
Woods

Terrarun River

Acropolis

CELESTE
KINGDOM

Nisha
Forest

ACHAZ
KINGDOM

Lake
Moonmist

Fae Estate

Arobell

OZUL
MOUNTAINS

ARIUS
HOUSE

CASTLE PINES

ROCKMOOR

SINVONS
LAKE

DARK
HAVEN

ARIUS
KINGDOM

HADE PLAINS

FRACTURED NIGHT WATERS
SPRINGS

ASNING
SEA

RAVEN HARBO

RIVER OF ENDINGS

DREAMLOCK
WOODS

SERAFINA
KINGDOM

FAE ESTATE

SANAL

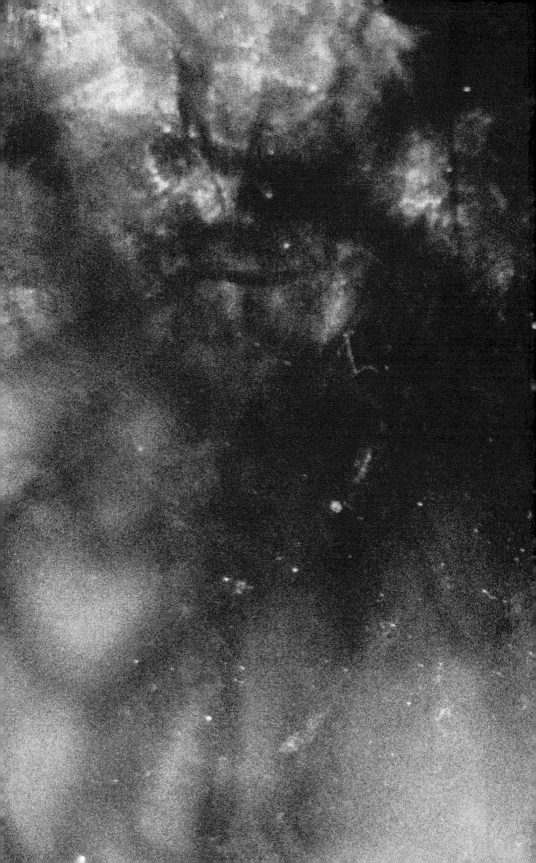

THE BEGINNING

I n all things there must be balance.
   Beginnings and endings.
   Light and dark.
Fire and shadows.
The sky, the sea, the realms.
The worlds are no different. Beings emerged from the Chaos to create such a thing.

Among those to emerge were six Firsts: Falein, goddess of wisdom and cleverness; Celeste, goddess of the sky and moon; Anala, goddess of day, fire, and the sun; Serafina, goddess of the stars and dreams; Achaz, god of beginnings; and Arius, god of endings.

Achaz and Arius emerged first. They became the most powerful of the gods, working together to maintain the balance. Beginning created. Ending judged.

The First gods created the Lesser gods. They went to various parts of the stars, setting up their own kingdoms among the realms and maintaining balance, and from them, worlds grew and prospered. Some grew faster than others. Some were favored more than others. Some were lost, and some were forgotten.

New beings were created and scattered among the realms. Other beings were created and kept close. But as more and more came into existence, tension bloomed among the gods. Power balances began to shift, and the gods began to create beings with mortals— demigods, whose descendants became their Legacy. Fear took root that one of those bloodlines would become more powerful than *the rest, so an accord was struck. There would be no more demigods created, and the Legacy across the realms were to be brought to one world. A realm created solely for them to grow and prosper and thrive. The Legacy were gifted mortals in their world to do the mundane tasks required for survival. They were also gifted the technologies from the most advanced of the worlds.*

And they were gifted the Fae.

Beings created to balance out the power of the gods that ran in the veins of the Legacy. Power that was too great to let go unchecked. The magic flowing in the blood of the Fae fed the power of the Legacy, forcing them to rely on the Fae. In exchange for being this source of power for the Legacy, the Fae were given their own gifts—one of four elements. They were granted enhanced senses and an extended lifespan. All of these were given by the gods so that the Fae could watch over their Legacy and keep their bloodlines safe.

Then the gods left that world, agreeing to never interfere there again.

Over time, Chaos descended among the stars. Wars raged, and the balance tipped. Some worlds were ended. Some were abandoned. Some were reborn.

But gods are fickle beings, and things meant to be forgotten never remain so.

PART ONE
LIFE MUST GIVE

1

TESSA

"Are you hiding in an alcove eating chocolate?"

Tessa froze at the sound of the low voice, said chocolate halfway to her mouth. She thought she'd been hidden well enough. Obviously not.

Damnit.

She quickly turned, hiding the chocolate behind her back. Which was stupid. He'd already seen it.

"I, um…"

She trailed off when her gaze landed on who had spoken to her. She could swear darkness swirled faintly in the dark emerald green eyes that were studying her, a slight frown on his full lips. His ebony hair was messy for the formal occasion they were about to attend, and a couple strands fell forward, brushing dark brows. His hands slid into the black pants that were clearly tailored to fit him perfectly, along with the black shirt and black vest that clung to his torso. He didn't wear the formal suit jacket that the other males had been wearing as she'd watched them slowly filter in. The top two buttons of his shirt were undone, and there was no tie in sight.

This night definitely called for a tie.

His head tilted to the side, and Tessa swallowed thickly, her mouth suddenly too dry. The *thing* inside her lifted its head, and she shoved it back down. That was the last thing she needed right now.

"Are you unwell?" he asked. Not because he cared about her wellbeing in any way. Very few actually cared about her, and that was defi-nitely a thread of annoyance in his tone.

That annoyance is what snapped her out of whatever trance she was in. She quickly dropped to a knee before him. Gods. He was a Legacy, and she'd just been standing there staring at him. Fantastic. Lange was going to laugh himself into tomorrow when she told him about this.

"My apologies," she murmured, making sure her tone sounded like she meant it with her eyes fixed on the male's black shoes.

"You may rise," the Legacy said impatiently.

Well, that was easier said than done. She was in a dress that clung to her figure as much as his own custom-tailored clothing. This was the only occasion she would likely ever wear something of such elegance. One sleeve flowed down her arm to her wrist, while leaving the other arm completely bare from her shoulder to her fingertips. It pooled at her feet, and she'd already tripped on the damn thing multiple times tonight. Her shorter than average height didn't help matters, even with the four-inch heels she'd been forced to wear. The dress was black with a sheer emerald green coverlet adorned with black beads that glittered in the flickering flames of the sconces.

Sconces, not lights and electricity like every other building had in the six kingdoms of Devram. Because... Honestly, Tessa had never really understood why the Pantheon was void of all modern advancements, save for cell phones. But even phones had to be placed on a special setting that only allowed for incoming calls. Nothing else. Something about wanting to honor the humble beginnings of the worlds. She'd always thought it rather silly. The gods didn't care about their world. Why would they care if there was basic lighting in the Pantheon?

A hand was suddenly in her face, and she glanced up at the Legacy in confusion.

"Well?" he demanded, wiggling his fingers. "I assume it will be diffi-cult to get up in that dress, especially as you seem unwilling to put down your chocolate."

Tessa felt her cheeks flush, but she slowly slid her fingers into his palm. His hand wrapped around them, tugging her to her feet. When she went to pull her hand back, his grip tightened.

"Why are you out here by yourself, away from the other Fae?" he asked, his voice deceptively low and innocuous. It wasn't quite as entrancing as the compulsions the Legacy could use, but it wasn't that far off either.

She knew she shouldn't be out here. Dex was going to be livid. Not so much at the fact that she had wandered off, but that she'd done so without telling him so he could join her.

"I was—"

"I would strongly suggest not lying to me," the Legacy said coldly.

"I wasn't going to lie to you," she retorted, and his brows rose at her address.

She sighed internally. This is why Dex never let her sneak off alone. She was remarkably good at moving about unseen and sneaking into places she wasn't supposed to be, but she was also rather impulsive at times.

Okay, a lot of the time.

"I was finding some place to eat this without having to share," she said, waving the chunk of chocolate in his face. Her other hand was still clasped in his.

He just stared at her like he wasn't quite sure what to say in response to that.

"Which is why I was hiding in an alcove," she added, beginning to fidget when he still didn't say anything. She hated enclosed spaces. The alcove hadn't been her first choice, but desperate times and all that. "I will just, um... Go back to the grand hall?" she said, trying to tug her fingers from his grasp, but his grip only tightened further.

"That would be the wise thing to do," he agreed.

"Okay, well, then I sort of need my hand back."

Instead of releasing her though, he stepped closer, crowding her back further into the alcove. "Are you slated to be Selected?"

"What?" she asked breathlessly. This was bad. So bad. Why in the world did she think she should come out here without Dex?

"It is the first time in a millennium that all six kingdoms have heirs selecting their Sources at the same time," the Legacy said.

"I know that."

"It is a historic night."

"I know that," Tessa repeated.

"Everyone is incredibly apprehensive. The Lords and Ladies are on edge, and their heirs are full of anxious anticipation. The Fae are allowed to join in the celebrations, and you are out here." His other hand came up and plucked the chocolate from her fingers. "Hiding and eating chocolate."

"Hey!" she protested, reaching for the sugar, but he held it out of her reach. She was shorter than average, sure, but he was also tall. Taller than Dex and Brecken, and they were over six feet.

"And arguing with a Legacy," he added harshly.

Tessa snapped her mouth shut. She was hungry, and he'd just taken the one bit of sustenance she was likely to get for the next four hours. He gave her a smug look as he set the chocolate on a ledge that ran above them near the sconces.

It was definitely going to melt up there.

She sighed, and he frowned at the petulance. "Are you slated to be Selected?"

"What?" Her breath hitched at the fact that he'd asked this question again. If she had been slated for such a thing, that would mean she had already been claimed, and he would not be allowed to touch her without offending one of the heirs and their parents.

But she was not slated to be Selected.

"Do not make me ask that question again," he said in a soft warning, leaning in and twirling a loose golden curl around his finger. "I am not a fan of repeating myself."

"No," she whispered, her eyes falling closed as she waited for whatever he was going to do to her.

"You are upset by that?"

"No," she said truthfully. Because she wasn't. It might have afforded her some measure of protection at this very moment, but she'd never wanted the *honor* of being Selected to serve as the personal Source of one of the ruling family members in any of the six Kingdoms.

"No?"

She shook her head, opening her eyes to meet his curious stare.

"Really?"

"You told me not to lie to you," she bit out.

"That I did," he said, his lips almost lifting into a smile, but it didn't fully form. "Do you always obey orders so well... What is your name?"

"Tessalyn," she answered bitterly, knowing she couldn't deny a Legacy.

"Do you always obey commands so well, Tessalyn?" he asked, stepping into her even more. She could feel a hard muscle brushing against her front.

"Rarely."

"Another truth," he said, that finger letting her curl go free and sliding along her jaw. She forced herself to remain still. "So you are either more obedient than you care to admit, or..." He trailed off, his fingers dropping to her bare shoulder and brushing down her arm.

"Or what?" she gritted out.

"Or it is just with me."

"It is neither of those things."

"Ah, now you are lying," he said, his lips finally turning up into a small smile.

She frowned. "I really should be getting back. I'm sure the Selection is about to start at any moment."

"It likely is."

"And I should be in there. So should you. To see your future Lord or Lady select their Source," she added, worrying her bottom lip. His eyes dipped to the movement.

"We definitely should be," he agreed, amusement seeming to flit across his features. "Be in there, that is."

"So..."

For a long moment, he didn't move, then he finally stepped back from her. She could have sagged with relief, but the surprise flooding through her was more overwhelming at the moment. As a Fae, she didn't really have the right to deny a Legacy. Fae could not deny a Legacy *anything* unless they were claimed and Marked. She could *say* no, but that didn't necessarily mean anything to them.

She slipped past the male and into the empty hall, pulling up the sides of her dress so she wouldn't trip on it. Her black heels clicked on the marble floor that was kept in immaculate condition, and she concentrated on not tripping yet again.

"It was a pleasure, Tessalyn," he called after her, and she knew she should turn and acknowledge him. She knew it would be seen as incredibly disrespectful not to do so, but she didn't. She hurried down to the small side door she'd found to slip out here and rushed back into the grand hall where the Opening Selections would be held. Fae and Legacy alike filled the vast space, although none of them mingled together.

"Where have you been?"

Tessa jumped at the familiar voice in her ear, spinning to find a tall male glaring at her with eyes such a dark shade of brown they were almost black.

Dex.

She pushed out a breath when he slipped an arm around her waist, pulling her back against his chest, and she relaxed into him.

"After the Selection is done, we're still sneaking out, right?" Tessa asked, scanning the other Fae who were of age for Selection as they milled about the grand hall.

"As long as we're not Selected," Dex replied, resting his chin on the top of her head.

Tessa huffed a laugh. "We both know we're not going to be Selected. We can sneak off as soon as the Selection is done. The gods know it'll be hours before we're offered any food, and I'm starving."

"I told you to eat before we left."

"I tried," she protested with a pout, shoving him off of her. Moving him wasn't the easiest thing she'd ever done. He was a good eight inches taller than she was, and while his muscles weren't as defined as some of the other Fae, they were definitely there. "Some Legacy prick took my chocolate."

"Wait, what? When?" Dex demanded, spinning her to face him and gripping her shoulders. The sleeves of his suit jacket pulled up just enough that a Mark was visible on the inside of his right wrist, the Celeste Estate symbol declaring which estate he was raised at. It matched the one on the inside of her own wrist. Eventually, two more Marks would join that one. One to declare their element and one to declare which kingdom they were assigned to serve.

"Five minutes ago," Tessa groused. "I was out in the corridor with a piece of chocolate I snagged off a passing tray—"

"The trays of food for the *Legacy*," Dex clarified.

"Yes, those trays," she said, rolling her eyes. "Anyway, I was caught, and he took my chocolate."

"He?" His eyes widened. "Are you all right? Did he—"

"I'm fine," she said, cutting him off.

"You shouldn't have gone off without me," he said tightly.

She sighed. "I know."

There was a tense moment of silence between them before he released her shoulders. "Who's sneaking out with us? Oralia and Brecken?"

Tessa nodded, her eyes continuing to roam around the room and searching among all the gathered Fae. There were more than she had expected, and they'd all been split up as they'd been herded down the various halls to this space.

"I'm sure Brecken will convince Katya to come," Tessa said. "Lange and Corbin will obviously come too."

Dex nodded. "Assuming none of us get Selected, you mean."

Tessa tsked under her breath, continuing to scan for any of their friends. "None of us are getting Selected, Dex. The heirs picked their Sources long before tonight. The Legacy ruling families have been watching us all for years. We know the Celeste Heir is choosing Jasper, and the Falein Heir is selecting Dade—"

"And the Achaz Heir is selecting Sasha. I know what we all think we know, Tessa. It's just..." Dex sighed, raking his hand through hair as brown as his eyes. "Until it's a done deal, anything could happen. And the Arius Heir is still unaccounted for." An emotion crossed his features Tessa couldn't quite read. Unease? Frustration? She wasn't sure.

It was true. The Arius Kingdom was incredibly private, and they rarely ventured out of their borders. When they did, nothing good ever happened. The Arius Kingdom was the definition of cruel and wicked, which fit, she supposed, since they were descendants of Arius, the god of death and endings. The Kingdom's ruling family embodied all of that and more with their power to command shadows and darkness along with other mysterious gifts that were not well known. Few outsiders were ever allowed into the Kingdom, and while it was known there was an heir of age there to Select a Source, he hadn't been visiting the various Fae estates the last several years to evaluate his options like the other heirs had.

Tessa reached over and grabbed Dex's hand, gently squeezing his fingers. "I know something unexpected could happen, but we both know the odds are low at this point. So let's just believe that none of us will get Selected, and that we'll all be drinking and, more importantly, filling our stomachs within the next two hours."

Dex gave her a lopsided grin, but it didn't meet his eyes. He reached over, tucking a curl of her honey-blonde hair behind her ear. "How many times do I need to tell you hope is pointless?"

"I don't waste my time on hope. Not when I have you to save me." He huffed a laugh at her teasing, and she pushed up onto her tiptoes to press a soft kiss to his cheek. "We're going to be fine, Dex."

He held her gaze for another heartbeat, then blew out a long breath. "I know, Tessie. I'm just ready for it to be over."

"I think we all are."

The Opening Selection Ceremony was just the beginning though. This was a year-long event that was just getting started. The Selection was held every five years. All the Fae who had come of age since the last

Selection were brought to the Acropolis. The Fae would have their gifts awakened during the Emerging Ceremony, then they would be put through various tasks and trainings while being observed by the Kingdoms. Eventually, they would be assigned to whichever Kingdom they were to serve in. If an heir was of age to Select a Source, it was done during a Selection Year. Once the heirs all chose their Sources, there would be a brief break of a few weeks to allow the heirs and their new Sources to get acclimated. Then they would rejoin the rest of the Fae back at the Acropolis. With only six kingdoms, that did not happen often with the extended lifespan of the Legacy. To have all six kingdoms with heirs of Selection age at one time?

A historic night, indeed.

She finally spotted Oralia's pale blonde head of hair making her way towards them. Brecken was following close behind her, and sure enough, he had Katya in tow.

"Nervous?" Brecken taunted when they reached their side. He waggled his dark brows up and down.

Tessa rolled her eyes. "No. Like I was telling Dex, we all know how this is going to go. The heirs have had their Sources chosen for the last year, if not longer. This is all formality at this point."

Despite that knowledge, there was a general sense of unease in the grand hall. What the Legacy in the alcove had said was true. Nervous laughter rang out from around the room, and everyone was fidgety. Couples held hands a little tighter, and conversations were hushed and whispered.

They were taught that being Selected was an honor. It was ingrained in them from birth that being Selected was the greatest role in society a Fae could ever hope to achieve, and that to be the Source of a ruling Lord or Lady was as good as nobility. Only those who were already tapped to be a Source truly believed that, and Tessa was pretty sure that was out of necessity to come to terms with their fate. Once they were fully bonded, they would believe it though. Their Masters' desires would become their desires.

The Legacy could fill their deep power wells naturally over time, but to fully refill them from a completely drained state would take weeks, if not months, to do so. They had the powers of gods in their veins after all. That took a while to recoup, and in the meantime, they'd be left vulnerable. But when they drew power from a Fae, it refilled their power wells instantly.

Which is why no other descendants of the gods were allowed a personal Source like the ruling families. It was a rite performed by a Priestess who bonded the Source and Master with four Marks that connected them as one. When all the Marks had been given, they could sense each other's presence, feel each other's emotions, and hear each other's thoughts.

Tessa hated the very idea of it. She didn't want to be in anyone's head, and she sure as shit didn't want anyone inside her head. She didn't even want to be inside her own head most days.

She was excited for her gifts to emerge, though. Unlike the Legacy, Fae gifts didn't emerge naturally. They had to be awakened by the Legacy, which would happen a few weeks from now for all the Fae in this room. Tessa had always dreamed of the fire element, but the Anala Kingdom didn't allow any other Kingdom to have fire Fae. They were all born and raised in Idalia, the Anala Kingdom capital. Instead, all of her aptitude tests were predicting air as the most likely element for her.

"Poor Sasha looks terrified," Katya said quietly to Tessa, drawing her attention to the brown-haired beauty standing at the edge of the group of five Fae who had been slated to be Selected. For all intents and purposes, they were already claimed by their heirs. They knew they would soon be unwelcome by their own kind. Everyone was already treating them differently. They would soon be bonded to a Legacy, able to be found at a moment's notice, and no secrets withheld from their Masters.

Sasha was a few inches taller than Tessa, and her hair hung down her back in loose waves. She looked stunning in a gown of amethyst against her bronze skin. She was wringing her hands together and worrying her bottom lip.

"I would be too if I knew the Achaz Heir would be Selecting me tonight," Tessa answered.

Oralia sighed. "This just needs to be over."

"I just need to eat an entire pizza. By myself," Tessa grumbled.

"I told you to eat," Dex taunted into her ear from behind her.

A grin tugged at Tessa's lips, but she didn't let it form. She took a small step back as she retorted, "And I told you I tried."

She felt Dex step into her, so close she could feel the small chuckle emanate from his chest. "Oh, Tessie," he murmured so that only she could hear. "What am I going to do with you?"

More of the Legacy were starting to arrive. They were dressed in their formal finery and gowns, just as the Fae were. Tessa watched as they interacted with one another. Family Guards, Fae chosen from their Kingdom's armies to guard the ruling families, were beginning to line the edges of the room. Some had bows and quivers full of arrows. Others had swords at their waists. The mortals of the realm had guns, but they did nothing against a Legacy or a Fae. Both races healed quickly, and unless those bullets were made of shirastone or nightstone —which were incredibly expensive and heavily regulated—they wouldn't do anything. Even then, they would have to hit the head or heart.

Servers were plentiful now, offering glasses of wine to the Legacy, and Tessa pouted. Now she was hungry *and* thirsty.

"Have any of you seen Lange and Corbin?" she asked, continuing to watch the Legacy move about the room.

Brecken snorted a laugh. "I'm guessing they found a room for a quick fuck before the festivities."

"They wouldn't," Katya gasped, her amber eyes widening in shock. "Here?"

"Oh, they totally would. Those two go at it whenever they can, and they like the thrill of forbidden places," Brecken answered with a wink.

Tessa was sure that was a blush at the implication of Brecken's words, and she was jealous that Katya's dark skin hid it so well. Brecken had had his eyes set on Katya for a few months, although Tessa didn't know why he bothered. The odds of them getting assigned to the same Kingdom were not great. She didn't understand why any of them formed relationships to be honest. If she got separated from her best friend, that was going to be hard enough. She couldn't imagine being separated from someone she loved so intimately.

But just as she thought that, she saw Corbin and Lange slip into the room, hand-in-hand. Corbin's shaggy brown hair was definitely disheveled, and Lange's shirt was mis-buttoned beneath his jacket and tie. The cocky grin on Lange's face said he'd definitely just gotten some.

"What's going on, guys?" Lange greeted when they reached the group.

"You tell me," Tessa replied, reaching to fix his buttons before straightening his tie. "Which room do I need to avoid the rest of the year we're here?"

Corbin and Lange exchanged mischievous grins before Corbin's hazel eyes met hers. "We'll never tell," he said with a wink.

"We're all getting drunk as soon as the Selection is done, right?" Lange asked, his sky-blue eyes wistfully following a server with yet another tray of wine.

"Yes," Tessa agreed. "And doughnuts. The ones with chocolate on them. Not the powdered sugar ones. Then drinking."

"For the love of the gods, Tessa. You're acting like you haven't eaten in days," Dex said with an exasperated sigh.

Tessa merely shrugged, shifting from foot-to-foot. These heels were killing her feet. She was used to sneakers. And pants. Not dresses. "I'm bored. How much longer until this thing starts?"

"Sweetheart, you need to find someone to take you to a coatroom. It makes time go by so much faster," Lange taunted, and Corbin elbowed him in the ribs.

Tessa rolled her eyes, but she couldn't hold back her grin. She planned to do exactly that tonight, only with a mortal. And not in a godsdamn coatroom.

The Lords and Ladies and their heirs had to be arriving any minute, and then this thing could get going. Maybe she could sneak a glass of wine somehow…

Her eyes fell on a couple of Legacy who were standing near the edge of the crowd. One had his back to the room, but the other seemed to be watching everyone intensely. He was slightly shorter than the one with his back turned but only by an inch, if that. He had dark brown hair that reached his jawline and piercing sapphire blue eyes that Tessa could see from across the room.

Then the other one turned to look out over the crowd, and Tessa sucked in a breath.

It was the Legacy from the corridor. The one who had cornered her in the alcove. He appeared to be watching everyone as intensely as the other male. Every once in a while, he would say something to the Legacy standing next to him, and he would be handed a folder of some sort after a moment. Where his companion got the folders from, Tessa had no idea. If they were outside the Pantheon, she was sure they'd be looking at tablets rather than paper documents. The two would look over the contents of the folder, heads close together, flipping a few pages, before the first would hand it back to the second and continue to observe the crowd. Tessa forgot about trying to steal the wine as she studied the two Legacy, trying to figure out what they were doing.

"You're staring," Dex murmured into her ear.

"He's the one who took my chocolate from me," she answered, the Legacy again being handed a folder.

"What are you going to do, Tessie? March over there and ask for it back?" he chided.

"No," Tessa admonished. "But I can certainly fantasize about ways to hurt him for it."

"Is that all you're fantasizing about?" he teased.

"Fuck off, Dex. You know I would never fuck a Legacy. Not by choice anyway."

Before Dex could respond, a commotion at the main entrance drew everyone's attention, and a moment later, the first of the ruling families came through the door. Of course, it was the Achaz Lord, his wife on his arm and his Source a step behind him. On his other side was the Achaz Heir, Dagian Jove. He had golden blonde hair, sharp cheekbones, and golden eyes. He was in a black suit with a white shirt. A gold vest was visible beneath his black suit coat, gold thread running along the cuffs and lapels. A gold tie matched his vest. His eyes went straight to the Fae slated to be Selected, and Sasha gave him a weak smile.

As the ruling families began parading through to the front of the room, Tessa's mind and eyes began to wander. She looked back to where the Legacy from the alcove had been standing, but the two were gone. She scanned the crowd, searching and finding no sign of them.

Dex squeezed her waist where his arms were still wrapped around her. "You're fidgeting."

"Bored and hungry will do that to a person," she muttered back. As the words left her lips, her gaze landed on the missing Legacy. They had slipped into the center of the crowd at the back of the room, almost as though they were trying to avoid being seen. The thing was, when Tessa had spotted them, she found herself looking straight into emerald green eyes. A roguish grin tilted up one side of his lips, and he nodded slightly at her.

Tessa quickly averted her eyes. She'd had a feeling he wasn't done with her. The male would likely try to seek her out at some point in the evening. Which was fine. She'd managed to avoid the untoward demands of Legacy for a few years now. Another skill she'd acquired. She would be long gone and stuffing her face with pizza by the time he was free to look for her.

As surreptitiously as she could, she glanced back at him. He and the other Legacy were bent over another folder, flipping papers and whispering back and forth. The other Legacy shook his head a few times, and the one from the alcove was pointing at various things on whatever it was they were looking at.

A resounding thud echoed throughout the room when the heavy main doors were thrown open, and a Legacy strode up the center of the room. He was tall with light-golden skin and thick black hair. He had hazel eyes, and everyone seemed to shrink back from him. A female of exquisite beauty was on his arm, dressed in a black gown that dipped low in the front. Her dark red hair was piled in curls on her head, and ruby drops hung from her ears and around her throat. Behind the male, a Fae followed, her eyes cast down at the floor and her hands clasped in front of her.

The Lord of the Arius Kingdom— Valter St. Orcas.

Then Tessa's legs nearly gave out and an audible gasp passed her lips when the Legacy from the alcove peeled away from the other, finishing knotting a black tie at his throat. He slid his arms into the sleeves of a suit jacket that was as immaculate as the rest of his clothing, buttoning it as he fell into step beside the Arius Lord.

But that couldn't be. That wasn't possible.

Because if he was walking next to the Arius Lord and Lady…

Emerald eyes cut to her, and the corner of his lips ticked up in a cunning smile.

He was the Arius Heir here to claim a Source.

2

TESSA

He was the Arius Heir.
    And she'd all but yelled at him.
    Over chocolate.
    Dear gods. She was lucky to still be standing, to still be breathing.
    They were such a private kingdom, Tessa didn't even know the names of the Arius Heirs, only the ruling Lord and Lady. She knew the heir had a brother, but that couldn't have been who he had been standing with earlier. If his brother was here, he'd be up on the dais with his family like the rest of the siblings, not standing among the other Legacy. She quickly scanned the room, trying to find the Legacy he'd been with, but it was impossible with everyone gathered together and focused on the dais now.
    "Tessa," Dex said slowly, his voice low. "Isn't that the Legacy you said took—"
    "Yes," she whispered, cutting him off.
    "The Arius Heir?" he hissed.
    "I didn't know that at the time. Obviously."
    "What did you say to him? Please don't tell me you did anything reckless."
    "Not really the time for a play-by-play of my conversation with him."
    Dex went silent, his grip around her tightening.
    This was fine. The Arius Heir asking if she was slated to be a Source didn't mean anything. It couldn't. She had done everything she could to

go unnoticed by the heirs when they'd come to the Fae Estates to observe potential Sources. So had the others. Her assessments were nothing extraordinary, and more than that, *she* was nothing extraordinary. Just another Fae among the masses. They had found their way off the estate more times than Tessa could count, getting caught for at least some of those escapades. They caused enough trouble to be worth minor correcting, but not enough to be sent to the Underground.

All the ruling families had gathered along the front of the room on a large dais that spanned the entire length of the hall. There were tables behind them, set with finery for the feast that would take place after the Opening Selection was completed. Tessa watched the Arius Heir slide his hands into his pockets, rocking back on his heels as his eyes slowly raked over everyone standing below him. His face was cold and impassive. Darkness incarnate, just like his father. His mother leaned over, and he bent down so she could speak into his ear. He nodded once, and she smiled serenely at him.

The Achaz Lord stepped forward, and the entire hall instantly fell silent. All the Fae dropped to a knee. All the Legacy, save for the Lords and Ladies, bowed at the waist, including the Heirs, before straightening again. The Achaz Lord cleared his throat.

"Welcome," he boomed, "to the five-thousand six-hundred twenty-second Selection. The Fae may rise."

Tessa pushed herself back to her feet, Dex helping her up just as the Arius Heir had done in the alcove. She brushed off the knee of her gown. Dex's arm slipped back around her waist, and she settled into his side, smoothing her hands down the sides of her dress. The Achaz Lord began droning on and on about the history of the Selection and the importance of the year-long event. The longer he spoke, the more her nerves settled and the shock of having spoken to and survived the Arius Heir wore off. Tessa was fairly certain she was about to find out if one could sleep while standing, in heels nonetheless, when the Lord finally said, "Let the Selection begin!"

"Thank the gods," she muttered, and Dex huffed a low laugh.

"Almost time for doughnuts," he whispered into her ear, pinching her hip.

"Don't remind me," she groaned. She was ordering a pepperoni pizza. No, wait. Sausage. No. Pepperoni *and* sausage. And doughnuts. She didn't care that they didn't go together. Doughnuts really went with anything. Yep, that's what she was getting. She wasn't sharing with anyone. Not even Dex. And if Lange tried to steal a doughnut, she wasn't above biting.

The Achaz Heir had stepped forward as he was asked for his selection. "I choose Sasha Roenya to be my bonded Source," Dagian announced, his voice as deep and booming as his father's.

Applause broke out again while Sasha was escorted up the dais by a Legacy of the Zinta bloodline, one of the sister goddesses of magic and sorcery, to stand behind Dagian. Legacy of the Lesser gods were all sworn to one of the kingdoms. The Zinta bloodline, along with the Sirana bloodline, goddess of love and fertility, were sworn to the Achaz kingdom. The most powerful of the Lesser bloodlines usually served as advisors on the High Councils of the Lords and Ladies.

All the Selected Sources would be escorted up to the dais to stand with their new masters. Before the feast began, the heirs and their new Sources would all leave to speak privately. Apparently that was when the bonding began, but the Selected wouldn't receive their first Mark until after the evening's festivities. They'd been told that the adjustment period to the Marks could take hours, so it was done at the end of the feast and ball, right before the heirs took their leave.

The Falein Heir, Prudence, was called forward next and was asked to Select her Source. Each Selection went as expected. There were no surprises, but when the Arius Heir was called forward, the entire room seemed to still.

"Theon St. Orcas," the Achaz Lord called, and the Legacy from the alcove stepped forward.

No one knew what to expect from him. All the Fae tensed, none of them breathing. Legacy watched with curious looks, and the ruling families appeared to be awaiting his decision as anxiously as the Fae were. The other heirs had laid claims to their Sources long ago. This was all tradition and ritual now, but the Arius Heir's pick could be anyone's guess.

Oralia had reached over, gripping Tessa's hand to the point of pain, and she wasn't sure she could get any closer to Dex. Lange's arm was draped tightly across Corbin's shoulders, and Brecken had Kat pulled back against his chest. She'd turned her face into his shoulder, eyes closed and lips murmuring a prayer to the gods that did not care.

"I choose Tessalyn Ausra to be my bonded Source," Theon announced, his voice skittering over her bones.

"No," Oralia gasped beside her, but it was muffled by the murmuring that broke out around them. Dex's hands tightened as Tessa's knees nearly gave out and she stumbled in her stupid heels. The Arius Heir couldn't have possibly said her name. There was no way she had been Selected. She hadn't been slated for Selection. She had been seen and dismissed so often at the estate, it hadn't even been a real possibility in her mind. No one wanted her. No one had ever wanted her. Nothing and no one. That's what she was. This… This was a huge mistake. A joke of some kind.

She glanced up at Dex to find his eyes closed and his features set in a way to suggest he had thought this was a very real possibility from the beginning, and when he opened his eyes and met Tessa's, she knew this was no ruse. Time seemed to stand still as she turned to look at Lange and Corbin, their eyes wide in horror. Kat had her hands clasped over her mouth, and Brecken's lips were pressed into a thin line, some kind of silent fury in his gaze. More and more eyes were coming to settle on her as she was pointed out among the Fae.

"Tessalyn Ausra," came a deep voice to her left. She turned to find the Legacy she had seen speaking with the Arius Heir. "Come with me."

He held out his hand to her, and all she could do was stare at him. This wasn't how this was supposed to go. None of them were supposed to be Selected. They were supposed to have at least another year together before they'd be separated and sent to the various kingdoms.

"Come on, little one," the Legacy said again, his voice soft and coaxing.

"You need to go," Dex hissed into her ear, shoving her lightly.

Tessa had never felt more alone than she did when his hands slipped from her waist. And that was saying something because she knew loneliness all too well.

She swallowed hard and willed her feet to move as she slipped her fingers into the Legacy's waiting palm. His hand slid to her lower back as they moved, and all she could think about was how hot his hand was, like a brand on her back. She kept her eyes forward and focused while he led her through the crowd and up to the dais. Her attention fell on a Fae standing poised and submissive behind Valter. His Source.

And she saw her entire existence from this point forward in that female.

Time was still moving so damn slowly. She knew her feet were moving. The sound of their footsteps echoed on the stone floor, but she felt like they were hardly making any progress forward. Her gaze slipped off the Fae for a split second, but that was all it took for it to land on Theon's dark emerald eyes. He held her stare, an unreadable expression on his face, and suddenly time sped up. She blinked, and she was standing behind him. The Legacy who had escorted her was gone. Tessa had no idea where he'd disappeared to.

"What an excellent round of Selections," the Achaz Lord was saying. She wasn't sure when he'd started speaking again. "I believe I speak on behalf of all the Lords and Ladies when I say I am immensely proud of all the heirs and the way they are growing into their positions. They will now be dismissed, along with their Sources, to begin the bonding before the feast commences. The rest of the Legacy are welcome to continue enjoying drinks as the tables are set. We will begin finding our seats shortly."

The heirs began filing off the dais, curious glances finding their way to her as they passed, but Tessa wasn't paying attention. Her eyes were fixed on Dex and Oralia and her other friends who were staring back at her, a mixture of shock, anger, and grief on their faces.

A hand at her elbow startled her, and she looked up to find Theon towering beside her. "Come, Tessalyn," he said in a soft command. "They have a room prepared for us."

She didn't know what that meant, but she allowed Theon to usher her off the dais, out of the grand hall, and into the corridor where they'd informally met a mere hour ago. What felt like ages ago.

They were escorted up a set of steps to a room at the end of another hall. Theon's hand never left her arm. His touch was somehow right and unnatural all at once, and she was fairly certain she hadn't taken a full breath since he'd called her name.

Tessa entered the room, stopping just inside the door. It wasn't just a room, she realized, but a small suite of sorts. They were standing in a small sitting room. The sconces were low, creating an intimate environment. A plush sofa sat along one wall with a couple of throw pillows. A small table and two chairs were against the opposite wall with a pitcher of water and two glasses atop it, along with a small covered tray. An ornate rug of earth tones ran along the center of the room atop the cold marble floor. There was a doorway that led into another room. She could see the end of a bed, and that was all Tessa needed to see to know she didn't want to step foot in that room.

"Do you have bags?" the Fae who had escorted them was asking, drawing Tessa's attention back to her and Theon.

"Luka Mors will be bringing them later. They can be left outside the room. I will retrieve them when it is time," Theon answered. "No one else is to enter this room. Am I understood?"

"Yes, my Lord," the Fae answered, her eyes fixed on the ground.

"You are dismissed."

The Fae bowed before taking her leave. Theon closed the door behind her, turning to face Tessa fully. She couldn't help but take a step back from him as his eyes slid over her from head to toe and back up again. He took a step forward, but paused when Tessa took another step back.

"You are frightened," he said, his head tilting to the side with a keen interest.

Tessa couldn't answer, her mouth too dry. She didn't know what to say anyway.

"If I were going to hurt you, I would have done so already," Theon added. "You do not need to fear me."

"I don't," Tessa finally managed to say.

He tsked at her, a knowing look entering his eyes. "We have already discussed you lying to me, Tessalyn."

"Tessa."

"What?"

"My name. People call me Tessa. Not Tessalyn."

A brow arched. "You do not like your given name?"

"It is fine enough. I just prefer to be called Tessa."

Theon's eyes narrowed as if trying to figure something out, but he nodded in acquiescence. "Tessa it is then. Whenever possible."

That was a weird caveat. Before she could dwell on it though, Theon took another step forward, and she took two more back. His lips pursed in frustration.

"You know we will need to get close to each other for the bonding to initiate, do you not?" he finally asked after several seconds of watching her warily.

She didn't know that. They were never told how the bonding actually took place. Only that four Marks were given over the course of a year, strengthening the bond and connection of the Source and Master.

Gods, she had a fucking Master now.

When she didn't answer, his brows rose in surprise. "You don't know, do you?"

It was Tessa's turn to purse her lips as she shook her head, her hands clenching at her sides.

"No wonder you are terrified," he muttered under his breath, running a hand through his hair. Then, a little louder, he said, "I am sorry, Tessa. I thought they prepared you better for this."

"They don't tell us much. I was not slated to be Selected, so I was not prepared like the other Selected Sources were," she answered. Theon took another slow step forward, and Tessa backed up again, but she bumped into the wall. She had no other way to put distance between them now. "Why do you need bags?" she asked suddenly, and Theon paused his slow advance towards her.

"We both need bags," he answered, continuing to observe her. "But mostly you do."

"Me? Why?"

"You will want to change before your first Mark. It will be...exhausting. Furthermore, I do not think you want to travel in that gown, no matter how stunning you look in it," Theon explained.

There was so much to unpack in that little explanation, but Tessa found herself saying, "I didn't pack any bags. Everything I have is in the rooms I was assigned. I don't have anything to change into. I was supposed to go get pizza and doughnuts after the Selection was done."

Gods, now she was rambling. To the Arius Heir.

His brows knitted. "You were to go get pizza and doughnuts dressed like this?"

"Yes. My friends and I were. We've had it planned for months. Years, really," she answered, lifting her chin slightly.

"You will not get enough to eat at the feast?"

"We weren't planning to eat at the feast. It will be at least three hours before the Fae are remembered and allowed to eat."

"So you were going to get pizza and doughnuts?"

"Yes."

"I see."

He'd somehow managed to get closer to her without her realizing it, and Tessa tensed. Theon noted the small movement as he said, "This works well for both of us. I was not planning on staying for the feast either."

"What?" Tessa said, taken aback by that news. "But we need to eat."

"You just told me you were not planning to eat here."

"That was before I knew I'd be served first. Right after the heirs."

"So…you are hungry?" Theon asked, cocking his head to the side and studying her as if he couldn't figure out a puzzle.

"Yes. I'm hungry. You took my chocolate," she snapped, and Theon's eyes widened at her tone. "My apologies," she added quickly, lowering her gaze to the floor.

"No need to apologize. It is good to know you get irritable when you are hungry."

Her eyes snapped up at his almost teasing tone, and she found him standing directly in front of her. She gasped in surprise, bumping back against the wall and tripping on her dress.

"Easy, beautiful," he murmured, reaching out to steady her. "Come sit. Have a glass of water."

Theon led her over to the small table and guided her into a chair before pouring her a glass of water from the pitcher. He handed it to her, and she took a small sip, wishing it was something with a much higher alcohol content. He continued to study her, and she shifted under his gaze, her eyes darting around the room. Why weren't there any windows in here?

"What do we do now?" she finally asked.

"We should discuss what is going to happen this evening."

"Which is?"

"The initiation of the Source bond and the first Mark."

"I thought the first Mark was the initiation," Tessa said, sipping the water again.

Theon shook his head slowly, holding her stare. "Your body is not ready to accept the Marks yet."

"Okay… How do I make it ready?" Her knee was bouncing, unable to contain her nerves, and Theon's attention flicked to the movement. She instantly stopped.

"I will help with that," he answered, stepping forward so their legs were nearly touching. He slowly crouched before her until he was looking up into her face. "Part of this bond is that you need to trust me implicitly, Tessa."

"But I don't even know you," Tessa argued. "And I definitely don't trust you."

"That was…blunt."

"You told me not to lie to you."

His lips twitched as if amused, which was good, because she was essentially talking back to the Arius Heir. She didn't give much thought to self-preservation a lot of the time, but this was pushing it, even for her.

"Indeed I did," he agreed. "But the bond tends to rush things like trust along. Once completed in its entirety, we will be connected so deeply, you will feel as if we are the same person. Our wants and desires will be the same."

Tessa knew that, and she hated it. The idea of it made her feel…used. Another thing she knew all too well, and something she'd sworn she'd never be again. Yet here she was.

"I know you do not trust me right now, Tessa, and what I am about to do will likely not help with that," Theon continued.

"What are you going to do?" she demanded, lurching back in her chair and knocking the water glass over.

"Relax, Tessa," Theon said, pushing to his feet and moving to grab a towel to soak up the water. Once cleaned up, he leaned back against the small table. "To prepare your body for the Marks, a tonic was created. It does a couple things, but the main thing it does is it allows my power to slip through the magical barriers you have no control over yet to allow my magic in."

"That doesn't make sense. I can't access my magic yet," Tessa said, her hands gripping the arms of her chair and her knee bouncing again.

"That is the whole point," Theon went on. "Because you cannot access your element yet, you cannot take down your own magical barriers. For the Marks to work, they need to get past those shields. The tonic creates a temporary crack in your shields that allows my magic to pass. Additionally, by taking the Marks before your magic is allowed to emerge, my magical signature will become intertwined with your own, which will allow me to draw on your magic once the bond is fully completed."

"Sounds great," Tessa muttered.

"Is it not an honor to be Selected as the Source of an heir?" Theon asked, shifting against the table.

Tessa's eyes fell to her lap. "For many, I'm sure it is."

"But not for you."

"I was not lying to you in the hall." She'd brought her hands to her lap now, playing with the beading of her gown.

Silence stretched on for what felt like minutes, neither of them saying anything. Tessa couldn't bring herself to look at him. She knew if he was going to go through with this, she'd have to take whatever this tonic was. Hopefully it tasted like chocolate because she wasn't even remotely hungry anymore.

He moved in front of her once more, and she felt his fingers gently grip her chin, tilting her face up to his.

"Tessa, look at me." He waited until her eyes came back to his. "I know this may not be how you envisioned your future, but soon enough it will be the only future you want."

There was a sharp stinging at her neck. Tessa cried out, her hand reaching up to grasp the spot, but Theon was faster. The hand at her chin snapped out to grip her wrist. His other hand lowered, and Tessa saw the syringe in his hand, a needle at the end of it.

"What did you do?" she gasped, trying to break free from his hold, but that was utterly futile.

"Tessalyn, *look at me,*" he ordered, and her eyes widened in horror as she felt the command slip under her skin.

Entrancing was a power gifted to all the Legacy. The ability to take complete control of another if they didn't have the mental shields to block it. Fae were only taught to shield against it if their assignments required such a thing, and even then, it wasn't something they could do until their gifts were allowed to emerge.

She tried to fight it, but her body worked of its own volition, her eyes sliding back to his at the order. He crouched before her once more, his free hand coming up to cradle her cheek. Power—dark and cold—vibrated against her skin at his touch, working its way inside her very being. She tried to scream. Tried to look away. Tried to *move* away from him. But she was frozen. An effect of the tonic, she suddenly realized. He began speaking in a language she shouldn't know, but her soul knew what he was saying as her heart thrashed against her chest, breaking and shattering with each word that fell from his lips.

"I am Theon St. Orcas, Heir to the Arius Kingdom. You are Tessalyn Ausra. I have Selected you to be my Source. You obey me above all others. My desires are your desires. You are mine."

3
TESSA

The finality of his words rang through the center of her very being, and although she couldn't move, two tears slipped down her cheeks. Theon wiped one away with his thumb, brushing the wetness along her cheekbone.

"Acknowledge that you understand what has just happened, Tessa."

Her lips parted as though released from a hold. "I understand... Master." She knew the word should taste bitter on her tongue, but to her horror, it was sweet and wanted.

"Good girl," he said, releasing her wrist and stroking her cheek once more. "When we are in private or with Luka Mors, and not in formal settings, you may call me Theon," he added.

Tessa could only nod, too stunned to do anything else. He stood then, pouring another glass of water and holding it out to her. "Drink, Tessa."

But she didn't reach for the glass. "I'm not thirsty."

"It will make you feel better. Help clear your mind," he insisted.

"No, thank you."

Theon sighed. "This is not going at all as I had imagined it would," he muttered under his breath. He rubbed his eyes with his thumb and forefinger before finally saying, "Tessalyn, *drink*."

She glared at him, having no choice but to take the glass and drink the entire thing before handing it back to him.

"Better?"

"Oh, yes. It fixed everything," she retorted, really not caring at all about self-preservation now as the *thing* beneath her skin grew restless.

His brows rose. "You are...unexpected."

"Then you should have selected someone else." Her tone was not as sharp as she'd intended. She hoped he didn't hear the small thread of defeat in it.

"I am certain I chose perfectly."

Silence settled thickly in the small room.

"What happens now?" Tessa asked, leaning back in her chair. Her limbs felt tired and heavy, but at least she could move them now. She needed to get herself under control.

Be what they want you to be now, so you can be who you were meant to be later.

That's what Dex always said to her. It helped. Sometimes.

"The tonic needs at least an hour to fully take effect before the first Mark can be given. That is why it is done now, before the feast," Theon said. He had retreated several feet away, giving her space but keeping an eye on her.

"So...we can go eat?"

Theon shook his head. "I already told you we are not staying for the feast. As soon as the hour is up, I will summon the Priestess, give you the Mark, and we will leave."

"Leave? To go where?" she demanded, sitting up straighter.

"Home. There are still a few weeks before the various Selection activities begin for the other Fae."

"And where in the Arius Kingdom is your home?"

He shook his head. "Not yet, Tessa. I will not tell you that until your first Mark is in place."

Tessa scoffed. "You can simply order me not to tell anyone," she countered scathingly.

So much for getting herself under control. Gods, she was better than this. She knew how to go unnoticed, and it certainly wasn't by talking back to a Legacy, especially the Arius Heir. Then again, she'd already been noticed, so what did it truly matter at this point?

"Tell me, Tessa, how long are you going to be this bitter about your fate?"

She crossed her arms, pursing her lips. "I want to eat."

"I will have food brought to you."

"No. I want to go to the feast. Give me one last night of normalcy. You owe me that, Theon," she pleaded.

Theon tsked. "I owe you nothing."

Tessa started, the words like a slap across her face. She wasn't even sure why his statement surprised her. She shouldn't be. He was a Legacy after all. Fae existed solely to serve his kind. Of course he would believe he owed her nothing for giving up her entire life for him. For giving up her entire *self* for him. She didn't have much, but what she did have she didn't want to give to a godsdamn Legacy.

Theon sighed as though he realized he'd said the wrong thing. "I did not mean—"

"Yes, you did, and it's fine," Tessa interrupted, pushing to her feet. She wobbled slightly, and Theon stepped forward, his hand outstretched to steady her, but she held up her own to stop him. "Don't." She took a few deep breaths before looking up at him. "I know you do not *owe* me anything, but I would really like to attend the feast and see my friends once more before you take me away to your home."

Theon held her gaze for a moment before nodding once. "I can agree to the feast, but we will not stay for the ball, Tessa. As soon as the feast is done, we are leaving."

"It is customary for the heirs to stay for the entire celebration."

Darkness flitted across his eyes. "The Arius Kingdom is not one for customs."

"But I—"

"The feast or nothing. Take it or leave it."

Tessa pursed her lips. "Fine," she conceded, crossing her arms.

She moved to the door, and Theon's hand came to the small of her back, his touch making her suppress a shiver. "Do not make it a habit to negotiate with me, Tessa," he murmured into her ear. "This is a one-time thing."

Tessa swallowed but nodded her acknowledgement, and he led her back down to the grand hall. Heads turned and eyes followed them as Theon escorted her to the dais. The other heirs were already present, their Sources seated beside them, all with bruises on their necks. It was the one and only time Fae would be given such a seat of honor.

Two empty chairs were at the end of the table, and Theon pulled one out for her, pushing it in as she sat. As soon as he took his seat, servers appeared, setting bowls of summer corn and herb soup in front of the heirs. Once the heirs were served, the newly chosen Sources were served before the staff moved on to the Lords and Ladies.

Tessa was too preoccupied searching the crowd for Dex and the others to eat, and Theon took notice. He leaned over, nudging the soup spoon towards her.

"Eat, Tessa," he said softly into her ear. "Do not make me force you again."

She stiffened at the implication of entrancing and clenched her teeth, picking up her spoon. She was on her fourth spoonful when she finally spotted them. All of their eyes were pinned on her, but it was Dex's gaze she held. Concern filled his eyes, and his lips formed a thin line, but there was nothing to be done.

Not right now anyway.

A salad followed the soup, and then a main course of roasted lamb, potatoes, summer vegetables, and bread. Tessa picked at her food, only eating because of Theon's threat, but he never said anything about it again. She could feel him watching her the entire time though, as if that wasn't unnerving. A couple of the other heirs tried to engage him in conversation, but his answers were curt and short. They eventually gave up.

When it was announced there would be a short reprieve between the main course and dessert, Tessa made to move back from the table to go see Dex. A hand landed on the back of her chair before she'd moved it more than an inch.

"Where are you going, Tessa?" Theon asked, his voice low.

"To see my friends before dessert is served."

"No."

"But the deal was we would attend the feast, and I could see my friends," she protested.

"I agreed to the feast. That was it," Theon said, his features hardening. They were starting to draw attention from both the heirs and the Lords and Ladies.

"Th—" But his name got stuck on the tip of her tongue. Her eyes widened as a smirk spread across Theon's face. This was a formal setting.

With no small amount of humiliation, she ground out from between clenched teeth, "*Master*, I would really like the opportunity to say goodbye to my friends since we will leave as soon as the feast concludes."

"No," he answered simply, sitting back in his chair and swirling his glass of whiskey.

"No? Just like that?"

Theon's lips pressed together, darkness seeming to seep from his skin before it disappeared just as quickly. He took a drink from his glass before setting it down and leaning in close to speak into her ear once more. "I told you our negotiation was a one-time thing, Tessalyn. Now, I highly suggest you stop making a scene in front of everyone." Tessa nodded once in understanding, but it wasn't enough for him. "Verbal acknowledgment, Tessa."

"I understand," she gritted out.

"Good," he said, leaning back and picking up his liquor once more, his legs spread wide in a purely arrogant male mannerism. Tessa leaned back in her own chair, crossing her arms. "Act properly, Tessa," he murmured over his glass. "I will not have my Source seen pouting and sulking about."

"Of course, Master," she answered with faux sweetness, sitting up straight and crossing her legs, placing her hands in her lap.

Another small smile played at his lips, and she could swear a spark of amusement shone in his green eyes. Pieces of some kind of divine chocolate dessert she would have devoured an hour earlier were placed in front of them a few minutes later, but each bite tasted like ash on her tongue. After three bites, Tessa set her fork down, pushing her plate back.

"For someone who was starving, you did not eat much," Theon said conversationally, spearing his last bite of dessert with his fork.

"I lost my appetite," she bit back.

"It is probably for the best. You will not want a full stomach when you receive the first Mark."

Her head snapped in his direction. "Why?"

Theon shrugged. "I am told receiving the Marks can be uncomfortable for the Source."

What the fuck did that mean?

"If you are finished, we can call for a Priestess," Theon continued, drinking the last of his liquor.

Panic roiled through her, and she was suddenly glad she hadn't eaten much as a wave of nausea came over her. "I…"

"Do not try to negotiate out of this, Tessa. It is time," he said simply, his glass making a slight thudding sound when he set it down.

He made to stand, but Tessa blurted, "I need to use the restroom first."

His eyes narrowed. "There is a bathroom in the Marking Suite."

Damnit. That wasn't what she wanted. She wanted to be left alone for five godsdamn minutes so she could think and come up with a plan. Looks like she'd be getting those five minutes in the bathroom.

"It can't wait," she replied, fidgeting and crossing her legs as though she were about to wet herself right there.

Theon looked sufficiently irritated as he said, "We can stop on the way to the suite."

She nodded in agreement and allowed Theon to pull her chair back and help her to her feet. She saw Dex, Oralia, and the others standing on the edge of the crowd, still watching her. The Fae hadn't been invited to eat yet. They wouldn't be until the Legacy were finished. The entire meal she had tried to come up with a way to get them a message, but Theon had been watching her like a godsdamn hawk.

As they descended the steps from the dais, Tessa knew this was her last opportunity. Theon's hand pressed to her lower back once more, and when they drew close enough to Dex, she said, "I didn't notice a restroom in the corridor earlier. Are you sure there is one on the way?"

Theon nodded once, his gaze fixed straight ahead. "There is one halfway down the hall to the right."

"Perfect," she replied, and she saw Dex slip away out of the corner of her eye.

Perfect indeed.

As they made their way out of the grand hall and into the corridor, Theon slid his hand from her back and pressed it to her neck, right over where he'd forced the tonic into her body. Tessa jerked back at the pressure on the bruised and tender spot, her eyes snapping to his accusingly. "What are you doing?"

"My power is healing the bruise."

"Arius Legacy don't have healing gifts."

"I will be able to heal *you*. It is a component of the Source Markings, and it is proof the tonic has taken effect, allowing my magic to slip past and heal you."

"Why didn't you do that to begin with?"

"Because it is tradition for Sources to bear the bruises for the evening until they receive their first Mark," he explained, reaching for her neck again.

She felt his dark magic rush under her skin, soothing the ache. "I thought the Arius Kingdom did not care for customs?"

"Careful, Tessalyn," he warned. "My patience will only be pushed so far."

When they reached the female restroom, Theon tugged her to a halt. "Five minutes, Tessa. If you are not back out here in five minutes, I will come in and get you."

"Understood, *Master*."

A growl rumbled from low in his throat. "We have much to discuss when we arrive home."

Tessa turned away from him, but before she could push the door open, someone else came out.

"Oh, pardon me," Oralia said, quickly offering a curtsy to Theon before hurrying off.

Theon didn't even acknowledge her. "Five minutes," he said, jerking his chin towards the door.

Tessa hurried in and immediately scanned the room. Five stalls were to her right, sinks on the left wall. A small window was high on the back wall, but not so small she wouldn't be able to squeeze through it if she could get up there. She took a step towards it when a humming sound caused her to pause.

She drew closer to the stalls and stilled outside the third one where the humming was loudest. Tessa pushed the door open to find a phone sitting on the back of the toilet, vibrating with an incoming call. The Fae did not generally have phones until they were working in their assigned kingdoms, but she'd lifted plenty of them from unsuspecting Legacy. Corbin was weirdly skilled with technology, considering they rarely had the opportunity to use such things, but he managed to wipe any security measures taken off the phones they had lifted in the past, leaving them untraceable. Their small group of six had two stolen phones they shared among themselves, this being one of them. And because it wasn't known they had the phones, they weren't checked to make sure the settings were changed in the Pantheon.

The call rang out and immediately started vibrating again. She snatched it up, connecting the call and bringing it to her ear. "Dex?"

"Tessie." Dex's relieved voice came through the speaker. "We're going to get you out. We're going to—"

"No, Dex. It's immediate death if you're caught. They will accuse you of attempting to kidnap a Source. You and anyone with you will be killed on the spot. We can't risk that," she argued, already knowing where he was going with this.

"So I'm supposed to do nothing?" Dex demanded. "We're supposed to just sit back and let you be turned into a Source? I can't do that, Tessa. Not after all we've worked for, and everything we've done to make sure this exact thing didn't happen. I won't be there to fix this."

"I'm not asking you to sit back and do nothing, Dex." She exited the stall, heading to the window again. "I think I have a plan."

"You *think* you have a plan?"

"It's sort of a make-it-up-as-you-go type of plan," she answered, reaching down and slipping off her heels. She somehow clamored up onto the basin closest to the back wall with the phone wedged between her ear and shoulder. "I have to go. I have two minutes to get out of this bathroom. Call me again in five. I'll have a more solid plan by then."

"Tessie, this isn't the time for your recklessness—"

But she cut the call before he could say more. Shoving the phone down the front of her dress, Tessa stretched out and unclasped the window. The bottom portion swung down just as a knock sounded on the door.

"Tessa," came Theon's voice, full of a dark warning.

"I'm just washing my hands," she called back, turning the faucet on with her foot.

Sucking in a deep inhale, she leapt from the sink to the window, cursing under her breath at the impact of her body meeting the wall. It had worked though. Her arms were gripping the windowsill, and she used her toes to climb her way up the wall, grasping for any type of purchase. This wasn't her first time sneaking out of undesirable situations. She could figure this out, even if the others weren't here.

She reached out with her fingers, feeling the window ledge on the outside and hauling herself up. As she pulled her torso through, she had the sudden crushing realization that she had forgotten one very important fact. The grand hall was on the third level of the Pantheon. She was three floors above the ground.

Fuck.

But the door banging open behind her left little room for rethinking her plan.

"Tessa!" Theon bellowed, footsteps thundering across the floor. "Get back in here!"

"Let go!" she cried, kicking out with her foot as a hand clasped around her ankle.

She heard Theon curse when her foot connected with his face, and his grip released. Pulling her legs through the window and up onto the ledge beneath her, she adjusted her positioning, not letting herself look down.

"Tessalyn—"

She threw her hands over her ears before his entrancing could reach her, but in doing so, she nearly lost her balance on the ledge. Reining in her breathing from nearly falling, she looked to her right. A balcony was a ways down. She could crawl along the ledge towards it. Going to the left wasn't an option as she'd have to cross in front of the window, and she could hear Theon cursing up a storm and slamming things around the bathroom. Pissing off the Arius Heir was not her finest moment, but her mind was quickly made up when shadowy mist started drifting from the window.

As quickly as she could without slipping from the ledge, she inched along towards the balcony. The wind had picked up, and the temperature had dipped as if a summer storm was moving in. Her hair fluttered across her face in the winds. She was halfway to the balcony when the phone began vibrating against her chest.

"Sorry, Dex," she muttered under her breath. "I don't have the plan completely figured out yet."

Theon was still yelling for her to come back to the bathroom window, tendrils of darkness seeming to search along the ledge, but the farther she moved along, the more her heart soared. Freedom was getting closer and closer. Of course, once she made it there, she'd need to figure out how to get out of the Pantheon and then the Acropolis undetected. Then she'd need to figure out some place to hide, but those were problems to worry about when she wasn't on a ledge. Right now, her focus was not falling. A fall from this height wouldn't kill her. Fae and Legacy were hard to kill, but the fall would certainly make her easier to catch.

A cry of relief left her when she leapt the final feet from the ledge to the balcony railing, clamoring over the top of it and sinking to her knees. Her entire body was trembling with adrenaline. She couldn't even get to her feet yet.

But she'd done it. For once in her life, she'd gotten out of her own mess.

Taking a minute to catch her breath and figure out her next move, the phone began vibrating once more. She'd done the first part by herself. Maybe now was a good time to let Dex and the others get involved with the rest.

She pulled the phone from her dress and was about to connect the call when the doors of the balcony swung open. Tessa gasped, dropping the phone as she looked up and met eyes of sapphire blue. A look of some type of annoyed acceptance came over his features.

"I told Theon you were going to be a handful," he muttered, striding towards her with purpose.

Tessa shrank back against the balcony railing, trembling for an entirely different reason now. When the Legacy reached her, he bent and retrieved the dropped phone. Snapping it in half, he tossed the pieces over the railing. Then he bent once more and slid strong arms under her knees and around her back, scooping her up.

"Come on, little one. Your Master is waiting."

4

TESSA

"What the fuck were you thinking?" Theon demanded when the Legacy carried Tessa into the small suite. He set her gently on the sofa and stepped aside as Theon dropped to his knees before her. He gripped her face in his hands, smoothing hair back from her face. "You could have fallen, Tessa. Someone other than us could have found you. Do you have any idea what could have happened?"

Tessa couldn't think of anything to say. She was too numb inside. All of that had been for nothing. That had been her last chance at escaping this fate. It had been her last shot at not becoming something to be used, to be drained of her strength and power whenever he wanted. It was her last opportunity to remain who she was and not be lost in who *he* was.

But all her chances were gone now. He would never give her this opportunity again. Even if she managed to run, the Mark she was about to receive would connect them so he would always be able to find her. She should probably be fearful of what he was going to do to her for the attempted escape, but she simply didn't care what happened to her. Certainly not now.

"She hasn't stopped shaking since I found her," the other Legacy said, slipping his black suit coat off and draping it around her shoulders.

"Has she said anything?" Theon asked, tilting her face towards his to look into her eyes.

"Not a word. She had a phone though," he answered, leaning his shoulder against the back wall, his hands sliding into his pockets. Theon's head whipped to him, and the Legacy gave him some kind of frank look. "What do you want me to do?"

"Tessa, are you all right?" Theon said, turning back to her and ignoring his question. Concern filled his features, but it was concern for his source of power, not for her. She knew that.

"Godsdamnit, Tessa," he swore, moving one hand to grip her chin and hold her in place. "Tessalyn, *speak*. Are you all right?"

"No," she answered, the entrancing pulling the word from her lips.

He leaned back to look her over. "Where are you hurt?"

His hands left her face, reaching under the jacket and running down her arms, turning her hands over. He instantly healed a small cut he found on her palm before continuing to check her over. She hardly noticed his hands brushing down her ribs and along her hips, moving her gown aside to check her shins and knees.

"Anywhere else?" he demanded, lifting her leg to check the soles of her feet.

Tessa shook her head wordlessly.

"I don't think her body is what she was referring to when she said she wasn't all right, Theon," the other Legacy offered from his spot against the wall.

Theon stilled, his lips forming a thin line as he lowered her foot back to the ground. He tilted his head up, looking at him. "Get things ready to go. We are leaving as soon as possible when this is done. Tell the Priestess to come here in ten minutes. Be ready."

He nodded in confirmation, pushing off from the wall, but he hesitated when he got to the door. "You are sure, Theon? There is no going back after this."

"The decision is already made, Luka. We cannot change the plan now. It will raise questions and draw unwanted attention," Theon answered, his gaze drifting back to Tessa. She hardly heard what they were saying, staring straight ahead, her fingers clenching and unclenching against the sofa cushions.

The Legacy, who was apparently the aforementioned Luka Mors, nodded once before he left the room, the door clicking shut behind him.

"Tessa, you need to change," Theon said, standing and moving to a small travel bag that was sitting on the small table. He pulled a bundle of clothing from it, bringing them back to her. Setting them on the sofa, he crouched before her again. "Tessa, look at me." Not wanting to feel the pull of his entrancing again, she dragged her eyes to his. "Do you need help getting changed?"

She shook her head.

"I will step out for two minutes, then I am coming back in," he said, pushing back to his feet. "Acknowledge that you heard me."

"I understand, Master," she said softly, reaching over and running her fingers along the clothing beside her.

He stiffened imperceptibly. "We are not... This is not a formal setting, Tessa."

She just stared at him, waiting for him to leave so she could change. After a few more seconds, he left the room.

Tessa stood on wobbly legs, the suit coat slipping from her shoulders. She pulled the sleeve of the gown down her arm, working the garment over hips before letting it slip down the rest of her body to pool around her feet. Naked save for her flimsy undergarments, she moved on to the pile of clothing. There was a fresh set of underthings nestled between black leggings and a black long-sleeve shirt made from some of the softest material she'd ever felt. She quickly dressed, just pulling the shirt over her head when Theon came back into the room.

He scooped up the dress from the floor and folded it, carefully placing it back in the bag. "You are going to want to pull your hair back, Tessa."

"I don't have any pins or a hair-tie," she replied quietly.

Theon dug through a side pocket of the bag and produced an elastic band, handing it to her. She didn't question him. Simply pulled her curled, honey-blonde hair into a high ponytail, quickly securing it.

Theon took the bag to the door, placing it on the floor, and came to stand in front of her once more. He slowly brought his hand to her cheek, pausing as though he expected her to flinch back from him. "I know you feel like you are being forced into this, but—"

"But nothing. I *am* being forced into this. I am not choosing this. You chose it for me," Tessa interrupted.

His eyes hardened. "This is what your kind were created for, Tessa. It is in your being to serve the Legacy. Any other Fae would be honored to be in your position."

"Then choose one of them! Choose anyone else who *wants* this! Please!" she cried, not caring that she was begging now.

Theon studied her, a muscle ticking in his jaw. He opened his mouth to say something just as a soft knock sounded and a female entered the room. She wore a white sheer gown that flowed down to her ankles. Gold sandals adorned her feet, and a gold belt was slung low on her hips. Her brown hair was braided in a coronet atop her head with strands of gold and ivy woven among it, the tips of her arched ears peeking out. A Priestess.

"I am told you are ready to bestow the first Mark to your Source, Heir of Arius," she said with a bow.

"Please, Th—" But the name got stuck on her tongue. Apparently the arrival of the Priestess made this a formal situation.

Theon looked at her a second longer before turning his back on her to face the Priestess. "Yes. That is correct. I am ready to proceed."

The Priestess nodded, moving to the small table. Tessa hadn't noticed the tray of items on it until now. They had been blocked from view by the bag earlier. She stood silently while the Priestess poured the contents of three vials into a small glass, stirring it with a glass stir rod. The liquid turned a shade of cerulean blue, fizzing with smoke wafting from it. Theon stood a few feet away from Tessa, his arms crossed and pointedly not looking at her.

A moment later, the Priestess picked up the glass along with a small black dagger and turned back to them. A serene smile spread across her lips as she approached Tessa. "You are going to want to sit."

"I prefer to stand, thank you," Tessa answered, clenching her hands into fists at her sides.

The Priestess glanced at Theon expectantly. Theon closed the few feet between him and Tessa, bringing a hand to her lower back. "Sit down, Tessa. This is going to be unpleasant."

Bringing his other hand to her shoulder, he gently guided her down to the sofa, lowering with her so he sat beside her. He was rigid, and Tessa couldn't help but wonder why. He wasn't the one about to undergo a Marking. More than that, he knew far more about what was going to happen than she did.

"You will drink this first," the Priestess said, holding the fizzing glass out to her. "You must drink it all. It is similar to the elixir injected earlier, but much stronger."

"Okay," Tessa said, tentatively taking the glass from her hand. It was warmer than she'd been expecting. "Then what?"

Again the Priestess glanced at Theon.

"Let's get through this part first, and then we will worry about the next step," he said, his hand still on her lower back. When Tessa didn't push the issue, he glanced at the Priestess and gave her a small nod.

"Theon St. Orcas, heir of the Arius Kingdom, you have come before a Priestess and requested the first Mark for your Source. Do you acknowledge your request?"

"I do," Theon said tightly.

"Do you understand your Source becomes yours and yours alone? You assume complete dominium. Once the first Mark is given, there is no undoing the bond that will be started. Only the death of either party can end it," the Priestess continued.

"I understand," Theon answered.

Tessa couldn't help but recognize the superiority playing out before her. These two Legacy spoke of her as a piece of property he was taking ownership of. The Priestess was asking him questions about her own existence as she sat silently, holding a fizzing cup of blue liquid and curling her bare toes into the rug to keep from fidgeting.

"You recognize that the Source bond connects you in all forms—physically, emotionally, and mentally, allowing you the ability to share power and life as one entity?" the Priestess asked.

"I do," Theon answered, flexing the fingers of his other hand.

"May Achaz bless this bonding, and may Arius offer judgment if it is ever broken," the Priestess intoned. "Theon St. Orcas, who do you Select as your Source?"

"Tessalyn Ausra."

Bile rose in her throat as the words left Theon's lips.

"Let the Selected drink the elixir to open the path for your claiming Mark."

The Priestess motioned for Tessa to drink, and she glanced once at Theon. His face was impassive as he nodded. She brought the glass to her lips, trying not to inhale the smoke drifting up from the glass. She didn't even have a moment to process the sweet taste because the liquid was like fire in her throat, burning as it went down. Her eyes widened, and she tried to pull the glass away, but Theon had moved his hand around hers, keeping the glass at her lips. Panicking, she jerked her head back, but his other hand was along the back of her head, holding her firmly in place. He'd known this would happen.

Her wide eyes met his, and that was all he needed. *"Drink, Tessalyn,"* he entranced, and she swallowed more and more as he tipped the glass up. Her stomach was burning with the liquid pooling in it, tears leaking from her eyes. The room was spinning, but she could hardly move, Theon holding her in place.

He removed the glass from her lips. "Good girl, Tessa," he murmured, wiping a drop from the corner of her mouth with his thumb and pressing it between her lips. "Lay down, beautiful."

He slid to the floor in front of her and helped her lift her legs to the sofa, easing her down and onto her side. She managed to drag her knees up to her chest, curling in on herself. The act took every bit of energy she could muster. "It hurts," she gasped out, more tears slipping down her face.

"I know it does, but what happens next will be worse."

How could what was going to happen next possibly be worse than this? Tessa wanted to vomit, but knew it would burn just as much coming back up. She also knew they'd force her to drink another glass if she vomited up this one.

"You have minutes to complete the first Mark, young Lord," the Priestess said from where she stood behind him. She was holding the dagger out to him, and Tessa's eyes widened in terror.

"Bring Luka in," Theon ordered, taking the dagger.

The Priestess crossed the room, and Tessa heard the door open over the roaring in her head. But her eyes were locked on Theon and the dagger. She didn't know what was about to happen, but she knew Theon hadn't been lying. This was going to be so much worse than the tonic she'd just choked down.

Luka came into her line of sight, and she began trembling as he moved to her side.

"Hold her down, Luka," Theon commanded, bringing the dagger to his palm.

Luka's large hands came to rest on her shoulder and hip, but he wouldn't look at her.

"Please, Luka," she begged, resorting to her last hope. She didn't know this Legacy, but if Theon wouldn't stop, maybe Luka would stop him for her. "Don't let him do this."

"I'm sorry, little one," he said, barely audible.

Her eyes went back to Theon, who had blood running down his arm from the slice in his palm. Luka took his hand from her shoulder and gripped her right wrist, holding out her arm to Theon. With his bloodied hand, he gripped hers, bringing the tip of the dagger to the back of it. The blade was so dark it seemed to absorb the soft light of the room.

He cut a deep gash into the back of her hand, and Tessa cried out. The Priestess was there, drawing some kind of Mark with the blood running out of the cut. In less than a minute she was done, clearly having done this before, and she nodded to Theon as she stepped back.

He locked eyes with Tessa. "Tessalyn Ausra, I have claimed you as my Source, to be bonded to me irrevocably. With this Mark, may the bond become physical, that we can always sense each other's presence and crave each other's closeness. *My power claims you as its own.*"

The last part was said in the language she didn't know but that her soul recognized. Theon dropped the dagger, taking her wrist from Luka and holding it firmly as he placed his bleeding palm atop the wound he'd created and the subsequent Mark.

Searing pain whipped through her veins as their blood mixed beneath her skin. It was unlike anything she had ever experienced. It was an agony that made her wish for death. His dark and cold magic crashed into her, invading every piece of her body and soul. She was screaming and arching off the sofa, Luka pinning her beneath him. It felt as if death itself were coursing through her over and over, and *gods*. She wished it would just take her. Theon only tightened his hand around her own, refusing to break the connection, and something in her was buzzing and thrashing, trying to rise up. But Theon forced more and more of his magic into her, and it was suffocating. She couldn't breathe, and that familiar sensation only made her panic more.

Theon's jaw was clenched, sweat beading on his brow, as he gritted out, "Just give in, Tessa."

But she didn't know what he meant, and another scream ripped from her throat.

Then a cord of purest gold was floating from her skin, rising up to meet one of obsidian black from Theon. The cords were twining around each other, tighter and tighter, and it felt as if they were wrapping around her chest. She thrashed beneath Luka, gasping for any amount of air. Darkness clouded the edges of her vision, and she thought for sure this was how she was going to die. His dark power was going to kill her. And she welcomed it. Welcomed any reprieve from this. She'd courted death for years. Maybe it would finally take her.

It could have been seconds, but it felt like hours later when a flash of silver erupted from the cords, and they settled back into Theon and Tessa. There was a tingling beneath her hand and a pull in the pit of her stomach, but she couldn't pay any attention to any of it. She was too focused on dragging air into her lungs.

Luka eased off her as Theon sat on the sofa and pulled her into his lap, cradling her against his heaving chest. Her own chest warmed at his closeness, and the pull in the pit of her stomach settled down, humming contentedly. Her entire body ached, but her head pounded as though she'd been out drinking all night.

"You're okay, beautiful," Theon murmured, like he thought he could soothe her. "I'm going to take care of you."

He seemed to sigh in relief while he held her, stroking her hair. Luka approached with a damp cloth, wiping sweat from her brow. She couldn't entirely comprehend what was happening right now. They likely thought she was too exhausted to care. They would only be half right.

"You know what to expect over the next several hours and days to come as she adjusts?" the Priestess asked.

"Yes," Theon answered.

The Priestess came forward and grasped Tessa's right hand. Tessa tried to look, but Theon held her head against his chest, not letting her see. When the Priestess dropped her hand, Theon snatched it up in his own.

"The Mark is in place. If she purges the tonic now, it will not matter. Your magic has settled into her. I have given the other necessary items to your associate and explained what must be done," the Priestess remarked, stepping back. "Do you require anything else of me this evening?"

"No," Theon said. "You are dismissed."

The Priestess bowed before exiting the room.

As soon as the door clicked shut, Theon said, "Get a blanket, Luka. She's shivering." A moment later, a thick fleece blanket was draped around her. Her head was throbbing, and the room was spinning. Every inch of her body felt as if thousands of shards of glass were embedded in her skin.

"How long before you think we can move her?" Luka asked, dragging a chair over from the table and sitting in front of them. His eyes were on Tessa, watching her carefully.

"I don't know," Theon answered. "I would like her to vomit first and see what after-effects are going to hit her."

Tessa whimpered at the mention of after-effects. What else could they possibly put her through?

"Shh," Theon murmured again, his hand rubbing up and down her back. "I've got you, Tessa." After a beat of silence, he added, "Clean up her hand, Luka."

Luka nodded, rising from his chair and returning with a wet cloth. Taking her hand from Theon, he gently dabbed at it. Tessa hissed, jerking it away.

"Let him clean you up, Tessa," Theon said softly, nodding at Luka to try again.

"Everything hurts," she rasped when Luka began dabbing and wiping at her hand again.

"I know it does."

She saw Luka's gaze flick to Theon, but she couldn't read his expression. When he finished cleaning her hand, Tessa tried to look at it, but Theon stopped her again. "Not yet," he said gently, guiding her head back to his chest.

Silence enveloped the room, and she let her eyes flutter closed, resting against Theon. Her body seemed to relax into him, but that wasn't right. He'd done this to her. She shouldn't be leaning into him. This was all wrong.

"We will see how bad the first wave is and then decide what to do from there," Theon was saying quietly, interrupting the confusion she was trying to process.

"If it's too bad to travel?" Luka asked.

"We will go to the townhouse. We are not staying here where everyone can see us and spies can learn too much."

"Agreed." Another beat of silence, before Luka added, "How bad do you think it will be?"

"I don't know," Theon answered. "She fought back. Way more than I anticipated."

She didn't know what to think of that because it had been impossible to fight against any of that.

She didn't know how much time passed when something began to happen. The aches in her body became more than tingling pinpricks. It was a burning that started at the back of her right hand and began radiating up her arm.

"Her heart rate is picking up," Luka murmured.

"I am aware," she heard Theon answer. "Take the blanket. She is getting hot."

She didn't feel hot. Her body felt freezing despite the burning overtaking her. Her eyes flew open, and she lurched forward as the blanket was removed. "You're okay, Tessa," Theon said, trying to pull her back into him.

She was okay? She was definitely *not* okay. This was all because of him. She was not *okay* because of him.

Tessa pushed away from him, tumbling onto the floor. "Don't touch me," she gasped, and at the words, something in her chest jumped and began vibrating violently within her. The back of her hand started throbbing, drawing her attention to it.

Like black ink against her fair skin, a Mark stood out. Swirling lines that wove together, and in the center sat three inverted, interlocking triangles.

The symbol of Arius.

Branding her.

Claiming ownership of her.

Her eyes dragged up to Theon from where she sat on the floor.

"Tessa, come here," he said, reaching for her again, but she scrambled back from him, her arms nearly giving out.

"No. Don't come near me," she rasped, but apparently that was the wrong thing to do. The cord that connected her to Theon jerked sharply within her, and she whimpered in pain.

Theon dropped to his knees before her. Luka was standing, watching everything warily.

"Tessa," Theon said, trying to sound reassuring. "The Source bond demands we are close, especially right now. When you tell me to stay away, it reacts poorly. Come here."

"No," she gasped, crying out as another jolt of pain ricocheted through her body.

"Tessa," Theon snapped in frustration. "You are about to experience something worse than the pain you are in right now. Let me near so I can help you through it."

"Don't growl at her, Theon," Luka cut in. "You know the adjustment will take time. She will need time to navigate this, and how it works. You both will."

"I am aware of that, but she does not need to be in pain," Theon argued. "I do not want to see her in pain when I can do something about it."

Luka opened his mouth to say something in response to that, but a wave of nausea washed over Tessa so strongly, she fell forward onto her hands and knees as she fought the urge to vomit.

"Get a basin," Theon said.

Luka was already moving and set a large bowl down beside her. "Don't fight it, little one," he said grimly, reaching to brush her ponytail back over her shoulder. "Let it out."

He stepped back, leaning against the wall, and when the next wave of nausea overtook her, Tessa took his advice. She vomited into the bowl, heaving over and over. It wasn't her dinner that came up though. It wasn't even the tonic. She assumed her body had burned through all of that already. It was thick, black shadows and silvery wisps of light. It poured out of her, and each time she heaved, pain racked her entire body, her stomach convulsing and her head throbbing. Tears were coursing down her cheeks, and she was gasping in between gags.

A hand rubbing up and down her spine told her Theon was back by her side. The cord in her instantly settled down at his touch. The vomiting, however, continued for the next several minutes. When it finally subsided, Tessa curled onto her side on the floor, her head coming to rest in Theon's lap. Luka handed him a cool rag, and he began pressing it along her forehead, then her cheek and down her neck.

"What was that?" she finally whispered. Her throat was raw from all the screaming and now the vomiting.

"My magic," Theon answered. "To give you the Mark, I had to pour some of my raw power into your veins so that your own magic would become overwhelmed by it, and, in turn, recognize it. Your body is trying to adjust to my magic in your system, along with the bond that is starting to form."

"It will…" She stopped and swallowed. "It will happen again?"

"Yes," he said. "The intensity will lessen over the next few hours, but it will take several days to adjust fully. All Sources go through the adjustment differently, but the general pattern stays the same."

This was going to continue for the next few hours? Days?

Luka crouched before them both with a glass of water in his hand. "Can you sit up?"

Tessa tried, but her body wasn't working right. It didn't feel like her own. Nothing felt right, and she didn't… She couldn't… She could swear she was screaming, but it must be in her head because Theon and Luka weren't reacting like she'd lost her mind.

Theon reached over, helping her sit up, and slid closer to her. He took the glass from Luka and brought it to her lips, tipping it up. When she drank the entire glass, her head fell against Theon's shoulder.

"I don't know if I can do that again," she whispered, her eyes fluttering closed.

"You can. I will be here. Helping you through it."

There was so much she wanted to say to him. So much she wanted to scream at him. She wanted to shove him away for doing this to her. But even the *thing* inside her had gone quiet, all the fight going out of her. So instead she sat with her eyes closed until the next round of vomiting and pain consumed her.

5
THEON

Theon sat in the back of the SUV with Tessa spread across the seat beside him. She was asleep, her head resting in his lap. She had vomited for nearly three hours before finally falling asleep. It had been the middle of the night when Luka had helped him change her out of her sweat-drenched clothing and dress her in fresh ones before Theon had scooped her up and carried her through the portal into the Arius Kingdom. They only allowed portals to open in specific locations within the kingdom, so they still had a good day of travel to Arius House. They'd arranged to have the vehicle waiting for them, and now they'd been driving for nearly two hours.

The Acropolis was in the middle of Devram, and all the kingdoms had portals to and from the sacred city. While the other kingdoms had several portals throughout their lands, the Arius Kingdom only had two; both of which were heavily guarded and monitored. If anyone was entering their lands, they were doing so on foot or by vehicle unless they had a direct invitation. And even then, his father tended to make them traverse the Ozul Mountains and Shade Plains rather than let them use the portals.

Luka hadn't said much from where he sat behind the wheel. The male was usually a broody ass, but this was more than that. He was clearly upset about how the evening had played out. He knew Luka thought he should have chosen someone else. Theon may not have visited the four Fae Estates to observe his options the last several years like the other heirs had, but he had done his research. They'd had information gathered and sent over on all the Fae that would be eligible for Selection, and Theon had poured over documents and reports for months, narrowing down options based on what he needed. He couldn't count how many nights he, Luka, and his brother, Axel, had spent holed up in his rooms, drinking and debating the merits of various Fae. At one point, an entire wall had been covered with photos and information about prospective Sources. His father had his opinions, of course, and Theon had pretended to take them into consideration.

Tessa thought their meeting in that corridor was random. It was anything but. He'd had his choices narrowed down to five, and he'd sought them all out in the hours before the Selection Ceremony. She had been the last one he'd tracked down. He'd never expected her to be hiding in an alcove out in the corridor. Then again, maybe he should have based on the number of times she sneaked off the Fae Estate in the Celeste Kingdom.

The Fae could leave the Estates, of course, especially as they got older. The Estates were essentially boarding schools for the Fae until they came of age for Selection at twenty-three years. It was just that few of them actually left the sections of the kingdoms where the Fae lived, and those who did were always tracked. Wards alerted the governing Legacy when they came and went. But when Tessa would leave the Celeste Estate, she somehow avoided the wards and left undetected. Numerous times. Sometimes with others, and sometimes by herself. It wasn't detailed in her file full of information. In fact, this particular skill was only mentioned in one small section in passing, which was curious in and of itself. It was a skill he was eager to learn more about though.

And it was a skill that would come in handy during the next year they would be spending in the Acropolis.

Theon had tried to sleep once they'd entered the Arius Kingdom, but he was too worried about the Fae sleeping beside him to let himself drift off. If she woke, he wanted to know. The faster this bond settled into place, the better. If there was something he could do to hasten it along, he'd do it. From everything he'd read about the bonding process, he didn't anticipate it taking long, and once her gifts emerged in a few weeks, they could really move ahead with their plans.

That first Mark though?

That had been unexpected. He'd anticipated some resistance from her dormant element, but fuck. He could still feel the shocks and flares of power as it had battled his own. It had drained him more than he'd liked, which meant he'd need to ask his father for an extra ration or suffer for the next two days.

He'd rather suffer.

He reached for a bottle of water and found Luka's sapphire gaze settled on him in the rearview mirror.

"You still think this was the best plan?" Luka asked grimly.

"Not much I can do about it now, is there?" Theon retorted, tossing the bottle onto the empty front seat.

"No, but how we carry on with everything else could still be changed," Luka said, switching lanes to pass a car as he reached for the water bottle.

"That won't be necessary."

"Theon," Luka sighed. "You should have Selected someone else if you wanted everything to go to plan. I've told you from the beginning she was not the one for this. You insisted on keeping her in the running. You found her hiding, away from the other Fae, eating food she'd obviously stolen. I told you she was going to be too hard to control, which will be a problem for you in and of itself."

"She will be fine. As the bond grows stronger, she will be more obedient. She will start to want what I want," Theon argued, looking down at the sleeping female. "Besides, she did not lie to me in the corridor before she knew who I was. You think she will start now that she knows I am the Arius Heir? She is not stupid, and I'm not going to base the choice of my Source on some intuition you think you have about her."

"It is not intuition when she has dozens of infraction reports from her Estate Mother. She is the exact opposite of stupid. She did not lie to you because she knows when and how to avoid making a scene. How do you think she avoided being looked at twice by the other heirs? She is clever, and she is too wild, Theon," Luka said, his eyes flicking to Theon's in the rearview mirror. "We needed someone with more self-control for this."

"We need a little wildness for this to work," Theon countered.

"I did not say her wildness was a bad thing. But to make her be what you need her to be…"

"It won't be like that," Theon insisted. "She will *want* to please me.

She will *want* to obey me, Luka. It is how the bond works. You know this."

"She pushed you away, Theon. She chose to feel immense pain rather than have you touch her."

"She is adjusting," he replied shortly, his fingers curling possessively around Tessa's shoulder. She'd been shivering when they had changed her clothing, so they'd added a thick sweatshirt over the shirt they'd put her in. He had the fleece blanket from earlier draped over her as well, since the air conditioning was on full blast to keep him and Luka cool. They may have been at a higher elevation, but the Ozul Mountains still saw the high temperatures that accompanied the end of the summer season.

Theon and Luka had changed out of their formal clothing before they'd left. Theon was in far more comfortable jeans and a t-shirt. He carved his hand through his hair, the cord connecting him to Tessa humming contentedly in his chest.

After several minutes of tense silence, Luka said, "She is fighting the bond, Theon. You would have been better off choosing a Fae who wanted this life. You should have dismissed her as an option the moment she told you she did not find being a Source the honor it is portrayed to be."

Theon ground his molars, a muscle flexing in his jaw. Luka had tried to tell him this on more than one occasion. He had sent Luka to look in on the various Fae when they had narrowed the list down. He had also had him gather information on the Fae the other heirs were leaning towards. That had to account for some of Tessa's resistance. The other heirs had spent the last few years building relationships with their potential Sources. Those Fae had been expecting this, already trusting their heir. It hadn't come as a surprise like it had for Tessa.

Luka had pointed out the various Fae to Theon as they'd watched them mill about in the hours before the Selection Ceremony. They left the Arius Kingdom so rarely that few would recognize him. And with the excitement of the Selection in the air, they easily went unnoticed.

Luka had pushed for him to choose a male named Jaxson Caeso. The only mark he'd had against him was that he was likely to emerge with the air element. Well, that, and he was male. Theon was leaning towards a water elemental, and a male Source wasn't ideal in his case. But he could get creative about the physical side of the bond if needed. They could bring others into the bedroom to satisfy that need. Even observing the male when he'd sought him out made him the more logical choice. He had a warrior's build, perfect for the role of protecting and defending. Theon knew the Falein Heir and the Serafina Heir had watched him for a while as well. Jaxson would be perfect for them, but Theon didn't need a guard of any sort. Not like the other heirs did.

He had been ready to agree with Luka, ready to make his choice, but he'd insisted on finding Tessalyn first. Just to make sure. She'd been the only one he hadn't been able to track down. It had been pure coincidence that he'd stumbled upon her on his way back from washing his hands after another Legacy had bumped into him and caused wine to spill over the side of his glass and all over his hand.

He'd watched as she'd slipped from that side door, looking stunning in that black and emerald gown that fit her body like a glove, showing off every dip and curve. And then she'd flitted into that alcove faster than a hummingbird, piquing his curiosity even more. She'd been tucked so far back that if he hadn't seen her go in there, he wouldn't have noticed her when passing by. He couldn't believe his eyes when he'd found her smuggling chocolate of all things. He'd been irritated when she'd acted surprised at getting caught. He'd been annoyed when she wouldn't speak, more than ready to walk away and choose Jaxson.

Then he'd been intrigued beyond all reason when she did open her mouth and wave that piece of chocolate in his face. Five minutes in that alcove with her and he'd known she'd be coming home with him.

He'd lost track of her when she'd gone back to the grand hall. When he'd told Luka of her, Luka had insisted they look over the files one last time. But when Theon's gaze had landed on her, when he'd found her leaning against another male and he'd felt the prickle of irritation at seeing another's hands on her, he'd known it was over.

He'd watched as a small smile had graced her full lips when she'd said something to the male, and then her eyes had connected with his. Turbulent grey eyes the color of stormy skies. He could see them clearly from across the room. They widened slightly at being caught not paying attention to the entering ruling families, and he'd smirked at her, giving her a slight nod.

Luka had pulled her file from the space between realms with his magic, opening it quickly while cursing under his breath about not being able to use their tablets in the Pantheon. It was tradition to keep the sacred ceremony as similar as possible to the first one centuries ago.

The Priestesses begrudgingly allowed phones to receive incoming calls in case of emergencies, but that was it.

He'd scanned the documents in the folder. Tessalyn Ausra. She'd come to the Celeste Estate when she was eight like most other Fae. Before that, she'd been housed in one of the estate group homes, which wasn't all that uncommon. Only a quarter of the Fae were raised in a familial home, and most of those were in the Anala Kingdom. Her marks throughout lessons were some of the highest among her peers. She was clearly clever to evade the wards. She had air element tendencies, which was disappointing. But if he had to choose between having a male at his side for the rest of his life or a female, the choice was obvious.

"I don't think it's a good idea, Theon," Luka had said. "She's not going to want this life. She told you that. She'll become a hindrance to the plans."

"How could she not want this life? She'll be provided with everything she needs. She'll be taken care of and protected. It is a Fae's greatest honor to be Selected as a Source," Theon had countered, his eyes landing on her once more. Ignoring the fact that she had told him just that in the alcove— that she did not wish to be Selected, would not find it honorable. They'd begun drifting towards the entrance, knowing his parents would arrive at any moment. Normally Axel would be here as well, but there was opportunity to be had when all the ruling families were preoccupied with this. Opportunity they planned to capitalize on, so Axel had been doing just that while they'd all been at the Acropolis.

"Go with Jaxson," Luka had hissed under his breath as they'd moved.

"No. I am going to go with her," he'd replied, pulling his tie from the pocket between realms and looping it around his neck.

"Fuck, Theon. Think with your head, not your dick. I get that she is more desirable than a male. Maybe you can still fuck her before we leave, but she is not the one for this," Luka had argued. "Think about this before you make your choice."

And he had. He'd thought about what he knew about the bond. He'd spent as many hours researching the bond as he had debating options. It would demand closeness— emotionally, mentally, and physically. He knew the Source and Master craved each other on an intense level. More than once he'd caught his father and his Source in…intimate situations. If this bond was going to come to that, he'd rather have it with

RAIN OF SHADOWS AND ENDINGS   63

her than Jaxson Caeso. The bond would make her want that too, so he'd Selected her.

And then she'd tried to godsdamn run from him.

He'd run into Luka in the corridor, two overnight bags in his hands. The male had arched a brow at Theon's obvious fury, and when Theon had told him Tessa had climbed out a fucking window, Luka had sighed, shoving the bags at him.

"I told you to pick Jaxson," Luka had said, before turning and setting off to track her down.

Staring out the window now, he watched the scenery pass by. Vegetation was green as one would expect at the end of summer despite the black mountains and grey plains. They just didn't have to endure the stifling heat some of the other kingdoms had.

Theon turned his phone over in his hand, finding no new notifications. "Have you heard from Axel?" he asked Luka, who was messing around with his own phone and switching the music.

"No."

"Are you going to be a moody bastard the entire drive?"

"Probably."

"For fuck's sake," Theon muttered under his breath, bringing up his message thread with his brother.

"Don't bother him right now," Luka said.

"What if something is wrong?"

"What are we going to do about it from here?"

He had a point. There was nothing they'd be able to do until they were back at Arius House. Axel could handle this, and if he was in the middle of something important, they didn't need to be interrupting him. He may be gone on business for his father, but he was also working on things for their own plans. If he got caught doing any of *that*...

Once this Source bond was in place, it wouldn't matter.

"Once we get home and get Tessa settled, I'll get in touch with him," Luka said after a tense moment.

"Yeah, all right," Theon muttered, flipping his phone over again and checking for any new messages.

Tessa began stirring beside him, and Theon tensed, preparing for the worst. "Get ready to pull over if needed," he said to Luka, who nodded in acknowledgement.

Tessa's eyes fluttered open, and she ran a hand down her face. Her makeup was smeared, and she had dark smudges of eyeliner and mascara across her cheeks.

"Where are we?" she murmured.

"We are on our way home," he answered softly. "How are you feeling?"

She was quiet for a long moment before she answered, "My entire body hurts, and my throat is on fire."

"Are you going to be sick?" Theon asked, helping her as she struggled to sit upright.

"I… I don't think so," she replied, pulling the blanket tightly around herself and putting space between them. The cord in his chest immediately tightened in protest at the distance. He knew they were both in the adjustment period, and that eventually they'd be able to spend periods of time apart without the bond being so intense. But right now, he just wanted her next to him. He wanted to feel her against him to appease the bond.

"Where are we going?" she asked, huffing a piece of hair from her face and pulling him from his distracted thoughts.

"Home," Theon answered.

"Where is your home located?"

Theon shifted, his fingers flexing as he fought the urge to reach for her. "The House of Arius is in the Ozul Mountains."

"I figured as much," she replied dryly. "*Where* in the mountains?"

"North of a small town called Castle Pines, which is about an hour from Rockmoor."

"Hmm," was her only response.

"But you are not allowed to reveal that to anyone, and I will need—"

"I am sure I will need to swear some type of oath to make sure I don't reveal your secrets," she interrupted, turning to look out the window. She was right, so Theon didn't say anything in response to that. "It's dark out," she muttered, frowning slightly.

"It is nearing dawn," Luka said.

Tessa nodded, wincing at the movement.

"You are in pain," Theon observed.

"I just said my entire body hurts," she said flatly. "How much longer will we be traveling?"

"Half the day at least, depending on how often we need to stop," Luka answered.

Tessa nodded again, sliding down the seat some more and resting her head against the window, her eyes drifting closed. Every inch she moved away from him, Theon felt the bond tighten in his chest. He wanted to tell her to come back to him, but thought better of it. He wasn't entirely sure how she would react, and if he were being honest, her lack of impulse control intrigued him. He needed to learn how to read her, to anticipate her actions.

Silence fell, and Luka kept glancing back at them in the rearview mirror. After a few minutes, she lifted her head and looked down, shifting the blanket. "I'm in different clothing."

"Yes," Theon confirmed. "Your other ones were soaked in sweat from the vomiting and...everything else. We thought you would want fresh clothing."

"*You* changed my clothing?" she gasped, clearly horrified.

"Luka and I did."

"Oh my gods," she moaned, dragging a hand down her face. "That crosses so many boundaries, Theon."

He couldn't help the shiver that ran down his spine when his name fell from her lips.

"You are my Source, Tessa. I am going to take care of you."

She stiffened at his words. Luka sighed from the front seat, shaking his head. Theon reached down to the small cooler on the floor, pulling out another bottle of water. He removed the cap before handing it to her. "Drink. You need to rehydrate after all the vomiting."

Tessa took the water without a word, sipping at it and wincing with every swallow. Eventually she handed it back to him and rested her head against the window, closing her eyes once more.

"You should lie back down. Rest some more," he encouraged.

"I need to get out and move around," she answered. "I need... I just need to get out."

"We can't stop—"

"There is a small town coming up," Luka cut in from the front seat. "We can stop there for a few minutes."

"Thank you, Luka," she murmured.

Theon glared at him, catching his gaze in the rearview mirror, and Luka gave him a look that said, '*Really, you jackass?*'

A short time later, they pulled into a small convenience station. This was a predominantly mortal town, and there were already people moving about before sunrise. This wasn't a total waste of time, he supposed. They could refuel the vehicle and get breakfast to eat as they continued on their way.

Luka slid out of the driver's seat, pulling open the back door and reaching for Tessa's hand to help her out. Theon exited out of the other side, quickly rounding the back of the vehicle to take her from him. She was weak from everything, and she practically fell into Luka's arms.

"Easy, little one," he murmured, his hands holding her tightly around the waist. "Let me know when you're steady."

Theon gritted his teeth, forcing himself to stay back and wait.

Until he saw the silent tears tracking down her cheeks.

"Tessa," he breathed, stepping forward and reaching for her, but she shrank away from him, recoiling into Luka's chest.

He stilled. He had no idea what to do. She was his Source. Why was she leaning on Luka? Why was she letting him support her? The bond was thrashing in his chest, demanding he take her back.

"Tessa, come here," he demanded, holding out his hand to her. "Luka needs to refuel the vehicle."

"Give her a minute, Theon," Luka said. "She is obviously in pain."

"And it would lessen if I were touching her. The bond would at least settle down, easing some of the discomfort," Theon retorted. "Give her to me."

"Give her a fucking minute. She doesn't even have shoes on to be walking around out here. Get yourself under control."

Theon glared at him before glancing down at her bare feet. His lips pursed, turning and stalking to the back of the vehicle. He opened the back, grabbing a pair of socks and sneakers from one of the bags.

When he rounded the vehicle once more, Luka was murmuring something too low for him to hear. Theon cleared his throat. "Shoes," he said, holding them up for her to see.

"I don't want to put on socks," she replied, shaking her head. "Don't you have a pair of sandals I could slip on? Flip-flops or something?"

Flip-flops? As if she'd ever be allowed to wear something so informal again. Not as an heir's Source. She was as royal as a Fae could get now.

"No," Theon answered. "All I have for you right now are these or the heels you wore for the Selection. You will have more options when we get home, although still no...flip-flops."

Fresh tears pooled in her eyes, and Theon could not understand for the life of him why she was crying about having to put on shoes. He sighed. "Tessa, just come here. You can sit, and I will put them on for you."

"Just go in and buy her a pair of flip-flops, Theon. It's a convenience store. I am sure they have a pair somewhere," Luka said, still supporting Tessa as she clung to him.

"I am not buying a pair of godsdamn flip-flops," he snarled. "These shoes are perfectly acceptable."

Luka bent his head, murmuring something into Tessa's ear. She nodded before he helped her back into the vehicle and shut the door. He stalked past Theon.

"What the fuck are you doing?" Theon demanded.

"I'm going to buy her a pair of godsdamn flip-flops, Theon," he retorted, not bothering to look back at him.

How in the fuck had he become the bad guy over a pair of godsdamn shoes? Flip-flops couldn't even be considered shoes.

He prowled to the backseat door and yanked on the handle, but she had locked it.

"Tessa," he called out. "Unlock the door." No clicking sounded to tell him she'd obeyed. "Tessa," he growled again. "Do not make me force you to do this."

Still silence greeted him.

"Tessalyn, *unlock the door now*," he snarled, forced to entrance her. A few seconds followed before a faint click sounded. He tugged on the door handle, but it was still locked.

Theon turned and yelled a curse to the sky as he realized she'd outmaneuvered the entrancing and unlocked the door on the opposite side of the vehicle. He slammed his fist into the windshield washer fluid container, knocking it clean off the pole it was poorly attached to.

"That will definitely make her more comfortable around you," came Luka's voice from behind him.

"Do not fucking talk to me, asshole. You are interfering with the bonding," Theon snapped, whirling on him. He held a pair of bright purple flip-flops in his hand.

"I hate to break it to you, but you're doing a fine job of interfering with the bonding all on your own, jackass," he retorted, brushing past him.

"Not with you being the fucking hero, coming to her rescue, and buying her godsdamn flip-flops."

"You could have been the hero and gotten her the godsdamn flip-flops yourself," Luka shot back, tapping gently on the window and holding said flip-flops up for Tessa to see.

He heard the lock click, and Luka pulled the door open. He slid the things onto her feet, then helped Tessa out of the vehicle once more. She seemed a little steadier, but she still clung to Luka, glancing at Theon nervously from behind thick lashes.

"Go stretch your legs with Theon while I refuel the vehicle," Luka encouraged gently, guiding her towards Theon. She resisted, but she was so weak, it did nothing. "I'll be right here, little one," he added, and Theon clenched his teeth at the fact that Luka had to persuade his own godsdamn Source to come near him. She was supposed to want this as much as he did.

Finally relenting, she allowed Theon to slip an arm around her waist, the bond immediately calming down in his chest and resuming its contented hum. She walked slowly, gingerly placing her feet down while she went. He couldn't help but think that the sneakers he had for her would be more comfortable than fucking flip-flops, but he bit his tongue, not wanting to drive her away from him again.

They didn't say anything as they walked beneath the obscenely bright lights, but she wouldn't let him steer her too far from Luka. When Theon couldn't stand the silence anymore, he asked, "Is it helping? Walking around and stretching your legs?"

"Mhmm," she hummed, stumbling a bit and causing Theon to tighten his grip on her.

"Careful, beautiful. You don't want to overdo it. Maybe we should head back to the vehicle."

"I need to use the restroom."

Theon sighed internally. Why hadn't he thought of that? They could have been making their way there. He whistled low at Luka and jerked his chin at the convenience store, and Luka nodded in acknowledgement that he'd meet them inside.

It took a few minutes to make it to the building and then make their way to the restrooms in the back. He opened the door to follow her in, but she pressed a hand to his chest.

"You're not coming in here," she said, her eyes saying there was no negotiating on this.

"Tessa, you cannot even stand on your own," he argued anyway.

"No. Absolutely not. It's bad enough you changed my clothes while I was unconscious. This is not happening." She may have been arguing with him, but she sounded utterly exhausted. Smoothing back her hair, the black Mark, *his* Mark, stood out starkly against her fair skin.

"Five minutes, Tessa," he finally agreed.

"Turtles move faster than me right now. I'm going to need more time than that," she sighed.

"Fine. Seven."

Tessa sighed heavily again, shrugging out of his hold. "Whatever."

The cord in his chest immediately went taut when the door closed behind her. He tried to keep himself busy, perusing the coolers and shelves of junk food, but still found himself checking his watch every thirty seconds. Luka showed up when she was four minutes into her allotted seven.

"Want one?" he asked, holding out a bag of doughnuts sprinkled with sugar.

"Those aren't good for you," Theon replied.

"Legacy," Luka said mockingly, jabbing a thumb into his chest. "This is not what's going to kill me."

He made a valid point. With their extended lifespans and self-healing abilities, Legacy weren't susceptible to the diseases and ailments that plagued the mortals. The Fae were generally healthy, too, as well as having extended lifespans, but they still fell ill from time to time. He'd make sure Tessa ate well and ate properly to ensure she stayed healthy. He told her he took care of what was his, and he meant it.

The seven minute mark hit, and she didn't emerge.

Then eight minutes.

Then nine.

At ten minutes, even Luka began looking concerned and agreed they should check on her. Theon didn't waste a second, knocking once before pushing open the door to the restroom.

"Tessa? I gave you ten minutes," he called out, immediately looking around for windows, relieved when there were none. He probably should have checked for those first given her earlier disappearing act, but since she could scarcely move, he hadn't been overly concerned.

The sound of sniffling and soft whimpering came from the last stall in the row, and he followed it. "Tessa?" he called again, pushing on the door. Of course it was locked. "Tessa, are you all right?" When she didn't answer, he sighed. "Tessa, unlock the door."

The sound of the latch sliding followed a moment later, and he pushed the stall door open. Tessa was sitting on the closed toilet lid with tears streaming down her face. Her arms were wrapped tightly around herself, and she was doubled over, rocking back and forth.

Theon lowered into a crouch before her, taking her face in his hands. "Tessa, what's wrong?"

"It hurts," she whimpered. "Everything hurts."

"Tessa," he sighed, pulling her into his arms, but she stiffened against him.

"My skin hurts. My hair hurts. I didn't know hair could hurt, but mine does. These tight clothes against my skin hurt. It's why I didn't want to wear the sneakers. I didn't want the feel of the socks on my skin. I wasn't trying to be a pain in the ass," she sobbed into his shoulder, her entire body tense and rigid against him.

"Shh," he said, trying to soothe her. "It's okay, Tessa."

"It's not okay," she cried. "None of this is okay. I'm miserable. I feel like I was hit by a truck. Now I have to travel for hours. Can't you use your magic and heal me like you did before?"

He shook his head, the bond humming at her closeness despite her obvious misery. "I can't, Tessa. Your body is reacting to my magic. If I flooded it with more, it would make it worse. *Any* magic right now would make it worse."

She didn't say anything. Just kept sobbing into his shoulder. He pulled his phone from his pocket, sending a quick message to Luka asking him to get his sweatshirt from the vehicle.

"We can stop as often as you need to if it helps to get out and move around," he said when he finished.

"Gods, Theon," she bit out. "Don't act like you actually care." She pushed off of him, struggling to her feet.

"Of course I care. I am here, aren't I?" he retorted, getting to his feet and backing up so she could exit the stall. When she made it past him, she moved to the sink, turning the tap on and splashing water across her face, wiping at the ruined makeup. Theon retrieved paper towels for her, handing them over.

As she wiped her face, he took a breath and tried again. "I care, Tessa. You are my Source. I take care of what is mine."

She whirled on him, nearly falling over as she lost her balance. Theon shot forward, catching her before she hit her head on the basin, but she shoved his hands off of her, backing up against the wall.

"I am not yours," she snarled, her features twisting into a fury that was really quite remarkable considering how weak she was.

"Of course you are mine, Tessa. I Selected you. You bear my Mark," he retorted, nodding at her right hand.

She looked down, staring at the back of her hand. Fresh tears fell onto the black Mark as she stared at it, slowly sinking down to the floor when it became too painful to remain standing. She didn't even look up when Luka came through the door, Theon's sweatshirt in his hand. He threw Theon an accusatory glare, coming to a halt at the sight of Tessa sitting on the dirty floor of a convenience store bathroom.

Theon sighed for the millionth time and pulled his t-shirt over his head. He lowered down before Tessa, reaching out to lift her chin. She winced at his touch, which was the exact opposite of how his body reacted to him touching her again. His bond purred and hummed in pleasure. He held up the shirt to show her.

"Let's put this on. It will be big on you, so the material won't rub on your skin. I do not have looser pants for you though," he said. Tessa just stared back at him, and something seemed fractured in the grey eyes that held his own. When she said nothing, he reached for the hem of the sweatshirt she was wearing. "Let's get this off, okay?"

As gently as he could and touching her as little as possible, he removed the sweatshirt, then the shirt beneath it. He didn't offer to remove the bra, assuming she wouldn't appreciate that after her reaction to them changing her clothing earlier. Theon slipped his shirt over her head, guiding her arms through the sleeves. Then he reached behind him for the sweatshirt Luka still held.

"Do you want this?" he asked, holding it up. She nodded once, and he helped her into it. "Are you ready to stand?" She bit her bottom lip, her eyes falling to the floor, and Theon glanced up at Luka who just shrugged, clearly not knowing what was going on either. "Tessa, are you ready to go?" Theon tried again.

"I'm tired, and my skin hurts," she murmured, drawing her hands into the sleeves of his sweatshirt that was far too big for her.

"I know. We can go," he replied. "I will help you up."

She let him pull her up and loop an arm around her waist again, but when she stumbled three times just crossing the restroom, Theon stopped and scooped her into his arms. She didn't protest, settling against his bare chest.

Luka helped him get her back into the vehicle. Theon moved to put the clothing she'd been wearing into the back and dug out another shirt for himself, then moved to get in on the other side. But when he opened the door, he froze. She was in the process of peeling the black leggings off.

"What are you doing, Tessa?"

"My skin hurts," she whimpered, ripping the material off her foot before moving to the other leg and trying to work the fabric down.

Luka was already sliding back out of the front seat and opening the back door, helping her slide the leggings the rest of the way off. She sighed in relief, Theon's sweatshirt pooling in her lap. Her bare legs captured Theon's attention, and all he could do for a moment was stare.

Luka reached over her, grabbing the fleece blanket and draping it over her lap. "Better?" he asked gently.

Tessa nodded, and Theon climbed into the backseat. They had been stopped longer than he'd wanted, and the sun was already breaking the horizon. They wouldn't be getting back to Arius House until evening at this rate.

Tessa leaned her head against the window again, her eyes drifting shut.

"Tessa, come lie down. You will be more comfortable," he said, reaching for her.

"No," she murmured, not even opening her eyes to look at him.

"Damnit, Tessa. It will help with the pain. It is part of the bond," he replied, trying not to lose his temper again.

"I'm fine, Theon."

"Tessa."

"Theon," she parroted.

He was done messing around. She made him feel like he had no control. The Source bond was jerking in his chest, demanding he close the distance between them, despite having just carried her to the vehicle minutes ago.

"Tessa, do not make me force this. Come here."

And that's when Tessa lost her fucking mind.

Her hands came up into her hair. She grabbed fistfuls of the golden locks and pulled, tilting her head back and screaming in utter rage and ruin to the heavens.

"Holy fuck!" Luka cursed, swerving over to the side of the road. Big, fat drops of rain had begun falling against the windows, sounding like rocks each time one hit. Theon's eyes were wide as he watched his Source utterly fall apart.

"Theon, do something!" Luka barked, staring at Tessa in disbelief. "She's going to rip her hair out."

"Tessa, stop it!" Theon snapped, flying across the seat and reaching for her wrists. But that caused her to grimace, and instead of screams of rage, she cried out in pain, keeping her hair firmly in her grasp. The rain was pouring now, making all the noise in the vehicle chaotic. Theon had to yell to be heard over her screaming and the pounding rain. "Tessalyn, *stop it! Stop!*"

Her screaming ceased immediately, and she released her hair, collapsing against him. He gathered her into his arms, leaning into the seat and resting his head back, closing his eyes as she panted against him. This would forever go down as being the longest day of his life, and he'd had some pretty shitty days.

Eventually, the rain let up some, and Luka eased back onto the road. Tessa's breathing evened out. He was exhausted. He couldn't imagine how Tessa felt. Although to be fair, Theon and Luka had made it a point to sleep most of the afternoon yesterday before the Selection Ceremony began. Neither of them had been entirely sure how the bonding would play out, but he knew neither of them had expected anything like this.

Mile after mile passed, and Tessa didn't stir in his arms. He couldn't get the image out of his head of her pulling at her hair and screaming. Every time he closed his eyes, he saw her doing just that, so he gave up on closing them, watching the familiar scenery pass by the window.

Tessa had become so still, he thought she had fallen asleep. So when her voice drifted up to him, hoarse from screaming, as they neared Sinvons Lake, he stiffened.

"Is this how it's going to be? When I don't act the way you desire, you will just entrance me?"

His jaw clenched. "If you would simply listen when I ask you to do something, this would not be an issue, Tessa," he finally ground out. He felt her tense at his words and try to push away from him, but he tightened his hold, keeping her in place. "Don't, Tessa. Don't do this. The bond wants us touching right now. It is how it strengthens and forms."

Still she struggled against him, and Theon couldn't believe she was fighting him on this yet again. "For the love of the gods, yes! If you are going to act like a petulant child, I am going to treat you like a petulant child. Stop or I will force you to stop."

She sucked in a sharp breath at the words and stilled in his arms.

After a full minute of silence, he heard her whisper, "As you wish, Master."

Luka was shaking his head, his shoulders tense and eyes fixed on the road, clearly disapproving of everything that had just happened. Theon rested his head back against the seat once more, closing his eyes. He had a Source, yes, but so far, that was the only thing that had gone according to his plans.

6

TESSA

She slept off and on for the rest of the drive. At least when she was sleeping, she didn't register the pain. When she was awake, she wanted to peel the skin from her bones. Tessa was certain that would be less painful than what she was currently experiencing. The sunlight hurt her eyes, and she longed for the darkness of night. She was freezing despite the layers she was wrapped up in, so she thought she might have a fever too. She didn't know for sure. Being Fae, she'd never experienced what true sickness felt like, but if it felt like this, she pitied every mortal in existence.

She'd stopped fighting with Theon. It was too exhausting, and he was right. Being close to him eased some of the physical discomfort. Internally, though, she was screaming at his touch. He made her drink water throughout the trip, insisting she needed to hydrate. He offered her food — fruit, cheese, crackers. She turned it all down. She said it was because she was nauseous, but she really just had no appetite. He would ask how she was feeling, but when her answer was repeatedly "fine," he eventually stopped asking.

She made no requests to stop again, but Luka made sure they did anyway. Every hour without fail, he'd pull into the next available stop. If she slept through the hour mark, he stopped as soon as he realized she had woken. Sometimes the stops were just pulling off on a side road. She would walk among the trees in only Theon's sweatshirt that stopped mid-thigh and the flip-flops Luka had purchased for her, clutching the blanket tightly around herself. Another time, they stopped in Rockmoor, one of the few widely known cities in the Arius Kingdom. Theon disappeared for a while there. The cord inside her may have had a fit, but she had breathed easier for the first time since her name had been called at the Pantheon. He returned with a pair of loose linen pants. He helped her slip them on, then slid the flip-flops back onto her feet. One would almost think he was trying to make up for being a complete dick.

The Ozul Mountains were beautiful though. Not bleak and dreary like she'd always assumed they would be. She couldn't remember being anywhere outside of the Celeste Estate and the surrounding forest it was nestled in. She'd been to Arobell, of course, the capital city of the Celeste Kingdom. But the Fae Estate was located on the outskirts of it, right on Lake Moonmist. She'd tried to breathe in lungfuls of the fresh mountain air whenever she could, but her throat and chest hurt too much, so she'd ended up just pulling the hood of the sweatshirt up to block the sunlight from her sensitive eyes. When they got back into the vehicle, she'd immediately fallen back asleep. Even ten minutes of walking made her exhausted.

"Tessa." There were fingers trailing along her cheek and jaw, and the blanket was being tugged off her. "I need you to wake up, beautiful."

Tessa forced herself to open her heavy eyelids and found Theon's emerald gaze fixed intently on her. She blinked at him, confused as to why he was waking her up when all he'd done the entire day was tell her she needed to rest. A soft smile tilted at the corner of his mouth. He brushed hair off of her face, tucking it behind her ear.

"What's happening?" Tessa murmured, her voice thick with sleep.

"We will be home in the next hour."

Home.

If she had the energy, she'd scoff at the term. Her home was with Dex and Oralia, with Brecken, Lange, and Corbin. Arius House would never be her *home*. Rather than say any of that though, she opted for silence and just stared back at him.

The small smile fell from his lips, and he shoved a hand through his dark hair. "My parents are going to be there. They will greet us upon arrival."

"Okay..." Tessa ventured, sensing there was more to this admission than that.

"There is a small shopping district in Castle Pines. You are going to need to change," Theon said.

Tessa held in the whimper. She could hardly stand the touch of these loose-fitting clothes against her skin. The thought of changing clothes made her cringe. Shaking her head, she squeezed her eyes shut. "No," she whispered past the burning sensation clawing up her throat. "It hurts too much. Please don't make me change right now."

A pitying look filled Theon's eyes. "My father will not react well to seeing you in this type of clothing. Luka and I are changing as well. As soon as we have greeted them, I will take you straight to our rooms, and you can put on more comfortable clothing again."

"I..." She squeezed her eyes tighter, feeling the tears well. Gods. She never cried like this. Lange would tease her relentlessly if he knew. Her heart squeezed at the thought, and she pulled the blanket up around her shoulders, wrapping herself up tightly. She'd lost her godsdamn mind earlier, crying her despair to the gods that didn't give a fuck about her or this world, the screaming in her head finally finding its way out. She couldn't do that again. Too many things happened when she lost control like that. It was why Dex hated it when she went off by herself.

Her entire body was trembling, and she'd never been more glad she'd refused food. The cord in her chest was getting agitated at the space she'd placed between her and Theon, and she wished she could reach inside herself and yank the godsdamn thing out.

"Take a breath, Tessa," Theon was saying, and she opened her eyes to find him reaching for her. She jerked back instinctively, and the bond shocked her. A godsdamn jolt went through her body that made her whimper and curl in on herself even more.

"Tessa." Theon's tone betrayed his exasperation as she felt the vehicle slowing and coming to a halt. He didn't say anything else, only stared at her.

"It will be best to meet his parents looking as presentable as possible," Luka said, twisting in the front seat to face her. His eyes held the same pitying look Theon had given her. "If you greet them in what you are wearing, the occasion will be drawn out longer than necessary, and you will suffer more."

They seemed to take her silence as acceptance, and they both exited the vehicle. Luka helped her out while Theon went to get whatever was considered acceptable clothing from the back.

"How do you have clothing in my size? Theon didn't even know who I was until he found me in the alcove," she said to Luka as he held her steady.

He seemed surprised by her question, but quickly wiped the reaction from his face. "When Theon took you to the room for the first dose of tonic, I left to get items for you from a list that Theon gave to me," Luka explained.

"Oh."

That still didn't explain how he knew her sizes when he'd only met her that night. She was also trying to figure out how Luka fit into all this. He wasn't a member of the ruling family, but was obviously close to them. A cousin of some sort? An Arius Legacy of lesser power to drive Theon around and run errands for him? But Theon seemed to value his opinion, and there was a quiet intensity about him that made Tessa wary, despite his somewhat gentle actions since she'd met him.

Luka led her around the vehicle to Theon. He had clothing in his hand, and he passed it off to Luka so that he could help her. They slowly made their way to a row of buildings along the road advertising various wares and services. Tessa was simply enjoying being out of the vehicle when another thought occurred to her.

"Your parents were at the feast."

Theon glanced down at her. "Yes, they were."

"Then how are they back already? They couldn't have gotten back that much sooner than we did."

"My father shadow-walked them back to Arius House."

"Shadow-walked?"

"It is best explained as his personal portal," Theon answered. "It is something he can only do when drawing from his Source, and it takes a fair amount of power so he does not do it often."

"And you... You will be able to do that? When you draw from me?" Tessa asked.

Theon glanced down at her again. "Yes. When you have all the Marks and the bond has been completed, I will be able to access all the gifts of Arius. Not often, and only for short periods of time. It drains both the Legacy and the Source to tap into the other gifts."

Tessa fell silent, not knowing what to say to any of that. She hadn't known that the ruling descendants could do that. They'd been taught that the Legacy were gifted one power from the strongest bloodline that ran in their veins. The ruling families were granted two or three gifts, but she hadn't known that they could access *all* of them. That was...

Tessa didn't have words for what that was.

Theon and Luka led her among the small collection of shops to a little clothing boutique. It was simple and elegant, nothing like what Tessa had been expecting, and Theon appeared to know the Fae behind the counter. She bowed to him, and when Theon requested use of one of the fitting rooms, she replied, "Of course, my Lord."

Theon took the clothing from Luka and led her to a room, the door clicking shut behind him. She should have argued about him coming in here with her, but she knew it'd be futile. He would insist on helping her change, and she knew it would take her far too long to do so by herself.

He set the clothing bundle down on a small chair and helped her remove the sweatshirt, his t-shirt, and the lounge pants. When she was standing in nothing but undergarments, shivering with the chills from her fever, Theon turned and picked up a dress. Tessa couldn't hold back the soft whimper this time. It was a deep amethyst and clearly form fitting. There was delicate silver beading woven throughout it. She could tell from the plunging neckline that there would be a lot of skin on display.

Theon stepped forward, and Tessa cringed.

"I know it is going to be uncomfortable, Tessa, but it is only for a bit. You can take it off at the first opportunity."

He crouched down so she could step into the dress, biting her tongue as he worked the fabric up her legs and over her hips. He gently turned her so her back was facing him, and she eased the bra off, breathing in through her nose and out through her teeth at the movements. When the dress was fully on, the brushing of his fingers along her spine as he zipped the back made the bond purr with pleasure, and she fought against the urge to step back into him, to feel him pressed up against her.

Theon turned her once more so she was facing the mirror that had been hung on the wall. She had to admit the dress was beautiful. If it didn't feel like she was wearing shards of glass right now, she would say she actually liked it. She met Theon's gaze in the mirror and found his eyes dark, his pupils dilated as he drank her in. They lingered on the plunging neckline before dropping to her legs. The dress stopped just above her knees, and she felt far too exposed. She had never worn anything like this.

When he finally dragged his eyes back to hers, his voice was thick as he said, "You are stunning, Tessa." His hands were still on her waist where he'd placed them to turn her, and now they slipped down a few inches to her hips, his thumbs running along the upper swells of her backside. "Simply stunning."

Her eyes narrowed on his in the mirror. "I look like a gutter rat, Theon," she replied, noting her limp and messy hair and tired eyes.

"No, beautiful," he said, shaking his head. "You look like salvation and temptation all rolled into one."

Tessa felt her cheeks grow hot, and she broke his stare, her eyes dropping to the floor. "Can you get me a brush? Hair tie? Hair pins? Things so I can at least look somewhat presentable for greeting a Lord and Lady?"

Theon nodded, and as she moved to sit in the lone chair, he went to the door and spoke quietly with Luka. When he came back, he crouched before her once more, picking up the flip-flops. "You will have to wear proper footwear when we get there, but you can put these back on for now."

"At least there are no socks," she muttered under her breath.

"Is your aversion to socks solely because of how you are feeling right now?" he asked, sliding the other flip-flop on.

"No. I mean, that is the biggest issue right now, yes. But I don't like socks in general. I don't like the feeling of them on my feet. It's just…gross."

He looked up at her, his hands coming to rest gently on her knees. "Socks are gross?" he asked, amusement in his tone.

"I wear them, obviously, but I take them off as soon as possible. I don't even really like shoes. I prefer to simply be barefoot."

"Socks are bad. You get difficult when you are hungry. What else do I need to know?" he asked, reaching up and tucking a strand of hair behind her ear.

She met his gaze at the question, his hand lingering on her cheek. "That I'm not your salvation or your temptation. I'm not *your* anything."

His features hardened at her words, and his jaw clenched. "We both know that is not true, Tessa," he finally said, brushing his thumb along her lower lip. Then he reached for her right hand and brought it to his lips, pressing them to the Mark there. Her breath hitched at the feel of his mouth on her skin. He rubbed his thumb along the Mark, studying it for a moment before he brought his eyes back to hers and said, "You can fight it all you want, but you are going to belong to me. Every piece of you."

A knock on the door had him rising to unlock it. Luka handed him a small brush and hair pins. She quickly brushed out her hair before twisting it into a quick and simple knot at the nape of her neck. She secured it with a few pins while Theon leaned against the wall with his arms crossed, watching and waiting. When she finished, he gave her to Luka, who had already changed into a black suit like he'd worn at the Selection Ceremony. While Theon was changing, Luka led her to a small bathroom where she quickly brushed her teeth and took care of personal needs.

Theon was emerging from the dressing room in his finery when she came out of the bathroom, and she was ushered back out to the vehicle. He tucked the blanket around her, pulling her into his side to lend her his body heat, and she blew out a breath as the bond urged her to take more. To touch more. To *want* more.

Tessa knew she should be nervous. Theon and Luka certainly made the Arius Lord sound intimidating enough, and she'd seen Theon's father at the Selection. She should be feeling all kinds of apprehension and anxiety, but she couldn't say that she felt much of anything beyond exhaustion at this point. A familiar numbness was settling into her soul despite her best efforts to keep it at bay.

The trek to the Arius House was beautiful. Twilight had set in, the sun low and nearly behind the mountains now. When Luka turned onto a road bordered by trees so thick it was like turning into a tunnel, Theon leaned down and grabbed the pair of black heels she'd worn the night prior. Tessa's feet hurt just looking at them.

Theon helped her change out of the flip-flops, then brought his hand to her cheek. "Do not speak unless spoken to, Tessa. He will expect you to kneel as is custom for the Fae before the Lords and Ladies, but you do not need to. You are in enough discomfort as it is. Do you understand?"

"I..."

It would be seen as incredibly disrespectful not to kneel when being presented to a ruling Lord.

"Do not fight me or push me away in front of him, and do not ask questions," he continued.

His features were tense and anxious, his eyes hard and urgent.

"I understand," she finally replied. He was her Master after all. What had he said? She obeyed him above all others.

"Good girl," he murmured, leaning forward and pressing a soft kiss to her brow.

Tessa pulled back from him and slid to the opposite door, looking out the window just in time to see Arius House come into view. It was massive. Made completely of grey and black stone, it was towering, even amongst the surrounding mountains. It was at least four stories high, more in some places. The west and east sides had towers reaching higher still. The length of the house itself twisted and turned amongst the mountains, making it impossible to see just how much land it occupied. Stone archways led off to various wings of the house, and she saw numerous staff, some Fae and some mortal, going about their tasks.

"You live in a castle," Tessa deadpanned, the vehicle coming to a halt in front of steps that led up to the large double entrance doors.

"It is not a castle," Theon replied.

"It has towers, Theon. It's a castle," she said, tilting her head to look up at the huge house again. "Do you live here too, Luka?"

"For all intents and purposes, yes," he answered. "I have a smaller estate an hour or so away, but I am rarely there."

"Hmm," Tessa hummed in answer just as the double doors to the house opened and two figures came striding down the front steps. She immediately recognized them. Valter looked just as he had at the Selection. His thick black hair was swept back from his face, and he was impeccably dressed in a suit and tie. His lips were curved in a vindictive smirk as he escorted his wife down the front steps.

She clung to his arm and looked exactly as a Lady should. She wore a lavender dress that showed just as much cleavage as her gown had last night. Her dark red hair hung down and flowed over her shoulders, but Tessa caught glimpses of the large diamonds that adorned her ears, matching the huge diamond pendant at her throat.

"Come, Tessa," Theon said. She hadn't realized he had exited the vehicle. So had Luka. She allowed him to help her down, and he placed her gently on her feet, letting her weak legs find their balance in the heels. "You good, beautiful?"

"As good as I can be," she murmured. He kept his arm firmly around her waist and escorted her forward. They met his parents at the foot of the stairs.

"Father," Theon said with a bow at the waist. She saw Luka do the same from the corner of her eye.

Gods. She should really be kneeling.

"Mother," Theon added with a nod of his head. "I trust your travels home were uneventful?"

"Indeed they were," Valter said, his voice deep and commanding. His dark hazel eyes were fixed on Tessa, and she dropped her gaze to the ground. "Was your Source not taught manners, Theon?"

"She was taught manners and knows she should be kneeling at the moment," Theon replied, his fingers flexing on her waist and digging painfully into her skin. "She is quite unwell after the first Mark and in a lot of pain. I ordered her not to kneel to keep her discomfort minimal."

"Is that so?" Valter asked. "And if *I* ordered her to kneel anyway?"

"I entranced her, Father." Tessa had to force herself not to react to the lie. "As she is my Source, and it is my magic that now courses through her, to try and overcome it with your own demands would be cruel."

"Indeed it would," Valter said, and his tone sent a shiver down her spine. "I guess the choice is yours then."

After a moment of tense silence, Theon gritted out through clenched teeth. "Kneel, Tessa." She lowered to a knee as quickly as she could, her dress riding up her thighs. "Is that sufficient?"

"Let's meet her then," was Valter's answer.

Theon helped her to her feet, his movements sharp and jarring, before ushering her forward. "Father. Mother. This is my Source, Tessalyn Ausra. Tessa, the Arius Lord, Valter St. Orcas, and my mother, Cressida."

Valter stepped forward and reached for Tessa's right hand, bringing it up to examine the Mark while Cressida said, "At least you have natural beauty, my dear. It overshadows the fact that your hair and face are a mess. Really, Theon? You couldn't make her at least a little presentable?"

Tessa felt her cheeks flush at her words, but before Theon could say anything in response, Valter dropped her hand, stepping back. His gaze slowly roamed over her, and Tessa had to fight to keep from cringing back from the Lord.

"I will admit, she is a beauty, son. Your mother is right. She is naturally exquisite," he finally said, and Tessa felt like she'd passed some sort of test. "I am glad you took my advice and chose an alluring one. I half expected you to choose a male Source out of spite." Valter chuckled at his own words, returning to his wife's side. His eyes never strayed from Tessa.

"While she is beautiful," Theon said curtly, "her beauty is not why I chose her, and as you both well know, she received her first Mark last night. Her simply standing before you now seems like more than should be required of her at this moment, let alone having her hair and face done."

And Tessa suddenly realized she had no idea why Theon had chosen her. She had never even thought to ask, but now that it had been brought up, she was curious. What had he seen in her in that alcove that had made him say her name? Why her out of all the other available Fae?

"I should hope her looks were not the only reason you Selected her, but a nice view by your side and keeping your bed warm doesn't hurt anything," Valter replied with a shrug.

Tessa felt her face heat once more but for an entirely different reason. She knew that Sources and their Masters often shared intimate relations as a result of the bond, but would Theon expect that of her? What was she thinking? Of course he would. Legacy took what they wanted, and he already viewed her as his. This would just be one more thing he took from her.

Valter glanced over his shoulder to his Source standing dutifully behind him. Tessa had been so preoccupied with the Lord and Lady, she hadn't even noticed the Fae. Her eyes were cast down, hands clasped before her as they had been at the Selection, but even from this angle, Tessa could tell she was pretty. Her black Marks stood out vividly against the backs of her hands. The female's red-brown hair hung loose down her back. It contrasted beautifully with her olive skin. She wore a fitted navy blue dress as low cut as Cressida's that offered the perfect view of the Mark over her heart, and Tessa knew if the female lifted her hair, a Mark would adorn the back of her neck as well.

"Eviana, come here," Valter called, and the Fae lifted her head, brilliant turquoise eyes going straight to her Master. She stepped to his side, and Valter looped his arm around her waist, tugging her close. She immediately turned into him, her hand coming to his chest.

"Yes, my Lord?"

"Meet Theon's Source, Tessalyn," he said, nodding towards Theon.

Eviana met Tessa's gaze and a flash of pity crossed her eyes before it morphed into indifference. "It's a pleasure," she replied dutifully, turning her attention right back to Valter. The Lord's hand slid from her hip to her ass, where it remained while he continued to speak to Theon.

"I bet you could still loan her out as a dam if you wanted. Make a little extra coin on the side," Valter said casually, and Tessa's head whipped to Theon.

What did that even mean? Loan her out?

Theon tugged her back to his side, practically crushing her against his ribcage. She bit down on a cry of pain.

"That will never be an option. Ever," Theon hissed.

Valter chuckled deep in his throat. "I am not surprised. Arius blood has always made us very possessive of our belongings. It was merely a suggestion. She almost certainly would have ended up one with her features, especially if she is even remotely powerful. After she had spent time in entertainment, of course."

"I guess we will never find out," Theon answered, his tone dangerously calm.

Valter smiled knowingly at his son. "She will, however, be expected to contribute to the Arius Kingdom as every other member of this household does."

"As my Source, I am sure her contribution will be sufficient."

Tessa was trying to follow what was being said between father and son, but her concentration had turned to not passing out. Her legs were growing wobbly in the shoes, and her head was throbbing. She could feel sweat beading on her brow and sliding down the nape of her neck, despite the fact that she was freezing and trying not to shiver violently against Theon. Black spots were appearing on the edges of her vision, and she was begging any god to care enough to put an end to this misery soon.

"Theon, dear," Cressida cut in smoothly. "The rest of your belongings were moved to the Source suite in the east wing, and Penelope went out this morning and gathered everything you requested for your new beauty." Her emerald green eyes flitted to Luka. "Your rooms were moved to that wing as well, Luka. I assumed that would be your desire?"

"It was. Thank you, Lady Cressida," Luka answered with a slight bow.

"Excellent," Theon chimed in. "If we are done here, I will take Tessa there so she can rest."

Thank the gods, Tessa thought, wondering just how far away this east wing was.

"I need to see you in my study, Theon," Valter said, beginning to turn away, taking Eviana with him. Cressida dropped her husband's arm, apparently content to let him go now that the show was over.

"I will come when I have gotten Tessa settled," Theon answered, starting to turn away himself.

"Now, Theon."

Theon froze. "She was just Marked last night, Father. You know the bond is still strengthening, and we are both adjusting. I would prefer to stay with her at the moment."

Valter looked over his shoulder with a smirk. "I remember the Markings well, son. Bring her with, or give her to Luka. I am sure he can take care of her until you return to finish *strengthening* your bond. Our discussion will not take long." Without waiting for an answer, Valter was striding up the steps, Eviana following him into the house.

"Don't make him wait, dear," Cressida said, reaching up and straightening Theon's tie before she turned and went up the steps as well.

Luka was already moving to Tessa's side. "I got her, Theon. Go see what he wants."

Theon looked down at her, running his hand along her brow and wiping away the moisture there before looking back at Luka. "The wards will recognize you. Help her change clothes. Everything she needs should be in the suite. If you come across something that is not there, make a list. I will send Pen out in the morning."

"I got it, Theon. Cressida is right. You don't want to keep him waiting," Luka answered.

"I will be back as soon as I can, Tessa," he said, tilting her chin up to meet his gaze. "Rest."

"I'll be fine, Theon," she sighed. "I really just need to sit down and get out of this dress."

Theon let Luka take his place beside her, and Luka instantly scooped her into his arms. Tessa sighed in relief as Theon slipped the shoes from her feet, and Luka hooked the heels on his fingers. With a tight smile, Theon turned and headed up the steps while Luka began walking along the drive.

"Where are we going?" Tessa asked in confusion.

"It's a faster route to the east wing," Luka answered. "We could go through the main house, but it's endless hallways and stairs. There is a door directly into the east wing through that archway."

Tessa followed his line of sight, noting the charcoal stones that created said archway. Silver dragons were etched into the stones. Arius was said to be particularly close with the dragons. Sargon, the god of courage and war, was also said to be able to shift into a dragon. With it being thousands of years since the gods had left this world, she had no idea what was real or legend.

"Thank you for carrying me," Tessa said softly, resting her head against Luka's shoulder.

"I'm sorry you had to endure that in your condition, Tessa," he replied. "But Valter is not a male to deny when he requests something."

"Valter does not seem like the sort of male who requests anything but rather demands everything."

"Indeed."

They passed under the archway and through a side door that led into a stairwell. As Luka started up the stairs, Tessa asked, "Was Theon lying to his father about why he chose me?"

Luka glanced down at her. "I would be lying if I said I didn't think your looks were part of it, Tessa, but I know it was not the entire reason."

"But what were the other reasons then?"

"There were several things he was looking for in his Source. Personally, I think there were better options, but when he spoke with you in that alcove, his mind was almost instantly made up."

"You make it sound like he was picking out an item at the market. *'I think there were better options,'*" she mimicked.

Luka sent her a dry look. "That mouth of yours is part of the reason I believe there were better options, little one."

Tessa glared at him as he pushed open a door. She felt wards brushing against her skin as they let them pass through. Then Tessa could only stare in shock at the opulent room before her. This wasn't a suite. It was an apartment and not a small one.

Before her was a sitting room. A large sofa, two armchairs, and a low table were to her right, facing an enclosed fireplace with a large TV mounted above it. To the right of the furniture was a billiards table, and on the wall was a dartboard. Next to the fireplace was a closed door. Off to the left was a nook nestled into a bay window that overlooked whatever was outside. On one side of the window, there was a large bookshelf in the corner with no extra space visible. On the other side was a desk, neatly organized with stacks of papers and books.

To her left was a dining table with seating for six, and running along the wall behind it was a full kitchen. A small island with two stools stood in the middle of it, and a door led to what she could only assume was a pantry.

Straight ahead of her was another doorway. It had to be Theon's bedroom. The entire space was decorated in a mixture of metal, stone, and opaque glass in varying shades of black, grey, and silver. Tasteful rugs ran in various places over the hardwood floor.

Luka lowered her onto a small bench just inside the door. She could tell he was trying to be gentle about it, but she still let out a hiss of pain at the movement. He removed his suit coat and tie, hanging them on a hook. As he began rolling back his sleeves, he said, "Right then. This is Theon's suite. There is a small bathroom through that door." He gestured to the closed door near the fireplace. "The kitchen is usually well stocked, but I don't know if the staff has done so yet. This was one of the guest wings until Theon requested his own wing when he obtained a Source." He motioned to the doorway ahead of them. "Through there is Theon's room and your room."

Tessa started at that. "My room is here? *In* his suite?"

Luka met her gaze. "You are his Source, Tessa. You will be within reach at almost all times, especially once all the Marks have been given."

"I know that. I just didn't think... I mean... I..."

Luka dropped to a crouch before her. She didn't know the male well, but she had a feeling he rarely spoke in the soft tone he used when he said, "It's going to be okay, Tessa. *You're* going to be okay. Theon will take care of you."

She said nothing, only reached up and began pulling the pins from her hair.

"I know you weren't expecting this, Tessa. I know you're miserable right now, but you can't change what's happening here. You know that, right? You need to figure out a way to live with this fate." His sapphire eyes searched hers, waiting for her to say something.

"I'm tired, Luka, and I want to get out of this dress," she finally said.

Luka sighed before pushing back to his feet. He helped her to her feet and walked her to the bedroom. It was just as grand as the sitting room had been. To the right was a large bed with grey sheets and a black comforter. A large portrait of four regal black horses hung above the bed and nightstands stood on either side.

Double doors ran along the back wall leading out to a balcony. Light grey curtains were pulled back, but it was too dark to see much of anything now. Tessa could just make out a seating area on the balcony though. A small sofa and a couple of chairs with a table between them.

To her left were two doorways. Another glass fireplace was set into the wall between them. There were two chairs before it with a small table. Luka led her over to one, and she lowered into the seat.

Pointing to the door on the left, he said, "Through there is the bathroom." He gestured to the door to the right. "Through there is your room. It's small, but it has a bed, a nightstand, and I believe a small desk. Between your room and the bathroom is a closet and dressing room. It should have all the items Theon ordered for you already in there."

Tessa nodded, too overwhelmed to do much else. When she didn't say anything, he slipped an elastic band from his wrist, gathering his hair into a small ponytail. "Let's get you out of that dress, little one."

He left her in front of the unlit fireplace, disappearing into the bathroom. When he came back a moment later, he held what appeared to be lounge pants and a male thermal shirt. "All of your clothes appear to be tighter fitting, so I grabbed one of Theon's shirts for you," he explained. Tessa only nodded again.

Luka helped her to her feet, and as tactfully as he could, helped her get changed. She gingerly lowered herself back into the armchair while he took the dress somewhere. When he reemerged, he crouched before her once more. "Tessa, tell me what you need right now. Do you need to rest? Eat?"

Tessa pulled her legs up onto the chair, wrapping her arms around them and resting her chin atop them. "I just want to be left alone for a bit."

"I don't think that's a good idea. You're still adjusting. Your body is going through a lot, and you're in pain—"

"Just a few minutes. Please, Luka," she said, staring at the glass of the unlit fireplace.

Luka was quiet for a few seconds before he said, "Okay. My rooms are in this wing. I'm going to go shower and change. I will be back in fifteen minutes. This room is warded. Only a select few can enter. You cannot leave this suite, Tessa. Do you understand? If Valter learns you are wandering the halls alone, it will not be good for anyone."

"I understand, Luka. Don't leave. I got it."

He stood at her words. "I will be right back. It...will get easier." When she still didn't say anything, she heard his retreating footsteps, and a moment later, she heard the door shut.

It will get easier.

Would it though? Would she eventually just accept her fate?

Maybe it would get better when they were back at the Acropolis. At least there, she would be able to see Dex and Oralia and the others. She would have activities to keep her mind occupied. She had never been one to sit idle, and she hated being alone. It was part of the reason she'd found her way off the Estate so often. Maybe she'd find a new sense of normalcy over the next few months.

And maybe she'd come to form some kind of...relationship with Theon. His father certainly made it clear enough that he expected their relationship to be physical. It obviously was between him and Eviana. Eviana looked like she was enamored with Valter. Was that just the bond? Or had she actually come to care that much for her Master?

And what had Valter meant when he said she would be expected to contribute to the Arius Kingdom? Not much was known about the intensely private kingdom and bloodline of Arius, but the things she had heard weren't particularly heartwarming. She had little idea of their gifts outside of the darkness they command and the apparent shadow-walking.

They were beyond wealthy, like all the ruling families, but how they amassed such wealth no one knew. The other kingdoms were all known for one thing or another. The Falein Kingdom was the scholars and healers, hiring out their services to the other kingdoms. The Anala Kingdom was the agriculture experts, helping the other kingdoms culti-vate their own food sources, for a fee, of course. The Celeste Kingdom was the peacekeepers among them all and was in charge of planning and carrying out the Selection every five years with all the kingdoms paying them handsomely for taking on the task. The Serafina Kingdom was the artists and architects, selling beauty and entertainment and designing the kingdoms' towns and cities. The Achaz Kingdom was the law. Each kingdom had their own forces and defenses, but the Achaz Kingdom upheld the established laws and accords of all the kingdoms, created new ones, and cast judgment on those who broke them. The Legacy themselves could live in whichever kingdom they wanted, provided it was approved by the ruling Lord or Lady of their bloodline's kingdom.

But Arius Kingdom? There were the mines in the Ozul Mountains, but what exactly they mined, Tessa didn't know. In fact, the only other thing she could really remember being said repeatedly in whispered words about the Arius Kingdom was that it was a kingdom you never wished to cross.

And now she suddenly found herself a part of it.

Question after question bombarded her. Maybe a quiet moment to herself had been a bad idea. She was too overwhelmed by it all. Too much had changed too quickly. She couldn't process it all. She couldn't decide if she wanted to scream or cry or rage.

When she heard the door open again sometime later, she hadn't moved an inch. Luka found her still huddled in that chair staring at an unlit hearth.

"Tessa," he sighed, coming to stand in front of her, "come and rest." When she didn't move, he tentatively reached out and unwound her arms from her legs, pulling her gently to her feet. The bond was becoming more frantic with each minute that passed and Theon did not return, and she gritted her teeth against the additional pain now coursing through her. Luka started to lead her to Theon's bed, but she resisted.

"No, not in his bed."

"He would prefer you rest there. It is far more comfortable than the one in that room," he protested.

"I'm not sleeping in his bed, Luka," she repeated, pulling her arm from his grip and making her way to what was apparently her bedroom. She stopped in the doorway. There were no windows in the small room, and she already felt suffocated just looking around it. The only light illuminating the space was what found its way in from the main bedroom. A bed for one was pushed against the wall to the right, a thin blanket across it. A little nightstand next to the bed had a small lamp, and a small desk stood on the back wall, scarcely two feet from the end of the bed. Tessa was positive that if she looked, she would find the closet four times bigger than this small room. At least there was no door. It made it feel bigger than it was.

"Tessa," Luka said from behind her, a hand coming to rest against her lower back. "Come and sleep in the other bed."

"No," she whispered, somehow finding it in herself to put one foot in front of the other. She pulled the thin blanket back and winced at the coarse fabric before climbing into the bed and curling onto her side facing the wall. She pulled the blanket up over her shoulder, effectively telling Luka to fuck off.

Footsteps retreated and returned a few seconds later, and she felt a much heavier, softer blanket being draped over her.

"Theon will not like this," Luka murmured as he left the room.

What did Theon care anyway? He had done this to her. He got what he wanted. He got his precious Source. He got his strength and his power, even if it meant putting her through agony. Then it occurred to her that she was going to have to go through this again.

And again.

And again.

She had to assume each new Mark would happen just like this. And what about when he drew power from her? Would that be as excruciating as being given the Marks? How often would he draw from her?

They kept telling her she was going to be okay.

They kept telling her that everything was going to be all right.

But they were liars.

7
THEON

Theon pushed out a breath, already restless at being so far from Tessa. Then he straightened his tie and tugged on his shirt cuffs before raising a hand to knock on the solid onyx doors of his father's study.

"Enter, Theon."

He opened one side of the double entrance doors and stepped inside. He knew this study like the back of his hand. This was where he'd been forced to spend countless hours being taught about the kingdom and its history after his private lessons were concluded for the day. This was where he was forced to sit through endless meetings that meant nothing to him at eight years. This was where he'd be lectured on how he wasn't doing enough, prepared enough, responsible enough to take over this kingdom. How he'd failed yet again. This was where his father made sure he remembered who was the more powerful of the two of them.

This was where his father assumed he would simply go along with all his plans.

Once they knew Tessa's element and the strength of her magic, everything would change. He could move forward with his own plans. For now, though, he was forced to fall into line.

The walls of the study were dark brown and lined with bookcases filled with books Theon knew were only found here. The floor was hardwood with blood red rugs adding to the darkness of the room. Red curtains were drawn over the windows. Normally they were wide open to allow sunlight in for the numerous plants throughout the space.

His father sat behind his desk, leaning back in his chair as he watched Theon with narrowed eyes. Eviana was curled up in an over-stuffed chair to his left under a window, toying with a small flower that was blooming and closing in her palm. Always nearby and within reach. Her piercing turquoise eyes were following his every movement, ready to intervene if necessary. Theon came to a stop in front of the desk and waited for his father to invite him to sit.

He never did.

"Tell me, son, how is the bond coming along?"

"You saw her, Father," Theon replied, forcing himself to still as his magic shifted beneath his skin. "She is weak as her body adjusts, but I am confident everything is going as it should."

"Her Mark was beautiful," Valter mused. "A beautiful Mark on an equally stunning girl."

"Her beauty has been established numerous times," Theon said sharply.

Valter smirked at him. "So it has. And how are you adjusting to the bond? Clearly the possessiveness has already settled into place."

Theon bit back a sarcastic remark. "It is more intense than I had anticipated, but I will adjust just fine."

"The intensity and need lessen some as the bond settles into place. She appeared to be fulfilling the urges. I can only assume the same is happening in your bed as the bond strengthens," Valter said, leaning forward and shuffling papers around on his desk. "You should be thanking me for the insistence of a female Source at this point."

Theon pressed his tongue to his cheek, refusing to respond to the comment. Mainly because he didn't think they would be sharing a bed the way his father was clearly referencing. They may end up sleeping beside each other, but the way things were going, she wasn't going to let him touch her in that way anytime soon. She could hardly stand to let him touch her to soothe her aches, let alone bring her pleasure.

But gods, he wanted to. This wasn't just some need for release either. The Source bond was creating a primal need to claim her and mark her as his in every way possible, not just with visible Marks on her skin. He wanted to taste her on his lips. Feel her tremble under his fingers from his touch rather than her fever. Feel what it felt like to be deep inside her. Fantasies weren't going to cut it. If the desire was this strong after one Mark, what would it be like after two? After she'd received all the Marks?

"Have you received word from your brother?" Valter asked, pulling Theon from his thoughts.

"Should I have?"

His father sent him a bland look as he settled back in his chair once more, his forefinger tapping on the desktop a few times. "Axel would contact you before me simply for the theatrics of it."

Theon shrugged, sliding his hands into his pockets and rocking back on his heels. "I have not heard from Axel since he left."

His father grunted in annoyance, his finger tapping again. "You have a few weeks until you, Luka, and Axel go back to the Acropolis. With your Source selection out of the way, you can begin to make progress with some of the other tasks I have for you. I do not want to spend weeks and months there. I will depend on the reports of you three when it comes time to select the Fae to serve this kingdom," Valter said, his demeanor becoming entirely business-like.

"This is what you needed to speak with me about so urgently?" Theon demanded. "Why could this not wait? Tessa—"

"Your *Source* is the reason this could not wait," Valter cut in, rising to his feet and leaning over his desk to leer at Theon. "I want to make myself perfectly clear. You are expected to do whatever is necessary to make sure our plans are seen through and so is your Source. And if that means you need to lend her out to make sure a deal is secured with the appropriate people, you will do so."

White hot rage ripped through Theon and before he knew what he was doing, darkness pooled in his hand, but his father was faster and stronger. Not only that, he had a Source that was fully bonded to him. Shadows like his own shot from his father's hand, wrapping around his throat and arms. The power threw him back against a bookshelf, and several books were knocked free and tumbled to the ground. Eviana had moved to his father's side faster than Theon could blink, vines reaching from the closest plants to take over for his father's shadows.

Valter removed his suit coat, handing it to Eviana without so much as looking at her. He didn't need to. He could speak directly into her mind. Slowly he strode towards Theon, rolling up his sleeves as he moved.

"While you know I enjoy seeing that wrath, Theon, you know better than to direct it at me," his father said calmly.

The fist to Theon's side had him grunting a curse before darkness was forced down his throat, cutting off his airflow. He strained against Eviana's vines, but they were too thick for him to do anything with his father's magic reinforcing the restraints.

"She may be your Source, Theon, and you may control the girl, but *I* control *you*," Valter snarled into his face. He slipped a black ring onto Theon's finger, spelled to not only nullify his magic but drain it. Without a Source, he wouldn't be able to refill his reserves as quickly, not without his weekly allocation of Fae blood, and he was already weak from the Marking ritual. But his father controlled the distribution of their supply and would withhold it from him to prove a point.

Valter turned away, ripping the shadows from Theon's throat and leaving him gasping as his father walked back to his desk. He rolled his sleeves back down and took his jacket from Eviana, shrugging it on while Theon gulped down air.

Grabbing his phone from his desk, Valter slid it into his pocket and made his way to the door. Pausing with his hand on the handle, he said, "Oh, and so we are clear, the next time she fails to kneel when it is expected, she will be kneeling in front of me for a different reason, and you can watch as a reminder for you both." His eyes went to Eviana. "Keep him bound for the next half hour, then come find me. All this talk of being on knees finds me wanting you on yours."

"Yes, my Lord," Eviana replied, bowing her head at the order.

"I need to go to Tessa," Theon snapped. He'd already been away from her far too long. His father's ministrations were nothing compared to the strain of the Source bond right now.

A cruel smile curled up on Valter's lip. "Oh, I know, son. I know *exactly* what that bond is demanding of you right now. Consider this a reminder of what is expected of you. Maybe I will go see how your little Source is settling in myself. Take care of her until you return."

The resounding click of the door shutting behind his father had Theon bellowing in fury, straining against the vines wrapped around him. Despite knowing Luka was with her and would protect her, he still raged at failing to protect what was his. He could feel his darkness drifting beneath his skin, just out of reach and slowly draining thanks to the dark ring on his finger. Eviana lifted a hand, tightening the hold of her magic before she drifted back over to her chair and curled up in it. Theon knew it was completely futile to beg her for help. She would never disobey her Master. She couldn't. It was impossible for a Source to disobey their Master.

Or so he had thought.

The relationship he'd witnessed every day between his father and Eviana had Theon believing that a Source obeyed without question. That the bond required such a thing. The few times he's seen the other Lords and Ladies with their Sources had only furthered that belief. The Fae were quick to obey, attentive, and wholly submissive. Not only that, but his father had always made it seem as if the bond made Eviana *want* to blindly obey him. That his desires had truly become her own. If he wanted it, so did she. One would certainly think that was the case at her quick agreement to go to him when she was done holding Theon prisoner.

But Tessa had disobeyed him at every turn. The only time she was obedient was when he forced her to be with entrancing or when she sensed a greater threat than him. It was not what he had been expecting. He had expected an immediate connection, accompanied by an intense desire to please him. Too much of his own plans hinged on having a Source. He needed her to submit, but he found himself wanting her to *want* him too. He wanted her to seek him out instead of having to demand she come to his side.

After several minutes, he said casually to Eviana, "How long did it take for you to completely give in to the bond?"

Eviana tilted her head to the side at the question, reddish-brown hair slipping over her shoulder. "Is your Source not pleasing you, Theon?"

"That is not what I said," Theon answered tightly. "I am simply wanting to be prepared for what comes next."

A small smile graced her lips that said the female knew exactly what he was asking, and wasn't that curious? Had she fought the bond in the beginning?

She tightened the vines, thorns forming that dug into his skin, and drops of blood fell to the floor. "You know if the bond were fully in place, she would be fighting her way to your side right now. The bond would require it of her."

Theon knew this. It was a side of the Source bond the Fae were kept in the dark about. One of the many things the Fae were kept in the dark about really. The final Mark would allow Theon to draw power from her, but it would also force her to defend him at all costs, even if that cost was her life. Because of the Kingdom Accords, there was rarely fighting amongst the kingdoms. The Sources rarely intervened, but they reacted to any and all threats. It was why Eviana had jumped up when Theon had drawn on his power at the mention of sharing Tessa.

Theon theorized it was an attempt to emulate the Guardian Bond that would sometimes be taken between the guardians of Arius and various gods and deities. He'd been enthralled by Marks, the magic behind them, and how they worked when he was younger. In the later years of his schooling, he'd spent hours researching and studying them, often to his father's annoyance. His father felt his time would be better spent learning the ways of the kingdom. Or rather, *his* ways of the kingdom. Hence the incessant lectures and *reminders*.

The Marks and how they worked had changed over the thousands of years this world had been in existence. Those of the Zinta bloodline with the strongest gifts could enact the magic used by the gods under the right circumstances. The Source Marks had been changed and perfected to make sure the Legacy remained as powerful as possible. Most of what he'd been able to find on the Marks was theory, but the idea of somehow incorporating this Guardian Bond seemed convincing enough, considering everything. The thing was, Theon didn't need that aspect of the Source bond, much to his father's chagrin.

"I am well aware what the bond will require of her," he finally bit out.

Eviana slowly made her way towards him, that small smile turning coy. "She is feeling the pull of the bond, even if she is trying to resist it. It is yanking her towards you. Calling her to you. It will not rest until she can feel your touch. When you give her the last dose of elixir tonight, the need will become stronger. Each new Mark will make the pull to you more intense. A thirst that only you can quench. The ache becomes unbearable. Worse than any pain she is currently experiencing." Vines coiled around his throat, and she yanked his head down as she pushed up onto her toes. She was so close to him now, her breath danced across his lips as her brow pressed to his. "She will crave you. Desire you. Want you with her entire being. Even if she fights, she will eventually give in. We all do."

"Did you resist him, Eviana?" Theon taunted. "Do you like getting on your knees and swallowing down his cock, or does the pleasure from the bond simply make you believe you love him?"

Her smile went wicked. "Careful, little heir. You are not like your father. Not yet anyway. You are so *noble*, so *virtuous*," she crooned mockingly. She ran her finger along his jaw, and Theon tried to jerk his head to the side, but her damn vines were still around his neck. A thumb brushed along his bottom lip as she leaned in once more to whisper, "When you take her, you will want to believe that she loves you too."

With those words, her vines snapped apart, and she stepped from his reach when his hand shot out to grab her.

Clicking her tongue, she tutted, "Now, Theon, what would your father say if you laid a hand on me?" Striding to the door, she stopped and looked back over her shoulder. "I look forward to getting to know Tessa more. Your father has big plans for us."

She was gone before Theon could answer, but he didn't want to waste any more time verbally sparring with her anyway. The tension of the bond was driving him mad. More than that, he couldn't take this fucking ring off himself. Not only was the Source bond having a fit, but so was his magic at being trapped beneath his skin.

He tried not to think about what Eviana had said as he made his way down the various hallways and up staircases. When he'd come of age to acquire a Source, he'd immediately requested that his quarters be moved to the east wing where a Source suite was located. His father had made him wait until right before the Selection before he'd actually let him move to this wing. He hadn't even had time to finish moving all his things before he'd had to go to the Acropolis. The staff had finished moving him in. The wing had been a guest wing, but there were only a handful of times another Lord or Lady had stayed here. It wasn't wanting a suite as much as it was about wanting to be out of the same wing as his father.

The wards around his rooms recognized him as he pushed the door open. He pulled his suit coat off as he moved. "Tessa? Luka?"

Tossing the jacket over a dining chair, he made quick work of his tie. He started unbuttoning his shirt as he quickly scanned the room, finding it empty.

Moving to the bedroom, he found Luka sitting before the unlit hearth, a glass of liquor dangling from his fingers. He was staring out the balcony doors where the cloudy sky was obscuring the stars.

"Where is she?" Theon asked. He knew she was here. The cord inside him certainly knew she was nearby. It was vibrating so much it felt like his skin was buzzing. He needed to shower and put on a fresh set of clothing after the events of the last two days, but he needed to see her first.

"Sleeping," Luka grunted, not even bothering to look at Theon.

Theon turned to the bed as he unfastened the final button, his shirt falling open. "Where?"

"In her bed."

Theon whipped his head to him. "Why the fuck is she sleeping in there?"

Luka dragged his eyes to Theon. "Because she refused to sleep in your bed."

"That's ridiculous. This bed is far more comfortable," Theon said, stalking towards the small attached bedroom. He hadn't requested anything be done to the room yet as he hadn't known who his Source would be or what they would want. It was a tiny room, and he hadn't really pictured his Source spending much time in there. At least not right away. Even if he'd Selected a male Source, he anticipated needing to sleep beside each other for the first several days due to the nature of the bond.

"I tried to tell her that, but she was adamant," Luka replied, bringing his glass to his lips.

Theon stopped in the doorway of the small room, the bond reaching out to her. He swore he could almost physically see the cord that connected them. Tessa was curled into a ball facing the wall, huddled under a blanket. He made his way to her, running his fingers along her cheek when he reached her side. The bond sent a bolt of pleasure through him, and he sighed as it settled. Stroking her hair a few times, he fought the urge to scoop her up, bring her to his bed, and climb in beside her.

"How is she?" he asked Luka when he finally forced himself to go back out to the bedroom.

"Well, she cried herself to sleep," Luka said grimly, motioning Theon to come closer.

Theon extended his hand, and Luka slipped the ring from his finger. A small shudder worked through him as the darkness sprang forth at the sudden freedom, and he let it remain for a moment, dark mist flowing along his skin.

"It is a lot to process, and she was not prepared for this. I think I would be more concerned if she wasn't emotional," Theon said, settling into the other armchair. He saw the bottle of liquor sitting on the table between the chairs and took a pull directly from it, resting his head back.

"She was not the one for this," Luka said.

"And what do you want me to do about that now?" Theon retorted, his shadows beginning to drift. "There is no second chance with your Source. You know that. Once this was set into motion, there was no going back. Not unless you want to kill her?"

Luka sent him an unimpressed glare, but didn't deign to reply to that. "We need to change how we're approaching this. We need to adjust our strategies. Gods, why couldn't you have just chosen someone else?"

"We are not changing the plans simply because you are having a sudden change of heart. Then everything we are putting her through is for nothing."

"No. We can still get the outcome we want. We just need to rethink our strategy," Luka protested.

"We can't simply change the plans," Theon scoffed, eyeing the darkness that seemed to reach towards the small room.

"That female just changed every godsdamn thing, Theon," Luka said, rage seeping into his voice. The blue of his eyes began to glow, his pupils shifting to vertical slits. "If you can't see that, then we are already fucked. She should not be able to resist the bond once Marked. You know this. Axel is out there busting his ass right now, and you're here fucking us over."

"You act as if I chose her at random," Theon spat. "She was one of the five remaining options."

"Only because you refused to remove her," Luka countered. "Both Axel and I told you repeatedly that she wasn't the one for this, and yet here we sit. All because you can't control—"

"Enough, Luka," Theon snarled, the shadows thickening around them and creeping towards the male now.

Luka only glanced at the darkness before taking another drink of his liquor. "You need to stop with your power unless you plan on taking something else from her tonight."

Luka may have been right about that, but he was wrong about the bond. It would settle into place. Tessa would come to terms with her new life. Their plans weren't ruined. They just got off track for a moment. She would rest, have some time to process, and then everything would be fine.

And if not, he had ways to push her along.

Luka dropped his now empty glass down on the side table and rose from his seat, going out to the other room. He returned a few moments later with a small leather case. "We should get this over with."

Theon nodded. "Let me shower and change first."

"I'll get things ready."

Theon made quick work of cleaning up and slipping into lounge pants and a black shirt. Before he left the dressing room, he did a quick check of the items he'd ordered for Tessa. From formal to everyday wear, there was something for every occasion. Shirts, dresses, skirts, sweaters, and everything in between were neatly hung and arranged with pants, jeans, leggings, and undergarments taking up drawers. Several dozen pairs of proper footwear were now displayed along one wall on a shoe rack. A jewelry stand had also been brought in. He opened the top to several watches, rings, and cufflinks, and he tossed the black ring in the back of it. Everything else in the stand would be for Tessa.

He retrieved the three rings he usually wore and slipped them onto his fingers. He'd only taken them off to blend in more at the Acropolis, which was something he wouldn't need to worry about anymore. Two of the rings wouldn't have been a big deal. One gleaming black and shaped like a wing that wrapped around his finger and the other a thick solid-silver band, he slipped them onto his pointer and ring finger of his right hand. The other, however, would have been noticed. A square black gem was set into a ring of onyx. It was large and chunky, and the stone was only found in a small section of the northeast part of the Ozul Mountains. Slipping it onto his left middle finger, he left the closet and went into Tessa's small room. She hadn't moved, save for slipping a hand under her cheek. He sighed, dreading what he was going to have to do to her next despite the necessity of it.

Luka was waiting for him in the same spot when he exited the small room. "Ready?" he asked, picking up a dagger.

"Don't really have a choice not to be."

"I suppose not."

Theon held his hand out, palm up, and Luka cut a line down the center. Theon tipped his hand so the blood ran down his palm, and Luka held up a small vial to collect it.

When the vial was full, the cut was already healing as Theon said, "Do you think I should wake her and tell her before we do it, or just…do it?"

Luka glanced up at him from what he was doing before refocusing on his task. He had pulled another vial from the case, and it was filled with a white liquid. Dumping the vial of Theon's blood into the other, he replaced the cork and gently began mixing the two. "I think she has had enough surprises," he finally answered, the mixture becoming a darker shade of red.

Theon pursed his lips and nodded, watching silently while Luka took a syringe from the case. He uncapped the needle before drawing the mixture into it. "You probably want to bring her out here though. That room is too small for both of us to be in there with her."

"Yeah, all right," Theon agreed.

Pushing out a heavy breath, he returned to where Tessa was sleeping. Pulling her hair back over her shoulder, he bent down and said softly into her ear, "Hey, beautiful. I need you to wake up for a bit."

When she didn't stir, he gently pulled the blankets back some and sat beside her on the small bed. Trailing his fingers up her arm, he tried again. "Tessa. Wake up. Just for a bit."

After several seconds, her eyes fluttered, and she rolled over gingerly, her brow pinching in confusion. "Theon?"

"Yeah, I need—"

But he didn't get to finish.

Tessa pushed herself up, and her lips landed on his. Theon froze, too shocked to do anything, but that only lasted for a second. The bond was humming away in excitement, and Theon slipped his hand into her hair and angled her head back just the way he liked it. Her hand came up and gripped the back of his neck, tugging him closer. Her lips tasted better than he had imagined, and he ran his tongue along the seam of them. She immediately parted, and she tasted like rain and pure light with a hint of something...darker he couldn't place. The cord in his chest was pushing him to take more and more, to claim her and make her his in every way, and he groaned low in his throat.

Tessa suddenly wrenched herself away, sliding up to the head of the bed and cringing against it. She pulled the blanket up to her chin, her eyes wide with horror. "I'm sorry. I don't know what I was doing..." She trailed off, her fingertips coming up to touch her lips. If they were tingling with pleasure the way his were, he understood why.

"It's all right, Tessa. It's the bond," he said, reaching for her, but she shrank back from him even more. He dropped his hand. "I was away from you much longer than I should have been. The bond demands our closeness right now. This is how it should be."

She stared back at him like that was not a justifiable explanation for what had just happened. Meanwhile, he was trying to stay focused on the task at hand instead of thinking about how he could get her to kiss him like that again.

He cleared his throat. "There is one more thing we need to do to complete the first Mark. Afterwards, you can rest and recover without interruption."

Horror filled her grey eyes for a completely different reason now. "What else could you possibly do to me?"

Something in his gut twisted at the words, any desire coursing through him quickly snuffed out. "Come out to the bedroom, and I will explain." When she didn't move, he reached out a hand to her again. "I can carry you if you are in too much pain to walk right now," he offered.

"I can walk fine," she retorted, but the bite of her tone, or rather lack thereof, betrayed how weak she was feeling.

Theon stood to give her room, and she slid carefully from the small bed.

A bed she would not be sleeping in again. Not when there was a bed ten times more comfortable in the other room with plenty of space for both of them. The bed was designed to comfortably hold a Lord or Lady, their Match, and their Source.

He followed her a step behind in case she stumbled. Luka was standing by the fireplace, sipping on another glass of liquor. He glanced discreetly at the mantle where Theon spotted the syringe. Theon nodded in acknowledgement while Tessa took a seat in the chair. Neither he nor Luka moved, and she looked between them, exhaustion heavy in her features.

"Can you just do whatever it is you're going to do to me so I can go back to my room and sleep?"

Theon let the comment about her room go for now as he came to stand before her. Crouching down, he peered up into her face. "To make sure your body fully accepts the start of the bond and the Mark, we need to give you an additional dose of tonic."

"Of tonic," she repeated. Luka had moved behind her and had drawn her hair back over one shoulder, exposing the column of her throat. She glanced back at him before returning her eyes to Theon. "The same tonic I drank before you cut me with a dagger?"

"It is a mixture of the tonic you were given by the Priestess and my magic."

Her eyes went wide again. She tried to lurch to her feet, but Luka's hands were on her shoulders, keeping her in place.

"What? No! Please don't! Theon, don't! My body is adjusting to everything fine. I feel the bond. The Mark is there. I will stay closer to you. I will do better with this!"

"This is the last thing. I swear, Tessa," Theon said, turning and grabbing the syringe off the mantle. When he turned back, tears were streaming down Tessa's face. He'd lost count of how many times he'd seen her cry in the last day.

She was pleading with him not to do this, and Luka's face was strained with effort not only to keep her seated, but to not hurt her while doing so. "We either need to move her to the bed so I can hold her down without hurting her further, or you need to entrance her, Theon," he gritted out.

Theon reached out and took her chin between his fingers, and she cried out in despair. "Please! Don't, Theon! It hurts so much," she sobbed.

"Do it, Theon," Luka demanded. "Get it over with."

Theon tilted her chin up. Her grey eyes were bleak and desolate. "Tessalyn, *be still.*"

She immediately ceased her thrashing, and Luka loosened his grip but kept his hands on her shoulders. Theon pushed her hair back again. She was trembling despite his command, and he knew it was uncontrollable.

"This is it. I promise, Tessa," he said, bringing the needle to her neck.

"Until the next Mark," she whispered back.

Theon paused, glancing down at her. He didn't want to think about the next time he had to do all this to her. The tonic wouldn't be needed with her magic freed, but the bestowing of the Marks would be the same. Clenching his jaw, he inserted the needle. He tried to be gentle about it, but there was really no way to gently insert a needle into someone's neck. As soon as he put pressure on the plunger, she screamed. Luka's hold tightened, but Theon couldn't simply inject it quickly. It had to be done slowly.

"It's almost over, little one," Luka said, trying to soothe her as he held her still, her cries of agony drowning out his words.

When the syringe was finally empty, Theon removed it, sliding a palm in place to heal the wound. It wouldn't take the pain away, but it would heal the bruising. Tessa had been right. Arius Legacy didn't have gifts to heal others, but a Source bond allowed them to heal each other with their connection.

Luka released her, and she collapsed to the floor. Curling into a ball on her knees, her hands dug into her hair as she cried out in pain, her face to the floor.

Theon tossed the empty syringe onto the small table and dropped down beside her, placing a hand on her back. "Tessa, breathe. Take a breath."

"It...hurts..." she managed between gasps, fingers clawing at her scalp.

"I know," he said, trying to pull her to him. He could at least placate the bond that was surely warring inside her now that he had given her a fresh surge of his own blood and magic. She stayed huddled in the ball against his chest, her hands clasped to her head.

"She is either going to pass out or vomit from the pain," Luka observed from where he still stood behind the chair.

"I am going to go with the latter if last night was any indication," Theon replied over Tessa's cries of agony.

"Agreed," Luka said. "Let's get her to the bathroom. Then I'll grab some blankets and pillows so she is not lying on the bare floor."

He picked her up from Theon's arms and carried her to the bathroom, murmuring low into her ear. Theon followed a step behind. He was exhausted. He hadn't slept in over a day, and it didn't appear he'd be getting sleep anytime soon. Legacy and Fae didn't require a large amount of sleep if they weren't using their gifts, but having to pour so much of his magic into Tessa last night and more now, not to mention the ring his father had shoved onto his finger, was taking its toll.

He took her back from Luka and lowered to the ground while Luka went to grab the blankets. He spread them out in the semi-private toilet area and then stepped back, leaning against the wall while they waited. Tessa's cries had become quieter, but that was most likely because her throat was raw from the screaming. It was about to get worse when she started vomiting again.

He ran his hand up and down her back, his other arm wrapped tightly around her waist. "I've got you, Tessa. We will get through this, and then you can sleep as long as you need to."

She didn't acknowledge him, and he got the distinct feeling he was attempting to soothe himself rather than her.

Minutes later, the first wave of vomiting hit. Theon helped her up, holding her hair back, while she heaved over and over into the toilet. Just like before, his dark shadows poured from her mouth. Some of the silver wisps were there too, but not as many as before. That was part of the bond. He'd seen it when their souls' essences had intertwined and flared silver before settling back into them when he'd given her the first Mark.

When the vomiting finally ceased, she collapsed onto him. He eased her down onto the blankets, pulling a pillow into his lap for her to rest her head on. Her eyes were closed, her breathing ragged. Luka passed him a damp cloth, and Theon wiped sweat from her brow and neck.

"Tessa?" Theon ventured softly.

She didn't answer, and he didn't push it.

The silence was deafening in the bathroom while they waited for the next round of nausea to consume her. Theon wasn't sure if she had fallen asleep or not, but her eyes never reopened while she lay there, whimpering in pain every once in a while and trembling from the heaving.

He glanced at Luka, who was watching her, pity and remorse in his eyes.

"You regret our decision," Theon said tightly, dabbing the cloth along her forehead again.

"Don't you?" Luka challenged sharply. "We have to do this to her again three more times."

"We knew that my Source would have to endure this," Theon answered after a moment. "We knew what to expect."

"But *she* didn't."

"She is a Fae. Designed for this very purpose," Theon said, annoyance edging into his tone. "And I'd be willing to bet the other heirs are not on the floor caring for a Fae."

"She was not made for this, and you know it," Luka retorted. "We could see that from the information in her file. Why do you think we told you to choose someone else?"

"You think she is not strong enough to endure this?"

"The exact opposite," Luka disagreed. "She has already shown she is more than strong enough to endure this. Her kind of strength is not the strength you need to succeed with your current plan. Her kind of strength will alter everything. We need to alter the plans to accommodate her, Theon. Not the other way around."

"We have already discussed this," Theon snapped, his voice rising. "The plan is not going to be changed now. It is too late."

Luka pressed his tongue to his cheek, his gaze flicking back to the female in Theon's lap. He finally pushed off the wall and said, "I'm going to get her some water," before leaving the room.

For the next few hours, Tessa vomited off and on, just like the night before. She didn't speak a word to him or Luka. She just reverted to closing her eyes and waiting in resignation while she lay on the floor. Luka had pulled the seat out from in front of the make-up vanity, lost in his own thoughts. Theon had maneuvered against the wall so he could sit against it, his head tipped back and his eyes closed. He was absent-mindedly stroking her hair, wondering how much longer this was going to go on, when she spoke.

"Theon?"

His head snapped up at her hoarse voice. Luka looked up too, both of them zeroing in on her. "Yeah, beautiful?"

"What did your father mean when he said you could loan me out?"

Her eyes were still closed, her hands clenched tightly around a blanket they had draped over her. But *that* was what she was contemplating in between bouts of hurling her guts up?

"That is something you never need to worry about, Tessa, because it will never happen," Theon finally answered, glancing at Luka. His lips had thinned because he knew the lengths his father would go to in order to get results just as well as Theon did.

"But what did he mean? He said I would have ended up one anyway if you hadn't chosen me as a Source," she pushed.

"We can't know which kingdom you would have been assigned to, Tessa. They assess that as you proceed through the Selection tasks. He was simply speculating. I do not want you to worry or think about it, all right?"

She was quiet for a long time. So long that Theon thought she had retreated back into herself, but then her voice came again, barely a whisper. "I just keep thinking that it couldn't have been worse than this. That I would have chosen just about anything over this."

Theon met Luka's gaze, finding it already pinned on him. He shook his head, silent communication passing between them. Now wasn't the time to tell her that being sent to serve in the Achaz Kingdom under the Sirana bloodline would have been much worse than what she was enduring right now.

"I want to go to my bed," she whispered a few minutes later.

"Okay. Let's just wait a little longer in case you get sick again."

She didn't reply, so Theon took it as acceptance, leaning his head back against the wall once more and closing his eyes.

This was worth it.

Putting her through this was necessary and would be worth it in the end.

8

TESSA

She slept for three days straight. When she managed to open her
eyes, Theon was always beside her.

The first time he'd been sleeping, his body curled lightly
around her own. Despite the ache in her bones, there was a calm that
enveloped her at having him so close. While she slept nestled next to
him, the bond rested in contentment too. No incessant pull or temptation. Her eyes had fallen on Luka, who'd apparently been tasked with
keeping an eye on her while Theon slept. He'd asked if she'd needed
anything, and Tessa had only shaken her head before she drifted off to
sleep once more.

Another time, it was midday judging by the light streaming in
through the balcony doors. Theon had been propped against the headboard looking over stacks of papers while referencing things on his
laptop. His hand resting on her shoulder, his thumb had made small
circles along her collarbone. He had immediately set everything aside
when he saw her open eyes. He'd offered to bring her food or water, but
she had fallen back to sleep again within minutes.

This time though, she could already tell it was different. There would
be no going back to sleep. She needed to use the bathroom, and she
could smell herself. She needed to get up and move around. A shower
and fresh clothing sounded divine. But more than any of that, the cord
inside her was back to tugging at her, pulling her awake.

She cracked her eyes open. Light filtered into the bedroom, telling her it was sometime during the day. Luka wasn't in the chair by the fire-place, and the bed felt suspiciously empty. She rolled over to find the space Theon had occupied every other time she'd woken vacant. Pushing herself into a sitting position, she slid a hand through her limp hair. It felt greasy and gross. Her tongue felt thick and tasted of bile. She could only imagine what her breath smelled like.

She was about to go in search of a glass of water when Theon came through the doorway. He paused when he saw her sitting up, clearly surprised, before hurrying to the bedside.

"Tessa, how are you feeling?" he asked, reaching out and tipping her chin up to study her face.

"Water," she rasped.

"Of course."

He left and returned a moment later with two bottles of water. He placed one on the nightstand before unscrewing the cap from the other, bringing it to her lips and tipping it so she could drink. She reached to take it from him, wanting to guzzle it down faster, but he stopped her.

"Slow down, Tessa. You are going to make yourself sick. You haven't eaten in four days, and you haven't drank anything in nearly as long."

He put the cap back on before placing it on the bedside table. Turning back to her, he reached out to cup her cheek, and she jerked back. The bond punished her with a jolt through her body, and she winced. Frustration clouded Theon's eyes, and Tessa dropped her gaze to the comforter.

"I need to take a shower and use the bathroom," she said, twisting the sheets in her fingers.

"Okay. I can show you where your things are," Theon replied, pulling the covers back so she could slide from the bed. He didn't reach for her again, but he stayed close as she stood on unsteady legs. She followed him into the bathroom, the lights automatically coming on when they stepped through the door. She had lain on this floor for hours a few nights ago, but she'd never actually looked around the space. No, her line of vision had been solely the inside of the toilet bowl.

She stilled while Theon went in ahead of her. The bathroom was as luxurious as the rest of the suite. The walls were entirely black tiled, the floor a white marble that was heated beneath her bare feet. To her right was a door that led into the dressing room. Directly ahead of her was a double sink vanity in dark wood tones. Copper faucets and fixtures adorned the space. Next to the dressing room entrance was a cosmetic vanity complete with a cushioned bench seat and mirror that would light up. Beyond that was the semi-private toilet space. In the back right-hand corner stood a large free-standing bathtub big enough for two, and next to it, spanning nearly the entire back wall, was a stunning, glass enclosed walk-in shower. Three large rainfall shower heads came from the ceiling along with various shower heads coming off different parts of the walls. A bench ran along the back.

Theon had gone to the far double sink and opened a drawer, pulling out a toothbrush and tube of toothpaste. "All your things are in these three drawers," he said, setting the items on the counter. "I had Pen get a hair dryer and other things. They're in this bottom drawer. If you need something else, let me know. There's a brush and comb here. Hair accessories and makeup are over in the make-up table for you," he added, gesturing across at the space.

He retrieved some towels from a tall cupboard beside the shower and placed them on the counter. "I have shower products in the shower for you, unless you'd rather take a bath?"

Tessa shook her head, hugging herself tightly. "A shower is fine."

"Okay," Theon nodded, running a hand through his hair. He had dark stubble running along his jaw, as if he hadn't shaved since they'd left the Acropolis. If he weren't forcing her into some kind of glorified servitude, she'd find it attractive. As it stood, it just made her scowl in annoyance.

"Do you want to see the closet for clothing now or after you've bathed?" Theon ventured.

"Can I brush my teeth first?" she replied, hating she had to *ask* that.

"Of course," Theon said, stepping aside. "I will meet you in there."

Tessa brushed her teeth. Twice. And even then her mouth still didn't feel quite clean. She figured she'd brush again when she got out of the shower. Finding a tie for her hair in the vanity table and pulling her hair up and off her neck, she walked into the closet.

It was huge. She'd been wrong. Six of those small bedrooms could fit in here. Theon's clothing took up one wall, while female clothing, shoes, and accessories took up the other three. In the center was an island with drawers on all sides. Theon had placed a pair of soft leggings and a long-sleeve shirt atop it.

"Does your skin still hurt, or will these be all right now?" he asked when she entered.

"I'm feeling better," she murmured, still taking in the massive amount of clothing and shoes. Theon walked to a section and pulled a pair of slippers from a drawer. She was going to have to draw a damn map of the dressing room to remember where everything was.

"You can wear these," Theon said, placing them atop the pile of clothes. "Since socks are not a viable option." His mouth twitched at the words, and Tessa gave him an unimpressed stare. "Do you need anything else?"

"I don't think so," she said, reaching for the clothing.

He held out the half-full bottle of water, but when her fingers wrapped around it, he didn't let go. "Drink it slowly," he warned.

"Yes, Master," she replied derisively.

His eyes darkened a shade, and a muscle in his jaw ticked. The bond in her chest gave a sharp jerk at her... What? Making him upset? Hurting his feelings? Whatever. Now that she wasn't vomiting magic or shivering with a godsdamn fever, her head felt clearer than it had in days. She was restless. And irritable. And hungry. And why were there no windows in here? It made the space feel too enclosed.

"Bathe, Tessa," he finally said, releasing the water bottle. "I will order you some food and have it delivered as soon as possible."

"Order food from where? Does anyone even deliver out here?"

"Our kitchen staff can make anything."

"Is there no food in the kitchen? I can just make something when I am done."

"Aside from the fact that you just woke up from sleeping for three days, my Source is not going to make her own food," Theon answered, heading for the door. "Yell if you need anything."

Tessa carried the clothing and the water bottle with her back into the bathroom, setting everything down on the sink beside the towels. She turned to the shower and realized she had no idea what buttons to push or knobs to use to turn anything on. After several rounds of trial and error, she finally got a few shower heads on and adjusted to a temperature that wasn't freezing. She found shampoo and conditioner that smelled like lavender and mint and a body wash that smelled like jasmine. She nearly moaned as she washed days' worth of sweat and grime from her body.

She didn't know how long she stood in the water, but the longer she did, the more her mind tried to wrap itself around her situation. None of this should have happened. She'd been told repeatedly no one would want her. She was scarcely glanced at when the other heirs would come to the Estate to observe them all. She was nobody and nothing, as the Estate Mother liked to remind her every time her behavior needed correcting.

"*You will be too much of a hassle for any of the royal households to want you. Don't you want to be chosen to serve in their houses, Tessalyn?*" Mother Cordelia chided, as Tessa sat in her small office for once again being beyond the yard. They kept telling her she would know when she'd gone too far, but she never did.

"*Why would I want to serve in a house?*" Tessa asked, her brow pinching. She was only six, but she was pretty sure that did not sound like something she would enjoy doing at all.

"*That is the best any Fae could hope for, child,*" Mother Cordelia said sternly. "*Other than being Selected as a Source, but you will never be that. You are too wild. Too disobedient. Too much of a hassle. No one will want to bother with you.*" The Estate Mother sighed, shuffling papers around on her desk. "*Off to bed. I do not want to see or hear from you the rest of the day.*"

"*But it's only high noon! I haven't had lunch. And dinner—*" Tessa protested, but her breath was stolen from her lungs. Mother Cordelia was a Legacy of the Sefarina bloodline, the goddess of the winds, and she currently had Tessa's air cut off.

"*And you will receive neither of those things until tomorrow,*" Mother Cordelia said curtly. "*Be grateful that is the extent of your punishment this time. Unless you would prefer the cellar again?*"

Eyes wide and lungs burning, Tessa shook her head, gasping when Mother Cordelia released her hold on her. Last time she'd been punished, she'd been shut in one of the small cellars. It'd been cold and dark, and she hadn't received food for two days. After that, it was only salty broth and crusty bread for a week straight.

"*Off to bed,*" she said again.

Tessa didn't linger, rushing out of the office and up the two floors to the room she shared with five other younglings. They shared this room, but none of them ever had anything to do with her. They were too afraid of getting in trouble like Tessa always found herself in, despite her best efforts. Always alone...

A tug on the bond pulled Tessa from her memories. She sighed, irritated at how much of a fit this thing inside her chest was throwing at being away from Theon. She couldn't even enjoy a long, hot shower in peace. Shutting the water off, she grabbed a towel and quickly dried off. She wrapped her hair up into another towel while she dressed, not bothering with the slippers. She would always choose bare feet when given a choice. The bond was becoming unbearable, and Tessa gritted her teeth against the demands. It yanked at her, aching to get back to Theon's side.

It terrified her.

If it was this demanding after the first Mark, what was it going to be like after the next?

She found a comb and began running it through her long hair. She could suddenly understand how Eviana could look at Valter the way she did. Her entire self was going to be wrapped up in Theon. She would become obsessed with him. Her world would revolve around him.

She brought the comb back up to work it through again, and her eyes fell on the Mark on the back of her hand. It seemed even darker against her skin now that it was freshly cleaned, seeming to taunt her. Arius's symbol for all to see. For some reason, her mind slipped to Dex and the look of dread and knowing he'd had on his face when her name had been called.

There was a soft rapping on the doorframe followed by, "Tessa?"

She didn't look up as Theon approached. She just continued to stare at the Mark on her hand.

The Mark that had stolen what little she had from her.

Theon didn't say anything else. He pried the comb from her fingers. She hadn't realized she'd still been holding it. He slowly began combing her hair for her. When he finished, he tilted her face up to his.

"Are you feeling all right?"

Tessa nodded, refusing to cry yet again.

"Do you feel nauseous? Headache? Body aches?"

She shook her head.

His piercing green eyes held hers, searching. "I wish I knew what was going on inside your head right now," he murmured, more to himself than her. "I wish I knew how to help you accept this." When she dropped her gaze at his words, he sighed and took her hand. "Come. They just brought up some food for you."

He led her out to the main room where the food was apparently broth and fresh bread. Fantastic.

"Can't I have, I don't know, doughnuts?" Tessa asked when Theon pulled a chair out for her.

"Doughnuts have no nutritional purpose."

"I know, but they're good," she replied, picking up the spoon and stirring it through the steaming broth.

"Even if you were feeling your best, I wouldn't let you eat doughnuts," Theon said, moving past her and into the kitchen area. She twisted in her chair and watched as he filled a kettle with water.

"You won't *let* me eat doughnuts?" she deadpanned.

He apparently didn't pick up on the pissed off part of her attitude until he turned and saw her face. He braced his hands on the island countertop, leaning forward. "Tessa, my part of this Source bond is to take care of you. Giving you doughnuts is not taking care of your physical or nutritional needs. Eat." He nodded towards the table.

Tessa turned around, mainly because she was too stunned by what he'd just said to do anything else. She scooped up a spoonful of broth and was about to bring it to her mouth when she just couldn't not say anything. She dropped the spoon back into the bowl with a clatter, broth splashing onto the opulent black surface of the table. Twisting to face him again, she said, "I'm sorry. Are you saying that even when you're satisfied that I am feeling one hundred percent better, I will not be *allowed* to eat doughnuts? Or pizza? Or fries?"

Theon glanced up at her. He was busy getting a tea bag placed in a charcoal grey mug as the teakettle began to whistle shrilly. He pulled it off the stove, pouring hot water into the mug. "Yes. That is exactly what I am saying. Allowing you to do so would be irresponsible of me."

Tessa really was at a loss for words this time. She could only stare at him in utter disbelief as he came to her and set the mug of tea down by her soup bowl before sliding into the chair next to her. He had a pile of papers in his hand that he set down on the table and began going through. When she didn't move, he reached over and slid her bowl forward an inch. "Eat," he said before returning to whatever he was reading.

Tessa dutifully ate the entire bowl of broth and two pieces of bread— a habit from not knowing when she would lose food privileges again. The moment she finished, Theon was clearing her dishes and sliding the tea forward. When he returned to the table, he reached to smooth back a piece of hair, and Tessa flinched away. He sighed, lowering into his chair once more and turning to face her.

"Tessa, you realize that the only reason you slept so soundly for three days is because I rarely left your side, don't you? If I did, it was for mere minutes. When I was beside you, some part of us was always touching, even if it was simply our arms brushing."

Tessa stared down at her mug, watching the steam rise. That made sense, she supposed. She vaguely recalled waking at one point and feeling nothing but complete calm and contentment despite the pain her body was enduring.

"Where is Luka?" she asked.

"Luka does not need to be here, Tessa. You are not his Source. You are mine."

Her eyes snapped to his, and she met emerald eyes bright with anger.

"Luka doesn't get frustrated with me for having trouble dealing with the fact that my entire life was just stolen from me," she retorted, glaring back at him.

"Can you just try, Tessa?" Theon said. "Can you try and let the Source bond do what it is supposed to do? Maybe you will find it is not nearly as bad as you are clearly envisioning. I have done nothing but take care of you and tend to your needs since Selecting you."

"You are the reason you had to take care of me, Theon!" Tessa cried. "If you had not Selected me, there would have been no reason to take care of me and tend to my needs."

"Aside from that unfortunate necessity, I have provided and will continue to provide everything you could ever need," he argued.

"Unfortunate necessity?" Tessa scoffed in disbelief. "Leaving that convoluted argument alone for a moment, you are literally deciding what I eat. How is taking away my choices not that bad?"

"I am keeping you healthy."

"You are keeping your prized pet in mint condition," she sneered.

Theon stared back at her for a long moment before he turned and began gathering his papers. His voice was tight and his words clipped when he said, "Luka needed to get some air, so he went to his estate for the day. He will return this evening. You are free to do as you wish in here, but it is imperative that you do not leave our rooms."

"Luka already gave me the lecture about not being allowed to leave the pretty cage," she snapped.

Theon's lips pressed into a thin line. He took a few moments, clearly trying to compose himself. "Rest. I am going to shower," he finally said.

He left the room, leaving Tessa sitting at the table, her tea growing cold.

Five days.

It had been five days of being cooped up in these rooms. Tessa had read several books from the bookshelves, all of them some sort of history or textbook. That was all Theon appeared to have in here. She'd also watched more mundane television than she cared to ever watch again. She couldn't even say she really watched it. She certainly hadn't been invested in any of the shows. Sitting idle had never been her thing, and being stuck in the same space for too long made her stir-crazy. It was part of the reason she so often found herself in undesirable situations.

Luka had returned, but he kept his distance, encouraging her to try and follow the lead of the bond and connect with Theon. That just made her more agitated, so now she only spoke to either of them when absolutely necessary. She had insisted on sleeping in the uncomfortable bed in that tiny room, much to Theon's annoyance and displeasure, and she took a small sense of satisfaction at denying the bond, despite the cord thrashing violently in her chest all night. Needless to say, she hadn't slept well the last five days. She'd taken to napping on the sofa when Theon joined her. He would sit at one end, reading through papers or working on his laptop. His nearness would calm the thing enough that she could slip into sleep.

Tessa stirred her fruit, granola, and honey that he'd ordered her for breakfast, wishing it was pancakes topped with bananas, chocolate chips, and whipped cream. She was nestled in the bay window she'd found herself in more often than not. It overlooked a huge garden area behind the house. The gardens appeared to have paths going off in various directions, and she wondered where they all led to. Did any go up into the mountains? Or did they all just loop back in one giant circle? And what did anyone need gardens this big for anyway? Were there hidden areas to get lost in? Were there actual gardens with food and herbs?

She heard the door clicking as she took a bite. Assuming it was Luka, she was planning on dutifully ignoring him, but when the door opened, it was not Luka who came in.

The male who walked through the door was devastatingly beautiful, as attractive as Luka and Theon. He had thick dark hair with auburn undertones to it rather than the inky black of Theon's hair. His hair was a little longer too. His eyes, though, were as green as Theon's. He was only an inch shorter than him and appeared to be close to her age of twenty-three. That meant he'd already undergone his Staying so she couldn't say what his age was for sure. Most Fae and Legacy went through their Staying in their early twenties, when the magic in their blood would keep their bodies from further aging. Tessa had undergone her own Staying at twenty years.

"Um, hi?" Tessa said as she swallowed a bite of blueberries, eyeing the newcomer. Luka had told her only a select few had access to these rooms, and so far, it had only been them.

The male had several small boxes in his hands as he studied her with curiosity in his bright eyes. He wore black pants and a white dress shirt with the top few buttons undone. His sleeves were rolled up, revealing muscular forearms dusted with dark hair.

"You must be Tessa," he answered.

Feeling incredibly uncomfortable, she started to call for Theon, but his name got stuck in her throat.

Because she wasn't alone with Theon or Luka.

Which was just fucking perfect.

"Master," she called with faux sweetness dripping from her tone. "You have a gentleman caller."

The male's brows rose in surprise, and amusement filled his features.

Theon came into the room shirtless, and Tessa felt her stomach dip and curl in all sorts of completely unacceptable ways.

This fucking bond.

He wore jeans that hung obnoxiously low on his hips showcasing the muscles that tapered and dipped below his waistband beautifully. He was toweling his hair dry, and his attention went to her first before shifting to the newcomer.

"Axel? What are you doing here?" he asked, coming to a stop in the doorway.

The male's gaze shifted from her to Theon. "I ran into Luka a bit ago. He wanted to get some air and asked if I could bring these to you." He walked further into the room, setting the boxes on the dining table.

"I'm surprised it's taken you this long to show up here. Pen said you returned two days ago," Theon said with a grin, tossing the towel across his desk chair and striding forward.

"You could have invited me sooner, jackass," the male said, crossing his arms over his chest and leaning against the table. "Apparently I should have waited longer. Things have clearly not settled into place here." An amused smirk tilted on his mouth again as his gaze shifted back to Tessa.

Tessa felt her cheeks heat under his scrutiny. Theon was going through the packages and glanced up at his words. "It's been...interesting," he said tightly, setting a small box back down. "Tessa, this is my younger brother, Axel. Axel, Tessa."

Brother. That made sense. She'd forgotten all about the fact that he had a brother.

"Pleasure," Axel said with a dip of his chin in her direction.

When Tessa didn't reply, Theon said, "Tessa, you can call me Theon in Axel's presence as you can when Luka is around."

"How generous of you," she snipped in response, turning back to the window and continuing to eat her fruit.

A chuckle came from Axel. "Oh, she is a delight. I think I like her."

"You would," Theon remarked. "You will have to excuse her. She's been in a mood the last several days."

"That will happen when you have magic shoved into your body, spend days in excruciating pain, and then be denied the pleasure of doughnuts and pizza," she called out sardonically.

"It also happens when you do not get adequate sleep and become obstinately stubborn," Theon retorted through gritted teeth.

"Obstinate and stubborn mean the same thing. Pick a different adjective," she shot back.

Axel fell into a fit of laughter as the door opened once more, and Luka entered.

She rolled her eyes. "Oh, look. Asshole number two has returned."

Axel's laughter only increased.

"Tessa, I see your mood has improved from unruly to bratty," Luka said in greeting.

She flipped him off over her shoulder.

"Maybe if you gave her some doughnuts, she'd be nicer," Axel suggested when he was able to form words again.

"Doubtful," Theon muttered.

Axel pulled a chair out from the dining table and took a seat, relaxing into it. "I hope you've warned her to keep her delightful comments to herself at dinner tonight? Could you imagine Father's face?"

At the mention of Valter and dinner tonight, Tessa whipped around to face Theon. "What is he talking about?"

A muscle feathered along his jaw as he met her gaze. "We are to have a family dinner this evening with my parents, Axel, and Luka," Theon said. "I trust you remember how to act in my father's presence?" She nodded mutely. "Good. Dinner is at seven and will be formal, so plan your day accordingly."

At the order, annoyance raced back through her. "Well, my day is pretty full between watching boring television shows, napping, and eating a salad, but I'm sure I can rearrange my schedule to fit in a shower before dinner."

"Please see that you do," Theon replied through clenched teeth.

"Will do, *Master.*"

9

TESSA

Tessa stood in front of the full-length mirror in the dressing room, staring at her reflection. She hardly recognized herself. She'd finally met the infamous Penelope, a sweet Fae with shining brunette hair and icy blue eyes. She came bustling into the suite in the late afternoon and ushered Tessa from the sofa to the bathroom to shower. Then she'd proceeded to do her make-up and dry and curl her hair, chatting away the entire time and telling Tessa she could call her Pen. Tessa could hardly keep up with the female, but she learned she was the personal servant of Theon and Axel. She could tell by the Markings on her wrist she'd attended the Falein Estate and had the water element. The female seemed happy enough, almost as if she *enjoyed* serving the Arius heirs.

Tessa's honey-blonde hair was now pinned half up, the rest cascading over her shoulders and down her back. The dress Pen had put her in was a shimmery-cream colored wrap skirt with a slit that went nearly to her hip. It had a split collar that rested down her shoulders, leaving her collarbone bare and sleeves that went three-quarters down her arms. She was sliding black stilettos onto her feet when Pen announced her work here was done before leaving her alone.

She tried not to worry her bottom lip that was expertly tinted a dark shade of red, not wanting to smear the lipstick. Tessa smoothed her hand down the dress again, her gaze snagging on the Mark on her hand. The next Mark would go on her chest, over her heart, and Tessa wondered if it'd be visible in this dress. It would look different. The first Mark designated the Lord or Lady they served. The other Marks...

Tessa frowned. She knew nothing of how the other Marks were chosen. Would they look like Eviana's?

She reached up, fingering the neckline. It covered all of her cleavage while still showing her collarbone, so maybe it would stay covered? Her fingers lingered, and she stared, wondering for the hundredth time in the last three hours how she'd found herself here.

She didn't hear Theon enter, and she started when he appeared in the reflection behind her. He looked stupidly attractive as always, dressed in a black suit clearly tailored for him. His tie matched her dress, and he'd shaved. Tessa found herself missing the stubble that had been present along his jaw the past few days.

He brought his hand up and brushed her hair over her shoulder, his hand lingering on the back of her neck. She told herself to flinch away, but she didn't. She hadn't seen him since that morning. He hadn't physically touched her since the day before, and she found herself leaning into him.

Theon didn't say anything, but she didn't miss the small shudder of relief that went through him in the reflection. His eyes closed briefly, reveling in the same pleasure the bond was currently giving her, and when they reopened, the emerald green was liquid as they met her eyes in the mirror. His thumb began moving tentatively on her neck, massaging sensitive points, and she drifted back a step, feeling his chest against her back.

Her eyes fluttered closed this time, Theon's other hand coming to rest on her hip and tugging her back into him even more. The cord inside of her was buzzing with excitement, and Tessa knew she was losing a battle she'd been fighting for days. A small voice in the back of her mind was screaming at her to move, but a much louder voice was whispering to her soul, telling her it could be like this all the time.

"This is how it's supposed to be, beautiful," Theon murmured into her ear, and goosebumps pebbled along her skin.

Her eyes snapped open to meet his in the mirror once more. He was leaning into her, his hand drifting up and splaying across her torso. The hand on her neck snaked around until he loosely gripped her throat. The metal of the rings he always wore now was cool against her suddenly heated flesh. With his thumb, he tilted her head to the side before slowly lowering his lips to her flesh, keeping his gaze on hers the entire time. He trailed lingering kisses up the column of her throat, and when he reached the sensitive area behind her ear, Tessa couldn't hold back the sigh of relief she felt at his touch.

"Don't move."

He stepped away from her, and she had to agree with the fit the bond was throwing, begging him to come back. What if she gave in? What if she gave in to the demands of this thing? Just this once? Would it satisfy it? Give her a reprieve from the constant desperation she felt?

Theon was back a moment later, stepping into her once more. He brought his hands over her head and laid a diamond choker against her throat, clasping it. Holding out a hand before her, Tessa looked down to find two diamond earrings lying in his palm. Wordlessly, she hooked them into her ears. Then he gently spun her, bringing her right hand to his lips. He pressed a kiss to the Mark before clasping a matching diamond bracelet to her wrist.

"This is all too much, Theon," she finally managed to get out. "I already feel far too...extravagant. Isn't this a bit overkill?"

"For a formal dinner with my father? No. But that truth aside, it is not too much, Tessa." His hands landed on her waist, pulling her into him. He brought his fingers to her chin, tilting it up. "Can you do something for me tonight?"

She got lost in the brightness of his eyes. The angle of his cheekbones. The curve of his lips.

"Tessa?"

"Hmm?"

The corner of his lips twitched up and a small dimple appeared. Without thinking, she reached up, tracing it with her finger. Theon groaned at the light touch, and his brow fell forward to touch hers.

"If this were any other dinner, I would say fuck it, and spend the rest of the evening standing here in this room with you. So I'll ask you again: can you do something for me tonight?"

"What?" she breathed, too lost in the sensation of having him so close.

"Can you remember this? What is happening right now? How you're feeling?" he pressed, the fingers of a hand trailing up her spine. "Can you pretend, just for the night, that you *want* this? And after dinner, we can come right back here and pick up where we left off?"

"I..." Tessa trailed off as his hand slid beneath her hair to her neck again.

"Just for one night, Tessa," he urged. "For one night, pretend you accepted this. Welcomed it. Just try. For one night."

She could do that for one night, right? She could try instead of focusing on everything he'd taken from her. She could let the Source bond take control for one night. Her eyes wandered to the Mark on the back of her hand, but Theon drew her back to him before her stare could linger.

"No, beautiful. Keep your eyes on me tonight, yes?" She nodded, not trusting herself to say anything. "And remember what I told you when we arrived: do not speak unless spoken to."

She nodded again, and Theon took her hand in his, leading her from the dressing room and out into the main living space. Luka and Axel were there and waiting, dressed in suits similar to Theon. Both of them stilled when they entered, sapphire and emerald eyes trailing up and down her body. She felt her cheeks flush at the attention, and her other hand came up involuntarily, clutching at Theon's arm.

Luka noticed immediately. His gaze bounced back and forth between her and Theon, but he didn't say anything.

Axel cleared his throat and gestured to the door. "Shall we?"

"Do you need anything before we go?" Theon asked, looking down at her.

She shook her head, and he led her to the door, removing his arm from her hold and settling his hand on her lower back as she stepped through the door in front of him.

"I asked Father if I could move to the east wing as well," Axel was saying as they traversed the various hallways. Tessa was only half-listening. She had never seen this part of the house. Luka had taken her in through a side entrance, and she hadn't left Theon's suite since.

While Theon's room was modern, the rest of the house felt like she had stepped into some type of dark castle. The walls were all dark stone with pictures lining them. She caught glimpses of dragons and serpents, a landscape of what she assumed was the After; or rather, what the artist envisioned it might look like. Dark red rugs ran the length of the hallways over smooth dark floors, and the windows had dark curtains pulled back. The sun was already setting, and lamps along the walls every few feet emitted low light, casting shadows on the various potted plants spaced along the hall.

"I'm sure Father was very open to the idea," Theon replied.

"Absolutely. He said he'd have my things moved to new rooms first thing tomorrow."

"You're full of shit," Theon said, guiding Tessa around a corner.

Axel chuckled. "You're right. He said when I was of age to Select a Source, I could move to that wing. Until then, he didn't want me in this wing *unsupervised.*"

Tessa scoffed. "What kind of trouble could you possibly get into out here in the middle of nowhere?"

Three sets of eyes settled on her. She'd already forgotten about the whole not-speaking-unless-spoken-to thing. Fantastic.

"Based on our earlier interactions, I am going to assume you could find trouble at the bottom of a soup can," Axel teased with a wink.

"That is...possibly accurate," Tessa conceded with a flash of a small smile.

"Those are stories I would love to hear sometime," Axel replied.

"You and me both," Theon said as they approached a large set of dark doors.

The males collectively slowed, and Tessa could feel the tension slither around them. Theon stepped in front of her, sliding a hand to her cheek. "Eyes on me tonight, yes?"

"Yes," she answered quietly.

He bent and pressed his lips to the top of her head before turning and entering the dining room, leaving Tessa to follow behind like the good little Source she was supposed to be. Valter was already seated at the head of the long table. High-backed cushioned chairs ran down each side. The table could easily seat twenty, more if needed. Cressida was seated to his left, and Eviana stood at his side.

Wait.

Would she be expected to *stand* beside Theon all night? In these shoes?

"Theon. Luka. How nice of you to join us this evening," Valter greeted them, a tight smile tilting his lips.

"Your wording left little choice, Father," Theon replied dryly, going around the table to the chairs at his father's right. He paused on his way to bend down and press a kiss to Cressida's cheek. "Good evening, Mother."

"Theon, you grow more handsome every day, dear," Cressida crooned, beaming up at her eldest son. As he moved around the table,

Axel bent and pressed a kiss to her other cheek before sliding into the chair beside her. Luka took the chair next to Axel.

Tessa dutifully followed Theon, who bypassed the chair directly to his father's right and took the next one. She paused, unsure of what she was to do. There were two empty place settings still on the table.

"Sit, Tessa," Theon said, motioning to the chair across from Luka. Tessa moved forward, silently thankful for the direction. As she took her seat, Theon snapped his fingers at a Fae along the wall, and a moment later, a glass of whiskey was placed in his hand.

"You allow her to sit before you even have your drink?" Valter quipped, swirling his glass of liquor.

"I saw no reason to make her stand," Theon replied, taking a long drink of his own.

"You could have allowed the rest of us to enjoy the view for a few minutes," Valter said with a smirk.

"I can see her pretty face just as well with her sitting," Axel cut in, winking at Tessa as he brought his glass of alcohol to his lips.

Valter's lips thinned at the comment, his eyes dragging to his younger son. Axel just tipped his glass in his direction in a mock salute and took another drink.

"Eviana," Valter said tightly, "you may sit."

"Thank you, my Lord," Eviana replied, moving gracefully to the seat at Valter's right.

The soup course was served, and small talk was had among the Legacy at the table. The Legacy were also given bread with their soup, while she and Eviana were not. Tessa frowned down at her bowl of vegetable soup, stirring around green beans and carrots. She cast a side-long glance out of the corner of her eye at Eviana, who was dutifully eating her soup, her eyes always either on her bowl or on Valter.

Theon leaned towards her, speaking directly into her ear. "Eat, Tessa."

His breath made her hair flutter against her cheek, tickling her skin, and a chill skittered along her spine.

"Why can't I have any bread?" she hissed back. Theon just gave a pointed look at her soup bowl before turning back to the conversation of his family. She gave a small sigh before bringing the spoon to her mouth. She was supposed to be trying after all, supposed to be pretending she'd accepted her place...beneath him. Apparently her place wasn't worthy of bread with her soup.

When the salad course was brought out, she was given a basic salad with a few cherry tomatoes and sliced cucumbers. The Legacy were given a strawberry-walnut spinach salad complete with cheese crumbles and strawberry vinaigrette. She scowled, stabbing pieces of lettuce forcefully and long fingers grazed briefly along her arm. A warning. She sighed, crossing her legs underneath the table and proceeding to eat her boring salad.

"Your Source is exceptionally fidgety at the dinner table, Theon," Valter said, and Tessa froze, her cheeks heating.

Theon, who had finished his salad, leaned back in his chair, picking up his refilled glass of whiskey. "This is the first time she has left our rooms since her arrival." His other hand came to her head, smoothing along her hair before resting on the back of her neck. He squeezed slightly. "She is eager to return." The smirk that crossed Theon's face and what that implied to his father had her fuming inside.

Valter chuckled, finishing his salad.

A foot nudged hers under the table, and she glanced up to find Luka staring at her. He shook his head slightly. Another warning. Tessa gritted her teeth.

She could do this. She simply needed to emulate Eviana, right?

She snuck another peek at the female who had already finished her salad. Her hands were folded in her lap, and while her eyes always went back to Valter, she still swept her gaze around the table at times. She was poised with her back straight, body always turned slightly towards her Master. Every once in a while her head would tilt as though she heard something.

When the main course was brought out, Tessa became excited as the Legacy meals were uncovered. Steak, roasted vegetables, mashed potatoes with gravy, and more bread. She was going to devour every bite. Theon never ordered her red meat.

And apparently this dinner was to be no different.

When her plate was set before her, she found a chicken breast, plain rice, and roasted vegetables. No bread. Biting her tongue yet again, she began cutting her chicken, and tuned into the conversation she'd been ignoring all evening.

"Luka, I just received word that you will be allowed to arrive early at the Acropolis with Theon and Axel and the rest of the heirs. After I explained the circumstances, they couldn't really deny the request," Valter was saying around his steak.

"Excellent. Thank you for your assistance in the matter, Valter," Luka said with a nod.

"I expect that to be a fruitful time for all of you. A chance to get to know the other heirs before the rest of the Legacy arrive," Valter went on. "I have received letters from several prospects seeking alliances."

"Must we talk about my darlings leaving for the next year?" Cressida cut in with a pout. "I'm going to miss them greatly."

"We will be home on holidays, Mother," Theon sighed, scooping up some potatoes.

"Yes, but a piece of my household will still be gone. That does something to a mother's heart."

"Get used to it, Cressida," Valter said, cutting another piece of his meat. "In addition to letters for alliances, I've received several proposals for Matches with Theon now of age. They've sent bloodlines and genealogies as well. There are a couple of decent options."

A Match?

For Theon?

Why hadn't she thought of this?

All the Legacy were given Matches— arranged marriages. They were carefully planned to ensure children produced were pure Legacy and only strengthened their bloodline, often matching a greater bloodline with that of a lesser god or goddess to make sure the greater bloodline's power ran true and as strong as possible. Why had she never thought of the fact that the reason she was given a small bed in Theon's suite was because he would eventually have a wife in his? He would be expected to produce the next heir for the Arius Kingdom. The Source bond would force Tessa to be his, but he would not be hers. That thought alone made her food lurch in her stomach. She didn't want Theon, but being forced to give herself to someone and receive nothing in return?

But then another thought hit her. He wouldn't make her stay in that room while... When they were...producing said heir. Would he?

At the thought, Tessa's fork slipped from her fingers. It hit her plate with a clatter, rice scattering across the table. Silence fell, all eyes coming to settle on her.

"My apologies," she said softly, beginning to clean up the rice, her cheeks hot.

"Theon, did we not have a discussion about your Source's manners?" Valter asked, his voice a steely calm.

"We did. It was unintentional and will not happen again," Theon said quickly, his hand coming to rest on her knee that had begun bouncing beneath the table.

"I should hope not, but you assured me of the same in our prior conversation. I clearly have a way of instilling obedience in my Source," he said with a nod of his head in Eviana's direction. She was eating her vegetables, eyes on her plate. "Perhaps you need assistance."

"She is not your Source to discipline. I will take care of it when we return to our rooms," Theon answered tightly.

Tessa didn't know how to react to anything that was being said, but at Valter's words of his "assistance," Eviana had glanced up briefly, her face paling, before she reached for her water glass and took a drink.

"That may be the case, but she will not be permitted to finish eating at my table," Valter said.

Tessa's eyes were fixed on Theon, who was staring at his father. His words ran through her head.

Keep your eyes on me tonight.

Theon would fix this. He'd promised to take care of her. He'd fix this, and she'd apologize profusely later. She'd try harder. She'd figure out a way to make this bond thing work.

She watched that muscle feather in his jaw. His knuckles were white around his glass. She was beginning to think it was going to shatter in his hand.

"Tessa, leave the table," he ground out. "Stand by the wall behind me until it's time for us to go. Do not make a sound."

She stared at him in complete and utter shock. "Because I dropped a fork?"

The words were out of her mouth before she had a chance to stop them. Theon's head whipped to her, his emerald eyes darkening a shade. No. They didn't darken. Darkness swirled in them.

"She speaks back to you too?" Valter asked, his voice tight with rage. "I swear to Arius, Theon, if she is not under control—"

"She is under control, Father," Theon interrupted, fury tinging his tone as he glanced over his shoulder at him. He brought his eyes back to hers. "Go, Tessa."

"Th—" she paused, his name getting stuck in her throat. "I didn't throw food across the table. I dropped a fork," she hissed indignantly, trying to keep her voice down.

Eviana's eyes had left her Master and were fixed on her, wide in horror at her outburst. Cressida was sipping on her wine, watching everything as if Tessa were the evening entertainment. Axel was giving her a pitying look, and Luka's glare was telling her to move to the fucking wall.

"Theon," his father growled from across the table, and that was darkness wreathing his hands.

"I have it handled," Theon snapped. "Tessa, we discussed the behavior that was expected of you tonight. Either move to the wall, or you will sit at my feet for the remainder of this meal."

"You cannot be serious," she balked, her eyes widening at the threat.

"Serious as the Pits of Torment," he replied coolly. Standing, he gripped her elbow, hauling her to her feet. He snapped his finger and a servant appeared. "Remove her chair."

Ice cold fury raced through her veins. Theon's eyes never left hers while his order was carried out. When the chair was removed, he said, "Kneel, Tessa, and not another word."

His entire demeanor was possessive and dominating, and as Tessa lowered to her knees, something snapped in her, just like the day she'd screamed to the gods on the drive here. It was a *thing* that lurked inside her, that only one other had ever been able to help her control. Her lips curled up in a smirk as she whispered mockingly, "Eyes on you. For one night. Right?"

"Enough," he snarled, the darkness in his eyes swirling faster. Dark mist appeared, hovering around him.

"Theon," Axel said quietly from across the table, and it seemed to pull Theon back from a brink, the darkness dissipating.

"Do not interfere with this, Axel," Valter hissed.

When Tessa was kneeling on the floor, Theon slowly sank back into his seat, finally pulling his gaze from hers.

"Must we really discuss Matches days before he is to leave this house?" Cressida asked, continuing their conversation as if nothing had happened. "At least when he has a Match, they will live here."

"I think it would be wise to discuss potential Matches," Valter countered. "Many will be at the Acropolis with him. He could get to know them there."

Tessa could hear the clinking of silverware and glasses as they resumed their meal while she stared at their shoes and legs beneath the table.

Beneath. The. Fucking. Table.

She gritted her teeth as her feet began to fall asleep in her shoes. She shifted so she was sitting, which was no easy task in this dress. Theon's hand came to her hair, running through the parts of it left down, and the fucking bond hummed in gratitude for his touch. It didn't care that she was sitting on the floor in humiliation. It only cared that she was touching him, even if it was at his feet.

"I do not think it needs to be discussed anytime soon," Theon was saying, twining a lock of her hair around his finger. "The law states there can be no Match unions made during a Selection year anyway."

"That does not mean an arrangement cannot be made and terms agreed to during the year," Valter answered. "There are three in particular I think would produce acceptable heirs. I can show you their reports tomorrow."

Theon sighed. "As you wish, Father."

Plates were removed, and dessert was brought out. Tessa was growing tired and restless, sitting on the floor. Theon playing with her hair was irritating, and she wondered just how long this meal was going to go on.

"Metias and Pavil will arrive tomorrow morning at ten," Valter was saying. "I want you and Luka at the meeting, Theon."

"Is that really necessary?" Theon asked, his fingers drifting over the diamond choker at her throat.

"I think it is. We need to get things finalized before you leave for the Acropolis."

"Everything is already finalized. I know what is expected of me when I get there," Theon said. His fingers grazed along her skin as he ran them along the choker, and Tessa suddenly saw it for what it was.

A collar.

A very pretty, very expensive collar.

A collar to control her and train her and subdue her. And she wanted it off. It was suffocating her. It was cutting off her air supply, little by little, until there would be nothing left. Until there would be nothing left of *her*.

The space beneath the table suddenly felt more like she was locked in a cupboard. Her breaths became shallow, and she couldn't get enough air down. She began to tremble. Her hand flew to her chest as if she could somehow force it to expand to allow more air into her lungs.

Theon went rigid beside her, his hand coming up to her cheek and stroking his thumb along her cheekbone, as if trying to soothe her. She squeezed her eyes shut tight, trying to focus on her breathing, but the necklace at her throat was digging into her skin. She swore it was becoming tighter and tighter. That it wasn't a collar at all but a noose.

She brought her hands up, trying to find the clasp at the back of the thing. Her hands were shaking, but she needed it off. Theon's hand landed on hers, and she gripped his fingers, digging her nails into his skin.

"Fine," Theon said, interrupting whatever his father had been saying. Tessa heard his glass plunk onto the table. "I will be in your study at ten tomorrow." He stood abruptly, his fingers sliding from her grip. "If that is all for the evening, then I am going to take my leave."

"You will leave the table with a half full drink?" Valter asked, his voice dangerously low.

"I have liquor in my room and a Source to deal with," Theon replied. Tessa heard chairs scrape, and from beneath the table, she saw Luka and Axel go to their feet as well.

"I will expect your presence at more family dinners before you go off to the Acropolis," Valter said.

"Noted," Theon replied, extending a hand to her. She looked up at him towering over her as she sat on the floor. When she didn't reach to take his hand, he said, "Come, Tessa."

Tentatively, she placed her fingers into his waiting palm, and he instantly closed it around them. He pulled her roughly to her feet, his face carefully void of any emotion. Crossing the room quickly, he towed her along behind him, and she nearly tripped in her heels. Luka and Axel trailed behind them.

Theon didn't slow until they rounded a corner. Then she found herself pushed up against a wall. Theon's hands were on her face, tilting it up to look at him. "What is wrong? Why are you pale as death?"

Tessa pursed her lips, refusing to meet his eyes. What did he care anyway? He'd made her sit on the fucking ground at his feet while they finished their dinner. She was trembling, but there were so many emotions rippling through her, she couldn't decide if it was from his closeness, her rage, or her feeling of utter helplessness. Her skin was buzzing, energy that needed to be expelled, and this fucking necklace needed to get off of her throat so she could fucking breathe.

"Tessa," he demanded, her name an order.

She dragged her eyes to his, glaring up at him. "Will I be made to kiss your shoes in punishment for something else I cannot control?" she sneered despite the tightness in her chest.

Someone sucked in a breath behind them. Luka or Axel, she didn't know. She also didn't give a shit. Theon's lips thinned. "Tell me what is wrong," he repeated, his tone deceptively calm. The same tone the Arius Lord had spoken in earlier that night. "Are you ill?" When she didn't respond, he gritted out, "How can I take care of you if you refuse to tell me what is wrong?"

"How can I trust you to take care of me when you place me at your feet like a godsdamn dog?" she spat back.

"Tessalyn, *answer me.* What is wrong?" he demanded, ire glittering in his eyes.

Unable to withstand the entrancing, she answered, "I want this necklace off."

Theon studied her for a moment, as if searching for a lie, but she couldn't fully lie around an entrancing. He reached up and unclasped the choker, slipping it into his pocket. "What else? Why are you so pale?"

"Why do you care? Because I was not the perfect doting Source like Eviana?" Tessa asked, her tone dripping with venom.

"Perhaps we should take this to your rooms, Theon," Luka suggested tightly from behind them. "Things will be reported back to the Lord."

"Fine," Theon snapped, reaching for Tessa's hand again. She jerked it back from him, crossing her arms over her chest. Theon's eyes darkened as his temper slipped, and he gripped her elbow, pulling her along.

A warning look from Luka had her swallowing down her protest.

The buzzing in her skin was increasing, and she could hear it in her head. Loud and incessant and needing out, out, out. The cord was vibrating too, relishing Theon's hand on her skin. And she couldn't handle it. She couldn't deal with all the emotions and the things that had happened during dinner and everything else that had been removed from her control.

When they finally made it back to his rooms, Theon opened the door, standing aside to let her enter first. She crossed the threshold, going straight through the main room.

"Tessa," Theon called after her as she walked into the bedroom. She heard the door click shut, and she heard someone else comment something about the thunder that was rumbling outside, but she didn't slow. Crossing Theon's bedroom, she flung open the double doors that led out to the balcony. She needed air. She needed to feel the wind on her face and to not be trapped inside those rooms. She paused only long enough to remove the shoes from her feet before stalking to the railing and hurling them both as far as she could, screaming defiantly to the sky in rage and releasing every emotion that was warring inside of her. Lightning flashed and thunder rumbled, the sound mixing with her screams, and as she sank to her knees, it started to pour. Big, cold drops splashed onto her face, into her hair. And gods, it felt amazing. Something wild and free. She was soaked in a matter of seconds, the beautiful dress she was wearing likely ruined.

Her face fell into her hands as she let herself cry all the tears of rage and anger, hurt and humiliation she had been holding back since dinner. Since she'd arrived here really. The diamond bracelet scraped against her cheek, and she fumbled with the clasp, throwing the thing across the balcony before all but ripping the earrings from her ears and doing the same. She briefly glimpsed the others standing in the doorway, staring at her in shock, clearly not knowing what to do with her.

No one ever knew what to do with her except shove her aside. Lock her away. Too wild to be something, so forced to be nothing.

When she began violently ripping pins from her hair and bringing strands with them, Theon finally moved forward. He slowly knelt down beside her and moved her hands away before beginning to gently remove the remaining hairpins. As he worked, the storm slowed. The downpour turned into a rhythmic rain, but it never stopped. It was a steady stream of something so cold, it numbed everything else inside of her.

When he finished, he took her hands, pulling her to her feet without a word and guiding her back inside. Luka was waiting with towels. He handed one to Theon before wrapping one around her shoulders.

He led her to the armchairs before the fireplace. Axel had turned it on and warmth radiated into the room, but she didn't feel any of it. The cold of the rain had settled in her soul, icy and unforgiving.

Theon went into the bathroom and emerged a few minutes later shirtless and in lounge pants. He came to her with another towel and began squeezing the water from her hair.

Tessa stared at the flames flickering behind the glass of the fireplace. Oranges and reds and hottest blues dancing together, tangling and fighting, loving and hating.

No, wait.

They weren't doing any of that.

Her head tilted to the side as she watched them lick against the glass that contained them. That stifled the wildfire they longed to burn. Her hand drifted up to her throat, her fingers grazing where the choker had sat. The fire just wanted to be free to do what its nature demanded of it, but it was stuck inside a glass box. It was contained so that others could harness its energy and stay warm or admire its deadly beauty. To be used and snuffed out with the flick of a switch.

"Tessa." Theon's voice was tentative. "You need to change out of your wet clothing."

Her gaze remained fixed on the flames for a few seconds longer before she dragged her eyes to his. He was watching her warily, clearly unsure of what she was going to do or say. She glanced at Luka, who was leaning against the wall near the door. He looked as though he were prepared to stop her. As if he anticipated she would try to leave. Axel was like a statue by the fireplace, his features a mixture of concern and shock.

She uncoiled from the chair she had been placed in, standing onto her bare feet. Theon stepped back, giving her space. She looked at the flames once more before turning and walking through the tiny room and into the closet. Peeling off the wet dress, she left it lying on the floor while she found a pair of leggings and a thermal shirt from the island dresser. She brought the dress into the bathroom and hung it over the tub. Then she removed her make-up—or what was left of it—and brushed her teeth, staring into her eyes in the mirror, red and puffy from crying. Broken and fractured and everything she'd tried to put back together over the years shattered once more.

She couldn't do this.

Theon had asked her to try for one night. She had barely lasted two hours before she was literally shoved under the table.

She crossed back through the dressing room and into the room she'd been given as her own space. Then again, nothing here was hers. She wasn't even her own self here. Crawling into the bed, she pulled the scratchy blanket up to her chin as she rolled over and faced the wall. She wished she could cry herself to sleep, but apparently she was fresh out of tears, so she stared at the wall, trying and failing to sort through all the turmoil roiling inside of her. She could still hear the rain splattering against the windows in the other room.

At some point, Theon came into the room. She felt him sit on the edge of the bed. He ran his hand over her still damp hair, and all she could think about was how he had done the same while she'd sat at his feet beneath a table.

"I know you do not want to, Tessa, but it would be best if you came to sleep in the other bed. Being near me will help...calm you," he said.

She didn't move, clutching the thin blanket tighter around herself, pointedly ignoring the joy of the bond at his touch. After a minute, he sighed, and she felt the weight of a heavier blanket settle over her. He left the room without saying anything else, and she heard hushed whispers as they moved out to the main room.

She refused to be like those flames in that fireplace. She refused to be collared and leashed and trapped. No. She was getting out whether this bond liked it or not. She'd go into hiding. Find a way to get in touch with Dex at some point. She'd figure out a way to stay hidden. She could blend in. Steal some money and buy a glamour so she could move freely among the mortals. Go somewhere in another kingdom, to the big cities where there were millions of people.

She wouldn't survive this. It would break her.

And she didn't burn when she broke.

She shattered, and the world shattered with her.

10
THEON

Theon was trying to stay focused on what his father was discussing with Metias and Pavil, but his mind was on Tessa. She had refused to sleep beside him last night, just like he'd known she would. He could have forced it, but after... Well, after her night, he didn't know if she'd give in or fight back even more. She hadn't spoken a word to him since the hallway after dinner. She hadn't uttered a word to anyone actually.

He'd slept like shit, the bond wanting her near. And while he'd lain there, unable to sleep, he'd replayed the night over and over in his head. How she'd dropped her fork when his father began speaking of potential Matches. How he'd been forced to somehow discipline her before his father decided to do it himself. He knew she'd been humiliated and hated him for forcing her to sit on the floor at his feet, but his father's punishments would have been far worse. He'd never been given the opportunity to explain though.

She had stiffened against him beneath the table. Then he'd felt her start to tremble, and he'd known something was wrong. When he'd stood from the table and looked down to see her pale as a spirit of the After, it took all of his self-control not to scoop her up and take her back to the sanctuary he'd created for her in their rooms, keeping her safely tucked away from his father and who he required Theon to be.

She'd learn that soon enough. Fuck, she'd already seen pieces of that façade, and if she didn't give into this bond soon...

He'd stood in stunned silence alongside Luka and Axel as she'd hurled her shoes over the balcony railing, proceeding to scream at the stormy skies. Memories of her doing the same in the vehicle on the way here came flooding back to him in those moments. He'd been frozen, unable to move as she broke in front of him, falling to the ground. The sound of her knees cracking against that marble balcony was a sound he couldn't turn off. It replayed on a loop in his mind. When she began yanking pins from her hair with such force and savagery, he'd finally made himself move before she hurt herself further.

Luka and Axel had little to say when he had emerged from her room after her clear refusal to come to his bed. They knew he'd had to do what he'd done at dinner. They knew what his father could and would do. Axel was visibly upset when Luka pushed a drink into his hand.

"I've never seen anyone lose it like that, but certainly not a Fae. Not a Source," he said, taking a long drink of scotch. "I didn't even know a Source could be like...that with their Master." He glanced at Theon over his glass, waiting for an explanation.

Theon had carved a hand through his hair, knocking back his entire glass of whiskey in one go. "I don't know what to do with her. I'm trying to give her space and time to adjust, but I don't understand how she can resist the bond so much. If she's feeling the pull like I do, it should be impossible to withstand it. I never thought we'd have to force this."

Luka had remained quiet, sitting on the sofa deep in some thought or another. They'd eventually all gone to their own rooms to call it a night. When Theon had finally gotten up just as dawn was breaking the horizon, he'd gone to her room to find her still staring at the wall. Had she even slept?

"I'm going to make coffee, Tessa," he'd said. "I'll order up some breakfast too."

She hadn't bothered to acknowledge his presence.

Breakfast arrived, along with Luka and Axel. Tessa didn't emerge. They ate without conversation. He had showered and gotten ready. Finally at half-past nine, he'd gone back to her room. She hadn't moved. Not an inch.

"I have to go to a meeting, Tessa, but Axel is out in the main room. He'll stay here with you until I get back." He was met with silence, and he didn't know what to do. Did he go to her? Force her to get up? Entrance her to at least say something so he knew...

Knew what? That she was all right? She clearly wasn't. Forcing her to speak would only make him feel better hearing her voice.

He sighed before he added, "When I get back, we need to discuss last night."

She didn't stir.

He'd deal with it when he got back. She needed to eat at the very least. She hadn't gotten to finish dinner. Maybe she'd get hungry enough to get up on her own. Gods, he hoped so. He was so fucking tired of fighting her on every godsdamn thing. He had not expected such resistance when he picked a Source, and it was becoming harder and harder to leash his temper the more she defied him and pushed him away.

"Theon," his father growled, bringing him back to the present. "Anything to add to what was just discussed?"

Theon glanced at Luka, the male giving him a frank look that told him he knew exactly what Theon had been thinking about. He gave a subtle shake of his head.

"No, that all sounds fine," Theon said smoothly. He honestly didn't even know why this meeting was happening. These plans had been perfected and finalized months ago.

"We were hoping to meet your new Source," Metias said, his voice as greasy as his slicked back hair. "We saw her at the Opening Selection Ceremony. She's a pretty little thing."

A possessive growl rumbled low in Theon's chest as something primal inside him raised its head.

His father chuckled from behind his desk. "The newness of the Source bond has made Theon a little territorial lately. I have scarcely seen her. Give it some time, and maybe he'll be more willing to share his things," he said, a hint of warning in his tone.

Theon blinked slowly, leashing his temper. The cord had been aching in his chest all morning, likely because he hadn't touched Tessa since last night. But now it was thrashing about in demand at someone even hinting at coming near her, let alone touching her. If anyone was going to be touching her, it would be him and only him. And that brought an entirely different memory surging to the forefront of his mind—the memory of how they'd connected last night before everything had gone to shit.

He had walked into their closet to see if she was ready to go and had been stunned stupid by what he found. Tessa had been standing there, studying herself in the full-length mirror. She'd had a slight frown on her lips and a crease between her brows, as if she didn't like what she saw in the reflection, which was absolutely ludicrous.

She hadn't heard him as he'd moved behind her, and he'd startled her when he came into view in the mirror. He'd brushed her hair back from her neck and had to keep himself from groaning at the first brush of his fingers against her skin. Every time he touched her, it felt like ecstasy. His skin had tingled with pleasure as she allowed him to let his hand linger. When she'd stepped back into him, it had taken every ounce of him not to push her up against the wall and press his mouth to hers. He'd been dying to taste her again since she'd kissed him. He'd brought his hand to her hip, greedily taking any bit of contact she'd allow. Why couldn't she just give in? She had to feel it, right? This couldn't just be him. How could she keep denying something when it could be like that all the time?

So he'd asked her—no, he'd *begged* her—to try for just one night. To pretend that she'd given in to the bond and accepted her place as his Source. He'd wanted her to get a taste of what they could be. He'd wanted her to experience pleasure at his hand. To become addicted to him. To crave him like he was craving her. This entire experience was the exact opposite of what he'd been expecting. *She* was supposed to be the one wanting him so incessantly, yet he was the one hoarding any bit of contact.

A sharp kick to his shin from Luka pulled him back to the conversation at the same time his father snarled, "Theon." He met his father's cool gaze. "I'm beginning to fear your Source's poor manners are rubbing off on you."

"My apologies," Theon ground out. "It was a rather long night of…discipline."

His father's gaze darkened with pleasure at the words. Theon knew all too well how much his father enjoyed correcting behavior.

He scratched at his chest as the cord continued to thrash about. The need to get back to Tessa was more intense than he had ever experienced. The pull seemed different, urgent, and he knew he was fidgeting. Even his magic seemed agitated beneath his skin.

"As I was saying," his father continued, "while I was able to get Luka early access to the Acropolis and Pantheon, that was not extended to you two. I did not want to cause too much more of a stir than we already have for now. We will let Theon, Axel, and Luka lay some foundations during the week they are allowed to be there early and go from there."

"We knew it was a long shot," Pavil said.

"That we did," his father said, shutting a folder that was open before him and getting to his feet. Eviana instantly rose from her usual chair and came to his side. "Unless there is anything else that needs discussion, I am afraid I must take my leave. I have another meeting to get to."

"Of course, Lord St. Orcas. We appreciate your time," Metias said, standing and bowing his head. Pavil did the same.

"Tavis will see you out," Valter said, gesturing for the Fae to step forward. The male had been his father's personal servant for as long as Theon could remember.

Theon and Luka followed them out, heading for the east wing while the others turned and headed for the main doors. Theon didn't know what his father's other meeting was about. Frankly, he didn't care.

"What the fuck is wrong with you?" Luka said when they rounded a corner. "You're acting like you rolled around in poison oak."

"The bond feels different today," Theon said, taking the stairs two at a time.

"What do you mean it feels different?"

"I don't know how to explain it. The last hour or so, it's been more insistent."

"Is it reacting to all the tension between you two?" Luka asked, genuine curiosity in his voice.

"There's been tension since the Selection Ceremony. That hasn't really changed," Theon answered, increasing his pace down the hallway. When Luka didn't say anything, he added, "I just need to see her. Explain why things happened the way they did last night."

"Sure," Luka said dryly.

Theon ignored the comment. Pushing through the door to his rooms, he immediately looked to the sofa hoping to see Tessa sitting there, but he only found Axel playing a video game of some sort.

"Did she come out at all?" Theon asked, dropping his phone onto the table and going to the fridge. He grabbed a water for himself and tossed one to Luka.

"Once. She didn't even look at me, let alone acknowledge me when I spoke to her. She rummaged around in the fridge for a second before going right back in there. Had a water and an apple in her hands," Axel answered, defeating an enemy and saving his game. "I did check on her though. She was curled on her bed, facing the wall," he added with a shrug.

"How long ago was that?" Theon asked, swiping a hand down his face.

Axel glanced at the clock. "Two hours ago, give or take."

Luka had taken a seat on the sofa, noticeably not saying anything. Again.

"You have nothing to say on this matter?" Theon asked, narrowing his eyes at his friend.

"Considering my advice and concerns have routinely been dismissed or ignored, I won't bother offering them anymore," Luka said, taking a drink of his water.

"For fuck's sake," Theon muttered, shoving a hand through his hair and setting his water down with a little too much force. He stalked off to go get Tessa. She needed to eat more than an apple and then they could talk.

"Tessa, I'm—"

But the words died on his lips. Her bed was empty. He looked around the small room before going into the dressing room and on into the bathroom. He must have missed her in his bedroom.

"Tessa?" he called, stepping into his room. His bed was perfectly made, and there was certainly no blonde-haired beauty in it. The chairs by the fireplace were empty, and one look out the balcony doors told him the balcony was vacant too. "Tessa?" he called again, mainly because he couldn't fathom where she could possibly be.

"What's wrong?" Luka asked, appearing in the doorway, Axel looking over his shoulder.

"She's not here," Theon said, still not able to fully wrap his mind around that statement.

"What do you mean she's not here?" Luka said, stepping fully into the room and going to her small bedroom.

"She has to be here," Axel said, looking around as if he might spot her when everyone else had missed her. "She only came out to the other room once. It's not like I could have missed her. She has to be here," he said again.

Luka came from the bathroom, clearly having taken the same path Theon had in his search. "Order her to come out. Entrance her," he said. "If she's hiding somewhere, she'll have to obey."

Jumping on that idea, Theon said, "Tessalyn, *come here*."

They all stood still and waited.

And waited.

"It's not possible," Axel said. "She couldn't just disappear. What'd she do? Climb over the balcony railing and jump down three stories?"

He scoffed at the absurdity of the idea, but Luka and Theon locked eyes before rushing out onto the balcony. Luka went to the left, and Theon went to the right.

"Here," Luka said. "This ledge leads over to lattice work and vines. Fuck!"

"You can't be serious," Axel said from the doorway. "She didn't actually... The wards would have stopped her from leaving without one of us."

"Oh, she did," Theon growled, going to Luka's side and looking down. "She absolutely did."

"Do you want to fly to find her?" Luka asked, looking out at the gardens that eventually shifted to forest as they climbed up the mountainside.

"No. My father might notice, and he cannot find out about this," Theon said.

This had to explain the shift in the bond. She was getting farther away from him. The urgency was still there, but it was becoming muted and muffled. "We'll take the horses and hounds. Axel, stay here in case she ends up coming back. Call me if she does."

"Got it," Axel said. "I'm sorry, Theon. I didn't know—"

Theon cut him off. "It's not your fault, Axel. She's..."

"Uncontrollable?" Luka supplied.

Theon was clenching his teeth so hard, he was surprised he didn't crack a molar. "Strong willed," he finally ground out. He snatched the thin blanket from her bed before stalking into the dressing room. "Call down to the stables and have them ready two of mine."

"On it," Axel called in to him.

Theon quickly changed into jeans, riding boots, and a thermal. He'd grab a heavier jacket from hooks by the door on his way out.

What the fuck was she thinking? Sure, it was decent during the day, but as soon as the sun started setting, the temperature in the mountains would plummet. What if this odd weather continued and it stormed? There weren't any jackets or gear in here that she could have taken with her. Had she taken any food? Water? And where did she even think she was going to go? Guards would see her trying to cross the gates or walls.

He had to assume she was going to attempt going up the mountain at the back of the property, where she would face not only the elements but the things that prowled the woods and Ozul Mountains.

Luka met him outside his rooms as he shrugged on his jacket, heading for the stairwell to take them out the side entrance of the east wing. Luka had changed as well, his face grim. They strode along the paths to the stables in silence, stopping to grab two of Theon's prized hounds on the way. These weren't your typical hunting dogs. They had sleek black coats, eyes that glowed like embers, and were as large as a small horse. They were more like wolves than hounds, he supposed.

He whistled sharply as he entered the kennels, and the howling and excited yips of his hounds immediately ceased. He unlocked the pens of his best trackers, Kacela and Rigel. They would make short work of finding her.

The hounds dutifully fell into step behind him as they continued on their way to the stables. When they arrived, two stable hands were finishing checking straps and buckles. Luka crossed to the small storage space to retrieve packs and fill them with water and a little food. Tessa couldn't have made it that far traveling on foot. She only had a few hours' lead on them. They ought to be able to catch up to her in an hour or two. At least Theon hoped so. That unnecessary meeting had gone on for hours.

While Luka put packs together, Theon tossed the blanket from Tessa's bed to the ground for Kacela and Rigel to get her scent. She wouldn't be needing the blanket anytime soon. She wouldn't be leaving his sight again until he was confident the bond was in place, and she was fully under his control.

Luka returned, tossing him a pack, and Theon moved to his favorite of his four horses, Osiris. They were giant black stallions named after some of Sargon's most famed warriors. Theon had searched tirelessly to find the horses and spent countless hours training them to his exact specifications. He mounted Osiris with ease while Luka pulled himself up into Zale's saddle.

"Ready?" Theon asked, moving Osiris's reins to one hand. The horse stamped his hoof and pawed at the ground, clearly ready to run. Kacela and Rigel were prancing around the horses, whimpering and restless with the excitement of the hunt.

"What are you going to do when you find her?" Luka asked, getting settled into his own saddle.

"I've been giving her space and time to adjust, but this is the second time she's run from me," Theon said, urging Osiris to walk from the stables. "And it will be the last."

He needed to bring the female to heel. Her wildness might intrigue him, but this was taking it too far. She could push him away and fight with him all she wanted in their private quarters, but not in public. Not in front of his father. She needed to accept her fate. Not only because his father would require it, but because Theon's own plans required her cooperation. He needed her willing to let him feed on her strength and power. When the time came, he couldn't be focused on forcing her to give it to him.

Tessa saw him as a merciless descendant of the gods who wanted to possess her and rule her, so that's what he would become.

He'd tried to ease her into her role, thinking it would build trust faster. But in doing so, he'd clearly given her the illusion that he wasn't in control of *everything*. That he wasn't in control of her. She'd learn why the Arius Kingdom was whispered about.

He'd become the nightmare she already thought he was.

11

TESSA

The sun had been high in the sky when she'd crept over the balcony railing and sidled along that narrow ledge to the trellis of climbing ivy. She'd prayed to anyone but the gods that it would hold her weight when she gingerly tested it and breathed out a sigh of relief as she shimmied down.

The wards had pressed along her skin, and these were strong. Some wards she could feel, but more in a she-knew-they-were-there sort of way. Few actually pressed to keep her out. Or in this case, keep her in. Weaker wards she didn't feel at all. Which is why she so often found herself in trouble for being in places she wasn't supposed to be as a child.

She'd never figured out how she could evade them. It was something she had just always been able to do. It had taken her a long time to figure out what was happening though, and by the time she fully understood it, she'd also long-since figured out how to sneak about without getting caught. Her ability to avoid the wards extended to whoever was with her, as long as they were touching. It was one of the things she never spoke of. One of the things they'd helped her keep hidden. If she was caught, Theon would question how she evaded the wards.

So she wouldn't get caught.

Theon's suite overlooked the gardens along the back of the vast estate. Knowing there was no way she'd make it past the guards at the front gates, she'd gone the only way she could go—into the forest that climbed up the mountainside. Their property couldn't go forever, right? Admittedly, she had not thought this plan through entirely. She rarely did. Usually there were others with her when things inevitably went to shit, but she could do this. She'd find her way to a road eventually, and then...

Well, she excelled at figuring things out in the moment. This wouldn't be any different, she supposed.

She'd waited until after Axel had checked on her. She'd heard him creep into Theon's room to make sure she was still...what? There? Breathing? Alive? Probably all three. He'd tried talking to her, but she'd ignored him just like she had Theon. As soon as Axel had gone back out to his video game though, she'd gotten out of bed. She'd already changed into jeans, a thermal, and sneakers so all she'd had to do was tie her sweatshirt around her waist and grab the small bag she'd found in the closet. She'd stuffed it with a couple bottles of water, an apple, cheese, and a bag of nuts she'd taken from the kitchen. That was all the small bag could hold. She likely wouldn't have been able to carry anything else down the trellis or through the woods.

The sun was setting, and she paused to untie her sweatshirt and slip it over her head. She hadn't taken into account how quickly the temperature would drop or how she would stay warm tonight. Where was she even going to sleep? She could find a cave or something, maybe?

What if there were bears in the cave? Or something worse? There were rumors of all manner of creatures in the Ozul Mountains. Creatures that could fly...

Tessa pushed those thoughts from her mind as she kept moving. She'd go until she couldn't see anymore, getting as far away from Arius House as she possibly could and figure the rest out as she went. She didn't really have much of a choice. She worked better under pressure anyway.

Her stomach grumbled loudly, and she sighed, reaching into the small crossbody bag and tugging out the apple to eat while she continued moving. She hadn't eaten since dinner the night before. Another thing she really should have thought about before climbing down a three-story drop. She glanced at her muddy sneakers. Boots of some sort would have probably been a good idea too.

But she hadn't been thinking. Her entire focus had been on getting out, getting away. Her entire world had revolved around that one goal. Nothing else had mattered. She couldn't think about anything else, too numb to really care. One step at a time. That's all she could do. And each step she took away from that house was her reaching that goal.

And gods. To be outside. Not cooped up in a set of rooms, but out in the open. No rules. No boundaries. Nothing to keep her contained. Space to breathe.

Each step also sent a resounding jolt through her limbs as the Source bond protested loudly, reminding her this still wasn't true freedom. It begged her to turn around and go back to Theon. It made her long for his touch and so much more. It pressed at her, pleading with her to give in, to serve him, to do everything in her power to please him. She gritted her teeth against the pain she'd grown used to as she'd run and eventually slowed to a walk. She'd become numb to that too eventually. At least she hoped she would.

The sounds of the woods as she'd made her way over logs and through muddy patches had become soothing. Animals rustled and insects buzzed. She tried to keep her mind busy as the sun sank lower.

Until she heard howling.

She couldn't ignore that.

Those were wolves.

Tessa picked up her pace, her legs burning at the nonstop incline. Maybe she could get out of their range? But as she worked into a jog, the howling got closer. Along with barks and snarls.

Fuck this. Wolves can't climb trees. If she had to spend the night clinging to a branch, then that's what she'd do.

She raced forward, the bag slipping from her grasp as she ran, but she didn't care. There wasn't time to stop. She slipped on the earth still wet from the storm last night, mud splattering as she stepped in puddles. Most of the trees here were pine trees, but she didn't register the stinging cuts she got from the needles as she raced among them. The first climbable tree she found, she started making her way up. How high could wolves jump? Four feet? Five feet? Six?

She went higher and higher until she was at least halfway up the giant tree just as two huge black wolves leapt from a clearing. She didn't know wolves could be that big, but they looked like they could jump higher than six feet. Orange eyes glowed as if they were embers. They prowled to the base of the tree she was in, and one stood up on its hind legs, placing its huge front paws on the trunk. It tipped its head back and howled to the ever darkening sky. The wolf beside it began circling the tree, joining its brother in the chorus.

How many more were they calling to join them? How long would they stay here trying to reach her? Would they eventually give up?

The sound of branches breaking and thundering paws had her trembling as she tried to climb higher. Weapons. A weapon of some sort would have been a good idea to bring with her.

Difficult. Impulsive. Reckless.

She cried out as her foot slipped, her torso scraping along the bark and pulling her from her spiral of thoughts. Clinging to the branch she was grasping, she pulled herself back up until she was resting against the trunk.

The thundering of paws slowed and then ceased, and Tessa held her breath. Had they decided not to come after all? But the two wolves still paced around the base of her tree, yipping and pawing at the trunk. The sound of more twigs snapping had her whipping her head in the direction of the sound.

But it wasn't wolves that emerged from between a cluster of trees. It was a massive black horse. It hadn't been paws but thundering hooves. The wolves at the base of the tree ran to the horse then back to the tree, barking in excitement. The black horse and the wolves weren't what held her attention though. It was the male on the back of the horse who was looking up at her with the rage of a thousand angry spirits from the depths of the Pits.

Theon brought his horse to a halt as another equally gigantic horse emerged from the opposite direction. Luka sat astride this horse, and when his eyes locked on Tessa, they seemed to glow faintly.

Theon gave a sharp whistle as he slid off the horse. The two wolves immediately quieted and sat at the base of the tree.

He reached into a bag tied to his saddle, and as he approached the wolves, he passed them each some type of meat. The wolves instantly tore into their rewards, soft snarling drifting up to her. Finally, he brought those emerald green eyes back to hers. She already couldn't move, but now she couldn't breathe either. The bond was having a fit in her chest, practically yanking her out of the tree to get to him.

"There are far scarier things in these woods than my hounds," his smooth voice crooned, carrying up to her.

"You don't scare me, Theon," Tessa retorted, grateful her voice didn't waiver because she was fucking terrified.

"I really, really should, beautiful," he answered, a cruel smile twisting on his lips. Darkness began to coil and swarm around his feet, creeping over the ground like a dense fog. It stood out starkly, even amongst the dimming light of dusk.

Theon lifted his palms, and Tessa's eyes widened as the darkness slithered from him like snakes. Shadows darker than night twisted and wound their way up the tree to her. She tried to scramble away from them, but where was she going to go? She was up a fucking tree.

Such a stupid move. Who traps themselves in a tree?

Someone reckless and impulsive. That's who.

The darkness wrapped itself around her waist before it suddenly jerked, wrenching her from the branch and suspending her fifteen feet from the ground. Tessa screamed as he held her there, Theon staring up at her with a satisfied smirk on his mouth. His wolves, having finished their treats, sat obediently at his side, and in that moment, all she could see was the God of Endings himself looking up at her. She saw everything his bloodline entailed. Power and death exuded from him in waves. And darkness. So much darkness.

As if the floor had been pulled from beneath her, Tessa was plunging to the forest floor. Another scream ripped from her throat, but she was yanked to a halt and placed on her feet by the shadows that clung to her waist. The wolves were on their feet, low growls sounding, but Theon strode purposefully forward. She backed up until she bumped into the tree she'd climbed. He didn't slow, coming right up to her and forcing her to tilt her head back to look up at him. What was he going to do to her?

"Are you physically hurt anywhere?" he asked, his tone formal and authoritative. His hands came to her face, where he tilted her head from side-to-side, before systematically working his way down her body. He didn't wait for her to answer, healing any scrapes and bruises he found as he went.

When he was satisfied she was fine, he gripped her elbow, hauling her over to his massive horse. With a flick of his fingers, his darkness again wrapped around her, and she gasped at the contact as she was lifted from her feet and onto the back of the horse. Theon hoisted himself into the saddle behind her, reaching around her to grip the reins. Tessa didn't know what to do or how to sit. She'd never been on a horse before.

As if he suddenly realized this, Theon spoke low into her ear. "Relax and sit back into me, Tessa. We have quite a ride ahead of us, and you will be incredibly uncomfortable if you sit like that the entire time."

His arm snaked around her waist where the darkness had been, and he tugged her back into the cradle of his hips. She couldn't hold in the soft moan that fell from her lips as pleasure darted up her spine. Without thinking, she pressed back into him even more, her back flush against his chest.

"My thoughts precisely," he murmured, his lips brushing the shell of her ear. "But this discussion will be had when we are back in our rooms."

Tessa stiffened at the implications of those words as Theon urged the horse into motion. Her hands flew forward, grasping the saddle horn to keep herself steady, despite his arm wrapped tightly around her. She'd like to think he wouldn't let her fall off the horse, but the one time she'd let herself trust him, he'd shoved her beneath a table.

Theon whistled sharply, and the wolves fell into step beside the horse, staying close to their master's side. Luka came to ride beside them, and they worked the horses into a steady trot.

They rode for over two hours, covering the same distance that had taken her an entire afternoon and into the evening to traverse. All of that work and effort for nothing, and despite trying to relax into Theon, she was tense against him. He was warm though…

No.

That feeling was the damn bond.

Arius House came into view as they crested a small hill, and Tessa sucked in a breath as they slowed the horses. The wolves panted, clearly as tired as she felt.

"We better walk the rest of the way," Theon said to Luka, speaking for the first time since he'd hauled her out of the tree. "The hounds need to rest."

"They did good work today," Luka commented casually. "It's been a while since I've hunted with them."

Tessa huffed. *Hunted.* She'd been hunted today. The arm that Theon still held tightly around her tensed at her disapproval.

"I thought of taking two of the younger ones, but I needed my best trackers," Theon replied.

Luka shrugged as he considered. "True. You should bring a pup out with Kacela some time though. He'd learn from her."

"Valid point. That is how Rigel became so skilled. I don't get out as much as I used to."

They rode in silence for a while longer until Luka said, "You know that Absko and Eyal are going to be upset they were left behind today, right?"

Theon huffed a laugh. "It isn't as if we could each ride two horses."

"They won't see it that way," Luka muttered. "They're going to be a handful for the stablehands until you take them out."

Theon was quiet for a few seconds before he said, "Maybe in a few days I can get back down here and take them out. However, the next couple of days are pretty full."

"Is that right?" Luka asked with exaggerated curiosity.

His tone snagged Tessa's interest, and she glanced at Luka, startled to find him staring straight at her. She quickly looked forward once more, swallowing nervously. The pace was more of a stroll now, and she was very ready to get off the horse and out of Theon's arms.

She jolted as the bond punished her for such a thought. It had been happily humming away for the last two hours. She'd forgotten the brutality of the thing that she'd dealt with most of the day.

"What's wrong?" Theon asked. She felt him dip his head to speak to her.

Refusing to look over her shoulder at him, she answered shortly, "Nothing. I'm fine."

"Then what was that? Why did you jump?"

She pressed her lips together and ignored him.

Before Theon could press her for an answer, Luka spoke again. "What's made your next couple of days so full, Theon?"

Theon sat up straighter. They had reached the paths of the gardens, and he turned the horse towards what Tessa assumed were the stables. "You know damn well why my next couple of days are so full," he said.

"I do, yes. But does *she*?"

Tessa stiffened. She didn't want to know what she had to do with Theon's next couple of days.

"She will find out soon enough," Theon replied.

Nothing else was said until they reached the stables. Theon slid down, landing gracefully on his feet. He dropped to a knee, leaving her atop the horse while he praised his wolves for their excellent tracking. They rubbed against him, licking his hands and face, and Tessa couldn't help but wonder how he'd trained *wolves*.

Luka had dismounted as well, untying a bag, and handing the reins off to a stablehand. "Make sure they get rubbed down well. They were worked hard today."

The Fae nodded, and as he led Luka's horse away, a loud huffing sound came from a pen. Another massive black horse stuck his head over a gate and began knocking on his stall with his hoof.

"Told you," Luka said pointedly to Theon.

Theon breathed out a laugh as he untied something from the saddle Tessa was still stuck in. How long was he going to leave her up here?

"Hold him steady," he said, handing the reins to another waiting stablehand. She watched in dismay as he left her there and strode over to the disgruntled horse. As he approached, yet another horse stuck its head out, huffing directly into Theon's ear as he passed by. It was as if the horse had planned a surprise attack.

"Hey, now," Theon scolded, but his tone was anything but upset. He pushed the horse away by his nose. "I'll take you out soon. I promise." The horse huffed again, and Theon reached into the bag, pulling out an apple. "Peace offering?"

At first, the large beast didn't seem like he was going to take the fruit, but then it swiped it quickly from Theon's outstretched palm. The first horse whinnied in displeasure. "Relax, Absko," Theon chided. "I have one for you too."

When the horses appeared satisfied, Theon returned to the horse Tessa still sat upon. He slung the bag over his shoulder, then flicked his wrist. Shadows appeared, winding around her again. They weren't as rough as when they'd ripped her out of the tree, but it still took everything in her not to scream as they lifted her from the horse.

When her feet hit the ground, she stumbled a bit at being on her feet again, but Theon caught her. His hands on her hips, he waited until she was steady, then one hand clamped onto her elbow.

"Can you take Kacela and Rigel to the kennels and make sure they are fed and given water?" Theon asked Luka.

"I can," Luka answered slowly, eyeing them both.

"Thank you. We will see you tomorrow for a late breakfast. Say mid-morning?"

Tessa started. No. Luka had to be there tonight. He wouldn't leave her to deal with Theon on her own, would he?

Luka was quiet for a long moment before he finally sighed. "Are you sure you do not want assistance tonight?"

"That won't be necessary," Theon answered curtly, tugging her along beside him as he headed for the door. "We will see you in the morning."

Tessa swallowed thickly while Theon led her through the garden paths and back to the house. He clearly knew the area well, but she stumbled along in the dark. She'd been dreading this moment. Not facing Theon and whatever consequences he may dole out for her trying to leave. But stepping back into this house? Two silent tears tracked down her face when Theon opened the door for her and motioned for her to enter first. His lips thinned when he noticed the tears, but he said nothing, following her through the side door of the east wing.

She dragged her feet as they climbed the stairs and went down the hall to Theon's suite. The wards pulled back, recognizing Theon, and he tugged her through the door. Axel immediately stood from the sofa.

"Thank the gods you found her," he said, coming over to them. Theon had finally released his hold on her and was removing his jacket and boots.

"Yes. Kacela and Rigel were exceptional as always," Theon replied.

Axel was looking at Tessa, worry filling his emerald eyes. "Do you need me to do anything or...?" He trailed off, his gaze flickering from her to Theon and back again.

"No," Theon answered, pulling his shirt from his jeans. "We are having a late breakfast tomorrow. You are welcome to join us mid-morning."

"Is Luka coming back tonight?" Axel asked cautiously.

"He is not," Theon said, crossing to the kitchen and pulling a bottle of whiskey from the liquor cabinet. "I need some time with my Source to discuss some things," he continued, pouring the liquor and taking a sip.

Tessa flinched back at the words.

My Source.

Not her name.

"Are you sure you don't want me to stay a little longer?" Axel pressed, clear trepidation lining his features as he cast another worried look at her.

Tessa could have kissed him for trying.

"Good night, Axel," Theon said firmly, glancing pointedly at the door. "Thank you for everything today."

Axel gave Tessa a pitying look before he scooped up his phone and a sweatshirt and left without another word. Tessa stood rooted to the spot where Theon had left her. Her sneakers were muddy, and her clothing was just as filthy. Her hair was a mess from the ride back, and her face was tear-stained from the events of the last two days. She didn't move as she waited for the barrage of questions and demands she was sure were coming.

What was she thinking?

Did she really think this would work?

Where did she think she was going to go?

How did she get past the wards?

Why couldn't she simply obey commands and rules?

Why couldn't she fall into line?

Too wild. Too disobedient. Too much of a hassle.

Theon drained the last of his whiskey, the glass settling back onto the counter with a faint clunk. He braced his hands against the edge of the countertop and stared at her. She couldn't read his eyes or his features, but she held his gaze, staring right back at him.

After nearly an entire minute, he began walking slowly towards her, and she couldn't help but take a step back. "What are you going to do?" she whispered.

"Oh, Tessa," he said mockingly. "There is so much that needs to be said. So much that needs to be discussed. So much that needs to be done."

With every step he took, the farther she stepped back until she hit the dining table. She looked around frantically, trying to find something to...what? Defend herself? It wouldn't matter. She'd seen his magic in the woods, but she knew that wasn't nearly the full extent of it. And when he could draw even more power from her? He'd be an unyielding force.

"But none of that is what I am going to do now."

"It's not?" she breathed.

"No, it's not." He stopped directly in front of her, his eyes roaming over her with an intensity she didn't know what to do with. "Right now, I'm going to count to three, and then I'm going to kiss you."

"You're going to..." She trailed off, sure she wasn't understanding what he was saying.

"If you do not want me to kiss you, say so before I get to three," he added with a casual shrug. "One."

He stepped further into her personal space. His hands came to her waist, lifting her smoothly onto the table, and Tessa's breath caught in her throat. She was too flustered to process what was happening.

"Two."

Theon slid his hands down her thighs to her knees, where he pulled them apart and stepped between them. One hand came to the back of her neck, and he leaned forward, lining his lips up with hers.

She opened her mouth to tell him to stop, but nothing came out. The cord inside her was frenzied with anticipation, and something unacceptable was curling low in her stomach, heat flooding through her.

"Three."

He didn't wait another second, pulling her the short distance that was left between their lips. This kiss wasn't soft and slow. It was hard and punishing. This kiss possessed her very being. His tongue pressed against the seam of her lips, demanding access, and she let him in. He tasted of night and smoke as their tongues tangled with each other. His hand held her in place at the back of her head, while the hand on her hip worked its way under her layers to graze bare flesh.

Her skin tingled wherever he touched, and tiny sparks of energy seemed to follow his fingers. She gasped when his hand reached her breast, squeezing it over her bra.

This damn bond.

Or was it the bond?

She couldn't focus enough to worry about it as his mouth left hers and began making its way down the column of her throat. Her hand sank into the silken strands of his black hair, while her other hand gripped the edge of the table. She was trying to remind herself that she was only feeling this way because of the bond. That if it weren't for that, she wouldn't be letting him touch her, but she couldn't focus on anything but his lips on her neck as they sucked and teased. He was going to leave a different kind of mark on her skin at this rate, and a part of her didn't care as she sank into the pleasure of it all.

When a soft moan escaped her lips, a dark growl came from Theon. His hands left her body, reaching for the edge of her sweatshirt and lifting it over her head in one swift movement. He wasted no time returning his lips to her skin, to her mouth.

His hands slid down her sides, over her hips, down her thighs, as if he couldn't touch her enough, and she couldn't get enough of his touch. Unable to stop herself any longer, her other hand finally wrapped around his neck, drawing him closer. He growled again in approval, and a hand slipped back under the thermal. Fingers dragged up along her spine.

Theon wrapped her ponytail around his other fist, yanking on it to tilt her head back. At her gasp, he drew back, nipping her bottom lip.

His eyes were darkened with want as he stared down at her, his breathing as ragged as her own. He seemed to search for something in her eyes, and she didn't know if he found it or if he gave up when he said with a voice like gravel, "Go and shower, Tessa. I'll have clothes laid out for you in the closet. You have five minutes, and I will be entering the bathroom."

Still trying to think through her lust-addled mind, Tessa blinked several times. "I...I can't be done showering in five minutes. I'm a mess."

Theon released her hair and straightened, forcing Tessa to crane her neck back even more to look up into his face.

"If you think I am letting you out of my sight for longer than five minutes in the near future, you are sorely mistaken. You are lucky I am not following you into the shower itself. If not to finish what we were doing here, then at the very least, to ensure you do not somehow figure out a way to slip down the godsdamn drain."

Tessa felt her face flush at his words, and she lowered her eyes, biting her bottom lip. Theon stepped back, and she nearly fell off the table.

"Go, Tessa. Your time is counting down."

She scrambled down at those words, rushing across the room and into Theon's bedroom. Lifting her shirt as she went, she kicked off her sneakers that had surely left a trail of mud. She undressed in the bathroom, not bothering to get her clothes to the laundry bin in the closet as she turned on a set of the shower heads to lukewarm. Despite how cold it was outside, her skin was on fire after what had just happened on the table.

What *had* just happened on the table?

She had expected rage and fury to be pouring off of Theon, and in a way, they had been. He had hardly spoken to her since finding her up a tree, and he'd seemed to take at least a small amount of pleasure from scaring her half to death when he yanked her off that branch with his magic. Luka had certainly hinted that Theon had plans for her, and Axel had seemed nervous about leaving her alone with him.

So why had he done *that?*

She was rinsing the conditioner from her long hair when movement caught her eye through the glass shower walls. Theon didn't even glance at her as he moved through the bathroom and into the closet. He'd removed his own shirt and his jeans were unbuttoned. He may not have looked at her, but she sure as shit watched him. Suddenly realizing her time was likely up, she quickly finished rinsing her hair before shutting off the water and grabbing her towels.

When she'd dried off and wrapped her hair up, she moved cautiously to the closet where he had indeed set out clothing on the island dresser. Theon was no longer in there though. She quickly dressed in the lounge pants and tank top he'd laid out for her. She knew she'd be grabbing a thermal to sleep in when she went to bed. The thin blanket she had would definitely not keep her warm enough, and that small room was drafty.

She went back to the bathroom to comb her hair, already dreading how long it was going to take to work out knots even after a conditioning treatment. Theon reentered as she was working the brush methodically through her strands. He stopped just inside the doorway, leaning against it and crossing his arms.

"I also need to clean up."

"Okay…" she said slowly, going to set the brush down on the sink.

"You are not to leave the bathroom while I do."

"I'm not staying in here while you shower, Theon," she protested.

"You are, Tessa. You will stay where I can see you the entire time," he replied, striding farther into the bathroom.

"I'm not going to go anywhere," she muttered.

Theon gave her a dry look that had Tessa shrinking back.

"Do not leave the bathroom, Tessa," he repeated before brushing past her. "If I have to chase you down while naked, I cannot be held entirely responsible for what will happen when I catch you."

Tessa walked to the bench of the makeup table as the sound of clothing being shucked off and hitting the floor reached her ears before the shower was turned back on. She kept her back resolutely to him, ignoring the annoying voice telling her to sneak a peek over her shoulder.

A few minutes later, the shower shut off, and he walked by with a towel wrapped around his waist. "Don't move," he said without looking at her as he made his way into the closet.

Tessa scowled, crossing her arms. He returned in less than a minute in lounge pants and no shirt. Her eyes raked over his muscled torso and along the tapering trail that disappeared into the band of his pants. Part of her wanted to touch. The other part of her wanted to stab him with something.

Or make him sit at *her* feet beneath a godsdamn table.

"Do you need anything to eat or drink before we go to bed?" he asked, drawing her from her thoughts.

She shook her head. It wasn't smart. Experience told her food would likely become sparse in the coming days. She'd hardly eaten, but she also had no appetite after how it had ended.

Theon nodded once before striding from the bathroom. Tessa sighed and stood, but instead of following him out to his bedroom, she crossed through the closet and into her small space. She frowned when she found the bed missing its blanket, but before she could ask about it, Theon called out from the other room.

"You are not sleeping in there tonight."

She went rigid and stormed to his bedroom. He was pulling back the blankets on his bed before turning to place his phone on a charger on his bedside table.

"Where is my blanket?" she demanded.

"It was in the stables so Kacela and Rigel could learn your scent to track you down in the woods. One would assume it is still there," he replied calmly.

"What am I supposed to use as a blanket?"

"There are plenty on the bed," he said, giving a pointed look at the comforter.

"I am not sleeping in a bed with you."

Theon's gaze snapped to hers, and Tessa cringed at the darkness that crept across his irises.

"You are sleeping in this bed with me, Tessa. You were gone for *hours*. The bond is demanding your closeness right now, despite riding so closely on Osiris and what we did on the table. So yes, you will be sleeping in this bed with me tonight. You will sleep in this bed with me for the foreseeable future because you are my Source and that is what is required of you."

Tessa opened and closed her mouth, not knowing what to say to that. She watched as he climbed into the bed.

With a sharp look, he said, "Come to bed, Tessa. If I am this tired, you are surely exhausted after traipsing through the woods for half a day." When she still didn't move, he sighed. "Do not make me force this. Tomorrow is going to be exhausting for both of us. It would do well for you to get a good night's rest."

"Why will tomorrow be exhausting?" Tessa asked, getting stuck on that one word.

"Because tomorrow we will discuss dinner last night, what happened today, how things will be different in the future, and everything in between. Now come to bed."

Theon watched her warily when she finally began moving. He trailed her all the way to the bed, and she settled down on the very edge as far away from him as possible. There was another audible sigh before his arm looped around her waist and pulled her across the bed.

She tried to stiffen against him, but her body didn't cooperate. Instead, all of her muscles relaxed, and she snuggled back against his bare chest. He worked his other arm under her, wrapping it across her shoulders, securing her to him. As she leaned her head back onto his shoulder, her eyes almost immediately closed, and she felt the barest touch of lips press to the top of her head.

Emotions roared inside of her, and for the life of her, she couldn't figure out which were her own and which were because of the bond that had been forced on her. She had the strongest urge to apologize to him for the day. If he felt half of the agony she'd felt with every step she took, she knew he'd been in pain. Although, the thing seemed to work differently for him. But then again, maybe an apology tonight would lessen the blows that were going to come in the morning. She always seemed to earn food privileges back faster at the Estate when she admitted fault right away, even if she didn't mean it.

Taking a deep breath, she whispered, "Theon?"

"Not tonight, Tessa. I don't have the energy to deal with this tonight," he murmured.

Tessa's lips tilted into a frown. What did that mean? He didn't have the energy for this conversation? Or to deal with her entirely?

You are too much of a hassle.

"But I—"

"Enough, Tessa," he bit out sharply. "This will be handled in the morning."

Tessa didn't answer. Only nodded her head once to convey her understanding.

She knew Theon had fallen asleep when his breathing turned deep and steady. But she was still awake, her mind wandering and conjuring all the ways Theon might punish her tomorrow. Her thoughts swirled, and she spiraled until she found herself counting.

One, two, three.

It was something she'd started doing when she was younger,

enduring whatever method Mother Cordelia was using to try to 'fix her.' It'd become a habit, always finding herself counting when she needed an escape. She'd count the seconds, telling herself she could do anything for one more second. And another. And another. One more second turned into one more minute, became one more hour.

But she hadn't needed to count much since Dex and the others had come around. They'd become the seconds, the minutes, the hours, helping her breathe until the light made it through the cracks in the dark.

Fifty-six, fifty-seven, fifty-eight.

She counted long into the night before sleeping finally claimed her.

12

TESSA

There were fingers combing through her hair. She was warm and calm and nestled back into the hard wall of muscle behind her. The fingers moved from her hair and began brushing up and down her bare arm, goosebumps pebbling in their wake. She felt... content? Safe? She wasn't sure. Both were foreign feelings to her.

When Tessa cracked her eyes open, there was a faint glow from beyond the balcony doors. It was barely dawn. She twisted to look at the clock on the nightstand, but her eyes settled on eyes of emerald green instead, and she got a little lost in them. She couldn't read any of the emotions playing out on his face because there really weren't any. In fact, his features were devoid of anything that would give her the slightest hint as to what his mood might be, and those fleeting feelings of safety and contentment quickly dissipated.

With a sigh, he pulled away from her, flinging the blankets off of himself. "I'm going to make coffee. When I bring it back in here, we will have the first of many discussions."

Without looking back, he padded barefoot from the bedroom. Tessa pushed into a sitting position, rubbing sleep from her eyes. That was the best sleep she'd had since she'd slept for three days straight. She knew it was because of sleeping curled up next to Theon, and despite knowing what was coming, she felt refreshed.

Climbing out of the bed, she went to the bathroom to brush her teeth. After she ran a brush through her hair, she found one of Theon's thermals to pull on. It was going to be a long day. She wanted to be in comfortable clothing, not tight fitting ones. She was just reemerging when Theon came back in carrying two mugs of coffee. He paused, his eyes sweeping over her, before he moved forward and set the mugs down on the small table between the armchairs.

"Sit," he said, nodding to the chair.

Tessa hesitated only a moment before lowering herself into the chair. She knew how to play this. The less combative she was today, the less severe the consequences.

The less time spent locked in the dark.

Theon picked up a mug and handed it to her. She instantly wrapped her hands around the hot ceramic cup, absorbing the heat.

"Tessa, I don't even know where to start," Theon said, beginning to pace back and forth before her, his hands running through his hair. "What happened at dinner the other night can never happen again."

"Agreed," she said, bringing the mug to her lips.

He paused his pacing, looking at her. "You agree?"

"Oh, yes," she continued. "I agree. I will never be made to sit at your feet again." She watched him carefully over her cup as she took another sip of caffeine.

"That is not..." He ran a hand down his face, and when he looked at her again, something had shifted in his eyes and features. They were harsher, darker. "No, Tessa. You can never disobey me like that again. Certainly not in public, and never in front of my father."

"I dropped a fork, Theon!" she cried. "I did not throw the fork across the room. I did not try to stab someone with it. I did not try to comb my hair with it. I. Dropped. It."

Theon's brow knitted in confusion. "Why would you try to comb your hair with a fork?"

"It has tines. Like a comb's teeth. Albeit a very small comb. But if one were in a bind, it would probably work," Tessa offered with a shrug.

Theon stared at her for a long moment. "I feel as though the similarities between a fork and a comb are not important at the moment..."

"No. They are not. What is important is that you made me sit at your feet like one of your damn wolves for accidentally dropping a fork."

Theon huffed a humorless laugh. "My hounds are far better behaved than you are," he muttered under his breath.

Tessa glared at him, unimpressed, as she raised her middle finger in his direction. Theon moved so quickly, Tessa jumped, coffee sloshing out of the mug and onto her pants. He was standing over her, his hands braced on the armrests on either side of her. He plucked her mug from her hand and set it on the table before returning his entire attention to her.

"Gods, Theon," Tessa snarled, bringing her hand to her chest. "What the fuck?"

"This behavior is exactly what cannot continue, Tessa," he said, and she stilled at his dark tone. "I have tried to give you time to adjust to this. I have let you have your temper tantrums and—"

"Temper tantrums?" Tessa repeated indignantly, sitting up so her face was inches from his. "You took *everything* from me!"

Theon tsked, stepping back from her. "Don't be so dramatic."

She shot to her feet. "I didn't even get to bring my own clothing with me!"

He waved his hand dismissively at the statement. "I have provided you with all the clothing you could ever need, and much better clothing at that."

"That is so not the point, Theon," she spat.

"Isn't it?" he countered. "If you weren't fighting so adamantly against your fate, you would see that I can provide you with everything you could ever need."

"You took me from everything I know, Theon. How can you not see that? My home. My friends. You stole my future from me." Her fists were clenching and unclenching at her sides, her skin beginning to buzz with something that needed out.

"You are wrong, Tessa," Theon said, shaking his head. "Your home? You'd already left it. You would be at the Acropolis until the Selection Year was over, and then you'd go to your assigned Kingdom. Your friends? You likely would have been separated from them when you received your assignment. Even if you were assigned to the same Kingdom, the Kingdoms are huge. You would have still been separated from them. And your future? You are Fae. Your purpose was always to serve the Legacy in one way or another. How that purpose was just altered was likely in your favor."

"How in the realm do you figure that?" Tessa balked, stepping back from him.

"You becoming my Source is better than any other fate you would have likely been assigned," Theon replied.

"Which is what exactly?"

He shook his head again. "That is not important, Tessa. Furthermore, none of that matters. When you became mine—"

"I am not yours!"

Theon's hand shot out, his fingers wrapping around her throat. "You are, Tessa. You are my Source."

"That doesn't make me yours," she snarled, trying to pull out of his grip, but his fingers only tightened until he yanked his hand back, as if he'd touched something too hot. Stalking from the room, he left Tessa standing before the fireplace, wondering what the fuck had just happened, but he returned a minute later with a tablet. Tessa narrowed her eyes as he turned the thing so she could see the screen.

It was a document on her. Her own face stared back at her from a photo in the upper right corner. The first page was details about her life: where she was raised, physical attributes, elemental predictions. Theon interrupted her view when he tapped something near the bottom of the screen.

Current Location: Arius Kingdom
Theon St. Orcas, Master, took possession at Opening Selection
Ceremony 5622, assuming complete dominium.

Theon had signed his name underneath in agreement.

Her hand shook when she moved to swipe the screen, but he pulled the tablet away from her before she had a chance to see anything else.

"What is that?" she rasped.

"Your documents. All the Fae have them."

"Documents for what?"

"To keep track of you and which kingdom is responsible for you."

She knew Fae were viewed as less than to the Legacy, but to have actual papers? Gods. The mortals had more rights than she did.

She couldn't stop moving, growing restless as something pressed at her being, aching to be let free. She was shifting from foot-to-foot, a hand raking through her long hair and tugging lightly at the strands. Theon was watching her warily.

"Before we left the Acropolis. I had to sign transfer papers before I could take you from the Pantheon," he said when she remained silent.

Documents. Transfer papers. He could call them something pretty, but it didn't change what they were.

Ownership records.

When he spoke again, his voice was still quiet, but there was nothing gentle about it. "You are *mine*, Tessa. What you say and how you act reflect directly on me, and while you might not see it this way, everything I do is to protect you and care for you."

"You only do so because I am your Source," Tessa spat. "You do not do it because you *care* for me. You do it because you need me."

"If that is what you choose to believe," he said with a shrug. "But, even if that was true, this can be a mutually beneficial exchange. You provide me with what I need, and I provide you with everything you need."

"And I am just to accept that I am a piece of property to be used and drained whenever you see fit?"

"It does not have to be that way. Why can't you see that?" Theon asked, moving forward and snatching her hands when she started to reach for her hair again. Sparks of pleasure darted through her body at his touch, and she shivered. "See, beautiful?" His tone had taken on a low tone, full of dark promises. "I know you feel what I feel when we touch, when we're close to one another."

"Only because I am forced to feel that way," she replied, trying to pull her hands from his, but admittedly not trying very hard. Theon tugged her closer instead, wrapping his arms around her waist and pressing his brow to hers.

"Let yourself be mine, Tessa. Give in to it. It will only get harder to resist, and eventually you will give in anyway. You will *want* everything I have to offer. Why put yourself through all this turmoil?"

Was he right? Would the pull get stronger and stronger with each new Mark? Would the agony of the bond become so great she would eventually just give in? Would this all be for nothing? Maybe he was right and this *was* her fate. Maybe it was all leading to this in the end...

"Stop thinking so hard," he whispered into her ear. "For a few seconds, just feel what it could be like." One hand slid up to her nape, while the other came to her lower back and pressed her flush into his body. She gasped as soft parts of her pressed into the hard planes of him. "It could be like this all the time," he murmured onto her skin, his lips skimming up her throat. "You and me, little storm," he breathed.

He was everywhere all at once, and she couldn't think straight. Not with this damn bond urging her to give in. Begging her to let him have her. "I..."

"No, Tessa," he whispered. "No thinking. Just feeling."

He brushed his lips across hers in a feather-light kiss. Then he did it again to one corner of her mouth. Then the other. He moved to her jaw. Just the slightest touch of lips to skin.

"I..." she tried again.

Was it all the Source bond? There was no doubt Theon was attractive. More than attractive. There had been something there from the moment she'd seen him at the Pantheon. Maybe her own attraction was compounding with the bond and that's what was making this so gods-damn hard. She just wished she could know for sure because he *had* cared for her. Granted, he was the reason she had been ill, and he'd taken her from all she'd ever known. It only seemed right that he provide her with clothing and a roof over her head. But he'd done other things too. He'd taken notice of her hatred of socks. He'd given her time and space, not forcing her to sleep beside him most nights and not entrancing her to obey him. He certainly hadn't tried to force her into anything physical to appease the bond. Even last night, he had given her an out. He'd counted to three and given her time to say no. So why hadn't she?

"I can hear the wheels turning in your mind," he murmured.

She opened her mouth, not even sure what she was going to say, but a knock sounded on the main door and she tensed. Theon swore under his breath as whatever spell they'd been under shattered.

"Stay with me, beautiful," Theon tried, long fingers gripping her chin and bringing her eyes back to his. "Ignore it. Stay where we were—"

The knock came again, sharper and more demanding

"Theon," Valter called from behind the door.

This time Tessa stepped back from him, feeling the color drain from her face.

Theon swore again, more colorfully than before. "Stay in here, Tessa. Do not come out to the main room. Do you understand?" She nodded mutely, gaze flashing to the door. "I'm going to need verbal acknowledgement."

"Yes," she whispered. "Yes, I understand."

"We'll continue this discussion in a moment." His eyes lingered on her, but when Valter pounded on the door again, he hollered, "Coming, Father," before turning and swiftly moving to let his father in. He pulled the bedroom door shut behind him.

Tessa turned and went back to the armchair, pulling her legs to her chest. She reached for her coffee, but it had grown cold.

"Good morning, Father," she heard Theon say. "What can I do for you at this hour?"

"You can start by answering the door the first time I knock," Valter answered, obvious annoyance in his tone.

"I apologize, Father. I wasn't expecting you, let alone so early in the morning," Theon replied.

"I came by yesterday afternoon, but you were not here. Axel said you'd gone for a hunt with Luka and taken your Source with you," Valter answered.

"That is true. Why were you looking for me?"

"I realized after our meeting with Metias and Pavil, I never gave you these to look over." There was a pause before Valter continued. "There are several options here, but I tagged the three I think would be most fruitful when it comes to heir production. Of course, I'm getting more offers every day, so something better could still come along."

And there it was. One of the many reasons she couldn't simply give in to the bond. Theon would be Matched with someone. He would have to take a wife to produce the next Arius Heir.

You and me.

That's what he'd whispered into her ear moments ago. But it would never be just him and her. It was just as she'd realized on the floor at dinner. She would be his, but he would never be hers. She might not want him, but this couldn't even be something to simply satisfy the bond. Theon would never let her seek out some form of companionship with someone else. That was becoming glaringly obvious.

"I will look over these later, but you could have simply forwarded them to me," Theon was saying. "Is there anything else you need?"

"Where is your Source?" Valter asked, and Tessa went still as footsteps neared the bedroom door. "Don't tell me she still sleeps while you are awake?"

"She is awake, Father. However, we were both still in the bedroom," Theon answered.

Valter chuckled, clearly assuming he meant they were both in the bed together. "I suppose I can forgive the delay in answering the door this one time then. But next time I expect the door to be opened the first time I knock, whether you are fucking your Source or not."

"Understood, Father."

"I'll let you get back to her then," Valter answered, footsteps fading away from the door. Tessa let out a long breath. "I'll expect you at dinner tonight." Before Theon could reply, he added, "You leave for the Acropolis next week. Your mother is going into hysterics. Expect family dinners for the remainder of your time here."

Tessa heard Theon agree, and she tipped her head back in dread, closing her eyes. She didn't know when they were leaving for the Acropolis, but days of formal dinners sounded like her own personal Pit of Torment. And this would be her life. Endless meetings and dinners, sitting silently at Theon's side.

The bedroom door opened a few minutes later, and she heard Theon's footfalls. When he didn't say anything, she opened her eyes to find him standing a few feet away. His hands were in his pockets, and he was studying her.

"When do we leave for the Acropolis?" she asked, void of emotion.

"Ten days. We are allowed into the ruling families' district of the Acropolis a week before the other Legacy," Theon answered.

Tessa nodded. Silence fell again for several moments before she said, "I am expected to attend your family dinners with you."

A statement, not a question.

"You are. Where I go, you go," Theon confirmed. "Which means we need to finish our conversation." He closed the few feet of distance between them, coming to stand over her. Her head was still tilted back on the chair so she could look up at him. He reached out to cup her cheek, but she turned her face out of reach. He sighed. "So you've decided then?"

"Decided what? I don't get choices anymore," she countered.

"You did, but you are correct in saying you do not get them anymore," Theon replied, that coldness slipping back into his voice as his hand dropped to his side.

"What does that mean?"

"It means that until you have accepted the bond and proven so through your actions and obedience, you no longer have choices," he answered matter-of-factly. "You will not leave my sight or my side for longer than a few minutes at a time. There is no more running; no more trying to escape this fate. When we get to the Acropolis, it means that when you are not in your scheduled trainings, you are with me. There are no negotiations. In public, you act appropriately—"

Tessa's mouth had fallen open more and more as he spoke, and she lashed out at him. "You already decide all of that for me, Theon! You decide what and when I eat. You lay clothing out for me. You—"

"I have given you time, Tessa," Theon interrupted, that darkness drifting across his irises. "I have given you time to accept this, but it has run out. This is your destiny. This is your reality. It could have been easier. It could have been pleasant. It still can be, but you have to accept the Source bond. You think I have taken everything from you? That I am your villain? I can be that for you."

"Why?" she whispered, unable to stop the tears from spilling over.

"Because I am out of options, Tessa. I need you to succumb to this. If this is how I will accomplish that, then I guess it is what I will do. Maybe seeing how bad it could be will make you realize that what I am offering isn't all that terrible," Theon answered. "There will be no more disobedience. There will be no more arguing with me, especially in public or in front of others. There will be no more pulling away from me when the bond demands our closeness," he went on. And when her eyes widened at that last part, he added, "I will not force anything on you, Tessa. You see me as a monster, and in many ways I am, but I should hope I have already proven I am not one of that nature."

He reached out, swiping the tears from her cheeks with his fingertips. She forced herself to remain still, resisting the urge to jerk away from his touch.

"Good girl," he murmured, cupping her chin. "Expect consequences for inappropriate behavior."

She stiffened at the words. "So I am to be trained like a dog now?"

Theon tsked under his breath. "Now, Tessa. If my hounds can learn such things, surely you will catch on much faster, no?"

"And how will you know that I have accepted this?" she demanded at his patronizing tone. "What shall be proof for you? When I obey your every command without question? When I act as I have been *trained* to?"

"I will know when you have accepted the Source bond, Tessa," was all he said. "Now go shower and make yourself presentable. Axel and Luka will be here for breakfast soon, and then we are going to Castle Pines."

"For what?" she asked, her fury banking as surprise coursed through her. They hadn't left the house since they'd arrived here days ago.

"Practice," he purred, letting go of her chin and turning to leave the room. "Makeup and hair, beautiful. My Source will not be seen in any way less than perfect outside of our rooms."

He left the door to the bedroom open as he strode out, leaving Tessa sitting there, not knowing what to say or do. Somehow this had all gone from bad to worse, and she didn't know if she could do what was required of her to survive it let alone fix it. This was no different than being locked away, so controlled she couldn't move, couldn't breathe.

She got up and went to the balcony doors, needing some air, but when she tugged on the handles, they didn't budge. She tugged again, the doors rattling, and her chest tightened when they stayed firmly shut. Her brow fell against the cool glass as a few raindrops began to fall, and she started to count.

At least she could still see the light, even if it was just out of reach.

13
THEON

Axel and Luka both arrived before the agreed upon time, just as Theon expected they would, and both were equally wary when they entered. They acted as if they were entering a battlefield, and maybe they were. Time would tell, he supposed.

The entire time he'd been on his horse, he had mulled over what to do with Tessa. He'd tried one last time to convince her with the pull of the bond itself. He'd prayed to the gods he could get her to just accept this fate after kissing her and sleeping beside her. She'd been so close until his father had shown up and ruined everything.

Again.

So it had come to this. It had come to him forcing her into submission. He'd looked at her indifferently as he'd rained down commands and orders. He'd treated her the way he'd seen other Lords and Ladies treat their Sources. Not like his father treated Eviana. He would never treat Tessa like *that*. Then again, he'd never planned on treating Tessa this way, yet here he was. But he had not anticipated her resisting the Source bond. That possibility had never crossed his mind once.

"How did everything go?" Luka asked, going straight to the kitchen and pouring himself some coffee. Theon had ordered food from the kitchens to be delivered shortly.

"If you mean did I lose control with her, no," Theon answered curtly, sliding his mug and Tessa's across the counter to be refilled.

"And how is she?" Luka pressed, filling a mug for Axel as well.

Theon drummed his fingers on the counter, his lips forming a thin line before he finally answered, "I'm hoping we came to an understanding."

Luka studied him, sipping on his coffee. There was a knowing look there that Theon both loved and hated. Part of being nearly inseparable while growing up meant the male knew him better than most.

"What does that mean?" Axel asked, coming over to grab his mug after letting the kitchen staff in, allowing them to set the table.

Theon glanced at his watch. Tessa knew what time breakfast was to be served. He wouldn't put it past her to test just how serious he was, but he was hoping *something* had come from making her sit at his feet a few nights ago. He added this entire debacle to the list of things he hoped would be worth it in the end.

Sighing, he answered, "It means I need her submission, and I'll do whatever is needed to have it."

Axel blinked at him. "You sound like Father when you speak like that."

Luka whistled low under his breath at the words, and Theon immediately went on the defensive. "It is nothing like Father. She is treated like a queen compared to how Eviana is treated."

"How he treats Eviana is not exactly a standard to measure against," Axel shot back.

Luka cleared his throat, his eyes flicking to the bedroom door, and Theon and Axel both turned. Theon's breath caught. He'd lain out a sleeveless red dress with white polka dots and a neckline that dipped low. The front hem of the dress fell to just below her knees while the back draped down to her heels where white stiletto sandals adorned her feet. She'd curled her hair so it fell in loose waves around her shoulders, and while she didn't need cosmetics, she certainly knew how to use them. Gold hoops hung from her ears, and a pendant necklace of some sort hung low, dipping into the neckline of the dress. Several gold bangles were on her wrists.

Axel gave an appreciative whistle, breaking the silence. "Look at you, baby doll. Did you get all dressed up just for us?"

Tessa looked pointedly at Theon before her eyes slid to Axel, and she said tightly, "I am told I'm going to Castle Pines later today and that my previous attire was not appropriate for such a trip."

Theon swiped up her refilled coffee and crossed the room, pressing the mug into her hand. As he did so, he gently touched her elbow and leaned in to kiss her cheek. "You look lovely, Tessa," he murmured.

She tensed, but she didn't pull back. He'd be lying if he said this wasn't part of the plan. He was hoping if she allowed him to touch her more in small ways like this, she'd give in to the pleasure of the bond sooner, realizing how much better it would be.

Her lips didn't so much as twitch when she met his gaze. Those grey eyes were a whirlwind of emotions he didn't know how to decode.

"Are you ready to eat?" he asked.

"I am told that is no longer my decision to make."

"Tessa," he warned in a low tone.

"Don't ask me questions like I have choices, *Master*," she replied quietly enough that the others could not hear. "You made it perfectly clear I do not."

He clenched his teeth at the response, but he nodded once.

"May I move to the table, or will that be considered pulling away from you?"

Theon glanced down to where his hand still cupped her elbow, and he dropped it, stepping aside for her to pass. When she reached the table, she paused, looking over her shoulder at him. He wasn't sure why until he realized she was waiting for permission to sit before the Legacy had taken their seats. His chest did something weird at the action.

She did this, he reminded himself, giving her a nod to take her seat. Theon glanced at Luka, whose brows were raised in surprise at the exchange as he came from the kitchen to join the table. Axel's attention was fixed on Tessa, his lips pressed into a thin line. He didn't know why they were so upset by this. They needed her to fall into line as much as he did.

Theon slid into the chair next to Tessa and reached to pour her a glass of orange juice. Axel and Luka glanced between the two of them as they began filling their own plates with pancakes, scrambled eggs, fresh fruit, and bacon, passing the serving dishes around the table.

"So...why are you going to Castle Pines, and can I come?" Axel asked, never one to let silence linger. He handed the bacon platter across to Tessa. She reached for it, but Theon beat her to it. He placed two strips onto her plate. Her lips pursed at the action, but she held her tongue.

"I have a few things to get for the Acropolis," Theon replied, taking the scrambled egg dish from him as well. "I just received an email with a few additional events that I need to prepare for. I also thought Tessa might want to get out of the house for a while. You know. Somewhere other than the woods."

Tessa paused her movement of bringing a piece of bacon to her mouth, but only for a moment. She didn't react in any other way to the comment as she took a bite.

That was unexpected. Even with the strict rules he'd lain down earlier this morning, he hadn't anticipated her giving in so quickly. He should feel elated at her behavior, instead he was...not. It was a marvel she was still somehow making things difficult, even following his own fucking rules.

"So can I join you?" Axel said after another moment of awkward silence.

"Of course," Theon answered, sliding a pancake onto Tessa's plate. "What flavor syrup do you want, Tessa?"

She slid her eyes to him. "Oh, Master," she said with a mocking sweetness, her lashes fluttering. "There you go with the illusion of choices again. I trust you to know what is best for me." She scooped up a forkful of fluffy eggs and smiled serenely at him as she brought the bite to her mouth.

"What exactly was said between you two?" Luka asked, his fork hitting his plate with a light clang. He leaned back in his chair, studying them both from across the table.

Theon gritted his teeth as he poured syrup onto the pancake. "Expectations were simply stated," he answered tightly.

"And said expectations were accepted?" Luka pressed, looking at Tessa.

"Mhmm," Tessa murmured, sipping on her orange juice.

"Really?" Luka asked, his tone saying how unlikely he found that. "Because this," he motioned between Theon and Tessa, "does not seem like something was agreed to and settled." When Tessa didn't respond, her eyes dropping to her plate, Luka shifted his gaze back to him. "Theon?"

"What do you want me to say, Luka?" he asked in exasperation, leaning back in his own chair. "She can't try running again. You know this. We were lucky it wasn't discovered this time. So yes, new rules and expectations were put into place after the events of yesterday."

Luka looked back and forth between Theon and Tessa a few more times before picking up his fork and digging into his breakfast without another word. Axel began speaking of a few places he'd like to stop at in Castle Pines, trying to ease the tension as he always did.

Theon watched Tessa from the corner of his eye while conversation took place around her. She silently ate her meal and replied with short, but polite, one-word answers when Axel or Luka spoke to her. They were clearly upset by her sudden reclusiveness. Theon was more than curious as to not only how this day would play out, but also how long she would be able to control herself. His greatest fear was her losing that little thread of control she seemed to have again tonight, and he made a mental note to be sure they were home well before dinner.

When breakfast was done, Luka and Axel went to grab a few things from their rooms before they left for Castle Pines. Theon had been clearing dishes and moving them into the kitchen. Pen would come and see to them while they were away. Now he went to his desk, pulling a small box from the drawer. He returned to the table, sliding his coffee mug out of the way. Tessa was still seated, staring out the bay window across the room and clearly lost to her own thoughts. Her hands were wrapped loosely around her coffee mug, and Theon almost snapped a photo. Unable to help himself, he reached out and brushed his fingers along her arm, and she jolted at the touch.

Her eyes snapped to his in a panic as she blurted, "You startled me. That wasn't me pulling away from you."

He frowned. "I didn't mean to startle you. I have something for you."

Her shoulders relaxed some, and she glanced down at the table, her brows arching in surprise when she spotted the box. "A phone?"

He nodded, opening the box to take the phone from it. It was the latest phone on the market. He'd had Luka pick it up for him a few days ago, and he'd spent his morning setting it up after his discussion with her.

When he held it out to her, she looked at him in confusion. "I don't understand."

He tilted his head at the statement. "You don't understand what?"

"Why you got me a phone."

"We leave for the Acropolis in ten days. My responsibilities are about to increase tenfold. There will be rare times, like when you are in trainings for your element, for example, that we are separated. I need a way to contact you, at least until the rest of the Marks are in place," Theon explained. He held it out for her again, and she tentatively reached for it, immediately setting it down on the table in front of her. "I got a case and screen protector for it," he added, at her reluctance to hold it. She nodded in acknowledgement.

Theon rubbed at the back of his neck. Why did this feel so... awkward? Most Fae had phones once assigned to their kingdoms.

"Tessa, I'm not really sure why you're so..." He couldn't even think of the word to adequately describe how she was acting because he didn't know. After nearly two weeks, he still could not read her even a little bit. He still knew nothing about her except that she hated socks and could find her way down from several floors above ground.

She didn't answer him, just stared at the phone. He'd turned it on when he'd taken it from the box, having charged it all morning. He cleared his throat. "Right then. The passcode is your birthday. I figured that'd be the easiest to remember..." He trailed off when she looked up at him.

"It's a four-digit passcode."

"Yes. Day and month," he replied, even more confused now.

Tessa glanced back down at the phone before clearing her own throat. "I do not know the day I was born. Only the month and year," she stated. Theon sat in stunned silence. "We do not celebrate our individual birthdays at the Estates," she went on. "All birthdays of a particular month are recognized as one on the first day of that month with cake. So I know my birthday is in the fifth month and what year I was born, but I do not know the day."

He had to take a moment before he was able to say, "Your birthday is the fifteenth day of the fifth month, Tessa."

She only nodded before returning her attention to the window.

Theon reached over and unlocked the phone, opening up her contact list. "I already programmed my number, Luka's, and Axel's numbers into the phone. We are the only people I want you contacting. There is an enchantment that will send me a message anytime you use it to communicate with anyone other than me or if someone else attempts to contact you. All content is blocked, other than the things I downloaded for you." Tessa nodded again, not even glancing at the phone. Not knowing what else to do, Theon kept talking. "I expect you to have your phone whenever I am not with you and to answer any time I call or text."

She nodded.

"I'm going to need verbal acknowledgement here, Tessa." Mainly because he didn't know what to do with her. Again.

"I understand the new expectations placed on me," she said quietly, nudging the phone aside. "I need to use the restroom before we go."

She looked at him expectantly.

"You do not need my permission to do so, Tessa. Certainly not in our own rooms."

"*Your* rooms," she corrected so quietly he almost didn't hear her.

He reached over and gripped her chin, drawing her eyes back to his. "I don't like this, Tessa. I don't like..." He trailed off when she seemed to stare right through him. "Grab a sweater in case you get cold in town," he finally said, releasing her chin.

She nodded, standing and disappearing into the bedroom. She'd left the phone sitting on the table, and he still could not figure out her odd reaction to it. He was no closer to understanding her than he was when she'd waved chocolate in his face.

He was still contemplating it when Axel and Luka returned a few minutes later, and just as Theon was about to go check on her, Tessa came back from the bedroom. She had a white cardigan over her dress, and she'd grabbed a small gold purse as well. Theon swiped the new phone off the table and handed it to her, and she immediately slipped it into her clutch without a word.

"Are we ready?" Luka asked, holding the keys to their usual vehicle.

"I think so," Theon answered, bringing his hand to Tessa's lower back to guide her forward. Axel and Luka bantered back and forth about the Chaosphere teams and the season that would start in the next week. Theon had never really understood why they cared about such trivial things like sports, especially Chaosphere.

They were just reaching the main foyer when his father's voice called out to them. Tessa went rigid beside him, and he heard her suck in a sharp breath. He slid his hand from her back around to her hip, tucking her into his side.

The males all turned to face the Arius Lord as he descended a set of stairs that led up to his study, Eviana falling from his side to a step behind him. He came to a stop before them, and they all bowed their heads in greeting, Tessa keeping her eyes fixed on the marble floor.

"Where are you three off to?" his father asked.

"I have some errands to run. I trust you saw the additions to the Acropolis agenda?" Theon answered. "Luka and Axel are just along for the ride."

"You're not going all the way to Rockmoor?" Valter asked, his phone in hand as he thumbed his screen, not bothering to look at them.

"No. Just into Castle Pines," Theon answered. "We will be home in plenty of time to get ready for dinner."

"See that you are," Valter said, his eyes lifting to Tessa in a way that made Theon want to shove her behind him. He nodded once to Theon, before turning and striding off, murmuring softly to Eviana, who had moved back to his side.

Theon ushered Tessa quickly out the door and down the steps, opening the back door of the vehicle and helping her into the backseat. Shutting the door, he turned to go around to the other side and nearly ran directly into Luka's chest.

"What did you do?" Luka demanded in a harsh whisper.

"Exactly what I said I was going to do," Theon answered, glaring as he put some space between them. "I ensured she never tries to run again."

"By taking away the little control she had? You, of all people, should know how quickly a person snaps when they have no control."

"No," Theon ground out. "As soon as she accepts the bond, I'll ease up on her. I need her to see how bad it could be so she'll appreciate the way it can be."

Luka scoffed. "That will never work."

"Then what, exactly, do you suggest?"

"Are we going or what?" Axel called, standing on the running board to look over the top of the vehicle at them.

"We're coming," Luka yelled back, but before he moved to get in, he pointed a finger at Theon. "This is going to bite you in the ass, Theon. Mark my words."

He sidestepped him and climbed into the driver's seat, leaving Theon to go around the vehicle and climb into the backseat behind Axel. Tessa had her clutch lying in her lap and was looking straight ahead. He could only assume she hadn't spoken to Axel.

Between the conversation this morning with his father and the confrontation he'd just had with Luka, he wanted her right beside him. Her presence was soothing, and her touch eased the constant tension in his chest. He could say the tension was from the Source bond, but the truth was that tightness had been there long before he found himself with a bonded Source. Reaching over, he grabbed her hand and tugged her towards him. He knew he was a bastard for it. This wasn't a power play or to show her he was in charge. This was him wanting comfort simply by touching her because somehow he could breathe easier when she was close.

She slid across the seat wordlessly, and Luka glared at him in the rearview mirror. Tucking her into his side, he pressed a soft kiss to the top of her head. He may have been a bastard for what he was doing to her, but for the drive to Castle Pines, he let himself forget about it all. He let himself forget she was his Source, and he was her Master. He let himself forget about his father's plans and his own plans. He let himself forget he was the heir of the Arius Kingdom and that she was forced to be by his side.

He let himself forget he was more like his father than he cared to admit.

Theon stood in his bedroom, sipping on the glass of liquor in his hand as he watched the female on the balcony. She sat on one of the balcony sofas, her knees pulled to her chest and a blanket wrapped around her, cradling a cup of tea in her palms.

She had been the portrait of obedience in Castle Pines, never straying from his side. She'd been utterly flawless in public, just as he'd told her she needed to be. When they spoke to her, her responses remained as few words as possible, even with Axel and Luka. He knew they were unhappy with the situation by the glares they threw at him all afternoon. Axel had tried to get her to go with him a few times, but she had shaken her head or politely declined, staying right by Theon's side. She'd acted like Eviana. Like a Source would be expected to act. It was what he'd demanded of her, so why was he hating every godsdamn second of it?

One of his stops had been to take Tessa to get a laptop and tablet. She would need them for her various training sessions at the Acropolis. While she wouldn't need to attend all the trainings the other Fae would go through, she would have to attend some of them. In addition, she would be attending various meetings and events with him. He needed her to have access to various information.

He had asked her to pick out the ones she wanted. She had scarcely glanced at the display models before saying she was sure he knew which were best while she stood with her hands clasped in front of her. He'd ended up just getting her the top of the line devices. Over the next few days, he would put the same blocks and enchantments onto them as he'd done with her phone before giving them to her.

When they'd arrived home and made it back to their rooms, he'd told her she could change into more comfortable clothing until it was time to get ready for dinner, but she'd declined, only removing her shoes. She'd asked if she could make a cup of tea and sit on the balcony. When he'd tensed at the mention of her escape route, her shoulders had curled in.

"I understand," she'd said quietly, moving to fill the teakettle with water.

But when her tea was done, he'd taken her out to the balcony himself and sat opposite her. Eventually, he'd gotten up to get his own drink and had left her to her thoughts. It wasn't as if she was speaking to him anyway. He had stayed where he could see her the entire time. He knew she wasn't happy, but she did seem...more settled after being out of their rooms for a while.

Now, however, he would need to interrupt her thoughts because she needed to get ready for dinner. He'd already laid out a black, flared cocktail dress with small hollow cut outs at the waist. She would look stunning in it like she did in everything else, but his mind kept conjuring the image of her in his shirt this morning. He found he much preferred that look on her— the messy hair, just woke up and hadn't had her coffee yet, simple and relaxed look. And yeah, her in his shirt, covered in his scent after sleeping beside him all night didn't hurt either.

Theon knocked back the last of his drink, setting the glass aside before walking back out to the balcony. He came to a stop beside her, reaching out and running his fingers along her hair and down her jaw. The bond tingled with satisfaction, sending a rush of desire through him. He'd promised her he wouldn't force anything on her physically— and he wouldn't—but fuck. He wanted to kiss her when she turned her head to look up at him expectantly, waiting for his next order.

True to his demands, she hadn't pulled away from his touch all day, and it had been pure bliss for the Source bond. He craved the day she didn't pull away because she didn't *want* to pull away almost as much as he was craving a taste of her lips right now.

He swallowed down his desire, and when he spoke, his voice was raspy and heated, "We need to get ready for dinner."

Tessa nodded once, then stilled again. Waiting, he realized. She was waiting for him to remove his hand so she wouldn't be pulling away from him.

He sighed, taking a seat beside her on the sofa. He took the mug from her hands, setting it on the table. "Tessa, can we talk?"

Her gaze met his, and he wanted to curse the gods at the lack of any type of storm in her grey eyes. "I don't get such choices anymore," she replied quietly.

Theon blinked. Those were the most words she'd said at once to him since this morning. Quickly shoving his surprise aside, he said, "I don't want it to be like this. Not here. In our own space."

Her lips thinned, and she broke his stare, fingers fiddling with her blanket. "Perhaps you can let me know how I need to adjust my behavior in your rooms tomorrow, but I really don't know that I can handle any additional expectations today."

"Tessa—"

"I need to get ready," she said, pulling the blanket from her lap and draping it over her arm. She stood and picked up the book and mug, carrying everything back into the bedroom with her.

Theon leaned back on the sofa, scrubbing his hands down his face.

Tomorrow.

He'd try again tomorrow. Tonight, he just needed to get through this dinner, and hope she could hold it together in front of his father. He wasn't sure he could stay his hand a second time.

An hour later, they were on their way down to the dining room with Axel and Luka. Tessa had pulled her hair up in a classic knot at her nape, leaving strands of honey-gold hair around her face. His hand was on the small of her back, and his fingers grazed the slivers of bare skin along the hollowed out slits on the dress.

As they approached the doors, she slowed and fell into step behind him, just as he'd seen Eviana do hundreds of times. He stopped, turning to face her, but before he could say anything, Tessa spoke first.

"I know what is expected of me."

"Tessa—"

"Your father is waiting," she interrupted, her eyes fixed on the floor.

"She's right," Luka said from behind them, and Theon clenched his jaw.

Turning, he nodded to the staff to open the dining room doors and entered to greet his parents.

The dinner was as all family dinners were. The air was filled with tension, and the conversation was dull. Tessa ate everything placed in front of her without fuss, sitting perfectly still. There was no fidgeting as there had been a few nights ago. No grumbling under her breath. He didn't miss his father's quick glances at her...or his lingering stares.

As dessert was being served, his father leaned back in his chair. "I must say, Theon, your Source is unexpectedly behaved this evening. I did not expect her to be broken so easily. Your discipline must have been highly effective."

"She is not broken," Theon replied tightly, meeting his father's gaze. "It has simply been a long day of adjustments."

"Call it what you want," Valter shrugged, taking a sip of his drink. "You seem to mistake me for condemning you. I'm impressed, Theon. I didn't think you had it in you to instill such submission."

Theon's fingers tightened around his drink, his knuckles turning white. Axel was giving him a knowing look across the table that seemed to scream, *I told you that you sounded like him.* Luka was sipping his own drink, his sapphire eyes on Tessa, whose attention was firmly fixed on her crème caramel.

"Seeing you take such control of your Source eases some of my worries about our plans while you are away at the Acropolis," his father continued.

"Please don't speak of the Acropolis," his mother interrupted, her lower lip trembling dramatically. "I'm trying to forget they are leaving in ten days."

"For the love of Arius, Cressida," Valter grumbled. "They will be home on various breaks and on holiday. It is not as though they are leaving forever. Soon enough there will be a new little heir for you to dote on."

Tessa stiffened imperceptibly beside him, and Theon reached over, placing a hand on her knee beneath the table. Her eyes flicked up to him for the briefest of moments before returning to her dessert. The rest of the talk around the table was idle chatter, his mother evidently content to imagine life with a grandchild running around this huge house.

As soon as dessert was cleared, Theon stood. Luka and Axel did the same, saying good night to his parents. He nodded at Tessa to follow, and the moment they rounded the corner and were out of sight of the dining room, he reached behind him and pulled her into his side, pressing a soft kiss to the top of her head.

"You were perfect tonight, beautiful," he whispered into her hair. Tessa said nothing, but he could see thin pools of silver in the corners of her eyes. "Tessa?"

"Walk with me, little one," Luka said, coming up beside them and holding out his arm to her. She glanced up at Theon, clearly asking permission. He didn't want to, but he nodded, releasing her to loop her arm through Luka's and let him lead her down the hall.

"How are these new expectations working out?" Axel asked, the sarcasm thick as he came to Theon's side.

Theon shot him a bland look. "It's only for a bit. Just until she accepts the bond," he insisted as he watched Luka and Tessa disappear around a corner.

"And if she doesn't accept the Source bond?"

"She will."

"When? After you've shaped her into—"

"Axel," Theon interrupted, rounding on his brother. "I am doing the best I can with a situation none of us anticipated, and something neither you nor Luka seem to understand."

Axel shoved his hands into his pockets, the muscle ticking in his jaw a mirror to Theon's. "She won't be the same at the end of this."

"Of course she will. I only need her to be this way around others. It just needs to be an act. When it's just us in private, she can be herself," Theon bit back. "This is temporary."

"She won't be the same, Theon," Axel repeated, shaking his head as they began moving down the hallway again.

"And what makes you so sure of that?" he asked, not bothering to hide his growing irritation with this conversation.

"Because you are different. When you started *acting* to appease Father, I told myself it was only temporary. I told myself you would go back to normal soon, but you didn't, Theon. You are not the same."

"Neither of us can stay the same after..."

"I know," Axel said, reaching to stop him from opening the door they'd come to. "I know why we are the way we are, but that doesn't mean we have to create more of us."

He pushed the door open, and Theon followed him into the suite. Tessa was standing near the bay window, looking out at the dark grounds. It had started raining again, this strange weather pattern appearing to continue. They didn't get much rain in the mountains at the end of summer, but at least this was a steady drizzle rather than a storm.

"Are we playing cards or something tonight?" Axel asked, stretching his arms up before pulling his dress shirt from his pants. He slid his jacket off, tossing it on the sofa, and loosening his tie.

"Sure. I'm just going to change," Theon answered. He crossed to the bedroom, motioning for Tessa to follow when she glanced at him.

As they stepped into the dressing room, he turned to her, caging her against the wall between his arms.

"What are you doing?" she gasped.

"Can I kiss you?"

Her eyes darkened some, her features hardening. "That's not my choice."

"It is," he replied, reaching behind her to pull pins from her hair. "I told you I wouldn't force anything on you, but today was intense. I know it was a hard day for you."

"How will kissing me change any of that?"

"It will appease the bond. Ease some tension," he answered, pulling the last of the pins free.

"I'd rather just change and go to bed."

Theon tilted his head to the side, twining a curl around his finger. "Axel and Luka want to play cards."

"I don't want to play cards."

"You can't be in the bedroom by yourself, beautiful." His other hand dropped to her hip, tugging her into him, and she sucked in a sharp breath.

For a long moment, she held his gaze, and Theon held his breath, waiting for her answer.

"I'd like to change," she finally said, breaking his stare.

"All right."

Theon stepped back, and she instantly wrapped her arms around herself.

He pulled out a pair of leggings and a tank top, adding one of his own thermals to the top. "In case you're cold," he said when she looked at him in confusion.

She nodded, moving forward to grab the clothing and retreating into the bathroom. Theon changed in the dressing room, giving her plenty of time to get changed in the other room. When he came out to the bedroom, she was sitting in front of the fireplace.

"You don't have to play cards, but I can't have you in here by your-self," he said, holding a hand out to her.

"I understand," she answered, reaching out and letting him pull her to her feet.

He tucked a piece of hair behind her ear, searching her eyes. "Tessa," he breathed. "Just accept the bond. This can all stop."

"Do you think I'm not trying?" she asked, her voice cracking the slightest amount, but he heard it. "Do you think I do not recognize how much simpler things could be? Do you think I enjoy the agony that comes from not fully submitting to this?"

"What is holding you back? What do I need to do? Tell me, Tessa. Name it, and it is done," he said, his hands framing her face.

She stared back at him, and for just a second, the façade slipped. He saw so many emotions swirling in her eyes, but there was something else there too. A flash of something. Before he could study it more, she blinked, and her newfound docile demeanor was back in place. The only sound was the soft pattering of the rain outside as they stared at each other.

"You've done enough," she finally said. "Please just let me figure it out on my own."

She pulled free of him and walked out to the main room. When Theon followed, she was already curling up in the bay window, staring out at the raindrops trickling down the glass. Luka was bringing her a blanket while Axel was shuffling cards at the table.

They hadn't even completed two hands when her breathing shifted. Theon glanced over to find her sleeping, her head propped against the glass.

"She was exhausted," Luka said, dealing the next hand.

"It was a long day for her," Theon confirmed. "A lot of adjustments."

"I told you on the drive here that this would break her."

"She is not going to break," Theon ground out. "I just wish I knew what was holding her back from accepting this."

"It's who she is, Theon," Luka said. "The sooner *you* accept that, the easier this whole thing will become."

"I don't know how many times we are going to have this conversation, Luka," Theon snarled. "We cannot undo this. The only thing that can break the bond is death."

"Would you undo it?" Axel suddenly chimed in. "If you could go back and change things, would you? Would you pick a different Source?"

Theon looked over at the Fae sleeping in the window. A female he'd only known a handful of days, but the mere idea of her not being here made him irrationally angry. Maybe it was the Source bond. It didn't really matter. He'd felt drawn to her the moment he'd stepped foot inside that alcove. Fuck, he'd felt drawn to her from the moment she'd become a possible Source option. Why else had he refused to rule her out despite Luka and Axel's very sound reasoning? He'd call it fate, but the Fates cared for their world as much as the gods did.

"No," he finally answered, picking up his cards. "No. I wouldn't pick someone else. Because just like she believes, I'm a bastard, and I can't let her go now that I have her."

14
TESSA

T hree days.

It had been three days of Theon's new expectations. Three days of going through the motions. Three days of doing as she was told. Three days of biting her tongue and keeping everything inside. Three days of barely speaking. Three days of being trapped in these rooms. Trapped in this house. Trapped in her own head.

Trapped.

So fucking trapped.

Theon had been true to his word. He didn't force anything sexual on her. There was often physical contact, but nothing overly suggestive. He hadn't asked to kiss her again since that first day. He would press soft kisses to the top of her head or to her temple, and his hand was always in hers or touching her in some way, but that was it. She'd admit she'd been getting the best sleep of her godsdamn life though. The bond was content sleeping next to him every night, but each day she found it harder and harder to resist the pull of the cord inside her that was pushing for more.

And each day she wondered if she was losing more and more of her mind. Of herself. Each day she wondered if this would be the day she finally gave up.

Theon tried at various times to engage her in conversation. So did Luka and Axel. She quickly lost interest in whatever they were saying.

No, that wasn't true.

She simply did not care.

Not only that, she was worried if she spoke too much, she'd say something reckless and make things even more unbearable.

She tried to read a book, but she couldn't focus on the pages for more than a few minutes at a time. Not that she minded reading. She just couldn't sit still long enough to focus on it, her mind constantly wandering. Suddenly she'd read five pages but had no idea what the pages had said.

Now she was lying awake in bed. For the first time ever, she had woken before Theon. His arm was draped over her waist, his features softer in sleep. That muscle that always ticked in his jaw relaxed for once. As carefully as she could, she slipped from beneath his arm, hoping not to wake him. She hadn't been in a space by herself for longer than five minutes for three days. A cup of coffee in the quiet morning hours sounded divine. No need to weigh every action and word. Not having eyes constantly on her. A few minutes when she could try to feel something other than the numbness settling over her soul. A few minutes to breathe.

Tessa slid on Theon's thermal shirt. He'd taken to leaving one out for her on the armchair by the fireplace. His body heat kept her plenty warm at night, but she was always chilled in the mornings. She tiptoed barefoot out to the main room, closing the bedroom door behind her so she wouldn't wake him while she made coffee.

A few minutes later, she settled into the bay window, a hot mug of coffee warming her hands. She loved dawn. Watching the sun start to climb. The promise that anything could happen. Nothing ever changed for her, but she liked the idea that something *could* change. Silly idealistic notions when she really thought about it. Hope never amounted to anything.

She stared out at the winding garden paths below. When she'd run through them in her escape attempt, she hadn't taken the time to look around. She had simply taken the main path that led straight into the mountains. But she had studied them from this vantage point in her hours of being trapped inside. There had been a constant gloomy drizzle for the last three days, so she hadn't even been able to sit on the balcony.

Movement caught her eye outside, and she found Axel running in the rain. Having never been awake this early, she'd never seen him out there before. She'd never been a runner. She didn't particularly *want* to be a runner, but she did want to be outside, even in the rain. Even if she had to run.

Tessa rose from her seat and retrieved the phone Theon had given her. It was on his desk, plugged into the charger. She hadn't touched the thing since they'd returned from Castle Pines and she'd handed it back to him. This phone was expensive. It looked like it was one of the latest models. She would have given just about anything to be holding one of the old, outdated phones she shared with her friends rather than this shiny new thing. This phone was just one more thing that separated her from who she had once been.

Returning to the bay window, it took her a minute to find Axel again. He was towards the back of the gardens now, almost out of sight. She didn't know much about running, but he seemed to be making pretty good time. Unlocking the phone, she pulled up Axel's contact information, quickly typing out a message.

Tessa: Can I go running with you?

She turned her attention back to the window where she saw Axel come to a sudden halt. He pulled his phone from his pocket, trying to shield it from the rain. Tessa watched the phone beside her as she sipped her coffee, waiting to see if he was going to answer. A moment later, her phone gave a soft ping.

Axel: One- I didn't know you were a runner. Two- I'm guessing Theon won't like that.

She pursed her lips, but before she could respond, another message came through.

Axel: You should ask Theon to take you running.

She'd never seen Theon run, and she was rarely away from him. Although, come to think of it, he must train at some point to maintain looking the way that he did. So when did he have time to do that? When he was gone for those meetings with his father maybe?

Her phone pinged again, and Tessa glanced down at the message. Axel had apparently taken her lack of response as her being upset.

Axel: If you can convince Theon to let you, I'll gladly run with you. Talk to Theon.

A door banging open made her jump as she clutched her coffee cup, trying not to spill any of it.

"Tessa?" Theon called, rushing into the main room. Upon seeing her in the bay window, he hurried to her side. "What are you doing out here?"

Tessa blinked up at him in surprise. "...drinking coffee?" She lifted her mug a little to further her point.

"Gods, Tessa," he breathed, running his hands through his sleep-addled hair. "I woke up to an alert that you were using your phone and then you weren't in bed... You know you're not supposed to be out of my sight."

"You were sleeping, Theon," she snapped, and his emerald eyes flared brighter at her outburst. "I've been out of your sight since you fell asleep last night," she added, rolling her eyes.

"Why are you texting Axel at dawn?"

"I saw him running out in the gardens. You said I could communicate with him and Luka."

"I know I did, but you haven't exactly been present the last few days."

"And whose fault is that?" she bit back.

His head cocked to the side. "Is this how I get you to speak to me? I must speak with you before you've had a full cup of coffee?" Tessa scowled at him, and the corner of his lips lifted the smallest amount. "What are you and Axel talking about?"

"That's none of your concern," she retorted. There was no way she was going to ask him if she could go running with Axel.

Theon's hand snapped out faster than she could track, scooping up her phone where it had slipped onto the window seat. "Wrong answer, Tessa. Everything to do with you is my concern."

"Give that back!" she cried, shooting to her feet and somehow managing not to spill her coffee as she set it down on the seat.

Shadows wrapped around her, holding her back while he unlocked the phone. His brows shot up as he read the brief text exchange before he shifted his gaze back to her. "You want to go running?"

"I want to go running *with Axel*," she retorted, giving up on trying to get the phone back and crossing her arms, his darkness drifting along her torso and tendrils winding into her hair.

"No," he answered simply, holding the phone out to her. "But like Axel said, I will take you running."

Not taking the phone back, she said, "I don't want to go running with you."

"Then you won't go running."

"Fine."

Theon sighed in exasperation. "Tessa."

"Theon," she parroted mockingly.

Theon's lips thinned, that muscle ticking in his jaw. "I'll have Pen go out and get you some running gear today. We can start running tomorrow morning."

"Did you go deaf overnight? I said I don't want to go running *with you*."

"Consider it a consequence then," he replied. He made his way towards the kitchen, pausing to place the phone on his desk. His shadows lingered a little longer before they pulled away from her, dragging along her flesh like they didn't want to leave.

"Consequence? For what?"

"You were not to leave my sight or my side for more than a few minutes at a time," he called over his shoulder.

"Theon!" she shrieked, stomping after him. "You were sleeping!"

He said nothing. Just poured himself a mug of coffee before turning back to her and arching a brow in question.

"You're serious?" she demanded.

"As the Pits of Torment," he replied with a nod. Tessa stared at him, completely dumbfounded. "I'll order up breakfast," he added after a moment, striding past her with his coffee in hand.

Tessa turned, following him into the bedroom where he'd gone to retrieve his phone. "I'm not going running with you," she said, all the emotions she'd been pushing down the last few days surging up in a torrent.

"We will discuss this later," he said, clearly not worried as he picked up his phone.

"We will discuss this now," she countered, reaching out and slapping the phone from his hand. It landed on the bed with a soft thunk. Theon dragged incredulous eyes to her, and Tessa forced herself not to shrink back from him. What was he going to do? That had been impulsive. She was arguing with him and fighting back. Two things he had said she wasn't to do anymore.

"Did you just slap my phone out of my hand?" he asked, his tone low and dangerous as he set his mug down.

"I...was trying to talk to you," she answered. She heard the slight tremor in her voice, so she could only assume he did too.

"Did you think I could not speak with you and order breakfast at the same time?"

"No. I just...wanted your complete attention," she said, finally managing to form the words.

"And now you have it."

Tessa swallowed, and he took a step towards her. She went to step back, but he reached out, twisting her so that the back of her legs bumped against the bed. One of his arms looped around her back, catching her, while the other held him over her when he lowered her onto the unmade bed.

"Theon, what are you doing?" she breathed. Her stomach dipped, and her skin tingled at the close contact. Sleeping beside him was one thing, but having him look at her like *this* was something else entirely. Faint wisps of darkness swirled across his heated emerald eyes. Eyes that dipped to her mouth.

"You wanted my attention," he said, his face coming close to hers. A lock of his black hair fell into his eyes, and without thinking, she reached up and brushed it back. The corner of his mouth quirked up. "You were saying?"

She had been saying something, hadn't she? His face moved an inch closer so that his breath danced over her lips.

"Tessa," he murmured, amusement flickering across his features.

"What?"

"What did you require my complete attention for?"

"To..."

He ran the tip of his nose down the length of hers, and her entire body flushed with heat and need.

"To what?" he whispered.

There had been something she'd been trying to tell him. There had been something she was trying to say. She mentally tried to go through her morning, but ignoring him on top of her was not easily done.

Coffee. Axel. Running.

Running!

"To tell you I'm not going running with you," she blurted at the sudden recall.

Theon pulled back a fraction of an inch. "You are sure?"

"Yes."

"Positive?"

"Positive?" Tessa repeated in confusion. "Yes, Theon. I am certain I am not going running with you."

"Hmm," he hummed. He'd worked his arm out from beneath her, and his hand settled on her hip. Now those fingers began slowly skating up her side, brushing across her ribs in a way that made her squirm.

"Theon," she breathed, trying to push against his chest, but he snatched her wrists with his other hand. Bringing them up, he pinned them above her head, and she went utterly still at being completely at his mercy.

"Did you know that you've said my name more times this morning than you have in the last three days?" he murmured, his hand skating along her ribs again. His gaze was fixed on his fingers, following their path.

She swallowed but didn't answer.

She did know that. Calling him by his name seemed too personal when they were not that. Source and Master. That was the extent of their relationship. Nothing more.

"I've missed hearing it on your lips, little storm," he continued.

"I don't care," she ground out.

"No, you don't," he said, more to himself than her.

His hips rolled against her. A small movement that had her sucking in a sharp breath because *gods*. If he was literally anyone else, falling headfirst into pleasure would be the perfect distraction from everything.

"What will it take for you to go running with me, Tessa?" he asked.

Her lip curled into a mocking smirk. "I don't negotiate with you."

He paused. "So mouthy this morning."

She scowled, turning her head to the side and averting her gaze. Mainly because if she kept staring at him, she was going to kiss him. And if this kiss was anything like the other two times they'd kissed, she didn't think she would be able to stop. Theon sure as fuck wouldn't stop.

"Would running with me versus Axel really be all that terrible?" he pressed, his fingers trailing along her torso again.

"Yes," she gritted out.

"Why?"

"Because he's not *you*."

He still held her wrists above her head, and his other hand came up and gripped her chin, forcing her gaze back to his. He didn't say anything for the longest moment, only searched her eyes. Finally, he said, "Axel can go running with us if you would like."

"No."

"I am trying to compromise with you, Tessa."

"And I am declining your proposal, *Master*."

His eyes flared brighter, that swirling darkness starker against them. "You do need to exercise. It's as important as proper nutrition."

"I'm fine," she bit out.

"Running or training in a gym. Your choice."

"I don't get choices."

"Both then."

"What? Why?" she cried in dismay. "As a punishment for being born? Or simply because you think I'm yours?"

His thumb brushed along her bottom lip, his features softening. "It's not a punishment, Tessa."

"Consequence. Punishment. They're the same thing, even if one word sounds prettier than the other. I would know."

At that, he stilled again. "What do you mean by that?"

Too much. She'd revealed too much.

"Nothing."

"I am going to need you to explain that statement."

"No."

"Tessa..." She could hear his irritation growing.

"Fine, we can go running," she said in a rush, if only to keep him from pushing her on this.

He eyed her for a moment before he released her wrists, but his body remained hovering over her as he braced his palms on either side of her head. She couldn't move. Parts of her would press against parts of him and—

A soft pinging sounded, and Theon's eyes darted to his phone where it still lay on the bed.

"Axel is on his way here with breakfast," Theon said, his eyes coming back to her. "Are you hungry?"

Tessa nodded mutely, and Theon slowly rose off her, taking one of her hands to pull her up with him. He didn't release her hand, and she tucked her hair behind her ear as he led her back out to the main room and to the dining table. While she was taking her seat, he went and retrieved her coffee mug from the window, going to the kitchen to refill it.

She frowned slightly. He was waiting on her. It was supposed to be the other way around.

The sound of the door drew her attention, and a moment later, Axel came through with a pastry box in hand. He was still in his running gear, a protein shake balanced atop the box.

"Morning, baby doll," he said in greeting, flashing her a grin.

She gave him a tight smile in return.

"Do I need to text you?" he asked, placing the pastry box on the table. "Is that the only way we communicate now?"

"I texted you once," she retorted. "The rest was all you because you talk incessantly."

"There she is," he said, his grin widening. He flipped open the pastry box. "They're bringing up eggs and sausage, but I thought these might be a good start."

She crossed her arms but leaned forward an inch to peer inside. There were a variety of muffins. It wasn't doughnuts, but they would do.

If Theon let her have one.

Her coffee mug appeared in front of her, and she could feel him standing behind her. This presence that both drew her in and made her want to scream.

"These look like Pen's doing," Theon said, reaching for the box and grabbing a muffin.

"You know Pen," Axel replied, dropping into a chair. He pulled a small mirror from his pocket that Tessa had seen him fiddling with every once in a while. She'd been curious, but not enough to ask about it. That would require speaking to them. The ring on his finger matched one of Theon's, the black stone in the center gobbling up any light.

Theon slid the box closer to Tessa as he lowered into the chair beside her. "Pen used to work in the kitchens before she was promoted to serve us."

"Promoted," Tessa deadpanned.

"Yes," Theon answered unfazed. "She is a talented baker though, and she still finds her way to the kitchens a few days a week. Apparently, this morning was one of them. Pick one."

She kept her arms firmly crossed, not wanting to take anything from him after he'd basically forced her to agree to running with him.

"There are all kinds," Axel said, rolling that stupid mirror between his knuckles.

"Blueberry?" Theon asked, his hand hovering over the box.

She pursed her lips, but when he started to reach for one, she blurted, "Chocolate chip."

"Good choice," Axel said with a wink.

"Whatever," she grumbled, snatching the muffin from Theon's hand.

Axel and Theon fell into conversation, and she sank back into herself. She may be with one of them at all hours these days, but she was more alone than ever.

One, two, three...

15
TESSA

"Why did I want to do this again?" Tessa moaned.

She was lying on the floor, and Axel was helping her stretch her legs and hip flexors. Theon had her up before dawn the last two mornings to go running. She liked dawn. While sipping coffee and watching the sun rise. Not dying and being unable to breathe while the sun was rising.

Theon made her eat a banana on their way out the door. They would meet Axel and proceed to run along the various garden paths. The first day she'd made it almost two miles before she was done. She may not have been athletic, but it wasn't as though she sat around all day at the Estate. She needed to keep busy, or she'd go half-mad if she was forced to stay indoors or in one place too long. And, of course, she'd had to run to avoid being caught a few times too. So she *could* run, but not for the *enjoyment* of it.

Today, Theon had made her go nearly three miles, informing her that her Fae body was more than capable of going that far. She wasn't fast, and they were clearly slowing their pace way down to stay with her. Theon and Axel were having godsdamn conversations during these runs while she was busy trying to suck down air.

And she was sore.

And hungry.

But mostly sore.

Theon had quickly showered and changed when they'd gotten back to the rooms. He had a meeting with his father and some others, and Axel had stayed behind to babysit her. She assumed Luka was going to be at the meeting with Theon. Tessa hadn't seen the male since the day they'd all gone to Castle Pines, but he was supposed to be back today.

"Don't whine," Axel said, pressing her leg up in the air. "I promise once you get through the first few weeks, you'll love it."

"First few weeks?" Tessa demanded, grimacing as he deepened the stretch.

"Come on. You don't hate it that much, do you?"

She didn't. Granted, it had only been two days, but it got her outside. If it's what she had to do to be outside, then she'd gladly struggle to breathe.

"No," she sighed. "I don't."

"Good," Axel said, stepping back and motioning for her to lower her leg. "Because I got you something."

Tessa sat up, sitting cross-legged on the floor. She grabbed her water bottle and took a long drink while he jogged over to his bag near the door. When he returned, he dropped to the floor beside her, passing her a small box. Setting her water bottle aside, she opened it to find two ear buds.

"I thought you might want to listen to music while you're running," Axel explained.

"That would be nice," Tessa admitted slowly, pulling one from the box and fitting it into her ear. "But I don't have anything to play music on."

She didn't want to tell him she didn't even know what kind of music she liked. She only knew a few songs. Ballads of Devram she'd been forced to listen to as part of her studies. Most of them didn't even have words.

"Sure you do," Axel said. "Your phone can play it. Get it for me, and I'll show you how."

"You get it," she whined. "I can't get off the floor right now."

"Get up, baby doll," Axel said, pushing on her back. "You need to move around so you don't get too stiff."

Grumbling, Tessa got to her feet and retrieved the phone from Theon's desk. Just as she was handing it over to Axel, a knock came at the door. They paused, waiting for whoever it was to announce themselves.

"Tessalyn Ausra?" came a voice that Tessa did not recognize, but Axel tensed. He brought a finger to his lips, signaling her to be quiet.

The knock came again.

"We were sent to retrieve you. The Arius Lord and Arius Heir have requested your presence in our meeting."

Tessa glanced at Axel, who shook his head. He leaned over, speaking directly into her ear, and even then, he spoke so quietly, she could barely hear him. "Go into the bedroom. Shut the door."

He pressed the phone back into her hand. She nodded, hurrying to do as he said. As she shut the bedroom door, the knock came again.

"Open up, Tessalyn. Your master will be very upset to hear you are disobeying a Legacy."

Tessa heard the door open, and she pressed her ear to the closed bedroom door.

"Metias. Pavil," she heard Axel say. "What are you doing in this wing of the house?"

Tessa had never heard Axel speak that way. His tone was low and dangerous and dark. The same tone Theon had spoken to her in when he'd yanked her out of a tree.

"Axel," came the greasy voice again. "My apologies. I thought these were Theon's rooms. We were sent to retrieve his Source for him."

"These are Theon's rooms," Axel answered. "His Source is in the shower. I can bring her to Theon when she is finished."

"Actually, we were coming to find you next. Your father has requested your presence as well," cut in another voice. "He was very insistent. Might I suggest you head down, and we can wait for Theon's Source to escort her when she is out of the shower?"

"I will need to check with Theon to confirm that," Axel said smoothly. "He is very protective of his Source, as you can imagine."

"Of course. It is his protectiveness that drove him to desire her next to him," the first voice replied. "Our meeting is going much longer than anticipated, so he would like her present."

"She just got in the shower, so she will likely be a bit," Axel said. "I can call down to the study and verify—"

"I really don't think that's necessary. We are allies now, are we not?" came the second voice. "I am starting to become offended at the obvious lack of trust you are displaying in us."

"We are allies, Pavil, but my brother entrusted the safety of his Source to me, and I take that responsibility seriously," Axel answered.

"More seriously than you appear to take your life when you interrupted an Arius Heir."

There was a long pause, and Tessa found herself smiling at Axel putting the male in his place.

And she wasn't entirely sure how she felt about that.

"It will only take a moment to confirm everything," Axel was saying.

"This is urgent business, Axel," the first voice sneered. "Your father is going to be very displeased if you do not go to his study immediately."

Axel went silent, and Tessa wasn't sure what to do. Suddenly, her phone pinged softly in her hand.

Axel: Run, Tessa. Theon isn't answering his phone. However you got down from that balcony, do it again and run. Theon will find you.

"Fine. I will head down there. Bring her straight to Theon as soon as she is done," she heard Axel saying. "But know if she arrives with a single hair out of place, you will deal with Theon, and we all know how that will go."

Tessa didn't linger any longer. She was still in her running clothes, but she had removed her shoes. Guess she was doing this barefoot.

With nowhere to put her phone, she tossed it on the bed and rushed over to the balcony doors, scurrying through and shutting them behind her. Darting to the left, she climbed over the balcony railing and onto the thin ledge that ran to the trellis. With her back to the wall, she slowly inched her way along, the wards pressing against her skin. She had moved faster the last time she'd done this, but the wind was picking up and some of the gusts were strong. Just as she was nearing the trellis, she heard the balcony doors burst open. She leapt the remaining distance, her hands slicing open on the wood as she caught herself. Her bare feet fought for purchase.

"What the fuck?"

Tessa looked over to see a shorter Legacy with slicked back hair and dark eyes watching her in shock. Another slightly taller Legacy came rushing up behind him.

"The side entrance," the second one said, pulling the other to follow him. "We'll cut her off in the gardens."

The two males disappeared as Tessa climbed down the trellis as quickly as she could. She jumped the last few feet and cried out as she landed wrong, her ankle wrenching to the side. Not giving herself a second to dwell on the pain, she took off running. Her ankle was throbbing, and the bond was growing more and more agonizing as she put distance between her and Theon.

The sound of pounding feet behind her had her putting on a burst of speed. Looking over her shoulder, she found the two Legacy easily gaining on her. She pushed her sore legs faster, but between her ankle and the bond, coupled with the fact she was already tired from their run a mere hour ago, she had already lost.

"It's okay, Tessalyn," one of them called to her, much closer than they'd been a moment ago. "We just want to get to know you better. We're going to be spending lots of time together."

Tessa followed the path that Theon had been taking her running on the last two days. It wound down farther into the gardens before it would eventually turn and take her past the kennels and the stables. She flung herself around a corner, and as she did, she tripped on a root in the path. She lurched forward, sprawling to her hands and knees. Before she could right herself, a hand latched onto her sprained ankle, and she cried out as pain and panic coursed through her.

"Such a pretty little thing you are," the one with the slicked-back hair crooned, dragging her along the stone path closer to him. Her arms and knees scraped on the stone.

"Let me go!" she cried, trying to find anything to grab onto as she was pulled backwards.

"Now, Tessalyn," came the second, walking up beside her. "Is that any way to speak to a Legacy? Although Valter did say you had an issue with manners." He crouched down before her, reaching over and running a single finger along her jaw. "He gave us permission to make sure those manners were corrected. Sadly, I am finding them lacking."

Terror and fear clawed their way up Tessa's spine, her already racing heart ramping up even more. The male who held her ankle began sliding his hand up her calf, and the other one tried to grab her wrist.

"No!" Tessa cried. She kicked out with her good foot, putting every bit of strength she could muster into the movement, and caught the one at her feet in the nose. He cursed as he jerked back from her, blood pouring out from behind his hand.

"You little bitch!" he spat, his voice nasally. "How dare you attack a Legacy!"

"Those manners definitely need correcting," the second male said through clenched teeth, fury lining his features.

"Don't touch me!" Tessa cried, scrambling away from him as he made another grab for her. A violent gust of wind tore through the garden path, knocking the second male back several inches, and Tessa used it to her advantage, crawling away even farther.

She shoved herself to her feet as the male came for her again, and she threw her hands out in front of her. "No!"

The word had barely left her lips when the ground beneath them shook. The first male, who had managed to get to his own feet, fell back onto his ass, and the second male dropped to his knees. Tessa pitched forward onto her own hands and knees once again, and when her palms met with the earth, light sparked and rippled, a large crack ripping through the path between her and the Legacy.

"What the—" the second male began to say, but he didn't get to finish. Gold mist began rising from the crack as a crevice took shape, widening the gap between Tessa and the Legacy. As thunder cracked, light so bright she had to turn away flared up from the ground. She was scrambling back, but not before she caught sight of something beginning to crawl up out of the crevice from the light.

No.

Not crawl.

It glided up out of the crevice.

Another appeared.

And another.

Tessa watched in utter terror as *bodies* rose up out of the crevice. But they weren't bodies of flesh and blood. They shimmered in the sunlight, their bodies nearly transparent. They floated a couple of inches off the ground, and they were all identical. Pale skin. Tall and lean, with sharp, angular features. Short hair as white as clouds.

They couldn't be real. She must have hit her head when she tripped on the tree root. Maybe none of this was real.

The first being that had appeared tipped its head back, inhaling deeply. His head turned. White eyes with no pupils settled on her. Could it actually see her?

Not real. This cannot be real.

The terror was paralyzing. She couldn't move, even as the other beings turned their heads to her as well. The two Legacy were just as frozen on the other side of the crevice, and when the first being lifted a hand, he drew a sword from the very air.

The others did the same.

Those were real.

Very real blades of gleaming gold.

The two Legacy lurched backwards as the beings turned back to them. The figures moved as if to leap across the crevice, but they simply floated over it.

And Tessa decided she had seen enough.

Whatever paralyzing fear she'd been under shattered, and she jumped back to her feet, running as fast as she could down the path. She stumbled more than once as her ankle protested every pounding step, rocks cutting into her bare feet. The cord was tightening around her chest, demanding she seek out Theon and making breathing even harder. She went around another corner, and the sound of barking told her she was nearing the kennels. She pushed herself faster until she was skidding to another halt as one of Theon's huge wolves burst from the kennels.

Its black fur gleamed in the morning sun, and its hackles were raised. Its ears were pinned back, and its orange eyes were glowing just like they had been when it had chased her up the tree in the mountains.

You have got to be fucking kidding me.

Frozen, Tessa didn't dare move as the wolf prowled forward. What would be a worse fate? Dying by a wolf or a being that had floated up out of the ground with a sword? She was trembling as the wolf neared her, but when it reached her side, it turned, nudging her hand with its nose. She was trying to hold her breath, but she'd just been running for her damn life and she was panting.

The wolf pushed into her hand again, then moved to nudge her behind the knees as if telling her to move. When she stumbled forward a step, the wolf leapt in front of her, pausing to look back over its shoulder at her.

I am losing my godsdamn mind. None of this can be real.

But as cries erupted from the Legacy behind her, she decided she would take her chances with the wolf over translucent figures with golden swords.

"Please don't kill me," she muttered as she darted after the animal.

The wolf led her past the kennels and down another path that she knew would eventually lead to the stables. As the wolf neared them, it darted to the side, and Tessa followed it off the path onto uneven ground. It went around to the backside of the stables, where it reared up onto its hind legs and began pawing at the door.

"Okay, okay," Tessa gasped, cautiously approaching the door. She unlatched it, pushing, but it wouldn't budge. "It's stuck," she grunted, throwing her shoulder into it again and again.

The wind was whipping wildly now, her hair flying in every direction, and thunder was continuing to rumble overhead as dark clouds continued to build. The wolf growled beside her and let out a loud bark. Startled by the sound, Tessa stumbled back just in time for the wolf to come leaping at the door. The impact of its paws hitting the door echoed around her.

The door flew inward at the weight from the wolf, and it barked again at Tessa. She stumbled across the threshold and into the stables. The moment she was inside, the wolf let loose a long howl before turning and going back the way they'd come. Not knowing what else to do, Tessa heaved the door shut behind her and turned to take in the stables. She was at the back of the building, and she bent over, hands on her knees, as she tried to catch her breath and figure out what to do next.

"She must have gone to the horses." The second Legacy's voice carried to her, and her stomach went to her throat.

Staggering forward, she looked for a place to hide, but all she saw were stalls. Down the way, one of the giant black horses had stuck his head over his gate, watching her.

That pen was definitely not an option.

Not wasting any more time, Tessa began climbing the gate to her right. When she reached the top, she jumped into the stall without thinking and bit down on the cry of pain. Tears of agony leaked out of the corners of her eyes, but the scream she let out wasn't from her ankle. It was from the giant horse she was suddenly face-to-face with.

Tessa slammed a hand over her mouth to muffle the sound as she slowly backed up from the creature. Her back hit the corner of the stall, and she stilled. The horse took a step forward, his large nose coming to her hair, and hot breath washed over her as he huffed.

The sound of the stable door creaking open had her stifling another scream, and she slowly sank down into the corner of the stall. If they came from the direction she had come from, they'd spot her immediately, but if they came from the other direction, she couldn't be spotted unless they searched each pen.

The horse's ear perked at the noise, and he moved to lift his head over the gate, apparently curious to see who else had entered his domain.

"Tessalyn," the second male called out. "Come out, come out, wherever you are."

One of the other horses let out a whinny while the one in the stall Tessa was in stamped his large hoof against the hay-strewn ground. Tessa's hand was still clamped over her mouth, trying to muffle the sound of her breathing. Dread crept up her spine, and terror coated her limbs.

"Valter will not be happy we lost her," the first male said.

Their footsteps sounded closer, and the horse shifted, almost as if it were trying to block her from view.

"Perhaps, but I think he will find what we saw very interesting," the second replied.

"Then let's go tell him before she summons any more of those things, or before Theon's damn hound shows up again," the first male answered. "I'm still struggling to heal the wound from that damn thing."

"I don't think she's in here anyway," the second said. "There's no place to hide unless she crawled into a stall, and Theon's horses would never allow that."

Their voices faded away as they exited the building, but Tessa remained frozen where she sat in the corner. Silent tears were tracking down her cheeks, and her entire body was trembling. The horse turned his head to look at her, and her heart ratcheted up again as he moved towards her. His head lowered, and his large nose nuzzled against her shoulder, before he lowered his massive body to the ground. His huge head came to rest on her legs, where he stilled.

After several minutes, Tessa slowly lowered her hand from her mouth. Extending trembling fingers towards him, she stroked the animal's cheek. He let out a soft huff, so she did it again. She stroked her fingers through his silky black mane and down his broad neck, but her trembling didn't cease as fresh tears coursed down her face.

She dropped her head to the animal's neck and sobbed.

16

THEON

T heon and Luka were making their way back to the east wing. Pavil and Metias had left a while ago, but his father had asked the two of them to stay behind. Luka had been gone the past few days, and his father wanted a report.

Theon needed the same, and they were heading back to the suite to discuss the other one with Axel. The report that would further their own plans and not just his father's. But as they were rounding a corner, the odd feeling from the bond started in his chest again.

The same way it had when Tessa had climbed down from the gods-damn balcony.

"You have to be fucking kidding me," Theon growled.

"What?" Luka asked, glancing up from his phone that he was powering back on.

"She's running."

He thought they'd finally made some progress. He thought they'd come to an understanding. He thought she was getting closer to accepting the bond. They'd compromised and gone running with Axel the last two mornings. She had been sleeping next to him every night without argument. She'd started speaking more the last two days, some of her old snark and temper breaking through every once in a while. He thought his plan had been working.

And now she was fucking running again.

"Are you sure?" Luka asked, his pace increasing to match Theon's.

"Yes," Theon snapped. "If she thought I was controlling after last time, she's not going to know what to do now."

Luka started to say something else as they turned down a hall, but they nearly collided with Axel.

"Theon," Axel said, coming to an abrupt halt. "Why aren't you answering your fucking phone?"

"It's off. You know how Father gets when we're in meetings," Theon retorted.

"I'm just seeing your messages," Luka said gravely.

"What the fuck are you doing out here, Axel? Where is Tessa?"

"Metias and Pavil showed up at your rooms," Axel answered, darkness swirling in his emerald eyes and wisps of the same winding through his hair. He was really worked up for his magic to be slipping. "They said Father had demanded my immediate presence, and that you had sent them to retrieve Tessa for you."

"Why would they say that?" Panic settled into his soul as Theon made to push past Axel, but his brother grabbed his arm.

"She's running, Theon. I told her to hide in the bedroom before I answered the door. When they were insistent, and neither of you answered my messages, I told her to climb down the balcony like she did before and run. I told her you would find her."

Theon spun on his heel, running down halls and stairs. If those motherfuckers laid a hand on her, they were dead. He didn't care what alliances his father had. No one touched her without his permission.

He burst through a door and out into the gardens where howling greeted him.

Kacela.

That was her tracking howl.

Theon raced towards the sound, Luka and Axel on his heels. Rounding a corner, he skidded to a halt at a large crevice that had appeared in the path. What the fuck? There was what appeared to be gold paint everywhere, and were those swords on the ground?

Kacela was on the other side of the crevice and barked excitedly when Theon came into view.

"Lightning strike?" Axel asked, coming to a stop beside him and eyeing the crevice before them. "The weather has been so odd lately."

"I don't care what it was," Theon answered, moving back a few steps before taking a running start and leaping over the expanse. His feet had barely touched the ground when he was running again, chasing after Kacela. How had she gotten out of the kennels?

Kacela led him past the kennels and to the stables, taking him around the back to a side door. Whining, she pawed at it. With a grunt of effort, Theon pushed the rarely used door open and stepped inside. Three giant black heads swung in his direction as he came in, hooves stomping the ground in agitation. Something had them worked up too.

"Tessa?" Theon called out. He could hear the panic in his voice. There was no place to hide in here. Not unless she crawled into a stall, and she had been leery of the horses when they'd ridden back from the woods. "Tessa? Are you in here?"

Kacela darted past him, going straight to Eyal's stall. He was the only horse not watching him as Theon moved down the aisle between the stalls. His horses were all impeccably trained, but Eyal was still the wildest. He could be temperamental and unpredictable. Theon slowed as he approached the pen, then came to a complete halt at what he found.

Tessa was huddled into a corner, visibly shaking. He couldn't see much of her, but what he could see was covered in cuts and scratches along her arms. Eyal was lying on his side beside her, his massive head resting in her lap while she cried into his mane.

All Theon could see was darkness as shadows clouded his vision. Pavil and Metias would pay for this. And his father? This only made Theon's need for her to accept the bond even stronger.

"By the gods," Luka breathed, coming up beside Theon and stilling at the sight.

Theon moved then, unlatching the gate and entering the pen. "Tessa?"

Eyal lifted his head, and Tessa raised her own as the horse shifted. Her grey eyes were wild with panic and terror, and she scrambled back farther into the corner, as if she could hide from them. Theon was forced to take a step back as Eyal got up before moving to the back of his sizable stall. Luka had come in behind Theon and moved to keep the horse back while he approached Tessa.

She was staring up at Theon. The dread in her eyes was palpable. She was pale and her leggings were ripped in some places. Her bare stomach had scratches and cuts too, as though she'd been dragged along the ground.

"I-I wasn't running from you, Theon," she stammered, shaking her head in emphasis. "Axel told me to run, and those Legacy were trying to get me. I don't know what they wanted, and I know I shouldn't have fought with them, but I wasn't running from you, Theon. I swear it!" She was speaking so fast, she was rambling.

He dropped to his knees before her, shrugging off his suit jacket before wrapping it around her shaking shoulders. "Shh, Tessa. I know. I know why you were running," he said, pulling her into him.

"I'm sorry," she whispered into his shoulder. "I'm sorry, Theon. I didn't know what else to do. I'm sorry."

She kept repeating the words over and over again.

I'm sorry. I'm sorry. I'm sorry.

He ran his hand over her hair, clutching her close. "Tessa, you have nothing to apologize for. Please stop saying that. I'm here. I'm here, little storm," he said softly, trying to soothe her as he spoke over her repeated apologies, but her trembling wouldn't cease.

"I'm sorry," she cried. "Please don't shut me in the dark. I can't breathe there. I'm sorry."

Kacela was whining from beyond the gate where she was locked out, and Axel stood just inside, his face as pale as Tessa's.

"I didn't know what else to do," Axel said when Theon met his gaze. "You know how Metias and Pavil are, and without knowing what had been said between you and Father, I didn't—"

"You did nothing wrong either, Axel," Theon said, cutting him off. "You kept her safe. That is what I asked of you."

"I didn't though," Axel said, guilt twisting his features as he gestured at them. "Look at her."

"You did the best you could in an impossible situation," Theon said firmly.

Silence fell among them as he held Tessa's shaking body close to him, but something else was wrong. The bond was writhing inside of him, pushing against his skin as if trying to get out. It should be humming happily at having her so close, even if she was sobbing.

"Let's get her to my rooms, and figure things out from there," Theon said, not wanting to say anything to alarm her further, but as he spoke, her trembling became violent thrashing.

"No, Theon! I'm sorry! I won't run again. I swear it. I won't. You don't need to lock me away. I'm sorry."

She was utterly frantic, not making any sense as her words tumbled over each other. He tried to speak over her, to calm her down, but she wouldn't listen, and the bond between them was taut and strained. What the fuck had happened?

Without another word, he stood. He had an arm wrapped around her waist, and he pulled her up with him; but as soon as she took a step, she was limping and whimpering in pain. A second later, he had scooped her up while she continued to whisper, "I'm sorry, Theon. I'm sorry."

"Something is wrong," he muttered over her head to Luka. "The Source bond is… Something is wrong."

"What does that mean?" Luka asked from where he still stood by Eyal.

"I don't know how to explain it. It's like… It's almost as if it wants me to push her away. Like it's rejecting her," Theon replied. At his words, Tessa began flailing in his arms to the point that he nearly dropped her. "Tessa, stop!"

"I need to breathe!" she cried. "I can't be locked away!"

"Give her to me," Luka said, coming over and reaching for her. "You need to make her answer a question."

Theon instinctively pulled her tighter against him, and Luka all but ripped her out of his hands. She buried her face in his chest, wrapping her arms around his neck. "I can't fix this," she sobbed into him. "He's going to lock me in the dark."

"I'm not—" Theon started, but Luka cut him off.

"Don't worry about that right now. Entrance her. Make her tell you if either of them touched her."

Realization crashed through Theon at the words. He'd been so overcome by panic, he hadn't even thought of that. Those two motherfuckers were the descendants of the lesser goddess, Gracil— goddess of emotion and empathy. Some of her descendants could amplify feelings. Metias and Pavil, in particular, could amplify fear and terror. Just being in their presence could increase feelings of panic and despair if you didn't have proper mental shields in place, but if they touched you, it was like opening a direct link between their gifts and your soul.

"Fuck," Theon cursed, reaching out to grip Tessa's chin. When her eyes met his, he could swear there was a faint violet ringing her pupils, but he didn't have time to study it. "Tessalyn, *answer me*. Did one of them touch you?"

"They both did," Tessa answered, the entrancing pulling the answer from her. "One held me by the ankle, dragging me backwards. The other ran his finger down my face."

"Fuck!" Theon repeated, raking his hand through his hair. They would have taken some of her worst fears and made them so great they'd be paralyzing. How she had even managed to run from them after being touched was a miracle in and of itself.

"I know it's not something you want to hear right now, but you're connected to her greatest fears, Theon," Luka said.

"She's my Source," Theon snarled. "She can't be— She's not...*scared* of me."

It wasn't possible. They were irrevocably bound together. Their souls and destinies were intertwined at this point. She couldn't *fear* him. Could she?

"I didn't say *you* were her greatest fear. I said you are *connected* to her greatest fears," Luka retorted. "Let me carry her back, and we can give her some space. Let their magic wear off a bit, and then, hopefully, she will be better able to fill us in on what happened."

Theon hated that idea. Even though the bond was pushing her away, he wanted her near. He wanted to make sure she was all right. To heal whatever was wrong with her ankle and all those godsdamn scratches and cuts. But instead, he bit out "fine" and began stalking towards the gate. Axel opened it, leading the way out, and Kacela whined, nudging Theon's hand with her nose.

He stopped to pet the hound while Luka maneuvered out of the stall with a still whimpering Tessa, and Axel replaced the gate latch.

"You did good today," Theon praised the hound in a wary tone. "Although how you got out of the kennels is beyond me."

"I will take her back," Axel said. "I'll meet you in your rooms."

Theon nodded, and he and Luka made their way to the house. With some type of luck, they managed not to run into anyone else. Luka walked Tessa straight to the bay window where she curled into herself, clutching her knees to her chest. He was speaking softly to her, and Theon couldn't hear what he said. Needing to do something, he went to the kitchen and filled the teakettle. He was placing tea bags in four mugs when Luka joined him.

"She is going to be fine," Luka said, leaning against the counter and crossing his arms. "She is already calming."

"Because I am over here. Away from her," Theon groused.

"Because you are doing what she *needs* and giving her space," Luka argued. "Metias and Pavil used their gifts on her, Theon. We are lucky we even got to her in time. It sounds like they weren't touching her for very long. Any more contact and…"

He trailed off, the tea kettle beginning to whistle shrilly.

"I know," Theon sighed, moving to grab the kettle. Pouring hot water into the mugs, he added, "My father had to be a part of this. It's why he kept us back when Metias and Pavil left the meeting. To give them time to get to her first. What does he want with her?"

"We will figure it out," Luka said, both of them watching her. She was staring out the glass across the gardens, her chin resting on her knees.

"If he expects me to work with those assholes, this can never happen again. Ever."

"Agreed," Luka said. "We can come up with a…tactful way to let your father know until we can take care of them."

"When that time comes, they are mine," he replied darkly, already debating how many ways he could draw out their deaths.

"Understood," Luka said.

"And my father won't give a fuck about anything we say," Theon growled as the door opened and Axel came in. Tessa flinched at the sound.

"You won't believe this," Axel said, closing the door softly, clearly having noted Tessa's reaction. "Kacela jumped over her kennel gate. There is no other way she could have gotten out of the kennels. All the pens, including hers, were securely locked."

"They can't jump that high," Theon argued, pulling tea bags from the mugs. "I made sure of it when I had the kennels remodeled when I got the hounds."

"I don't know what to tell you, brother. I couldn't see any other way she got out of her pen," Axel replied. "She also had that golden paint all over her paws and muzzle. But it was more like…"

"Like what?" Luka asked when Axel hesitated.

"It was like golden blood, but that doesn't make any sense, right?"

None of the events of today were making any sense. Like everything else in their lives, they needed to consider every possibility before they decided how to proceed. Their father clearly had a hand in all of this. Theon just needed to figure out why.

Axel grabbed one of the mugs. "Want me to take this to her?"

"I guess," Theon muttered, bringing his mug to his lips.

Tessa lifted her head when Axel approached. He said something to her as he offered her the mug, and she took it without any type of reaction before turning back to stare out the window. He then wandered off to the bedroom.

Theon turned back to Luka, taking another drink of his tea. "When she lets me near her again, she needs any wounds healed, and she needs to bathe."

"How do you think she did it?" Luka mused, ignoring everything Theon had just said. "How do you think she managed to run after Metias and Pavil touched her?"

"Maybe they didn't use their gifts to their full extent? She is an heir's Source after all," Theon replied. Luka didn't answer, telling Theon exactly how likely he thought that idea was, especially if his father had a hand in this. Theon didn't bother saying anything else. They'd know soon enough once she calmed down.

Some time later, Axel emerged from his bedroom. He was carrying Tessa's phone and some earbuds in his hand.

"I got her these to use while running," Axel said by way of explanation as he held the items out to him. "I don't know what kind of music she likes, so I set up a bunch of playlists for her and paired the earbuds with her phone." Theon nodded, taking the items. "Should we do something?" he asked, his gaze drifting back to Tessa.

"I need to check her injuries," Theon sighed.

"Do you want me to do it?" Axel asked.

"No," Theon bit back harshly. Axel's brows rose. "I mean, I'll do it. I should be able to heal most of them with the bond between us. Just give her a few more minutes."

Axel nodded. "Are you going to confront Father about this?"

"Eventually," Theon answered. "I haven't decided how to handle it yet. I need more details first."

"You think she'll be fine by dinner? Father won't excuse her," Axel continued.

Fuck.

Dinner.

"I guess she'll have to be," Theon said tightly.

They fell silent, all eyes on the female in the window for the next ten minutes. The bond was slowly shifting back to desire and craving her touch rather than wanting him to push her away. He wasn't focused on that though. He was contemplating the fact that he was related to her biggest fears.

In some way or another, she was scared of him.

A part of him was satisfied with that response. He craved control and instilling fear was definitely one way to obtain that. He had a hard time believing she was that terrified of him though, and maybe that was his own fault. Maybe all of this was his fault, his failure. In trying to make her comfortable, he'd shielded her too much from their true natures.

He finally pushed off the counter and made his way towards her. She turned and met his gaze, dread still filling her grey eyes.

"What happened to your foot?" he asked roughly.

She flinched back, her eyes dropping to her feet. "I didn't mean to. It was an accident."

"I'm not upset, Tessa. I want to heal it for you."

He saw her throat bob when she swallowed. "I landed wrong when I jumped from the trellis. I twisted my ankle."

"You ran all the way to the stables on a sprained ankle?" Theon said stiffly, looking at her feet. One ankle was definitely swollen.

"I... Axel told me to run. I thought you'd want me to follow his orders since you weren't here. I'm sorry," she whispered.

"I'm not... Godsdamnit, Tessa. I'm not mad that you ran from those fuckers," he said, reaching out and gently placing his hand on the swollen ankle. His magic swelled, the darkness pressing against his skin, flowing from his hand to her. It was different using his shadows for this, and without all four of her Marks in place, it was more draining than other times he used his gifts.

His gaze raked over the cuts and scratches crusted with dried blood all along her arms and abdomen, along with the bruises beginning to blossom on her skin. In a tight tone, he said, "I cannot heal everything at once. Tomorrow I will be able to do more, but I want to check them all. See if there are any that may need a Healer."

Tessa nodded once, returning her attention out the window. The sky was the same color as her eyes. She tensed as his hands slid up her legs and over her bare stomach, cataloging every scratch. The bond began humming once more between the physical contact and the effects of Pavil's and Metias's gifts beginning to lessen, and he couldn't help but wonder if it was doing the same for her. The way her limbs were tight and coiled beneath his hands, he would guess not, but that's how she always seemed to be around him. Unless they were sleeping. When she slept, she looked like a goddess to be worshipped.

"Nothing seems extensive unless I missed something?" he asked.

She shook her head. "No. You've done far more than I deserve."

Theon pushed his tongue into his cheek. What was he supposed to say to that?

"Why do you think you don't deserve care for injuries? Did I miss any?"

"I disobeyed you, Theon. Leaving my injuries would be a justifiable consequence."

Gods, that was something his Father would say.

"I will heal them tomorrow, Tessa. Our bond is simply not strong enough yet to take care of them all at once. Are there any others I need to be aware of?" When she remained silent, he added, "Tell me, or I will force you to do so." He didn't think it was possible, but her face paled even more at the mention of entrancing. He went preternaturally still, his voice dark when he asked, "Did either of them entrance you?"

"No," she answered, turning her arms over and holding them out to him. Scratches ran all along her forearms, some of the cuts still bleeding.

"Anywhere else?" he asked through gritted teeth. She shook her head, and Theon pushed out a long breath. "Come into the bathroom. We can clean those up, and you can bathe. Then you can rest for the afternoon before we need to get ready for dinner."

She winced at the mention of dinner, but obediently got to her feet. He glanced over his shoulder to Luka and Axel, who were watching them silently, concern on their features.

"Can one of you order up some lunch?" Theon asked. "Something warm."

"On it," Axel said, hooking his phone from his pocket. "I will have it delivered in an hour."

"Thanks," Theon replied, following Tessa through the doorway to the bedroom. She moved straight to the bathroom and reached to pull her torn running top over her head. Then she disappeared into the closet, and Theon moved forward to fill the giant bathtub.

He heard her come back into the bathroom, and her voice carried to him.

"A bath?"

"I thought it would be more calming than a shower," he answered, turning to face her, "but if you would rather—"

The words died on his lips. She stood before him in lacy red underthings that matched the red sports bra she'd worn running that morning. Despite the dried blood and dirt on her skin, the bond spiked with desire at the sight of her.

He cleared his throat. "If you would rather take a shower, I can get that set up for you."

"A bath is fine," she said, moving forward and reaching for her sports bra.

"I will check on you in a few minutes," he said, turning quickly to leave.

"Wait," she called out, and Theon turned back to her.

She was worrying her bottom lip, and her hands had dropped to her sides where her fingers were curling and uncurling into loose fists.

"What do you need, Tessa?" he asked when she didn't speak after several moments.

She still didn't look at him when she said, "Can you stay? I don't want to be alone right now."

17
THEON

"You want me to stay in here? While you bathe?" he asked slowly, sure he was misunderstanding what she wanted.

"If you don't want to, can Luka or Axel? I don't want to be alone," she repeated. "The quiet is too loud sometimes, and I feel trapped in it," she added in a whisper.

Fuck if he was going to let Axel or Luka in here while she was naked.

"I can stay," he said. "I will just step out while you get in."

He waited in the bedroom for a full two minutes, trying to get himself under control. His mind was flooding him with all kinds of filthy fantasies, and the bond was capitalizing on them. It liked the idea of her wet and naked.

It liked that idea a lot.

When he re-entered the bathroom, Tessa was just coming back up from under the water, her hair plastered to her head and water dripping down her skin. He'd put jasmine and lavender scented soap in for her, so at least the suds obscured her naked flesh from his view. She leaned her head back against the tub and closed her eyes.

"You can't sleep in the bathtub, beautiful," Theon said softly, moving to stand next to her with his hands shoved deep into his pockets.

"I know," she answered, her fingers skimming through the bubbles.

"We need to talk about something."

Her eyes opened at that. "I don't know what those things were that came up out of the ground. I don't know what that was or how it happened."

That statement was definitely something he would be revisiting later on this afternoon, but he needed to get this bond sorted out first. It wasn't supposed to be like this, and after today, he needed it firmly in place.

"Let's come back to that," he replied. "Why are you terrified of me, Tessa?"

"I'm not scared of you," she answered defensively.

"Pavil and Metias have gifts that can amplify certain emotions. When they touched you, they used their power to amplify your greatest fears," Theon said, pulling his hands from his pockets and rolling back his sleeves. He lowered to his knees beside the tub. "When I found you, you were terrified because of what had happened, yes, but you were also terrified of what I was going to do to you."

Tessa was silent as he took the cloth he'd set out for her and dunked it into the water. He gently began cleaning dried blood from her arm. "I don't want you scared of me, Tessa. I just need your submission."

"I'm trying, Theon," she said, so quietly he barely heard it.

"Are you? Because it shouldn't be this hard to give into a bond. Once you do, things can be different. This would have never happened," he replied, dunking the cloth and guiding her forward so he could run it down her back. He slid her long hair over one shoulder.

"How do you figure that?"

"You would have been with me. I wanted to wait until you'd adjusted and accepted the bond before requiring you to attend meetings with me, but it appears that can no longer be the case."

"Maybe if you would tell me things instead of keeping me in the dark about everything, I'd be more prepared for these types of situations."

"I *want* to tell you things, Tessa, but I can't. Not until the bond is fully in place. I need to know I can trust you."

"The bond does not equate to trust, Theon," she replied, then she slid under the water once more.

Theon could hardly see her beneath the bubbles. He waited until she resurfaced, and as she pushed her hair off her face again, Theon said, "Can I ask you a question?"

"You are the Master," she answered dryly, taking the cloth from him and beginning to scrub at her legs.

"What does the bond feel like to you?"

She paused. "What?"

"I'm trying to understand. Because if it feels anything to you like it does to me, I cannot for the life of me figure out how you are resisting the thing."

Tessa resumed the scrubbing of her legs, and it took a moment before she said, "It feels like an ache in the pit of my stomach when I am away from you. It is a constant buzzing, like an itch that won't go away. If it goes on too long, I feel like vomiting. When I actively resist and pull away from you, the bond punishes me for it."

"And when you let me touch you?" he pressed.

She wouldn't look at him, but she'd stopped washing. "I'm ready to get out," she said suddenly, setting the cloth along the edge of the tub.

"I will get you a towel in a moment," Theon said. "Answer me first. What does the bond feel like when you let me touch you?"

She swallowed audibly, but she didn't offer anything else. He wasn't letting this go that easily though. He wanted an answer to this one question, and he was prepared to draw it from her lips if needed. Before he could entrance her though, she tossed a question back at him.

"Did you send them to collect me like they said you did?"

"No, Tessa. I would have called Axel if I had wanted you brought to me."

"They said…" She pursed her lips, drawing her knees up to her chest, and Theon's gaze snagged on more bare skin.

"What did they say, Tessa?"

"They said that your father had given them permission to make sure my manners had been corrected, and then when they couldn't find me, they said he was going to be upset they had lost me. What does your father want with me, Theon? Is he the reason you chose me to be your Source?"

She finally met his gaze, and her eyes were filled with a desperation to understand.

"No, Tessa, my father did not decide you were to be my Source. The relationship between a Master and Source is too fragile for anyone else to choose it for someone," he replied.

"You chose it for me," she countered.

"I meant it is too important for another Legacy to choose someone's Source for them," he amended.

"Then why did you choose me? We'd never met before. You'd never visited the Estate. Why did you pick me out of the hundreds of eligible Fae at Selection?"

Her voice was strained with that same desperation he could see in her eyes, but Theon didn't have a suitable answer for her. He wished he could explain it, but the truth was he couldn't adequately describe it himself. Finally, he said, "When I spoke with you in that alcove, I wanted you and only you."

She pressed her lips together at the answer, and he wasn't sure what that meant. He expected her to ask another question about it, but she said, "Can I get out now?"

Fully aware she hadn't answered his own question, he stood and grabbed two towels from beneath the sink. Returning to the side of the tub, he said, "Up."

She looked up at him from beneath her wet lashes. "What?"

"Up," Theon repeated. "I'll wrap you in a towel."

He expected her to resist, but a quick look of determination filled her face before she gripped the edge of the tub and pulled herself up. Theon didn't even try to hide the fact that he was looking at her. Her long hair covered most of her breasts, but the apex of her thighs was fully exposed, and his entire being was well aware of that.

As she stepped over the edge of the tub to the bathmat, he draped a towel around her shoulders. She gripped it between her fingers, covering herself, and he unfolded the second towel to squeeze the water from her hair. When he was done, he went to the closet while she dried off. He didn't grab her clothes though. He came back with a warm, black fleece bathrobe.

He turned her so she was facing away from him before he pulled the towel from her body. His eyes dropped to her ass as he held the robe open for her to slide her arms into it. Tessa quickly pulled it closed around herself, tying it at the waist. When she reached up to tuck a lock of hair behind her ear, the sleeve slid up her arm.

"Many of your wounds are already healing," he noted, one of the surface scratches nearly faded.

She sent him a bland look before she stepped around him and moved to the vanity. "I know I am not a Legacy, but I *am* Fae. We do heal faster than mortals," she retorted, digging out a comb from the drawer and beginning to run it through her hair.

As soon as she finished, he was behind her. He braced his hands on the counter on either side of her body, caging her in. Startled, she met his gaze in the mirror.

"You never answered my question, beautiful," he murmured into her ear, and he watched the faint pink color creep into her cheeks. "What does the bond feel like when you let me touch you?" He brought his hand up, trailing the tips of his fingers down her neck, barely touching her. She shivered against him. "I have other ways of discovering the answer to that question if you will not tell me."

Her face instantly hardened. "You will entrance me over this?"

He gripped her hips, turning her in his arms before lifting her up and setting her on the vanity counter. She gasped as he stepped between her legs.

"I do not need to entrance you for this," he purred sensually.

"You said you'd never force this," she rasped, that flush returning as he held her gaze.

She was still so off balance from the events in the garden, she couldn't hide her emotions as well, and he hated that he didn't know how to read everything playing out on her face. Soon it wouldn't matter. The Mark she would receive on the fall equinox would allow him to feel her emotions, and if she somehow had still not accepted things by then, this would all be much easier to navigate.

"I will not force anything, Tessa. You are free to tell me to stop whenever you wish. Or in the alternative, answer my question, and I will stop immediately," he replied, his fingers skating up her calves. She was practically eye level with him when she was sitting on the vanity, and he slowly brought his mouth to hers. "I will kill those motherfuckers for touching what is mine," he murmured, his lips feathering across hers as he spoke.

She sucked in a breath. "I'm not yours."

"Lie to yourself, but not to me," he murmured, his fingers slipping behind her knees and under the robe. Another shiver rolled through her at the touch.

"I'm not lying." Her voice was breathy and not at all convincing.

"Your body says otherwise," he argued, running his nose along the length of hers.

"It's just this bond," she gritted out, her hands gripping the edge of the counter, knuckles turning white.

"Is it?" He began trailing his lips along her jaw until he reached the space beneath her ear. "What does it feel like when my fingers trail up your thighs, Tessa?" She tried to hide it, but he heard the soft whimper that escaped from her. "Or when my lips touch here?" He pressed his lips to her throat, sucking lightly and scraping his teeth along her skin.

Her breathing was becoming ragged as he trailed his lips lower, and she leaned forward when he began dragging them along her collarbone. His fingers were crawling ever so slowly up her thighs, and for a heartbeat, he thought she was finally going to give in. For a fleeting moment, he thought she was finally going to give the bond exactly what it wanted, but then she spoke.

"It feels like coming up for air when I've been shoved underwater for too long." Her voice was thick with desire. "When you touch me, it feels like pleasure igniting under my skin. When you touch me, it feels like nothing else matters as long as you never stop. It feels like safety and warmth and light." The last words were such a soft whisper that Theon barely caught them, but he had halted his movements the moment she had started speaking. Not because he had told her he would, but because he couldn't believe what he was hearing.

"If that is what it feels like, why do you resist it so adamantly?"

"Because it's not real, Theon," she blurted, the desire in her voice shifting to frustration. "It's just the Source bond making me feel that way. My body responding to physical touch. It's not *real*."

"It could be," he argued.

"Even if that were true, how would you know? How would you know what is the bond you forced and what is real? How could you tell the difference?"

"Is this what is keeping you from accepting this?"

"Yes. No. Part of it, maybe? I don't know," she answered, her eyes darting away from his. His hands were still beneath her robe, halfway up her thighs.

"You know if you would accept the bond, you wouldn't think about any of that, right?"

"That's not the... Forget it," she said suddenly, leaning away from him. "What do I need to wear this afternoon?"

"You need to rest this afternoon."

"Understood. What should I wear to do so?"

"What were you going to say?" he countered.

"Theon?" Axel's voice carried in from the bedroom. "Lunch has been here for ten minutes. It's getting cold."

Theon held Tessa's gaze for a moment longer before he left her sitting on the vanity to retrieve some clothing for her. He stepped out of the bathroom while she dressed in loose pants and a long-sleeve shirt, and then he led her out to eat. She ate her soup and hot turkey sandwich without a word, and when she finished, she went straight to the sofa. The rest of them weren't even halfway through their meals, but they had also eaten at a much slower pace between light conversation and their gazes constantly cutting to her.

"Were you able to meet with her?" Axel asked Luka, tipping his bowl to get the last of his soup.

"No," Luka said grimly. "It was too risky for Cienna this time."

"You were covered in blood when you got back," Theon said. "If not Cienna, who?"

"The three Legacy your father sent me to take care of."

"Godsdamnit," Theon muttered, sitting back in his chair and tossing his napkin on the table. "When was the last time we talked to Cienna?"

Axel had pulled a small mirror from his pocket, fiddling with the thing. "She made contact when I was there during the Opening Selection Ceremony, but I didn't see her. Only received her message."

"It's something, I guess," Theon said, tapping his finger on the table. Axel gave him a pointed look before he realized it was the same mannerism his father always made. A muscle ticked in his jaw as he swiped up his water glass.

"We should discuss how to handle tonight," Luka said.

"I say we let it play out naturally. See if he mentions anything or what he brings up."

"That could work," Luka answered, rubbing his hand along his jaw in thought.

"Father isn't going to bring this up," Axel argued. "There is no way he would implicate himself."

"He won't give a fuck about implicating himself," Theon replied. "He's going to be far more worried about revealing a plan before he is ready to do so. He is up to something, and he doesn't want me to know what it is yet. He will be expecting me to confront him. If we say nothing, it will keep him guessing."

"But if Pavil and Metias had succeeded today, you would have found out anyway," Luka cut in. "Did she tell you anything about what happened?"

"She wasn't ready to talk about it yet," Theon said, not revealing that was likely because he was pushing her thoughts elsewhere with his hands halfway up her thighs. "She said that my father had told them to make sure her manners had been corrected. She also mentioned something about things coming out of the ground and not knowing what they were or how it happened."

"What things?" Axel asked.

Theon shrugged. "She was pretty shaken up. I didn't want to push the subject yet, but we need to look into it, along with the swords and gold paint or blood or whatever the fuck it was." He got to his feet. "We can continue this conversation, but I want to be near her. Her sleep will be more restful, and I need her to be at least partially functional for dinner."

The others nodded. Axel went to the kitchen and poured them all some liquor before joining them. Tessa was already fast asleep on the sofa, and Theon carefully repositioned her so she rested on a pillow in his lap. He pulled the blanket she had covered up with higher over her shoulder and stroked her hair back.

"I don't blame you, Axel," Theon said, taking a glass from him. "There is nothing you could have done differently. You telling her to run was the best thing you could have done, and I'm grateful. But until we know what Father is planning, she needs to be with me whenever possible."

Luka and Axel didn't look thrilled by the idea, but they didn't broker any arguments against it either.

"So you are going to have her attend meetings with us?" Luka asked.

"Unless you have a better idea? She'll need to start attending them when we get to the Acropolis anyway," Theon answered.

"What happened to easing her into this?" Axel asked.

"That changed when he came after what is mine," Theon replied.

Axel was staring at Tessa's sleeping form, a slight frown on his face. "Do you think Eviana was like her? Before Father…"

He trailed off, both Theon and Luka understanding where he was going with that statement.

"I don't know," Theon answered. "I have a hard time picturing her any other way. She was Father's Source long before we came along. He Selected her before he was Matched with Mother."

"Maybe it's because we've never interacted with the Fae until they are in service to the kingdom, but she's just…," Axel started, trailing off while he studied the sleeping female. "It makes me wonder if they are all like this before they are forced to become what they are assigned to be."

Theon shrugged. "We wouldn't know. We've never visited the Estates, and we only observe them during trials in Selection Years."

"I've been to the Estates a few times," Luka said. "The younger Fae are more carefree and free-spirited, but that's to be expected before they are assigned to their kingdoms and duties."

They were quiet for a moment before Axel asked, "So any ideas which heirs we're going to try to befriend when we get to the Acropolis?"

"Father has already demanded I am to make alliances with Celeste and Falein. He believes Anala to be a lost cause," Theon replied, bringing his drink to his lips. Tessa shifted slightly beneath his hand, and his fingers flexed around her shoulder.

"And in the meantime, who do you think our best bets are to forge true alliances with?" Axel pushed.

"We didn't get a lot of time to watch them at the Selection Ceremony," Theon answered. "Luka has been doing some digging and gathering information, but I think the week at the Acropolis with just the ruling families will give us the best idea of that. I'm hoping for Falein and Anala. Serafina would be ideal, but that kingdom is fiercely loyal to the Achaz Kingdom."

"So much depends on her," Luka cut in, his sapphire gaze fixed on Tessa. "You should have chosen someone else, Theon." He stood at the words, setting his empty glass on the coffee table. "I will see you all at dinner."

He left, the door banging shut behind him, and Theon let out a long sigh, closing his eyes and leaning his head back against the sofa.

"He is worried," Axel said after a while.

"He thinks Tessa isn't the one for what must be done. That she's too unpredictable. It is why I require her complete submission. It is why I am pushing her so hard to give in to the Source bond. I need the loyalty the bond creates. We can't tell her everything without it," Theon answered.

"Perhaps your time would be better spent focusing on a real bond rather than a forced one?" Axel ventured.

"We don't have the time for that, and you know it," Theon retorted. Axel was fixing him with a knowing glare. "Do you no longer agree with the plan and what needs to happen?"

"Of course I know what needs to happen, Theon," Axel bit back. It took a lot to rile Axel, but when you did, his rage almost made him more formidable than Theon.

Almost.

"We have planned this for too long. Too much hangs in the balance for her to mess with the plans. She will fall into line. If she had accepted this fate, nothing like today would have happened," Theon retorted. "You and Luka need to get it through your heads. This is happening. We cannot change it. So either help me convince her to accept this, or stop coming around until she has. You can pass the message on to Luka."

"I think Luka realizes that, Theon. It's why he wishes you'd have chosen someone else."

"And you?" Theon challenged.

Axel leaned forward, his forearms braced on his knees. A muscle feathered in his jaw the same way Theon's did when he was irritated. "She'd be safer if she accepted it," he finally conceded. "She'd be safer, and our plans could move forward."

Thank the fucking gods. Finally, they were understanding what he had been trying to get across to them since she came into their lives like a tempest.

"Can you grab my laptop? I have work to do this afternoon," Theon said, nodding towards his desk.

"Sure thing," Axel answered dryly, getting up to retrieve the computer. He placed it down on the armrest next to Theon. "So we're going to do this then? We're really going to let our monsters out of their cages? Show her what the rest of the realm sees?"

"Sometimes we need to become a monster to kill one, Axel," Theon said darkly. "I've shielded her as long as I could. She was going to see us for what we are eventually."

"And when she becomes one of us?" Axel asked, his hands sliding into his pockets.

"She won't."

"Theon—"

"She won't, Axel," he cut in sharply.

Axel didn't say anything else. Simply turned and left, just as Luka had.

She wouldn't end up like them. They had been raised to be this. She had been raised to be... Well, she had been raised to serve the Legacy. Other than what was in the file of information he had, he really didn't know anything else about how she'd been raised on the Estate. Born at one of the Sirana Villas of the Achaz Kingdom, she'd been sent to the Celeste Estate the moment she was born. That was likely the real reason she hadn't known her birthday.

Sirana. Goddess of love and fertility. Her Legacy were all sworn to the Achaz Kingdom.

Theon huffed a humorless laugh. They had the fertility part down. Not enough Fae had families of their own. Some by choice; most due to the duties they were assigned. On top of that, it was difficult for Fae to conceive in general. Numbers had started to diminish despite the extended lifespans they shared with the Legacy, so centuries ago, the kingdoms all met and agreed that something needed to be done. A new accord was made, and some Fae were assigned to the Achaz Kingdom to "serve" under the Sirana bloodline. And the love part of their duties? Escorts and entertainment.

The decision had been unanimous among the kingdoms, but even if Arius Kingdom hadn't agreed for whatever reason, it wouldn't have mattered. There had forever been a divide between them and the others. It stemmed from a disagreement between the Achaz and Arius Kingdoms centuries ago, and over time, Arius Kingdom had become more and more withdrawn from the rest of Devram. That was fine with Theon. They had more than enough resources within their borders to provide for their people. They had defenses. They had wealth. They had the Ozul Mountains.

And they had the Underground.

But while Theon was fine with remaining the nightmare kingdom of Devram, his father wasn't. Things had escalated between him and Rordan Jove, the Achaz Lord, over the last several decades, and now his father wanted more. Achaz Kingdom had long been the law of Devram, upholding accords and handing out judgment for those who broke them, despite Arius being the god of judgment and endings. And while those with the gravest offenses were sent to them to be held in the Underground, his father was no longer happy being the shunned kingdom only good enough for those Devram didn't want to deal with. Now that his heirs were coming of age to claim Sources of their own, his father was ready to put plans into motion that had been in place since before Theon was born. His father may be the biggest godsdamn dick known to Devram, but he was smart and cunning and willing to wait for opportunity.

The thing was, he'd instilled those same qualities into his children.

He'd created monsters that were equally cunning and willing to do whatever was necessary to get what they wanted. The difference was they didn't have the luxury of time. Their father'd had centuries of time to craft his plan. They'd had to get there faster, and while they were advancing their father's plans, they were also furthering their own. Every move they made put them at risk of being caught. Of the wrong thing getting back to his father.

All the more reason Tessa needed to accept this Source bond.

Theon sighed, clicking open a message from Bohden, his father's Commander-of-Forces, skimming the message regarding the new males and females being received at the Underground this week. None of them were of interest to him, and he moved onto the next message. Eventually he stopped reading them all together and opened a locked folder of research he'd been putting together on getting past wards.

The thing was, he was fairly certain the key to that was sleeping in his lap.

18
TESSA

The balcony she stood on was high above the ground, overlooking fields of green and gold. Grasses swayed gently in a breeze under a grey sky that somehow didn't feel gloomy considering the color. In one direction, far off in the distance, she could make out mountains, lightning flashing periodically as if a never-ending storm hovered. In the other direction, there was a sprawling city. Buildings obscured the skyline, and she couldn't tell where the city ended. This was clearly a country manor of some kind.

A noise behind her had her spinning around, and she found a stunning female emerging from a set of double doors. Tessa went still, unsure of where she was or what she was supposed to do. The female's hair was nearly the exact shade of her own. Loose and wavy, it flowed down around her shoulders, reaching nearly to her navel, the tips of her arched ears peeking through the strands. Her lips were painted blood red, and she moved with an ethereal grace not even the Legacy possessed. She was dressed in an elegant ivory dress that was sheer to the point of indecency. Gold jewelry adorned her ears and neck, matching the gold belt slung around her hips. Even her fingers had gold rings. Except one. That one was silver and onyx.

The female moved to stand beside her, leaning on her arms she had folded along the balcony railing. She stared out across the expanse before them, and Tessa wondered if the female even knew she was there. She hadn't acknowledged her. She hadn't even looked at her.

Her question was answered a moment later, when the female turned and eyes of grey settled onto Tessa. Tessa could swear there were even glimmers of gold swirling faintly in her eyes. She did not speak. Just looked at Tessa as if she could see through to her very soul.

Another female appeared, as if she stepped from the air. If the first female was stunning, this female was beautiful in a terrifying sort of way. Her dark skin seemed to glow with a silver aura, and her raven black hair floated around her on phantom winds. She had vivid violet eyes and wore a white gown that was stark against her complexion.

"It worked," the second female said, her voice both melodic and dark as night all at once.

"It appears it did," the first answered. Her eyes did not leave Tessa, as if she physically couldn't drag them away from her.

Tessa still couldn't wrap her mind around what was happening. Should she speak? Drop to a knee? Move? Stay still?

"Does he know?" the second asked, tilting her head as she studied Tessa.

"I sent word with Altaria," the first answered in confirmation. "He was unhappy."

The second tsked under her breath. "This is why I do not mess around with males."

The first smirked at her. "After his temper tantrum, he agreed that the reasoning was warranted."

"Of course he did," the second replied, rolling her eyes. Then she added, "You do not have much time, Akira. I can only hold her here for so long."

"She called the Hunters today," the first, Akira, said suddenly, an emotion Tessa didn't know how to read flickering in her eyes. Pride? Maybe. No one had ever looked at her like that.

"Did she now? And they responded? How interesting." The second female's curiosity seemed to triple as she continued to study Tessa. "And the Huntresses?"

Akira's features darkened. "They only answer to him. No one else can summon them. But he will send them. Like he did for me." There was a short pause, and then, "The wild and untamed answered her call as well."

"Her father's daughter," the second said. "She will be powerful."

"She already is. It will only grow. My father thought he could use her against me. Use her to seek his petty revenge. She will be an unyielding storm in that world. A tempest of wrath and vengeance."

"It is time, Akira," the second said. "The enchantment fades. Anala is entertaining him, but he will sense her presence any moment."

Akira took a step forward, and Tessa gasped when she reached out and took her face between her hands.

"Know that sometimes we must break to be forged into who we were meant to be," she said, streaks of violet flickering in her eyes like lightning cutting through the flecks of gold. Then she bent and pressed her lips to Tessa's brow. "You will break, Tessalyn. Make sure you get back up and take what is yours."

19
TESSA

Tessa sat at the vanity table, staring at her reflection. She was supposed to be getting ready for dinner, but all she could do was think about the strange dream she'd had. The dream that hadn't felt like a dream at all. Yes, she'd been sleeping, but everything about that encounter had felt very real.

Which was silly. Because how could she have been there and here at the same time? It wasn't possible. A dream was the only plausible explanation, but still…

She'd jolted awake after the blonde female had kissed her brow, and she'd nearly knocked Theon's computer to the floor. Still here. Still on the sofa in Theon's suite. She'd stared at him, swallowing thickly when he'd only stared back at her, not saying a word. She'd bit her lip, tucking her hair behind her ear.

Theon had started to reach for her. Some part of her had wanted him to because that entire thing had been unsettling, not to mention everything that had happened with Pavil and Metias. But he'd stopped himself, and for the life of her, she couldn't figure out why. Why did he suddenly have an issue with touching her whenever he wanted?

After she drank an entire glass of water, he'd sent her off to get ready for dinner. She really just wanted to curl up in his giant bed under blankets with a cup of tea and watch the Chaosphere game that was on tonight, but that clearly wasn't an option.

"Tessalyn, are you ready?"

She looked over her shoulder to see Theon dressed in a black suit. He wore a black shirt underneath along with a black tie, and he looked like Arius himself. Or what she imagined the god of endings would look like. Tessa's mouth dried out as she met his gaze. Something in his eyes was different too. The shadows were thicker, making his emerald eyes too dark.

"Why aren't you ready?" he asked, his eyes narrowing in clear annoyance.

"I am," she replied, swiping up a tube of red lipstick and quickly applying it. He had set out a black floor-length dress for her tonight. It was sleeveless, with an extended plunging neckline and a slit up one side that went nearly to the top of her thigh. She had left her hair down, but had curled it so it fell in soft curls around her shoulders. Pen usually did her hair for dinner, and Tessa hoped it was adequate.

She stood, and Theon said nothing when he took her hand and hauled her quickly out to the main room. Luka and Axel were waiting as usual, and Tessa tensed at the looks on their faces. Something was different about them, too.

Theon stepped into her line of sight and brought his hand to her cheek. "You know how you are expected to behave tonight?"

"Have I not been meeting expectations at dinner, Theon?" she replied with faux sweetness.

Theon's lips formed a thin line. "Careful, Tessalyn, or you will find greater expectations placed on you."

He leaned forward and brushed a light kiss to her lips. She felt her face flush. He'd never kissed her in front of the others. Not on her lips anyway. She jerked back from him on instinct, stumbling in her heels, and his arm shot out, snaking around her waist. He tugged her close, whispering into her ear, "That is considered pulling away. Do not do it again."

Tessa stiffened in his hold, her eyes coming to his. His darkness coiled, tendrils of it reaching out to brush along her jaw, and she sucked in a breath at the feel of it.

"Do we have an understanding?" he pressed.

She nodded mutely.

"I am going to need verbal confirmation, Tessalyn."

"Yes. I understand," she whispered, that darkness tracing down the column of her throat before dissipating. It felt...familiar. Which made sense, considering Theon had forced his magic into her being.

"Good." He reached up and adjusted a lock of her hair before releasing her. But gods, it also made something in her soul stir.

She glanced at Luka and Axel. Their features were as hard as Theon's. They were also entirely in black, and while darkness didn't swirl in their eyes, power and violence emanated from them in a way that had her stepping closer to Theon.

"Theon—" she began as he pulled her forward.

"Hush," he said harshly, Axel opening the door for them. Axel hardly glanced at her as she was led into the hallway.

Uncertain what was going on or how to react to it, she remained quiet all the way to the dining room. In fact, no one spoke. The males acted like they were going to their death. Or rather, like they were going to defeat death.

As they approached the dining room, Theon dropped her hand, striding ahead of her without a word. Valter and Cressida both sat up a little straighter when they entered the room. Tessa was apparently not the only one who noticed something different about the three of them this evening.

"Father," Theon greeted curtly, with the smallest bow possible. He bent and kissed his mother on the cheek before moving to his seat. Tessa moved behind him as usual, but unlike every other night, he did not immediately tell her to sit.

She was utterly baffled. Was he truly upset with her about earlier today? But he'd sworn to her over and over before she'd fallen asleep that he didn't blame her for that. Her confusion only escalated as drinks were ordered and Eviana was allowed to sit while she remained standing. Theon didn't look her way and neither did Luka nor Axel. Valter, however, was shooting her curious glances every so often.

When the first course of a chilled soup had been placed before each seat, Theon casually said, "Tessalyn, sit and eat," before resuming the conversation he was having with his parents.

She moved forward cautiously, taking her seat and picking up her spoon. She was just lifting the first spoonful to her mouth when Valter apparently couldn't keep his curiosity at bay any longer.

"Trouble with your Source, son? You do not appear nearly as affectionate tonight," the Arius Lord said.

Thank the gods someone had said it, because she clearly wasn't allowed to voice her confusion.

"Everything is fine," Theon said dismissively, taking a bite of bread.

He didn't elaborate further, despite Valter clearly expecting more of an explanation.

"Is there anything else we need to take care of before we leave for the Acropolis in a few days?" Luka cut in before Valter could pose further questions. Cressida let out a muffled sob at the words.

Tessa tuned out the dinner conversation as they fell into mundane small talk once again. Everything was certainly not fine. Ever since she'd woken up, Theon had been different. His tone had been harsher, and his demands had become firmer. Theon was treating her like—

Like a Source.

She nearly dropped her spoon at the realization and sat back in her seat abruptly. The few bites of soup she'd taken churned in her stomach. Theon's gaze shot to her. She thought she saw a flicker of concern flash across those emerald eyes, but if she did, it was gone a moment later.

He leaned over to speak into her ear. "Are you unwell?"

She shook her head, despite the tightening in her chest.

"Then eat."

He returned to his soup, and Tessa swallowed hard, sitting forward once more. Her hand was trembling as she brought her spoon to her lips.

She managed to finish her soup and her salad, forcing down the food. She was halfway through getting her main course of steamed fish and rice down when she heard her name. It took a moment to realize she was being addressed directly.

By Valter.

"Tell me, Tessalyn," he was saying, "which element are you predicted to emerge with?"

She froze, looking at Theon. She had never once been spoken to during dinner conversation by anyone other than Theon. He wasn't looking at her though. His eyes were narrowed on his father as he answered for her.

"You know her assessments all report her most likely to emerge with the air element."

"Can she not speak for herself? You have kept her sequestered away nearly the entire time she has been here. Your mother and I have not been given an opportunity to get to know her, and in five days you leave for the Acropolis," Valter admonished.

"I did not realize you had any interest in getting to know her in such a way," Theon answered tightly.

"I assume she is going to be in our lives for the foreseeable future. Surely we should get to know each other a bit, no?" Valter countered, taking a sip of his liquor.

"Perhaps."

Valter returned his full attention to Tessa, who had set her fork down beside her plate to avoid accidentally dropping it again. Her hands were clasped tightly in her lap to keep from wringing her fingers. She couldn't falter here. She had quickly learned there was no room for mistakes when it came to the Arius Lord, and she certainly didn't need Theon even more upset with her.

Theon reached over under the table and placed a hand on her knee, squeezing it as if in warning. Was she not supposed to speak? Her chest tightened more, and she tried to control her breathing. She didn't know what she was supposed to do.

"Which Estate did you reside at, Tessalyn?" Valter asked, settling back casually in his chair. Eviana was still eating. So was Cressida. The males, however, were all focused on her.

Tessa glanced at Theon again, and he gave a nod to answer. She cleared her throat quietly before saying, "The Celeste Estate, my Lord."

"And the Priestesses performed the assessments for your element there?"

"At the nearby health compound, yes, my Lord."

"How many times? How many tests were done?"

She swallowed, her heart beating so rapidly she was sure everyone at the table could hear it. "Tests were performed once a year from the time we turned ten years until we turned eighteen. Then they were performed seasonally until the Selection," she answered, barely suppressing the shudder that wanted to go down her spine. The tests were not pleasant. Over five years of seasonal testings had been agony.

"And you scored highest in the wind and air element every time?" Valter continued, his hazel eyes watching her closely.

"From what I was told, yes. I have never seen the actual reports."

"You have seen her results, Father," Theon cut in. "Why are you interrogating my Source regarding her element? We will all know the answer in a few weeks' time."

"Because I was given very interesting information today that suggests she will *not* emerge with the air element, and I am trying to figure out how such a glaring mistake could have been made on her assessments," Valter answered tightly.

Tessa glanced at Theon, finding his eyes were fixed on his father. She looked across the table to Axel and Luka, but their attention was on the Arius Lord as well.

"And what information is that?" Theon asked.

"I am told she created that crevice in my gardens with her bare hands, which would highly suggest the earth element," Valter replied.

"That's impossible," Theon scoffed. "She has not emerged yet. She couldn't display any sort of magic."

"Do you know how the assessments are performed, Theon?" Valter asked condescendingly, a cruel smile turning up the corner of his mouth.

Theon gritted his teeth, that muscle feathering in his jaw. "Yes."

"Then one could assume the events of today would have elicited such a display of power," Valter concluded, bringing a bite of meat to his mouth with a smirk.

Theon slowly set his drink down. A dull thud sounded as it hit the table with force. "Tell me, Father. Why were Pavil and Metias chasing my Source through the gardens?"

Valter scoffed dismissively. "They simply want to get to know her as your mother and I do, Theon. We are all going to be working together closely after all."

"And coming to my rooms uninvited to meet her without my presence was the appropriate way to get to know her?"

Theon's voice was low and dripping with venom, and Tessa shrank back in her chair as inky shadows drifted around him. Eviana was instantly at Valter's side, a snarl on her lips, as she placed herself between the Arius Lord and his son.

"Not necessary, Eviana," Valter purred, running a hand down her back. When he came to her hip, he tugged her down into his lap. His gaze returned to Theon. "Control yourself, or you will be reminded why control is important," he ordered sharply.

Tessa watched as Theon took several deep breaths, that darkness slowly fading. His fingers flexed on the table, the light glinting off his rings. When Valter was satisfied, he said, "As I was saying, the reports I received from Pavil and Metias today suggest one of three things: either the assessments performed at her Estate were not done properly, the reports in her file are false copies, or your Source found a way to hide her true abilities."

Valter's gaze settled back on her as he said the last words, and Tessa couldn't get a breath down. Air couldn't get to her lungs, and her chest wouldn't expand to take any in.

The assessments were torturous. They were put in situations that elicited natural self-preservation responses and were intended to push dormant magic to the surface. When they were young, the assessments were mild, but for the last five years, the tests had been excruciating, involving everything from physical pain to mental distress. It would have been impossible for her to somehow hide her abilities. She didn't even remember displaying any actual magic. More than that, they were not one hundred percent accurate. They were only a series of educated guesses.

"Did you know?" Valter demanded so loudly Tessa jumped in her seat.

"I do not know what you are asking, my Lord," she answered softly, twisting the fabric of her dress in her fingers.

"Did you somehow hide your abilities during your assessments to remain unseen by the other heirs?"

"No, my Lord. That would not be possible." Her voice had risen an octave, her fear seeping into her tone. She may have hidden other things, but there was no way she could have hidden any elemental magic during an assessment.

"Then explain the gardens, *my dear*," he hissed.

"I do not know what happened in the gardens," she said, failing to keep her voice even. "I do not know how the crevice appeared or what the things were that crawled up from it. I swear it."

"Calm down, Tessa," Theon ordered from her side, his hand squeezing her knee again in emphasis.

She swung her gaze to him. "I swear it, Th— I swear to you. I don't know what happened in the gardens."

Theon stared back at her, his features hard and tense. "We will discuss this later," he finally answered tightly.

He returned his attention to Valter, and her heart fell. He didn't believe her.

"This entire conversation is irrelevant. In less than two weeks, she will emerge along with all the other Fae of age, and we will know what her element is," Theon said.

"I have made arrangements for her to be reevaluated by a Priestess in Rockmoor in two days," Valter answered.

"That is not your decision to make," Theon spat. "She is mine, not yours."

"I will not be caught off guard at the Emerging Ceremony, Theon," Valter barked. "You should be the one demanding this, not me. Your Source has kept secrets from you."

"How I deal with my Source is not your concern," Theon countered.

"Wrong, boy," Valter growled, his fist slamming onto the table so hard the cutlery rattled. "She will reflect upon this kingdom as much as you and your brother do. We cannot appear weak. Ever. And certainly not right now."

"How would her having the earth element versus the air element change anything?" Axel cut in, sounding bored.

"The more intensive assessment the Priestess will perform will not only assess her probable element but also her power level. Something not routinely done in the generic assessments unless requested," Valter replied. "The other heirs would have had these advanced tests done before they chose their Sources. It will put us on a more even playing field."

"Tell him the other good news," Cressida suddenly chimed in, her hand coming to rest on her husband's arm.

"A potential Match is visiting Rockmoor and will be at the Acropolis all year for the Selection proceedings. I have arranged for you to have lunch with her after the assessment is finished," Valter replied, pushing his plate back for a Fae server to remove.

"For fuck's sake," Theon spat, sitting back in his seat and taking a long drink of his whiskey. "Is that really necessary right now? We have far more important things to be focusing on."

"I did not say the Match was decided," Valter went on, his fist tightening around his glass. "I said you were going to meet her."

"I can meet her another day."

"You will meet her in two days in Rockmoor. It would be ideal to have a Match arranged before the end of the Selection year," Valter replied while everyone else's plates were cleared from the table.

Tessa hadn't finished her food. She was too shocked by the conversations taking place around her right now.

"Yes, I would love some time to get to know my future daughter-in-law before a union ceremony, Theon," Cressida agreed, bringing her wine to her lips. It was red. Dark red. Blood red. She had never drank from a clear wine glass before. It had always been a silver or gold chalice. This was crystal though, and Tessa had never seen wine that color.

"You can at least meet her," Luka suddenly said, speaking for the first time in a while.

"Perhaps *you* should meet her," Theon bit back. "You will need a Match, too."

Luka smirked at him. "Maybe she has a sister."

"Fuckwit," Theon grumbled, flipping him off.

"Theon!" Cressida chided.

"Enough!" Valter barked. "Taking a Match is part of your responsibility as an heir. The sooner an agreement is reached, the sooner our focus can be moved to other things."

The table fell silent as desserts were placed in front of everyone. Tessa reached for her fork, but Theon lifted his hand from her knee and slid her plate over beside his own. Was he seriously depriving her of dessert now too? This was the only sugar he ever let her have, and only when they dined with his family.

Theon pushed his chair back slightly before reaching over and tugging on Tessa's hand. She glanced up, his eyes dark with fury as he tugged her a little harder. Getting to her feet in resignation, she moved to stand behind him at the wall. She certainly wasn't going to risk sitting at his feet again, but before she could take a step, he pulled her to him and down into his lap. Surprise coursed through her as his arm wrapped around her waist. Her heart leapt, and pleasure darted up her spine.

"What is her name then?" Theon asked through gritted teeth, picking up a fork and cutting off a piece of the chocolate and caramel cream pie.

"Felicity Davers," Valter answered.

Theon didn't respond, lifting the fork. But instead of bringing it to his mouth, he raised it before Tessa's lips. Confused, she met his eyes. The anger still glimmered in them, along with that new hardness that had appeared this afternoon, but something far more primal was there too. Without breaking his stare, she opened her mouth and let him slide the fork between her lips. His eyes dipped to the movement, that primal thing flaring brighter.

"Davers?" he questioned conversationally, going for another piece of pie.

"Yes," Valter answered. "Of the Gracil bloodline. I gave you her file the other morning. Have you looked through any of them?"

"No," Theon answered dismissively, still not looking at his father. "I have been busy." He fed another piece of pie to Tessa before taking a bite of his own.

Tessa was so flustered she didn't know what to do with herself. After the gardens, he had taken care of her. Then she'd woken up, and he'd given her the cold shoulder. Now he was feeding her dessert? He was going from hot to cold to hot again so quickly, she didn't know what to expect from one moment to the next.

"Then I suggest taking a break and looking them over before you leave for Rockmoor," Valter replied tightly. "Unless you wish for me to simply make the decision for you?"

"Of course not," Theon snapped. "If someone is going to be required to be by my side for the rest of my life, I will damn well be deciding who that someone will be."

"Just make sure the contract is contingent upon production of an acceptable heir," Valter went on. "I want a clause in there stating if she cannot produce a sufficient heir within a certain timeframe, the contract is null and void, and you are free to pursue another Match."

"There will be far more contingencies than that in my Match Contract."

"And there should be," Valter agreed with an arrogant smirk. "No one gets to simply join the Arius ruling family without proving their worth."

"Agreed," Theon answered, bringing another bite to Tessa's mouth. She couldn't help the soft hum that escaped her at the decadence hitting her tastebuds again, and Theon's eyes went even brighter, some of that darkness leaving them. He set the fork down and brought his thumb to the corner of her lips, swiping up a drop of caramel that had landed there before pushing it into her mouth. He held her gaze as she swiped her tongue along the pad of his thumb, then he was suddenly pushing her to her feet.

"Anything else this evening, Father?"

"Make sure you review those files, Theon," Valter answered pointedly before waving them off in dismissal. Theon didn't reach for her. He simply left her to follow him as he moved to the door. Luka and Axel got to their feet as well. A Fae opened the double doors, but before Theon exited the dining room, he paused and looked over his shoulder.

"Just so we are clear, Father, if anyone lays a hand on what is mine without my permission again, they will beg for Arius to come for them before I am through, whether or not we have an alliance with them." Theon's voice was low and dangerous and full of dark promises. Valter narrowed his eyes at his son. "They will wish for the Pits over what I will do to them."

Tessa expected Valter to become angry at being told such a thing, but instead, a cruel grin curled at the corner of his lips. "I would expect nothing else from the Arius heir, Theon."

20

TESSA

Tessa followed Theon out of the dining room, Luka and Axel brushing past her without a word or glance. Seriously, why was she getting the cold shoulder from all three of them? Luka was a broody ass, so he didn't particularly surprise her, but Axel?

"I thought you were going to lose it in there," Axel said when they reached the stairwell.

"I nearly did, but it wouldn't have done any good. Not yet anyway," Theon answered. His entire body was tense. She could see his muscles coiled and tight beneath his suit jacket while she followed behind him. He was back to cold again, and she didn't know if she should speak or not. She hated feeling so godsdamn unsettled.

"I think he got the message," Luka said grimly.

Axel huffed a laugh: "You think? The look on his face when Theon pulled Tessa into his lap was priceless. He knows Theon will be just as powerful as he is soon, if not more so. That is why he is so concerned about her element. You know it. I know it. The fucking Fates know it."

There was a spring in Axel's step, as if this was the most exciting news of the evening. But *that* was why Theon had pulled her into his lap? To make a subtle jab at his father that he would soon be more powerful as soon as he could draw power from her?

"What are you doing, Tessa?"

She looked up to find the three of them standing in front of the suite door. Theon's eyes were narrowed on her. She had stopped moving when they'd turned down their hallway. All she would ever be to him was a pawn in a game among the Legacy. A piece of property to be used however her Master saw fit. The documents Theon had shown her days ago flashed through her mind, and she was suddenly crushed under the weight of missing Dex and Lange and her friends. People who wanted her for her, not what she could give them.

"Tessalyn," Theon snapped again.

She drew in a deep breath, pushing it out as she forced her feet to move. They stepped aside to let her enter first, none of them saying a word.

"Cards tonight?" Axel asked, immediately stripping off his suit jacket and loosening his tie.

"I can't do cards. I need to look at those fucking files and figure out who this female is I am to meet in a couple days," Theon groused, going straight to the kitchen and pouring himself another glass of whiskey.

"Pool or darts then?" Axel asked, grabbing a bag by the door and moving towards the bathroom.

"Either is fine," Theon replied. "Tessa, come change."

She followed him through the bedroom and into the closet. He pulled out leggings and a thermal before turning to face her. Crooking a finger in her direction, he beckoned her closer. She pursed her lips, her hands going to her hips as she glared back at him. When she didn't move, he said in a low tone, "Come here."

"I don't need your assistance to change," she retorted.

"Come here, Tessalyn," he growled again, his eyes darkening at her defiance.

She rolled her eyes and moved towards him. As soon as she was within reach, Theon snatched her off her feet and lifted her onto the island dresser. She gasped at the unexpected movement. His hands lingered on her hips before he slid them down the outside of her thighs, her calves, all the way to her feet. He unbuckled her heels, sliding them off. When both of her shoes were removed, he braced his hands on either side of her, caging her within his muscular frame.

"I need you to accept this Source bond, Tessa," he said, his voice low and heated.

"I don't care what you need, Theon," she replied, steeling herself to face his fury at her words.

To her surprise though, he didn't immediately snap back at her. He leaned forward, bringing his nose to the crook of her neck and inhaling deeply. "I want to hunt down Pavil and Metias and peel the flesh from their bones, then make them eat every piece of it," he murmured against her skin. "Then I want to break each bone in their body in multiple places before taking them up the mountain and leaving them there for the beasts of the woods to pick off piece by piece." Tessa sucked in a breath at the violence he was describing. "No one touches what is mine," he snarled, his lips brushing her throat as he spoke. "I said I would take care of you, Tessa, and I know what you need. You need to accept this bond."

"You don't know anything about what I need," she breathed, her heart pounding out a weird rhythm at his closeness.

"No?" he questioned, pulling back and bringing a hand to cup her cheek. "Then enlighten me, little storm. What do you need?"

"I need to go home." It was the first thing that came to mind, and she didn't give herself a chance to hesitate when saying it.

"You are home," he answered, that dangerous note sounding in his voice once more.

"This isn't my home. My home is with Dex and Oralia and—"

"I do not know how to make this any clearer to you, Tessa. You were going to be separated from them eventually," Theon interrupted, his hand falling from her face. "Do you know what it means when I signed those documents assuming complete dominion?"

"I know what you think it means—"

"Complete possession and retention. They are no longer yours, and you are no longer theirs. You are certainly no longer *his*."

"What the fuck does that mean?" Tessa demanded.

Theon huffed a humorless laugh. "I saw you wrapped up in that Fae's arms at the Opening Selection Ceremony. I can only assume that was this *Dex* you refer to so often. If you are expecting me to apologize for not giving you a chance to say goodbye to your lover, you are not going to get it. You are *mine*, Tessa."

"He is not my lover, you arrogant son of a bitch," Tessa snapped, and Theon's brows shot up at her words.

"Care to say that again?"

His voice was barely a whisper as he stared her down, and Tessa didn't give a shit anymore. This day had been pure and utter torment. She had been chased through the gardens, had barely escaped Pavil and Metias getting a hold of her, had dealt with Theon's on-and-off again moods this evening, and had been used in a power play against his father.

"Which part?" she purred back, bringing her face right up to his. "The part about Dex not being my lover or calling you a son of a bitch? Because both are true, and I will gladly say them both again."

Theon's hand shot out, gripping her by the throat, and he was pushing her down onto her back. Her hands flew to his wrist, wrapping around it and trying to pull his hand away, but it was no use. She would never be any match for his strength.

"Theon," she gasped, squirming to try to get away from him, but he held her firmly in place with that one hand.

He smirked down at her as she struggled, his dark magic coiling like snakes around his forearm. "Tell me this, Tessalyn: Did your precious Dex ever touch you?" His hand wasn't tight enough to cut off air, but he made it clear she would not be moving until he allowed it. His eyes slowly raked over her, and his other hand came up, his fingers trailing along the flesh exposed by the slit of the dress.

"No," she rasped, shaking her head in emphasis. "Never like that. He's never been that."

"So who has touched you?" he asked, his head tilting to the side as his gaze followed his fingers skating up her leg. More and more dark shadows were drifting around him, tendrils reaching for her, and she tried to flinch away from his power. "One of the other Fae with you that night?"

Tessa shook her head, but when she didn't speak, his fingers flexed around her throat, air getting trapped. "No," she gasped, and he immediately loosened his grip. "Fae have never touched me."

Theon's eyes snapped to hers. "You are untouched?" She shook her head again, and his eyes narrowed. "A Legacy touched you? Who?"

"No," she rasped. His fingers had tightened again, and she wasn't even sure he knew he was doing it. She dug her nails into his skin, trying to suck down air. "I've only ever been touched by mortals," she managed to gasp out.

He couldn't hide the shock at that admission, and his fingers slackened around her throat. "Why the fuck would you let mortals touch you?"

"Because I didn't know where I was going to end up after the Selection, and I didn't want to have an intimate relationship with someone when I would likely be separated from them. So we would sneak off the

Estate on a regular basis, and I fucked around with mortals," she snapped in reply. "No attachments made, and no feelings required."

Theon stepped back from her, his hand dropping to his side. Tessa slowly pushed into a sitting position, her hand massaging her throat where he had gripped her.

"Despite what you think, Theon, I am well aware that I would have likely been separated from the majority, if not all, of my friends after Selection. However, I would have had time to prepare for that. I had an entire year. Instead, I was ripped from everything I knew by a bastard who only views me as a piece of property to be used as he sees fit."

The muscle in his jaw ticked as he stared at Tessa for a long moment without saying a word. Then he stepped forward, caging her between his arms once more. "You are forcing me to treat you as property, Tessa."

"How do you figure that?" she balked.

"You need to accept this bond."

"This fucking bond! It's all you care about!" she cried, shoving hard at his chest. Not that she moved him even an inch. "As long as you get what you want, fuck whoever suffers because of it, right?"

Theon lurched back from her. "Change," he snapped, grabbing a pair of his own lounge pants and swiping up his drink before he stalked to the bathroom.

Tessa changed quickly into the clothing Theon had set out for her before she made her way back to the main room. Theon still hadn't re-emerged. She eyed Luka and Axel warily. Axel was racking the balls, preparing for a game of pool. They had both changed as well, but neither of them acknowledged her.

She went to the fridge to retrieve a bottle of water before going to the bay window. The moon was a faint crescent amongst the stars. She could see nothing else out in the darkness.

You are forcing me to treat you as property.

Theon's words kept ringing in her ears. She leaned her head back against the cool window, closing her eyes as the words played on repeat over and over. How could he blame her for this? She hadn't asked for any of this.

And what had that even been in the dressing room? He'd gone from speaking softly to her to demanding to know who had touched her to snapping at her to get dressed in the span of five seconds.

"I need to know what happened in the gardens, Tessalyn." Theon's voice broke through her thoughts.

She opened her eyes to find Luka and Axel staring at her. Both of them had their arms crossed, leaning back against the billiards table. Theon stood nearby, another drink dangling from his fingertips at his side. The coldness on his face told her she was dealing with the heartless Arius heir.

"Did you create the crevice?" Theon asked.

"No. I don't know how that happened," she answered, her hands tightening around the water bottle. The plastic crinkled beneath her fingers.

"Were you there when it appeared?" Luka asked, addressing her for the first time since that morning.

"Yes."

"And?" Theon pressed.

So Tessa told them how she had tripped while she was running and how one of the Legacy had dragged her back along the stone path by her ankle. She told them how she'd broken his hold on her, and when they'd tried to come after her, the ground had shaken beneath them. She told them how she'd stumbled, falling to her hands and knees, and how the crevice had appeared to separate her from Pavil and Metias. Then she told them about the beings that had drifted up out of the crevice before she'd turned and ran.

Theon, Luka, and Axel didn't say a word the entire time she spoke, and when she finished, they were all staring at her. She couldn't read their expressions. All of their faces were masks of stone. Theon drained the last of his drink before he turned and went to his desk. He grabbed his tablet, his finger swiping and his eyes rapidly skimming the contents.

"You never once exhibited earth element tendencies, Tessa," he said, swiping again. "Your results were almost unanimously air with a slight affinity for water." He lifted his eyes to meet hers, waiting expectantly.

"I don't know what you want me to say, Theon." She gestured to the tablet. "You clearly know more about me than I do. I didn't even know my birthday until you told me."

"Did you find a way to hide your true abilities, Tessa?" Luka asked, cutting into the conversation.

"No!" she cried, her heart rate picking up at the mere mention of the assessments. "That's not possible."

"I wouldn't say it is impossible," Theon ventured with a shrug, pausing his swiping.

"I would say it is impossible," Tessa seethed. "You think you are prepared for those tests, but you never are. They are never the same."

"So you tried to prepare yourself for them? Why? If they are merely to estimate your element, what would you need to do to prepare?"

"Do you know what they do for those tests?" she demanded, her hands tightening further around the water bottle. Rain had begun falling again. Big drops plinking against the glass panes surrounding her.

"Yes," Theon answered tersely.

"Do you really?" she demanded again, not bothering to check her anger at this point. "Because if you did, you'd know why we tried to prepare ourselves for them. You'd know that those tests are designed to push you to the edge of breaking to see what inherent magic resides inside you. You'd know that I have endured physical pain to the point of losing consciousness, only to be healed just enough to continue. You'd know that I have been made to watch those I care about most being tortured in front of me, and I have been tortured in front of them. You'd know that one time, they had me convinced that I had parents and siblings, that I had a fucking family who loved me for no other reason than because I was breathing. But when I couldn't display an element on command, they killed a member of my mythical family until none remained; then berated me for failing my own flesh and blood until I wanted to take my own life. You'd know they layer grief and pain and fury on top of each other. They do anything they can to drag magic from you, and for what? So the Legacy can have a really good guess as to what element we'll have when we emerge. So they can figure out the best way to use us."

The silence was thick in the room when Tessa finally stopped speaking until a flash of lightning was followed by a crack of thunder that rattled the windows. Tessa flinched at the sudden sound, turning to look out the window again. "You are not focusing on trying to control an element in those tests," she said quietly as she watched the rain fall in the darkness. "You're too busy trying to separate lies from reality. You're too busy trying not to break so completely that you can't be fixed. But that's impossible. You always break. We help each other glue the pieces back together, but it's never quite right. The pieces of yourself never quite fit back together the way they once did. Until eventually, you don't remember what it was like to not feel cracked and scarred. Until eventually, you are just a shell of what you once were, but you know there's no way to go back, so you just move forward, even if death's song sounds sweeter and sweeter every time."

Tessa got lost in the memories of her assessments. She remembered the six of them huddled in Corbin and Lange's room, all of them on one small bed after a brutal round of testing. Dex had held her close while Brecken had gripped her hand tightly. When the assessments started happening seasonally, they got drunk every night after the tests were completed. Those were the nights she ended up in a mortal's bed trying to forget everything she'd endured that day, seeking any type of escape from it all. The Priestesses always healed them of any physical injuries they received during the tests, but the mental wounds scarred, often ripping open at inopportune moments. The invisible marks were far worse than any physical ones.

"Come sit with me, Tessa." Theon's voice had softened a touch, and Tessa turned to find him sitting on the sofa. Axel and Luka had started their game, Luka lining up a shot while Theon had a stack of files beside him.

"I would prefer to go to bed," she said, wanting nothing more than to curl up under a pile of blankets and sleep so she didn't have to feel.

"In a bit," Theon answered. "Come and sit with me for a while first."

Reluctantly, Tessa vacated her seat in the window and moved to sit beside him, her leg butting up against his. He wordlessly passed her a blanket before wrapping an arm around her and nestling her into his side. She instantly felt calmer as the cord settled in contentment at being next to him, and she sighed. She hated he could soothe her just by touching her all because of a stupid Mark on her hand.

Theon flipped open one of the folders beside him and began reading through the contents. Axel and Luka fell into their game, light conversation taking place between the three of them, and before she knew it, her eyes were drifting closed.

They clearly thought she was asleep when Axel said, "You know she created that crevice, right?"

"It certainly sounds that way," Theon answered mildly.

"Whatever beings crawled out of it certainly didn't sound like earth magic," Luka cut in, swearing under his breath at whatever was happening in the game. "I searched the gardens, but there was no sign of any beings. Even the swords were gone by the time I got back there. Since your Father did not bring them up at dinner, I am assuming he is in possession of them for his own purposes."

"The beings sounded like something Pavil and Metias would create," Axel replied, the sound of pool balls clinking punctuating his words. "Things of nightmares."

"They don't have that kind of power," Theon said. Tessa was focusing on keeping her breathing even as they spoke, not wanting them to know she was listening to every word. She felt Theon adjust the blanket. "The only plausible explanation is that she did it."

"How do you explain the beings then? What do you think they were?" Axel asked.

"I don't know. She might know, but after hearing about the assessments, I didn't want to push her anymore tonight."

"That is fucked up," Axel replied. "I knew they were put in stressful situations to see if their magic surfaced, but I didn't know it was anything like that."

"Me either," Theon said, and Tessa felt his fingers run over her hair, then along her arm.

"If their gifts were allowed to emerge naturally around ten years, they could emerge sooner, and none of these aptitude tests would be necessary," Axel mused.

"They are designed that way," Luka said. "The Fae were designed to be completely controlled by the descendants of the gods. That is why their magic has to be awakened by the Priestesses for it to emerge completely. It gives Legacy a chance to master their gifts before the Fae can come into theirs."

"Still fucked up," Axel answered before declaring a victory in their game.

"They were designed to serve the Legacy," Theon said dismissively. "I doubt any thought was put into how uncomfortable the Fae were made in doing so."

Tessa couldn't help but stiffen slightly at his obvious indifference to what she and the other Fae had been put through. She'd always envied the mortals in that way. The Legacy could really care less about the humans. They just existed in their towns and cities, rarely looked at twice, and there to carry out the mundane tasks of the realm that did not require magic.

Theon's hand ran down her hair again, and she forced herself to relax.

After several minutes of a new pool game being the only sound, Luka said, "It explains why she's so resilient. Why she hasn't broken yet."

"Partly, I suppose," Theon agreed, his fingers stroking lightly up and down her arm. He often did the same in the early hours of the day when she was just waking up.

"I don't know," Axel said. "The way she spoke, she's broken so many times she just figured out how to hold the pieces together."

"She was put through the same assessments as the other Fae, other than those tagged to be Sources early on," Theon said. "But she is still stronger-willed than most other Fae. The assessments cannot be given all the credit for her tenacity."

"What else do you think she's endured?" Axel asked, his tone ringing with a touch of sorrow.

"I wish I knew," Theon answered. "I don't want her to break. I just need her to bend."

"Careful, Theon," Luka said. "Something can only bend so far before it snaps."

21

TESSA

Tessa spent the entire next day being ignored by Theon, Axel, and Luka unless they wanted something. Thankfully, Theon had let her sleep in and didn't make her get up to go running, and she'd been perfectly content being left to herself all day. She spent the entirety of it trying to meld the Theon who had taken care of her after the Source bond had been initiated with the Legacy who was her Master now. Really, the same could be said for all three of them.

Theon always had a temper that he worked hard to keep under control, not to mention how possessive he was, but now? Now there was a darkness that seemed to constantly linger around him. Literally. Whatever dark magic he possessed was often coiling around him or trailing his footsteps. Now he was cold more than he was hot. She was rarely allowed out of his sight, and he would randomly summon her to his side, seemingly just to have her near.

Even more confusing were the random times he would corner her and kiss up her neck or trail his fingers along her body. The cord in her chest would flare to life with renewed vigor. Apparently it could sense when he was being aloof with her, and when he gave her attention, it did whatever it could to keep it. The sensations were sharper, and the pleasure was deeper…but then he'd flip that switch again, leaving her practically panting and unable to focus on anything else.

Luka and Axel were just as big of a mystery. Their own demons seemed to peer out from sapphire and emerald eyes. Axel's carefree mannerisms were few and far between, his darkness making an appearance every once in a while, and Luka seemed to be more brooding and aloof than before. Neither of them spoke to her unless necessary. The days of conversation around the table while eating breakfast or playing cards together were clearly over. Everything had changed since the incident with Pavil and Metias, and Tessa couldn't figure out why for the life of her. All she knew was her world was a little darker, and she found herself caring less and less every day.

"Hey, beautiful," came soft words whispered into her ear. "You need to wake up."

Tessa groaned as she came up out of the deep sleep she'd been in. She grabbed a pillow and pulled it over her head. "I'm not running today, Theon," she mumbled back, praying to the gods he would let her sleep again this morning.

But her prayers went unanswered as usual when he pulled the pillow from her hands. "We are not going running, Tessa. We need to be on the road to Rockmoor in an hour. You need to get up and get ready."

She went rigid at the words. She'd adamantly ignored any thoughts of the aptitude test she was going to be forced into today. No one said anything about it to her, and whenever it tried to cross her thoughts, she immediately put in earbuds and turned up one of the playlists Axel had set up for her. She didn't think she was going to be able to sleep last night, but when Theon had crawled into the bed and tugged her back to his chest and began making slow circles with his thumb along her stomach, she found herself asleep within minutes.

"Come on, little storm," he murmured, and she felt the blankets being pulled off of her before hands were on her shoulders and rolling her to her side. "Look at me, Tessa."

She took a deep, steadying breath and opened her eyes to find him staring back at her with concern. "I do not know…" He trailed off for a moment before clearing his throat. "I do not know what the best clothing options are for the assessment today."

"My running clothes will be best," she answered, pushing herself up before him. He lifted a hand as if he were going to touch her, but he dropped it back to his side instead, nodding once in confirmation. He moved to get off the bed but paused when she said, "I'll need a change of clothing for afterwards."

That muscle in his jaw ticked, and darkness appeared in his irises.

"Understood. Get up and get ready. Axel and Luka will be here in a half hour. We will eat breakfast on the way."

Forty minutes later, they were piling into the vehicle, Luka behind the wheel as usual. As they were pulling out of the gates, Theon handed her a banana and a yogurt with granola.

They'd been driving for nearly twenty minutes when Theon said, "You need to eat, Tessa."

She looked down at her lap where she still held the breakfast in her hands. He could be right. She could need the sustenance, but he could also be very wrong. Having food in her stomach could be the worst thing to do depending on what the assessment would entail. Opting for middle ground, she set the yogurt in the cupholder and slowly ate the banana as they drove. Theon didn't mention finishing her breakfast again, and she found herself grateful he had momentarily paused being a dick for the day.

Then she wondered at what point *that* had become her standard of something she was grateful for.

The trip to Rockmoor went by quickly, and before she knew it, they were pulling up in front of a towering white building. There was a smaller version of this building in Arobell near the Celeste Estate. A health compound for various procedures, including element assessments.

Try as she might, Tessa couldn't help the trembling that had started in her limbs as Axel and Luka climbed out of the vehicle. The banana she had forced down was already threatening to make a reappearance, and she swallowed hard against the bile rising in her throat.

"Tessa."

She brought her eyes to Theon's. He said nothing else as he stared back at her. She could swear the cord was vibrating so violently between them, it was going to rise up out of their skin. He reached out a hand to her, and she took it, allowing him to pull her along the seat. He pressed his brow to hers, his hand slipping to the nape underneath the high ponytail she'd put her hair in.

"I will be there. As soon as it is over," he murmured. "I will be there to take care of you."

And even though she knew it was because she was his Source and not because he actually cared about her, she nodded her head, forcing back the tears threatening to pool in her eyes. She would need him. She would need the bond. She would need something to anchor her if she could not have her friends, her real family, surrounding her afterwards. A part of her broke at knowing it'd be him that would hold her together after this.

She didn't beg him not to make her do this. It wouldn't change anything. She knew that even though his father had ordered this, he wanted it done too. He wanted to know just as much as his father did.

Theon brushed his lips lightly against hers before turning and opening the car door. He led her over to where Luka and Axel were waiting near the entrance.

"Ready?" Luka asked, glancing from her to Theon.

Theon nodded, and Luka pulled the door open. The inside was as white as the outside of the building. Bright lights glared off the white marble floor. A white marble desk rose up in front of them, a Fae sitting behind it. She wore a black business suit, her brown hair twisted into a tight bun at the back of her head. She stood and bowed immediately in the presence of the Legacy, then realizing that the Arius heirs stood before her, she dropped to a knee.

"Forgive me, my Lords," she murmured to the ground.

"Rise," Theon answered, his tone severe. "You know why I am here, yes?"

The Fae nodded. "I will call for a Priestess at once."

"Do so."

Tessa looked around the lobby. There wasn't another piece of furniture in the entire space. Theon's fingers tightened around her hand as the sound of clicking heels sounded from behind them. They turned to find another Fae walking towards them, dressed the same way as the one who had greeted them. She dropped to a knee in front of Theon immediately. When he had bid her to rise, she said, "Heir of Arius, it is an honor. The Head Priestess is preparing the assessment. If you would follow me to an exam room, they will collect your Source from there."

"My associates will join me."

It wasn't a request.

"Of course, my Lord," she answered, her eyes staying fixed on the ground.

She led them through a door and down a corridor with more doors on either side of it before she opened one and let them all enter.

"The wait should only be a moment," she said, before shutting the door behind them.

This room had a small sofa and padded chairs in it. There was an exam table of some sort against one wall. Axel set the duffel bag he was carrying onto a chair, his gaze flickering over Tessa.

There was another door opposite the one they had entered, and when it opened, a muscular Fae male came through. He wore a loose linen tunic and pants. Tessa immediately unzipped her jacket, shrugging out of it and handing it to Theon. She only wore a sports bra beneath it.

"Tessa, what are you—"

But he stopped speaking when she held out her hand for a heart rate monitor to be placed on her finger. The Fae said nothing as he attached sensors to her chest and side, but she caught a glimpse of the markings on his inner wrist. He'd attended the Falein Estate, was assigned to serve in the Arius Kingdom, and his element was water.

"Left or right?" he asked in a deep tone.

"Right," she answered, moving back and hopping onto the table before lying back. He nodded, moving to a cabinet on the wall, pulling down supplies to start an IV line.

The Fae met her eyes as he wrapped a band tightly around her arm, and she made a fist. He glanced once at the Legacy in the room, before returning his attention to her arm. When he was bent over her to insert the catheter, he asked quietly, "Do you want to know?"

"Yes," she whispered.

"A Level Five room," he replied, and Tessa closed her eyes, sucking in a breath as the needle went into her arm. She knew deep down that she would be going into the worst rooms. The young Fae who were first starting assessments went into Level One rooms. As they got older, they progressed to Levels Three and Four with the horrors faced more terrifying the higher the level. She had only heard of Level Five rooms, never been in one.

"What does that mean?"

Tessa opened her eyes to find Theon standing on the other side of the table. She hadn't realized he'd moved so close to her.

"What does a Level Five room mean?" he demanded.

Neither the Fae nor Tessa said anything as the Fae wrapped her IV site.

"You'll need to remove your socks and shoes," the Fae said to Tessa before he retreated out the door he'd entered through.

"Tessa, what does that mean?" Theon repeated, knocking her hands out of the way as she sat up and reached for her sneakers. He undid the laces and pulled them from her feet, stuffing her socks inside of them.

"It means you should have a fairly accurate answer to your question of my element when I am done," she replied in a monotone voice. She didn't have it in her to fight with him. Not with what she was about to face.

The door opened again, and a Legacy came through. Her copper hair was braided over a shoulder and gold ivy was woven through it. A golden circlet sat low on her brow. She bowed to Theon before coming to stand beside them at the table.

"Heir of Arius," she said in a melodic voice that all Priestesses seemed to have. "My name is Zefira, and I am honored to be performing your Source's assessments this morning."

"Thank you for seeing us on such short notice," Theon answered, lingering by Tessa's side.

"While unconventional, the Arius Lord was rather insistent," she answered, leaning forward to check Tessa's IV. Seemingly satisfied, she asked, "Do you have any questions before we begin?"

"How long will the assessment take?" Theon asked. He'd shoved his hands deep into the pockets of his suit pants.

"Lord St. Orcas indicated you wanted the advanced assessments done, correct?"

"Yes," Theon answered tightly.

She nodded. "They will take much of the morning, and she will need an hour of recovery afterwards. You are free to stay in this room during the tests. There is a television in that cabinet and refreshments will be provided." The Priestess motioned towards a freestanding armoire across from the sofa.

"I cannot be with her?" Theon asked, his tone betraying how unhappy he was with that.

Tessa sat quietly, already knowing the answers to everything he was asking.

Zefira shook her head with a sympathetic smile. "I am afraid not, my Lord. We rarely do such assessments on Sources because the bond makes the Master particularly...protective. We made an exception because of your situation, and I did caution Lord St. Orcas about this. You may watch from an observation deck if you insist, but I would highly suggest making yourself comfortable here."

"When can I be with her again?"

"When the tests are concluded, she will be moved to a recovery room to be monitored while her results are compiled. You can be with her there if you would like, or we can bring her back to this room when the recovery period is over," Zefira explained.

"You will take me to her as soon as she is in the recovery room. Is that understood?" Theon snarled, darkness appearing to thicken around him. Zefira flinched back, her eyes widening.

Luka was suddenly there, placing a hand on Theon's shoulder. "She understands, Theon. I think it is best if we stay in here during the assessment."

"We will go to the observation deck," Theon ground out, shaking off Luka's hand.

"I will request your associates join you in that case," Zefira said, her lips pressing into a thin line.

"Fine," he snapped.

"I will have someone escort you momentarily," she said with a nod. "Any other questions?"

Theon looked at Tessa, that muscle ticking in his jaw again, before he turned back to the Priestess. "No. No other questions."

"Wonderful." She moved gracefully back to the door and opened it. "We are ready, Rhett." The same Fae from before came back into the room, handing Zefira a tablet. "I will need you to sign this, giving us permission to perform the assessment as her Master."

Theon took the tablet stiffly, scribbling his signature with a finger, before shoving it back at her. She gave it to Rhett and pulled a syringe from the pocket of the gown she wore. Golden liquid swirled inside of it, and Tessa immediately started trembling again, her breathing turning ragged. Theon's gaze flashed to her. She saw him start to lift a hand towards her, but the Priestess stepped in front of him. She quickly injected the golden liquid into the IV line.

"What is that?" Theon demanded. "What did you just give her?"

"Nothing to worry about, Heir of Arius," Zefira said soothingly. "It helps prepare her body for the tests. A variation of the initial Source elixir you injected her with. It simply makes her more compliant until we are ready to begin. She knows how uncomfortable these assessments can be, and this ensures she does not fight when it is time."

Zefira stepped aside, nodding to Rhett, who came forward and easily lifted Tessa into his arms. A snarl ripped from Theon, and Luka was holding him back.

"He's taking her to the assessment, Theon," Luka said.

"If you still wish to observe, I will send someone to escort you,"

Zefira said with a disapproving look. "But know that the discomfort you are feeling now will only increase."

Tessa's arms and legs felt too heavy to move, and her head dropped forward against Rhett's chest. The Fae squeezed her gently where he held her, offering silent camaraderie to a fellow Fae.

"I will watch," Theon gritted out.

"Very well. I will send an escort," Zefira conceded.

With that, she turned and walked out, Rhett following obediently behind her. She heard Theon snarl again as the door closed behind them, and Rhett carried her down a hallway. They climbed two sets of stairs before they entered a darkened room, and Tessa was placed into a chair. Rhett strapped her arms to the armrests and her legs to the bottom before the chair was reclined back.

She stared up at the ceiling, trying to regulate her breathing. No windows. Never any windows.

There were mirrors lining the upper half of one wall, and she guessed that was where Theon would be watching. Zefira's pretty face appeared in Tessa's line of vision, her rich brown eyes trying to appear kind, but Tessa knew better.

"Today may be a bit more uncomfortable than you have experienced in the past, Tessalyn," she said, pulling something from her pocket. "I just need you to let your body naturally respond to everything. Do not fight it."

The same instructions they were always given.

A mask was fitted over her mouth and nose, and soon a sweet smelling gas filled her senses. The room swam around her before burning, hot pain was searing up her spine. She screamed around the mask, thrashing against the bindings that held her in place as the burning intensified. Tears leaked out of her eyes and ran down the sides of her face, mixing with the sweat already beading there and pooling into her hair.

She couldn't scream anymore, the burning in her lungs too much to let her elicit any noise. She couldn't feel the straps biting into her skin as she strained against them. She couldn't hear the noises of the machines she was hooked up to, or see the various Legacy monitoring her. As if the pain weren't enough, the cord inside her chest was having a fit of its own at being so far from Theon. Shocks erupted from her nerve-endings. She closed her eyes against the agony, and once again, she begged for death to come for her.

As suddenly as it had started, the pain stopped. Tessa opened her eyes, blinking against the sunlight. She wasn't bound to the chair anymore but standing in the middle of some woods. Birds fluttered from a tree to her right, and she spun around at the noise.

This isn't real, she told herself, but the cord inside of her reacted as if it were definitely real. The jolts of pain it elicited through her body at believing it was so far from Theon almost knocked her to her knees.

"It's not real," she reminded herself.

"Of course it is real."

A tall male with golden hair and eyes stepped from the trees. She immediately recognized him as Dagian Jove, the Achaz Heir.

"What are you doing here?" Tessa gasped, dragging her hands through her hair and tugging.

"I heard Theon's Source was on the run. I thought I would see if I could track you down first," Dagian said with a shrug as he casually strolled closer.

"I'm not running from him."

"No? Then what are you doing out here in the Dreamlock Woods so far from him? It is well known you have tried to run from him before. Quite the embarrassment for the Arius Kingdom, really."

"I... I don't know. I've never been to the Dreamlock Woods," Tessa stammered, looking at the trees around her. The Dreamlock Woods ran between the Achaz and Serafina Kingdoms along the Wynfell River.

Dagian tutted under his breath. "You know I am more powerful than he is, right?"

"I did not know that, my Lord," she answered, trying desperately to get her bearings. How had she traveled to the Dreamlock Woods?

"What do you mean you did not know?" Dagian spat. "I descend from Achaz, the ruler of the gods. Of course I am more powerful than an Arius descendant."

Tessa was quiet, trying to figure out the best way to navigate this particular part of the assessment, but the pain from the bond was excruciating and making it too hard to focus. She pulled at her hair again, trying to stay grounded.

"Look at me when I am speaking to you, Fae," Dagian snarled. "Tell me, how did the Heir of Arius get a more powerful Source than I did?"

"I'm not... I'm not that powerful," Tessa said, stumbling over her words as she slowly backed away from him.

"I heard what happened in those gardens. We all did," he sneered.

She shook her head. "That wasn't me. I didn't do that."

"Maybe. Maybe not. Either way, I cannot take that risk, can I?" Golden light crackled between Dagian's fingers. "How did you manage to evade the rest of us when we were looking at Source prospects? How did you manage to evade *me?*"

"I don't know," Tessa pleaded, wincing as another shock ravaged her body. "I didn't do anything."

"You know, since I couldn't get a private moment with you, I had to track down your Fae friends from the Celeste Estate," Dagian said nonchalantly, taking another step towards her.

"What?" Tessa gasped, going utterly still.

"It is a shame, really. That was a nice group of Fae. They would have served their kingdoms well once assigned." Then he shrugged. "But none of them could answer my questions either."

This isn't real, Tessa's mind was screaming at her, but the pain whipping through her body said otherwise.

A bolt of power straight from Dagian's palm suddenly knocked her onto her back. Tessa screamed as pain shuttered through her before she rolled onto her side and vomited.

"I can do this all day, Tessalyn Ausra," Dagian said, crouching down beside her and brushing a stray piece of hair from her face. His fingertips dragged along her cheek. "I need to know what those things were that you created in those gardens."

"I didn't create anything," she rasped, pushing herself up onto her hands and knees.

She immediately collapsed back to the ground as another bolt of power slammed into her. She screamed when Dagian didn't let up, hitting her again and again.

One, two, three—

"Will you last longer than your friends? What were their names again? You Fae all tend to bleed together after a while."

"Please stop!" Tessa gasped from the ground, unable to even move her arms to lift herself up.

"Answer my questions, Tessalyn, and this all stops," Dagian purred. "Serafina's heir is en route, by the way. Lealla will enjoy helping me pry answers out of you. There is no way in any of the realms we will allow the Arius Kingdom to regain power in this world."

"I don't know what that means. I don't know anything," Tessa sobbed, her heart breaking for Dex and Lange. For all of them. She'd never gotten to see them again after the Opening Selection. She'd never gotten the opportunity to say goodbye, to feel one more of Corbin's comforting hugs. She'd never gotten to hear Dex's voice one last time.

"You are his Source, Tessalyn. Surely he has shared secrets with you," Dagian sneered.

"He tells me nothing!"

Another bolt of power had Tessa screaming again, and the bond amplified the sensations. She tasted blood in her mouth, felt it trickling from her nose, her ears.

"Please, stop," she whimpered. "I don't know anything."

"I do not believe you. No one believes you, Tessalyn," he whispered harshly into her ear. "You are just another Fae. Expendable to us. Perhaps Theon will be glad to be rid of you. He can Select a new Source that can actually please him. One that isn't too much of a hassle."

Thunder rumbled overhead, and Dagian glanced at the sky, a look of confusion passing over his features. Tessa had managed to push herself to her knees, her body shaking violently.

"I need to see your power, Tessalyn," Dagian said, returning his attention to her.

"It hasn't emerged yet. I can't access it," she pleaded, the world spinning around her as she fell forward onto her hands once more.

"You can under the right conditions," Dagian replied, a cruel grin filling his features. He raised his hand once more, golden light crackling at his fingertips, and Tessa braced herself for the burst of power.

But it never came. Instead, another crack of thunder sounded, followed by a female voice that somehow sounded both horrific and cunning all at once.

"Do not touch her again."

Tessa opened her eyes and gasped at what stood before her.

She had midnight hair that flowed around her, and what appeared to be ashes flitting among the black strands. The black pants and tunic were fitted with some type of leather armor strapped atop it, but her feet were bare. Vambraces adorned her arms, and she held a bow at her side. Her eyes were a dark grey, smoke swirling in them. A quiver full of arrows was at her back, but she didn't reach for one. Instead, she drew one from a flurry of ashes, nocking it loosely to her bow.

Dagian had gone still, his mouth falling open at the being that had placed herself between him and Tessa.

"Not real," Tessa murmured, wrapping her arms tightly around herself. "This can't be real."

The female began circling Tessa, ashy footprints left in her wake, as she smirked at Dagian.

"Your move," she purred, another burst of ashes leaving a black dagger hovering at her shoulder.

Dagian didn't move, and then Tessa was gasping as her eyes flew open to find herself staring up at the ceiling of a room, still strapped to a chair.

"What did you do?" Zefira snarled at her, her hands gripping Tessa's face too tightly. "Who was that? How did you call her?"

"I didn't do anything," Tessa cried, jerking against her restraints, breathing hard. She could still feel Dagian's magic coursing through her body.

Not real, she told herself over and over. *Dex is still alive. They are all fine. None of it was real.*

Zefira pushed away from her, pacing back and forth. "You are proving far more difficult than I anticipated," she said condescendingly, as though this were all Tessa's fault. She snapped her fingers at Rhett, and he appeared a moment later with another syringe. This one was filled with a dark black liquid.

"This will sting," Zefira said, uncapping the syringe.

In a matter of seconds, Tessa was screaming again as pain tore through her. It felt like daggers were being driven into her stomach, while her skin was simultaneously being peeled from her body. The pressure in her head was unbearable, and she could feel blood trickling from her nose, her ears, the corner of her mouth. There was no counting to endure this.

The last thing she remembered was Zefira asking for another syringe before darkness dragged her under.

22
THEON

Theon lost his godsdamn mind when Tessa started screaming again. For a few minutes, her cries of pain and torment had ceased.

He'd forced himself to watch everything they were doing to her. He'd watched as they'd strapped her to a chair. He'd watched when they put some sort of mask over her mouth and nose. He'd forced himself to keep his eyes on her when they pushed more and more things into her body, trying not to think of how he'd done the same. He'd thought they were done. There had been no sign of her element that he could see, but he also didn't know how this worked. Tessa was clearly experiencing *something* though.

But right now, Luka and Axel were both holding him back as he strained against the observation window, slamming his fists against it again and again. He watched his Source at the mercy of the Priestess, who was injecting more of the black elixir into her. Tessa was screaming, blood running from her nose and ears. The cord in him was vibrating and tightening around his chest, making it hard to breathe. Was she dying? Is that why it felt like this?

"Theon," Luka growled, straining to hold him back. "There is nothing we can do."

"It has to be over soon, right?" Axel gritted out, his brother's hold just as tight as Luka's. "It's been over three hours."

Shadows were pooling in Theon's hands, seeping from his skin and thickening around his body. It began filling the entire room, forcing Axel to use his own power to counteract it.

"Theon!" Luka barked again as Tessa's screams echoed up to them, his sapphire eyes beginning to glow faintly.

Theon closed his eyes and tilted his head back, roaring into the room at not being able to get to her. The bond was panicking at having his Source of power in danger, and he was up here instead of down there with her, unable to protect what was his. He knew now that was why he hadn't been allowed to be in that room. He would have let his darkness feast on everyone in that room the moment Tessa had even whimpered in pain.

Except he hadn't.

He'd done absolutely nothing while she had tried to prepare herself for this. Sure, he'd left her alone for the most part yesterday, tried to take her mind off it when he could tell her thoughts had drifted there. He'd held her a little tighter while she'd slept, letting the Source bond offer whatever comfort it could. But he hadn't done anything on the drive here when she couldn't stomach breakfast. He hadn't done anything when she'd shed her jacket and sat back to have the IV placed in her arm as if this were simply routine. He'd done nothing when Zefira and that Fae had taken her from him, despite her obvious panic over what was about to happen.

And now he could do nothing but watch.

"I think she is done," Axel said, yelling to be heard over Theon's bellowing. "The Priestess is giving her something else."

Theon opened his eyes to look down into the room again. The Fae was wiping the blood from Tessa's ears and nose. The Priestess was pressing her hand to Tessa's forehead, clearly healing whatever the fuck she had done to her. Tessa's eyes did not open though.

The door to the room opened behind them, and Theon whirled. He grabbed the Fae by the throat, lifting her off of her feet. Her eyes widened in terror as her hands flew to Theon's, trying to dislodge his fingers. He only flexed them more, her pulse thrumming wildly. He caught a glimpse of her element marking. Air. She wouldn't dare use it against him.

"How long until she wakes?" he snarled.

The female was gasping and shaking her head, writhing against the wall.

"Theon," Axel interjected, placing his hand on Theon's arm. "She is going to take you to her, aren't you?"

Axel's voice was low and threatening, and the Fae began nodding as much as she could beneath Theon's hold. He released her, and she sank to the floor.

"Get up," Theon snapped.

She scrambled to her feet, coughing as she dragged air into her lungs. "This way, m-my Lord," she rasped.

They all followed her from the room to a stairwell. When they'd gone down two floors, she paused, turning to Axel and Luka. Her voice trembled with nerves as she said, "The Priestess requested only her Master come to recovery. If you continue down another flight, you will come to the hallway that will lead back to the exam room you were in. It will be the fourth door on your left."

"Theon?" Luka questioned, his voice wary.

"I will be fine," Theon bit back. As long as she took him directly to Tessa, they had nothing to worry about. "Take me to her."

The female nodded, picking up her pace as she led him through a door and down yet another hallway. At the end, she pushed through two swinging double doors. The Fae who had been assisting Zefira was just placing Tessa down onto a bed. Theon pushed past the female who had led him here, stalking over to Tessa's side. He shoved the male Fae out of the way with a snarl, leaning over Tessa and smoothing hair back from her face. She was pale and sweaty and vomit was on her clothes from when he'd watched her retch during the assessment.

"When will she wake?" he demanded.

"Soon, my Lord," came Zefira's melodic voice from behind them. She was pushing something clear into the IV tubing. Theon hadn't even registered she was standing there, all of his focus on Tessa. Zefira glanced around the room and said loudly, "Leave us."

The room immediately cleared out.

"We need to discuss her results."

"What of them? I did not see her display any magic from where I stood," Theon replied, his tone icy and deceptively calm. His dark power was hovering just beneath his skin. "Before you deliver those results, Priestess, be warned: if she went through all of that and you did not get the answers I seek, my reaction will be unpleasant."

Zefira paled and she swallowed thickly. "I got results, but not what I was expecting."

"Explain that," he said darkly.

"You are correct. She did not display any magic. That should not have been possible. We used our strongest methods, my Lord."

"Then why didn't it work?"

Zefira seemed nervous as she glanced at Tessa's still sleeping form. "Because she is strong, my Lord. She is undeniably powerful. Whatever element she emerges with, she will, without a doubt, be the most powerful Fae with that element."

Theon was silent as he processed that news. It didn't matter what element Tessa emerged with, she would be the most powerful. Even if she emerged with earth magic like his father clearly feared she would, Tessa would be stronger than Eviana.

"If the tests you performed today are the strongest ones available, why were her assessments at the Estate able to predict the air element?"

"They didn't. Not in the way you are thinking," Zefira answered. "I reviewed the reports sent to me to prepare for today's assessment. While her results tended to be mostly air and wind, those are just estimates. I pulled up the detailed reports of her past assessments. She never actually exhibited any magic like we normally see. The results in her records were our best guesses based on performance. Her lineage is unknown. We cannot even factor in genetics at this point."

His brow furrowed. "What do you mean her lineage is unknown? She came from one of the Sirana Villas. I have documents that name who sired and birthed her. Her lineage played a role in why she was Selected."

Zefira shook her head. "Based on what I have seen today, those are not accurate, my Lord. The two listed as her sire and dam would not have produced someone this powerful. It would simply not be possible. "

"Are you saying her documents were fabricated? Why?"

The Priestess glanced down at Tessa once more before meeting Theon's gaze again. "If I had to guess, it was done to hide her in plain sight."

Theon let that knowledge sink in, turning it over in his mind. Fae offspring were closely monitored, both those born in the Villas and those born to Fae serving other kingdoms. For Tessa to have been hidden among them...

But by who? Someone who clearly knew how powerful she would end up being.

Then another thought occurred to him.

Had Tessa known this entire time? Had she truly been hiding her abilities? She could get past wards with ease. She had appeared truly shocked when she was Selected, as if she'd never thought it in the realm of possibilities.

His father had been right.

She was keeping secrets.

"So what you are telling me," Theon said, "is that she could, essentially, emerge with any of the elements? One is no more likely than the other?"

"Correct, my Lord," Zefira answered.

A soft moan came from Tessa, and his eyes snapped to her. "Do not send the report to my father," he commanded Zefira. "This type of news should be delivered in person."

"As you wish," she said with a bow of her head. "She will be in some discomfort as she wakes."

"Can I touch her?"

"Yes. The Source bond will help ease that discomfort, I am sure. I will have Rhett fetch her some water. I healed her, but her throat will still be parched from the screaming," Zefira said. "Do you need anything else?"

"No," he answered, grabbing Tessa's hand.

Zefira left him standing beside the bed, and he heard her summon the Fae back to the room. Rhett soon appeared, a cup of water with a straw and a damp cloth in hand.

"I can clean her up some for you," he said, his eyes downcast.

Theon nodded, wanting to take care of her himself, but knowing that such a thing would appear odd to everyone in here. He may clear her dishes, serve her food, and give her freedoms in their rooms, but that could never carry over into the outside world.

He watched as Rhett gently wiped the damp cloth down Tessa's face and neck before cleaning as much of the vomit from her clothing as possible. When done, he left and returned with a fresh cloth, laying it across her brow.

"Do you need anything else, my Lord?" Rhett asked, stepping back from the bed.

"No, but stay close."

"Yes, my Lord," he answered, moving to stand against a nearby wall.

Theon reached to run his knuckles along her cheek. "I need you to wake up now, beautiful. I need to see those stormy eyes," he said softly, brushing his thumb along her bottom lip. There was no reaction. No moan or flinch.

Ten minutes later, she still hadn't made any indication she was waking. Rhett had retrieved a stool so Theon could sit next to the raised bed, and Theon had it as close to her as he could get. His phone buzzed in his pocket, and he took it out irritably to see a message from Felicity Davers.

Fuck.

He'd forgotten all about the fact that he was supposed to have lunch with her later today. In fact, he was supposed to be meeting her in an hour, and Tessa hadn't even woken up yet. He quickly tapped out a message to Luka, telling him to get in touch with Felicity and let her know it would need to be postponed at least an hour.

He had just shoved his phone back into his pocket when Tessa's hand moved a little in his own and another low moan passed her lips again. Theon shot to his feet, knocking the stool over in his haste. Leaning forward, he ran his hand along her brow.

"Tessa?"

She whimpered softly, wincing in pain.

"Tessa, I'm here. Wake up."

"Water," she rasped.

"Open your eyes first," he begged. Actually pleaded with her. It had to be the bond making him act so irrationally, just as it had been doing since the thing was initiated weeks ago. He was reacting to a threat against his power Source. His apparently *very* powerful Source. "Tessa, open your eyes, godsdamnit."

But she didn't, and that one act of disobedience had him calling for Zefira.

"Why won't she wake up?" he demanded

"She will, my lord," the Priestess answered, checking the bag of fluids dripping into her IV line. "Her last round of the assessment was very intense."

"I need to hold her," Theon bit out.

"I do not think that would be a good idea until she has completely woken up," Zefira said with a slight frown.

"It is not a request," Theon snarled, darkness snaking out from him and reaching for her.

"Of course, my Lord. I will have Rhett fetch a chair," Zefira answered, backing away from the pooling black around Theon's feet.

A minute later, the Fae was planting an armchair he'd gotten from gods-knew-where beside the bed, and Theon scooped Tessa into his arms before settling down into it. Rhett adjusted the tubing connected to her so it laid atop the blanket. She nestled into his chest, her hand coming up to clutch at his shirt, and the cord finally—*finally*—settled down in his chest. She was back where she belonged. His phone buzzed again, but he didn't bother trying to fish it out of his pocket.

"Tessa," he murmured into her hair. "I need you to wake up. I want to get you out of here, but I can't until you open your eyes."

She sighed against him before her body tensed for a few seconds, then relaxed into him once more. Why wouldn't she fucking wake up?

It was one thing to know how the Fae were assessed for their elements. It was another thing completely to witness it. He did not know what she had experienced to scream like she had. Those screams would echo into his dreams. She would certainly not be sleeping anywhere but in his bed for a good long while.

And what had he even learned? He still had no idea what her element would be. Had it been worth it to learn that her power would be unmatched? It made him an even bigger bastard to say that it was. It was worth it to know his Source would be more powerful than his father's, just as it would be worth it to put her through the next three Marks to make sure he could access that power.

Zefira came over and checked on them, again reassuring Theon that Tessa would wake up any time. He was about to simply get up and take her out of the damn place when she let out a soft groan, flexing her fingers against his chest.

"Water," she rasped again, and when Theon looked down, he found grey eyes staring up at him, faint traces of violet shimmering around her pupils that he'd never really noticed before. He would have studied it more, but there were unshed tears pooling.

"There you are," he murmured in relief, pressing a kiss to her brow.

He felt her sigh deeply, shuddering against him. He reached for the cup of water that had been moved within reach and brought the straw to her mouth. She took a sip, immediately coughing and sputtering.

"Easy, beautiful," he soothed, pulling the cup back. When she finished her coughing spell, she leaned forward again, taking the straw between her lips. She took another couple of sips, wincing with every swallow, before settling back into Theon, her eyes falling closed. "Don't go back to sleep, Tessa."

"I'm tired," she mumbled back.

"I know, but let's get out of here first. Then you can sleep."

She blinked her eyes back open, but he knew she wouldn't last long. He sent Rhett to get Zefira immediately.

"She's awake. Wonderful," the Priestess cooed as she glided over to them. She reached into a drawer near the bed and produced yet another syringe.

"What is that?" Theon barked when she moved towards Tessa with it.

"It's normal," Tessa said softly, pulling her arm out from beneath the blanket.

"What is?"

"It is a contraceptive, my Lord," Zefira said. "The elixirs used for the assessments have been known to remove prior contraceptives from the body before they are technically due for their next dose. It is merely a precaution."

A contraceptive?

That had never even crossed his mind. He knew the Fae were given them every season, of course, but it just hadn't even been on his list of things to worry about. No one was going to be fucking her. No one but him was going to be laying a godsdamn finger on her.

Tessa whimpered, and he realized it wasn't from the injection. His arm had tightened around her. He immediately loosened his grip, and she released another shaky breath.

"All set," Zefira announced, pulling the needle from Tessa's arm and tossing the syringe into a bin. She turned back to face them. "Rhett can carry her back to your waiting room."

"I have her. For the bond to soothe her," he added when Zefira gave him a quizzical look.

"I would like to leave her connected to the fluids a little longer. There is a tonic mixed in to speed up the recovery process," Zefira was saying as she led them out of the recovery room. Rhett trailed after them, carrying the bag of fluids. "Once that bag is depleted, the IV can be removed, and you will be free to go."

"Is there anything else I need to know?" Theon asked. "Anything I need to be prepared for? Is it normal for her to be...like this?"

Zefira waved a hand dismissively. "Fae are resilient, Lord St. Orcas. That is how they were designed by the gods. She will be fine. She can certainly resume her required duties today."

She couldn't be serious. He was certain Tessa wouldn't even be able to stand if she tried right now. Her head was resting against his chest again, and he was sure if he looked, her eyes would be closed.

"Here we are," Zefira sang, turning a knob and pulling a door open for him. Axel and Luka lurched to their feet as he entered, their gazes going straight to Tessa. Zefira handed a folder to Luka. Theon hadn't even realized she'd been holding one. "If you have any questions before you leave or in the future, please do not hesitate to contact me."

"Noted," Theon said stiffly, lowering onto the sofa. Tessa whimpered as he got comfortable, and Zefira and Rhett left the room. The door hadn't even clicked shut when Luka was opening the folder and skimming over the report.

"There is nothing in here about her element," he said, flipping pages back and forth.

"There won't be," Theon answered. "The tests were inconclusive for her element."

"You are telling me we put her through *that* for nothing?" Axel asked, the horror at that idea evident in his tone.

Theon glanced down to find Tessa sleeping once again, and he ran a hand down his face. "The tests were inconclusive as to which element she is going to emerge with," he explained. "However, they were incredibly useful in estimating her power level."

"Holy fuck," Luka breathed as Theon finished speaking. He looked up, his eyes wide when they met Theon's. "They are certain?" He'd clearly just come to that portion of the report.

"According to the Priestess, yes," Theon answered. He looked at Axel. "If the tests are correct, she will be the strongest Fae in whatever element she emerges with. No one with the same element will be stronger. No Fae will be more powerful than she is."

"So if she emerges with earth…"Axel trailed off as the realization came over him.

"She will be stronger than Eviana. And even if she doesn't have earth, her power will still be stronger than Eviana in whatever element she does have," Theon confirmed.

"Holy fuck," Axel said, echoing Luka as he sank into a chair. His gaze swung to Luka, and a smirk turned up one side of his lips. "Still think he should have chosen someone else for his Source?"

Luka was still flipping through pages. "I would be a fool to say this isn't very good news for us and our plans, but with power like that…" He snapped the folder shut. "She is already a handful. Controlling her will be difficult, especially when she can fight back more than she already does."

"Better us have her than another kingdom," Theon argued. "Plus, once she is fully Marked, I will be able to access and use that power. And when she finally accepts this bond, control will no longer be an issue."

"Can you imagine if no one had claimed her?" Axel mused, propping his head on a fist. "She would have emerged, and the kingdoms would have fought over her. Blood would have been spilled for sure, Kingdom Accords be damned."

"There is more I need to tell you, but I would rather not do so here. However, we do need to discuss the matter of her safety," Theon said. "I know I have been somewhat possessive of her since Selection—"

"*Somewhat* possessive?" Axel interjected, arching a brow.

"The point is," Theon pressed on, pointedly ignoring his brother. "No one gets near her without one of us with her. This stays between us for now. I have already informed the Priestess not to forward the report to my father. That I would deliver the results myself."

"He is going to see it when he reads the report," Luka said. "It plainly states it."

"Then I will have a false report made while we are in Rockmoor. We must have some forgery connections here, don't we?"

"On it," Axel said, pulling his phone from his pocket.

Theon nodded a thanks to his brother before he continued. "Anyway, while her safety is obviously important now, after the Emerging Ceremony, it will be a top priority. Being my Source should go a long way in keeping her safe, but that kind of power will draw people to her like a moth to a flame. Not to mention Father will be livid."

"Agreed," Luka said. "What are your thoughts for the Acropolis?"

"She is never left alone," Theon said. "I know you will have your own suite in the apartment lodgings there, but I would feel more comfortable if you spent the majority of your time at the Arius townhouse with me and Axel."

"I will be with you two most of the time anyway," Luka replied with a shrug.

"I also want you to start training her." Theon's phone buzzed in his pocket again, and he carefully fished it out, trying to avoid waking Tessa. "Why is Felicity Davers confirming our change of plans from lunch to dinner?"

"Because if you were still going to meet her for lunch, you would have needed to be there ten minutes ago," Luka answered. "When you messaged me that Tessa still hadn't woken yet, I had a feeling it would go like this. I arranged for a dinner reservation rather than lunch." Theon narrowed his eyes at his friend, and Luka held up his hands placatingly. "You are already going to be keeping something major from your father, Theon. You don't need to piss him off more by telling Felicity to fuck off today."

He was right. Theon needed to do whatever possible to keep his father's suspicions low right now. He sighed, sending a quick message back to the female confirming the change of plans.

"How long until we can get out of here?" Axel asked, looking up from his phone. "I have a guy that can meet with us in an hour to get us a fake report. He lives in the suburbs though. It will take at least a half hour to get there."

Theon glanced up at the fluids bag. "The Priestess said once these are gone, her IV can be removed, and we can go."

There was a lull in the conversation before Axel said, "Are you going to tell her the results?"

And Theon didn't know the answer to that. Did he tell his Source that she was going to be the most powerful Fae in Devram? Would it make her resist everything even more? Make her think she could fight it harder once her element had emerged? Or would it make her give in? Knowing she will be hunted and fought over, and that by giving in to the bond, she would be safer. More protected.

Or did she already know? Had she known all this time, and *that* was why she'd been resisting everything so adamantly? Had she thought she had gotten away with it, only to be caught off guard in the end?

"I don't know," he finally answered.

And he hated it. He hated that he didn't have an answer. That he didn't have control over this entire situation.

But the well of power sleeping in his arms?

He would soon have control over all of that, and then he could take control of Arius Kingdom.

23
THEON

A moment later, the door opened, and Rhett came into the room. He paused for a moment when he saw Tessa curled in Theon's lap, a brief look of surprise passing over his face before it quickly vanished.

"I'm here to take out the IV," he said, looking up at the empty fluid bag.

Theon nodded once, and the male moved forward. As soon as he began unwrapping the IV site, Tessa stirred awake. He gently pulled the catheter from her arm, his eyes meeting with Tessa's as she watched him.

"Do you need a restroom before you go?" Rhett asked her.

"That would be great. Thank you," she replied, her voice hoarse from screaming and disuse. She shifted her gaze to Theon. "Do you have my clothes? So I can change too?"

"I am coming with you," Theon answered.

Tessa sighed as she pushed off of his chest. "We've discussed this before. Boundaries."

"You cannot even walk right now," he argued.

She hauled herself to her feet, her face pure determination. Theon quickly got to his own, reaching for her, but she pulled away. She grimaced as she did and stumbled a step. When he reached to stabilize her, she pulled away again.

He gritted his teeth. "Godsdamnit, Tessa. Just let me help you."

"I don't need your help, Th—" She pressed her lips together in frustration as his name stalled on her tongue. "I'll be fine."

"Fine isn't good enough," he retorted, stalking across the room to grab the duffel bag from the floor.

"The restroom is just across the hall," Rhett supplied slowly, his gaze flicking from Tessa to Theon and back again. "I can help her walk—"

"If you lay a finger on her without permission, it will be the last thing you do," Theon said darkly, and inky shadows began creeping towards the Fae.

"Theon," Axel cautioned from where he stood, and Theon could feel it. He was on the brink of losing complete control.

Rhett cast a worried look in Tessa's direction, but she simply gestured for him to lead the way. Theon followed them out the door, staying close in case she stumbled again. Rhett led them across the hall, where he opened a door and flipped a switch on in a small bathroom.

"Sorry there isn't a shower in there," he said, looking at Tessa.

She smiled softly at him, her eyes seeming to warm a touch, and Theon ground his teeth together. She'd never offered him that look or that smile.

"This is more than enough," Tessa replied. "Thank you, Rhett."

"Get out," Theon ordered, stepping into the bathroom behind them.

Rhett glanced at him before turning back to Tessa. "I did track down a toothbrush and toothpaste for you though. It's by the sink."

"Thank the gods," Tessa replied, instantly moving in that direction. Theon hadn't even thought to pack such things for her. He'd only packed her the change of clothing she'd requested.

Rhett left the small bathroom, and Theon moved to shut the door behind him.

"You can get out, too," Tessa said, bracing her hands on the sink, clearly using it to hold herself up.

"I am not leaving you alone in here, Tessa."

"Are you afraid there are vampyres lurking in the corners of the bathroom, Theon? I will be fine," she replied, rolling her eyes.

"Why would there be vampyres in here? Is that a common thing after an assessment?" he asked, looking around the small bathroom.

"There are not..." Tessa gave him a perplexed look, as if she were at a loss for words. "There are not routinely vampyres in the bathrooms after assessments, Theon. I was being a smartass. What kind of childhood did you have to think vampyres are real?"

Theon ignored her question, instead staying, "Either way, you can hardly stand. Someone needs to help you."

"*You* are the reason for that, Theon!" she cried. "You are the reason someone needs to take care of me. *Again.*"

Something deep inside his chest flinched back at the words, and it wasn't the cord that connected them. He'd never felt the bond that deeply before. This was something else.

Tessa was glaring at him, her eyes the color of a stormy sky. When he didn't say anything, she rolled her eyes again, turning to the sink. "Whatever, Theon."

She unwrapped the new toothbrush and reached for the toothpaste. While she did that, Theon pulled her change of clothes from the duffel bag. He knew she'd be uncomfortable, but also knew they'd be attending a lunch with Felicity. He'd packed her a sundress, which now wouldn't be appropriate for a dinner. They'd have to stop and pick her up something else after they were done with the forgery expert.

Theon turned back to Tessa to find she hadn't started brushing her teeth yet. She was staring down at the sink.

"Tessa, are you all right?"

She jumped as though she'd forgotten he was in here with her. "I'm fine," she answered quickly, bringing the toothbrush to her mouth.

When she had finished, she brought the items over and put them into a side pouch in the duffel bag, zipping it shut. She peeled off the leggings and sports bra she was wearing, and Theon didn't bother to look away. She was his, after all. If he wanted to look at her, he was going to.

No one else though.

Not Luka or Axel.

Or *Rhett.*

Rage coiled through him at the look that Fae had given her.

He felt the sundress being ripped from his hands, and Tessa glared at him as she slipped the cerulean blue garment over her head. She pushed him aside to pull out fresh undergarments and gold sandals. When she stood back up from buckling the straps on the sandals, she was breathing hard, and perspiration beaded on her brow.

"You should have let me help," Theon said, stooping down to pick up the discarded clothing and stuff it into the bag.

"You've done plenty today, Theon."

She winced as she said it. She had mentioned the bond punishing her when she actively pulled away. After everything she'd been through today, why would she choose to incur more pain?

He carved a hand through his dark hair. "I feel as though we need to have a discussion to remind you of what is expected of you."

"What were my results?" she asked instead, moving to lean against the wall.

"Inconclusive."

She stared back at him. He could see the emotions warring in her eyes, and for once, he could read every single one of them. Disbelief. Anger. Pain. Frustration.

"Come. We need to be somewhere," he said, holding his hand out to her.

She took it wordlessly, and he led her back across the hall to the exam room. Luka and Axel were on their feet and ready to go. The Fae female who had escorted them in when they'd arrived was waiting near the door.

"How are you doing, baby doll?" Axel asked, stepping forward to take the duffel bag from Theon.

"I'm fine," Tessa answered shortly, her fingers flexing in Theon's hand.

"She is not fine," Theon drawled. "She is, however, back to her delightful, obstinate self."

"Is that so?" Luka asked, studying Tessa in that unnerving way of his.

Tessa huffed and tried to pull her hand from Theon's, but he tightened his grip around her fingers. She wasn't going anywhere.

They followed their escort back to the main lobby, and when they stepped outside, Theon had to blink against the natural light after being inside the compound all morning. The sky was cloudy, as if it might continue the trend of raining off and on all day. He helped Tessa into the vehicle, climbing in after her. She had already slid to the other side of the vehicle, her brow pressing to the cool glass of the window.

"Tessa, what do you need?" Theon asked, forcing himself not to reach for her. Axel twisted around in his seat to look at them, and Luka was glancing in the rearview mirror as he pulled into traffic. They'd all been treating her... Well, they'd been treating her differently, and after what she'd just been through, even Theon could agree that it wasn't working. For any of them.

Tessa brought her finger to the glass, tracing a raindrop that was sliding down the window. "That's a loaded question," she finally answered softly.

The guidance system sounded through the vehicle with directions to the forgery expert.

"Do you need healing anywhere?" he asked.

"No."

He spread his arm along the back of the seat, but before he could try to persuade her to come closer to him, she was already moving. She slid along the seat and nestled into his side, her head dropping to his shoulder and eyes falling closed. He glanced at Axel, whose brows were arched in surprise. The bond was buzzing, aching for more from her and wanting to soothe away everything she was feeling.

"Tessa?"

"I'm tired, Theon," she said, snuggling in closer. "And the bond helps... It helps me remember that everything I just saw and heard and felt wasn't real. Well, the physical pain was real, but the rest..."

She trailed off, falling silent again, and Theon shifted, wrapping his arm around her. "Rest, Tessa," he murmured as she settled against him. Her hand came to rest gently on his chest, her fingers curling into his shirt directly over his hammering heart, and he pressed his lips to the crown of her head. Within minutes, she was sound asleep.

When he was sure she was truly in a deep sleep, he told Luka and Axel everything the Priestess had said about Tessa's lineage.

Axel had pulled the small mirror from his pocket and was fiddling with it as he said, "Who would have had the means to hide her heritage? And why? Hiding her may have protected her for a while, but the moment her element appears in full strength at the Emerging Ceremony, the Pantheon would have turned into a battlefield to be the first to claim her."

"Yes, but by that time, no one would have been able to claim her as a Source," Luka countered. "Any heirs would have already chosen."

"We all know that doesn't mean anything," Theon cut in. "Anyone with a Source can suddenly find themselves without one to make room for another."

There were laws against such a thing, of course, but those didn't necessarily mean anything either. An investigation was always done in the event of a Source's death, and while the investigation was going on, if the lord or lady had already Selected another Source, that Fae was held for them until the investigation was completed.

"Then we come back to who has the ability to hide her?" Axel said.

"Whoever it is would have been around her from the beginning," Luka mused. "They would have constantly been altering reports. Nothing like this was ever mentioned in any of the information we have on her."

"But the Priestesses performing the assessments would know. None of them ever reported it either? It was never noticed that her reports were being changed? None of it adds up," Axel murmured, flipping the mirror in his hand again and running his thumb along the smooth glass.

Luka was eyeing Theon in the rearview mirror. Theon knew he could see the tension in his features, the darkness starting to drift around him.

"What are you thinking, Theon?" Luka asked.

"That she has to have known this entire time and has said nothing."

Axel twisted around again. "You cannot possibly believe that."

"How could I not? How could *she* not know?"

"Her magic hasn't emerged, Theon. It is bound until the Emerging Ceremony in a few weeks. How could she know?"

"She knows she can get past wards without issue," Theon countered. "She's proven that time and again."

"That doesn't mean she knows *why* she can do that," Axel shot back. "Have you even asked her about it?"

Theon scoffed. "Yes. We had a rather heartfelt conversation about it in between all the bickering and power struggles."

"You've made this a power struggle," Axel retorted. "She gets along with Luka and I just fine when we are not being dicks to her."

"Because she doesn't view either of you as the ones to have ruined everything for her. You know what I ruined? Her ability to stay hidden."

"You're a delusional idiot," Axel muttered, turning back to face the front.

"Am I? It would explain why she is so resistant. She thought she had succeeded until I found her in that alcove."

"Don't kid yourself, Theon," Luka cut in. "You were always going to choose her."

"There were four other options. I was going to choose Jayson."

"Right. You were going to select a Fae whose name you can't even remember," he replied dryly. "You left *Jaxson* and the others as options to humor us. We are not dense."

"And thank the gods I did choose her," he snapped, his arm around her tightening a fraction. He wasn't in the mood to argue about this yet again. The other options no longer mattered.

"What are you going to do now, then?" Luka went on, smoke beginning to furl from his mouth as he spoke. He was getting pissed. "Continue to try to force submission? Because that's been going so fucking well."

"No," Theon gritted out, the darkness thickening around him and reaching for Tessa. He had to actively hold it back from drifting along her arms. "I will wait her out. Now that we know what she's hiding, we can wait for her to slip-up. Reveal what else she is hiding."

"She is not Father," Axel drawled, lifting a hand as his own power worked to quell Theon's. "You do not need to develop some elaborate scheme to draw her out."

"Obviously we do if she has managed to stay hidden this long."

"Luka?" Axel pressed.

The male was quiet for a long moment before he sighed. "I think we get through this trip. This dinner with Felicity. Give Tessa a day to recover from the assessment, and deal with this when we are back at Arius House."

"Fuckwits. The both of you," Axel grumbled, pulling earbuds from his pocket.

"Have you heard from Cienna?" Theon asked.

Axel flipped him off over his shoulder while fitting the earbuds into his ears.

"Axel," Theon growled.

"He will tell us when he hears from her," Luka said. "Let him be."

Not another word was said the rest of the way to the forgery expert's house.

When Luka pulled up in front of a two-story house, Tessa was still sleeping against him. He didn't want to wake her and make her come into the house, but he didn't want to leave her out in the vehicle either. If she woke and he wasn't here...

It seemed as though she was finally starting to put a little trust in him, and even if she was keeping secrets, he didn't want to jeopardize anything if she was starting to give in.

"I will stay out here with her," Luka said, turning off the vehicle. "You two go in and get this done."

Theon nodded. "Contact The Palace. We will spend the night if I have to go to a dinner. When we are done here, we can stop and get Tessa a dinner dress, nightclothes, and whatever else we might need."

Axel didn't say anything. Just opened the door and slid out, putting his earbuds away as he made his way up to the house.

Theon gently extracted himself from Tessa, prying her fingers from his shirt, and quickly exited the vehicle.

"I want this done as fast as possible," he snapped at Axel as they made their way up the front walkway.

"I am aware," Axel replied shortly. "You can tell him what you need and come back out here."

A moment later, it swung open and a mortal of average height stood before them. He had thick black-rimmed glasses and dirty-blonde hair tied back at the nape of his neck.

"Hey," he said, reaching out to grasp Axel's hand. "Long time no see."

"Tucker," Axel replied, shaking the guy's hand. "Thanks for seeing us on such short notice."

"For the kind of coin you offered, I'd see you in the middle of the night," he answered with a chuckle.

"This is my brother, Theon," Axel said with a nod in Theon's direction.

The mortals knew who the governing Legacy were of their town and knew the names of the ruling families. Other than that, Theon wasn't sure they could distinguish Fae from Legacy without seeing the Markings the Fae had on their wrists. They both had the arched ears, slightly elongated canines, and a natural grace about them. As long as the mortals took care of the mundane jobs that kept their societies running, the Legacy left them alone. They were more focused on the Fae.

Theon shook the man's outstretched hand, curious how, exactly, Axel knew this mortal who did not tremble or bow before them.

"I don't mean to be a dick, but we are in a hurry," Theon said.

"Of course," Tucker said, stepping back to let them inside.

Theon looked back over his shoulder at the vehicle before Tucker shut the front door. He led them down a hall to what was apparently his office, and Theon quickly explained what he needed. Tucker took the file and set to work, not asking a single question about what the report said or meant. Theon figured the guy forged documents for a living. He'd probably seen things just as strange if not stranger. Axel plopped onto a sofa sitting off to the side, thumbing through his phone, but

Theon paced back and forth while Tucker worked. If it bothered the guy, he didn't let it show.

Twenty minutes later, Tucker was handing documents across the desk to him for approval. Theon read them over, then passed them to Axel to double check. The man had to make one minor change, and then Theon was out the door, leaving Axel to take care of payment.

"The Palace is making sure the penthouse suite is ready for us," Luka said when Theon opened the back door. "And rather than stop anywhere else, I placed an order for what we need and am having it delivered there."

"Good thinking," Theon replied, tossing the folder to the front seat. "Did she wake?"

Luka shook his head. "Whimpered a couple times in her sleep, but never opened her eyes."

Theon gently lifted her head so it rested in his lap, letting his fingers move up and down her arm. Luka got them on their way to The Palace when Axel returned. It was the most elite hotel in Rockmoor, and Theon's family owned the penthouse at the top. His father used it most when he stayed in the city for business, but Theon, Luka, and Axel had spent their fair share of time there as well. Tessa woke when they pulled up at the valet parking.

"Where are we?" she murmured, her voice thick with sleep.

"We are spending the night in the city. We are at the hotel. You can rest before we have to go to dinner," Theon said, opening his door and sliding out. He reached for her to help her out.

As soon as they entered the penthouse, Theon steered Tessa towards the primary bathroom. "Shower, and then you can sleep or eat. Whatever you need to do."

She said nothing, only started stripping out of the sundress, looking relieved. Theon exited the bathroom to get her clothing, only to realize he didn't have any for her yet. Luka and Axel were looking over a room service menu in the sitting room.

"Does Tessa want anything?" Axel asked, barely glancing at him.

"Not sure. I will check with her when she gets out of the shower." Theon crossed to the small refrigerator and grabbed two bottles of water. On his way back, he paused beside his brother. "We can't be on opposite sides, Axel," he said quietly, Luka wandering away to the room he usually slept in. "We survive together."

"I am not against you, Theon," Axel replied. "But I am always going to call you on your shit. I am telling you, she is being used in all this."

"You cannot know—"

"I *can* know," he interjected. "While you and Luka spend your time pacifying Father, I spend my time in the Underground. I know you and Luka think I am not as experienced because I am a few years younger, but I have gone through the same shit you have. While you are brushing elbows with the elite, I'm sharing drinks with the depraved. I am telling you, she is not that. She does not have some nefarious agenda, but she is going to if you don't back the fuck off of her."

"I am doing the best I can, Axel."

"Then let us help one godsdamn time, Theon," he retorted. "I know you have this obsessive need for control, but control does not mean you have to do everything yourself."

"I am aware."

"Are you?"

Theon swiped a hand down his face, letting out a long sigh. "I know we need to continue this conversation, but Tessa—"

"Go," Axel said, flipping the room service menu open again. "We're good."

Theon nodded. He knew his brother well enough to know he meant it. They would continue the conversation, but Axel wouldn't hold it against him until they did.

He went back into the bedroom, and when he could still hear the water running, he set the bottles of water down and crossed to the window overlooking downtown Rockmoor. He didn't want to go meet this female. Eventually he'd need to take a Match, but that had been so far down his list of priorities, he hadn't even entertained the idea as of late. He was still trying to adjust to having a Source and getting her under control, let alone focusing on building something with a potential Match.

He grabbed one of the waters, twisting the cap off and taking a drink. He didn't want to be hauling Tessa out to a dinner, but there wasn't anything he could do about it. She needed to be with him at all times, and not just because of the results they got today. He couldn't be seen without his Source, and this female would be at the Acropolis. He didn't want to give her the wrong impression.

He heard the shower shut off and turned to face the bathroom. A few minutes later, Tessa emerged, a white, fluffy robe tied around her waist.

"I didn't know what I was supposed to wear," she said timidly, fiddling with the sash in her hands.

"We are having clothes delivered, but they will not be here until later," Theon replied, taking a step towards her. "Are you hungry? Do you want to order food?"

"Can we just sleep some more?" she asked, her eyes fixed on a spot on the floor.

"We?" Theon asked, his pulse jumping at that one word.

"I…" She pushed out a defeated breath. "I need you right now, Theon. My head is all wrong, and I saw things…" She pursed her lips, twisting the sash around her hand.

She needed him.

She hadn't said those words once since he'd Selected her. He'd known there had been times she'd needed him—after the first Marking and after the shit with Pavil and Metias—but she'd never actually said it out loud. What those words did to the bond had him crossing the room in three long strides.

He took her hand and led her to the bed, pulling back the bedding. "We will sleep as long as you want, or until we must get ready to go," he said, stepping back so she could climb in.

While she was getting comfortable, he sent a quick text to Luka and Axel declining food and letting them know they were going to nap before silencing his phone. He shed his suit jacket and shirt, kicking off his shoes and stripping down to his undergarments before climbing in beside her. She immediately rolled into him, her head resting on his chest and a leg coming over the top of his. Her soft skin against his flesh had him instantly hardening, but there was fuck all he could do about that. She was in a robe, for fuck's sake.

"Do you want to talk about it?" Theon asked, running his fingers through her damp hair.

"No," she whispered. "I want to sleep so I can forget everything. Just for a little while."

"Okay," he answered, pressing another kiss to the top of her head. "Sleep, little storm. I'll be here when you wake."

Silence fell and Theon moved his hand from her hair to her back, rubbing up and down her spine, feeling her relax into him.

"Why do you do that sometimes?" she asked into the quiet room.

His hand stilled. "Do what?"

"Sometimes you call me 'little storm.'"

"Because your eyes remind me of a thunderstorm," he answered, revealing only part of the reason.

"When you say it, you make it sound…intimate."

"A Source bond is supposed to be intimate," he countered.

"So it's because of the bond?"

"Yes and no," he answered honestly.

She didn't say anything else, and a little while later, her breathing had shifted enough to tell him she was asleep again. He didn't sleep though. When he closed his eyes, he saw her strapped to that fucking chair, screaming in agony, with blood dripping from her nose and ears. And this docile creature sleeping on his chest was the result of that. She'd retreated into herself, battling her own nightmares and not letting him help. A part of him wondered if she would ever let him help her. A part of him wondered if that was where she hid her secrets.

But something else had come from this whole fucked up day too. Tessa was responding to the Source bond. She was using it, seeking him out, and asking him to comfort her. And if she ended up giving in to the bond because of today, he didn't regret a single thing about it.

24
THEON

He let Tessa sleep until Luka knocked softly on the door. Luka had bags of clothing and other items in his hands that he set on the small table near the window. He hung a garment bag in the closet as well, which Theon assumed held Tessa's dress for dinner tonight.

"How is she?" Luka asked, his eyes going to where she still slept on his chest.

"I don't know," Theon sighed, his fingers brushing gently up and down the sleeve of her robe. "She hasn't said much. She only asked me to sleep with her, that she needed the comfort of the bond."

"You think she is accepting it?" Luka asked, his brow arching.

"Gods, I hope so. I'd hate if this is what it took, but if she is finally accepting the bond and welcoming it, it was worth it."

"Perhaps," Luka said, crossing his arms and leaning back against the table.

"You think otherwise?"

"I think her time with Pavil and Metias was just as traumatizing, if not more so judging by her display of power, and that didn't cause her to accept a godsdamn thing."

Theon mulled that over a moment before he replied, "Maybe it's been building and building, and today was the final push she needed."

"Perhaps," Luka said again.

"What are you and Axel going to do while we are at dinner?" Theon asked, changing the subject. Debating this wouldn't serve any purpose at this point.

"He is bringing his laptop. We will work on alliance possibilities out in the vehicle. Do some research on what these things could be that crawled out of that crevice. If we can figure out what they are, maybe we can figure out Valter's angle," he answered with a shrug. "Then there's a Chaosphere game on."

"Sounds exhilarating."

"Considering we are not quite sure how the evening will play out, we didn't think it would be a good idea to leave you without a ride."

Theon nodded in agreement. "I better wake her so we can get ready. Dinner is in two hours," he said, wishing they could simply stay in this bed until morning.

Luka took the hint, leaving the bedroom. Theon let out a long breath, then gently shook Tessa's shoulder. It only took a moment, and she was blinking open her eyes, tilting her head to look up at him.

"We need to get ready for dinner," he said by way of explanation.

"Okay," she rasped, her voice still somewhat hoarse from sleep and the events of the day.

Neither of them made to move.

After another five minutes, Theon said, "Ready?"

She nodded mutely, pushing herself off of him and clutching the robe closed before it could gape open. Theon slid from the bed, following after her. He had packed some cosmetics for after the assessment, or rather Pen had, and he pulled them from the bag along with various hair items.

"Do you want my hair done a certain way tonight?" she asked.

"You can decide what would look best with the dress. It is hanging in the closet." He nodded towards the open door. He never gave Pen instructions on how to do her hair, so he wasn't going to start now.

She crossed the room silently, forgetting about the items he held, and unzipped the garment bag. He couldn't see much of the dress, but she apparently saw enough, and he followed her into the bathroom, setting her things on the vanity. He left her to it, going back out to the bedroom and putting his suit back on. Luka had ordered him a black tie to go with his entirely black suit and shirt. He took the dress from the closet and brought it to the bathroom.

She was perched cross-legged on the counter. He hung the dress on a hook before approaching, stopping directly behind her.

"Am I taking too long?" she asked, looking down to dig through the bag.

"No, beautiful," he answered, pressing his lips to her neck, unable to help himself. She leaned back into him, her head immediately falling onto his shoulder, allowing him better access to her throat. He groaned at the action. "Why do we always have some place to be at times like these?"

Stormy eyes met his in the mirror, and a soft, almost-smile tilted up the corner of her mouth. That smile nearly undid him, and it could scarcely be classified as a smile. He'd never been on the receiving end of the real thing from her.

"Are you even a little interested in meeting your potential Match?" she asked, leaning forward and digging through her bag again.

"No," Theon answered instantly, watching her dust some sort of shimmery powder on her eyelids.

Her eyes flicked to him briefly in the mirror before she returned to digging through the bag once more. "Why?"

"I have other things to worry about right now. My Match is not at the top of that list."

She pulled some contraption from the bag and squeezed her eyelashes in it. "What other things?"

He paused for a moment. She'd never been interested in what he did or what he was working on. This was new. It was almost as if she was… trying. Trying to build something between them.

"Work for my father. My own plans," he answered vaguely.

"You don't have time to invest in a relationship then. That is what you're saying?" Tessa asked, lining her eyes in black.

"No. I do not have the time to invest in a relationship with a potential Match right now," Theon answered. "I have business alliances to focus on. Not to mention you."

Tessa stilled at the last word, slowly dragging her eyes back to his in the mirror. She stared at him for a moment before not saying anything and applying mascara. When she was done, she spun around on the vanity, hopping down and walking over to the dress. She unzipped the garment bag, and before Theon had a chance to realize what was going on, she dropped the robe she was wearing. He could only stare at her as she stood naked before him, pulling the dress from the hanger. He had already been half hard just from sleeping beside her, but this added a whole new level to his arousal. It was almost painful.

Theon swallowed thickly, his voice gravel when he said, "Undergarments. I forgot to grab them for you."

He made to leave the bathroom, but Tessa looked at him over her shoulder, that same almost-smile tugging at her lips as she stepped into the gown. "This dress isn't made to be worn with undergarments, Theon. Lines would show."

Fuck. Me.

He watched as she shimmied the dress up and over her thighs and hips. She rolled it up her torso and over her chest, sliding her arms into the fitted sleeves that stopped just above her elbows.

"Zip me?" she asked, pulling her hair off her neck so it was out of the way.

He stepped forward wordlessly, his fingers brushing bare skin as he zipped the dress. She turned when he was finished, looking up at him beneath her lashes. "I just need a few more minutes to do my hair."

He reached for her, his hand cupping her cheek. His other hand gripped her waist, tugging her into him. She gasped when her front collided with his, his now fully hard cock pressing into her stomach.

"Are you really going to make me sit through an entire dinner I do not wish to be at knowing you are not wearing anything beneath this dress?" he asked, his voice low and rough because he sure as fuck wasn't going to be able to think about anything else the entire night.

She sucked in a sharp breath, her eyes darting to the side. "I don't have any other dress options here."

"Indeed," he answered, releasing her. "Come out to the sitting room when you are ready. I will set your shoes out for you."

She nodded, and he took a step away from her, backing slowly out of the bathroom. Theon finished getting ready, forcing himself to calm down before he went out to the living room to find Axel and Luka dressed in jeans and button-down shirts.

"So fancy, brother," Axel teased with a smirk.

Theon raised his middle finger, walking to the liquor cabinet and finding a small bottle of whiskey. He downed the entire thing.

Axel tsked at him. "You are so dramatic sometimes."

"Talk to me when Father is sending you to meet your first potential Match," Theon answered with a growl. His attention was fixed out the window, and he was contemplating getting another bottle of liquor.

"I don't know why you are complaining," Axel retorted. "Not when you get to spend the evening with this exquisite creature at your side."

Theon turned and found Tessa standing there, a slight flush to her cheeks at Axel's words. The black heels raised her up several inches, her gown just brushing the floor now, and her hair was braided in some intricate way over her shoulder. He didn't know how she'd managed to do something like that to her hair in just a few minutes. Her lips were painted bright red, and she slid her eyes to Theon before looking at the floor.

Axel had crossed the room to her and held out his hand. "Spin, baby doll. Show us everything." A small huff of laughter left her, and she let him spin her in a slow circle. He dramatically clutched at his chest before leaning in and pressing a soft kiss to her cheek. "You look stunning, Tessa."

"Thank you," she said softly, giving him a small smile.

"How are you feeling?" Luka asked from where he sat on the sofa. His eyes were roaming slowly over her too, but his brow was furrowed, as if he were confused or contemplating something.

"I'll be fine," Tessa said nervously. She reached up as though she was going to fiddle with her hair, but then seemed to remember it was styled. "We all found our ways of dealing with the assessments."

"And how do you deal with them?" Luka asked, his head tilting as he continued to study her.

She shifted her weight from foot-to-foot, and beneath it all, she still looked tired. Theon hated that he had to force her to go out tonight.

"In the past, my friends and I would sneak off the Estate to deal with them, but since I doubt you all are going to let me sneak off, I'll figure out some other way," she answered, glancing at Theon.

"That would be an accurate assumption," he replied, finally moving from where he'd been rooted to the spot. When he reached her side, he slid an arm around her waist, his hand resting on her hip, and she immediately leaned into him. He could have sworn he felt her let out a little sigh of relief at the contact. "Are we ready?" he asked, looking at Luka and Axel.

They all filed out of the room, and Theon didn't miss the various looks Tessa received while they stood in the lobby waiting for the valet to fetch their vehicle.

"I'm not going anywhere, Theon," Tessa whispered.

"What?" he asked, glaring at a guy who was blatantly staring at her, his eyes roving freely.

"If you tighten your grip on me any more, you're going to leave bruises," she teased, and he snapped his gaze to her at the tone. He hadn't realized he'd been pulling her in closer and closer the longer they stood there.

"I don't like them looking at what is mine," he ground out.

Again that almost-smile graced her lips, and she turned into him. She reached up and straightened his tie before she tilted her chin to meet his eyes. "Let them look," she replied. "You are clearly the only one who gets to touch."

Theon bent down so his mouth hovered just over her lips. "How much will you let me touch tonight, Tessa?"

Her eyes widened slightly, but she didn't pull away. She didn't even flinch. "I told you the other night, Theon, only mortals get to touch me like that."

With that, she pushed away from him just as the doorman pulled the door open. She didn't wait for him as she followed Luka and Axel down the steps to the vehicle. He hurried after her, slipping into the backseat.

Only mortals get to touch her?

Fuck that. That wasn't an option. Not again. Never again. If that was her wish, she was never going to be touched again. She had told him she would sneak off the Estate regularly to meet up with mortals, but she'd also just said the same thing about dealing with the assessments.

Tessa hadn't slid across the seat like normal, instead scooting into him as soon as he entered the vehicle. He brought his lips close to her ear, his arm holding her to him. "You do know that no mortal will ever touch you again, right?" Her lips pressed together tightly, and when she didn't speak, he went on. "How did you deal with assessments before, Tessa?" But she didn't answer. She just shook her head a few times in refusal. He would get the answer from her sooner or later, but right now, he needed to cover something else. "You know what is expected of you tonight?"

She stiffened beside him, and he knew if he hadn't been holding her so tightly to him, she would have pulled away.

"Yes, Theon. I know what you desire of me tonight," she answered, her eyes falling to her lap.

"If you need the comfort of the bond at any time—"

"I won't," she interrupted, sitting up straighter. "I'll be fine. I will figure something out."

He reached up and gripped her chin, forcing her eyes to his. "Tessa, you told me earlier the Source bond is helping. Are you going to try and tell me that is not true now?"

"I am telling you that I know what type of behavior is expected of me, and I will not do anything that may result in me possibly spending the evening sitting at your feet," she retorted.

Axel glanced back over his shoulder, quickly looking forward again. They were clearly listening to their conversation.

"That..." He paused, forcing himself to take a deep breath. She had yet to let him explain his reasoning for the events of that dinner. They'd been too busy struggling for the upper hand ever since. "We will finish these discussions later," Theon finally said, and Tessa crossed her arms.

The rest of the ride was silent, a tenseness emanating from the back-seat that even had Luka and Axel holding their tongues. When they pulled up to the restaurant, Theon got out and reached for Tessa's hand. As she stepped to the curb beside him, he leaned down to whisper, "Behave."

She frowned up at him. "What, exactly, do you think I am going to do?"

Theon arched a brow as he escorted her into the elite restaurant. "I never know what you are going to do. It is infuriatingly intriguing."

The hostess informed them Felicity was already there and waiting at their table, leading them through the restaurant to the back. As they approached a table, a place setting was being added on a second table that had clearly been brought over to go with the table for two.

A beautiful female with shining chestnut brown hair stood as they approached. Her brown eyes held a warmth Theon hadn't been expect-ing, and her dress was tasteful. There wasn't an overt amount of skin on display, but what was on display was golden-tan, suggesting she had spent lots of time in the sun this summer. That made sense since she lived in one of the Southern cities of the kingdom. She was a few inches taller than Tessa, and she bowed deeply to him.

"Heir St. Orcas, it is an honor," she greeted, her voice as warm as her eyes. She stood and stepped forward, her hand outstretched. "Felicity Davers."

"Theon," he replied, taking her hand in his and squeezing it. His other hand was still on the small of Tessa's back, and he ushered her forward. "This is Tessa, my Source."

"It is a pleasure," Felicity said, reaching to shake Tessa's hand. "Your dress is stunning."

Tessa smiled politely but didn't say anything in return, for once appearing to remember how a Source was to act in public.

Felicity returned her attention to Theon. "I hope I did not overstep, but they did not have a place set for your Source. I know the bond is new, and I did not think you would want to be too far from her, so I arranged for another table to be brought over."

She was watching him somewhat nervously, clearly unsure whether she should have interfered. Theon was more surprised than anything. He hadn't expected her to think of his Source at all. To be honest, he had anticipated her trying to flatter and seduce him in an attempt to worm her way into a Match contract. But she actually seemed...pleasant.

"That is very considerate of you," Theon answered. "Thank you."

Faint color flushed along her cheeks, and she cleared her throat softly, clasping her hands in front of her.

"Sit," he said, gesturing to the table.

Her eyes widened. "Oh, I could never sit before you, my Lord."

"I insist," Theon answered, ushering Tessa to the table. He slid into his own seat across from Felicity before he added, "You as well, Tessa." She nodded, slipping into the seat beside him, and he could almost feel her relief at being off her feet.

A server appeared instantly to take drink orders. He ordered himself a whiskey on the rocks, and Felicity ordered a glass of wine.

When the server turned to Tessa, she glanced at Theon. "I would love a glass of wine tonight," she said tentatively.

"I do not think that would be wise. Not after the day you have had," Theon answered, returning his attention to his menu.

"Water please," she replied tightly to the server, who nodded and left to get their drinks.

"Have you been unwell today?" Felicity asked, directing the question to Tessa.

Tessa glanced at Theon again, and he stepped in. "She had some assessments done at the health compound today," he explained. "The assessments can be intense, and she has slept most of the day. It is why we needed to change this meeting from lunch to dinner."

"My goodness," Felicity replied, her hand fluttering to her chest. "We could have rescheduled for another time, my Lord. The health of your Source is more important than this dinner."

Theon sat back in his seat as the server placed his drink down in front of him. This was unexpected. The Legacy notoriously cared little about the Fae. Fae were servants, created by the gods to serve a Legacy's every whim and desire. Rarely was their comfort considered.

"Tell me about yourself," Theon said, taking a drink of his liquor.

Felicity flashed him a pretty smile as she set her wine down. "I was born and raised in Raven Harbor. My father is of the Gracil bloodline, but my mother is of the Rai bloodline."

"Your father is the governor of Raven Harbor," Theon said, having learned all these details from the file his father had put together.

Raven Harbor was their port city located at the mouth of the Night Waters where the small river of dark water met the Asning Sea. No one knew why the waters of the Night Waters turned dark as the night sky when they flowed east from the Fractured Springs, but they returned to the blue of the sea the moment they met with the Asning.

"He is," Felicity answered. She shifted, flipping her hair over her shoulder. "I have two younger sisters as well."

"Will they be at the Acropolis with you?" Theon asked.

"No. They will stay back. They will attend the next Selection year," Felicity confirmed, sipping her wine once more.

"And if you and I are Matched, who takes over for your father when the time comes?" Theon asked.

For a split second, Felicity's smile faltered, but her bright smile was back in place a moment later, and she answered, "Whomever my middle sister, Eleanor, is Matched with."

"You are upset by that?"

"Of course not, my Lord," she answered quickly. "It would be the greatest of honors to be your Match."

Before Theon could ask another question, Tessa shifted beside him, drawing his attention to her. "Are you all right?"

Tessa nodded, but Theon could see her white knuckles as she clenched the arms of her chair. He reached over and pried off the hand closest to him, intertwining his fingers with hers. The cord sparked between them, and she visibly relaxed a touch.

Felicity asked, "Are you looking forward to the Selection rounds this year?"

"I attended the last Selection with my father," Theon answered, trying to shift his focus back to her, but the bond had other ideas. He found his thoughts wandering to the lack of undergarments beneath the dress Tessa was wearing. He cleared his throat. "He will not be attending the entire year, as he has other matters to tend to. He has entrusted the task to me and my younger brother."

The server returned to take their orders, and he ordered an herb-crusted steak for himself and a shrimp pasta dish for Tessa along with salads. She had tried to tug her hand back, but he'd tightened his fingers around hers. She clearly needed this, whether or not she wanted to admit it.

When the server left, she said, "I need to use the restroom." He moved to stand, but she tsked under her breath. "I am simply going to the bathroom. Stay and visit with Miss Davers."

"Ten minutes, Tessa. Do not make me come looking for you," he conceded, but he didn't like it, especially not after everything she'd been put through today. He watched her make her way across the restaurant.

"It is admirable how much you care for her," Felicity commented, finally drawing his gaze back to her. If she was jealous or feeling slighted by the lack of attention, she didn't show it.

"She is my Source. I take care of what is mine," he replied, grabbing his glass and taking another drink.

"Out of duty or because you care for her?" Felicity questioned, bringing her wine back to her lips.

"Can it not be both?"

"It can be, but is it?" she asked, with a tilt of her head.

"Are the Fae at your family home taken care of out of duty, or because you care for them?"

Felicity shrugged. "There are a few I am fond of," she answered. "I think we all have favorites when it comes to those who serve our families, but I would say the Fae are cared for primarily because it would be an inconvenience to have to care for ill Fae or find replacements."

"Fair enough," Theon conceded.

"But," Felicity went on, "I can only assume it is different with a Source and the bond. What is it like? Having a Source?"

"I do not think I can accurately answer that seeing as we only have the first Mark," Theon answered, glancing at the time. Tessa had six minutes left.

"What has it been like so far?" Felicity pressed.

"Very different from what I thought it would be," he admitted. "And I do not know if that is simply because we are not completely bonded yet, or if it is because of something else."

"It is not going well?"

"No, that is not what I mean," Theon amended. "I thought the Source bond and everything it entails would instantly snap into place as soon as everything was initiated, but it does not."

"Maybe you are right," Felicity supplied. "Maybe once the Marks are in place, and she has emerged, it will be different. Easier. For all involved."

Not wanting her to think he wasn't in control of his Source, he took another sip of his drink before saying, "They come to love the hand that feeds and cares for them."

"I suppose that is one way to look at it," Felicity said thoughtfully, her eyes flicking to something over his shoulder. "Like your famed hunting hounds in a way."

"My hounds cannot talk back to me," Theon muttered.

Felicity let out a soft laugh at that. "I am sure you took care of any resistance quickly and effortlessly." She paused before adding, "I thought maybe it would be different since you will eventually be able to read her emotions and thoughts. Is it not odd to have someone constantly with you at all times?"

Theon shrugged a shoulder. "Perhaps, but considering I will be able to draw from her power after the bonding is completed, I would rather have her with me than anywhere else."

"Of course you would want to protect one of your most valuable assets," Felicity said with a nod.

"She is definitely that," he agreed, sinking the last of his drink.

The server arrived with the salads and bread, and a moment later, Tessa was sliding back into her seat beside him. He turned to speak with her and found her pale, her cosmetics too dark against her skin. There was almost a greenish hue to her skin tone.

Theon leaned towards her. "Are you all right?"

"Fine," she answered tightly, pulling her napkin into her lap. She reached for her water glass, her hand trembling slightly.

"Tessa." He brought his hand up to touch her, and she closed her eyes, clearly fighting the urge to pull away from him. Her entire body was rigid and taut. Her breathing was shallow. What the fuck had happened while she was gone? "Did someone do something to you?"

She shook her head.

"What do you need?"

He shot a quick glance at Felicity, who was politely trying to look anywhere else as she ate her salad. Beside him, Tessa took in a deep breath and held it for a moment before pushing the air back out of her lungs. She finally opened her eyes again, her gaze fixed on the salad plate before her.

"I apologize," she said. "It has been a long day, but I am fine...Master."

The muscle ticked in his jaw at the title, and he sat back some. Gesturing to her salad, he said, "Eat, Tessa. You have not eaten all day."

She dutifully picked up her fork and stabbed some lettuce and croutons, bringing the bite to her nearly bloodless lips. He reached for the bread, buttering a slice and placing it on her plate. She glanced at it briefly before bringing another bite of salad to her mouth. If possible, her face turned a little more green, and she reached for her water once more.

"Tessa..."

"I'm fine!" she snapped, and her eyes widened as she lost control of her tongue. Her gaze dropped to her lap. "My apologies," she gritted out.

But it was a lie. Her tone told him she wasn't sorry at all. Theon's eyes narrowed, and he glanced at Felicity out of the corner of his eye. She was eyeing them now, her fork halfway to her mouth with her last bite of salad. He couldn't let this go. He couldn't let a public outburst at him go without consequence.

But what was he to do with her here?

He reached over, his hand capturing her chin and turning her face to his. "Do you not remember our discussion of stated expectations, Tessalyn? Particularly the portion of what will happen if those expectations are not met?"

Her eyes went wide. "I— Yes, of course," she replied, stumbling over her words. A mixture of panic and fury entered her eyes.

"And would you agree expectations are not currently being met?"

Thin pools of silver began to well in her eyes, and he knew they were not tears of regret but anger as she blinked them back.

"Answer me," he ordered.

"I would agree."

"And when we discuss the repercussions later tonight, you will remember this moment?"

He could see all of her rage and humiliation and helplessness playing out in her stormy eyes, and when faint traces of violet sparked across her irises, it took everything in him not to react. He had not been imagining it all those times. What kind of power would make her eyes do that?

"Verbal acknowledgment, Tessa," he murmured softer than he'd intended, his thumb gently sweeping along her jaw.

Her throat bobbed. "Yes, I will remember. I will remember all of it."

She held his stare, her eyes hardening. The traces of violet were gone, but the storm of malice remained.

He released her chin as he said, "You look unwell. I will have soup brought for you."

She shifted in her seat, her teeth clenching as she worked to control herself this time. "I am fine, but that would be lovely."

That would be lovely?

Why did those four words make him feel so...unsettled?

The server appeared to clear their salad plates, and then nodded when he reached for Tessa's with a questioning glance. "Was the salad not to her liking, my Lord?"

"The salad was fine. She is feeling unwell. Can you cancel her order and bring a soup instead? Some type of broth, if possible."

Tessa stiffened beside him.

"I am sure the kitchen will prepare something for you, my Lord."

Theon nodded in acknowledgment, and as Tessa reached for her water again, he leaned over to whisper, "When we have our discussions later tonight, you would do well to remember not to lie to me."

She opened her mouth to speak, but immediately snapped it shut.

And that was all the confirmation he needed to know she was keeping even more secrets.

25
TESSA

She wasn't fine.
She was the farthest thing from fine.
Then again, she couldn't really say she'd been *fine* in years.

She wasn't ill as Theon believed her to be, although she definitely felt sick now. Well, sicker than she'd felt since she'd woken up in Theon's lap in the recovery room at the compound. If Theon would have entranced her to tell him what was wrong, they'd have been here all night because there was so much wrong, she wouldn't have known where to start. She'd never had to function this quickly after an assessment. Despite what that godsdamn priestess had told Theon, they did not "resume their regular duties" within hours of an assessment. Certainly not after a Level Five assessment. They were always given an extra day of recovery time. No lessons or required attendance at anything else. She slept or fucked or drank. Or all three. But the only one she'd been able to do today was sleep, and that hadn't been nearly as helpful without the alcohol to make her forget or the pleasure to drown in.

The server appeared sometime later, placing food before Theon, then Felicity, before finally setting a bowl of steaming broth before her with a side of crusty bread.

Broth.

Fucking great.

It was probably too salty too. Just like she was forced to endure at the

Estate where broth had been her meal for weeks when other food was withheld.

"You are so good to her, Theon," Felicity praised again when Theon ordered a bottle of ginger ale to be brought, still believing Tessa to be ill. Tessa had to fight the eye roll.

"As I said," Theon was saying, cutting into his steak, "I take care of what is mine."

Tessa stiffened at the words, reaching for her water again. She took a sip and jolted when she felt Theon's fingers on the back of her neck, water sloshing out of her glass and down her dress.

Gods, his touch today. She hadn't been lying when she'd told him she needed it. The bond was comforting and soothing and all the things she didn't want it to be. It had kept the nightmares away when she'd slept. It had calmed her when all she could see in her mind was that final vision they'd forced on her. The one where Theon and Axel and Luka had—

"Here you are."

Tessa jolted again when the bottle of ginger ale and a glass were placed in front of her. Theon was making slow circles on the back of her neck with his thumb, but even that didn't seem to be enough right now. Not that she could do anything about it in a public restaurant. And maybe she was grateful for that because she knew if they were alone right now, she'd let him do pretty much anything to her to keep the memories from swarming up and dragging her down again.

"Thank you," she replied quietly, giving the Fae server a small smile.

"You are very jumpy tonight, Tessa."

And good gods, she jolted again at Theon's whispered voice near her ear. He reached across her, picking up the small bottle of ginger ale and pouring it into the glass for her. Then his lips were at her ear again. "It makes me think there is something, or perhaps several things, you are keeping from me."

Tessa resisted the urge to swallow, reaching for the glass of ginger ale. "It has just been a long day," she replied softly.

She could feel his eyes on her for a long moment, but he finally sat back, returning to his meal and the Legacy he was supposed to be getting to know. Knowing he was paying very close attention to her though, Tessa picked up her spoon and began stirring the broth.

"Tell me, Felicity, what gift did you end up with?" Theon asked.

"Was that not in the information my father sent over to you?" Felicity asked, and Tessa could feel her eyes on her too.

"It was, but powers manifest differently for everyone. I found it interesting you ended up with gifts of Gracil rather than Rai. How, exactly, does the power of creating conflict work?" Theon answered.

The female could create conflict? That seemed fitting.

"I can sense conflicts among people," Felicity replied. "And from there, I can fan the flame, so to speak."

"That could be useful," Theon mused, sitting back in his chair and taking a sip of his fresh drink.

"It certainly can be, and a gift I would be more than delighted to share with the Arius Kingdom and bloodline," Felicity said with a small smile.

"Indeed."

Tessa snuck a peek from beneath her lashes as she brought a spoonful of broth to her mouth to find the two Legacies' gazes locked on each other. She forced the mouthful of broth down her throat before setting her spoon back down. Maybe it wouldn't be so bad for him to take a Match. Maybe it would take his focus and attention off of her all the time. Would she be expected to serve his Match, too, though? She had never seen Cressida giving orders to Eviana. Granted, she hadn't been around Eviana or Theon's parents much, but she had never seen Cressida interact with Eviana at all.

"Will you tell me of Arius House?" Felicity asked, breaking the silence and dropping her eyes to her plate as if suddenly shy. Tessa dipped her head to hide the eye roll she couldn't stop this time. "Who resides there with you?"

"The house is big enough that I have an entire wing to myself. My parents have a wing as well, and my brother's rooms are in that wing of the house. Mine were there until I took my Source. Luka, who will be my advisor when the time comes, also has rooms in my wing," Theon answered.

"And your mother runs the household?" Felicity asked. "Would that be expected of me?"

"Eventually, I suppose," Theon answered. "However, I do not see my mother giving up control of that anytime soon. So you would have time to pursue other interests for a while if you desired."

"What do you want out of the Match agreement, Theon?" Felicity asked, picking up her glass of wine. "Are you wanting a companion to share this life with, or someone simply to produce your heirs?"

Tessa sat up straighter at that question. That... That was a bold question to ask upon a first meeting.

Theon was quiet for a long moment, taking a sip of his drink before he answered. "I suppose it would depend on the person I enter into the agreement with. Could a true relationship form? Perhaps. Will I force something? No. Will I appease my father at the moment and meet with potential Matches? Yes."

"And what will be your biggest factors for choosing?"

"Bloodline. Power. If I can stand being around the person for longer than ten minutes," Theon said with a smirk.

Felicity glanced at the delicate timepiece on her wrist. "Considering we have been dining together for well over an hour, and you have not attempted to leave, despite your Source clearly being ill, I would say I am doing fairly well on all three."

"Perhaps," Theon conceded.

Tessa didn't finish her broth.

It had been one of the longest evenings of her life. She was exhausted—physically, mentally, emotionally. She nearly cried in relief when Theon and Felicity finally called it an evening…when it was nearing midnight. Theon had made it a point to touch her at various times throughout the evening, but Felicity had captured much of his attention. She had been so clever about it, too, never appearing desperate or demanding. She asked the right questions, provided the right answers, and in the end, they had already made plans to go for dinner when Felicity arrived at the Acropolis.

Which was great. Just fucking great.

After making sure Felicity was safely tucked away in her vehicle, Theon reached out a hand to Tessa where she was waiting for him near the doors. He could have let her get into the vehicle with Axel and Luka, but no. She had to stand here and wait for him. Trying to brush past him, she ignored his outstretched hand, but then his hands were on her waist, spinning her and pushing her up against the side of the vehicle. He rested one of his arms above her, leaning in close. His other hand stayed on her waist.

"We have much to discuss tonight, Tessa." His voice was low, and the cord was vibrating wildly after having been ignored for much of the night.

She swallowed thickly. "One would think you're talked out after so much conversation with Miss Davers."

Theon's head tilted to the side, a lock of dark hair falling over his brow. "Are you jealous, beautiful?" He brushed his nose up the length of hers.

"No, I'm not."

"You're not?"

"I'm tired, Theon. This day was... Well, it was uncomfortable."

Unbearable was more like it, but she already knew he was upset with her small outburst at dinner.

Too wild. Too impulsive.

"Hmm," he hummed, running the tip of his nose along her jaw. "Do you want to tell me about that?"

"On the side of the car outside of a restaurant? Not particularly," she rasped, tilting her head back as his lips brushed along the column of her throat. She was trying to ignore the heat coursing through her.

"Then I suppose we will need to finish this...discussion back in our rooms," he replied, his teeth grazing her collarbone.

Tessa fisted her hands beside her, pressing her body back against the vehicle to support her trembling legs. "I would rather just go to sleep when we get back," she managed to get out as that hand on her waist began roaming lower. And gods, she hated that she thought about urging him to take more. Just so she wouldn't have to *feel* anything right now.

She felt him smile against her flesh. "I am sure you would, but that will not happen. You have some secrets I need to know."

He pulled back, reaching over and opening the door to the backseat, leaving her breathless. The bond was like a magnetic force inside of her, trying to pull her back to him.

"I don't know why you think I'm keeping anything from you," she retorted, pushing off the vehicle and climbing in.

"Mhmm," he murmured, sliding smoothly in beside her. She tried to move across the seat to put distance between them, but his arm snagged her around her waist again. "Don't even think about it."

He didn't even leave her on the seat. He pulled her directly into his lap, one hand coming up to her nape and beginning to massage the muscles there.

"So…" Axel started, dragging out the word. "How did it go?"

He and Luka were both twisted around in their seats, looking at them, and Tessa felt her cheeks heat. Did she really need to be in his damn lap?

"It went fine," Theon answered. "Felicity is quite…unanticipated."

"Unanticipated?" Axel repeated. "That's how you're going to describe her?"

"She just wasn't what I was expecting," Theon said.

"She was like Tessa then?" Axel asked, his gaze darting to her quickly before focusing back on Theon again.

"What? No. She was nothing like Tessa," Theon said, his hand stilling on her neck. "Why would you think that?"

"Because you described Tessa as being unexpected. And unexpected and unanticipated mean the same thing," Axel said, arching a brow that Tessa could barely make out in the glow of the dash.

"I know what unexpected and unanticipated mean," Theon snapped.

"So…she was like Tessa then?" Axel repeated, and Tessa heard Luka snicker as he turned back and put the blinker on to merge into traffic. Was Axel really teasing Theon over this?

Theon kicked the back of Axel's seat with his foot as he muttered, "Prick."

Axel laughed. "Tell us about her then, brother."

As Theon started telling them all about Felicity Davers, Tessa closed her eyes, leaning into him and thinking about all the *agaveheart* she was going to drink tonight.

Agaveheart was made from the center of the agave plant that had been roasted, crushed, and fermented. It tasted both sweet and spicy, and it burned on the way down in the best way.

But that's what she had really done when she'd gone to use the restroom. As soon as she was out of Theon's sight, she had discreetly made her way back to the hostess. She had swiped a couple of large notes from Theon's rather impressive stash when she had finished her hair that evening, and she had pulled one from where she'd stuffed three down the front of her dress.

She had asked the hostess to send a bottle of top shelf *agaveheart* to their hotel and have it left at the front desk for her with strict instructions to let them know *not* to send it up to their room because it was a surprise and that Tessa would pick it up in person. She'd only ever had the cheap *agaveheart* they'd stolen. If Theon would not let her drink wine at dinner, he could certainly pay for her to drink afterwards. She would do at least one of the things she always did after the power assessments and that was getting drunk and repressing the memories. Not particularly healthy, but what was that mortal saying? Make lemonade out of lemons or some shit? And when you're desperate and have no lemons? You make lemonade out of *agaveheart*.

She still hadn't quite figured out how she was going to get out of the room tonight to get said *agaveheart*, but as usual, she'd figure it out as she went. It's not as if things could get any worse. She huffed a small laugh at the thought, but apparently everyone in the vehicle heard it, because silence fell. Theon's hand that had again started massaging her neck stilled once more.

"You find that amusing?" he asked.

Her brows knitted. "Find what amusing?"

"What I just said about Felicity."

"I wasn't listening to your conversation, Theon. I listened to you and Miss Davers talk enough tonight. I do not need a play-by-play of the evening. I was there for every dull moment of it."

"You did not enjoy the evening?"

"Aside from the fact that today was agony and I am tired?" Tessa retorted. "No, Theon. I did not enjoy the evening. I was bored out of my mind, and we were inside for hours."

"You should have stayed out here with us, baby doll," Axel chimed in. "We watched the Chaosphere game. The Sunstars slaughtered the Firewings."

"I would have chosen to watch paint dry over sitting there and listening to those two dance around topics all night," she replied, and Axel barked a laugh. "He wouldn't even let me have wine to get through the evening."

"Why would I give you wine when you are not feeling well?" Theon cut in.

"I never said I wasn't feeling well," she bit back.

"That's beside the point," he argued. "You looked as though you were going to vomit with each bite of salad. Why would you ask for wine when you are not feeling well?"

"Likely because I choose inappropriate methods of dealing with emotional issues and trauma," Tessa muttered.

Axel barked another laugh.

"I can actually see that," Luka commented as they came to a stop at a red light.

"I cannot tell if you are joking or serious," Theon said, pushing her away from his chest to try to see her face in the dark interior of the vehicle.

"I can't tell if you are going to be amicable or a dick from one minute to the next lately, so I guess we're even," she retorted with a shrug. "Then again, that goes for everyone in the vehicle these days."

"Gods, you're mouthy when you're tired," Theon sighed, tipping his head back.

"I'm kind of like one of your hounds, but I can talk back," she sneered, and Theon stilled against the seat.

"What did you just say?" he demanded in a low tone that had Luka and Axel stiffening.

"You heard me, Theon," she sneered again.

Theon had been eating out of her godsdamn hand and couldn't see how he was being played. But Tessa saw it. Tessa saw it the moment the female flicked her eyes to her when she was returning from the restroom and compared her to one of Theon's hounds knowing Tessa could hear. The female knew she paused, almost causing a server to run into her with a tray full of drinks, when Theon commented about how his hounds couldn't speak back to him.

When Theon had called her a *valuable asset.*

The silence in the car was deafening for a long moment before Theon said, "We have much to discuss tonight."

"Oh my gods," she groaned, dragging a hand down her face. "You really are going to repeat every conversation you had tonight, aren't you?"

"What are you talking about?"

"We already had this conversation outside after dinner. You said those exact words to me."

"A conversation is not what appeared to be happening after dinner," Axel muttered from the front seat.

Theon ignored him, his entire focus on her, and the restless thing inside her raised its head. She didn't care. She didn't care that she was poking the monster, that she was likely making Theon incredibly angry. She didn't care that there was definitely going to be a consequence for her actions. She was exhausted and feeling so many emotions, she couldn't separate them out to deal with them if she tried.

"Then let's have a different conversation, Tessa," he said, his voice turning dark, and Tessa tensed at his tone. "What happened when you left the table tonight? And do not tell me nothing. You were fine when you left, and pale as moonlight when you came back."

Tessa leaned in close to him, her lips feathering against his as she spoke, and she felt him suck in a breath. "I bribed the hostess at the front of the restaurant to get me a bottle of *agaveheart* and have it sent to our hotel," she simpered.

"Are you really going to make me entrance the truth from you?"

"Are you really going to continue to argue with me tonight after the day you put me through? For nothing, I might add. Since my results were apparently inconclusive," Tessa retorted, leaning back.

Axel coughed, trying to cover it up with a huff of laughter. "Tessa takes that round."

"Shut up, Axel," Theon snapped, his eyes never leaving her.

"We're here," Luka announced, throwing open his door and climbing out. Axel got out, leaving Tessa alone with a monster in the dark.

"We need to have a conversation about what you overheard tonight."

"Sure, Theon," Tessa replied, patting his chest patronizingly. "Right after we have a discussion about the three of you being assholes lately."

A growl emanated from deep in Theon's throat, and Tessa had the good sense to jerk back from him, but his grip on her waist tightened, keeping her in his lap. "Just so you are aware, the behavior you are displaying right now falls under the arguing with me category."

"Just so you are aware, I don't give a flying fu—"

The door of the vehicle opened abruptly, cutting Tessa off.

"The valet is waiting," Luka said tightly. "I am sure whatever is going on in here can be continued inside."

"It most certainly will be," Theon said, sliding Tessa from his lap and handing her out to Luka.

"We should make arrangements for the vehicle to be here and waiting in the morning," Luka said while Theon climbed out and shut the car door. "Axel went inside to take care of the departing details so we don't have to mess with it. He's also arranging for breakfast to be ready to take with us."

Tessa shivered against the chill of the night, and Theon glanced at her. "Go inside and stay by Axel. We will be right in."

She didn't hesitate, turning and rushing up the steps while rubbing her arms to create some warming friction. A Fae at the door let her in, and she immediately spotted Axel leaning against the front desk. There was a small seating area to the left, so she plopped down on a leather sofa to wait for them. She rested her chin on her hand, taking in the opulent lobby. It wasn't as if she could head up to the private floor their penthouse suite was located on anyway. The floor was keyed to their magical signatures.

"Do you normally get all dressed up to sit in hotel lobbies after midnight?"

Tessa looked up to see a handsome mortal in jeans and a button-down shirt looking at her, a light amusement in his russet colored eyes.

"Always," she answered. "It's one of my favorite pastimes. There is just something about a hotel lobby that soothes the soul."

"Maybe it's the music?" the man supplied, the amusement forming into a small grin now.

"It's no elevator music, but it's the next best thing, I suppose," Tessa said, exaggerating a wistful sigh.

The man chuckled, holding out a hand to her. "I'm Tristyn."

"Tessa," she replied, slipping her hand into his. He squeezed it warmly. "And what about you? What are you doing down here in the hotel lobby after midnight? Aside from striking up random conversations with Fae females."

"Female," Tristyn corrected. "Only one incredibly stunning female."

Tessa felt her cheeks flush slightly. "That's…"

"Accurate?"

"I was going to say cliché, but sure, we can go with accurate," she said, her smile growing as he dropped onto the sofa beside her. He wasn't close enough to touch her, but he was close enough that she forgot about the shit her life had become for a moment.

"So what's the real story, Tessa? Have a date tonight?" he asked, settling into the sofa and draping his arm along the back.

"You're incredibly forward," she remarked, angling her body a little more towards him.

"One would assume that if you are dressed like that," he gave her a pointed look, "you were at a rather important event. Since the Opening Selection Ceremony is over and not held in the Arius Kingdom, the odds of you being at said function alone are slim to none."

She let out a small huff of laughter. "I was at a function, and I was not alone. But it was not a…date or whatever," she admitted, glancing at Axel, who was still at the front desk.

Tristyn followed her gaze. "With him?"

"No. I mean he was there. Kind of. He stayed in the vehicle."

"He stayed in the vehicle?" Tristyn repeated, his brow furrowing. "Why?"

"It's rather complicated."

"You are incredibly vague and hard to get information out of," Tristyn remarked, steepling a finger along his temple as he watched her.

"What information are you trying to get out of me?"

"At the risk of sounding even more forward, I am trying to work out if you are with someone," he answered, that grin kicking up again.

"You are asking if I am Selected or bound to someone?"

He frowned. "No, Tessa. I am asking if you are involved with anyone. In a relationship. There is no union Mark or other symbol of commitment…"

He trailed off, and Tessa dropped her gaze. A mortal wouldn't understand the Source Marks, so it made sense he didn't recognize the one that marked her skin. "I am not involved with anyone, but—"

"You are going to tell me no before I even get to ask? That is mighty presumptuous of you," Tristyn said, leaning in a little closer and a mischievous smile growing.

She smirked at him, enjoying their banter, but before she could open her mouth to say something in reply, Theon's voice drifted to her.

"This looks cozy."

Tessa lurched back from Tristyn, her eyes flying up to meet emerald ones as she shot to her feet and nearly tripped in her heels. Luka and Axel flanked Theon on either side, their arms crossed over their chests as the three of them stared at the man still seated on the sofa.

"Ah," Tristyn said, rising casually to his feet. He was obviously unconcerned with the fact he was a mortal and they were Legacy, and Tessa couldn't help but wonder if he knew he was speaking to the Arius Heir. "This must be the 'but' part of your statement."

Tessa swallowed hard as Theon's stare slid to her. "Don't go quiet now, Tessalyn," he bit out. "You were quite chatty a few moments ago."

She shook her head, not daring to glance at Tristyn.

"We were just talking," Tristyn said, his hands sliding into his pockets as he rocked back on his heels. "Nothing more."

"Tessa," Theon said tightly.

She took a deep breath before turning to Tristyn, finding concern etched into his warm russet eyes. "It was nice to meet you, Tristyn. Have a good night."

She turned to walk toward the elevators, but a light grip on her elbow had her pausing. More than that, the touch had the cord in her thrashing because it wasn't Theon who was gently holding her in place. His gaze darted to the three Legacy before settling back on her. "Are you all right, Tessa?"

And oh gods, what it did to her to have someone actually *care* about her wellbeing just because he was a decent person had her blinking back tears. He wasn't asking to ensure that she was in prime condition. He was asking because he was genuinely concerned for her. A complete stranger that she had only met a few minutes before cared simply because she was breathing, and not because of a dormant power he would one day be able to tap into.

The possessive rumble that came from Theon had her swallowing down all that emotion as she brought her fingers up to gently brush across Tristyn's hand on her elbow. She forced her voice not to tremble as she replied lightly, "That's kind of you, Tristyn, but yes. I am fine. They are simply a little...protective."

Theon pulled her from Tristyn's grip, his arm sliding around her waist and tugging her into his side. She could tell from Tristyn's face he didn't believe her, and he stepped forward again, reaching for her hand.

"Touch her again, and you will find out just how *protective* we are," Theon said darkly, and Tessa looked up to find shadows wisping across his eyes.

Tristyn took a step back, his features losing the playful nature she'd experienced moments ago.

"I assure you, Tristyn, I am fine," Tessa said, and Theon's fingers dug into her waist. "Have a good night." She looked up at Theon, biting her bottom lip nervously.

He spun her so her chest was pressing against his, and his hand came up to her face, his thumb pulling her lip from her teeth. "We have so much to discuss, beautiful," he ground out.

"So I've been told," she answered tightly.

His gaze dipped to her lips. "So mouthy tonight," he murmured.

"So possessive without Felicity to talk to," she crooned back.

"You have no idea how possessive I can be, Tessa."

"I think she has a pretty good idea," Axel murmured from behind them.

Theon turned to him incredulously. "Are you trying to get me to punch you tonight?"

Axel shrugged, unfazed. "I am simply saying the entertainment you two have provided in the last half hour has been better than the Chaosphere game, and that was an epic game. I have missed this. Can we go back to it?"

"Axel," Theon growled in warning.

"No, I'm with him," Tessa interrupted. "Do I get a vote?"

"No," Theon snapped, whipping his head back to her. "You need to stop talking. That mouth of yours has gotten you into enough trouble this evening."

"Weird. I hardly said anything for almost *four hours*," Tessa drawled.

"Tessa!" Theon barked. "By Arius, what is wrong with you tonight?"

"You two are causing a scene," Luka interrupted, and Theon seemed to suddenly remember they were indeed standing in a public hotel lobby. Tristyn was looking back and forth between them, a slight smirk on his lips as he observed their exchange.

Theon started leading her to the elevators, and Tessa couldn't help herself. She knew it was a bad move, impulsive one might say, but she looked back over her shoulder, her gaze connecting with Tristyn's. She winked at him. "Older brothers, am I right?" she said with an eye roll and a jerk of her thumb at the three Legacy. "Maybe I'll see you around, Tristyn."

"Do you have a death wish?" This time it was Luka chastising her as Axel's brows rose in utter shock.

Tristyn visibly relaxed, and that flirty grin from earlier returned. "I'm staying here for a few more days. Room 608," he called after them.

Theon turned to say something to him as the private elevator opened, but Luka and Axel both pushed him inside. Tessa stepped from Theon's grip, leaning against the back of the elevator wall, and as soon as the doors closed, Theon rounded on her. And because she was apparently all out of fucks to give, Tessa smirked up at him.

"I kind of wish we had snacks for this show," she heard Axel mutter to Luka from where they stood against one side of the elevator.

"For the love of the gods, stop talking, Axel," Theon spat.

"Perhaps you should sleep on everything that has happened tonight, and deal with it in the morning, Theon," Luka cut in, shooting a pointed look at Tessa. She read the warning in it, the order to stand down, and she huffed, crossing her arms over her chest.

The elevator doors opened with a soft ding, and Theon stepped to the side to let her pass, never taking his eyes from her. As soon as they entered the suite, Theon strode straight for the liquor in the minibar.

"Go to bed, Tessa. I will deal with you in the morning."

Deal with her.

Such a hassle.

Such an inconvenience.

"Sure thing, *brother*," she retorted, spinning on her heel to retreat to the primary bedroom.

"Good gods, Tessa. You *do* have a death wish tonight, don't you?" Axel barked, his tone somewhere between shocked and amused.

Tessa let out her own humorless laugh. "Compared to these last few weeks, death would be a welcome reprieve at this point."

"You don't mean that, Tessa," Theon said, plopping his drink down and stalking towards her, but Luka grabbed his arm, holding him back.

"Do not push her anymore tonight, Theon."

Theon turned to him incredulously. "Are you seriously telling *me* not to push *her* any more tonight?"

"I have been warning you about this from the very beginning," Luka retorted. "Let her go tonight."

"She is not your Source. This is not your call to make."

"Deal with it in the morning, Theon," Luka insisted, not letting go of his arm.

Theon's gaze drifted back to where she stood, and she couldn't read the look that passed over his features. "Did you mean that, Tessa?" he demanded.

She pursed her lips, breaking his gaze, and glancing from Axel to Luka. They were all looking at her expectantly.

"These last few weeks have been what I imagine the Pits of Torment to be like. Pure and utter agony, and you do not seem to care as long as I am obedient and behave properly. Have I thought death might be a kinder option a time or two? Yes. When I was experiencing the pain from the first Mark or the torture of the assessment today, did I wish for death to finally claim me and just put me out of my fucking misery? I'd be lying if I said no. But not even death wants me, even when handed to her willingly."

Silence rang in the room, and it was Axel who spoke first. His eyes were wide in disbelief, and he stumbled over his words in a way she had never heard before when he said, "Tessa, are you saying… Have you tried to— In the past…"

He trailed off when Tessa held his gaze, her lips pressed together in a tight line. It was answer enough for tonight. They didn't get to have her secrets. They didn't get to have her past.

"I have done nothing but try to care for you, Tessa," Theon said, his tone too calm and even. Too forced. "If you would just accept this fate, you wouldn't… I wish I could figure out how to make you understand that acceptance of this would take care of all of this."

All of this.

What did that even mean?

But there it was. She'd laid it all out there. All but told him she would rather death come for her than live out the life fate had dealt her.

And he'd come back to the fucking bond and her unwillingness to accept it.

A soft, broken laugh of disbelief came from her as she whispered, "Good night."

As she was shutting the door to the primary bedroom, she heard Luka's voice carry to her down the short hall. "I told you this was going to bite you in the ass."

Tessa paused to listen.

"I don't know what got into her tonight," she heard Theon reply, his voice thick and tired sounding. "I thought she was getting closer to accepting this. She's been seeking me out all day, needing the bond, and then it's like a fucking switch flipped."

That had been part of the plan, though. Sure, the bond had been soothing and comforting to her, but she had also wanted Theon to think she was starting to accept it. Because maybe if he thought that, he'd put a little more trust in her and give her a little more freedom.

And she planned to use that extra freedom to get down to the lobby and get her bottle of *agaveheart*, especially after how the night had played out since they'd left the restaurant.

"I warned you she would not be the same," came Axel's voice. "Not after the way we've been trying to force her to accept this."

"What would you have me do?" Theon snapped.

"Let's sleep on it," Luka said again. "Give her some space for a little while. We'll all get some sleep, and maybe things will be…better in the morning."

Doubtful.

26

TESSA

It had to be over an hour later when she finally heard the door to the bedroom open. Tessa had been starting to worry she was going to fall asleep and miss out on her *agaveheart* all together. She had been close to getting up to see if Theon had ended up sleeping out in the sitting room, but that was highly unlikely, especially with them not in his suite at Arius House. And if he saw her up, she could only assume another round of verbal sparring would ensue, and her *agaveheart* dreams would be gone.

She focused on keeping her breathing even, not wanting him to know she was still awake. She heard him sigh and felt the air stir as he stopped near her. Then she felt his thumb brush lightly over her bottom lip, and she couldn't help the shiver that raced down her spine.

"Even in sleep you react to the bond," he murmured, brushing his thumb along her lip again. "What am I going to do with you, little storm?"

His fingertips brushed down her bare arm as he moved away from her and began getting ready for bed. She felt the mattress dip when he climbed in, and she could have sighed in relief when he didn't tug her back against his chest for once. All he did was trail his fingers down her spine before he settled in and got comfortable. It took a while before his breathing evened out and for her to know he was in a deep enough sleep to even attempt this. If she got caught sneaking out of this room... Well, it couldn't be much worse than it already was, right?

Carefully, she slipped from the bed and padded barefoot to the door. She had dug out a pair of leggings and tank top from the clothing that had been delivered, and Luka, bless his soul, had also gotten her a pair of flip-flops. She was already chilly as she pushed her feet into them, but she didn't want to wear Theon's shirt that he still left out for her every night. She wanted nothing to do with him at this point, and she ignored the small jolt the bond gave her for that thought, gritting her teeth in annoyance.

As quietly as she could, she eased the door open, and the sound of the television greeted her. Shit. If Luka or Axel were still awake, there was no way this was going to work. The door that led to the other suite across the hall was closed, so it appeared at least one of them was in bed. She crept down the small hall. If someone asked, she'd say she was coming to get some water.

Slowly peeking around the corner, she found Axel sprawled across the sofa. He had apparently fallen asleep while watching Chaosphere highlights. Suddenly, the television being on was a blessing. It would cover the sound of her movements. She wasn't worried about getting back to the room. She knew he'd find her soon enough.

She slipped silently out the door. Letting out a breath of relief, she practically ran to the elevator, and the grin that spread across her face when the doors slid shut was one of manic delight. She didn't know how long this would last. She could already feel the bond stretching and panicking, but she was going to enjoy every second of freedom.

When she stepped off the elevator, she made her way directly to the front desk. The concierge eyed her, but also knowing she was the Source of the Arius Heir, he handed the *agaveheart* over reluctantly. Tessa immediately opened it and drank down what had to be three or four shots. The alcohol warmed its way down to her belly, and she strolled casually over to the main doors, the world suddenly a little brighter. Or darker? It was night, after all. Light. Dark. Didn't matter. Nothing mattered as she downed another shot. It was all the same to her.

There wasn't a doorman at this hour, so she let herself out and breathed in the cool night air. Goosebumps pebbled her skin, but she hardly noticed. For these few precious moments, she was going to pretend she was free. She was going to pretend she wasn't some possession owned by a descendant of the god of endings. That she was free to speak to whomever she wished. That she was free to eat whatever she wanted. Wear whatever she wanted. Fuck whoever she wanted. That she wasn't an inconvenience to anyone or a hassle too wild and uncontrollable to deal with.

She snorted a laugh that became a ridiculous giggle, but not as ridiculous as the thought of all these fucking Legacy thinking they were superior. Descendants of the gods? How far back would they have to trace their bloodlines to even come close to one of the gods? They were probably more closely related to the mortals. The original Legacy were half-god, half-mortal anyway. The Legacy fancied themselves gods in Devram, when in reality? They had a fraction of the power they descended from, even if they did strategically arrange Matches to strengthen bloodlines.

"You've taken to drinking outside the hotel lobby now? Can your *brothers* not find you out here?"

Tessa nearly choked on the shot she had just sucked from the bottle. She turned to find Tristyn off to the side, leaning against a wall and puffing on a cigarette. He still wore the same jeans and shirt, although he'd added a jacket to his attire.

"Oh, he will definitely find me out here," she answered with a flirty smile, sidling up to him.

He took another toke off the cigarette and smiled down at her knowingly. "They're not your brothers."

Her smile faltered. "No, they're not."

"Are you okay? They're not...assaulting you or anything? Right?" Tristyn asked, watching her carefully.

"Oh gods, no," Tessa replied, her eyes widening. "I'm fine. I swear. It's...complicated." She didn't particularly feel like explaining the inner workings of the Legacy society to a mortal at the moment.

"It seems more than complicated," he said, holding the cigarette out to her. She took it with a coy smile.

"I don't smoke," she said, pinching it between her fingers and holding it away from her body.

"It's lull-leaf," he said by way of explanation. "Completely natural and calms anxiety."

"Are you saying I appear anxious?" she asked, studying the roll in her hand. Then she shrugged and took a long drag, blowing the smoke out into the night because fuck it at this point. She didn't care about anything anymore.

"Things seemed pretty intense with them," Tristyn said.

"I guess you could say they are charged with my safety."

"Like bodyguards?" he asked, arching a brow as he took the lull-leaf back from her.

"Something like that."

He leaned forward, tucking stray hair behind her ear. "Makes sense. You are definitely important enough to need three bodyguards."

She huffed a laugh. "I am the farthest thing from important."

He hummed in contemplation before asking, "Are you with any of them?"

"One wants to be, but no. I'm not," she answered, taking another drink from the *agaveheart* bottle. "Do you think they're still making food in the kitchens here?"

"Probably not," Tristyn said with a shrug. "You hungry, wild fury?"

Her brows knitted. "Wild fury?"

He winked at her. "I did witness that entire exchange in the lobby. He was pissed. You, however, were full of fury, and wild enough to push him even further."

Tessa felt her face heat and was suddenly grateful for the darkness surrounding them. "I can be impulsive," she murmured, crossing her arms tightly, suddenly cold. The *agaveheart* bottle dangled from her fingertips.

"Nothing wrong with a little chaos," he said with another shrug.

"Most would disagree with you."

"I'm not most."

She cleared her throat. "Well, I'm currently drinking my dinner, so food wouldn't hurt," she said, tipping the liquor bottle his way in a salute.

"I bet we could get a pizza delivered."

"You think so?"

He shrugged again. "I can go check with the front desk."

"You just might be an angel, Tristyn."

"Definitely not," he snickered as he turned to head into the lobby. "You coming in with me or...?"

"Actually, while you're doing that, could I borrow your phone to make a quick call? I left mine upstairs," she added hastily.

"Sure, but if you're staying out here, you should take this, too," he said, shrugging off his jacket.

"The *agaveheart* is keeping me plenty warm."

He huffed a laugh. "I'm sure it is, but it is brisk out here." He held the jacket out to her, and she took it with a nod of thanks. After she'd maneuvered it on, he unlocked his phone and handed it to her. "Don't run off with this," he said with a half-grin.

"I wouldn't dream of it," she returned. "You've been far too kind to me today."

She could just make out his slight frown. "All I've done is talk to you and share some lull-leaf."

"And you're about to get me pizza."

"That's basic decency."

"One would think," she muttered.

"I'll be right back," he said, slowly backing away from her.

"I'll be right here."

With a last look, he turned and quickly jogged up the steps back into the hotel. When the doors had closed behind him, she looked down at the unlocked phone, marveling at another small freedom she'd managed to steal. She quickly dialed one of the two numbers she knew by heart.

As it was ringing, she wandered over to a small bench and sat down, taking another swallow of *agaveheart*. She was feeling all sorts of happy now. The lull-leaf had more than relaxed her, and if she weren't positive Theon would likely find her within the next hour, she may have even entertained heading up to Tristyn's room with him if he hinted at the prospect.

The line picked up on the other end, pulling her from her thoughts.

"Hello? Who is this?" the male voice on the other end demanded.

Her voice caught in her throat, and she swallowed down the tears that were threatening to pool.

"You're a real dick to be calling at this hour—"

"Brecken?" she choked out. "Brecken, it's me."

Silence greeted her for a few long seconds before he said, "Say it again."

A small laugh escaped her. "It's me, Brecken, but I don't have a lot of time. Is Dex—"

"Tessa?" Dex's voice came down the line, and the tears she'd been fighting spilled over.

"I miss you so much," she whispered.

"Tessa, where are you? Are you okay? I can't believe he let you call us."

He was speaking so fast, and Tessa had to cut him off.

"I'm in Rockmoor, but only for a few more hours. I persuaded a mortal to let me borrow his phone for a minute. Theon doesn't know I'm calling."

"Are you going to get in trouble if you get caught?"

"Definitely," she confirmed. "But I am well on my way to being too drunk to care right now."

There was a long pause before he said, "Tessa, are you okay?"

"I had to do an assessment today," she informed him, her voice slurring slightly. "In a Level Five room."

"Fuck," Dex hissed. "Gods, Tessa. I'm so sorry that we—that I—can't be there with you right now. What happened?"

"It was bad, Dex," she answered, her tone softer as the memories crept up on her. "They had me believing you were all killed. They think I somehow hid my true abilities in all my previous assessments."

"You couldn't hide your abilities."

"I know. I tried to tell them that, but..." She shrugged even though he couldn't see her.

There was another beat of silence. "I'm sorry, Tessie. I'm so fucking sorry."

"What do you have to be sorry for? It's not you who Selected me and forced me into a life of being invisible except for when I'm needed for my power," she replied bitterly.

"Is he... Is he at least treating you all right? Is he taking care of you?"

Tessa snorted a laugh. "He controls everything, Dex. What I eat. What I wear. Where I sleep."

"Does he hurt you?"

"Physically? No. Mentally and emotionally?" She swallowed thickly as she fought off another bout of tears. "I'm not okay, Dex," she finally whispered.

"A little over a week," he said, his tone slightly desperate. "A little over a week, and we can see you. I need you to hang on just a little longer. I'll be there. I'll fix this for you. We can—"

"He won't let me be with you, Dex. He has it in his head that we're involved. He doesn't believe that we have never been that," she replied, trying to keep the panic from her tone. "He just..."

"He what, Tessa?"

She sighed. "He's convinced that once I give in completely to the Source bond, everything will be better. That I will want what he wants and—"

"You've been fighting the Source bond?" Dex interrupted.

"I've tried to give into it, but I can't, Dex. No matter how hard it tugs at me. No matter how much it strains and pulls me in that direction. I just can't, and gods, I wish I could. It's just one more thing that makes me too much of an inconvenience."

Tears were coursing down her cheeks again. She wiped them hastily away, brushing her fingers on her leggings.

"We will find a way, Tessie. We will find a way to talk and see each other. I promise," Dex said, his tone telling her just how determined he was to make that happen. She knew it was unlikely, but she didn't want to talk about that right now.

"There's really no way for you to get in touch with me until the Acropolis," she replied. "He got me a phone, but he monitors everything on it."

"We'll figure it out," he repeated.

Tristyn came into her line of vision, and she gave him a small smile. "I have to go."

"I'll see you soon, Tessie."

"Tell the others I miss them."

"I will. We'll figure it out. Just hang in there until I can get to you and fix all this."

"You can't fix this."

"Just hang in there a little longer," he repeated. "I'll see you soon, Tessie."

"Bye."

She cut the call, knowing if she didn't do it right away, she'd stay on the phone with him until Theon came and dragged her kicking and screaming back to the suite to punish her somehow. She wordlessly handed the phone back to Tristyn.

"You all right?" he asked, sliding it into his pocket before he sat down on the bench beside her.

"Yes," she answered quickly, swiping at her cheeks again. "That was a friend I haven't seen in a while."

"I'm glad you were able to talk then," Tristyn replied. He reached over and dug into the pocket of his jacket, extracting two more rolls. "You look like you need another."

"Do you always carry these around with you?" Tessa asked as she took one.

"No. Only when I know I'll be needing them. I'm in town on business and had a rather stressful day," Tristyn replied, reaching over with a lighter. "Pizza should be here shortly. They weren't very busy at this hour."

"I don't have any way to pay for my half," Tessa said, her cheeks flushing again at the admission.

"Don't worry, fury. I got it," he answered, settling back against the bench and blowing out a puff of smoke. "I hope you like pepperoni."

"Who doesn't like pepperoni pizza?"

He chuckled. "I figured it was a safe bet."

She held out the *agaveheart* to him. "You're buying me pizza and giving me lull-leaf. The least I can do is share my liquor."

He took it with a nod of thanks before taking a good pull from the bottle. "You're going to be hurting in the morning," he observed, holding the bottle up to see that it was nearly a third gone already.

She shrugged. "It'll be worth it."

"You had a rough day as well, I take it?" Tristyn asked, handing the bottle back to her.

"You could say that."

Silence fell between them, somehow comfortable.

It was a few minutes later when Tristyn said, "This probably isn't my place, but I'm going to say it anyway: It's okay not to be okay, Tessa."

"You don't know me, Tristyn," she said softly.

"Doesn't change what I just said."

The pizza arrived a few minutes later, and Tessa devoured her first slice. Tristyn held the box open to her so she could grab another, his first slice only half gone.

"Did you not eat at whatever function you were at?" he asked.

"You know how food can be at those things," she said, waving her hand dismissively, glad to have something to focus on after that phone call.

"Fair enough," Tristyn conceded, closing the pizza box. "What kind of function was it?"

She took a bite to give herself time to come up with a plausible lie. "A meet and greet for one of the males I'm with. He's pretty high up in his field. I was his plus one in a way."

"His plus one? You mean his date?"

"No, I wasn't his date. That was someone else. I was just there. In the background."

"In the background?" he repeated. "Are you telling me he took you with him while he was on a date with another?"

"Kind of. It's really hard to explain."

"I don't think you could provide me a good enough explanation in the end anyway," Tristyn said, reaching for the *agaveheart* bottle.

Tessa laughed as she opened the pizza box to get another slice. "And tell me, Tristyn…"

"Blackheart."

Tessa snorted a laugh. "That is not your surname."

"Swear to the Fates."

"Well, Tristyn Blackheart, what would an outing with you look like?"

"Pizza and *agaveheart*. Obviously."

She huffed another laugh. "Idiot."

"And if I wanted a proper date?"

Her smile fell. "That wouldn't be possible."

"Because of the bodyguards?"

"One in particular."

"The one who wants to be with you."

"Yes."

"But you don't want to be with him."

"No."

"Why?"

"Because—" She paused, trying to figure out where to even start. "It's complicated," she finally said.

"So I hear."

She could just make out his faint smirk.

"You could still give me your number. Just in case," he added.

Tessa stilled. She didn't even know the phone number that was connected to the phone Theon had given her.

"I'm leaving in a few hours, and you're not from here either," she said, forcing a bright smile to her face. "It's not like we could arrange such an outing anyway."

"Perhaps," he replied. "But we could talk. That's what phones are for, you know."

She laughed lightly. "This is rather embarrassing, but I just got a new phone and number, and I don't have it memorized," she admitted. "So you'll have to give me yours, and I'll text you from mine."

"I feel like you're giving me an excuse to not have to give me your number."

"I swear I'm not," she insisted, giving him a light shove in the shoulder. "I really don't know the phone number. I could make one up if you prefer?"

He barked a laugh, producing a business card from somewhere and handing it to her.

She couldn't read it in the dark, but she tucked it into the waistband of her leggings. They sat in silence for a few moments, then she asked, "What kind of business are you in Rockmoor for?"

"I'm on the board of a rather large company," Tristyn answered, reaching for another lull-leaf smoke from his jacket she was still wearing.

"As a mortal?" Then she realized how rude that was and quickly added, "Not that— Sorry."

"While admirable that you would apologize to a mortal, there is no need," Tristyn replied, lighting the lull-leaf and extending it to her.

"Do you get to go home after you're done in Rockmoor?" she asked, quickly changing the subject.

"I'll be going to the Acropolis, actually."

"No shit?" Tessa took a drag and exhaled. "I'll be leaving for the Acropolis in a few days."

"Really?" There was a heightened interest in his tone. He took the lull-leaf back. "How old are you anyway?"

A burst of laughter escaped her. "You've been drinking with me for the last hour. It's a little late to be concerned with age issues, isn't it?"

Tristyn chuckled under his breath. "I'm not worried about that at all."

"I'm twenty-three years. I'll be twenty-four after the spring equinox," Tessa answered. "You? You seem young to be on the board of a big company."

Not to mention he was mortal.

"When you are part of starting the company, they force you to be on the board," Tristyn replied, glancing at her sidelong.

But before she could reply, she felt the bond jump in anticipation. She'd been ignoring the thing, aided by the *agaveheart* consumption and the effects of the lull-leaf, but that excitement could only mean one thing: Theon was close. She straightened a little, sucking down a drag from the lull-leaf Tristyn had handed back to her.

"You started the entire company? That's impressive," she said, trying to keep her tone casual. Her eyes darted to the hotel doors.

"Depends on who you're asking," Tristyn replied.

"I think that's rather impressive no matter who you're asking," Tessa argued, bumping his leg with her own. "What kind of company is it?"

Tristyn was about to reply when he arrived.

She heard the lobby doors fly open.

She heard heavy footfalls on the steps.

She stared straight ahead, taking another toke of the lull-leaf.

He came to a stop a few feet away from her, directly in her line of sight.

It may have been night, but that was definitely darkness pooling around his feet and gathering around his arms. If she could see his eyes, she was certain they would be swirling with that darkness too.

She could feel Tristyn's eyes on her as she met Theon's gaze in the dark and puffed out the smoke she'd inhaled.

"What. The fuck. Are you doing?"

Theon's voice was low and dangerous and sent small tremors down her spine, but she smirked up at him. "I don't know why you're surprised. I told you what I really did when I said I went to the restroom at the restaurant. *Agaveheart*, remember?" She held up the now nearly half empty bottle of liquor before she took another pull from it.

"You are outside. In the dark. Drinking and smoking," he ground out from between his teeth with barely contained rage.

"And eating pizza. The horror." She cut in with mock dismay, taking the final drag from the lull-leaf before stubbing it out on the arm of the bench.

"With…" She saw his head turn so his focus was on Tristyn now. "*You.*"

Not wanting him to do anything to Tristyn, Tessa lurched to her feet. Which turned out to be a bad idea because she didn't realize just quite how much *agaveheart* she'd had to drink. Fae and Legacy metabolisms were much faster than mortals, so it took more to get them intoxicated. She'd clearly reached that threshold. Or maybe the lull-leaf added to everything. Either way, she stumbled, and Tristyn reached out to catch her before Theon could. Before she could thank him, she was ripped from his hands.

"What did I say about touching her again?" Theon snarled, holding Tessa tightly to his chest.

"We were just talking," she scoffed. "Relax."

"Relax? Did you seriously just tell me to *relax*?" Tessa couldn't help but tense at his soft tone. That tone scared her more than when he raised his voice. "I woke up to find you *gone*. I could tell you hadn't gone far, but the fact you were gone at all—"

"Clearly I'm fine," she replied, trying to push off of him.

"Clearly our definitions of 'fine' differ," he bit back.

"She's not lying," Tristyn cut in. "All we did was sit out here and talk while eating pizza and—"

"Smoking and drinking. Yes, I can see that," Theon snarled. "Are you aware she is a Fae in service to this kingdom?"

"I did not summon her to my side. I did not provide the alcohol to her," Tristyn retorted dismissively. There was no way he knew he was speaking to the Arius Heir. "She got that all by herself. Apparently she already told you how."

Tessa tried—and failed—to hide her smirk.

"I think it's best if you fuck off now," Theon growled, tightening his hold on Tessa. Then he jerked her back, looking down at her. "What are you wearing?"

Tessa looked down too, realizing she was still wearing Tristyn's coat. "Um, a jacket?"

"Take it off. Now."

He didn't even give her a chance to take it off herself before shoving it down her arms. Tessa caught it before it fell to the ground, holding it out to Tristyn with a small grin. "Thanks for letting me borrow it. And for the pizza and lull-leaf."

Tristyn took his jacket back, draping it over his arm. "I really should get going anyway. I have an early meeting. You good?" He gave a pointed look over her shoulder at Theon.

"I'm good. Thank you for the last hour. It was nice to…talk to someone," she admitted, and Theon's fingers on her tightened even more as he began tugging her towards the stairs.

"Night, fury," Tristyn called after her, and she offered him a little wave.

Theon didn't say a word, leading her to the private elevator. When the doors opened, he pulled her roughly in, and in her drunken state, she stumbled against the back wall, gripping the railing when the elevator began its ascent. She opened her mouth to say something snarky, but before a word could form on her tongue, Theon spoke first.

"Tessalyn, tell me everything that you have done since you left our bed. *Speak.*"

Her eyes flew wide at the unexpected entrancing, and words

tumbled from her mouth as she tried to work around the order the best she could. "I came downstairs and collected the *agaveheart* I had sent here. I went outside for fresh air, and Tristyn was out smoking. We started talking and shared lull-leaf and the *agaveheart*. I mentioned wanting pizza. He went and ordered some while I borrowed his phone. When he came back, we sat and talked until you showed up."

The elevator came to a stop, and the doors slid open. Before she could take a step to exit, Theon was in front of her, crowding her against the wall. "Before I address everything you just said, did he touch you?" His eyes were manic and desperate, dark wisps swirling among his irises while tendrils of dark shadows reached for her.

"No."

His entire body relaxed a fraction, and he slid a hand around to the back of her neck. He pushed her ahead of him, steering her towards their room. "Do not make a sound when we get inside. If you wake up Luka or Axel, you will be in even more trouble."

"I mean, does it really matter at this point?" she drawled.

The grip on her nape tightened as they came to their door. Theon reached around her, gripping the handle, but before he pushed the door open, she felt his breath on her ear. "I just want to make sure you are aware that had you accepted this godsdamn bond, I'd be finding a much better use for that mouth of yours tonight."

Tessa stilled, heat flooding through her at his words, but she scoffed, "Too bad you're not mortal. I'd show you all kinds of things with my mouth."

"Fuck me," she heard him mutter a moment before the door clicked open, and Theon pushed her forward. Axel was still sprawled across the sofa, the TV still on. Theon left her standing near the short hallway, plunking the half gone bottle of *agaveheart* onto the coffee table and grabbing a couple bottles of water.

When they were in the bedroom, he handed her one of the bottles. "Drink this. You are going to need it."

"I have a high tolerance," she bit back, taking the cap off the water anyway and taking a sip.

"I am gathering that, considering over half of that *agaveheart* was gone. Go shower," he added with a jerk of his chin towards the bathroom.

"What? Why?"

"Because I will not have you smelling like another male and certainly not like a *mortal*," he snarled. "So either go wash his scent from your skin, or I will do it for you." Tessa huffed under her breath as she turned to the bathroom, quickly knotting her hair up on the top of her head. "I'll bring you something to sleep in," he called after her.

She stripped down, burying Tristyn's business card in the bottom of her cosmetics bag before she climbed into the shower. Although fell into the shower was probably more accurate. She was definitely feeling all the *agaveheart* now. Perhaps the lull-leaf had been a terrible decision. An impulsive one.

She scrubbed herself down as quickly as she could, and when she climbed back out, she found Theon's long-sleeve thermal waiting for her. There weren't any bottoms of any kind to be found, and she grumbled as she slid his shirt over her head. It fell midway down her thighs, and she tossed her towel to the floor as she went back out to the bedroom, finishing off the bottle of water Theon had given her.

"I need pants," she demanded, tossing the empty bottle into the trash.

"They are being laundered. The front desk assured me they would be back in time for us to leave in the morning," Theon answered from the armchair he was sprawled in, his legs spread wide and a finger steepled along his temple as he studied her.

Tessa crossed her arms. "And undergarments?"

"Also being laundered. Luka neglected to order any extras when he purchased your clothing this afternoon."

"Are you serious?"

"Mhmm," he confirmed. "Come here."

"No," she scoffed.

"Tessa." Her name was laced with warning. "Come here, and we can speak about this."

"I can speak with you just fine from here."

"Tessalyn—"

"For the love of the gods," she grumbled, stalking over to him.

The moment she was close enough, he reached out, grabbing her bare thighs and pulling her between his legs. Looking up at her, he asked, "What, exactly, is the problem with your sleeping attire?"

"I'm not sleeping next to you in just a shirt, Theon," she replied, adamantly ignoring the sensations of his hands where his thumbs were making sweeping circles on the backs of her thighs.

"You're not?" he asked, pushing to his feet. His hands slid over her hips as he moved.

"No, I'm not," she insisted. "We need to figure something else out."

"Hmm," he hummed, reaching to take her hair out of the knot on her head. "There are no other options, Tessa. Luka is in the other bedroom, and Axel has commandeered the sofa so…"

"So nothing. It's not happening," she snapped, slapping his hand away as he began twining a lock of her now loose hair around his finger.

"You slept by me all afternoon in nothing but a robe," he pointed out.

"That was different."

"How was that different?"

"I needed you then. I needed something to block out the shit I was forced to endure today because I don't have access to the people and things who could actually help me deal with it."

Tessa slapped her hands over her mouth. She had not meant to say any of that, to reveal that much of her desperation.

"*Agaveheart* almost works better than entrancing," Theon said, his arm winding its way around her waist. "How did you deal with the assessments in the past?" She shook her head, refusing to give him any more of herself. "Tessa," he coaxed, stepping further into her and forcing her to take a step back. "I'm ready to hear all those secrets."

"I have nothing to say to you."

"You have nothing to say to me? Only to the mortal downstairs?" His nostrils flared when he brought up Tristyn, ire flashing in his eyes, but he seemed to push it back down just as quickly.

"He fed me pizza, so he automatically ranks higher than you on that action alone," she retorted, stepping back when he stepped forward again.

She felt a growl emanate from deep in his chest as he muttered, "This fucking mouth of yours is going to be the death of me."

"You sure seem obsessed with my mouth tonight."

"Beautiful, I'm constantly obsessing over your mouth. Over what's going to come out of it next. What it tastes like when you let me kiss you. What it would feel like around my cock," he replied, his gaze dipping to her lips as he spoke. She swallowed thickly as he moved into her again, and when she stepped back, the backs of her knees hit the bed. She hadn't even realized they'd moved this far across the room. A slow grin spread across Theon's face. His arm was still wrapped around her waist, and he leaned into her, forcing her back down onto the bed.

She tsked at him. "It's just the bond, Theon," she said, trying to ignore the feel of him as he pressed his body into hers.

"You say that a lot," he replied, reaching up and trailing his fingers down her cheek, her jaw. "I'm not entirely sure why you think that—"

"Because you didn't even know who I was a few weeks ago," she interrupted, slapping his hand away from her face. "You're telling me you suddenly care for me? Want me for more than a fuck? In that short amount of time? And it is not because of a bond?"

"Even if that were true, why would it bother you so much?" he pushed, his eyes searching hers.

"It's not real, Theon!"

"What makes you think it is not real? The bond did not simply create something out of nothing. It amplifies what is already there," Theon argued, his hips pressing down onto her own in a way that had her thoughts scattering. "Why do you think the other heirs spent the last few years building a relationship before they Selected their Sources? It was so the bond had something to build on."

"I don't understand," she rasped, not daring to move and cause more friction between them.

"The bond builds on what is already there," Theon said again, his power snaking along her bare thighs. "There was something instantaneous between us whether you want to admit to it or not, and the bond increases that desire. If you find you are seeking comfort from me, then the bond is building on something that is already there."

"I was seeking comfort from the bond, Theon, not you."

"And yet you said you needed *me*."

"Semantics."

"There is some part of you that already feels safe with me."

"You don't know what I'm feeling," Tessa bit back.

"You are right. I don't," Theon answered, his fingertips running delicately along her cheekbone again. "That is, admittedly, the Mark I am most looking forward to you receiving. I want to know what you are feeling when you shut down and refuse to tell me." Tessa tensed beneath him. "Like that right there. Why did you do that?"

"Because I don't want you knowing what I'm feeling all the time or what I'm thinking. Just like I don't like you knowing where I am all the time," she retorted. "I don't like needing you. I *don't* need you."

"You are telling me this entire day, you saying you needed me, initiating all the physical contact, the compliant nature, all of that was an act?" he demanded.

A sneer curled up on her lip. "Yes. I knew if you thought I was starting to embrace the bond, you would let your guard down a bit. I could tell it was working when you let me go to the restroom by myself at dinner, so I ordered the *agaveheart* to be sent here."

"Because you deal with the assessments by getting drunk?"

"I deal with assessments by getting drunk and fucking mortals to make me forget everything I had to endure," she spat back.

"What did you experience today, Tessa? Aside from the physical pain?" Theon's tone had softened some, his emerald eyes watching her intently.

She shook her head. "I may be drunk and telling you way more than I ever planned to share with you, but I won't be giving you any more pieces of my soul tonight."

He cocked his head to the side, a smirk tipping up on the corner of his mouth. "Would you like me to distract you in other ways?" His hand dropped to her thigh, and his fingers began trailing through his shadows. "You claim this entire day was a ruse, but I bet your body says otherwise. Tell me, beautiful, will I find you soaked and ready for me?"

"Does it matter? Did you suddenly become mortal while I was out fraternizing with one?" she ground out.

"A mortal is never going to touch you again," Theon snarled, his hand stilling. "I've told you this." Tessa rolled her eyes, and he gripped her jaw, forcing her to look at him. "No one else will ever touch you in such a way again, Tessa. No one."

"Then I guess it'll be me and my own hand for the rest of my miserable life, Theon. Because if you think you'll ever fulfill such needs for me, you can go fuck yourself," she spewed, and the bond shot a jolt through her body that had her arching into him and wincing at the pain.

Theon stared at her, seeming to search for something in her eyes. "Little storm," he sighed.

"Don't call me that," she sneered.

"Is this life really so bad? To be cared for? All your needs provided? Do you truly hate the three of us that much?"

"I don't feel the need to respond to that. The fact that I made such an elaborate plan to sneak out and get drunk to get away from all of you should be clue enough. The fact that if I hadn't known you'd come for me in less than an hour, I would have absolutely gone to Tristyn's room with him should be answer enough," she retorted.

Theon's hand came down beside her head, slamming into the mattress, and Tessa froze, her eyes widening. "I have been incredibly patient with you tonight, but if you make one more reference to anyone else touching you, you will not like the consequences."

She clenched her jaw, forcing herself to hold her tongue. She was suddenly too tired to fight anymore. For a brief hour, she didn't have to pretend to be something she wasn't. Trying to force herself back into that role now was too exhausting, and she had nothing left.

"Can we call a truce for tonight and continue this verbal sparring match in the morning?" Theon finally asked. "We need to be up in a few hours, and you are not going to be feeling well."

"Hopefully I'll still be drunk," she muttered under her breath. Theon pushed off of her, grabbing her hand and tugging her to her feet. He began leading her around the side of the bed, and Tessa stumbled as the room spun around her. He steadied her before he pulled the blankets back.

"I'm still not sleeping next to you in just a shirt," she insisted.

"I hear you, Tessa," Theon replied, gently pushing her down so she sat on the edge of the bed. "I will sleep in the armchair." He lifted her legs up into the bed.

"You will? Why?"

He helped her lie down before leaning over her, his face hovering inches from hers. "Because despite what you seem to have convinced yourself of, it is more than a bond, Tessa." He brushed a soft kiss to her cheek before pulling the sheets and comforter over her.

She watched him cross the room and lower himself into the armchair, stretching his legs out in front of him. With a huff, she rolled over so she wouldn't have to look at him, and she prayed the *agaveheart* and lull-leaf would be enough to keep her nightmares at bay.

27
TESSA

Tessa woke to the blankets being ripped off her as Theon said far too loudly, "Rise and shine. We need to go."

She pulled the pillow over her head and tugged her legs up to her chest, curling in on herself. Theon's shirt bunched around her thighs, and she groaned as she realized she had no pants or underwear on and now no blankets.

"Tessa, get up," Theon said again, and she heard him moving around the room. Something bounced on the bed, and she peeked out from under the pillow to see a bottle of water lying beside her.

How long had she been sleeping? It couldn't have been that long. She was pretty sure she was still somewhat drunk. She pushed herself up into a sitting position, and the room tilted. Definitely still drunk. Grabbing the bottle of water, she twisted off the cap, taking a big gulp.

Theon came out of the bathroom. He was in jeans and a long-sleeve thermal. He started to say something, but stopped when his eyes landed on her sitting in the middle of the bed. His gaze roamed over her, and she glared at him, twisting the cap back on the water bottle.

"I need clothes," she rasped, her mouth too dry.

"I was just going to get them," he answered, crossing to his bag and stuffing the clothing he held inside. "I did not expect you to be awake yet."

"You woke me up."

"Yes, but you drank half a bottle of *agaveheart*. I thought it would be more difficult to rouse you," he replied, zipping the bag shut.

"I didn't drink half the bottle," she retorted with an eye roll. "Tristyn drank some of that."

He stiffened at the mention of Tristyn and yanked the duffel bag off the small table. "I packed all your things other than your toothbrush. It is in the bathroom," he said tightly. "I will be back with your clothing."

He wrenched the door open and stalked through while Tessa took another drink of water. Glancing at the clock, she found she'd been right. She'd only slept for two hours...which meant even as a Fae, there was still plenty of alcohol in her system.

She groaned when she pushed to her feet, steadying herself against the bed. Her stomach lurched. She usually slept through this part of the hangover.

Making her way unsteadily to the bathroom, she brushed her teeth and pulled her hair into a messy bun on top of her head. She splashed some water onto her face, trying to wake herself up, but it was no use. She was supposed to be passed out right now. She wasn't supposed to be feeling anything. Instead, she was feeling *everything*. She was picturing all that she'd been forced to endure at the assessment yesterday. Dagian telling her Corbin and Oralia and Dex were dead, tortured because of her.

Not real, she reminded herself, gripping the edge of the counter, the water continuing to run into the drain. *None of what you saw was real.*

But she could feel it.

She could feel each bolt of power as it raced through her body. She could hear Dagian laughing as he told her he'd killed Dex the same way. She could taste the vomit and blood in her mouth, despite having just brushed her teeth.

Not real, she told herself over and over. *You talked to Dex a few hours ago. He's alive. They all are.*

"Tessa?"

Theon's voice carried in to her from the main room, and she straightened, turning off the faucet.

"I'm coming," she called back, but her voice held a touch of emotion she couldn't hide.

He appeared in the doorway, her leggings in his hand. "Are you all right?"

Not trusting herself to speak again, she nodded, still gripping the counter. He tossed the clothing onto the vanity.

"Get dressed," was all he said before turning and walking out of the bathroom.

She glared at his back as she reached for the clothes. He clearly assumed she was in this state solely from the alcohol, that she'd brought this on herself.

She slid on the black underthings, but she couldn't get the images out of her mind. She couldn't get Dagian's laughter to stop ringing in her ears, couldn't get the taste of blood out of her mouth.

But *agaveheart* could.

Agaveheart could get that taste out of her mouth and drive everything she was feeling back into oblivion. She could sleep in the vehicle. She could sleep the entire day away.

She made her way out of the bathroom, not bothering with the leggings. She'd come put them on once she had that bottle back in her hand.

"Theon?" she heard Axel call out, but she was zeroed in on the liquor bottle on the table where Theon had set it a few hours ago. With a grin of victory, she scooped it up. But before she could bring it to her lips, it was yanked from her grip.

"What the fuck are you doing?" Theon demanded, holding the bottle out of her reach.

"I just needed a drink," she bit back.

"What you need to do is go put on fucking pants. You drank plenty last night."

"Hold on," Axel cut in. "*She* brought the *agaveheart* here last night? I was wondering who drank without me."

"I do not know why this is such a surprise to everyone," Tessa replied. "I told all of you on the way here that I bribed the hostess to send a bottle to the hotel last night."

"None of us thought you were serious," Theon said, handing the bottle off to Axel and gripping her arm.

"Why? I'm not supposed to lie to you, remember?" she retorted.

Axel was holding the bottle up, peering at the liquid. "You really drank all of this after we went to sleep? That was only a few hours ago."

"I didn't drink *all* of it," Tessa said. "I shared with Tristyn."

"I think this is a story we all need to hear," came Luka's voice from the hallway.

"There is nothing to tell," Theon ground out. He was clenching his jaw so hard, Tessa thought he might crack a molar. "I woke up to find her gone from the room. When I finally tracked her down, she was sitting outside with the mortal from the lobby, smoking, drinking her weight in *agaveheart*, and eating pizza."

"How did you get out of the hotel room?" Axel asked, peering at Tessa now. "It's warded."

"I walked on my own two feet." Then she looked up at Theon with a smirk. "And the *mortal's* name is Tristyn."

"Gods, Tessa," Luka muttered, running a hand down his face. He muttered something about it "being too early to deal with this shit," then he looked at Theon, who was clenching and unclenching his free hand. "Are you going to heal her hangover?"

"You can do that?" she gasped, looking back at Theon.

"I can," he said. "But I feel more inclined to make you suffer through it."

"She will probably vomit in the vehicle," Axel pointed out.

"I will deal with it eventually," he replied. He met her gaze then, and a smirk of his own crossed his lips. "But right now, she still has quite a bit of alcohol in her system. She's quite the talker when she has been drinking, and I need to know who she called when she borrowed the *mortal's* phone last night."

Tessa's eyes widened. She forgot she'd told him she'd done that. Godsdamnit.

"But first, she needs to go put on pants," he said, tugging her back to the bedroom once more. He marched her straight into the bathroom and stood watch while she pulled the leggings up her legs, then he tossed the flip-flops at her feet.

He didn't say another word to her as he led her from the room, stopping only to grab a bag from the floor near the door and slipping the strap over his shoulder. His hold on Tessa's hand didn't lessen as the elevator descended, and when they stepped into the lobby, he pulled her closer to his side. The concierge met them at the doors, handing a paper bag to Axel.

Tessa had just stepped off the last step when she was pressed up against the outside of the building, Theon's mouth crashing into hers. She was so caught off guard, she found herself kissing him back before she could get her defenses up against the bond. His tongue swept in, clashing with her own, and his hands slipped under the hem of his shirt she still wore as her own hands slid up his muscled stomach and chest. She'd been chilled when they'd stepped into the morning air, but not anymore. Heat flooded through her, and she arched into him. The need to drown in pleasure came rushing back in full force.

He pulled back as suddenly as he'd started, a wicked tilt to his lips. She stared up at him, her breaths coming far too fast and her thoughts a complete and utter mess.

"Not just in the background today, are you, fury?"

Tessa jerked around to find Tristyn standing several feet away, his eyes on her and Theon, and she understood. Theon had never kissed her so thoroughly in front of others, not even Axel or Luka. But this morning? He had a claim to stake.

Theon was still smirking like a jackass as the valet pulled their vehicle to the curb.

"Don't let him fool you," she called back to Tristyn. "He just doesn't want anyone else touching."

"So he doesn't want you, but he doesn't want anyone else to have you?" Tristyn asked, his head tilting with the question.

"You got it," she tossed back with a wink before she moved to climb into the back of the vehicle. "See you around, Tris."

"Looking forward to it, Tessa," he called after her.

She slid all the way across the backseat and could feel the tension radiating off Theon as he snapped the door shut. She bit her lip when she met his stare. His entire body was taut and practically trembling with rage. Maybe she'd finally pushed him too far.

Did she care?

She probably should, but try as she might, she couldn't muster up an ounce of fear or panic or anything really as she stared back at him.

Luka and Axel were just as tense in the front seat, and Axel kept glancing back at them nervously while Luka pulled the vehicle onto the road.

After several minutes of utter silence, Axel slowly ventured, "Theon?"

"Fine," Theon hissed from between his teeth. "I am fine." Tessa snorted, leaning against the window, and his head whipped to her. "Who did you call, Tessa?"

She pressed her lips together, turning to look out the window. They were still deep in the city, and it would be a good hour to get out, even with little traffic.

"Do not make me force you," he said. "You will tell me one way or another."

Still she said nothing.

"Tessa, after last night and this morning, you really should not push him right now," Luka warned, glancing at her in the rearview mirror.

"You should mind your own business," she retorted, crossing her arms. "You all should."

"*You* are my business, Tessa," Theon snarled. She hadn't realized he had slid across the seat. He gripped her chin, forcing her to meet his gaze. "Everything you do is my business. Who you speak to is my business. Who touches you is my business."

"That's just it, Theon," she sneered. "It isn't. None of it is your gods-damn business."

That hand gripping her chin slipped to her throat, jerking her forward so her lips met his again. The kiss was hard and punishing, and fire flooded through her veins. Her hands slipped into his hair, and she tugged hard. Theon let out a growl in response, and he pulled back. Anger radiated in his emerald eyes, but lust emanated even more.

"Why do you think it is appropriate to keep kissing me this morning?" she breathed.

"Why do you think you can continue to be mouthy without consequences?" he countered, an arm snaking around her back and tugging her down the seat so she was lying beneath him.

"We are not alone, Theon," she rasped.

Between the buzz of the alcohol and the sensations of his body pressing into hers, her head was spinning. She was trying, and failing miserably, to keep her wits about her. The bond certainly wasn't helping as it drank in the contact.

"Mmm," he hummed against her skin, sliding his lips to her neck. "They are wisely keeping silent and pretending they are not watching." He dragged his mouth up to her ear, where he whispered, "But they are definitely watching, Tessa. Make no mistake."

Then his lips were slowly trailing back down the column of her throat, but that wasn't what made her gasp. His magic pressed against her skin, cold and dark. His presence was everywhere at once, and oh gods, she couldn't think straight. The bond reached for him. She was sure she could actually see the silver cord straining towards him as all the sensations overwhelmed her.

"Who did you call, Tessa?" he murmured, his lips coming back up to trail along her jaw. His shadows trailed up her thighs, under his shirt she still wore. "Tell me," he pushed. "Or Luka and Axel are going to get quite the show. Who did you call?"

"Dex," she gasped, but his darkness didn't pull back.

No, it skated up her torso as if it were his own hands, and his lips brushed the shell of her ear when he whispered again. "The not lover?"

"Yes," she rasped, her back arching off the seat as his magic caressed her breasts.

His arm was still looped around her back, holding her in place against the seat, and his knee came up, working its way between her thighs. The fingers of his other hand trailed up her throat until he cupped her jaw, his thumb running along her bottom lip. "Why did you call him?"

"I had to hear his voice. Make sure he was alive," she breathed out, his magic raking over her skin again and making it impossible to focus.

"Why?"

Gods, even his voice was sensuous and only added to everything else bombarding her.

"Because a vision at the assessment tried to convince me he was dead," she cried, his shadows climbing further up her thighs and making wet heat pool in her core. "The Achaz Heir was in my vision. He tortured me with his magic and said he did the same to my friends. That he killed them. All of them. Because of who I am to you."

"Why is Dex so important?" Theon pushed. His finger traced around her lips, his eyes on hers as his dark magic brushed against her center, making her grind herself against his leg that was forcing her thighs farther apart.

"He keeps me from going over an edge," she gasped, pleasure flaring out as she ground her clit against him again. "He helps glue the broken pieces back together, even when I don't think it's worth it anymore."

Everything stopped. Theon's fingers. His lips. His magic. It all stilled against her flesh at her words. She was panting beneath him, and he slowly brushed his thumb along her cheekbone, almost tenderly.

"Good girl," he praised softly. "Thank you for telling me."

He was still pressed against her, and her mind was reeling. She couldn't get coherent thoughts to form, and it was utter bliss to not be able to godsdamn think. To just feel pleasure. There was movement in the front seat, but Theon leaned forward, running the tip of his nose along the length of her own, and by the gods, she wished they were anywhere private.

She wished he hadn't stopped.

His lips hovered over hers, and she felt his breath as he whispered, "This is going to hurt."

"What?" she started, her eyes widening, but his mouth pressed to hers and his magic poured into her and down her throat. It seeped into her being, burning a path along her veins. She arched against him for a completely different reason, but there were hands, physical hands, holding her down. Her eyes locked on Axel, who was gritting his teeth as he held her in place.

She writhed beneath Theon, screaming against his mouth as he continued to press his magic into her. It was almost as bad as when she had been given the Mark. Her entire body felt like it was on fire, and she was just as helpless.

Finally, Theon pulled back, pushing off of her. Axel released her, and she scrambled up. Luka had pulled the vehicle into a vacant lot on the outskirts of the city at some point. Axel had already exited the vehicle and was reaching for her, but she shoved his hands aside as her stomach lurched. Her legs gave out when she tried to step out of the vehicle, and she fell out instead, her leggings and knees ripping open on the pavement.

"Gods, Tessa," Axel muttered, reaching for her again at the same time Theon came up beside him and began to crouch beside her. She threw up her hand to keep them away, and the St. Orcas brothers went flying across the lot. Tessa didn't have time to process that as she pushed herself back to her feet. She stumbled a few more steps from the vehicle before she dropped to her knees again and heaved.

"That was *not* earth magic," she heard Axel snarl from wherever they had landed.

"No shit," Theon growled.

"Did you see—"

"I saw."

"I thought a Source couldn't attack their Master," Axel said. She could see them prowling back towards her from the corner of her eye as she heaved again. They both had darkness wreathing them, their faces as dark as the shadows at their command. She had no idea where Luka was. She couldn't lift her head enough to look for him.

"They are not supposed to be able to," Theon replied tightly.

When they were a few feet from her, Axel stopped, but Theon continued towards her cautiously. He slowly crouched before her and tilted her chin up. Shadows swirled tightly around him, as though they were acting as a shield or some kind of armor. "I'm going to heal you, Tessa."

"Once again, you are the reason I need healing," she tried to snarl, but there was no bite to her tone.

"I had to get the alcohol out of your system," he replied. Her confusion at that statement must have been evident on her face because he added, "I sent my magic into your body to burn it all out. That is why it felt like that."

"You are an asshole," she added, hardly feeling the jolt the bond gave her for calling him such. "And so are you," she growled, her gaze lifting to Axel.

"I'm sorry, Tessa," Axel replied, true remorse ringing in his voice.

"I don't want your apologies," she spat. "I don't want anything from any of you."

"Tessa—"

"Axel," Theon warned as he pressed a hand to her cheek. She felt his magic kiss her skin, cooling and tender this time, and the headache that had started throbbing at her temples instantly ceased. "Help her stand."

Axel came to her side and helped her up, and Theon healed the scrapes on her knees, looking her over carefully for any other sign of injury before he rose to his feet. "Anywhere else?"

Tessa only held his stare for a moment before she shrugged out of Axel's grip and made her way back to the vehicle. Luka was leaning against the side of it, his arms folded over his chest.

As she drew near, he straightened, his arms dropping to his sides. "Are you—"

"Fuck off, Luka," she snarled, climbing into the backseat and snapping the door shut behind her. She had her knees to her chest, leaning her head against the window and refusing to acknowledge the others as they climbed into their seats, and Luka started the engine. She heard Theon moving around, and a moment later, a blanket was draped over her.

Now she was stuck.

She was trapped in her thoughts of the assessment and Theon and the bond and Tristyn and everything. There was no alcohol to make her forget. There was no mindless sex to get lost in. Even worse, she could feel Theon on her. She could feel his hands and his lips and his magic. All of it had the bond pulsing through her, urging her to go to him, to seek out his comfort and more.

She was alone. Stuck in her own head.

And that was a dangerous place to be.

28

THEON

Tessa wouldn't look at any of them, let alone speak to them. He tried to offer her food or water. So did the others. She just stared out the window. He could have entranced her, he supposed. He could have forced her to move closer to him, to rest against his own body rather than the godsdamn window. He could also feel remorse for what he'd done to her, but he didn't. That information was necessary and remorse wouldn't change anything anyway. He'd needed to know who she'd called and why. And he certainly didn't regret having her pinned beneath him. Just the thought of his magic raking along her body had him pressing against his jeans, and gods, he was so sick of fucking his own godsdamn hand. He'd told her he wouldn't force her, but something was going to have to change and soon.

His magic was as drawn to her as he was. It constantly strained beneath his skin, curious tendrils of darkness trying to break through. Always trying to get to her. When it could mingle with her own power? It would call to her magic as the Source bond called to her soul, and he didn't know what he was going to do if she still resisted.

He readjusted himself at the thought, glancing at her again. Her eyes were closed, and he couldn't decide if she was truly sleeping. He had watched her sleep the rest of the night after she'd passed out in their bed. Sipping on a glass of whiskey, he'd pondered what he was going to do with her. This couldn't keep happening. Maybe it'd get better when the other Marks were in place, but he couldn't wait that long. This needed to be under control. *She* needed to be under control.

At least in public.

She feared him to some extent. She knew he was dangerous, knew a monster lurked beneath his skin. He'd tried to keep it from her. He hadn't wanted her to see it until she was irrevocably devoted to him and him alone. But she was always one extreme or the other. She was either completely submissive or utterly uncontrollable. And while he knew there were other ways to instill obedience, he also refused to become the kind of monster his father was. Then again, maybe the monster he actually was wasn't any better than his father in the end. He did know that while her wildness drove him mad, he also craved it in a way he couldn't explain.

He stole another look at her and found the blanket had slipped down her arm. Reaching over, he tugged it back up. She hadn't so much as sighed in the last hour. She had to be asleep.

"What are you going to do now?" Axel asked.

"What do you mean?"

"Obviously what you are doing isn't working," he replied, twisting around to look at him.

"I've repeatedly told you it wouldn't work," Luka chimed in.

Theon pressed his tongue to his cheek, sitting back in his seat once more. "I have a plan."

"Does it involve us getting blasted across a fucking parking lot again? Because if so, count me out," Axel said.

"She was clearly in some sort of…distress to make her magic break through like that," Theon replied, running his hand through his hair. How had the assessment not produced anything, but him burning the alcohol from her body had? Surely the assessments were worse than that? She'd been bleeding from her nose and ears, for fuck's sake.

"Right. And what's your explanation for her eyes?" Axel asked dryly.

Theon had cut him off when he'd tried to bring it up earlier, not wanting Tessa to know they had noticed.

But they had definitely noticed.

Axel had been reaching to help her up when Theon had come around the vehicle. Theon could tell she was about to vomit as he'd crouched beside her. Her eyes had connected with his for the briefest of moments before her magic had sent him and Axel flying, highly suggesting the wind and air element as her prior assessments had always predicted.

But there had been flashes of violet in her eyes, much like darkness would swirl in his own. Except this was more like energy flickering. It was as if there was lightning being reflected in her stormy eyes when blasts of power had slammed into them. When Theon had made his way back to her, it had been gone, along with her fight. She was once more resigned and withdrawn.

"It's not the first time I've seen it," Theon admitted.

"Care to repeat that?" Luka said, casting a quick glare over his shoulder at him.

"It had never been that pronounced," he said. "It had been quick glimpses in the past. I wasn't even sure I'd seen it."

"Seen what exactly," Luka gritted out. Theon could see his fingers tightening on the steering wheel, his knuckles turning white.

"When she's feeling a lot of emotion, her eyes almost seem to glow a faint violet color."

"This wasn't some faint glow," Axel cut in. "She blasted us clear off our godsdamn feet, Theon."

"I am aware."

Axel turned to Luka. "What are you thinking?"

"That we need to talk to Cienna," Luka answered grimly.

Axel was already fiddling with the small mirror, and he paused his movements to glance down at the reflective surface. "We can't exactly summon her."

"Which is annoying as fuck."

"She's in hiding because of you," Axel retorted.

"There has got to be a better way to communicate than that fucking mirror."

"This is the only way Father cannot track her down."

Theon didn't answer. They'd had this debate several times before. It was pointless to argue about it again. He was on Cienna's shit list. So was Luka. And that was not a pleasant place to be. She would only communicate with Axel, so he was forced to let his brother handle all correspondence with her. Which is why he was spending more and more time in the Underground lately. There likely was an easier way to communicate with her, but this was the only option she provided.

"What do we do until then?" Axel asked.

"I'm working on a plan," Theon said, his focus wandering back to Tessa. "I'm still figuring out the final pieces," Theon muttered.

"And we will get to know this plan when?" Luka asked flatly.

"When we get home," he answered, tipping his head back against the seat and closing his eyes.

This would work.

It had to.

When they pulled up at Arius House, he tugged the blanket from Tessa's body, his fingers grazing her arm.

"Tessa?" he murmured softly, trying to keep his distance. "Tessa, we're home."

Her eyes slowly fluttered open and met his briefly before she came fully awake and broke his stare. She sat up, grabbed the door handle, and climbed out without a word. Not even waiting for them to grab the bags, she began walking up the drive to the east wing entrance.

"Go. I've got them," Axel said, watching her go. If their father saw her walking away from them like that, he'd be livid. Theon knew there would be no saving her from that wrath.

He jogged after her, slowing when he fell into step beside her. "You can't just take off like that, Tessa."

She said nothing, her eyes resolutely focused on the path ahead of her.

"You can't stop talking to me either."

Still nothing.

They continued in silence, but when they reached the door and she brought her hand up to pull it open, Theon leaned casually against it. She slowly slid those stormy eyes to his, leveling him with an unimpressed stare.

"I have a proposition for you."

Tessa blinked once, the only sign of acknowledgment she gave.

"I will tell you what it is after you've showered," he continued, and her lips pursed slightly. Her hand still rested on the door handle. Luka and Axel were almost upon them now too.

"We also need to eat," he said nonchalantly. "Tell me what you'd like, and I'll order it up so it'll be waiting for you when you get out of the shower." She arched her brows as if to say '*Really?*,' and the accompanying lip curl told him how unlikely she found this to be. "Anything you want, beautiful," he coaxed, trying to get her to say one godsdamn word to him.

Still nothing.

"Tessa," he growled, unable to keep his frustration buried any longer. Darkness floated from his fingertips, reaching towards her, and she glanced down at it, stepping back from him. He forced himself to breathe deep. In an hour, this would be taken care of. In an hour, she'll have heard his proposal, and everything will be fine.

He hooked his phone from his jeans pocket, pulling up the text thread with the kitchens. "Cheeseburger and fries it is then," he said calmly. "Anything I should leave off or add to your burger?"

He saw her press her tongue to her cheek. It wasn't a word, but at least it was a reaction other than nerves or anger.

"Last chance," he prompted, his thumb hovering over the send button.

"Bacon on the burger," she blurted before crossing her arms with a huff.

His lips curled in a half grin. "Will do, little storm," he said, reaching for the door and pulling it open for her. She didn't look at him when she strode past and began the trek to their rooms.

He let her walk ahead of him, giving her space as he hung back to walk with Luka and Axel.

"Food?" Axel said doubtfully. "That's your big plan?"

"No, that's not the plan," Theon retorted. "I just wanted her to say something."

"Because…?" Luka asked.

"Because we have a meeting with my father this afternoon, and I can't have him picking up on tension between us."

"Right. That's why," Luka said knowingly.

Theon didn't say anything else. When they reached their rooms, Tessa had stopped outside, waiting for one of them to unlock the wards for her. Ironic, since she could easily pass right through them. She pushed by them all and went straight into the bedroom. Theon followed and heard the shower turn on before he even entered the room. He pushed out a long breath before going through the dressing room to pull out clothing for her. He pulled his shirt off, tossing it into the laundry bin. Then he slipped his shoes off and waited barefoot in the closet for her.

He heard the water shut off some time later, and she paused when she entered the dressing room, a towel wrapped tightly around her. He swallowed thickly, pushing the memories of his mouth on her skin away so he could focus.

"We have a meeting with my father later this afternoon, but I thought you'd want more comfortable clothing for now," he said with a nod to the jeans and shirt he'd set out for her.

"We?" she asked, tilting her head to the side.

"Yes. We," he confirmed. "You will be required to attend such meetings with me from here on out."

"Who else will be there?" she asked, moving towards the clothing.

"Luka. Axel. Some associates." When she cast him a dry look, he sighed. "Pavil and Metias."

Her eyes widened, and he took a step towards her. "I will be there the entire time."

"That is somehow not comforting in the slightest," she muttered, expertly sliding undergarments on while managing to keep her towel in place.

"I will always keep you safe, Tessa."

"Forgive me for calling bullshit on that statement based on my experiences these last weeks."

"Food should be here," he ground out, pushing down the retort on the tip of his tongue. He needed her open to hearing him out. He couldn't afford for her to go back to not speaking to him right now. "Come out to eat after you've gotten dressed. And make sure you have pants on."

Tessa smirked at him as he left the room. Luka and Axel hadn't changed yet and were sprawled across the sofa. A few minutes later, Tessa emerged and made her way to the table.

They joined her, and Theon let her take a few bites before he cleared his throat. She glanced up at him. "As I said, I have a proposition for you."

Tessa carefully set her cheeseburger down, wiping her fingers on her napkin before leaning back in her chair, looking at him expectantly.

"I know you do not want this bond. You've made it more than clear you will not give into it anytime soon," he said, and her eyes narrowed in suspicion. "The problem is you've already been Selected. There is no undoing that."

Theon glanced at Axel and Luka across the table. They were watching them closely, obviously curious to hear what he had to say as well. He'd purposely kept them in the dark on this. They were going to be pissed.

"So here is my proposition to you: when we are with others, outside of the people in this room, pretend you have accepted and embraced the bond."

"Pretend," she repeated dryly.

"Yes, pretend. When it is just us, when you are alone with me or Luka or Axel, I will require nothing of you," he continued. "You will be free to do what you wish. Ignore us. Speak to us. Don't speak to us. Whatever you like."

"Let me get this straight," she replied, pushing her plate back and planting her palms facedown on the table before her. "You want me to *pretend* that I have become enamored with you. That my world revolves around you. You want me to dote on you, call you Master and *pretend* I *want* this so it makes your life easier, and I— What, Theon? I get what from this arrangement?"

"Before I answer that question, I need to clarify something," Theon answered. "I do not want you to pretend to be enamored with me, Tessa." Her brows knitted together in confusion, and he pressed on. "I want you to pretend to have accepted this fate. Embraced it. I want you to pretend that we are so in tune with each other that others take notice. I want others to fear what we are, Tessa. I want others to fear *you*, to fear what they think we will become when the final Mark is bestowed."

"When you can siphon power off me at will," she sneered.

"No, beautiful," he countered, leaning in towards her. "This is what you get out of it. If you pretend, if you are convincing enough, then when I run this kingdom, when my father no longer rules, you will be given an entire wing of this house. You will be protected and cared for, and you will get to decide if and when I get to draw from you."

"Theon—" Axel started, but Theon held up his hand to silence him.

He knew what this sounded like, but he had thought about this for hours. By the time she got the final Marks, it wouldn't matter. She'd want this as much as he did.

"If you never want to see my face again when my father is gone, I won't enter your wing of the house. You will be as free as possible," he finished.

She was staring at him, and for the millionth time, Theon found himself wishing he could read her emotions.

"Why?" she finally asked. "Why don't you just force me to submit?"

"Because constantly trying to control you is exhausting, and it obviously isn't working," he replied, sitting back in his chair and taking a drink of his water. He picked up a fry, dragging it through some sauce before popping it into his mouth. "But that outcome for you is likely some years away, so allow me to make it worth your while now," he continued, and Tessa's eyes widened. "Prove to me you can do this. Prove to me you can be convincing at this meeting with my father in a few hours, and I will let you call your beloved Dex and speak with him."

"You're going to reward me like a hound?" she challenged, her lip curling in disgust.

"No," he countered, shaking his head. "Be convincing, and we can discuss how things will go from here on out. Give me a little, and I'll give back."

"Give and take," she clarified.

"Exactly," he confirmed, swiping up another fry and swallowing it down before he leaned towards her. He gripped her chin between his thumb and forefinger. "Let me be very clear, Tessa. I do not want an Eviana. I do not want a pet who follows me around and caters to my every whim. I want someone people fear as much as they fear me. Do we have a bargain?"

Her eyes widened at the formal words. If she agreed to the bargain, they would both bear Bargain Marks. If either of them broke the deal without the other releasing them, there would be unspeakable consequences, some type of curse.

"Theon!" Luka barked, but before he could say another word, Tessa cut him off.

"It's a bargain," she said quickly, and he felt a prickling along his torso. He looked down to find a sun and stars along one side of his ribs. He glanced over to find Tessa had her shirt raised with a similar Mark along her torso. She met his gaze once more and swallowed thickly.

He nodded towards her plate. "Finish eating, then you need to get ready."

She held his gaze a moment longer, suspicion still shining in her stormy eyes, before she pulled her plate back to her and took another bite of her burger. Luka and Axel were staring at him from across the table. Axel looked shocked, and Luka's shoulders were rigid, his mouth a thin line.

No one spoke for the rest of the meal, and when he'd finished his own burger, Theon pushed back from the table to go shower. He let the

hot water run over his body, bracing his hands against the tiled shower
wall. This was going to work. It had to. This wasn't him forcing her
into submission. This was her choosing it when it mattered most. This
was her meeting him halfway, and in the process, she'd unwittingly
feed the bond, little by little until she'd given into it without even realizing it. She'd never want him gone. She'd crave him the way he
craved her.

And gods, did he crave her. He couldn't understand how she was
resisting any of this. Every minute of every day was an exercise in
control, and every time he slipped up, it only made him want her more.

When he truly kissed her for the first time atop the dining table.

When he had her beneath him, arguing about running.

When he'd helped her wash after the gardens.

His hand was already wrapped around his length, a groan of frustration slipping from his lips as it grew impossibly harder in his hand with
each image.

Holding her in nothing but a robe.

No undergarments under that godsdamn dress.

Caressing her thighs while she stood between his legs in nothing but
his shirt.

The tendons in his forearm flexed as he pumped, gripping himself
harder. Tighter. The ache in his balls was nothing compared to the
agony of not being able to claim her in every possible way day after day.

She had been so fucking mouthy last night, and he hadn't been lying
when he'd told her he wanted his cock down her throat to silence her.
Her hand. Her tongue. Her cunt. He'd settle for anything she'd give him
at this point. Anything to not be coming in the godsdamn shower yet
again.

His cock throbbed in his hand, precum leaking from the tip and
mixing with the water dripping down his flesh. There was no rhythm to
his movements anymore, each stroke of his hand harder and more
frantic than the last.

Water cascading down her body when she stood from the tub.

Sitting in the middle of the bed this morning, his shirt bunched
around her thighs, glaring at him.

The feel of her grinding herself against his thigh.

The moans of need as she gripped his hair.

The feel of his power running over her, searching for her magic,
feeling it just out of reach.

But none of that was what had his balls drawing up even tighter, his breathing so fast he was practically gasping.

That was her willingly curling into him, her fingers brushing along his skin.

That was the quiet mornings when she slept on his chest, seeking him out in her sleep.

That was when she said she'd needed him. Because whether or not she wanted to admit it, that hadn't been a lie.

He slapped his other hand against the tiled wall, water spraying into his face, and a low moan rumbled from deep in his chest as he came, his entire body seizing with release. His cock pulsed in his hand, his abdomen caving in, and he wrung the last of his orgasm from his shaft, squeezing.

"Godsdamnit," he growled, his brow dropping against the wall as he tried to catch his breath.

So godsdamn tired of fucking his own hand, but the mere thought of finding another female to sate the need made something in his heaving chest twist.

The sound of movement made him straighten, and he found Tessa sitting at the vanity, digging through various drawers for whatever she needed. How long had she been sitting there? Had she watched that entire thing? That thought was enough to make his spent cock twitch.

Gods-fucking-damnit.

He finished showering quickly, and when he shut the water off, she waited until he had a towel wrapped around his waist before meeting his eyes in the vanity mirror. If she'd witnessed anything, she didn't let on.

"I feel like there's a catch," she said.

"No catch," he replied, coming up behind her. "This makes sure of that." He ran his thumb along the sun on her skin, once again unable to resist touching her. When she didn't reply, he started moving to the dressing room. "I'll set a dress out for you."

"Can I pick it out?" she asked in a rush. He paused, looking over his shoulder at her. "Let me pick it out. If you don't like it, I'll change," she pushed.

"All right," he conceded. "You have an hour."

He left her to it and got dressed in black pants and a black button-down shirt. He was rolling the sleeves back as he wandered back to the main room. The staff had come by and already cleared the lunch dishes.

He pulled his laptop from his bag, standing at the kitchen island going through correspondence. There were several from other heirs, and he clicked open one from Tana Aithne, the Anala Heir. He was reading through the email when Luka and Axel returned, the door clicking shut behind them.

"What the fuck were you thinking?" Axel demanded after doing a quick scan of the room and finding Tessa not present.

Theon glanced up from his computer. "I was thinking I need submission and forcing it wasn't working."

"You don't think you should have run this by us first?" Axel asked, making his way over to where Theon stood.

"I wasn't aware I needed to," Theon replied slowly, his tone holding a warning. "Besides, you're the one who said you wanted it to go back to how it was. This way that can happen."

Axel turned to Luka. "What do you think of this?"

Luka rubbed the back of his neck. "Actually, I think it's a good idea."

Axel was about to argue when the bedroom door opened. They all turned to face it and found Tessa standing there looking like a dark goddess. She wore a long, black lace dress that hugged her hips and had a deep slit up the front of the right thigh. The front dipped low between her breasts and tight sleeves ran the length of her arms. She had blood red rubies around her neck and hanging from her ears, and her golden hair was curled and pinned over one shoulder. Black heels made her a couple inches taller, and when she slowly turned, the open back of the dress made Theon grip the edge of the counter. It stopped just above the swell of her ass, and his fingers itched to run her spine. That would definitely be happening at some point this evening. His release in the shower was, once again, utterly pointless.

She glanced back at him over her shoulder. "Is this sufficient?"

He met her gaze and found her cosmetics as dark as her dress. She had dark color on her eyes and thick liner around them. Her lips matched the rubies at her throat.

"Tessa, you look like darkness itself," he managed to get out, his voice thick and gravelly.

"How fitting that I am the Source of the Arius Heir then," she replied, slowly coming towards them. She stopped beside him and reached up to brush a lock of his hair back.

Luka cleared his throat. "We should get going."

"You know what is required of you to have that phone call?" Theon asked, his eyes roving down the front of her dress again. Always some-where to be when she was like this.

"I know exactly what I need to do, Theon," she replied, her hand sliding down the front of his shirt, her fingers brushing along his belt.

And fuck. The way she said his name with that sensual lilt had his hand shooting out when she made to turn away from him. His fingers closed around her wrist, and he tugged her back to him. She peered up at him from beneath long lashes, a slight pout on her full lips.

"I am glad to hear that, beautiful," he said softly into her ear, and she shivered against him. His lips lifted into a satisfied smile. "But I will be expected to treat you a certain way."

"You said you didn't want me to be like Eviana," she protested.

"I did, but my father will still find a need to punish you if you are too...disobedient," he continued. "I need you to be careful. Be smart about this and know that how I speak of you to him is not how I feel about you. Understand that any actions I take are to protect you, not punish you." She nodded, but doubt flickered in her grey eyes. "Keep your eyes on me. I will warn you if things are going in a direction we do not want to travel."

"The last time you told me to keep my eyes on you, I ended up kneeling at your feet," she retorted, and he tugged her into him further, pressing his front to hers.

His tone dropped an octave as he whispered into her ear, "Would it make you feel better to keep your eyes on me while I kneel at your feet later tonight?" She sucked in a sharp breath and tried to move back from him, but he held firm. "Our agreement allows you freedom in the privacy of my company or that of Luka or Axel, but in front of others, appropriate behavior is still required."

"So that's the catch?" she breathed.

"No, beautiful, that is just the bargain we agreed to," he replied. He stepped back from her as he said, "Shall we?"

She stared at him for a moment longer before turning away without a word and making her way over to Axel by the door.

This was already working out better than he'd hoped.

They quickly made their way to one of the lounges in the house, his father's study too small for the number of people that would be present this afternoon. As they approached, voices carrying from the room indi-cated Pavil and Metias had already arrived. He felt Tessa stiffen behind him where she was walking with Axel, and he quickly turned to her. He beckoned her forward with two fingers, and she narrowed her eyes but obediently came to him. His hands settling on her hips, he pressed her back against the wall, hearing her breath hitch again at the closeness.

"Keep your eyes on me, and no one else. Do you understand?" She tipped her head back against the wall, closing her eyes and taking a deep breath. "They will not touch you." She nodded, her eyes still shut tight. "I'm going to need verbal confirmation here, Tessa. There is no room for error with my father. Can you do this or not?"

She took another deep breath before she opened her eyes and met his own. "Eyes on you," she whispered.

"Good girl," he murmured, pressing a soft kiss to her cheek before tucking her hand into his and leading her into the meeting room.

All chatter ceased when they entered. Eviana was nestled into a chair near the window, and she sat up straighter, eyeing them curiously. His father's lip curled up when he saw him holding her hand, and Pavil and Metias smirked, their eyes roaming over her appreciatively.

She stepped closer to him, her other hand coming up and gripping his forearm. He looked down to find her eyes fixed firmly on him, and he smiled darkly at her. "Get me a drink, beautiful," he said, tracing a finger lightly along her jaw. "You know what I need."

He saw the shift in her eyes, a dark, cold indifference, as she stepped away from him, her fingers dragging down his forearm. While everyone in the room watched as she made her way to the alcohol cart, he walked to a nearby armchair and sat across from his father. Tessa poured him a measure of liquor before coming back to him. She perched herself on the arm of his chair before leaning over and lifting the glass to his lips. Unsure of where she was going with this, he met her stormy eyes and held them as he took a swallow.

Then she brought the glass to her own lips and downed the rest before giving him a grin that told the rest of the world to fuck off.

His father cleared his throat. "You let her drink your own whiskey. Does she not yet know her place?" he asked, clearly disgusted by the display.

"Father, I assure you, drinks are not the only thing we share," he replied, his gaze still fixed on hers. "She knows her place is beneath me, right where she belongs."

Her eyes flared with a flash of ire, but it was gone just as quickly. "Refill?" she purred softly.

"In a bit," he answered, and she held the empty glass out to the staff.

The Fae glanced around the room, clearly unsure what he should do, before he stepped forward and took it from her.

"The two of you are not alone in this room, Theon," his father ground out from between his teeth.

"I am well aware," Theon replied. "If we were, she would certainly not be silent right now."

She brought her hand to his chest where her finger traced along the collar of his shirt, dragging her nail sharply along his collarbone. Theon smirked at her before finally breaking eye contact to look back at his father. "Let's get on with this."

"Tessalyn, I don't know that you have been introduced to Pavil and Metias," his father said smoothly, lifting a glass of liquor to his lips.

"Actually, we've met briefly," she replied, glancing dismissively at the two males seated to the right of his father before bringing her eyes back to Theon. "They found me in the gardens when I was walking with one of my Master's hounds. Unfortunately for them, his wolves are as protective of me as he is."

The corner of Theon's lips tilted as the males scowled and shifted in their seats. He chuckled softly under his breath. "Kacela, along with all my hounds, has been trained extensively to protect what is mine." He reached up and began twirling one of her curls around his finger.

Pavil cleared his throat. "Yes, well, that was all just a misunderstanding. We simply wanted to get to know your Source since we will be working together at the Acropolis."

"By lying to me about her being summoned?" Axel cut in, his tone low and dark as a Fae handed him a glass of whiskey. He was leaning against the wall near the window, Luka nearby doing the same.

Pavil and Metias shifted again, glancing at his father. Theon pretended not to notice as he gave a sharp tug on the hair wrapped around his finger. Tessa had stiffened slightly when Pavil had spoken about getting to know her better, and she was starting to wring her fingers in her lap. His father would notice that tell in a heartbeat. At the pull of her hair, her eyes snapped back to him.

"It was all a misunderstanding," his father repeated, his tone making it clear this subject was to be dropped. "There was no harm done. We can move on."

"Actually, that's not entirely the case," Theon replied, snapping his fingers at one of the Fae along the wall. "They stalked my Source through the gardens. They attempted to see her without me present, and they tried to make her believe I had instructed such a thing be done. In turn, she was forced to question my ability to keep her safe, which has caused a trust issue with our bond."

As he finished speaking, a drink was passed to him by the Fae he'd snapped at, and he smoothly passed it over to Tessa, meeting her stare. "Now I find myself forced to prove to her I can indeed care for her as she deserves to be cared for." He brought a single finger up and trailed it down her jaw. "Tell me, beautiful, what will be proof enough for you?"

He lifted his other hand, and a whip of darkness exploded from his palm. It coiled tightly around Metias's throat. The male's hands flew to his neck, but there was no way to grab purchase on shadows. Pavil tried to lurch to his feet, but Axel flicked his fingers almost lazily, and darkness of his own had Pavil pinned to his seat.

"Enough of this, Theon," his father growled, slowly rising from his seat. Eviana was by his side in a matter of seconds, waiting for her next order.

"You wish for me not to defend what is mine?" Theon demanded, pushing to his own feet. "These two touched what belongs to the Arius Kingdom. You expect me not to punish crimes against me? Against *us*?"

"We were acting on orders," Pavil cried out in dismay.

A cruel smirk filled Theon's face as he dragged his eyes back to Pavil. "I do not give a fuck," he replied, his voice dark and low. He took a step towards him, actively ignoring the blue shade Metias was turning. "I do not care if Arius himself appeared to you and told you to come for her. The moment you laid a fucking finger on her, the second you looked at her without my permission, your life was put in jeopardy."

"Do it, Eviana," his father ordered, but before Eviana could lift a hand to cast any type of magic, Luka strolled casually between her and Theon. His pupils had shifted to vertical slits, his sapphire eyes glowing brightly. Smoke flowed from his nose as he exhaled deeply.

Valter's features contorted with fury. "Stop this, Theon. You have made your point."

"Have I?" Theon asked as Metias slid from his seat to the floor, his eyes beginning to roll back in his head. He could not kill a Legacy by mere strangulation, but his darkness was doing far more than cutting off air supply as it sank in deep to the male's soul. Torturing. Burning. Making him wish for death.

He looked back at Tessa, who, to his absolute delight, was still casually sitting on the arm of his chair, sipping on the whiskey he'd given her. She looked bored out of her godsdamn mind, her eyes fixed on him.

"What do you think, beautiful? Do you think I have made it clear what will happen should anyone other than me touch you again?"

Tessa shrugged her shoulders dismissively, cocking her head to the side. "That one certainly seems to have gotten the message," she answered, her eyes darting to Metias, who was now still on the floor.

Theon smirked at her, finally releasing his magic from the male's throat, and turning back to Pavil. Another whip of darkness shot from his hand, wrapping around Pavil's wrist and snapping it back before anyone could blink.

"In case the message is not clear enough," Theon said nonchalantly over Pavil's cry of pain, "if you, or anyone else, ever interferes with the relationship I have with my Source again, your life will instantly be forfeit. If it weren't for my father, you would be dead. Next time, not even he will be able to save you."

"Un-understood, m-my Lord," Pavil stuttered, grasping his broken wrist to his chest.

"I trust you will relay the message when he comes to," Theon said with a sneer towards Metias's still form on the ground, veins of black running across his flesh. There would be no healing that.

He turned his back on them, strolling back to where Tessa sat. He leaned in close, his breath dancing over her lips when he spoke so softly, he knew only she could hear him. "Have I made it clear what will happen to anyone who touches you without my permission?"

The storm in her eyes flashed with defiance before she quickly schooled her features. "I think your message is crystal clear," she said with a tight smile.

"And you?" Theon asked, pulling back a fraction. "Do you find your faith in me renewed?"

Her smile turned coy. "I trust you as much as I ever have, Master."

His eyes narrowed, but he took his seat, taking the drink from Tessa's hand.

"Now that that's settled," his Father bit out, "can we get on with our business? Some of us do not have all day."

"Of course, Father," Theon replied, taking a sip of liquor.

"The three of you leave for the Acropolis tomorrow. We will all join you in a week for the Emerging Ceremony," Valter said. "I expect this week with the other heirs to be fruitful. I want new alliances in the making."

Theon listened to his father go over the details they'd discussed numerous times, again wondering why they were even having this meeting. After an hour, he dismissed Metias and Pavil, but when Theon made to stand, he halted him.

When the door had shut behind their supposed allies, Valter said, "I have not received the report from the assessment yet."

"Her testing did not yield completely accurate results, but they were in line with air and wind tendencies," Theon said darkly, images of being thrown across the parking lot this morning flashing through his mind.

"How is that possible?" his father demanded. "How could they not be completely accurate? Was the proper testing done?"

"Yes," Theon answered, reaching up and bringing his hand to Tessa's nape. She had tensed beside him, her breathing shifting. He began making slow circles with his thumb, feeling her relax some beneath his touch. "I observed the entire thing. The most advanced assessments were done."

"And her power level estimates?" his father pressed.

Luka came forward, handing Valter a folder that contained the false report. His father flipped the pages, his face impassive as he skimmed the documents inside.

Tessa was still tense, and Theon dropped his arm to her waist, tugging her off the arm of the chair and pulling her into his lap. She came easily, leaning back into him. His hand skimmed up her exposed spine, and she arched subtly.

"This says she will be quite powerful," his father said, snapping the folder closed.

"It does," Theon agreed. "She tested on the higher end of the power scale."

Tessa's head tilted at the information, and he felt her eyes back on him. He didn't look at her, but he could feel the anger simmering under her skin as he ran his hand up her spine again.

"It will be an exciting Emergence then," his father was saying, passing the folder back to Luka.

"That it will," Theon said, locking eyes with Axel across the room. "Is there anything else? Or can we head down to dinner? I would hate to keep Mother waiting."

"She will likely draw out this dinner the way it is," his father grumbled. "She has been in tears all godsdamn day about you leaving tomorrow."

When he urged Tessa to stand, he finally met her gaze, her eyes still fixed on him.

And the storm of emotions that stared back at him told him it was going to be a long night.

29
TESSA

Tessa went straight through the main living space, through Theon's bedroom, and out to the balcony when dinner was over. She needed to breathe. Needed to be outside.

She had made herself focus on the dinner conversation, picking up bits and pieces of interesting information, but most of the evening was Cressida spontaneously breaking into tears about her sons being gone for the next several months. In those moments, Theon's words from the meeting with Valter would play through her mind.

She tested on the higher end of the power scale.

Inconclusive.

That's what Theon had said her test results were. And they had been for her element, she supposed, but he'd told Valter even that was still estimated to be air. He hadn't told her any of that, even when she had specifically asked what her results had been.

She tested on the higher end of the power scale.

He had lied to her. They had not been *inconclusive*. All the talk this morning about working together. Each of them surrendering a little. Give and take.

Nothing but lies to get what he wanted from her.

Why had she even entertained the idea of trusting him? And now she had this godsdamn Bargain Mark on her skin. Because one Mark binding her to him hadn't been enough apparently. What had she been thinking?

She'd hadn't been. Always so impulsive. Always unable to control herself.

Too wild. Too much of a hassle.

"Tessa?"

She turned to find Axel standing in the doorway, watching her warily. Darkness floated around him like a light mist. It was the first time she'd ever seen him let his power be seen for more than a few seconds.

"What?" she demanded.

"It's raining, baby doll," he said softly.

She hadn't even noticed the gentle rain that had indeed begun falling. She wrapped her arms around herself, squeezing tightly, pretending it was Dex or Corbin or Lange.

Old insecurities and feelings clawed their way up from the depths of her soul.

Too much of a hassle.

"Tessa." There was a soft touch to the small of her back. "Come in out of the rain."

She looked up into emerald green eyes. "You should have told me," she whispered, the rain beginning to fall harder.

"You were just waking up, still in pain..." Theon trailed off, his hair becoming plastered to his head.

"You should have told me."

"It does not change anything, Tessa. You have already been Selected, already claimed. It is not as if this changes anything."

"Did you know before? When you Selected me? Is there something in those fucking documents you have full of information about me that I do not even know? Is that why you chose me?"

"No, Tessa," Theon said, shaking his head. "I knew you were predicted to emerge with air. You had a slight affinity for water, but the Priestess yesterday told me you have never actually displayed any elemental magic in any of your assessments. They were just guesses based on your reactions during the tests and bloodline."

"Bloodline?" Tessa repeated, lurching back as if he had shoved her. Her back hit the balcony railing. "I was alone, Theon. Always alone. I was raised in an Estate home until I was old enough to begin my instruction at the Estate school. They would have to know who my parents are for bloodline to play a role in my predictions."

Something akin to pity crossed Theon's features. "Come away from the railing, Tessa," he coaxed, holding out a hand to her.

"Do you know who my parents are?" she demanded, the bond in her chest reaching for him while she held her breath, waiting for his answer.

"Come inside, Tessa. We can talk," he said, taking a step towards her.

"Do you know?" she demanded again.

Lightning flashed across the dark sky, and thunder cracked.

"Tessalyn." Her name was a warning. He would entrance her next.

She did not care.

"Why did you choose me?" she asked instead, her thoughts and emotions all over the place.

She couldn't focus on anything when he clearly knew so much about her and who she was, while she'd been raised in the dark at an Estate with other parentless Fae. Repeatedly told that she wasn't good enough, wasn't compliant enough. That no one would want her unless she had something to offer them. That she was too much of a hassle for anyone to bother with otherwise. That she would forever be nothing, too much of a disappointment to be something.

That was how they had found each other. Dex and Brecken. Oralia. Lange and Corbin. The Celeste Estate was different from the others. The other three Estates were more akin to small cities where Fae resided. The Celeste Estate was where the Fae who did not have homes went. Those without families to raise them. But Tessa had been there first. Alone for years.

Dex had been the first to find her when she was scarcely eighteen years. He was older than her by nearly five years and had missed being eligible for the most recent Selection by a mere month. He'd been sent to the Celeste Estate along with a few others to wait for the next Selection Year.

He had found her hiding under a set of stairs that led off of the kitchens. It was the place she had always hidden when she was younger, hoping to steal any scraps leftover from meal preparations. Over time, it became the place she went to escape...well, everything. Except her own thoughts. There was never escaping those.

A head of dark brown hair suddenly appeared, eyes so dark they were nearly black in the shadows of the nook under the stairwell. "What are you doing under here?"

"What am I doing under here?" Tessa had asked. "What are you doing under here?"

The male slipped farther into the shadows, dropping to the floor beside her. He had a small paper bag in his hand. Bending a knee, he rested an arm atop it. Then he held the bag out to her. "Want one?"

She narrowed her eyes. "No."

"You don't even know what's in here," he countered.

"I don't need to know. I am not going to help you."

"Help me? With what?"

"Who are you?" Tessa asked.

"Dex. Who are you?"

"I've never seen you around here before."

"Just got here this morning. Came from the Serafina Estate."

"Why?"

Dex shrugged. "They needed somewhere to keep me until Selection, I guess." He reached into the sack and pulled out a doughnut, taking a bite. "You going to tell me your name?"

"No. How did you get those?"

Dex glanced at her out of the corner of his eye. "The doughnuts?"

She nodded. She was starving. Mother Cordelia had found some reason to withhold her meals today. She couldn't even remember what she'd done this time.

"Bought them in Arobell before coming here."

"Oh."

He held the bag out to her again. "Want one?"

She shook her head.

"What are you doing under here?" he asked again, looking around the cramped space. She hardly fit in the small space, let alone a full-grown male.

"How old are you?" she blurted before she could stop herself. No surprise there.

"Twenty-three. How old are you?"

"If you are twenty-three years, why are you not assigned to a Kingdom?"

"Born days too late, I guess," he answered with a shrug, finishing off his doughnut.

She took a deep breath then, tipping her head back against the wall and closing her eyes. "Well, Dex from the Serafina Estate, whatever you have heard about me, it is not true, so you can kindly fuck off."

"I don't even know your name."

"Leave."

"I didn't mean to make you upset."

She didn't say anything.

"My apologies if I offended you."

There was rustling, and a moment later she heard him leave. When she opened her eyes, she found he'd left the paper sack. Glancing around to make sure he'd truly left, she pulled out a doughnut with chocolate frosting and took a bite.

"Tessa?"

The sound of Theon's voice jerked her back to the present where it was now pouring rain. Icy drops slid down her exposed back. He was standing directly in front of her, his hands shoved in his pockets. "Where'd you go, little storm?"

She brought her eyes to his. "Tell me why you Selected me. No bullshit. Tell me what you want from me."

"Why is this so important to you?" Theon asked, his suit soaked through and clinging to his body.

She didn't even feel the chill against her skin.

"Tell me."

"Tell me why it matters," he countered.

"Tell me!" she screamed, but her voice was carried away on the howling winds. "Tell me what it is you want from me so godsdamn badly that you took me from those who actually cared about me."

"Why do you insist I do not care for you?"

"Why can't you answer the godsdamn question?" Her hands came up, shoving against his chest, and to her surprise, he moved back a few steps.

"Wind," Theon murmured, meeting her gaze. She didn't actually hear him over the driving rain, but she read his lips. He looked up at the sky for a long moment before he stepped close to her once more. "Come inside, Tessa. I will answer your questions."

"Answer them now," she demanded, digging in her heels when he reached for her and tried to tug her to the doors.

He spun back to her. "Tessa," he said incredulously. "You need to get out of the rain."

She reached behind her, gripping the railing in clear refusal.

"Fine," Theon snapped, a hand carving through his dripping hair and pushing it out of his face. "You want to know what I know? You want to know why I Selected you? You were one of five options. I did not go to the Estates like the other heirs, but I was still watching all of you from afar. The Arius Kingdom has people everywhere. I had people reporting to me. I wanted someone clever, and I don't mean book smarts. I mean cunning. I wanted someone who wasn't afraid of bending the rules. I desired the fire element, but Anala Kingdom refused all offers, so I was willing to settle for another element if they were likely to be powerful. I did not want a meek, timid Source. Obedient, yes, but not someone who would cower. I was not lying earlier today when I said I want others to fear what my Source and I will become.

"I had it narrowed down to three females and two males. I sought you all out before the Opening Selection Ceremony. I actually couldn't find you. Because you, Tessalyn Ausra, you are clever and cunning and have so many *secrets*." Tessa sucked in a breath as he moved even closer. "I was going to pick someone else because I couldn't fucking find you. Not until I happened upon you, completely by chance, in an alcove with stolen chocolate. You did not appear to fear me, not completely anyway judging by the way you waved that chocolate in my face, but you also did not lie to me when I warned you not to." Tessa swallowed thickly. "And I knew. I knew in that moment that I would pick you. Because your marks were high in every lesson you completed. You like to break the rules, but you know how to do so without getting caught. And these secrets..." He reached out, fingering a wet lock of hair.

"I don't have secrets," she whispered, the rain having lessened to a steady drizzle. "You know my secrets, not me."

"Don't start lying to me now, Tessa," he said sensually, his face angling down towards her.

"I'm not."

His mouth came closer. "Are you sure about that?"

"Yes," she breathed, knowing if he tried to kiss her, she would let him. *Wanted* him to.

"There is one secret in particular I don't know," he said, his breath dancing over her lips.

And tonight, if he asked, she'd let him have that secret too. She'd let him take what he wanted. Because for one night, she needed an escape from all of this. She wanted to drown in pleasure, letting it overpower the pain and loneliness and—

"How do you get past the wards?"

"What?" Tessa blurted, blinking hard, sure she couldn't have heard him properly.

"You have some very unique skills, Tessa."

"I have... *That's* why you chose me?"

"It was not the only reason. I told you some of the various factors that played into my decision."

"Some of the various factors," she said softly. Then she was stepping around him. She moved to the middle of the balcony before spinning back to face him again. "So I simply checked the most boxes on your checklist?"

"No. I mean—" Theon pushed out a harsh breath. "Why does any of this matter? What is it going to change? It is done. You were Selected. We need to figure out how to move forward with this together, Tessa."

"It matters because very few *want* me, Theon!" she cried. "They want what I can give them, what I have to offer, but never *me*. And you have just told me you are no different. So I am trying to figure out what exactly it is you want from me—"

"Everything, Tessa," Theon snarled, moving so quickly, Tessa didn't register he'd even moved until he was before her once more, his hand loosely gripping her throat. "I want everything you have to give, and then I want more. I want every piece of you— every secret, every tempest raging in those stormy eyes. I want all your fear and all your pain, all your smiles and all your laughter. I want all your mornings and all your nights, all your days and months and years."

"You can't have them," she sneered.

"I can have them," he countered. "I will have them. Even if it takes our entire lifetime together, you will give them to me. Each and every piece. You can hate me for it, but it won't change it."

"You will take everything from me?" she asked, her voice barely audible.

"I will. I want it all."

"And what will you do when there is nothing left, Theon?" She heard him suck in a sharp breath. "What will you do when you have taken everything and left me with nothing?"

His eyes darted over her shoulder, and she glanced back to see Axel and Luka standing in the doorway. One look at their faces told her they'd been watching everything play out and had heard every single thing that had been said between them.

She turned back to Theon. "What were my results today?"

He opened his mouth, then closed it again.

She huffed a laugh of disbelief. "The joke's on you, Theon. I have nothing left to give. What little I had, you already took. Congratulations. You already won."

His hand slipped from her neck, and she took a step back from him. "As for the wards, I don't know how I do that. I didn't even know I was doing anything out of the ordinary until I was *punished* for it by the Estate Mother when I was five years. It is something kept hidden because she enjoyed handing out consequences for inappropriate behavior. Something you and her seem to have in common. But I should have known that is what you desired from the beginning. It is all anyone ever wants from me. All that I am useful for. The only reason anyone bothers with me."

She turned then, Luka and Axel stepping to the side when she neared so she could enter the bedroom. She went straight to the bathroom, peeling off the sopping wet dress. Stepping into the shower, she turned the water so hot she could hardly stand it. Then she sank to the floor and pulled the pins from her hair while the water beat down on her, wishing it could wash away the emptiness of her soul. But all she was left with were her thoughts, swirling in her mind like the water down the drain.

She was up before Theon the next morning, having slept in the bed in the small room. Theon hadn't argued with her. He hadn't even tried to convince her to sleep beside him. The sun hadn't risen yet, but she couldn't sleep. She was surprised she'd managed the few hours she had gotten. She sat in the bay window, sipping on coffee, watching the rain drizzling outside and wondering if it would rain like this at the Acropolis.

They would drive to Dark Haven before using the portal there. The other Fae had never left the Acropolis. They had used these last few weeks to get assigned to dormitories and go through an orientation of sorts of what to expect throughout the Selection Year. As a Source, she knew she wouldn't have to go through all the various lessons and trials the other Fae would undergo, but she also wasn't exactly sure what she would be doing there now. These last few weeks had been so chaotic between her and Theon and this damn bond. She just assumed she'd be told what she needed to know when she needed to know it at this point.

Just do as you're told and stop being a burden.

Be what they want you to be now, so you can be who you were meant to be later.

But did it matter when she just didn't have it in her to care anymore?

Maybe she'd been going about this the wrong way. Maybe she could find some sort of purpose in this. Some sort of…contentment in the fate she'd been given. Fighting against it was getting her nowhere.

The sound of footsteps had her glancing over in time to see Theon emerge, shirtless and wearing only his lounge pants. She looked back out the window, utterly annoyed at how her heart rate had picked up at seeing him, the cord stretching and reaching for him. She hadn't gotten dressed yet herself, unsure of what she'd be required to wear. She was hoping she'd at least be able to be comfortable while traveling. So her hair was up in a messy bun on her head, Theon's thermal over the tank top she'd slept in. He'd draped a heavy blanket over her after she'd fallen asleep, so she hadn't been cold.

She heard him getting coffee in the kitchen, then she felt rather than heard him approach her in the window.

"I don't believe the townhouse at the Acropolis has a bay window overlooking gardens," he said. "I wonder, where will you perch there?"

She slowly turned to look up at him.

"So we are back to not speaking?" he asked when she didn't reply.

She frowned. "No. I have just never been to a townhouse, so I don't know what to expect or where I will…perch."

"I haven't been there since it was updated after the last Selection, but I imagine the layout will be the same."

"They update them after every Selection Year?" Tessa asked.

"They do."

"That seems excessive."

"It probably is."

When he didn't say anything further, Tessa said, "Do I need to pack anything in particular to bring with me?"

"Pen left two days ago to get everything in order. We will have clothing and necessities upon arrival. Anything else we might need, we can find in the city," Theon replied.

"Penelope will be there with us?"

"She is the only staff that will be there with us, per our request," he said, taking a drink of his coffee as an almost fond smile crossed his lips. "Anyway, I have your computer and tablet already packed. We can go over passwords and whatnot on the drive. You just need your phone and any personal—"

He cut himself off when he realized what he was saying.

She cleared her throat. "As was stated last night, I have nothing, so I have nothing to pack other than what you deem necessary."

"Can we talk about...all of that?"

"No."

"No?"

She turned to look at him once more. "Our deal was that I would be compliant and help you with whatever it is you need my help with as your Source. When we are alone, I am not required to be such a thing."

"You no longer want your questions answered?" he asked, his head tilting as he studied her.

"Nope."

"You were very insistent last night."

"And you were correct. It does not matter. It changes nothing, so we are moving forward," she replied, standing from the window seat. "What do I need to wear today?"

Theon was quiet for a moment, still studying her. "I am unsure of what this is," he finally said.

"Unsure of what *what* is?"

"This mood of apathy."

"Whatever. Just tell me what you want me to wear today so I can get ready to go."

He was quiet for another few seconds before saying, "Be comfortable for travel. We will change before we go through the portal."

Tessa took her coffee cup with her into the dressing room, a little surprised he didn't have clothing picked out for her. She changed into a pair of jeans and pulled on a tank top, planning to wear a comfortable sweatshirt if she even had such a thing in this giant closet.

She brushed her teeth and applied light cosmetics before brushing out her hair and tying it up in a proper ponytail. She was slipping sneakers on when Theon came into the dressing room, a towel around his waist, apparently fresh out of the shower. Her mind immediately went to walking in on him in the shower yesterday.

Godsdamnit.

Trying to focus on anything other than what he had looked like with his cock in his hand and his release painting the shower wall, Tessa asked, "When you have a Match someday, where will her clothes go?"

Theon cursed when he slammed a drawer shut on his fingers. "What?" he asked in a low growl.

She eyed him warily, flicking through hangers. "Your Match. If you and Miss Davers are Matched, where will her clothing go?"

"Is that really something we need to discuss right now?"

"I was just curious," she said with a shrug.

"She will have her own rooms with her own closet," Theon said tightly.

"Her own rooms? She won't stay in your rooms?"

"She will stay in *our* room at times, I suppose. Other times, she might want her own space."

"Hmm," was all Tessa said as she finally settled on a long-sleeve shirt, unable to find a comfortable sweatshirt.

She slid the shirt on and turned to find Theon watching her while he buttoned his shirt. He'd also gotten dressed in jeans, and when he finished with the buttons, he rolled the sleeves up to his elbows. She left him in there to finish packing whatever else he might need and wandered out to the main room, finding Axel there. Her brows rose in surprise.

"You're early."

"I am just that excited to watch you and Theon on a day-long road trip."

"Funny," she deadpanned, then she stilled when she saw a pastry box on the island counter.

"Doughnuts," Axel said with a grin, following her gaze.

"Does Theon know?"

Axel shook his head slowly, his grin turning mischievous.

"I'm still pissed about you holding me down on the way back here yesterday," she said warily, making her way to the pastry box.

"I know. You should be."

Her hand stilled as she reached to open the box.

He'd followed her into the kitchen, sliding onto a stool. He opened the box for her, and she could have cried to see six different kinds of doughnuts. She picked up one with chocolate frosting on top, taking a bite.

"I'm sorry, Tessa," Axel said, pushing the lid closed.

"It's fine. It doesn't matter."

"It does matter. We have decades, centuries possibly, of being around each other. I don't want..." He trailed off, as if he didn't know how to finish his thought.

Tessa swallowed her second bite before she said, "As was stated last night, none of it matters, does it?" Axel opened his mouth, but she kept going. "Besides, soon enough you will have your own Source and a Match. I'll be in the background, just there when Theon needs power. That's my purpose, right?"

"Tessa, we don't want it to be like that. We've never wanted it to be like that. We've never wanted—"

"It doesn't matter what anyone wants," she sighed. "Again, as was stated last night, nothing can be changed."

She set the half-eaten doughnut down on a napkin she'd grabbed. It just…didn't taste right.

"Nothing can change you being his Source, that's true," Axel said carefully. "But that doesn't mean you need to be miserable, Tessa. He just…" He pushed out a long breath, swiping a hand down his face. "You've seen Eviana. We don't leave the kingdom much. The Arius Kingdom is private for various reasons you will soon learn. The relationship between my father and Eviana is all we really had to go on when it came to Sources. Theon thought—well, we all thought really— that it was just…automatically like that."

Tessa was quiet, fidgeting with the napkin beneath her fingers. "I am well aware that I am…a disappointment in many ways, Axel. Despite my best efforts to not be that, I know I can be a hassle."

"You're not, Tessa. You're—"

"I know I am different from other Fae."

"Theon wants different. He doesn't want—"

"I know what Theon wants," Tessa cut in. "He told me his entire godsdamn checklist last night. I just so happen to check all the boxes except the easy one."

"He doesn't want easy."

"I don't care what he wants. I don't care what any of you want."

"Okay, that's fair," Axel said, nudging the half-eaten doughnut forward with his fingertips. "Then what do you care about, Tessa?"

"Nothing," she answered. "Why would I bother caring about anything? It won't make a difference."

"What about this bargain with Theon?" he countered. "You obviously care about something to make a bargain."

Tessa brushed her fingers along her ribs, where the Bargain Mark now marred her skin. "The bargain was impulsive. Something I'm told I am often. It was pointless and simply tied me to him in yet another way. But I will uphold my end. I will be his perfect little Source in public. The gods know I don't need to be any more cursed than I already am."

Axel frowned, and he opened his mouth, about to say something else, when Theon strode into the room. "Luka is waiting for us down at the vehicle," he said, glancing once at the doughnuts. He grabbed Tessa's coffee mug, and she watched him pour what was left into a travel mug, topping it off with what was left in the pot. He twisted the lid on before passing it back to her without a word. Then he scooped up a messenger bag and looped it over his shoulder. "Ready?"

Axel swiped up the pastry box, closing the lid. "For months away from this place? Absolutely."

Both of their gazes settled on her. She made her way to them, following the St. Orcas brothers out the door and leaving the half-eaten doughnut sitting on the counter.

PART TWO
DEATH MUST TAKE

30
TESSA

Tessa had the earbuds in that Axel had given her, listening to a playlist he had set up. Her back was to the door against the window. She'd long since lost her socks and sneakers, and her bare feet were on the seat between her and Theon. The laptop Theon had purchased for her was propped against her bent knees, and she was playing around with the various features. Theon had shown her the basics of the tablet and computer. They'd had access to basic technology at the Estate, but, like her new phone, this was the best on the market. Corbin would be beside himself. He was usually reserved and stoic, except when it came to technology.

They'd been traveling for a few hours when there was a lull between songs, and Tessa caught a few words of the conversation taking place around her.

"I don't know how she can focus on the screen with it constantly bouncing like that," Axel was saying.

"She has become increasingly fidgety," Theon replied.

"Probably because she hates confined spaces and has been trapped in a vehicle for hours," Tessa muttered under her breath, instantly ceasing the tapping of her feet. She began drumming her fingers lightly on the laptop keys as the next song started up, staring at the screen. She hadn't really been doing anything for the last hour. Nothing but trying to keep her mind busy so she could forget about being cooped up in a vehicle. They just kept moving her from one place to another, but that was to be her life now, she supposed. At least there'd be new scenery to stare at. See? She could find the silver lining or whatever it was the mortals said.

Fingers brushed along the top of her foot, and her stomach dipped. How could a single touch do that to her?

This fucking bond.

So why didn't she pull away from him? She could. She didn't have to follow all his ridiculous commands anymore when it was just them. But gods, did that single touch calm her restlessness just enough to make it bearable.

He kept his hand there, making small circles with his thumb, and she leaned her head back against the window, closing her eyes. Moments later, she felt the vehicle slowing, and she twisted to look outside as Luka pulled to a stop in a small town.

"Why are we stopping?" Tessa asked, pulling the earbuds from her ears.

"I need to get a phone charger, baby doll," Axel said before sliding out of the vehicle.

"You don't have an extra charger?" she asked Theon.

"No, but while we're here, do you want to get out and walk around?"

"It can't take that long to buy a phone charger," she said doubtfully.

"We're not in a hurry. There are no required engagements until tomorrow," Theon said, opening his door. "Come on."

Her eyes narrowed, but she reached for her socks and sneakers, quickly lacing them up and sliding across the seat. She immediately tipped her face up to the sky, breathing in the fresh air. When she reopened her eyes, she found Theon leaning against the vehicle, his hands in his pockets, watching her.

"What?" she asked, suddenly self-conscious as she wrapped her arms around herself.

"Nothing," he said, pushing off the vehicle. He held out a hand to her. "Shall we?"

Not letting herself think about it, she slid her hand into his and let him lead her down the sidewalk. They passed a few shops until they came to a small park, an empty Chaosphere field stretching out behind them. It wasn't in the best shape. The grass was overgrown and the boundary lines were faded, but it was something she would expect of a small community, she supposed. Theon took a seat on a bench and looked at her expectantly.

"I'm not sitting down."

He arched a brow. "Why not?"

"I've been sitting in a vehicle for hours," she replied, hopping from foot-to-foot. "And other than running with you, I've been cooped up in your rooms for weeks."

"You forgot about your little rendezvous through the woods."

She shot him a dry look.

A half-smile lifted on his lips. "Well, little storm, what would you like to do?"

She glanced behind her at the empty Chaosphere field. "Can we buy a ball?"

Both brows shot up at that. "You want to play Chaosphere?"

She shrugged. "You think you can score against me?"

"Doubtful," came Axel's voice behind them. "Theon never played Chaosphere. He was always too busy studying and researching."

Tessa turned back to Theon. "You never played?"

"You did?"

"Of course I played. What child didn't play Chaosphere? I mostly played by myself, but—" She cut herself off, then cleared her throat. "Yes. I would play. I took every opportunity to be outside."

"I'll go get a ball," Axel said, dropping a bag near the bench.

Luka was standing nearby, an expression Tessa couldn't read on his face as he looked between her and Theon. She kicked her foot back, grabbing her ankle and stretching.

"You're really serious about this," Theon observed, that small smile quirking on his lips again.

"I'm very competitive," Tessa retorted, switching to the other leg.

"This is going to be very interesting," Luka muttered, folding his arms across his chest.

"Did you play?" Tessa asked him.

"Of course I played. I'm fairly certain everyone *but* Theon played Chaosphere as a child," Luka answered, and Theon flipped him off.

A minute later, Axel showed up with a black ball, tossing it back and forth between his hands. "You ready for this, baby doll?"

"Does Theon even know how to play?" she teased, easily catching the ball when Axel sent it her way.

"I know the basics," Theon said indignantly, swiping the ball from her as he strode past.

"You and me versus Theon and Luka?" Axel asked, coming up beside her.

"Deal," Tessa replied, and something she hadn't felt in weeks blossomed in her chest.

"What position are you best at?" Axel asked.

"Ground offense."

"Really?"

"Mhmm," she hummed, tilting her face back to the sky where the sun was trying its damnedest to peek out from the clouds.

"I feel like we should get some bonus points or something. I'm at a clear disadvantage with Theon," Luka said from the center of the field.

"Fuck off," Theon muttered. "It's not that hard."

Tessa and Axel exchanged grins before getting into position. The ball always started on the ground where it could only be moved with feet. Once it left the ground and was touched by someone's hands, it couldn't touch the ground again during that round.

"I'll take Luka, and you'll cover Theon?" Axel asked.

Tessa nodded as Theon placed the ball in the center of the field, and the four of them got ready. Axel counted down, and Tessa shot forward, kicking the ball to Axel before Theon had even moved. She wasn't a fast runner, but she could handle a Chaosphere ball better than most. There wasn't much for entertainment on the Estates, and most of the other children stopped wanting to be around her when she was constantly being reprimanded for something or other. Anyone with her was usually punished as well, and they learned quickly it was better to simply avoid her. She spent hours alone with a Chaosphere ball, usually off in a secluded area. The other children were always on the fields, so she would find her own space.

She ran down the field as Axel sent the ball her way again, and she laughed when Theon made the most pathetic attempt to steal the ball she had ever seen. She kicked the ball back into the air at Axel, who caught it with ease. He made it to the end of the field, dodging Luka and tossing the ball into the goal pit.

"You weren't kidding about ground offense, baby doll. That was fancy footwork," Axel said, gripping her around the waist and spinning her in a circle. Another laugh bubbled up her throat. It felt weird. When was the last time she'd truly laughed?

"Yeah, yeah," Luka grumbled, stalking back to the middle of the field with the ball. "I still think I should get a few bonus points for having Theon on my team."

"I am not that bad," Theon protested.

"You kind of are," Tessa replied, getting into position for the next round.

Luka got the ball, kicking it up to Theon, who caught it. She raced down the field beside him, and he glanced at her side-long.

"You're going to defend against me? I tower over you," Theon said with a smirk. He wasn't wrong. Defensive players were usually muscled, built for tackling whoever had the ball.

"I don't need to defend against you," she replied, keeping pace with him as he made his way down the field. "I just need to defend the goal pit."

Theon tossed the ball over her head to Luka, who barely avoided Axel's attempt at intercepting the ball. While Theon was focused on Luka and watching the ball, Tessa went for the goal, where she prepared for their attempt to score. Luka tossed the ball back to Theon, who tossed it towards the goal pit, and Tessa easily blocked the shot, catching the ball.

"You really are terrible at this," she said with a laugh.

"I am not that bad," Theon grumbled.

By their ninth round, Theon and Luka had managed to score one point, while she and Axel had scored the other seven. She was racing down the field, preparing to receive the ball Axel had just kicked her way, when an arm looped around her waist, lifting her off the ground.

"Theon! You're cheating!" she cried through a bark of laughter as he intercepted the ball and kicked it to Luka.

"I am," he agreed, spinning her around and setting her back on her feet, blocking her path to go after the ball. "I'm becoming a touch insecure with myself after being out maneuvered every round, beautiful."

"You almost scored a point that one time."

"And now you are teasing me," he admonished.

She bit her lip as she stared up at him.

"Let's go, guys," Axel hollered. "We have one round left!"

With a small smile at Theon, she turned and jogged to the center of the field for the final round.

"We ready?" Luka asked her.

"Don't look at me," she said. "Theon's the one who needs all the help he can get."

Axel snickered as Luka set the ball in the center of the field. Axel managed to gain control of it, and Tessa whooped in triumph as she took off down the field. Luka leapt to tackle Axel, and he sent the ball in the air to Tessa, but as she jumped to catch it, darkness swarmed above her head. Shadows caught the ball as though they were hands, and Tessa landed on the ground, turning to face Theon with a disbelieving look on her face.

"That's not fair!" she protested, her hands on her hips.

"It has already been established that I do not play fair," he conceded, his shadows flinging the ball to Luka, who took off in the other direction, Axel chasing after him.

"You're being a sore loser," Tessa chided as Theon came to a stop in front of her.

"I am," he agreed, grabbing her hand and tugging her into him. His other hand reached around and wrapped around her ponytail, pulling gently and tilting her head back. "You never cease to surprise me."

"Because I can play Chaosphere?" she breathed, his heated eyes holding hers.

"Because you are...just not what I expected."

"It's not that hard to play Chaosphere, Theon." When he just stared back at her, she asked hesitantly, "Why are you looking at me like that?"

"Because you are smiling, and I rarely see such a thing."

Her breathing had been evening out after the exertion of the game, but now her breath hitched again. She didn't know what to say to that, but as he continued to hold her gaze, the rest of the world slowly faded around her. She got lost in emerald irises and black hair that brushed his brow. In that dimple that appeared when a slow grin began to fill his face. At some point, she'd reached up and gently curled her fingers into his shirt. She had no idea when she'd done that.

"I am going to kiss you, Tessa," Theon said, his voice low in a way that had heat pooling low in her belly.

"Okay," she whispered.

He wasted no time bringing his mouth to hers, as if he thought she would change her mind at any moment. But as soon as his lips touched hers, pulling away from him was the last thing she wanted, and in that moment, she wasn't sure if it was all the bond.

Theon had kissed her plenty of times over the last few weeks. Heated kisses. Punishing ones. Desperate kisses and claiming ones, but none had been like this. This kiss was slow and languid, his tongue gently rolling against hers. His hand was still wrapped in her hair, but he used it to tip her head back a little more as he deepened the kiss. She found herself pushing up on her toes, trying to get closer to him as his other hand cupped her cheek.

She couldn't decide if she was relieved or disappointed when he broke the kiss first, his breathing as ragged as her own. He rested his brow against hers, his eyes falling closed. Is this what it would be like if she gave in? If she let herself find... Well, not happiness, but some type of contentment with them? With him?

"I am beginning to think you plan these things, little storm."

"Plan what?" she asked, too distracted by the way his lashes fanned across his cheekbones with his eyes closed.

"You only let me get this close to you when we are in public or have some place to be," he replied, his eyes opening and connecting with hers. His palm still held her cheek, and his thumb brushed along her bottom lip. "I would ask you to remember this moment, to remember how you are feeling right now so we can revisit it when we are at the townhouse, but I know that request would be futile...right?"

"Right," she whispered, unable to break his stare.

"Can I ask something else of you then?"

"I think you ask enough of me the way it is."

Her fingers were still clutching at his shirt, and she felt him tense beneath her hand.

He cleared his throat as he straightened, his hands slipping from her face and hair. "We should get going. Do you need anything else before we go back to the vehicle?"

Tessa shook her head, quickly uncurling her fingers from his shirt and taking a step back from him. She looked around the field, but Luka and Axel were nowhere to be found. The lightness she'd been feeling was already lessening, and she wrapped her arms around herself as the sun slipped behind clouds once more.

Theon glanced up at the sky, then back at her, his brow furrowing as if he couldn't figure something out.

As if he couldn't figure *her* out.

She fell into step beside him, and neither of them spoke as they made their way back down to the street. Theon did not reach for her hand, and for once, the cord that connected them did not seem to mind.

Axel and Luka were waiting for them at the vehicle, both of them looking from Theon to her and back again. She saw Theon shake his head the smallest amount when Axel opened his mouth to say something, and his brother quickly snapped it shut again.

"Are we ready?" Luka asked, keys in hand.

She didn't answer, dread already filling her at having to go back into the vehicle. She was trying to soak up every bit of being outside.

It wasn't until they were back on the road, her earbuds back in place as she scrolled through playlists that she realized Theon had not been holding her to him the entire time they'd kissed. There had been no arm looped around her waist. She could have stepped away at any time. In fact, *she* had been clinging to *him*.

Startled by the realization, she glanced up at him. He was looking at something on his phone, his features tight and mouth set in a thin line. There was space between them, and he'd hardly spoken since they'd all climbed back into the vehicle. He'd hardly looked at her.

And as she returned her attention to the music on her phone, she wondered what he had wanted to ask of her.

"Can I ask you a question?" Tessa said, pulling an earbud from her ear.

The entire vehicle fell silent, all eyes settling on her. Axel reached over and turned down the music, and they all waited. It was rather unsettling.

When Theon nodded at her, she cleared her throat softly, pulling out her other earbud. "What is a Guardian Mark?"

"What?" Theon said, obvious shock in his tone.

"I was looking through some things on the computer, and I found some of your old lesson papers," she replied, skimming the one she currently had open.

Axel twisted even more in his seat to look at Theon. "Seriously? You have old lesson papers still saved on your computer?"

"I never clean my files out," Theon retorted. "I gave Tessa access to my entire network. Some files are password protected. Obviously those are not." His attention returned to her. "Why are you looking through those anyway?"

She shrugged. "I'm bored."

"We only have about an hour left," Luka said.

"Great," Tessa replied. "So about this Guardian thing. This paper Theon wrote says it's a Mark of some kind."

"It is," Theon answered slowly.

"Like the Source Marks?"

"Sort of."

"According to your paper, they incorporated the Guardian Mark into the Source Marks somehow."

"It is a theory."

"Right. A theory…" she murmured, continuing to skim through the document again. "But what is it exactly?"

"How much do you know about Arius and Sargon?" Theon asked instead.

Tessa glanced up at him. "Arius is the god of endings and who you descend from. Speaking of which, how far back does that go? Like a few generations up your family tree, and we'd find Arius or…?"

Theon barked a laugh. "No, Tessa. The original demigod our family is descended from lived literally thousands of years ago. Before this world was even created. I don't even know how many generations back we'd have to go to even come close to figuring that out. Likely hundreds."

"And Sargon is the god of war and courage," she said.

"Yes," Theon replied, his eyes flicking to the front seat where Axel and Luka were listening intently. "He also commands Arius's armies, including his elite guardians."

"Elite guardians? And what do you mean by Arius's armies? Wouldn't Sargon ultimately answer to Achaz since he is the ruler of the gods?"

"Why the sudden interest, little one?" Luka asked, and she was surprised it came from him. He tended to let Theon and Axel deal with her, only interfering if Theon was being a special kind of asshole.

"It's just this Guardian Mark thing…" She paused as she read more, her feet beginning to tap on the seat again. "I don't understand why they would incorporate it into the Source Marks. How would that work?"

"There are different types of magic throughout the worlds, Tessa," Theon said, watching her closely. "Some are not as readily found here because the gods do not interfere with our world, but that does not mean our own magic hasn't evolved in various ways. We have found ways around that."

"What does that mean?"

"How do you think advancements are made with tonics and technology?"

"We were taught the gods gave their Legacy the best from all the worlds before they dumped you all here," she replied, her eyes going back to the screen.

"You phrase it so eloquently, baby doll," Axel teased.

Tessa shrugged. "So the Guardian Mark was a real thing?"

"It *is* a real thing," Theon answered.

"In theory."

"It is a theory that the Guardian Mark was somehow incorporated into the Source Marks, but the Guardian Mark itself is not a theory," Theon clarified.

"How did it work?"

"Guardians are always of the Sargon bloodline. They were often bonded to Arius descendants, but the strongest of Sargon's bloodline were bonded to gods or deities to protect them."

"Deities?" Tessa asked, glancing up at him.

Theon gave her a soft smile. "Deities were the result of a god having a child with a magical bloodline."

"A magical bloodline? Like the Legacy?"

Theon shook his head. "The Legacy all have mortal blood. We are descended from demigods, the result of a god and a mortal. We may have worked hard over the many centuries to make the mortal blood as insignificant as possible by carefully arranging Matches, but it doesn't negate the fact that we will always have some mortal blood, even if only a drop at this point."

"So what kind of magical bloodline then?"

"The gods created worlds," Luka chimed in. "You think they only created a few forms of life and only in this realm?"

"I guess that makes sense," she mused. "What other magical bloodlines are there?"

Theon shrugged. "Who can really say at this point? With the gods agreeing to not interfere in this world, it is not as if we can know of anything going on in the other realms. It is said Legacy could once travel between places by simply willing it, as if they walked through the air. But they took that ability from us when they brought all their Legacy here."

"Travel between places? Like between kingdoms?"

Theon shrugged. "Between kingdoms. Between worlds. That is something we will likely never know, I suppose. I've found texts that suggest more than the gods emerged from the Chaos."

"So back to this Guardian thing," Tessa said, sitting up a little straighter because this was truly fascinating. Of course she'd known there were other realms, but she'd never really thought much about it. What would be the point when her entire purpose was to serve the Legacy? But entire other bloodlines and races? Even though it made complete sense, it was still hard to wrap her mind around. "Gods and deities just picked a Guardian? Then they were given this Mark and what? How did it work exactly?"

"They didn't just pick a Guardian," Luka said. "Some tried to replicate it and force such a thing, but it never worked the same. The Guardian Mark had to be agreed to by both parties, or it wouldn't function as it was created to."

"And it was created to...?"

"The Guardian and the Ward's lives became connected. The Guardian could sense when their Ward was in danger, and the bond created required the Guardian to do whatever was necessary to protect their Ward, even if that meant giving their own life," Luka answered. "That is why it did not work when forced. When forced, the Guardian could, and often did, become resentful of their Ward. But when the Guardian *chose* the Guardian Mark and subsequent Guardian Bond—"

"Wait, Guardian *Bond*?" Tessa interrupted. "Like this Source Bond thing?"

"Source bond thing," Theon repeated dryly.

She gave him a simpering smile. "Don't pretend your feelings are hurt. I have made it perfectly clear how I feel about this *Source bond thing*."

Theon clenched his jaw but didn't say anything else.

"The Guardian Mark creates a bond of sorts. As I said, the Guardian can sense when their Ward is in danger and is driven to protect them," Luka said into the tense silence.

"And this was incorporated into the Source Marks how?" Tessa asked, scrolling down on the document.

When no one spoke, she glanced up to find the three of them looking between one another.

"For those who believe I have a lot of secrets, you lot certainly seem to have a lot of your own," she said casually.

"If you'd accept this bond, I could share all my secrets with you, Tessa," Theon said.

"Right. Before you can trust me, I need to blindly trust you and accept the bond. Got it."

"Tessa," Theon sighed, running his thumb and forefinger along his brow.

"What is the theory of how this was incorporated in the Source Marks?" she asked.

"It—" Luka started.

"Luka…" Theon warned, causing Tessa to glance up again.

"She deserves to know, Theon. She *should* know."

Theon began to say something, but Tessa cut him off. "I don't *deserve* anything, Luka. You should know that by now."

"Tessa, we're trying here," Theon said.

"No, Theon. Luka is trying. Axel is trying. You are just demanding. Much like your father."

The vehicle fell quiet, all the males going still. After a long, tense moment, Tessa put her earbuds back in, closing out of the document and shutting the laptop. She'd closed her eyes, leaning her head back against the window when an earbud was plucked from her ear. Theon was leaning over her, but before she could snap at him, he spoke first.

"How much do you know of the Marks, Tessa?"

"What?"

"When this all started, you told me you didn't know as much as the other Sources. That you hadn't been prepared for what's happening like they were."

"Because I haven't been."

"So what do you know?"

"There are four Marks."

"Do you know what each of them does? The order they are given?"

She blinked at him because she didn't know. She knew what the Marks would do, but not the order or which ones would do what.

A finger brushed over the Mark on her right hand. "This one allows us to feel each other's physical presence. It's why the bond craves close-ness right now. It's our essences getting to know each other, and it's why…"

"You're annoyingly needy?" she supplied, and Axel snickered from the front seat.

"Yes," Theon said tightly. "You are supposed to be feeling the same way, but obviously are…not."

Tessa flashed him a sardonic smile.

His finger left her hand and came to her chest, brushing over her heart. "The next one will go here. On the fall equinox," he continued softly. "It will allow us to feel each other's emotions."

She swallowed as he held her gaze, something in her stomach unacceptably fluttering. "And if I don't want you to know what I'm feeling?" she breathed.

He didn't answer, his finger trailing up along her collarbone, around her throat until he brushed down her nape. He leaned forward to whisper in her ear. "And on the winter solstice, you'll get the third Mark here, allowing us to hear each other's thoughts."

"And if I don't want you in my head?" she whispered back.

"I am praying to any god that will listen that you will feel differently by that point," he answered.

"How unfortunate for you the gods can't hear those pleas. And if they can, there's nothing they can do about them."

Heated emerald eyes met her own. He lifted her left hand, his thumb brushing over the back of it. "The final Mark will go here. On the spring equinox."

"And will allow you to draw power from me."

"Yes," Theon agreed, that heat in his gaze dying out a little and being replaced with something Tessa couldn't quite put her finger on. "Each Mark adds another layer to the bond, but the final Mark... You will feel driven to react against any threat against me."

She jerked back from him. "What?"

"That is where the theory about the Guardian Mark somehow being incorporated into the Source Marks comes from."

"So let me get this straight," Tessa said. "Not only will I lose all sense of self, all privacy, all of *me*, I will also be forced to give my life for yours if the situation demands such a thing?"

Theon opened his mouth but closed it again, saying nothing in response.

"You will literally take everything from me," she whispered in realization.

"No," Theon said, shaking his head, still gripping her left hand. She tried to pull it back, but he squeezed her fingers. "No, Tessa. That will never happen."

"What do you mean that will never happen? Do you not intend to force the rest of the Marks?"

"No. I mean, yes. You will receive the rest of the Marks," he amended quickly at her arched brows. "But you will never be required to give your life for mine."

"You can't say that, Theon. If the situation—"

"It won't happen, Tessa."

"How can you be so sure?" she demanded, her voice rising.

His hand came to her cheek. "Because I already have a Guardian, Tessa. A full Guardian. With a Guardian Mark and a Guardian Bond."

"What? Who? How?" she asked, stumbling over her words as she tried to digest what he'd just told her.

"I already have a Guardian," Theon repeated. "It's how we know so much about the Guardian Bond."

"Who?" she repeated.

"Luka."

Tessa's head whipped to the front seat. She pushed past Theon to lean over the center console. "You're his Guardian?"

"I am," Luka agreed.

"How?"

"I willingly took the Guardian Mark when we were sixteen years," Luka answered. "We both have one."

"Where?" she demanded, sitting back and looking expectantly at Theon.

"We both have Guardian Marks on our backs."

"I've never seen it," Tessa argued.

"You wouldn't," Theon said. "Guardian Marks are magic of the gods, Tessa. It's called many things in various texts— Blood Magic, magic of the gods, the Celestial Language. The point is, you can't see them unless you have the blood of the gods in you. Although, there are some texts that suggest you will be able to see them once you have all the Source Marks."

Tessa could only stare back at him. He reached out, tucking a stray piece of hair behind her ear.

"Do all the heirs have Guardians? Lord St. Orcas?"

Theon shook his head slowly, his eyes never leaving hers. "Guardians must be descendants of Sargon."

She turned back to Luka. "You are a Sargon Legacy?"

"I am."

"How?"

"What do you mean *how?*" Luka said dryly. "I've seen your lesson marks. I know you were taught basic anatomy, Tessa."

She rolled her eyes. "I mean there aren't any Sargon descendants anywhere. That line hasn't even pledged to a Kingdom."

"Because Sargon is loyal to Arius. There was no need," Luka answered.

Tessa was quiet, trying to process everything, but she couldn't. It was all too far-fetched at this point. So instead she turned back to Theon and said, "That doesn't explain why the other heirs don't have a Guardian. Or why your father doesn't have one. He's the Arius Lord."

"Sargon descendants are few and far between," Theon replied.

"Why?" Tessa asked, her brows knitting.

"No one really knows. Some believe he was far more...selective about who he sired children with so he doesn't have as many descendants," Theon answered.

Her nose wrinkled at that, but it kind of made sense. The gods were eternal. She imagined living for an unlimited number of millennia allowed time for various...experiences. But still. Just how many children did the gods have? Sure, they created various bloodlines, but they hadn't *physically* created them all *that* way. Right?

"What are you thinking?" Theon asked.

"That the other gods are kind of...promiscuous?"

"Promiscuous," Theon repeated, his lips twitching.

"I'm trying to be respectful."

His brow arched. "That's new." She gave him a dry look while flipping him her middle finger. "And that's rude," he added.

She was about to respond when something else occurred to her. "Wait. You're a descendant of Sargon?"

"Yes," Luka sighed.

"Then what are your gifts?"

The three of them looked between each other again.

"You really don't know?" Axel asked.

"Why would I know? I thought he was an Arius Legacy. I thought he was your cousin or something."

"Luka can shift his form," Theon said slowly.

"I don't understand."

"Luka can shift into what it is believed Arius's elite guardians were created in the image of."

"Which is what?"

A wry smile curved up on Axel's lips. "Luka can shift into a dragon, baby doll."

31
THEON

"A dragon," Tessa repeated.

"You really didn't know?" Axel asked.

"No!" Tessa said incredulously. "How would I possibly know that Luka can shift into a *dragon*? Wait. No. Better question. How could you assholes not tell me this before now?"

Axel shrugged. "His eyes change when he gets irritated. And when he's really mad or if Theon is being threatened, he'll breathe out smoke. He did it at the last meeting with our father. You didn't see that?"

"Oh, sorry," Tessa drawled. "I was too preoccupied with Theon torturing someone with his shadows or darkness or whatever the fuck it is you two control." She smacked Axel on the shoulder. "No, I didn't see that."

"You're not very observant then," Axel retorted.

Theon held in his bark of laughter at the look Tessa sent his way. She was still leaning over the center console between the front seats, and she twisted back to Luka. The whole Luka-can-shift-into-a-dragon thing seemed to have distracted her from the Source Marks and what they would require of her. But he'd also spoken the truth. Luka would defend him before either of them would let Tessa put herself in harm's way for him.

Which was exactly the opposite of his father and Eviana, and not for the first time, Theon wondered if something had gone wrong with his bond with Tessa. Had the Priestess made an error with the Mark somehow? Had he not invoked the wording correctly? Magic was finicky and needed to be done precisely.

She had air magic. There was no doubt about that. When she had shoved him on their balcony last night, he had felt the force of it. He had felt her power wrap around him, and he had felt his darkness rise up to meet it. Just as quickly, her magic had dissipated, but for that split-second their magic had touched, he'd felt...so much he hadn't been able to process it all.

Pleasure.

Desire.

Euphoria.

Her.

He'd felt Tessa in a way he never had before. He'd felt her strength. He'd felt her power.

He'd felt the storm he often glimpsed in her eyes, and he wasn't entirely sure he was prepared to harness that power when he could access it. He was going to need her help in controlling it, but to get that to happen, he needed her to trust him.

But if she had air magic, how had she created that crevice in the gardens? And what about the things that had crawled out of it? That was not air and wind, and her assessment had given them nothing else to go on aside from her power level. He'd been researching possibilities, but so far, he'd found nothing to explain it. Luka had searched for hours trying to find traces of the things, but it was as if they'd just disappeared.

He glanced out the window again. The gathering clouds seemed to have lessened some, sunlight breaking through. His eyes flicked back to Tessa, who was still leaning into the front seat.

"This actually explains a lot," she was saying.

"What does that mean?" Axel asked.

"Luka is always so brooding. I imagine dragons are broody."

"I am not broody," Luka muttered.

"Uh-huh," Tessa said. "Do you have scales?"

"Yes, Tessa," Luka sighed.

Theon reached for her, gently pulling her back from between the seats as she said, "Do you have wings? Can you fly?"

"I have wings, and yes, I can fly," Luka answered.

Ten minutes later, Tessa was still asking questions, but she had also settled into Theon's side, much to his surprise. He hadn't initiated it, and he could only assume she was so engrossed in this conversation with Luka, she hadn't realized what she was doing.

Or rather, what the bond was naturally doing.

"Why doesn't Lord St. Orcas have a Guardian?" she asked.

"Luka was supposed to be his," Theon replied.

"Aren't you two the same age?"

"We are," Luka supplied, glancing at Theon in the rearview mirror.

Theon nodded subtly, curious how much of his past he was going to share with her. Tessa was right. He was a broody ass, and he didn't care for people in general. But he'd been different with Tessa from the very beginning. It was in things others wouldn't notice, but Theon had. And he couldn't decide if it was because she was his Source, so his friend was making more of an effort knowing they would forever be in each other's lives, or if it was something else.

"My parents died when I was young," Luka answered. "I barely remember them. I was only five years."

"I'm sorry," Tessa whispered.

Luka cut her a quick look in the mirror. "Why? You weren't there."

"I know, but I can still be sad that you lost your parents. Had to grow up alone."

"He wasn't alone," Theon cut in.

She glanced up at him before her gaze dropped to her lap. "Yeah. I guess not."

"As was stated, Sargon's bloodline is rare. So rare, in fact, with my parents gone, I am the only known descendant in all of Devram," Luka supplied.

"But how is that possible?"

He shrugged. "We've searched for answers over the years, but have found nothing of value."

"That's not true," Theon cut in.

Axel snorted a laugh, but before Theon could say anything in response, Luka spoke over them.

"Few know my true lineage. Most believe me to be an Arius Legacy, and we simply don't correct them. But to answer your original question, Valter took me in because of my bloodline. I was to become his Guardian when I turned sixteen years. While the Guardian Bond can be forced, that was never the intention. When chosen by both parties, the Guardian relationship is stronger and more powerful.

"Theon and I, along with Axel, had been raised together. All of us trained and raised to further the Arius Kingdom, but we have…differing views from Valter on the best way to accomplish such things. On my sixteenth birthday, there was a ceremony planned to create the bond between Valter and me."

"But in the early morning hours of his birthday, we were prepared to do the ceremony ourselves," Theon supplied.

"How?" Tessa asked.

"Little Theon here is quite the academic," Axel said teasingly. "He'd been studying that bond for years. You know, instead of doing normal things like playing Chaosphere."

"But I thought a Priestess had to bestow Marks?" Tessa asked.

"They are trained extensively to do so, and they are the only ones trained for the Source Marks. In fact, there are very few who know how to give the Source Marks to deter lesser Legacy from taking their own," Theon explained.

"I don't understand," Tessa said. "If the Guardian Bond is not well known, how would you have found a Priestess to give the Mark?"

"We are a very private kingdom, Tessa."

"The Priestess who did my assessment?"

Theon shook his head. "No. She may work in our kingdom. But like every other Zinta Legacy, she is first and foremost loyal to her blood-line, and the Zinta bloodline is loyal to the Achaz Kingdom. She took a blood vow regarding your assessment, but we would still never trust them with something like this."

Her brow furrowed. "Then who would have given the Mark?"

"A Witch."

Her eyes flew wide as she stared up at Theon. "A Witch? But they are banished to the…" She trailed off, horror filling her grey eyes as she whispered, "The Witches are confined to the Underground."

Theon nodded. "They are."

"You went to the Underground for this Guardian Mark."

"Do you know where the Underground is located, Tessa?"

She shook her head. "No one knows where the Underground is. Only that you do not wish to find out."

A dark smile tilted on his lips. "For some, that is certainly the case."

He saw her throat bob as she swallowed, edging away from him the smallest amount. "And for others?"

"For others, it is a place to find what they need."

He watched her debate her next question. Saw the resolve fill her eyes before she asked. "Where is the Underground, Theon?"

"In the northern part of the Arius Kingdom. Beneath the Ozul Mountains."

"The Arius Kingdom controls the Underground?"

"I don't know that control would be the best word choice, but we oversee it, yes," Theon confirmed.

Tessa went quiet, turning to look out the window, but she didn't move any further from him. Not like he'd expected her to. They were all quiet, waiting to see what she said next. This was information she would have been learning soon enough. He didn't think it'd be like this, with her still resisting the bond, but they were out of time. Along with everything she'd be doing at the Acropolis, she'd be getting detailed history lessons from them on the Arius Kingdom. She may not have to go through the Selection process and trials like the other Fae, but she would be just as busy.

"Do you go there often?" she finally asked.

"Not as much as Luka and Axel do," he answered.

Her eyes darted to the others. Both of the males were staring ahead, letting Theon tell her what he wanted her to know for the moment.

"Why do they go there?"

"Sometimes on business for my father."

"And other times?"

"Business of our own." She turned away to look out the window again, but not before he saw the flash of acceptance on her face. When she didn't ask another question, he found himself adding, "There are things I need to share with you—things I *will* share with you—but I would prefer to do so later tonight. Once we are settled."

Tessa only nodded, her attention now fixed out the window.

After several minutes of silence, Axel said, "Luka can breathe fire."

"What?" Tessa's head swung to him, her eyes wide, and she was once again leaning between the front seats. "You can breathe fire?"

Luka threw Axel an irritated glare, but he answered her. "I can breathe fire, but it drains my magic reserves faster."

"How long does it take to refill your reserves?" Tessa asked, reaching forward to take a doughnut Axel was handing to her.

Theon met his brother's eyes and gave him a small nod of thanks. Tessa hadn't eaten all day. They'd offered. Multiple times. She'd declined all day other than the few bites she'd taken of the doughnut this morning. He didn't really care what she ate at this point, just that she was eating.

"Naturally, it would take several weeks," Luka answered.

"How else would you refill them if not naturally? You don't get a Source, right?"

"No, Tessa. I do not get a Source. Only the ruling Lords, Ladies, and their heirs get a Source. You know this."

Luka glanced at Theon in the rearview mirror, and he steeled himself for what she was about to learn.

"Fae blood can refill Legacy power reserves, Tessa," Theon said. His arm was still spread along the back of the seat, and he resisted the urge to pull her back to him when she twisted back to face him.

"What do you mean Fae blood can refill Legacy magic reserves?"

He pushed out a breath, swiping his other hand down his face. "All the Legacy, save for those with Sources they can draw from, are given a ration of Fae blood each week to use as they see fit. So they do not need to wait for their power reserves to refill naturally."

The doughnut she'd taken a few bites of was now forgotten in her hand. "But where do they get this Fae blood?"

"After Selection, when Fae are assigned to their kingdoms, they are required to donate blood weekly as part of their duties," Theon answered, not breaking her stare.

"Donating," she scoffed. "Why aren't we told about this?"

"You are. During the Selection year process, Fae are told."

Tessa nodded, her eyes falling to her lap. After a long minute of silence, Theon reached over and took the half-eaten doughnut from her hand. She slid along the seat, back to the opposite door, and he let her go.

He'd let her sleep in that small godsdamn room last night, draping a heavy blanket over her after she'd fallen asleep. He hadn't slept at all, the bond making him agitated, and he'd had the entire night to let her words replay over and over.

What will you do when you have taken everything and left me with nothing?

I'm a nobody with nothing to give.

Congratulations. You already won.

And again he wondered what had she experienced in her life at the Estate? What had pushed her to this point? To believe she was nothing?

He could try to tell her that wasn't true. That she was more than power to him, but she had refused to speak about it this morning. He had a feeling she would refuse now. Tonight. Tomorrow. He'd lost control and said too much last night.

And now?

Now she had no reason to believe anything he said.

When they reached Dark Haven, they all changed into appropriate clothing. Luka, Axel, and Theon donned black pants and button-down shirts. Tessa slipped into a simple sheath dress of emerald green that clung to all her curves. She slid on black heels before he took her hand and led her through the portal where they emerged at the Acropolis portal station.

The guards were all from the Celeste Kingdom, extra sentries brought into the Acropolis during Selection Years, and they all bowed to him and Axel as they came through. Others would be required to provide identification, but not the Arius Heirs. One looked as if he was going to ask Luka for papers, but one glare from Theon as he handed over the documents for Tessa had the male dropping his gaze. He hardly glanced at Tessa's papers before handing them back to him, the guard's hand shaking slightly.

Another vehicle was waiting for them, along with a driver. Luka had stalked towards him and only held out his hand. The driver wasted no time dropping the keys into his open palm before backing away. There was no way they would allow a driver to accompany them. Anyone could have paid the male to spy on them and report back on their movements and conversations.

The trip to the Greater District of the Acropolis wasn't long. The Greater District was where all the ruling families and upper council members had townhouses. The ruling families also had manors on the outer edges of the Acropolis, but Theon had wanted to be closer to the Pantheon. The townhouses were a ten minute walk. Not only that, when his father did visit throughout the year, he'd be staying at the family manor.

They pulled into the drive of the three-story brick townhouse. Although, to be honest, it really couldn't be considered a townhouse. It was bigger than the document forger's two-story house had been. The main level consisted of a full kitchen with a pantry and wine cellar. A formal dining room, sitting room, and lounge were also on the floor, along with a study. The second floor held two rooms with their own bathrooms. The primary bedroom and bathroom took up the entire third floor.

As he'd told Tessa, the entire place had been renovated since he'd stayed here five years ago with his father. Even then, it had only been to observe some of the Selection proceedings. He hadn't been permitted to stay the entirety of the year. Axel hadn't been allowed to attend at all.

Theon helped Tessa out of the vehicle once Luka had parked in the attached garage, and they entered through a side door into a small foyer. Tessa was looking around, Luka and Axel brushing past her with small bags in hand that housed their computers and whatever other personal belongings they'd brought along.

"Pen?" Axel called, dropping his messenger bag just inside the hall and undoing the top button of his shirt. None of them had donned a tie, but that was as informal as they dared let themselves get.

"It's about time you younglings got here," Pen called out, and a moment later she appeared, a tray of fresh fruit in her hands.

Axel swiped up a piece of melon, dropping a kiss to Pen's cheek before he popped the fruit into his mouth. "No cookies?"

She tried to give him a stern look of disapproval, but it morphed into a smile a moment later. "In the kitchen," she answered, waving him off.

"You spoil me, Pen," Axel said, dropping another kiss to her cheek before taking off to the kitchen.

Tessa was staring after him, clearly uncertain as to what had just transpired. Luka stepped forward then, plucking the tray from Pen's hands and carrying it farther into the house. She clucked after him, but let him take it. Then she turned back to Theon and Tessa, her hands going to her hips.

"Any troubles, Pen?" Theon asked, his hand landing on Tessa's lower back to usher her forward.

"No, dear," she answered, looking him up and down. "You need to sleep more."

He sighed. "I know, Pen."

"Have you slept at all since I left?"

"Of course." Her eyes narrowed, and he sighed. "Not as much as I should."

She hummed in disapproval. "Dinner will be ready in an hour. Then you can all turn in early before your busy week."

"Yes, Pen," he said with a smirk, bending to press a soft kiss to her cheek when he passed her.

"Do not try to placate me, Theon St. Orcas."

"Wouldn't dream of it."

"Mhmm," she hummed, turning and making her way to the kitchen. "I swear to Anahita, Axel, if you've eaten that entire platter of cookies, I am not making more our entire stay here."

Theon turned to Tessa. "Ready for a tour?"

She blinked up at him before slowly answering, "Sure."

He only made it through the formal sitting room and lounge before Tessa was blurting, "What was that?"

He paused at the entry of the lounge. "What was what?"

Gesturing back the way they had come, she said, "That. With Penelope."

"You know Pen is assigned to serve me and Axel."

"Yes, but…"

He slid his hands into pockets. "Pen once had a lover. Her name was Caris. She was what one would consider our nanny, I suppose. She was more of a mother to us than Cressida ever was. When Pen wasn't in the kitchens, she was with us and Caris. We could…be a handful."

"What happened to Caris?"

"She died."

"That is why Pen was assigned to you?"

Theon nodded.

"Your father allowed a Fae to have so much sway over your upbringing?" she asked curiously, shifting her weight and wincing.

"He trusted Fae under his control more than he trusted another Legacy who might try to use us against him. Take those off," he said, nodding at her shoes.

She quickly slipped the heels from her feet, sighing in relief. "Thank you," she said softly.

He nodded. "Come. I'll show you the rest of the house before dinner."

He wasn't surprised to find her on the balcony.

She'd thought they hadn't heard her when she'd muttered about how she hated being cooped up in the vehicle. He'd never realized how much she hated confined spaces. He'd never stopped to consider why she always wanted to be on the balcony back home or why she got so fidgety when required to sit for extended periods of time.

After he'd shown her around the townhouse, he'd had Luka come back up here and make sure there was no way she could get down from this balcony. Sure, there were wards around the townhouse, but that didn't mean anything with her. Which was also why he was up here now.

Theon leaned against the doorjamb, watching her as she stared out across the Acropolis. It had the perfect view of the Pantheon with its surrounding security wall, Fae sentries stationed along it. Off to the left were the high-rises where the Fae of age for Selection were being housed in dormitories. Where Tessa would be now if he hadn't Selected her.

"Little storm," he said after a few moments.

She started, clearly not having heard him come up behind her. "I assumed it was all right for me to be out here," she said hurriedly, tucking a piece of hair behind her ear.

Theon nodded. "It is."

"I just needed some air."

"If you would have mentioned it, we could have gone for a walk."

"It is demeaning to ask to go for a walk like a hound," she retorted. "None of the other Fae are required to be with a Legacy every second of the day. I saw them on the drive here."

Theon sighed. "It is inappropriate for a Source to be seen without their...bonded Legacy."

She huffed a humorless laugh. "You can say Master, Theon. It's what you are."

"You can't be alone for your own protection as well, Tessa," he said, ignoring her little outburst. "It is a crime that sends one to the Underground for judgment to kidnap a Source, but that doesn't mean it won't happen. They could take you to use against me, my family, and the Arius Kingdom. We are not well-liked, and they would make sure you were kept alive somewhere, away from me. We cannot bond with another Source unless death takes the first."

"I will be sure to ask my mythical kidnappers for death then," she retorted. "Maybe then you can have a more compliant Source."

"Why do you have to make everything an argument?"

"It's that whole hound-who-can-talk-back-thing, I suppose."

"You're like a difficult child when you get in these moods."

She smirked. "A child doesn't do this," she said, raising her middle finger at him.

"You didn't know me when I was a child," he returned with a mocking smile.

She barked a laugh. An honest-to-the-gods genuine laugh, and the feeling in his chest at the sound was one he didn't recognize.

"It sounds like Caris and Pen kept you all in line," she said, finally turning to face him fully.

"They did their best," he agreed. Then he cleared his throat. "I thought you might want that phone call."

Her eyes went wide. "Now?" He nodded, pulling his phone from his pocket. "On your phone?" she asked doubtfully.

"Yes," he answered, holding it out to her. There was no way he was letting her call from her phone and giving that Fae her number. If he ever tried to contact her, he would reach Theon directly.

"I would rather not," she said, wrapping her arms around herself tightly and turning back to the balcony.

"That was our deal, was it not?"

"Yes."

"And now you do not wish for the phone call?"

"Can I see them? Tomorrow?"

"No." When she only nodded, he added, "We have things to do tomorrow." She said nothing, strands of her hair fluttering in the breeze. Autumn weather was moving in which made the constant rain more odd. Even more bizarre was that the rain seemed to have followed them.

Or followed her.

He hadn't told Axel and Luka of that observation yet. Not until he had more proof. They constantly teased him about his research and theories. He'd learned long ago not to say anything until he could fully back it up to avoid being the constant subject of their jesting.

"Tessa?"

"Hmm?"

"You should call them."

"No."

"Why?"

"Because I do not wish to," she said.

"You wish to see them."

"Yes."

"How would that be different?"

She slowly dragged her eyes to him. "When you can hear my thoughts, will you be content to do simply that? Or will you insist on laying eyes on me?"

Valid point.

"You can video call him," Theon offered.

She blinked.

"On the phone," he added, extending his phone to her once more.

Still, she did not reach for it. "Why are you so insistent about this?"

"Because that was our deal. You upheld your end. I wish to uphold mine."

"Consider it upheld."

"Just call him."

"No."

"Then why make the deal?"

"Because I am impulsive and did not think it through."

"You regret it?" he pushed, his head tilting as she became more agitated and lost a little more control. She always revealed little pieces of herself she kept hidden when she got like this.

"Yes," she ground out.

"Why?"

"Because it was just one more way I tied myself to you."

Her eyes fell closed in regret when she realized what she'd said, and she turned back to the balcony once more.

Theon moved to stand beside her, sliding his phone back into his pocket. "You will be tied to me in every way, Tessa. That Bargain Mark does not make a difference, and taking what is yours will not make a difference either."

"I do not want it."

"The phone call?"

"Sure. We'll go with the phone call."

He reached out, unable to stop himself as he took her chin between his thumb and forefinger, forcing her to look up at him. "I know it makes me a bastard, but I stand by what I said. I will have each and every piece of you. I can wait until you are ready to give some of those pieces."

"And the pieces I won't give?"

"I always find a way to get what I want, Tessa."

Her lips pressed into a thin line, but she held his gaze. A faint ring of violet glowed around her pupils, and it was not fleeting this time. It stayed, staring back at him.

"What are you thinking right now?" he murmured. When she didn't answer, he stepped into her, his front brushing hers.

"That I do not know how I will survive a lifetime with you," she answered.

"You survive it by not being stubborn simply to prove a point."

Her grey eyes hardened, the violet flaring a little more. "What is that supposed to mean?"

"It means if you are refusing this phone call simply to prove that you can, you are only hurting yourself. Dig your heels in on things that matter, Tessa. Be smart about it," he replied, releasing her chin as a gust of wind swept around them. Thunder rumbled off in the distance, and Theon watched the violet flash like a streak of lightning across her irises.

What Fae element did *that*? He'd be spending some time researching tonight, but all the texts that would likely help him were back at Arius House.

"Why are you telling me this?" she asked.

"I already told you. I want us to be feared, Tessa. Your lessons and training here won't just be in your element. I need you to be smart about when and where you exercise your obstinate tendencies."

She stared back at him, and he could practically hear the debate playing out in her head.

"If declining this phone call will serve a purpose beyond thinking you are proving something to me—which I assure you, you are not— then by all means, dig in those heels, Tessa. Or take what you earned. Take what's yours to claim."

He let silence fall between them for a full minute before he pulled his phone from his pocket once more. "I will ask you once more. After this, consider it forfeit. Would you like to make the phone call you earned?"

She swallowed thickly, scowling as though she hated that she'd let him talk her into this when she reached for the phone. "Can I still video call them?"

"Yes," he said, fighting back his smile of victory.

"Can I speak to them privately?"

"No."

"Fine," she huffed, brushing past him and moving into the room. She dropped onto the sofa in the bedroom's small sitting area, where a television hung above the fireplace.

A moment later, she had her knees pulled to her chest, his phone balancing atop them as he dropped down beside her. He wouldn't sit here the entire time. Just until he got what he wanted. He may have just told Tessa to take what she'd earned, and he'd meant it, but he would also teach her to take advantage of every opportunity presented to her. Some of those opportunities would be shit, but there would always be a way to take something away from it.

And right now, he was going to get what he wanted from this opportunity.

The voice call rang out, and she bit her lip as she thumbed open his messages. She sent one to the same number. It was only two words.

Theon: It's me.

Then she sent the video call through again.

It was answered immediately.

A Fae with messy dark brown hair and brown eyes so dark they were nearly black appeared on the screen.

"Tessie?"

She had the phone angled so Theon wasn't on the screen, and that was fine for the moment.

"Hi, Dex," she said, a small, sad smile pulling at her lips.

"How are you calling me?" he asked, a mixture of relief and suspicion in his voice.

She cleared her throat, glancing at Theon out of the corner of her eye. "I am borrowing his phone."

"Borrowing?" the Fae repeated skeptically.

He appeared to be walking down a hallway of some sort, and he stopped at a door, knocking twice.

"He knows I am using it," Tessa answered, glancing at Theon sidelong again.

Understanding flashed across the Fae's face. "How long?"

"Thirty minutes."

A grin filled the Fae's face. "That's more than enough time."

Tessa's brow furrowed. "For what?"

The door the Fae had knocked on opened then, another Fae appearing, and Tessa's face lit up. The Fae's sky-blue eyes blinked once in surprise as Dex flipped the phone so he could see Tessa. The new Fae had hair so blonde it was nearly white. His surprise was replaced by a wry smile a moment later.

"Hiya, Sweetheart," he crooned with a wink.

"Hi, Lange," she breathed excitedly, sitting up a little straighter. "Corbin?"

Another Fae appeared over the blonde Fae's shoulder. This one had warm, brown skin, shaggy brown hair, and hazel eyes. He was slightly shorter than the blonde one, and he rested his chin on Lange's shoulder.

"Tessa? Are you all right? We've been worried," the Fae said, far more serious than the blonde Fae had been.

Theon propped his elbow on the arm of the sofa, steepling his finger along his temple as he watched Tessa. He could still see the screen for the most part, and while he had wanted a visual of her so-called family, he also wanted to observe her with them and them with her.

"I miss you all," Tessa said in answer to his question.

Theon could see the brown-haired male—Corbin she had called him —about to say something else when Dex's voice sounded.

"She's not alone. Someone call Brecken and Oralia, and tell them to get their asses over here fast. She only has thirty minutes."

Corbin disappeared, and Dex entered the room as Lange snatched the phone from his hand. The Fae moved to a sofa as he said, "Did you catch the Chaosphere game the other night?"

Theon rolled his eyes. Fucking Chaosphere.

But Tessa was shaking her head. "I was...out and missed it. Fill me in?"

Theon tuned out Lange's run-down of the game, his eyes bouncing from Tessa to the phone and back. He watched her relax more and more with each passing minute. Watched that smile never leave her face. Watched a side of her come out he'd never fully seen before, only glimpsed on a Chaosphere field earlier that day.

Corbin had returned, sitting close to Lange. Lange's arm came around him, settling on the back of the sofa. A couple of some sort then. Tessa had been smart about that, at least. The odds of those two ending up even remotely close to each other was slim. Tessa had said she wouldn't sleep with other Fae because she didn't want that kind of relationship until she'd been assigned to her kingdom. How had she worded it? No attachments made, and no feelings required.

Lange was still going on about the game, Tessa clinging to every word and laughing at his animated play-by-play, when there was commotion in the background.

"Give me that," came a female voice, and Theon leaned in a little to see the female that had appeared. She was pretty with pale blonde hair similar to Lange's, but her eyes were as dark as Dex's. "Tessa?"

"Hi, Oralia," she said with a smile.

"Thank the gods. Dex said you called a few nights ago, but it's not the same as talking to you myself," the female said, nudging Corbin's knee so she could take the seat next to him on the sofa. "Are you here yet?"

Tessa glanced at Theon, a clear question in her eyes, and he nodded, giving her permission to share.

"Um, yeah," Tessa said, tucking her hair behind her ear. "Arrived today."

Dex appeared on the screen, perching on the arm of the sofa beside Oralia. "Staying at the townhouses, I assume?"

"Mhmm," Tessa answered.

"What does Dex need to fix for you?" Oralia asked, and Theon's brow furrowed at the question. Tessa's cheeks flushed a light pink, and Theon sat up straighter. That relaxed state she'd been in while talking to Lange and Corbin disappeared.

"I don't think even Dex can fix this mess," she answered.

The female laughed, a high thing that grated on Theon's ears. "Sweetie, Dex has been cleaning up after you for nearly five years now. You should know better than to doubt him."

A weak smile appeared on Tessa's lips, and she cleared her throat. "Is Brecken around?"

Oralia rolled her eyes. "He's still chasing after Kat."

"He's always been persistent," Tessa mused, seeming grateful for the change of subject.

"That he is," the female agreed. Then she tilted her head, looking up at Dex. "I suppose you want to monopolize the rest of her time?"

Dex smirked, taking the phone. "Best friend privileges."

"Whatever," Oralia grumbled, sitting back against the sofa.

Dex's attention refocused on Tessa, and Theon pushed to his feet. Tessa watched him, confusion in her eyes, but he moved to the closet, unbuttoning his shirt as he moved out of her sight. He could still hear everything though, and the placement of one of the mirrors in the large closet allowed him to still see Tessa.

She sighed, tipping her head back against the sofa.

"You're not strong enough for this, Tessie," Dex was saying.

"I know, Dex," she whispered. "Oralia was right. I've never been able to fix my own shit, and this... I need you."

"I know, Tessa," he answered, and now Theon was more than curious. This Fae didn't know her nearly as well as she claimed if he was telling her she wasn't strong enough.

His shirt hanging open, he crossed his arms over his chest and leaned against the wall, watching her in the mirror.

"I know it is hard for you, but you have to curb that impulsiveness," Dex was saying. "It will only get you into more trouble."

"I'm trying, Dex," she answered.

"Try harder."

She nodded mutely, and Theon's jaw nearly dropped. Who the fuck was this docile creature?

"Lighten up, Dex," came one of the other male Fae. "She doesn't need your deprecating shit right now."

"You know what happens when she loses control, Lange," Dex retorted.

There was a snicker. "Yeah. Shit gets a lot more exciting."

"You call it excitement. I call it another thing I have to take care of."

And Tessa winced at the words.

A godsdamn grimace.

He'd pushed her to take this call so he could observe her with them, and he'd seen enough the moment she'd winced. He was about to go out there and end that godsdamn call himself, but he stopped when he heard—

"Fuck off, Dex. Give me the phone," Lange said.

"Tessa, you can do this. We've survived worse," came Corbin's voice.

"But I was with all of you," she whispered.

"We're always with you," Corbin said. "Is it like two years ago?"

Two years ago? What the fuck happened two years ago?

"Some days," Tessa answered, and Theon could see a tear slipping down her cheek in the mirror.

"You're a survivor, Tessa," Corbin said.

"What if I don't want to be one anymore?"

Theon stiffened at the words. This wasn't the first time she'd spoken this way. She'd basically told them she'd attempted to take her own life, but Fae were like Legacy in that a simple dagger wouldn't do it.

"You can shatter, Tessa," Corbin said solemnly. "We'll put the pieces back together just like we've always done."

"What if there's nothing left of me?" she asked, tears coursing down her face now.

"Then we'll help you find yourself again. Just like before. Just like you've done for us."

"You can do this, sweetheart," Lange chimed in.

"They're right, Tessie," came Dex's voice. "I'm sorry about what I said. I just... I'm worried about you."

Theon moved then, appearing in the doorway of the closet and leaning against the doorjamb. Tessa glanced at him, swiftly wiping at her face.

"I have to go," she said.

"We'll find you. At the Emerging Ceremony, if not sooner," Dex said. "Even if we can't speak, we'll see you. In person."

"Tell Brecken hi. And Kat too."

"We will."

Then she quickly cut the call, tossing Theon's phone onto the sofa cushion. She stared straight ahead, her hands resting on her knees where his phone had been.

She didn't speak another word the rest of the night.

32
THEON

She was back on the balcony this morning, a mug of coffee clutched in her palms. Already showered and dressed, she was wearing a casual long-sleeve dress with some basic heels. Pen had set the outfit out when Theon had asked her to pick something simple yet classy for a day of meetings and preparations.

Tessa had slipped into bed without fuss last night. Theon had stayed up another few hours, sipping on a glass of liquor and going through correspondence. He'd wanted to research the phenomena with Tessa's eyes, but, of course, shit was happening in the Underground now that he was here. There were three urgent messages from Bohden that his father had forwarded to him to "handle."

Just like he'd been sent to *handle* the Selection.

To *handle* the other heirs.

And after *handling* the situations, he'd been too exhausted to look into the Fae elements anymore.

Sighing, he finished knotting his tie before he rolled back the sleeves of his shirt. He'd need to wear his suit jacket later, but for now, breakfast was ready and Tessa needed to eat.

"Tessa?" he said as he approached the balcony doors.

She turned to him, her hair fluttering in the fall breeze. She'd left it down today, the ends curling softly where it hung down her back. Still, she did not speak. Only looked at him, waiting for his demands.

"We have some things we need to discuss."

"All right," she answered hesitantly, and the relief that flooded through him at the sound of her voice had him breathing a little easier.

"Luka and Axel are waiting for us downstairs."

A wary look of resignation filled her eyes. "So I'm to be ganged up on by all three of you this time?"

"What do you mean?"

"I can only assume you are going to lay out *expectations* for our time here."

"No," he countered, and she arched a brow.

"No? You are not about to tell me all the rules for being here? What is expected of me? What I can and cannot do? Where I can and cannot go? How I must always be with you?"

What was he supposed to say to any of that?

A sardonic smile flashed across her face. "Thought so."

She came into the room, closing the double doors behind her. He silently followed her out of the bedroom and down the stairs to the dining room.

"Morning, baby doll," Axel greeted with a grin when they entered.

Tessa nodded, pausing as she waited to be told where to sit. Axel's smile faltered, and he shot Theon a glare as though he had caused this. Pressing a hand to the small of her back, Theon nudged her to the seat across from Axel before he took the chair beside her. Luka strolled in a moment later, his sapphire eyes taking them all in.

"Did you see those emails from Bohden?" Theon asked him.

Luka nodded, piling bacon onto his plate before he was even fully seated across from Theon.

"And?"

"And what?" Luka asked. "What are we going to do from here?"

"We have to do something," Theon argued.

"No," Luka countered. "We're going to tell Bohden what to do and let him handle it."

"That's a shit plan."

Luka shrugged. "Until you can come up with a better one, that's the plan we're going with."

Theon muttered a curse but dropped it, scooping fresh fruit onto Tessa's plate as she reached for a glass of juice.

"What's your plan today?" Axel asked.

"Meetings with the other heirs and the Pantheon," Theon answered. "Dagian Jove also requested a lunch meeting, but—"

He lurched back from the table when Tessa knocked over her juice.

"Sorry," she stammered, shooting to her feet and reaching for napkins.

"It's fine, Tessa," he said, snatching up his coffee mug as the juice spread across the table. "Pen will get it."

"I can clean up my own mess," she replied, her napkin already soaking up some of the juice, and Theon nodded, letting her do just that.

When the table was cleaned, and she'd settled back into her chair, Theon said, "We need to discuss what your days will look like during the Selection Year."

She nodded, pushing the fruit around her plate with her fork.

"You do not need to attend the same trainings as the other Fae. You will have your element training, of course, after the Emerging Ceremony. There is also a training solely for the newly Selected Sources."

Her head snapped up. "Why?"

"Because none of the heirs trust the other Fae around their Sources," Theon answered. "It's a training all the other Fae go through. The six of you will just do so separately."

"You all decided this? All the heirs?"

"Yes."

"What happened during the years only one or two Sources were Selected? It's been centuries since six were Selected at one time," she argued.

"They were given private instructors from my understanding."

"Why can't we do that now?"

"It seemed like a waste of resources," Theon answered. "Why find six different instructors when we can just use one?"

"But—"

"Additionally, as future rulers of the Kingdoms, the heirs are all supposed to get along and work together. In theory, we will be spending a good amount of time with the other heirs and Sources. It would be good to get comfortable with them."

"In theory," she repeated dryly.

"According to the Kingdom Accords, that is how Devram operates. Working together for the greater good of the realm," Theon replied.

"And yet Arius Kingdom is rarely heard from and is intensely private," Tessa mused.

Theon's lips curled darkly. "We were forced to be."

They all fell silent when Pen bustled in with a plate of fresh waffles.

Tessa glanced at him, and Theon nodded. She immediately grabbed two, pouring syrup atop them. Not his first choice, but at least she was eating.

When Pen left the room, he said, "Do you know what the Kingdom Accords are based on?"

"Of course," she answered, starting on her next waffle. She'd already devoured the first. "The Revelation Decree."

"Decree is a generous term," Theon muttered.

Tessa paused with her fork halfway to her mouth, turning to look at him. "What does that mean?"

"Not the time for a three-hour history lecture, Theon," Axel cut in before Theon could say anything.

"I wasn't going to—"

"Yes, you were," Axel retorted. He fixed his attention on Tessa. "There is a lot of speculation around the Decree and where it originated from, particularly how it was interpreted. But if you let him, Theon will go on and on about this for days. In fact, you will likely get to enjoy that soon enough, but we really don't have the time today."

"The point is," Theon cut in, "we need to get on amicable terms with the other heirs. This was a step towards that goal."

"Why?" Tessa asked, now sounding bored as she returned to her breakfast.

"Because my father wishes to take over Devram."

Tessa's fork clattered to the table, and Theon snatched up her glass before juice was spilled again.

"Your father... He can't... What?" she sputtered, clearly trying and failing to process what he'd said.

"My father believes we have been forced to the far corner of the realm long enough. He wishes to seize control of Devram," Theon answered.

"You cannot speak so cavalierly about overthrowing the other kingdoms, Theon," Tessa hissed, her voice low and quiet as though she were afraid of being overheard. Then her eyes went wide, and Theon was glad he was still holding her juice glass when her hands landed on the table. "Wait. Is that what you need my help with? Aiding your father in taking over the realm?"

"Yes and no," he said, setting the juice aside and wiping his hands on his napkin.

A laugh of disbelief left her. "You said when you ran Arius Kingdom,

I could have my own wing and be rid of you, but if your father succeeds, you will not run Arius Kingdom. You will be heir to the realm." She sat back in her chair, and Theon didn't need to know her at all to read the fury in her eyes. "You played me."

Theon said nothing, sipping at his coffee. She was only partially correct, but she didn't need to know that yet. *Couldn't* know that yet. Not until the bond was in place could he fully trust her with all of their plans.

"What about the Revelation Decree?" she demanded. "It clearly states that the Achaz Kingdom must rule."

"As Axel said, the Decree is open to interpretation."

"How else do you interpret *'For Dark must bow, And Light must rule?'*"

"We prefer to focus on the *'Life must give, And Death must take'* portion of the Decree."

Tessa only blinked at him, for once at a loss for words.

"We will have plenty of time to discuss the Decree and what it may or may not mean," Theon added, frowning at her plate. She'd only eaten a waffle and a few bites of fruit. "You should eat more."

"I'm not hungry," she stammered, sitting back in her chair.

"We have time. There is more we need to go over."

"*More?*"

"We will resume your morning runs, and then you will train with Luka for two hours every morning," Theon said, cutting into his sausage and taking a bite.

She glanced quickly at Luka. "What do you mean train with Luka?"

"Physical training. Combat training—"

"*Combat training?*"

"You need to learn to protect yourself, Tessa," Theon said. "Metias and Pavil will not be the last ones to come for you, despite the obvious threats and consequences of such actions. While you are to always be with us, things happen that—"

"Things happen," she said, interrupting him yet again, and it had him setting his silverware down sharply on the table. "What does that even mean?"

He turned to lean towards her, and he heard her sharp inhale at the action. "It means, little storm, that if Luka, Axel, and I can gain private access to someone's Source, then someone can get access to mine, even with every precaution in place."

She lurched back from him. "You've... But the Accords—"

"To many, the Accords are simply pretty words meant to make the realm feel safe and protected."

"But not to the Arius Kingdom?"

The cruel grin returned. "Beautiful, if you think Arius Kingdom is the only one that operates outside the Accords and makes deals in the shadows, you are sorely mistaken. Some would argue that the other kingdoms can be even more cunning and ruthless. Personally, I think they tell themselves that for a sense of security because they still send their cursed to the Underground, so I think that proves which kingdom is feared the most."

"And you believe that being the most cunning and wicked is something to boast about?" she challenged, leaning in towards him once more, that spark of defiance flashing in her eyes.

Theon reached over, tucking her hair behind her ear. "You will learn soon enough that being the most cunning and wicked is the only way to survive in a realm of villains, little storm."

For several minutes, the only sound was silverware and chewing as the males finished their breakfasts. Tessa was silent, absent-mindedly eating pieces of fruit, and he let her sit with her thoughts. He wasn't stupid. She might not have the wicked part down yet, but the cunning part of survival?

Tessa was more cunning than anyone realized. Her type of cunning was the most dangerous.

She cleared her throat when they were all finishing up their meals. "Is there anything else I need to be aware of?"

"You will need to clarify that statement," Theon replied, placing his napkin on the table.

Tessa glared at him. "Is there any other information you've withheld from me to trick me into bargains?"

"The bargain was your choice, Tessa. You were not forced into it."

She scoffed, pushing her plate back. "Whatever you need to tell yourself, Theon."

He took a deep breath, pushing down the urge to argue with her about this, but he couldn't keep his dark shadows from appearing. They coiled around his arms, and it took everything in him to hold them back when they tried to reach for her. "Today," he gritted out, "the Keeper requested the other heirs and I have meetings with the Pantheon Priestesses and Sentinels to ensure the Selection Year goes smoothly."

"Will the Keeper be there?"

"Of course not," Theon said. "The Keeper never leaves the Inner Sanctum of the Pantheon."

"Right," Tessa said, her gaze fixating on a point over his shoulder as she mulled something over.

The Keeper of the Decree was the most revered person in Devram. Residing within the Pantheon itself, even the Kingdom Lords and Ladies were leery to cross them. No one knew if the Keeper was male or female. They were rarely seen, and they always wore robes that completely hid all features. Theon had glimpsed them twice in his life. The one time he'd dared to ask his father about the Keeper, his father had only said, *"We will worry about the Keeper once we have secured our rightful seat of power."*

Of course, that hadn't been what Theon had been asking. He'd wanted to know *about* the Keeper. While perfection was demanded in all areas, including academics, he'd learned quickly enough that his father became annoyed when Theon chose to spend hours researching various things instead of focusing on his "duties as the heir." His days had become doing what was expected of him to appease his father while simultaneously keeping his father's attention off Axel. His nights had become hours spent in the library with his shadows obscuring the light so he wouldn't be caught.

He'd discovered many things in those late hours— texts about the Guardian Bond, historical accounts of past Selections, a few mentions of other worlds, notes about the gods, theories of Chaos. But what Theon had found most intriguing hadn't been discovered in the Arius House libraries. It had been found here, in the Acropolis. Specifically in the Pantheon.

And it had been confiscated from him by the Keeper itself.

When Luka and Axel stood from the table, Tessa asked, "So what will be required of me?"

"Today?" Theon asked, arching a brow.

"In...all of this," she clarified. "What will be required of me to aid you and your father?"

"*Me*, Tessa," he said in a tone that made her flinch when his shadows reached for her. "You aid me, not my father."

"But aren't I aiding him by extension? Didn't he say—"

"It does not matter what he said."

"But—"

"Do you know where the Keeper resides?"

She blinked at the sudden change in subject before she answered. "At the Pantheon. In the Inner Sanctum."

"And do you know what they guard so obsessively?"

"They are the Keeper of the Decree."

"A Decree that everyone is taught and has memorized by their second decade of life," Theon countered. "They guard more than that, Tessa."

Her brow pinched together. "Like what?"

He shrugged. "No one knows."

Her eyes narrowed. "But you have ideas?"

"Oh, he definitely has those," Axel said, rolling his eyes.

"They are not all unfounded," Luka interjected, distracted by something on his phone.

"None of my ideas are *unfounded*," Theon said in irritation.

"Right." Axel smirked. "Like the female in the mirror?"

Theon scowled at his brother. "She was there."

Tessa was looking up at him in confusion. "You saw a female in a mirror?"

"Yes."

"Or so he says," Axel said.

"What did she look like?" Tessa cut in before Theon could reply to his brother.

"Allow me," Axel drawled dramatically, and Theon sent him a dry look as he sat back in his chair, crossing his arms. "She had silver hair and silver eyes. More weapons than he could count. She had gifts of shadows but also fire as bright as the stars, and Theon saved her from imminent death when another in all black approached to kill her."

"I *did* save her from imminent death," Theon ground out from between his teeth.

"And yet no one else has seen her," Axel countered, propping his head on his fist with a mocking grin.

"Where is this...mirror?" Tessa interrupted, a crease forming in her brow.

"The Underground," Theon answered.

"So it's a cursed mirror?"

"Not everything in the Underground is cursed, Tessa. Some would even argue such curses are blessings."

"I will take your word for it," she muttered. Then she added, "Is there something special about this mirror?"

"Yes," Theon answered at the same time Axel said, "No."

Tessa glanced back and forth between them before turning to Luka. "Do *you* believe there is something special about this mirror?"

"I believe everything is not always as it seems," Luka answered, finally looking up from his godsdamn phone. Sapphire eyes connected with hers as he added, "Whether that be mirrors, traditions, or people." Tessa held his gaze but didn't say anything, and Luka's eyes slid to Theon. "I just sent you something you may find of interest, but read it later. We should be going."

Theon glanced at this watch and nodded. "Can you walk to the Pantheon in those?" he asked Tessa with a quick look at the heels she was wearing. They could drive, but it seemed pointless when they were only blocks away.

"We're going to walk? Outside?" she asked, her eyes brightening, and Theon couldn't help the grin that played on his lips.

"As opposed to walking inside?" he asked, pushing to his feet and beginning to roll down his sleeves.

"You've forced me to stay inside for weeks, Theon."

"So you will be fine walking in those?"

"Yes," she answered immediately.

The males grabbed their suit jackets, and a few minutes later, they were on their way to the Pantheon. The clouds provided a chill to the air, but Tessa didn't seem to care as she tipped her face to the sky as they walked. None of them spoke much, and ten minutes later, they were showing their phones to Pantheon sentinels to show they had been set to the appropriate mode.

Everyone except Tessa.

"You do not have your phone," Theon demanded, gripping her elbow and spinning her to face him.

"It was dead," she replied.

"What part of 'have your phone on you at all times' was unclear?"

She glanced at the sentinel before she stepped closer to him and hissed, "What difference does it make if I am to be with you at all times?"

"Because you will not be with me at all times today. You have to meet with the private Source instructor at the end of the day."

"You didn't tell me that."

"I am not required to tell you everything. You, however, are required to have that phone at all times. I made that abundantly clear."

"I didn't—"

"Enough. I will deal with this later," he snapped, pulling her past the sentinels and into the Pantheon. He couldn't even send Luka or Axel to get her phone. They had tasks to tend to while they were here. He nodded to them as they peeled off to do just that while he led Tessa down the opposite hallway.

"Where are they going?" she asked, looking back over her shoulder, and that had him dragging her into an alcove and crowding her against a wall. "What are you doing?"

"Reminding you we are in public," he replied in a low, harsh tone.

"I know that," she snapped back.

"Do you? Because your place at this moment in time is not ask questions. This is where you pretend, Tessa. This is where you prove to me you can do this, because by the gods, there are other ways I could be handling this."

"Handling *this*," she repeated.

"Yes, handling this. And they would be far easier than a godsdamn Bargain with you."

Her lips thinned, all her features going taut. "I understand."

"The stakes are higher than ever. There is no room for error. Not in front of these people. Not anymore."

"I got it, Theon."

"I hope so because you can expect harsher consequences for failures," he replied, stepping back. Her eyes widened, but she smartly held her tongue. "We are about to walk into a room full of other heirs and their Sources. Do not speak without permission. Remember what I require of you."

"I remember," she said bitterly.

He gripped her chin between his thumb and forefinger, tipping her chin up and forcing her to look at him. "Tell me."

"Someone they fear as much as you."

"I want them to fear what we are *together*. I want them to believe our bond is different from theirs. Better in every possible way," he corrected. "The meeting with my father was a test-run. Do not fail at this, Tessa."

"I understand," she ground out again.

He released her chin, brushing her hair back over her shoulder. "You don't fully understand yet, but you will."

He could tell she wanted to ask what that meant, but she didn't. Instead, she pushed off the wall and straightened her dress. He reached out then, grabbing her hand and intertwining their fingers. Sources usually walked behind their Masters, but he hadn't been lying. He wanted the other heirs nervous that he treated her differently than they treated their own Sources. It was a fine line he was asking her to walk, and she needed to walk it perfectly.

His strides were long and purposeful, forcing her to work to keep up with him in her heels, but she did not complain. And when they walked into the large stateroom, all chatter ceased. All eyes turned to them, and from the corner of his eye, he watched her chin tip up a little more. Everyone else was already here. One might think him late, but he'd wanted to be the last to arrive.

His cold gaze swept over the others dismissively until he settled on Dagian Jove, heir to the Achaz Kingdom. His golden hair was swept back, and his golden gaze held his, but Theon didn't miss the quick glance at Tessa. Dagian's Source stood a step behind him, off to his left. She was pretty. Brown hair and eyes. Bronze skin. Sasha Roenya. Predicted to emerge with wind and air like Tessa. He knew all about the new Sources. He'd studied them as much as he'd researched his own options.

Next to Dagian stood Lealla Isleen, heir to the Serafina Kingdom. Her silvery-blue gaze narrowed on him, and her sharp smile told Theon she was still the heartless thing he knew her to be. Then came Mahina Candra, heir to the Celeste Kingdom. Ebony hair framed a pretty face, but jade green eyes bounced between him and Tessa. He could sense the nerves she was trying to hide, and he let his darkness out to drift around him and Tessa. Mahina flinched. It was nearly imperceptible, but it was there. Beside her was Prudence Farhan, heir to the Falein Kingdom with her ashy-brown hair and hazel eyes that watched him curiously. And last was Tana Aithne, heir to the Anala Kingdom. Her bright red hair hung in tight curls down her back, and amber eyes flickered with flames as they met his own.

"Heir St. Orcas, welcome," came a melodic voice, and Theon dragged his gaze to the Priestess at the front of the room. "My name is Sancia, one of the High Priestesses of the Pantheon. This is Evander, our Head Sentinel. We welcome you to the Acropolis and the Pantheon."

Theon bowed his head the smallest amount in greeting. "Your grace."

"If everyone takes a seat, we can get started. We have much to discuss today," Sancia said, gesturing to several chairs and settees that had been artfully arranged in the space. Nearby were much less extravagant chairs, and Theon led Tessa to one. Bringing his lips to her ear, he whispered, "Watch. Listen. Learn everything you can about the people in this room. Do you understand?"

She gave a small nod, and he let his lips brush lightly along her temple as he stepped back. Unbuttoning his suit jacket as he walked, he moved to an armchair next to Mahina. He heard her audibly swallow, but he paid her no mind. His gaze was back on Dagian, who was seated across from him. And when Theon took the drink a Fae brought him, Dagian lifted his own to him in greeting. Theon didn't return the gesture, instead bringing his drink to his lips and taking a sip, internally smirking at the look of superiority that filled Dagian's features.

They might all be forced to sit here and be amicable, but the pretense was just that. Every heir here had an agenda, whether their own or their parents'. Likely both. But only he was going to be the one to walk away with everything he wanted. He smiled at the thought as he took another drink, and Sancia began her opening greeting.

He didn't care who became a casualty for the cause. Like he'd told Tessa, failure wasn't an option.

33

TESSA

She was the last of the Sources to be meeting with the private instructor. She'd learned the Arius Kingdom was always last. Theon had been last to select his Source. He'd been last to receive his drink among the heirs, and now she was last to meet with this private instructor. It hadn't escaped her that he'd embraced being last. *Owned* being last by making a statement when they'd entered that state room earlier today.

She'd seen the way the heirs had watched him. Just like he'd told her to, she'd observed them and the Sources. She knew them all, of course, but only Jasper, the Celeste Heir's Source, and Sasha, the Achaz Heir's Source, had resided at the Celeste Estate. Dade, the Falein Heir's Source, had been there for a few years, but when Prudence had started watching him more, she'd had him moved to the Falein Estate.

For hours, she had been forced to sit and listen to the High Priestess and Head Sentinel discuss procedures for the year, what was expected of each kingdom, changes from the previous Selections, and more. Her head hurt from it all, but she'd also watched Theon absorb it all with ease. How many times had he been forced to sit through such things? He was clearly practiced at it, knowing what to say and when to say it. Pointed questions were posed to Sancia and Evander with just enough respect to pass as...well, not pleasant, but acceptable.

Watching Theon here was different all together. She was beginning to realize that he had been keeping parts of himself hidden from her, trying to…make her more comfortable? Lure her into a sense of safety? She didn't know, but this? This was the Arius Heir. This is what she had been expecting of the Arius Kingdom. Cold-hearted. Cunning.

The heir of darkness, death, and endings.

At midday the Legacy had been served a fine lunch in the stateroom. Afterward, the Sources were provided with sandwiches, an apple, carrots, and water. Theon had taken her outside the Pantheon to eat so he could check things on his phone. Not that Tessa had minded. He'd hardly spoken to her while she sat on a bench, watching the people pass by. A small part of her had hoped she might spot Dex or Corbin, but hoping never did anything for her.

The break was short-lived, but on their way back into the Acropolis, Theon had filled her in a little more on what to expect for the afternoon. They'd be escorted around the Acropolis and the surrounding area where the trainings were being held so they could observe the other Fae at their leisure. The private instructor had also requested individual meetings with each Source to get a better understanding of what needed to be covered. Sasha went first, right after they'd finished lunch, and from what Tessa could tell, it was roughly an hour before she reappeared and Maxson, the Serafina Heir's Source, disappeared for an hour.

It had been dusk when she had been escorted by a sentinel to one of the marble buildings outside the Pantheon. She could tell Theon didn't like that she was being separated from him, and who knew where Luka and Axel were.

This was probably why he'd wanted her to have the phone he'd given her.

She hadn't left it behind on purpose, and she hadn't lied. It *was* dead. She rarely used it and often forgot about it. Even when she'd wanted to use it for her phone call with Dex, Theon had made her use his. What was the point of her even having one?

This. This was obviously the point, and she made a mental note to make sure she charged the damn thing tonight.

The sentinel knocked once on the intricate oak door before pushing it open and gesturing for Tessa to enter. With a weak smile, she walked into what appeared to be a study.

And went utterly still.

There was a Legacy sitting behind a large, mahogany desk. Her back was straight, hands folded on the desktop before her. Her dirty blonde hair was pulled into a tight bun at the back of her head. Dark navy eyes narrowed on Tessa, her sharp features already making her disapproval clear.

"Sit, Tessalyn," the Legacy said, giving a pointed look at the chair before the desk.

"What are you doing here?" Tessa blurted, her feet rooted to the spot.

Mother Cordelia couldn't be here. She'd known she'd come for the Emerging Ceremony at the end of the week, but Tessa had planned to avoid her at all costs. It shouldn't have been too hard. Tessa would be up on the private Arius observation deck with Theon and the others. Mother Cordelia would have been on a separate viewing deck. It was perhaps the only time Tessa had been grateful to be a Source.

Somehow Mother Cordelia's eyes narrowed even more. "Sit down, Tessalyn."

It was instinct when she scurried to the chair, conditioning from years at the Estate.

From years of being summoned to her private study. That study was nearly as grand as this one.

Tessa sat perfectly still, back straight, hands folded in her lap. Her knee gave a small twitch, her foot trying to bounce, but at the quick flick of Mother Cordelia's gaze to the action, Tessa forced the movement to cease.

You fidget too much. No Kingdom will want a Fae who draws so much attention to herself, Tessalyn.

That's what Mother Cordelia would say while a Fae with earth magic would bind her tightly to a chair. So tightly that she couldn't bounce her knee. So tightly that she couldn't move an inch.

So she'd learned not to fidget in her presence.

But Mother Cordelia couldn't punish her anymore, right? Not without Theon's permission. To use gifts against a Source was an action that would send one straight to the Underground. Which wouldn't be so bad for Mother Cordelia now that she thought about it...

"This is not where I expected to be seeing you, Tessalyn," Mother Cordelia sighed, opening a thick folder in front of her. Technology was allowed outside the Pantheon, but Mother Cordelia had never liked computers and tablets. She preferred to dramatically add papers to an ever-expanding file of why Tessa would never be wanted or good enough.

"I'm sorry," Tessa replied without hesitation. She'd learned long ago to take the blame for anything and everything. Arguing with her only made things worse.

"Yes, well, if the Arius Heir had bothered to observe his options like the rest of the heirs, this could have all been avoided. That Kingdom does like to be difficult," she muttered.

Tessa sat quietly, knowing better than to speak unless spoken to. Mother Cordelia flipped several pages in the silence. Finally, she flipped the folder closed, folding her hands once more. "I was asked to oversee the instruction of the new Sources given this Selection Year's historical circumstances."

Tessa swallowed, her interlaced fingers tightening in her lap. Of course Mother Cordelia saw it. Tessa could practically feel the vines binding her wrists, thorns digging into her flesh as she *learned* not to do that too.

"However, you were not prepared for this role as the others were," she continued. "As such, Heir St. Orcas has requested an additional three hours each week for private instruction to make up for the inadequacies."

"He what?" Tessa stammered. When Mother Cordelia's brow only arched at her outburst, Tessa said, "Why can't he...instruct me himself? Surely that would strengthen our bond more than—"

"An heir has far more important things to be tending to," Mother Cordelia interrupted. "Dealing with you is not a hassle he needs to be burdened with, especially during a Selection Year. Since you resided at the Celeste Estate, it is only logical that I am your instructor, since I am well acquainted with your shortcomings."

"Surely three hours a week is unnecessary," Tessa argued, her voice becoming more shrill with each word. There was sweat beading on her nape, and gods, she wished she'd worn her hair up today. Instinctively, she glanced around the room, noting all the small nooks and crannies. The tall cupboard in the corner. The open chest of books that could easily be emptied. The space beneath the desk where a foot could easily connect with flesh.

All the spaces she could be shoved into the dark to be dealt with later.

"On the contrary," Mother Cordelia said sharply. "I argued five hours would be more conducive, but your Master decided three would be sufficient. One hour. Three days each week."

"Can't we do all three hours at one time?"

"No."

"But—"

"Enough," Mother Cordelia snapped. "I will not spend our time together debating with you. You have too much to improve on to waste time on such frivolities."

Had Theon told her? Had he told her she'd tried to run more than once? Had he told her she argued with him constantly? Had he told her how she'd been forced to sit at his feet beneath a table? About her last assessment?

The Estate Mother never let on how much she knew until it suited her, and now was no different. Her face held the same slight sneer it always did as she shoved the thick folder to the side and grabbed another stack of papers.

"Are we done?" Tessa bit out, suddenly needing to move. This wasn't just restlessness. This was feeling like she might actually die if she couldn't get up, move, run, breathe fresh air.

Scream to the sky.

"No."

"What else do we need to do?"

"We have until the top of the hour."

"To do what?"

It was becoming too hard to breathe, and why was it so godsdamn *hot* in here? There were windows, but they were closed up tight with the curtains pulled shut.

"To do as you are told," she retorted. "I don't know why this is so hard for you to understand, Tessalyn. That is your purpose. Do what you are told by the Legacy. Aid them. Give them what they want and don't be a hassle about it. Now sit until our time is up and prove to me that these last two decades have not been a complete waste of my time and effort."

She felt it then. The quick pull of air from her lungs. Tessa blinked, and it was gone. Withholding oxygen wouldn't kill her, but it was certainly Mother Cordelia's preferred way to get a point across. Giving her just enough air to stay conscious, but withholding enough to make her feel like she was suffocating.

So she sat silently, forcing herself not to move. But instead of counting, she found herself going through lyrics for the songs Axel had put on those stupid running playlists. She could make it through one more song.

One more second.
One more song.
One more day.
One more year.
It didn't much matter in the end.

She stumbled down the marble steps as she gulped down the night air. Her hairline was damp with sweat, and her entire body was trembling from sitting for an hour, still and unable to move. When Mother Cordelia had finally given her permission to leave, she'd all but bolted from the room. She would likely be punished for such an action at her next private session with her.

There hadn't been a sentinel waiting for her outside the room like she'd anticipated. Maybe she should have waited for one, but she couldn't stay inside one second longer. She felt like she'd just run for an hour with Theon, and her chest wouldn't expand enough to take in the air she was trying to draw in.

Dex.

She needed Dex. He was the only one who could help her through this. He was right. She wasn't strong enough for this. Not by herself.

But there was no one. Only her and the night that had fallen, blanketing the world in darkness.

And there wasn't enough air even out here.

And she couldn't just stand here.

Kicking off her heels, she started walking down the sidewalk. She couldn't think about anything but getting out of the towering buildings that trapped her. And then she wasn't walking, but running through the streets. She had no idea where she was going. No one called out to stop her. Fae were free to move about here, and few would immediately recognize her as the Arius Source right now. Soon that would all change. So much had already changed, and yet she was the same. Still being shoved into nothingness. Still being trapped in a study with the Estate Mother. Still being a hassle. Still somehow creating chaos she couldn't handle herself.

She ran and ran, briefly thinking she could probably outrun Theon right now. Never once did it register how much trouble she was going to be in because all she could think about was open spaces and fresh air not tainted with expectations and demands.

It wasn't until she was dropping to her knees on the banks of the Wynfell River that she realized just how far she'd run.

It wasn't until then that she felt like she could breathe.

There was a scattering of trees around her, and she found herself on her back, staring up at the sky. The stars stared back, glittering and uncaring of a world the gods forgot.

The river ran through the Acropolis, but she had to be a good mile or two outside the outer walls. She wasn't entirely sure how she'd evaded any patrolling sentinels, but she didn't know how she evaded the wards either. She didn't know how long she had, but Theon would find her. He always did. He'd drag her back to the townhouse and rain down his consequences. She'd slip into the role he demanded of her until she fucked up again. If anything, it was a familiar cycle, and at this point, she'd accept any semblance of routine in her life, even if she suffered every time. Was it even worth it to keep trying?

The bond inside her was silent for once, and she sucked in another deep breath, the air shifting and a breeze cooling her skin. The only sound was the river for several long minutes until a low whining had her sitting up, her gaze connecting with eyes of glowing orange. She swallowed her scream as she scrambled to her feet. But that low whine came again as a large silvery-grey wolf took a few steps from the trees.

Was it...hurt?

She had never seen wolves in the forest around the Celeste Estate, and Tessa hadn't known there were wolves around the Acropolis. This wolf was as big as Theon's were with those same glowing eyes. Something had its ear perking, and the wolf's nose went to the sky. With a parting look, it darted back into the trees, but before Tessa could contemplate the absurdity of that entire scene, a female voice sounded.

"A Source all by herself? What will the Legacy say?"

Tessa spun to find a female dressed entirely in black from head-to-toe. She even had a hood up, concealing her features.

"Are we sure this is her?" came another female voice that had Tessa spinning around once more. This one was dressed the same, prowling towards her with purpose. Black gloves. Black boots. And was that...a dagger in her hand?

Tessa took a step back, her heels forgotten somewhere on the ground. The two females had her trapped between them and the river.

"Looks like her," the first said with a shrug.

"We've never seen her before," drawled the second.

"Exactly," said the first. "But if you're unsure, I could taste her first. Surely her blood would be divine."

"Do you wish for death, Risna?"

"It would certainly add some excitement to our lives."

Tessa wasn't sure what to do as she watched the two exchange words. It wasn't as if she could run. These two were clearly skilled in stealth. Not even the wolf had heard them until the last minute.

"Let's grab her and take her back. Even if it's not her, we'll be rewarded for collecting a Fae outside the boundaries," the second one said.

"No, wait!" Tessa stammered. "You can't touch me."

"And why is that?" the one called Risna asked, and even with her hood up, Tessa could tell she'd tilted her head in curiosity.

"Because I am the Source of the Arius Heir."

"Thank you."

"...for what?"

Tessa could hear the smile in Risna's voice when she answered, "For confirming you are the one we were looking for."

They both lunged for her, and Tessa screamed. She lurched backwards, her feet landing in the icy waters of the Wynfell River at the same time thunder cracked and streaks of lightning illuminated the night.

Illuminated the two figures dropping from the sky.

One had dark-leathery wings. The wings of a dragon.

The other had wings of nothing but shadows that dissipated into the night the moment his feet hit the ground.

Luka and Theon were here, and she wasn't sure if she should fear them more or the two who were trying to take her.

Theon stepped forward. Even in the night, Tessa could see the darkness floating around him.

Floating around *her*.

Like a shield, the shadows clung to her.

"Who sent you after her?" Theon demanded, his voice nothing but the icy promise of death.

"You know we cannot tell you, Heir of Endings," Risna replied, two daggers in her palms. "So just kill us and be done with it."

RAIN OF SHADOWS AND ENDINGS

"Daughter of Night, you of all people know there are so many things worse than death," Theon said.

"We had no choice," the second female supplied. "Surely you know this as much as I know you will not let us go free."

"What is your name?" Theon demanded.

"Does it matter? History will not remember me."

"Who else is with you?"

"No one. Only us," Risna cut in.

"Lies," Theon snarled, his darkness surging around her.

The female let out an agonized scream, dropping to her knees. Her hands clawed at her arms, her chest, her face.

"She tells the truth," Tessa cried, the female's screams filling the night. "It is only them."

Theon whirled on her, his shadows tugging her forward out of the water and onto the riverbank. "Do not say one more word," he spat, his darkness yanking her hands behind her back and binding them there.

But Luka had stepped forward, black flames appearing in his palm, and the second female was suddenly begging, pleading. "Two!" she cried. "There are two others likely already halfway back to report what they've seen."

Luka was in the sky before she finished speaking, flying low over the tops of the trees, and Theon was stalking forward. The second female tried to run, but his shadows wrapped around her, dragging her back to him. Tessa had no idea where he got the dagger. Perhaps he used the female's own, but that was a blade slicing across her throat. That was blood spraying in the moonlight. That was Theon bringing the blade down into her chest, directly into her heart.

Tessa was too shocked to do anything but stare at him as he tossed the female aside. Literally *tossed* her still bleeding body onto the river-bank. He couldn't just...leave her there, could he?

Risna was still writhing on the ground, screams still pouring from her as Theon approached. He held another dagger, and Tessa again wondered where the fuck he was getting all these godsdamn blades. Pulling his darkness back, he crouched beside the female and growled, "Tessa, come here."

But she was still staring at him in disbelief. She couldn't comprehend his demand, even if she wanted to.

"Tessalyn, *come here*," he said again, the entrancing forcing her feet to move, but her entire body was trembling as she lowered to her knees beside him, her wrists still bound. Risna was whimpering, and she could see rips in her sleeves, along the body of her tunic, even her pants. Streaks glimmered in the moonlight against the dark fabric. Blood. His darkness had done *that*?

"Do you know what she is?" Theon demanded.

She shook her head, staring down at the female.

"*Speak, Tessalyn.*"

"N-no," she whispered.

Theon yanked the female's hood back, and even with her injuries, she lurched forward, hissing as she lunged for Tessa's throat, and—

Those were *fangs*.

"She is a Night Child," Theon said, gripping the female by the hair and yanking her back. He held his dagger at the female's throat and tipped her head back farther. She bared her fangs again, a crazed sort of mania in her eyes as she tried to reach for Tessa once more, but Theon's grip was solid. He wouldn't let the female touch her. But the black streaks running through her skin, spider-webbing across her cheeks, down her throat...

"I don't understand," Tessa rasped.

"A vampyre, Tessa. She is what you would call a vampyre, and she was sent to take you."

"Vampyres aren't real."

"And yet you look upon one."

She shook her head, mainly because she couldn't wrap her head around what he was saying.

And then Theon slid the dagger across the female's throat.

Tessa lurched back as warm blood sprayed across her face, her neck, her chest. It was too familiar. Except this wasn't the blood of her friends. This wasn't the blood of other Fae being tortured to force her magic to surface.

Just like with the other female, the other *vampyre*, Theon brought the dagger down into her heart.

"Night Children can only be killed with blades made of certain material. This one," he said, yanking the dagger free, "is made of nightstone. It must go through their heart."

"I don't know what nightstone is." It sounded stupid, but that was the only thing she could think to say.

"I know, but you will soon," he answered, and he was far too calm for a male who had just killed two people.

He cleaned his dagger off on the female's cloak, leaving Tessa kneeling beside the corpse while he retrieved his other blade. His shadows loosened, freeing her wrists. She watched as both daggers disappeared among shadows, and then he came to a stop before her. He said nothing else, his hand appearing in her line of sight. He wiggled his fingers impatiently, and she placed her shaking hand in his palm.

With a sharp jerk, she was on her feet, and then an arm was wrapping around her waist, pulling her into his chest. Black wings of shadows appeared behind him, and she tried to push out of his hold. But he was already hauling her into the sky, a hand clamping onto her mouth to stifle her scream.

His lips brushed her ear as he said, "We have to fly low to avoid being seen right now. When we near the townhouses, I will use my shadows to shroud us. Do not scream. Do you understand, Tessa?"

She nodded. He released her mouth, only to slide an arm beneath her knees. She buried her face into his chest so she couldn't see the land passing by below her, and when she felt his magic slide around her, she leaned into the darkness.

Let it calm her.

Let it soothe her.

Let it caress her.

She didn't care that it was an extension of Theon. She didn't care that the bond was using it to draw her to him more and more. Too much had happened in the last few hours. Seeing Mother Cordelia again. Sitting in a state of panic and memories for an hour. The run to the river. The vampyres. Watching Theon kill them. She could still feel the sticky blood on her face, her neck. She felt like she did after an assessment with too many emotions to process and too much shit to sort out. There were so many questions, but she didn't know where to begin. She needed to clean this blood off her, but she also knew Theon was pissed. Consequences for her impulsiveness were coming, and maybe he wouldn't give her the time to shower or think or—

The spiraling of her thoughts was cut off when they landed in the yard behind the townhouse, and Theon lowered her to the ground. The grass was cold beneath her feet, and a light rain was falling. The double veranda doors were thrown open, and Axel was there, taking her from Theon's grip. She didn't understand why until she saw Theon stripping off his suit jacket, followed by his tie and shirt.

"Where are your shoes?" Theon asked, glancing down at Tessa's bare feet as he removed his own black shoes.

"By the river," she rasped out.

"The river?" Axel repeated, grabbing her wrist. She hadn't realized she'd been twisting her fingers into his shirt. "The Wynfell River? What the fuck were you doing there?"

"Call Luka. He shouldn't be fully shifted, so he should answer. He's taking care of bodies. Make sure he finds her shoes," Theon said, stepping forward and taking her back from his brother.

She hardly noticed that she was being passed back and forth. Not with the familiar numbness settling in. Not as she felt herself shutting down. Not as she felt herself slipping into nothing where she didn't have it in her to care about anything. Where she didn't know how to hold herself together.

Where it was too exhausting to try.

"Stay with me, little storm," Theon said softly, guiding her into the house and out of the drizzling rain. It wasn't much, but it was enough to mix with the blood on her skin. She could feel drops of it slowly sliding down her flesh, and she raised her fingers to wipe at one.

They came away stained in red.

And she was immediately pulled into memories of assessments.

Of visions they forced her into where *she* killed her friends. Killed her family that didn't exist.

Of choking on her own blood while she was tortured in front of her friends.

Of watching her friends be tortured.

"Please stop!" she cried as the small knife was stabbed into Lange's side again and again.

He groaned with every strike, his body marred with small deep cuts. When this was over, all traces of the abuse would be gone. No scars on the outside. What Legacy would want Fae marred with imperfections to serve in their kingdoms?

"You can make it all stop, Tessalyn," the Priestess replied calmly. "Just show us your element.

"I can't!" she wailed. "I'm trying, and I can't!" She was chained to a wall, forced to watch.

And when Lange lost consciousness, they brought in Corbin.

"Tessa. Tessalyn, *look at me.*"

The entrancing forced her gaze to eyes of emerald green. Theon was gripping her face between his palms, his thumb grazing back and forth across her cheekbone, smearing the blood splatters.

He had blood on his face too. More than she did. Little spots and larger smears. And he looked…tired. His eyes weren't as bright.

"Are you back, Tessa?"

She nodded mutely, leaning against the wall.

The wall?

Her eyes darted around. They were upstairs in their bedroom, but even the small familiarity of it wasn't enough to ease the tension in her body. What she needed was—

"Here."

Theon was before her once more. When had he left her? But he was pressing a glass into her hand.

A glass of amber liquid.

She swallowed the entirety down.

"By the gods, Tessa," Theon muttered.

But she didn't care as the liquor warmed her belly, her arms loosening a fraction.

More.

She needed more.

She needed to drown in it.

No, she needed to drown in—

"I know what you need, Tessa."

His dark voice cut through her thoughts as she raised her eyes to his.

"You know nothing," she retorted, but her voice cracked.

Something akin to relief flashed in his eyes, but it was gone just as quickly. He'd retreated several steps from her, standing halfway across the room, as though he wasn't sure what she would do next.

"You told me how you deal with things like this," he said.

"Things like what?"

"The assessments. I know this wasn't that, but I get the feeling this was similar in many ways. At the very least, I would guess it brought up memories," he added when she opened her mouth to argue.

She snapped her mouth shut, pushing down said memories. But it was no use. They surged back up faster than she could shove them down.

Another drink.

She needed another drink.

She needed the bottle.

She needed to drink so much that not even her nightmares could haunt her.

She needed to feel something other than the numbness of nothing.

"I don't need to physically touch you to give you what you need, Tessa," Theon said, his hands sliding into his pockets as he watched her from across the room.

She felt his dark magic sliding across her skin. It seeped through the fabric of her damp dress. It was feather light, the barest of touches, as it trailed down her arms, across her torso, down her legs. Her knees gave out the smallest amount, and she leaned harder into the wall. And gods, she wanted this. She wanted to tumble into the oblivion that pleasure held, even if it came from him. Something inside her raised its head at the thought of letting him give her this, and she refused to admit that she *wanted* it to come from him. *Needed* it to.

"Will you finally let me take care of you, Tessa?" he asked, his voice low and rough as he took a single step towards her.

Was she finally going to give in?

Was it giving in?

Maybe it was simply her taking something she needed from him the same way he was going to take her power from her.

The way he was going to take everything from her.

That's what she told herself as she nodded her head once, squeezing her eyes tight at letting this happen.

"I'm going to need verbal confirmation here, beautiful. I want to hear you say this is your choice."

Her head tipped back against the wall. His magic had stilled while he waited for her answer, and she needed that darkness more than she needed to breathe at the moment.

"Yes," she rasped.

34
TESSA

His dark shadows immediately slid up her torso, fingers of darkness grazing the undersides of her breasts, and she sucked in a sharp breath, ready to let the sensations drag her under. But again his magic stilled.

"And your eyes. I need those too." It was a whisper she felt ghost across her lips. Her eyes flew open, and she gasped to find Theon right in front of her. "Good girl. Eyes stay on me."

This close, she could see the specks of blood in his dark hair glimmering in the soft glow of the dim lighting. She could smell the tang of blood, but maybe that was the blood on her own skin. There were smears of red across his cheek and down his throat where he had tucked her in close while they had flown here, which meant there was likely blood smeared in *her* hair. He wasn't touching her, but his body was mere inches away. She could feel the heat of him as much as she could see the want in his eyes.

She nodded again at his demand, and then a throaty moan escaped her when his darkness flicked over her nipples before kneading her breasts.

"Some day you are going to let me touch you in all the ways I am longing to, Tessa," he said, his voice as dark as the shadows continuing to caress her breasts, drag along her ribs, across her torso. A tendril of darkness glided across her throat, another brushing along her bottom lip. "Some day you are going to *ask* me to touch you." A small whimper came from her, and

Theon's eyes somehow went even darker at the sound. His mouth moved a fraction of an inch closer to her ear but still did not touch her, just as he'd promised. "You will beg me for it, Tessa, and I will enjoy every second of your pleading before I finally take everything that is mine to have. Because someday you will realize this is far more than a simple Source bond."

A sound somewhere between want and dread came from her as those hands of darkness slid over her hips and down her thighs. She couldn't think around it all. All she could do was *feel*. Then he drew that darkness right over her center, and she cried out, tension building and pooling low in her belly.

"We have always been more," he continued. "From the moment I saw you slip into that alcove with stolen chocolate, I knew you were mine. The Fates always have their way, Tessa, and this will be no different."

She could feel him all over her, his shadows coating every inch of her flesh. It was too much and not enough all at once. And when that darkness pressed on that bundle of sensitive nerves, she gasped again.

Theon moved as though he was going to swallow the sound with his mouth, but he stilled. His features twisted, as if it physically pained him not to have his lips on her right now. He didn't say anything else. He just watched her, holding her gaze, as his shadows and darkness brought her to ruin. She was writhing. Her hips bucking and searching for more as his power played with her, pulsing against her clit. Every time her eyes fluttered, he would pull his magic back and shake his head, reminding her to keep her eyes on him.

It didn't take long to find herself at the edge, and she didn't want it to end. She knew what this was. A temporary distraction from her life, but godsdamnit, she would cling to this distraction with all that she was.

The bond that connected them was going wild. Each stroke of his dark power electrified every nerve of her being. She gasped again, her entire body beginning to tremble as his magic intensified. Tendrils of shadows trailed along her ribs. Working her breasts. Pressing at her center. Stroking her cheek. Winding through her hair. They were everywhere.

He was everywhere.

"Give it to me, little storm," Theon demanded. Darkness wrapped around her throat, forcing her chin up. His hands were braced on the wall on either side of her head, holding him a breath away from touching her. "They're all mine anyway."

She shook her head in denial at his comment, and his magic stilled.

She nearly sobbed at the loss, her entire body shaking with want and need.

"Hear me well, Tessa. Everything you are is mine. Everything you have to give, I will take, including your pleasure."

Then his magic pressed in on her, that darkness going icy cold as it circled and worked those nerves between her thighs, hurling her over the edge before she could brace herself for it. She cried out, but it was quickly muffled by Theon's hand slipping over her mouth.

"Shh, little storm. Axel is just below us," he whispered, but the thought of his brother hearing them somehow only intensified the orgasm. She was falling into nothing as release tore through her, spreading out sweet and sharp from the center of her body. Her eyes finally fluttered closed, and waves of pleasure pulled her under.

As she drowned in it.

And when she surfaced from the ecstasy, she was leaning against Theon, his arm wrapped around her waist, clutching her tightly, while his other hand wound into her hair. She could feel his length pressing against her stomach, and she was curled into his bare chest, her nails digging into his flesh. She slowly raised her eyes to his. He brought a hand up to smooth back hair from her brow. His fingers and palm were stained red, his hand still bloody from the vampyres he'd killed. Somehow, she didn't care. Not right now. Not as she clung to the weightless feeling in her limbs, to the weightless feeling in her soul.

He dipped his head so he could speak into her ear once more. "You are absolutely stunning, Tessa. I could watch you come for me a thousand times over and never grow tired of it. Just imagine what I will do when you let me have all of you."

She was still trying to catch her breath, but it caught in her throat at his words. Her achingly empty core clenched weakly again, and she forced herself to inhale deeply before she did something truly stupid. She couldn't let him have all of her. Not now. Not ever. Because if it was anything like what he'd just done to her with his power, she couldn't wrap her mind around what that would be like.

But it was never going to happen.

The bond hissed at the thought, but she was still too high on her release to register its dismay. This high was better than alcohol ever was. It's why she desperately sought out mortals after assessments. But sex with mortals had never been like *that*. And what Theon had done to her wasn't even sex. It was…

It was only like that because of this fucking bond. That's what she was going to tell herself until she believed it.

Theon's hands slid to her hips, and he took a step back. He still held her steady, his eyes sliding over her. She could swear he let his shadows follow his gaze, ghosting over her one final time.

"Can you stand?" he finally asked after several moments of silence. His voice was hoarse and gravelly.

"Yeah. Yes," she rasped, clearing her throat. "I need to wash up."

Theon nodded, releasing her from his hold and taking another step back. To her credit, she only stumbled a bit as she pushed off the wall behind her.

She made her way to the bathroom, feeling Theon's gaze follow her the entire way before she shut the door. Bracing her hands on the counter, she let her head fall forward.

Shit. Shit. Shit.

She looked up, staring back at her reflection in the mirror. Her cheeks were still flushed. Her limbs were still heavy. She wasn't entirely sure how her legs were holding her up. That was definitely blood smeared across her face and throat. There were streaks of red down her hair where Theon had touched it.

How had she just let that happen? What had she been thinking?

And why the fuck was she contemplating asking him for more?

She didn't need him. He didn't know what she needed. This was just another way he was binding her to him. Strengthening this fucking bond.

Stupid.

Impulsive.

Reckless.

But as she stepped under the hot spray of the shower, watching pink-tinged water flow down the drain, all she could think was that it had been worth it.

It had been worth it to not be able to think about anything else while Theon had brought her to ruin. She didn't care what that said about her. Drowning in rapture kept her from shattering, and she wasn't about to apologize for how she held the pieces of her soul together.

"Let's go, baby doll."

Tessa groaned as curtains were thrown wide. She pulled the blankets over her head, curling tightly into herself.

This day could already go fuck itself.

She hadn't stayed in the shower long last night. The moment her thoughts and memories had started to surface again, she'd only wanted to sleep. Not because she was exhausted or tired. She definitely should have been after the events of the day. But when it came down to it, she just didn't want to be awake.

She didn't want to be awake now either.

It was coming. The dark was coming at any moment, and she couldn't decide if she even cared.

She'd expected to face Theon's wrath when she got done cleaning up last night, but when she'd exited the bathroom, it hadn't been Theon waiting for her. It had been Axel. Theon had apparently needed to go with Luka to "take care of some things" leaving Axel to watch over her. Tessa had been both relieved and disappointed. Relieved because it had delayed facing Theon and whatever consequences were surely coming for her, but disappointed because she'd needed the bond.

The bond. Not *him*.

She'd wanted to ask where exactly Theon had gone, but she hadn't. And Axel hadn't provided any more information either. He'd only settled onto the sofa with his computer and a drink, looking so much like his brother it was almost comforting.

Almost.

"Tessa. Let's go. I want to get a run in before I have to drop you off with Luka," Axel said again, tugging on the blankets.

A run with Axel?

She threw the blankets off, pushing her hair out of her face as she sat up. Looking at the other side of the bed, she could tell Theon hadn't slept here. Had he even come back?

"Where is Theon?" she called to Axel, who had disappeared into the dressing room.

"Out," he called back.

"Still?" She was climbing out of the bed when Axel reappeared, running gear and sneakers in his arms.

"Yes, still," he answered, holding out the items. "Go change. We leave in five minutes. Eat this too," he added, swiping a banana off the coffee table and piling it atop the clothing.

"But—"

"Go, Tessa. I have shit to do today."

"You're in a good mood," Tessa griped, snatching the clothing from him.

"Don't start with this, Tessa," Axel sighed. "We've been up all night doing damage control, and Theon had to—"

Her eyes narrowed when he abruptly stopped speaking. "Had to what?"

"Nothing. Just change. You don't want to be late for training with Luka. He'll be an ass."

"As opposed to...?"

A dark grin tipped at the corner of Axel's lips. "Baby doll, Luka is a Sargon Legacy. The god of war and courage. Remember *that's* who is going to be training you."

"Where did he learn it all?" she asked, going into the bathroom. She left the door open so she could hear Axel's response.

"Father sent him to several trainings. He'd be gone for months. Theon would be a prick the entire time, but that was when Father was preparing Luka to be *his* Guardian, not Theon's," Axel explained. "Still, I think a lot of it is natural instinct. Theon and I attended a few of the trainings with him and didn't pick up on things half as quickly."

"Luka had fire. But it was black," Tessa hollered, her words garbled while she brushed her teeth.

"Well, yeah. It was dragon fire," Axel called back. "Three minutes, Tessa."

She spit into the sink before quickly shucking off the pants and tank she'd slept in, shutting the door to take care of personal needs. Slipping on her running clothes and sneakers, she had the banana stem clenched between her teeth when she emerged while tying her hair back. Sighing, Axel grabbed it, peeling the banana and handing it to her when she finished her hair.

"What's dragon fire?" she asked.

"The fire of a dragon," Axel said dryly, grabbing her phone from

RAIN OF SHADOWS AND ENDINGS

where it was charging. Theon must have plugged it in because she hadn't even thought of it after the events of last night. "Let's go."

"Your answers are as helpful as your brother's," she retorted, taking a bite of the banana.

"Ask Theon about dragon fire in your lessons with him. I'm sure he'll talk about its properties for hours."

"What lessons?"

Axel glanced over his shoulder. "He probably hasn't had time to tell you yet, but part of your lessons include ones with him. Detailed history of Arius Kingdom. I'm sure you'll get hours of him talking about all his ideas and theories."

Pen was at the door with two water bottles in hand, holding one out to each of them. "Your protein shake is in the fridge, Axel."

"You're too good to me, Pen," Axel teased affectionately.

Pen rolled her eyes, but smiled as she pulled the door open for him. "See you in a bit."

There was no more talking after that. Axel pushed her even more than Theon did, and after running through the Acropolis bare foot last night, her legs and feet were already sore. By the time Axel let her stop, she wanted to vomit and her muscles were burning.

"I...hate...you," she gasped out between dragging in lungfuls of air as she plopped to the ground, her head hanging between her bent knees.

"You're acting like you're dying," Axel chided, kicking an ankle back to stretch.

"I *am* dying, you ass."

"Not yet, but you will be after Luka's done with you."

"I need food."

"He has some for you," Axel replied. "Get up. We'll walk there for a cooldown."

"Walk where?" she grumbled as Axel pulled her back to her feet.

"The training arenas."

"I'm training *there*?"

"Mhmm."

"But that's where they train the Fae assigned as warriors and sentinels."

"Sure is."

"I am...not that."

"No, but you need to train in combat, Tessa. We already told you that. Then you would have at least been able to defend yourself last night until Theon could find you."

Axel's tone was sharp and accusing, and it made Tessa wince. He never spoke to her this way.

"I didn't run from him," she answered defensively.

"I should fucking hope not, but I'll let you work that out with Theon."

"Should I be worried?"

"Do you care?" he countered.

Fair point.

They didn't speak the rest of the way to the training arenas. Axel led her through the building and down hallways until they came to one of the private training rooms, and he pushed open a door, standing aside to let her enter first.

And her jaw dropped.

Luka was here. Shirtless. And by the gods. She'd known he was fit, but she'd had no idea *that* was beneath the suits he always wore. Those were defined muscles that disappeared into the waistband of loose linen pants. He had clearly been here a while. His brown hair was tied back in a barely there ponytail, and a fine sheen of sweat covered his body.

Axel chuckled beside her, reaching over and touching her chin with his forefinger, closing her mouth. "Careful, baby doll," he said with a wink. "Don't let Theon see you looking at him like that."

She tried to swallow, but her mouth was too dry as Luka finished up...whatever it was he was doing, and turned to face them. He jerked his chin towards the wall and said, "Eat that."

Tessa turned to find a table with various things atop it, including a small bowl of yogurt with berries. She snatched it up, partly because she was starving, but more so because she knew a consequence was coming. It was instinct to eat as much as possible right now, even if she knew Theon wouldn't do that to her.

Probably wouldn't do that to her anyway.

"You have this handled?" Axel asked Luka, watching her inhale the yogurt. His brow furrowed. "It's not your last meal, Tessa."

She felt her cheeks flush, but she didn't care as she looked between him and Luka.

"I have her. Theon will be here in a bit."

Tessa paused with the spoon halfway to her mouth.

"Do I need to be here for that?" Axel asked, raking a hand through his hair.

"No. Not until you track down what we need."

Axel nodded, suddenly avoiding eye contact with Tessa. She had lowered her spoon back to her yogurt, and Luka said, "Finish that, Tessa."

"I'm not hungry."

"Your days are going to be long. You need to be fueling your body, especially once your element emerges. Training with me and training with your magic is going to deplete your energy stores quickly. You need to eat multiple times a day."

"You're acting like I'm going to be fighting for my life."

"That's exactly what you would have been doing last night. Finish that," he ordered again, jerking his chin at the forgotten yogurt. She huffed, but brought another bite to her mouth. She turned to say something to Axel, but he was already gone.

Luka was grabbing some more mats and making the training area bigger. Tessa didn't know what was happening here, but she got an uneasy feeling in her gut.

"Luka?"

"What?"

"Where has Theon been?"

He paused for the briefest of moments. "We've been trying to figure out who the Night Children were working for."

"Did you figure it out?"

"No."

"He told Axel you were taking care of the bodies of the two he killed."

"I did."

"What did you do?"

"Burned them to nothing."

It took her a moment to move past that statement before she could say, "I didn't... I thought vampyres were made up to keep us in line at the Estates as children," she said, setting aside her empty yogurt bowl.

"Night Children are not allowed to roam freely. Most are sequestered to the Underground," Luka answered, motioning for her to join him in the center of the mats where he stood waiting.

"One said she wanted to drink from me," Tessa said, dragging her feet as she made her way towards him.

He huffed a dark laugh. "I'm sure she did. Fae blood is like a drug for Night Children."

"But..."

"But what, Tessa?" he asked with a resigned sigh as he began adjusting her feet and back and arms.

"Don't the Legacy drink blood? How are they different?"

Luka was behind her, his hands on her shoulders, pulling them back so her spine straightened. "The Legacy are rationed blood to make sure they don't become like the Night Children."

"What?" Tessa gasped, spinning to face him.

He growled—an honest-to-the-gods growl—in irritation.

"Tessa," he snapped. "Focus."

"On what? Where to put my feet?"

"Yes. Form is everything when it comes to proper training. It's all about control, and you have none."

"Don't sugar-coat it or anything," she grumbled, letting him adjust her positioning all over again.

"Are you going to try to tell me you have a shred of self-control?"

"I have more self-control than you know," she retorted.

"Says the female who spent a dinner beneath the table because she couldn't keep her mouth shut."

"Fuck you, Luka."

"No, fuck you, Tessa," he snapped, jerking her shoulders back harder than necessary. "How have you not realized nearly everything Theon has done, including making you sit beneath a table, was to protect you?"

"Protect me? The one I need protecting from is Theon," she cried, again turning to face him.

"I swear to Arius, Tessa. If you move out of position before I tell you to again—"

"You'll what? Punish me? Can you even do that without Theon's permission? Come to think of it, can you do anything without his permission?" she sneered.

"Oh, little one," Luka replied, his voice laced with warning. His eyes were glowing brightly, and his pupils had shifted to vertical slits. "This attitude of yours is delightful as always—and Theon finds it twistedly endearing for some godsforsaken reason—but if you cannot get yourself under control, Theon will be the least of your worries." He kicked her feet into position again. "Tell me, Tessa, what do you think would have happened if Theon hadn't forced you to sit at his feet that night?" When she didn't answer, he continued, his tone patronizing, "Come now, surely you must know since you've never let Theon explain his actions."

"Explain his actions? He shoved me under a table, Luka!"

He was in front of her faster than she could blink, his hand gripping her jaw, and she winced. Not because he was gripping her hard, but because his hand was *hot*. "Would you rather be shoved to your knees, Tessa? Forced to take a cock into that smart mouth?"

She jerked back from him. "Theon wouldn't do that."

The sardonic smile that filled his face was terrifying. "If you only knew the *behavior corrections* we've witnessed and endured over the years, Tessa. The kinds of things he has saved you from. Things he wouldn't tell you because he was trying to ease you into this, trying to protect you even in that. From his father. From us. From himself. Sitting beneath a table was a fucking luxury. But I think even if you let him explain himself, you'd still see him as your villain, wouldn't you?"

Suddenly bands of black flames were around her ankles, and she flung her arms out to keep her balance as her feet were yanked back into place.

"If you move out of position again, those flames will burn you."

"You cannot be serious."

Then she yelped when the flames flared for a blink, biting into her skin.

"The two of you are so godsdamn exasperating," he snarled, once again yanking her shoulders back. "He's too controlling, and you're not controlled enough. I told him over and over this would be a disaster. You're two forces that should repel each other. Fire and shadows. Light and dark. Beginnings and endings. Instead, you're drawn to each other."

"I am not drawn to him," she seethed, forcing her feet to stay planted.

"Refusing to acknowledge something doesn't make it non-existent."

"Acknowledge this," she spat, raising her middle finger.

He opened his mouth to respond, but stopped himself. For a long moment, he just held her gaze, as if searching for something.

Finally, he took a step back and said, "Memorize this position. It needs to become second nature. Every single thing I teach you will start from this position."

"This is stupid. If I'm being attacked, they won't wait for me to assume this position."

"Stop talking back, or you'll find flames in your mouth, little one."

Her eyes narrowed. "You wouldn't."

"He certainly would."

She jerked at the sound of Theon's voice, briefly wondering why she hadn't felt him approaching, but then she let out a curse as the flames on her ankles singed her skin when she moved out of position again.

And they didn't stop burning.

"Luka!" she cried, hopping from foot-to-foot trying to put out the flames.

"Get back into position," the dragon said, crossing his arms over his chest, the dragon fire intensifying.

"I can't think around the burning!" she cried again, trying to make her feet move, but she hadn't been paying attention to how he'd constantly arranged her.

"Luka, her eyes," Theon said cautiously.

"I see them," Luka replied. "She's been on that edge for a few minutes now."

She had no idea what they were talking about, but apparently she found the correct foot placement because the burning ceased. Except when she glanced up, Luka was rolling his eyes, and Theon looked like he was moments away from stepping in.

As soon as Luka removed the flames from her ankles, Theon visibly relaxed. Folding his arms across his chest, he leaned back against the table, his emerald gaze sliding over her.

"This is why Theon won't be present during training," Luka said in a low voice from where he stood beside her. "He'll get over-protective."

"Then why is he here?"

Luka arched a brow at the question, but instead of answering, he turned to Theon and said, "I wasn't expecting you for at least another hour."

"I know," Theon answered, a hand raking through his dark hair. He still looked tired. Had he truly not slept? "Axel found what we needed."

"Already?"

Theon nodded. "He's on his way back."

"Did he find extra supply as well?" Luka pressed.

"No."

"What are you going to do?" Luka asked, looking pointedly at Tessa.

"Not until after."

"As your Guardian—"

"My Guardian, not my keeper," Theon cut in sharply.

"For fuck's sake, you need both most days," Luka grumbled.

When silence fell, Tessa tentatively asked, "Do I have to keep standing in this same spot, or can I move now without obtaining more burns?"

"Don't move," Luka snapped.

She huffed in annoyance, but kept her feet planted. His eyes had finally shifted back, and she didn't want to piss him off again. More than that, Theon still hadn't spoken to her or approached her, and she didn't know what to make of it. She felt off balance and on edge, not knowing what to expect, and the cord in her chest was oddly still and silent.

When the minutes passed by with no one speaking, she couldn't take it anymore. "If Night Children are supposed to stay in the Underground, why were they here? Why were they..."

"Coming after you?" Luka finished. "Theon has already explained this to you. You can be used against him, and by proxy, against the Arius Kingdom. You will forever be hunted, Tessa."

"By vampyres?" she balked.

Luka shrugged casually. "Vampyres bound to a particular kingdom. Mercenaries. Someone trying to gain favor with a Kingdom Lord or Lady. Whoever is hired by another Legacy to do their dirty work."

"I am supposed to just accept being hunted?"

"No. You're going to learn to defend yourself," Luka retorted. "You're going to learn to control your element when it is revealed. And you're going to harness some of that wildness."

She didn't bother telling him it wouldn't work. Didn't bother telling him that Mother Cordelia had tried for years to *teach* her self-control. Didn't bother telling him she wasn't worth the energy, the hassle. He'd figure it out soon enough himself.

The door opened, and Tessa forced herself not to spin at the sound, instead looking over her shoulder to find Axel strolling in. He was still in his running gear and had a half-empty protein shake in hand.

"Let's get this over with," he grumbled. "I have shit to do."

Seriously, what had crawled up his ass today?

"You have it?" Theon asked.

"I said I did," Axel retorted, producing something from a burst of shadows that Tessa could only describe as a stick. A thin, black stick. "You're sure about this?"

"It was your idea," Theon replied.

Axel winced, his gaze cutting to Tessa before looking away quickly. Then he held the stick out to Theon. Her Master didn't hesitate, snatching it from him and moving towards her. And suddenly Tessa felt the full force of their Source bond. It was as if she was feeling the hours they'd been separated all at once, and it was too much. She sucked in a breath, her knees buckling. She dropped to her knees. The cord inside her was frantic, and her skin was buzzing, something trying to claw its way to him. Memories of last night surged up. Of him touching her with his magic. Of him knowing exactly how to bring her body to ruin.

She didn't register that Luka was holding her down. Not until Theon's fingers brushed along her torso, tugging down the waistband of her running leggings to expose her hip.

"Theon," she gasped.

He still said nothing to her. He only brought that stick to her skin. But it wasn't a stick she realized far too late. It was a scion. The same thing the Priestesses used to give Marks. They were the only ones sanctioned to do so, but they'd already told her they'd found ways around that. It was how Luka had become Theon's Guardian.

"Theon, stop!" she cried. She didn't know much about the Marks, but she knew they had to be drawn precisely. One error, one minor imperfection, could change the Mark's purpose entirely. "Theon, please. I'm sorry. Please don't!"

But black flames around her throat, her chest, her legs had her stilling, and she realized that once again she was helpless. There was nothing she could do but let this happen. No one would save her. No one would protect her. No one would stop them, just like no one stopped Mother Cordelia. No one stopped the Priestesses.

And another piece of her soul shattered as she went lax in Luka's hold.

The dragon's brow immediately furrowed, his eyes snapping to her. "Tessa..."

But she was already going through song lyrics, waiting for it to be over.

One more second.

One more minute.

One more song.

That's what she told herself as she felt the burning of the scion when Theon drew on her skin. There was no flinching. No screaming. No tears.

There was just nothing.

There was nothing when he passed the scion to Axel and let him draw a Mark on his hip in the same spot. There was nothing when the same was done to Axel and Luka. Three identical Marks that she could only assume matched the one Theon had given her.

There was nothing when Theon produced a dagger and reached for her arm.

There was nothing when he dragged the blade across her skin, and Luka caught her blood in a cup.

There was nothing when he passed the cup to Theon, and he drank the whole thing down, his entire body seeming to shudder in relief.

"It's a Tracking Mark, Tessa," Luka said, finally snuffing out the black flames that were still keeping her immobile. "Last night, I came to collect you from the instructor, but you were gone. I had to waste time tracking down Theon so he could use the bond to track you down, and even then... This will be faster. For all of us. Axel and I can find you now too."

Her gaze slid to Axel. "This was your idea?" she asked, her voice hollow.

"To better protect you, Tessa," he answered helplessly.

"I didn't ask you to make it pretty for me, Axel. I asked if it was your idea."

His features went tense, his eyes shuttering with a mask she rarely saw from him.

"Yes," he answered.

She only gave a sharp nod.

"Tessa, you need to calm down," Luka said carefully.

Her head tilted as she met his gaze. "I am calm."

"I know, but..." His eyes dropped to her hands, and she followed his gaze.

There was faint light flaring from between the fingers of her clenched fists. She slowly raised her hands, uncurling her fingers, and light seemed to crackle and spark at her fingertips. Not like fire, but like—

"You're too calm, little storm."

Theon's voice cut through her thoughts, and her head snapped up, meeting his gaze. There was more color in his features, and he seemed more awake. With a start, she realized it was because of her blood. Legacy needed Fae blood to replenish their magic. He'd used a lot of his gifts last night with the flying and the killing and the apparent shadow fucking.

"One wants me calm. One wants me wild. Your expectations are becoming impossible, Master," she said, getting to her feet, and her voice sounded strange even to her. It was laced with something dark.

It was laced with something powerful.

The three of them were surrounding her, but they were all also several feet away, as though afraid to come closer.

As though they knew something she didn't.

She met Theon's gaze once more when she asked, "What element am I going to emerge with?"

"We don't know, Tessa. Your assessments were inconclusive."

"And you will use me to help your father take over Devram?"

"No, beautiful. You'll help me kill my father."

"So you can have Devram?"

Darkness hovered around him like a faint mist, and she could swear it reached for her when he said, "No, Tessa. So I can have the Underground, and *they* can have Devram."

35

TESSA

"Who are *they?*" she asked, her fingertips still tingling with the crackling light, "Night Children?"

"Gods, no," Axel barked. "While plenty of Night Children are decent enough to work with, they could never be entrusted to rule over entire lands."

"Then who?"

"There are plenty of Legacy there from the various kingdoms," Theon supplied.

"They were sent there because they were a threat to Devram," Tessa said incredulously.

"A threat to Devram? Or to the ruling Lords and Ladies?" Theon countered.

"Does it matter? The ruling families have ruled since the world was created. The ruling families were selected by the gods themselves."

A dark look crossed Theon's face. "So much history gets lost when a select few choose what gets to be remembered."

Her focus dropped to her hands again. Her palms glowed as though she was holding sunlight in her palms. It reminded her of Theon's shadows, the way it moved and swirled, only bright and full of life rather than dark and full of death. But the light crackling at her fingertips?

Her gaze connected with Theon's when she raised her palms, and all three of the males took a step back from her.

"What is this?" she demanded.

The three of them exchanged looks, Luka sliding closer to Theon, before Theon answered, "We don't know."

"I don't believe you."

"That's fine. It won't change my answer."

"How do I make it stop?"

"You let me help you."

"I don't want your help," she gritted out.

"And yet you need it."

She curled her fingers in, fists clenching. "Why is it manifesting now? When I haven't been through the Emerging Ceremony?"

"I don't know," Theon said.

"You don't know," she repeated flatly. When he only shook his head, she said coldly, "Give me your best guess. I am told you are full of theories."

"My best guess is that you are so powerful it is breaking through the binding on your power," Theon answered. "But that is only a theory."

"What binding?"

"I will not explain that until your power is under control. You have to let me help you, Tessa," Theon insisted.

"Either that or I restrain you until it dies out," Luka added.

"How can you—" Tessa started.

"I thought we agreed Luka and I were handling her for a while," Axel cut in.

"*Handling* me?" Tessa repeated, the power in her palms flaring brighter.

"Axel, shut up," Theon snapped. "Don't you have shit to do?"

Axel gave him a mocking smile. "Sure do, *my Lord.*"

"Axel—"

But he was already leaving, the door banging shut behind him.

Theon exhaled a long breath, trying to brush past Luka and approach her, but Luka gripped his arm. "There is a reason we agreed to Axel and I handling this right now."

"She can't be walking around like that, Luka," Theon said, darkness wreathing his hands as he tried to jerk his arm free. "It's going to be bad enough after the Emerging Ceremony."

"And we're preparing for that, but I can't let you near her right now. You know what almost happened in Rockmoor when she threw you across that parking lot. We are in a small space. I will shift if she loses control. Do you want that?"

Tessa watched as Theon swiped a hand down his face, the tiredness she'd glimpsed earlier already returning.

"What happened in Rockmoor?" she asked, trying to ignore the lightning sparking at her fingertips.

"I almost shifted and attacked you. I was seconds away from seriously injuring, if not killing, you, Tessa," Luka snapped.

"Fae aren't easy to kill. Just like Legacy aren't."

"Few things can counter dragon fire, and nothing in Devram can withstand it."

"Oh," was all she could think to say, her eyes falling back to her hands.

"Our magic mirrors our emotions, Tessa," Theon cut in. "Your magic has its own personality. It will try to control you unless you control it. These are things you learn in your element lessons after your element emerges, but—" He sighed again. "You may need a private instructor for that as well."

"Like who?" she asked.

"We're still working on that. For now, you need to focus on your training with Luka, and work on keeping yourself under control."

"Because that's worked so well in the past," she murmured.

"Why were you by the river last night?" Luka suddenly asked, and the light in her palms flared.

"Luka!" Theon snapped.

"We need to know. What's the point in calming her down if she's just going to get like this again when we discuss it?"

Theon rubbed at the back of his neck. "Fine." His eyes came back to her, waiting for an answer.

"I didn't mean to."

"I will need you to clarify that statement. You didn't mean to disobey direct commands? Leave the Acropolis boundaries unattended and without permission? The private instructor said you were uncooperative," he said, his voice growing harsher with each word.

"Of course she did," Tessa muttered.

"Tessa," he growled in warning. "I know I have been explicit in my expectations of you, as well as the consequences for failure. You have repeatedly told me you understand."

"What do you want me to say, Theon? The private instructor ran the Estate where I was raised. There's history there."

"I know. It's why I thought you'd be the most comfortable with her."

"Be the most..." She trailed off, biting down on the hysterical laughter threatening to escape her.

"I recognize you weren't prepared for this role like the other Sources were," Theon said. "That weakness needs to be taken care of, and none of us have the time to deal with it."

Too disobedient.

Too much of a hassle.

No one will have the time to bother with you.

"Of course," Tessa said, the light in her palms dying out.

"Tessa?" Theon asked, both he and Luka tensing as if preparing for her to— What? Attack them?

She almost laughed at the thought.

She'd have to care, and Theon's words had effectively reminded her why she didn't.

"None of this explains why you ran all the way to the river last night," Luka said, having stepped in front of Theon once more.

And Tessa couldn't help but wonder if that would be her soon? Placing herself between Theon and danger. They told her they wouldn't let that happen, but the bond seemed to control Luka's actions, even if he didn't realize it. How could they know it wouldn't do the same to her? She'd seen Eviana leap to Valter's defense.

"I was in a panic," she finally answered. "Mother Cordelia and I do not have a pleasant history. I do not enjoy spending time in her company, as it was usually followed by being shoved into small spaces and being hungry for days afterwards."

"Explain that," Theon said, his words steely.

"No," she answered, her arms wrapping around herself.

"She would keep you inside?" Luka asked, his penetrating stare on her. "That is why you prefer being outside?"

"Something like that."

Theon was about to say something else, but his phone buzzed with a notification. Pulling it from his pocket, he said, "It's my father."

"Go," Luka said. "I've got her, and we will meet up with you for this afternoon's meetings as agreed."

Theon looked her over one last time before he muttered, "Fine."

He was already lifting the phone to his ear as he left the training room.

"Get back in position," Luka ordered.

"That's it?" she asked, her arms dropping to her sides.

"What do you mean that's it?"

"I thought there would be...some other consequence."

"The Tracking Mark wasn't enough for you?"

Luka was circling her, once again making small adjustments to her form.

"No, I just...thought there would be more."

Bands of black flames appeared around her wrists and ankles.

"I told Theon I had it covered with training," Luka said, his pupils shifting to vertical slits when he came to a stop in front of her.

The dark grin he sent her told Tessa she was going to hate every second.

Theon reached for her hand to help her from the back seat. While they waited for Luka to round the vehicle, he buttoned his suit coat, and Tessa stood quietly beside him, going through song lyrics in her head.

Theon had hardly spoken to her the last two days. She ran with Axel, not Theon. Axel handed her over to Luka, who proceeded to make her learn "how to fall correctly" by knocking her on her ass for an hour before he would work with her on different blocking techniques. Luka enjoyed it far too much, and while her Fae body healed her eventually, she still sat with sore muscles for hours in meetings with Theon in the afternoons. He'd say the same thing to her then that he was leaning down to speak into her ear now:

"Watch. Listen. Learn everything you can about the people in this room."

So he could use her to take over Devram. Whether his father took it over or the people of the Underground, the end result would still be the same. Theon would either be heir to the realm, or he would rule those he let take over the realm.

Either way, she could do nothing to stop any of this from happening. As soon as the Source Marks were in place, he'd take whatever he wanted from her whenever he wanted. He already had this godsdamn Tracking Mark, allowing even more people to find her whenever they wished. More than that, she was pretty sure he'd found a way to control the Source Bond. She couldn't feel his presence like she could before.

He'd come to their room at night, and suddenly she'd feel the full weight of the thing after not feeling so much as a tug from the bond all day. She'd soak it up, her soul needing to know he was still there. Like he knew she needed that daily reminder.

And she didn't know what to make of it all.

Surely the Tracking Mark couldn't have been her only consequence for that night by the river. But he'd said nothing. Done nothing. And her nerves were so frayed, every little thing was making her jumpy. Luka was frustrated with her during training, not only because she was a novice, but because she couldn't stay focused. Axel disappeared after their runs, not to be seen again until dinner. Anytime she asked either of them where Theon went in the morning, neither deigned to answer. She was told what she needed to know when she needed to know it.

So she sat and watched.

She sat and listened.

She sat and learned everything she could.

Like the fact that Theon gave more attention to the Anala and Falein heirs than he did the others. That he enjoyed making the Celeste heir nervous and seemed to make a sport of snubbing the Achaz and Serafina heirs. That he never took the same route through the Pantheon, as if he were trying to memorize the various hallways and passages.

She observed the other heirs. How the Achaz and Serafina heirs seemed to always be whispering to each other. How the Anala heir seemed annoyed by everyone, especially Theon's extra attention, and it made Tessa smile on the inside.

But more than any of that, she watched how the other heirs interacted with their Sources. Sasha was much like Eviana. Quiet and submissive, always a step behind Dagian. Even during the meetings, she sat in the chair closest to the Legacy. The male Sources seemed to dote on their heirs, and Tessa wondered if it was real. Was she truly that defective as a Source?

Her silver heels clicked on the marble steps, the skirt of her deep red gown parting at the slit up her thigh as they climbed the steps to the second floor of the lounge, where they were attending a social event. It was the first event where other Legacy would be present. She'd noticed more and more of them arriving throughout the day. Most appeared to be Legacy who served on the kingdoms' councils, advisors to the Lords and Ladies. Thankfully, none of the actual Lords and Ladies were arriving until the day of the Emerging Ceremony, which meant Valter wouldn't be here for another three days.

Theon walked ahead of her, side-by-side with Axel, both of them dressed in all black, and the lights glittering off their matching onyx rings. Luka walked with her. When they reached the top of the stairs, Theon didn't even look at her as he gestured her over to his side, sliding his arm around her waist.

He bent to speak directly into her ear, "There is no room for error, Tessa."

"I understand."

She could feel eyes on them, and she leaned into him a little more, trying to calm her sudden nerves.

"This is a night to learn how the heirs interact outside their pampered little circle," he went on, his tone hard as he focused on something across the room.

Not something.

Someone she realized as she followed his gaze.

Dagian Jove stood with two other Legacy she did not recognize, but Theon clearly did.

"Where is Sasha?" she asked, noting she wasn't within reach of her Master.

"Traditionally, Sources are given a little more freedom at events like this," Theon replied tightly. "Fae are allowed to congregate on the first level. The Legacy stay up here." He finally met her gaze as he added, "As do the Sources."

"Why are the Fae here?"

"It allows the Legacy to observe them if they wish, but most use this night as a last chance to let loose before the Selection events get fully underway."

"Oh," was all she said as she tried to push the thought of Dex and her friends being so close while she was stuck up here. She stared into emerald eyes that had scarcely glanced at her lately when she asked, "And where am I to be?"

The corner of his lips curled, a small dimple appearing. "You are to be where I can see you at all times."

"Am I to stay by your side?"

"As much as I would prefer that, it will appear that I do not trust you if I require that of you tonight. The other Sources will be given extended freedom to show their bonds are settled into place."

"Oh."

"Do not fail tonight, Tessa," he said in a low voice, winding a loose curl around his finger.

"I won't."

With that, Theon released her, the three males crossing the room to join some other Legacy. Tessa turned to find the other Sources all congregated together around a small table, and she sighed, making her way over. Sasha gave her a small smile, sliding over to make room for her. These Fae were used to being separated from the rest. They'd been segregated since they'd been marked to be Selected. They hadn't exactly welcomed Tessa, especially with her being an Arius Source, but Sasha was kind enough. It probably helped that they knew each other from the Celeste Estate.

Gatlan, the Anala heir's Source, looked her up and down before sliding a bowl of pretzels towards her, and Tessa nodded in thanks. The other Sources didn't acknowledge her, but she knew they were watching her as much as she was watching them.

"How are you?" Sasha asked, grabbing a pretzel from the bowl. She didn't eat it though. Just began breaking it into pieces.

"Tired," Tessa answered with a weak smile.

A snort of laughter sounded, and Tessa looked up to meet Jasper's gaze. "I bet you are," he sneered, bracing his hands behind his head and leaning his chair back on two legs.

"What is that supposed to mean?" Tessa asked, her head tilting as she watched him. His light brown hair was clean cut, and his brown eyes narrowed on her.

"I was on the same Estate you were, Tessa," he replied. "I know all about you and your activities."

"What sort of activities?" Maxson asked, a knowing smirk filling his face.

"She was always finding her way off the Estate to find other company," Jasper replied.

"I thought she was with that other Fae. What's his name? Felix?" Dade chimed in.

"Dex. How do you even know about him? He came after you were moved to Eridis in the Falein Kingdom," Tessa said through gritted teeth.

"I told him," Jasper offered.

"But I know all about you," Dade interjected. "The night you were

Selected, my Mistress made it a point to learn everything she could about you."

"I've lived a fascinating life," Tessa muttered, watching as Sasha reached for another pretzel, breaking it into tiny pieces just as she had with the first.

"Just preparing for the life you were destined to have until Arius Kingdom fucked it up," Jasper said with a cruel smirk.

"Shut up, Jasper," Gatlan cut in.

"No, it's fine," Tessa said, returning Jasper's cruel grin. "Jasper is just a little jealous."

"Jealous?" Jasper repeated incredulously, his nostrils flaring as his hands came down flat on the table. "Of *you?*"

Tessa shrugged, sitting back in her chair. "While you had to stay back like a good little boy, I got to go out and live a little."

Jasper was suddenly leaning towards her. "You think I'm jealous that you were constantly in Mother Cordelia's office being reprimanded? You think I'm jealous that you fucked your way through mortals like it was a sport?" he spat.

"I think you're jealous that the only pussy you'll ever know is Mahina's," Tessa returned calmly. "The gods know you weren't allowed to fuck anyone else."

"You little cunt," Jasper was snarling, and Maxson and Dade were both resting hands on his shoulders while Sasha looked around nervously.

"Do not make a scene," Sasha hissed, reaching for another pretzel.

Jasper shrugged the others off. Sitting stiffly in his chair, he adjusted his shirt cuffs as he said casually, "I forget how little you know, Tessa. How little you understand. The rest of us were made privy to kingdom secrets years ago. Entrusted with the secrets of our Mistresses long before we bore their Marks."

"Coddled and pampered," Tessa sneered. "I'm aware."

"We were being prepared for our roles just as you were."

"No one knows where any of us would have ended up if we weren't marked to be Selected," Gatlan said, sipping from his drink. He was the only Source at the table who had been allowed alcohol by his heir.

"None of *us* know because we were chosen so early, but Tessalyn?" Jasper snorted another derisive laugh. "It's no secret where she was going to go." He held her gaze when he added, "Serving the Sirana bloodline."

The confusion must have been evident on her face, because Maxson was suddenly leaning eagerly forward. "Oh, that's right. She has no idea what purpose they serve," he said, full of mock pity. "Is that what we're supposed to be jealous of? Your naivety? Hasn't your Master told you anything?"

"With those tits and that fuckable mouth?" Jasper said, his hands braced behind his head once more. "You'd have been a plaything for the Legacy. When you weren't with child, of course."

"Don't," Sasha said forcefully, snapping another pretzel in half.

"Once her element was known, she'd have been paired with every powerful Fae of that element hoping for powerful, desirable offspring," Maxson pushed on, popping a pretzel into his mouth. "You know they get rewarded for that, right?"

"Rewarded for what?" Tessa ground out, her hands clenched tightly in her lap. She tried to tell herself what Maxson was describing wasn't true, but she knew it was. The Legacy valued power above all else. It's why assessments were done. It's why Matches were made. Why wouldn't they force the Fae to do the same?

Maxson's face was pure amusement as he watched her, clearly enjoying this. "All the Sirana Legacy will be at the Emerging Ceremony to see which Fae emerge the most powerful. Those who created the five most powerful are rewarded. Coin. Status elevation. A powerful Match of their own." He shrugged as if this wasn't some disgusting practice. "You would have been sent to a Sirana Villa, fucked until you carried a child, and then done it over and over, especially if you're even semi-powerful. What element are you expected to emerge with anyway? Clearly not fire," he added, glancing at Gatlan. "Anala Kingdom has those Fae locked down tight."

Tessa went utterly still, suddenly realizing exactly what this was. An attempt to gain information about her. None of the other heirs had looked at her twice, and she was sure that the moment Theon had Selected her, her files became entirely confidential and made unavailable to anyone else. Mother Cordelia was smart enough not to share information without permission from the Arius Kingdom, so their only source of information on her would be the other Fae at the Celeste Estate. It was well-known she was impulsive and reckless. Jasper would have known that getting her worked up would make her more apt to say something without thinking.

And that one question made it clear what their Mistresses had asked of them tonight.

Tessa crossed her leg, the deep slit of her dress revealing her thigh. Every male eye dropped to it. Then she leaned forward, propping an elbow on the table and resting her chin in her hand. "Tell me, Maxson, what will be your punishment for failure tonight?"

The brief look of panic was fleeting in his steely eyes, but it was there, confirming everything.

"What the fuck are you talking about?" Maxson asked, sounding bored.

"What will your Mistress do to you for failing to gather her requested information?" Tessa repeated.

"You don't know what you're talking about."

"Should I say something false just so you have something to report back?" she went on. Then she grimaced. "Although, the punishment for providing wrong information will probably be worse, right?"

"Don't speak about her like that."

Tessa clicked her tongue in mock sympathy. "Unless you enjoy her punishments?"

"Shut. Up."

"No judgment if you do. Sometimes punishments make you feel alive, right? Like you're not simply going through the motions of survival."

Sasha was breaking more pretzels. Dade and Jasper were rigid. Gatlan was smirking into his drink.

Tessa got to her feet, leaning over the table towards Maxson. "My tests were inconclusive. We have no idea what I'll emerge with."

"You fucking liar. The assessments can't be inconclusive," Maxson spat, his face turning red with his anger.

Tessa shrugged, swiping Gatlan's drink from his hand and knocking back the last of it. The other Sources all went still. Dropping the glass to the table with a soft thud, she said, "If you prefer a harsher punishment for inaccurate information, you can tell Lealla I'm predicted to emerge with water and almost no power."

"Fuck you, and fuck your fucking kingdom," he seethed, shooting to his feet.

"Oh, Max, if only you were mortal. Then maybe you'd have a chance at that," Tessa simpered as she straightened and ran her hands down her dress, smoothing it out. "Then again, I still would never touch Serafina seconds."

She was walking away before she could hear Maxson's response, knowing he wouldn't dare cause a scene in front of all the Legacy here. Keeping her chin high, she glanced around the space, spotting Theon and Luka deep in conversation with some other Legacy. Axel was beside them, whispering into the ear of a female whose lips lifted into a grin.

Not knowing where else to go, she made her way to the railing overlooking the first floor. The other Fae were filtering in, laughing and happy. They had drinks in their hands, and they were waving each other down across the room. She scanned them all, searching for just a glimpse of Lange or Dex, but there were so many down there, it was impossible.

"Look at you, wild fury. All dressed up once again."

Tessa turned to find Tristyn Blackheart leaning back on his elbows against the railing, a drink dangling from his fingertips.

"What are you doing here?" she blurted out.

"Attending the social, apparently," he replied, gesturing out towards the Legacy.

"But you're...not mortal," she said in realization.

"I am not."

"But you said you were."

"I never actually said that."

"You never corrected me. It's the same difference," she said flatly, turning back to look over the lower level once more.

"It's not the same difference," Tristyn argued, bumping her with his elbow. "Controlling information is controlling power."

"You're a Legacy. You have enough power," she muttered before sighing. She couldn't talk to a Legacy like that. "I apologize."

"Don't," he said, taking a sip of his drink. When she didn't say anything else for several moments, he turned to look out over the lower level as well, holding his drink out to her. "It's not *agaveheart*, but it's a peace offering nonetheless."

"I can't drink tonight," she replied.

"Because of Theon."

It was a statement, and she felt herself flush at the realization he must have known all along who she was. But if that was true, he also knew who Theon was, and he hadn't backed down an inch from the Arius Heir.

"Yes, because of him," she answered tightly.

"And yet you were just drinking with your friends."

"That was… They're not my friends."

Accepting she wasn't going to take his drink, he brought it back to his lips and took another sip before he said. "That's too bad. You need to let a few people into your chaos."

"Let me guess. Someone like you?" she asked with a coy grin, glancing at him sidelong. He was too easy to talk to, too easy to fall into idle conversation with. She didn't need to be told how dangerous that was, but she couldn't figure out which bloodline he was from.

He huffed a laugh. "I have enough chaos of my own, fury."

"I have friends," she said defensively. "Or I did… I do."

She could feel Tristyn studying her before he jerked his chin at the Fae below. "Down there?"

"Maybe? I haven't seen them yet."

"They were with you at your Estate?" he asked, subtly offering her his half-empty drink again.

She took it without thinking. "Yes. Not right away. Only in the last few years, actually."

"Interesting," he mused. "And they're not here?"

"Wouldn't matter if they were. I can't go down there."

"You only break the rules when *agaveheart* is involved?" he asked, his lips twitching when her head whipped towards him.

"I only break the rules when it's conducive to my own agenda," she retorted. Then she added with a small smirk of her own, "And when *agaveheart* is involved."

He huffed a laugh as she took a swallow of his drink before handing it back to him.

"We should go dance," he said, scanning the Fae below once more.

"I just told you I can't go down there."

"There's a dance floor up here."

"I know, but—"

She didn't want to tell him that Theon wouldn't be able to see her on the dance floor in the back corner.

"I'm not as appealing when I'm not a mortal?" he teased, and she felt her cheeks flare bright again.

"That was— I was very drunk that night. I apologize if I offended you."

"Offended? Fury, I was flattered," he said with a wink. Then he pushed off the railing, slowly backing away from her. "If you change your mind, I'll be waiting for you."

She watched him disappear into the Legacy milling about before turning back to look out at the Fae below yet again, wishing she was down there instead of up here. Wishing she could go have some fun with Tristyn. Wishing she could be anywhere else.

Instead, she had to stay here and watch the people in this room. Listen in on conversations. Learn everything she could. The only person she wanted to learn more about was Tristyn.

She straightened at the thought.

She *should* learn more about Tristyn. Who was he? He had made not only her believe he was mortal, but Theon, Axel, and Luka had thought he was mortal too. What Legacy power could do that? And what did he do that made him not fear Theon, or any of the other heirs, for that matter? Wasn't this exactly what Theon wanted her to do? Learn secrets to be used later?

She didn't give herself time to second guess her decision. Following the same path she'd seen Tristyn take, she made her way to the edge of the dance floor. He said he'd be waiting, and a moment later, he appeared before her with a grin.

"Is this conducive to your agenda?" he asked, extending a hand to her.

"Perhaps," she agreed, letting him pull her onto the dance floor just as a well-known ballad began to play. "I don't know how to dance to this."

"I'll guide you," Tristyn said. "Do you know the words to this song?"

"There are no words to this song," she said with a laugh. "It's simply a ballad for dancing."

"See, that's where you're wrong."

"Are you going to serenade me?"

"I am an excellent singer."

"Prove it."

Tristyn twirled her under his arm as he cleared his throat dramatically before pulling her back into him and bringing his lips to her ear. "In all things there must be balance. Beginnings and endings. Light and dark. Fire and shadows. The sky, the sea, the realms."

"That's not a song," she interjected. "That's the Revelation Decree."

"It is many things," he countered.

"I don't know what that means," she said with a laugh as he spun her under his arm again.

"Shh," he hushed. "Just listen. It goes with the ballad perfectly." She nodded in acquiescence, and then Tristyn was speaking low into her ear again. He wasn't exactly singing, but the tone of his voice was smooth and her entire body relaxed into him.

> *"In all things there must be balance.*
> *Beginnings and Endings.*
> *Light and Dark.*
> *Fire and Shadows.*
> *The sky, the sea, the realms.*
> *But when the scales tip,*
> *And Chaos rains,*
> *Who will fight?*
> *And who will fall?*
> *For Dark must bow,*
> *And Light must rule,*
> *But Chaos does not choose.*
> *Control the uncontrollable,*
> *Or to fury they both lose.*
> *Life must give,*
> *And Death must take,*
> *But Fate requires more.*
> *Destiny beckons,*
> *And sacrifice demands.*
> *Who will be left standing,*
> *When Chaos comes to reign?"*

By the end, she was hypnotized, a little lost to his voice and his russet-colored eyes. Tristyn held her gaze as he dipped her back, the final words lining up perfectly with the final stanza of the ballad, just like he'd said they would.

"How do you know the Decree is many things?" Tessa asked, letting Tris lead her into another dance, completely oblivious to the Legacy dancing around them.

"I know the one who gave the Decree."

Her brow furrowed. "The Decree came from the gods."

"Did it?"

"You're confusing."

"I know. It's incredibly frustrating."

Another bark of laughter escaped her. "How is it frustrating for you?"

"Because I do not always wish to be confusing," he replied.

"Only some of the time?"

"Exactly."

Silence fell for a minute before she said, "Can I ask you something?"

"I won't stop you."

"You're not mortal."

"That's not a question," Tristyn teased.

"How did you make me think you were? Make *them* believe you were?"

"People see what they want to see, fury."

"But you weren't fearful of the Arius Heir."

His features seemed to darken some. "There are far scarier things in the realms than a Legacy so far removed from Arius it is laughable to call him such a thing. He is no more related to Arius than I am at this point."

"But he is powerful," Tessa stammered, a little dumbfounded at his nonchalance.

"There are far more powerful beings in the realms."

"You speak as if the rest of the realms care about us."

"You speak as if they don't."

"They can't," she argued.

"They *shouldn't*," he countered.

Tessa clicked her tongue. "This conversation is getting stupid."

Tristyn laughed, his fingers giving her hand a quick squeeze. How long had they been dancing?

"Can I ask *you* a question?" he asked.

She sighed with mock dramatics. "I suppose."

"How are you?"

She was so taken aback, she missed her next step, Tristyn keeping her on her feet. "What?"

"The last time I saw you, you were not doing well."

"I was fine."

"You were not fine," he said pointedly. "You made an elaborate plan to secure *agaveheart* and drown in the bottle."

"I didn't—" She rolled her lips together, suddenly remembering they weren't alone on the dance floor. She plastered on a fake smile. "I'm great."

He gave her a frank look. "You're a terrible liar."

"I'm an excellent liar."

"Mhmm," he hummed. "Are you with him yet?"

"What?" she stammered at the sudden change of subject.

"Theon. Are you with him yet?"

"That's not your business."

"Debatable."

"Debatable?" she repeated. "Nothing about that is debatable. It's none of your business."

"So that's a no," he said.

"I didn't say that."

"You don't have to," Tristyn said with a slight shrug. "But that aside, I want you to know you are strong enough for this, Tessa."

She couldn't speak around the sudden lump in her throat as she swallowed back the tears threatening to well. "You still don't know me," she whispered.

"If you knew—" A frustrated sound rumbled from him when he cut himself off.

"If I knew what?" she pressed.

"If you only knew what I knew," he said, something Tessa could only describe as a mixture of longing and pain sounding in his voice. "It's something you can't learn until you're forced to walk through it, but you'd know that strength grows in the moments you think you can't go on, but you do anyway. Strength is fighting back. Strength is doing whatever it takes to claim what is yours, even if others try to convince you it is not yours to take."

"What if I'm not? What if I'm not strong enough for any of that?"

"You are, Tessa. If you are weak enough to fall, you are strong enough to rise back up. Weakness and strength come from the same place, and both are necessary. Both provide purpose, and both can lead to destruction or salvation. You just need to embrace a little chaos," Tristyn said, a fierceness filling his features. "And when you come out on the other side of this, the Heir of the Arius Kingdom won't be the nightmare. You will be."

36
THEON

"Gods, you're pissy," Axel mused.

Theon could feel his gaze on him, and he resisted the urge to flip him off. Tonight was about appearances and making connections. He'd been drawing lines among the other heirs for two days, and now it was time to move beyond them. Alliances needed to be formed within the other kingdoms, not just with the ruling families. None of the plans would work if there weren't established relations on the inside, but more than any of that, they needed to make it known that Arius Kingdom would no longer be pacified staying in their corner of the realm.

When Theon remained silent, Axel continued, "I know things aren't ideal with Tessa right now, but for the love of Arius, go find someone to fuck, Theon," Axel added, taking another drink.

"I don't want to find someone to fuck," Theon bit out.

"You need a good fuck," Axel said pointedly. "Let off some steam. Clear your head so you stop biting off everyone else's. You're not making any relations being a constant dick."

That was easy for him to say. He'd been chatting with the same dark-haired female all night and didn't have a godsdamn bond interfering. Theon had tried to be somewhat pleasant tonight, but Axel was right. He was pissy, and it had everything to do with the Fae he wanted to fuck.

Because he certainly could force her. He was willing to cross a lot of lines. Fuck, he had done a lot of unforgivable things. Killed people. Set others to take the fall for his actions. Fucked people over to gain information. None of it kept him up at night. Necessary actions to get what he wanted.

But this? He couldn't do it. Because for some fucked up reason, he thought this was the one thing keeping him from turning into his father completely.

"A good fuck would get you out of your head for a while," Axel mused knowingly, the teasing gone from his tone. If anyone would understand being in your own head, it was his brother.

"You think I don't want to?" Theon retorted, signaling to a passing Fae for another drink. "This fucking bond won't let me *want* anyone else right now. The gods know I've fucking tried."

Axel arched a brow. "Are you serious?"

"Yes," Theon grumbled. "Meanwhile, Tessa can tell me all about how she would rather fuck a mortal or her own godsdamn hand instead of me, and I'm left jacking myself in the shower."

Axel huffed a laugh but quickly covered it with a cough at the glare Theon threw at him. "But you said the other night—"

"The other night was about keeping her from going over an edge," Theon said, taking the drink off the tray the Fae was holding out to him. "She was spiraling. From the things I have managed to learn about her, I could piece together that it was probably similar to what happened after an assessment."

"When she would go off the estate to find mortals," Axel said in realization.

Theon nodded. He hadn't told them much of that night, only that she'd finally let him help her. But he'd wanted to keep that night for himself because it might be the only thing she ever let him have, and if it was, he didn't want to share it with anyone.

He'd spent as little time as possible with her the last two days, mainly because he knew he wouldn't be able to control himself around her. After he'd made sure she was all right, he'd left Axel with her while she'd showered. He'd met up with Luka to make sure the Night Children were taken care of. Luka had already found the other two, and they'd spent the rest of the night cleaning up the mess of it all and trying to figure out who had sent them after Tessa.

It could be anyone, really. A Lord or Lady. One of the fuckers in this room looking to move up in social status. It could simply be someone with a vendetta against Arius Kingdom. The gods knew there were plenty of people with those.

But he'd been drained. Between using his magic to find her, defend her, and then basically fuck her, he hadn't experienced power levels that low in a long time, and he'd been four days away from his allotted ration of Fae blood. Luka had all but forced him into taking blood from Tessa because he was starting to draw power from him. That's how the Guardian Bond worked. When Theon ran out of his own magic, he began drawing from Luka. It wasn't ideal to have either of them low on power for any amount of time, even if Axel was here with them. Luka had given him until mid-day to take blood from Tessa, or he was going to do it himself.

But gods, Tessa's blood? That was the most divine Fae blood he'd ever tasted. He'd never noticed a difference in the blood he was given weekly. Fae blood was Fae blood, but not this time. This had made his entire being feel chaotic and out of control. It had to be because of their Source Bond. Or maybe it was because she was going to be so powerful once her gifts emerged? A combination of the two? He didn't know, but it had taken every bit of his self-control not to take more.

Just like it'd taken every bit of his self-control not to follow her into the shower to take more when he'd made her come with his shadows.

Axel cleared his throat. "Did you learn any more about her time at the estate?"

"No," Theon answered shortly.

That was a lie. After her refusal to explain her history with her Estate Mother, Theon had gone to speak with Cordelia himself. He just hadn't decided what he wanted to do with the information yet, mostly because he was too close to losing control right now. Too many things were spiraling, leaving him riding a dangerous edge. Anger at Tessa for leaving the Acropolis. Anger at those godsdamn Night Children for trying to take her. Anger at whoever had sent them after her. Anger at the Estate Mother for hurting her. Anger that he was in this situation to begin with.

But mostly he was furious with himself.

For failing to keep her safe yet again.

For failing to figure out who wanted her.

For failing to control his Source.

For failing at all.

He failed at something he didn't know a person could fail at. That had to be the epitome of failure. To fail at something that was impossible to fail at.

So he'd let Axel and Luka deal with her the last few days because it was the only way to protect her from himself.

He'd tried to stop himself from watching her all night. They'd agreed Luka would be the one to handle her at this social, but he found himself looking for her yet again. The last time he'd seen her, she'd been sitting with the other Sources. He wasn't blind. They clearly hadn't accepted her as one of them, likely because of whose Source she was. She didn't fit in with them. She couldn't fit in with the other Fae. She only had him, Luka, and Axel, and she couldn't even be with them tonight. Not that she'd want to be. She was still pissed at all of them.

No, pissed wasn't the right word.

She had become...apathetic. As though she suddenly didn't care about anything, resigned to simply accept whatever was required of her and being done to her. He started at the sudden realization. She'd been different since the night in the rain on the balcony when she'd told him he'd already won. He'd told himself it was her slowly giving into the bond. That he hadn't completely failed. That it was because she hadn't been adequately prepared for her role. Any excuse to justify why this had gone so horribly fucking wrong.

But this was worse. Her not caring was worse than her hating this, and how the fuck did that work?

And where the fuck was she?

"I have some things to tell you."

Theon looked over to find Luka sliding into the chair next to him.

"It better be where Tessa is," Theon snapped.

He saw the look exchanged between Axel and Luka and downed the rest of his drink when Axel said, "This isn't fucking working. Something has to change."

Luka raked a hand through his hair, and it made Theon pause. He was agitated, and Luka rarely showed any emotion. Theon braced himself when he said, "What do you need to tell me?"

"I already told him he needs to find a good fuck," Axel offered.

"Fuck off, Axel," Theon said, dropping his now empty glass on the low table before him. "Spit it out, Luka."

"Axel has a point, and the first thing I have to tell you could help with that. Felicity Davers is here," Luka said.

"How does that help with anything?"

Luka shrugged. "You could find out if you're compatible."

"By fucking her?" Theon replied flatly.

"How else do you plan on producing an heir?" Luka asked, and Theon saw the slight twitch of his lips.

This fucker was teasing him.

"You can both fuck off. Where is Tessa?"

The small bit of mirth on his face instantly vanished, and Luka pushed out a harsh breath, raking his hand through his hair again. "Before I tell you that, I need to tell you something else. And before I tell you *that,* I need you to remember we are in public with dozens of Legacy who will take any chance they can to observe weakness."

"This sounds ominous," Axel muttered, setting his drink aside and leaning forward, bracing his elbows on his knees.

"What is it, Luka?"

"Tristyn is here."

"Who the fuck is Tristyn?" Axel asked.

But Theon knew *exactly* who the fuck Tristyn was.

"The mortal is here?" Theon demanded.

"Oh, fuck," Axel hissed under his breath, and Theon felt it then. Both of their powers subtly pressing against him. Axel's shadows were a mist that was unnoticeable, and Luka's was a low black flame that blended in with the low lighting of the lounge. Both of them prepared to combat his power if he lost control.

"There's more," Luka said.

"Where is Tessa?" Theon gritted out, his darkness pressing at his being and shadows clouding his vision.

"Tristyn is not a mortal."

"What?" Theon hissed. "How in the realms do you figure that?"

"For starters, he's here. On this level. At an event for *Legacy.*"

"Don't be a smart ass. If he's a Legacy, why did we all assume he was mortal when we ran into him in Rockmoor?"

"I don't know. Perhaps Tessa will have some insight. She's been dancing with him for the last ten minutes," Luka answered.

Theon was already on his feet, striding straight for the dance floor across the room. "Why are you just telling me this now?"

"Because she seems to have some sort of connection with him. Maybe she'll get us information—"

"I don't want her to get anything from him," Theon snarled, already spotting her golden hair where Tristyn was indeed twirling her around the dance floor to some fast-paced number. Her eyes were bright as she tipped her head back in laughter, and the pair had gathered quite a crowd.

Luka and Axel were both gripping his arms, tugging him to a stop.

"We need to decide how to handle this," Axel murmured.

"I will handle it by making him choke on darkness before hauling him to the Underground for tampering with a Source," Theon said darkly.

"*Or* we think about this rationally. Which bloodline is he from? Which kingdom is he loyal to? Can we sway him?" Axel countered.

Godsdamnit. Theon knew he was right, but all he could see was the male's hands on what was his. All he could hear was her laughing with a male that wasn't him. All he could feel was the failure weighing down on him.

"If we charge in there and use our power, not only will everyone assume you do not have control of your Source, but the extent of our powers will be revealed," Luka murmured in a low voice. "Your father will not be pleased."

"And you think he is going to be pleased by this?" Theon demanded, his hands clenching into fists in his pockets.

"I am saying we need to be smart about this."

"They know we can control shadows," Axel muttered, and Theon could hear the calculation in his tone. "So we play both parts. We let them see the power they know we have while also looking like we let this happen. Make it appear we already have an alliance in place."

"What if he doesn't go along with it?" Luka asked.

"He will," Theon said, his fury lifting just enough to think semi-rationally. "He has an interest in Tessa. We need to figure out what that interest is."

"Do you think he knows about...well, her?" Axel mused, watching as Tristyn spun her around.

"He knows something," Theon said, squaring his shoulders. "But his time with her is up."

He strode forward, shadows trailing behind him with every step. He sent some of his darkness to Tessa, letting it wind around her like ivy, claiming her as much as reminding her who she belonged to. She stiffened for the briefest of moments before she relaxed into Tristyn once more, her movements becoming more fluid, if such a thing were possible. It was all he needed to see to know she was going to put on this little show with them.

The song finished at the same moment they reached the edge of the dance floor but no one dared move. The other Legacy, including the other heirs, were looking on with interest. Dagian was sipping a drink, his eyes fixed on Tessa in a way Theon did not like, while Lealla was watching Theon with a smirk. Tana's Source was at her side, murmuring in her ear, and Mahina and Prudence were across the dance floor, their eyes glowing softly as if preparing to defend themselves.

"Theon St. Orcas," Tristyn said, stepping toward him.

No hesitation. No hint of trepidation. Just the same arrogance the male had displayed in Rockmoor. At least now Theon understood why to some extent.

"Tristyn," Theon replied, and he really wished he knew the male's surname. It would give him a clue to his bloodline and what he was doing here. Judging by the small smirk on the male's lips, he knew this. "Thank you for keeping Tessa company this evening."

"Always a pleasure. Although I will say I preferred our time in Rock-moor over this," he said with a wink at Tessa.

She looked at him with a coy smile. "I was thinking the same thing. There's just something about hotel ambiance."

"And that elevator music," Tristyn added wistfully to which Tessa let out a genuine laugh.

Theon cleared his throat, his shadows thickening and beginning to creep along the dance floor. There were sharp intakes of breath and people taking a step back as Luka and Axel stepped to his side.

"It's time to go, Tessa," he said.

"Of course," she replied, the picture perfect Source as she turned and bowed her head to Tristyn. "Thank you for the evening."

Tristyn, however, reached over and tipped her chin up. "We're far past this nonsense," he said, his voice so low Theon could hardly hear the words spoken. "Destruction or salvation, wild fury. Your choice."

With those parting words, Tristyn nodded at Theon before he turned and walked off the dance floor, the crowd parting around him. Theon could feel every eye on them, waiting to see what happened next, but before Theon could decide what to do, Tessa moved.

She sauntered over to him, reaching up to straighten his tie. Then she let her fingertips drag down his torso until they rested against his stomach. She looked up at him from beneath her lashes, biting her lower lip. With a dark smile, he thumbed her lip from her teeth and leaned down to speak low into her ear, "Failure was not an option, Tessa."

"I've failed at nothing," she returned, a cruel smile of her own forming as she pushed up onto her toes and slid her hand back up his chest and around to his nape, digging her nails in. Her lips trailed along his jaw as she continued, "Does everyone not see a bond different from their own? Is that not what you demanded of me, Master? Do you see another Source speaking to anyone else? Do you see another heir so *trusting* of their Source that they let them dance and converse with another Legacy?"

The recent apathy seemed to have dissipated, replaced by something new. Something he'd glimpsed in that training room when she had seen her power manifest and hold. When she'd gained an idea of just how powerful she was going to be.

He slipped an arm around her waist while his other hand slipped into her hair, his fingers tangling in the golden strands. He tugged, pulling her head back to look into her eyes. There was no glowing violet ring, but that familiar storm was there, just beneath the surface.

"I suppose we should dance then," he returned, glancing up and signaling whoever was in charge of music to play something.

"What?" she stammered, her eyes widening in surprise.

"I can't have you dancing with other Legacy and not me. We're putting on a show, aren't we?"

"A bond that is superior in every way," she replied, her breath catching when he dragged his fingertips down her spine before taking her hand in his and pulling her flush against his front.

He let himself focus on the feel of her beneath his hand. Let himself feel the way she moved against him as he led her around the dance floor. He didn't even register which dance they were doing. They were all muscle memory, ingrained in him from a young age, but he felt each of her sharp inhales, despite her best attempts to hide them.

He didn't pay attention to the shocked looks from the Celeste and Falein heirs. He didn't notice the scowls from Dagian or Lealla or the narrowed gaze of Tana. Theon let the rest of the room watch on as he took this moment with Tessa, even if it was an act. He'd pretend it wasn't. For the duration of the song, he'd pretend he wasn't what he was in the same way she pretended to be what he demanded of her.

He'd steal this moment, wishing the song would never end, because when they got home, everything would change.

37
THEON

He waited until they were upstairs in their room.

They'd left the social an hour later. Axel had stayed behind, back to whispering in the ear of the dark-haired female. Luka had driven them home, but he hadn't even come into the house. He was already stripping off his jacket, tie, and shirt, clearly planning on flying under the cover of night.

Which left Theon completely alone with Tessa.

Her display of newfound fierceness had instantly vanished as she'd slid across the seat, giving him her back and staring out the window for the short drive home. She hadn't said a word, and she wasn't saying anything now as she strode straight into the dressing room.

Theon followed her, finding her struggling to reach the zipper on the back of her dress. He brushed her hands out of the way, and she immediately tensed. Leaning in close, his lips brushed her ear when he asked, "Ready to tell me what the fuck you were doing with him?"

He let his fingers graze her skin as he slowly slid the zipper down.

"You saw us. We were dancing," she answered, her tone clipped as she held the front of her dress against her chest.

"For the sake of clarity, you allowed another to touch you without my permission. Was I not clear what would happen if that occurred?"

"And yet Tristyn still breathes," she retorted.

"For now," he agreed, his hand falling to his side when she spun to face him.

"You can't just kill him, Theon."

"The events at Wynfell River suggest I could do just that."

"He's not just some vampyre. He's a Legacy, same as you."

Theon reached out, fingering a lock of her hair. "Oh, little storm. Do you think I have not shed the blood of a Legacy? For things far less than touching what is mine?"

"I am not yours," she gritted out, moving to shove past him, but he gripped her arm, spinning her once more and moving her against the wall. He moved with her, his chest to her back as she gasped.

"What were you doing with him, Tessa? In front of dozens of Legacy looking for weaknesses?" he demanded.

"I was doing exactly what you asked of me," she bit back. One hand was braced on the wall, keeping her face from pressing into it. Her other hand was still clutching her dress to her front.

"How do you figure that?"

"Watch. Listen. Learn everything you can about the people in this room," she spat. "So I was learning everything I could about Tristyn."

That godsdamn smart mouth. That's all Theon could think, and he couldn't decide if he was furious with her or proud of her for finding a workaround. It was that kind of cunning he needed from her, but not to be used against him.

"Do you have any idea what that looked like to the other Legacy?" he asked, his voice far too calm. He could tell she felt it too, her body going even more rigid.

"I swear, Theon. I was only trying to find out information for you."

He hummed at her non-answer. "And what did you learn for me?" While he spoke, he brought a hand to her shoulder, slipping the strap down and running his fingers along her flesh.

"I...I found it odd none of us realized he was a Legacy in Rockmoor. I was trying to figure out how that was possible," she answered, her voice breathy as he did the same thing to the other strap.

"And what did you learn?" he repeated.

"I—" Then with a burst of strength he wasn't expecting, she twisted in his hold, spinning to face him. "Stop," she snarled. "I can't think when you're doing that."

"Maybe you can understand a fraction of what it was like to learn you were with him then," Theon retorted, bracing his hands on the wall beside her head, caging her in. "The fury that made it impossible to focus on anything else."

She smirked. "Oh, I understand helpless fury just fine, Theon."

"Do you, little storm? Because lately it's just been indifference." Her lips pursed, her gaze darting to the side, and he gripped her chin, forcing it back to him. "Luka and Axel said the latest arrangements haven't been working, and I'm inclined to agree."

"That's on you," she sneered. "I don't get a say in the *arrangements*. I'm told where to go and when, what to say and how to say it."

"And yet you continuously do the opposite. You know what I think, Tessa?"

"I don't care what you think."

He released her chin, letting his fingers drag down her throat before he traced them along the neckline of the dress she was still clutching to her chest. "I think you enjoy toeing the line. It makes you feel alive."

"You know nothing about me, Theon. *Nothing*."

"I know you hate socks." She clicked her tongue, turning away from him again, but he kept going. "I know you love food that is terrible for you. I know heels hurt your feet."

"Heels hurt everyone's feet. Anyone who tells you otherwise is a liar," she grumbled.

"I know you'd rather be on a Chaosphere field than stuck inside. You prefer mornings over nights. You've discovered a love of music. You hate running, but love it at the same time. You're impulsive and reckless, and your *friends* use that against you, but pretend they are doing you favors."

Her eyes snapped back to his. "They do not do that."

"No, perhaps not all of them. I'll give you that," he conceded. "But I know more than that."

"I can't wait to hear it," she said with derision.

He leaned in close, bringing his face a mere inch from hers. "You didn't want to be Selected as a Source, but a part of you is glad you were because it means you're not as worthless as you've clearly been told you are. That someone just might see some value in you, even if you can't see it yourself. It's a little bit of hope you're too afraid to cling to, so you let yourself sink instead. But that's not what scares you the most. No, the thing that scares you most is that you *want* this life. You *want* to be more than forgotten. You *want* to be more than just another Fae assigned to some menial task in the kingdoms. I know you're simply too afraid to admit you want it, let alone claim it. How did I do, little storm? How close am I? How well do I *not know* you?"

She was staring at him, and even with everything he did know about her, he still couldn't read any of the emotions swimming in her eyes. He'd known this would go one of two ways. She'd either shut down or she'd fight, and gods, he hoped she was going to fucking fight with him because she needed to let out all that rage before it consumed her. A person could only push that down so far before it boiled over.

Or in Tessa's case, before he found himself being blasted across a fucking parking lot.

Her chest was heaving, and he waited, watching her every move. He'd moved back a fraction, just enough to give her a little space to breathe, but not enough to go anywhere.

Her lips suddenly curved, the smile so dark and wicked he didn't think she was capable of such a thing. "You think I *want* this life?" she asked, and the chill of her tone sent the same through him. "Oh, Theon. Why in the realms would I *want* to be bonded to you for the rest of my years?"

A bark of incredulous laughter fell from her lips, and Theon almost smiled at the viciousness of it.

"You, Theon St. Orcas, are *exactly* the reason I didn't want to be Selected. Who in their right mind wants to be chained to someone who craves control because he doesn't have any?" He unwittingly took a step back from her, and that maniacal smile only grew, violet rings sparking in her eyes. "You think I haven't noticed? You think I haven't *watched? Listened? Learned everything I can* about the people I am forced to spend every wretched minute with? Axel deflects anything and everything, pacifying someone just enough until he can figure out how to get what he wants. Luka acts broody and apathetic, but in reality? He's searching for himself and how he fits into all of this fuckery. And you?" A pointed finger landed on his chest, a nail digging into the fabric of his shirt. "You think you have control because your father gives you the illusion that you do. You force everyone to bend to your will because you are forever forced to bend to his. You demand perfection. Tell me failure is not an option, but you are the biggest failure of all, aren't you? Because you are exactly like your father, despite every effort not to be."

His hand was around her throat before she could blink—before *he* could blink—shoving her back against the wall once more.

She didn't even flinch.

Instead, she continued to smirk at him, her eyes glowing brightly as she said, "How did I do, *Master*? How close am I? How well do I not know you?"

"Tell me why I shouldn't hunt down Tristyn right now and make him pay for touching what is mine? To show just how *in control* I am, Tessalyn."

"You call this control? Your hand is on my throat," she tossed back.

And a dark smirk curved on his own lips as he answered, "If I wasn't in control, Tessa, I'd be squeezing. You know that's why I've left you to Luka and Axel the last few days, right? So I could make sure I was in control when I'm around you."

She scoffed. "And you think you're in control when you constantly need keepers to keep you in check?"

"I don't need keepers," he snapped, his fingers flexing the barest amount.

"You have no control, Theon," she repeated. "They call me reckless and impulsive, but I can take control from you with one hand."

"Is that so?" he countered.

"Yes."

"Then do it."

And she did.

With one hand, just like she said.

She released the dress she was still managing to clutch to her chest. The fabric slid down her body like water, pooling at her feet so she was left standing before him in barely there underthings and six-inch heels.

"Tessa." Her name was a growl as his fingers flexed around her throat again.

"Tell me again about that control, Theon," she taunted with malice. "You can't even control me, the one person in the entire realm you're supposed to have complete dominion over."

Everything in him was reaching for her— his magic, the bond, his entire being in a need to... He didn't even know anymore. Claim her? Show her who was in control? Give her control?

His breathing was ragged as he drank in all the skin bared to him. Golden hair spilled over her shoulders, concealing her breasts, and without conscious thought, he was brushing it back.

He felt her tremble beneath his hand, could feel her pulse beneath his fingers still wrapped around her throat. He regained the space he'd put between them, his front brushing against her bare torso.

"You're regretting that impulsiveness right now, aren't you?" he whispered, the same derision she held dripping in his tone. Not at her, but because of just how right she was.

"My life is one big regret. Why would this be any different?" she tried to retort, but it was breathy without the bite.

They stared at each other. This stand off of wills that seemed as though it was never going to end.

Until it did.

He didn't know who moved first. Maybe it was her pushing against his hold on her throat. Maybe it was him sliding his palm around her neck to drag her into him. But her soft lips were on his, and his tongue was in her mouth. There was no explanation for why she was wrapping her legs around his waist, her heels slipping from her feet, or why he was pressing her into the wall, his hips thrusting into her.

He was suddenly furious at the fact that he was still fully dressed while he had her like this. He wrenched away, his shadows twining around her wrists and bringing them above her head, holding her in place.

"Do not move," he said, yanking at his tie while simultaneously trying to shuck off his suit jacket.

"Theon, I—"

But her words dissolved into a low moan as he let his shadows play, rolling over her peaked nipples, down her torso, her thighs, but never where she wanted them.

No, he'd told her she'd beg for that, and after everything she'd just said to him, she'd be doing exactly that.

He took a deep breath, getting himself back under the control she'd fleetingly stolen. He forced himself to undo each button of his shirt rather than just rip the fucking thing off. His darkness was still keeping her where he wanted her, thighs rubbing together, hands above her head. For once—for fucking *once*—they had nowhere to be when she was letting him touch her.

He kicked his shoes off as his shirt slid to the floor before he lost his belt and undid his pants. They were still hanging off his hips when he stepped forward, unable to wait any longer. He could feel her trembling beneath his power, but he needed to feel her beneath his fingers.

Tell me again about that control, Theon.

Her taunt echoed in his mind, and he choked down the growl that crawled up his throat.

He was in control.

Of this.

Of her.

Of himself.

He pulled his darkness back, all of it but the shadows keeping her wrists secured above her head. Heated eyes watched his every move, and he smirked at her unwittingly following his demand from the other night. She knew what she wanted and remembered how to get it.

But he wasn't going to make it that easy. Not this time.

He brought the tip of his finger to the hollow of her throat, and she sucked in a sharp breath.

"Theon."

"Shh, Tessa. Unless you are going to tell me to stop, not a word." She swallowed, and he felt it beneath his fingertip. The motion had his hand back around her throat. "Do that again."

"What?"

"Do that again. Swallow."

"Why?"

He leaned into her, feeling the gasp as his bare chest pressed to hers. "Because I want to imagine what it's going to feel like when my cock is in your mouth, little storm." Whether or not on purpose, he felt her swallow, and he groaned, pulling back. She was squirming against the wall, tugging at the shadows keeping her arms suspended, and a knowing smirk tugged at the corners of his mouth.

Releasing her throat, he let his fingertips drag down her chest between the valley of her breasts. Let his thumb scrape along the underside of smooth flesh. Her thighs were clenching, and he kicked her feet apart, not allowing her any relief as he slid his fingertips to her other breast, circling around the peaked nipple.

She whimpered when his touch left her breast, moving back to her torso and continuing their path down her stomach, the curve of her hip, around her thigh where he began brushing them back and forth lightly along her soft skin.

"Tell me again about my lack of control, Tessa," he murmured, his eyes fixed on his fingers as they slid up her inner thigh. Watched as she bucked her hips forward, chasing his touch when he dragged them back down.

"This isn't control," she rasped. "It's nothing but another way to make me miserable."

"You don't appear too miserable right now," he replied, letting his little finger skate along her center just enough to make her whimper again. He leaned in, his lips feathering along her cheek when he whispered, "You're soaked, little storm."

"It's the bond," she gritted out. "Nothing else."

His fingers stilled, his teeth nipping at her jaw when he said, "Then there is no reason to continue this, is there?"

"W-what?" she stammered.

It took everything in him, but he took a step back from her. His gaze slid from her bound wrists to her heaving chest to her writhing hips as his darkness kept her feet where he wanted them.

"Nothing else happens until you admit this is more than a fucking bond."

"It's not."

Another sharp inhale when he shot forward, an arm braced above her head and his finger drawing light circles on her stomach. "So godsdamn stubborn," he mused.

"What happened to not lying to you? I'll be lying if I tell you this is something more than a physical need," she retorted. This time when her hips thrust forward, he pressed his own to hers. The resulting moan from her lips mixed with his own groan as his cock pressed against her.

"Then lie to me, Tessa. Lie to me, and tell me it's more," he rasped.

"You're asking me to lie to you now?"

"Yes," he said, the word desperate and heady as he ground against her again.

"It's more than a bond," she gasped.

"Tell me you're going to let me touch you."

"As if you'd let me stop you," she bit back, still fighting him, and why did that only make him harder?

"Maybe you're right, Tessa," he murmured, his lips working their way to her neck, his tongue tasting her as he moved. "Maybe I don't have any control, but in this? This is the one place I won't cross a line if you tell me to stop. So tell me. Tell me to stop if it's nothing more than the bond." But nothing but the sound of her ragged breaths reached him. "I'm waiting, little storm."

After what felt like an entire minute, she whispered, "Please don't, Theon. Please don't stop."

His lips at her throat went from a light caress to sucking kisses, and he released her wrists, needing to feel her hands on him. She didn't disappoint. Her nails dragged along his back before she was shoving at the pants still clinging to his hips.

"Don't do this if you're going to ask me to stop," he snarled, helping her remove the rest of his clothing.

"I already sacrificed my dignity and said please, Theon. May as well make it worth it," she sneered, her head tipping back when his lips returned to her throat.

"Will it always be like this, little storm? A constant battle with you?" he asked, pushing her undergarments down her legs.

"Yes," she rasped when his fingers found their way back to her thighs.

"Good," he replied, before he finally sank two fingers into her. There was nothing slow and tender about this, about them. There never had been. It had been a never-ending fight from the moment he'd snatched her chocolate in that alcove.

"Gods," she gasped.

Her shoulders curled inward as her brow fell to his shoulder and her legs buckled, but he already had a thigh wedged between her legs, keeping her upright. Theon knew then this would forever be his favorite way to see her— writhing and needy for him and him alone. And he needed more of it.

He pressed his thumb to her swollen clit, feeling her clench around his fingers as he pumped them in and out. Her breaths were nothing but sharp, staccato fricatives, her hips moving with every thrust of his fingers.

"Your eyes, Tessa. Give them to me," he demanded, and her head snapped up. Her grey eyes were glazed with want and desire, and fuck, he was nowhere near done with her.

"Ask me for it," he ordered.

"Please, Theon," she cried in frustration, her hips never ceasing their movement as they chased the pleasure from his fingers.

"Please what?" he pushed, pressing his thumb to her center again.

"Fuck!"

"Oh, we will, Tessa. Make no mistake about that," he replied, a hand coming to her hip and forcing her to still.

The whine that came from her had a dark chuckle rumbling from his chest.

"Theon, please."

"Please what?"

"Please let me come."

The begging.

It did more to him than he thought it would.

He slid his fingers in and out once. So torturously slowly that she cried out in anguish.

"Tell me you're mine, Tessa. Tell me that, and I'll make you come. Now. Later. Whenever you want."

"No," she ground out, attempting to move her hips again.

His hand stilled, his fingers deep in her soaking center.

"You'll *lie* to me about everything else but that?"

But she turned her head to the side, breaking his gaze, and that just wouldn't do. He'd never wanted an answer more in his life.

"Tell me why, Tessa," he said, cupping her cheek and bringing her face back to his.

"No."

"Tessa—"

"No," she interjected. "I'm not yours, but I'll use you the same way you'll use me."

"I'm not going to use you."

"Now who's the liar?" She was squirming against his hand again, trying her damnedest to rock her hips, and he lightly slid his thumb over her clit. "You can call me yours, but that won't make it true," she panted.

He pressed down more firmly, moving his thumb in a tight circle, and she cried out when he pulled back just as quickly. "Beautiful, you'll always be mine. Just because you refuse to accept it doesn't make it false."

"But you'll never be mine!"

Her head tipped back, her eyes falling closed, and he could tell by the look on her face she hadn't meant to say that. That it had slipped out of her because she was a mess of want and denial.

"Tessa—"

"Gods, Theon," she snapped, her eyes flying back open and flaring brightly with streaks of violet. "Either fuck me and give us what we both want or just let me go. Please."

He stared at her for a long moment, the echoes of her anguished words ringing in his ears, before he pulled his fingers from her. He saw the flash of disappointment before it morphed into acceptance. Then he was scooping her up and hauling her out of the dressing room.

"Theon—"

But she was cut off when he tossed her roughly onto the bed.

He'd been right. Everything had changed when they got home, but not in the way he'd been expecting.

Not as he looked down at her naked with her hair fanned across their bed and eyes wary but still a little glazed with unsated need.

He curled over her, bracing himself with one hand while the other gripped her chin. "The next time we do this, you will tell me you're mine, Tessa."

"There won't be a next time," she spat, her hips already rising and seeking him out.

He hissed as he felt her slick cunt slide along his length. "There will be, Tessa, but not until you believe this is more than a bond. Not until you fully understand that you are mine."

"Then there will never be a next time," she repeated.

"We'll see," was all he said, before he gripped her thighs and yanked her to the edge of the bed. He pulled them wide before finally sinking into her.

38
TESSA

Her breath stalled in her chest as Theon filled her without warning.

But gods, was it everything she had been needing for weeks.

The burn of being stretched. The feeling of being full. The pleasure that drowned out *everything*.

"Breathe, little storm."

The words were murmured into her ear and had her sucking in a sharp breath as he smoothed hair back from her brow. She hated she was swallowing down tears to keep them from pooling. She hated herself for finally giving him this. For being so godsdamn weak that she'd given in. For being so desperate to not feel after the events of the last two days. Mother Cordelia. The river and the vampyres. The constant guilt and embarrassment of Theon and his fucking shadows. The running. The training. The sitting through endless events with Theon. Being shunned by the other Sources before they tried to use her. The confusion and turmoil over what Tristyn had said to her.

Destruction or salvation. Your choice, wild fury.

This could destroy her or save her, and tonight, she'd let it save her. Tonight she'd take from Theon, and she wouldn't regret it when it was over.

"Are you all right?" he asked, some type of concern filling his emerald eyes as he straightened. He still stood at the end of the bed, towering over her, his cock deep in her aching center.

"I've fucked plenty before, Theon," she replied, rocking her hips in a testing movement.

He hissed, his brow pinching. "Stop moving, Tessa."

"Why? You said tonight I get what I want."

"I just need to make sure you're fine before—"

She bucked against him again with more force. "As I said, I've done this plenty."

"With mortals," he retorted, a hand gripping her hip to keep her still. "It's different with a Legacy."

She snorted a laugh. "Sorry to be the one to tell you this, but mortal and Legacy cocks are exactly the same. The blood of a god does not make your dick more special."

She was prepared for the darkness that crept across his irises at the mention of being the same as a mortal. She was not, however, prepared for the shadows that sprang to life around him, twining around her arms, caressing her breasts, her hips, her thighs. She wasn't prepared when Theon's touch followed his magic, and she wasn't prepared when something beneath her skin started pressing at her being, trying to claw its way out.

She was already arching off the bed, and he hadn't even godsdamned moved yet.

"It's different with a Legacy," he murmured again, his voice as sensual as his touch where he was toying with a nipple. Then his head tilted to the side as he studied her. "You feel it, don't you? You feel your power trying to get to mine."

"I— I don't know what it is," she rasped, pressing against his hold on her. It had to be the bond. There was no other explanation. "Theon, I need you to move."

"I know what you need, Tessa," he replied, pulling out a fraction before pressing back into her.

"Do you?" she snapped. "Because it's more than that."

He huffed a laugh. "Still fighting me, even with my cock buried inside you."

"I'm beginning to wonder if you know what to do with it," she bit back.

His small smile fell, and then his mouth was on hers, his tongue swiping at the seam of her lips. He didn't need to try too hard. She immediately let him in, moaning as he claimed her mouth the way he tried to claim every piece of her.

Bending her knees, she moved to wrap her legs around his waist, but then he was pulling back and pulling out, and she was cursing in frustration.

"Godsdamnit, Theon!"

"Hush, Tessa," he snapped, gripping her hips and flipping her over, tossing her further up the bed. "I told you I know what you need."

She felt the bed dip as he climbed up behind her, his knees pushing her legs wider. Then he was hauling her ass up before he slid all the way into her again, and she was moaning into the blankets, her face buried.

Taunting. That's what made him do this to her.

She tucked that away for future use.

His hand was in her hair, pulling until her back bowed, and she was hissing at the sharp sting in her scalp. He pulled out and slammed back into her again as he growled, "Is this what you're wanting from me, Tessa?"

"Gods, yes," she moaned, arms stretched before her and fingers curling into the blankets. The buzzing beneath her skin increased, and whatever it was, it was as desperate for release as she was. Heat speared out from her center, her entire body sparking with need. The tension was becoming too much as he continued to hold her on the brink of pleasure, knowing exactly how to move to give her what she wanted, but not enough to let her grab it. And in this moment, she both hated him and needed him, and it wasn't fucking fair.

He thrust into her again. Then his chest was flush with her back when he curled over her to speak again. "Do you feel that, Tessa?" He punctuated his question with another thrust of his hips as his shadows continued to rove across her flesh. There one moment and gone the next, the thing inside her was chasing it all, like lightning trying to catch the darkness it eclipsed. "It's not the bond. I know you think it is," he continued, low and dark in her ear. "But it's *you*, Tessa. It's *us*. So much more than a fucking bond."

And then he was pressing her down to the mattress, his hand on her neck, holding her in place as he lost any semblance of control. The angle made him go deeper, his cock hitting the perfect spot every godsdamn time. She was coiled so tightly, it wasn't going to take much more, so she let herself sink into the sensations of his cock plunging in and out of her. His shadows pressing against her clit with every thrust. Of his heavy breaths and her ragged gasps. Of his fingers flexing on her hip as he steadied himself. The sweat beading on her brow.

"Give it to me, Tessa. Now," he demanded with another hard thrust.

She shook her head against the hold he still had on her neck. "Not yet," she pleaded, wanting to cling to this all-consuming pleasure just a little longer.

"It's mine. I decide when I get to have it." Then there was a snarled, "Fuck! I can feel your power, Tessa. Just beneath the surface. When it is set free—"

She stopped listening. She didn't want to hear yet again what her power was going to do for him. To hear yet again just another box she checked on his list.

So when his shadows pressed into her clit, vibrating against her, she let herself fall into oblivion as release tore through her. It wasn't until she was coming back down from the high that she realized her hands were clenching the blankets so tightly her knuckles were white. That Theon had removed his hand from her neck. That he was pulling her back into his chest, dropping little kisses to her head, her temple, her jaw. She hadn't even realized he'd come while she'd been lost to her own euphoria.

"You're perfect, Tessa," he murmured.

"You already got to fuck me, Theon," she sighed. "You can stop trying now."

"Tessa—"

"Please just...stop talking."

To her surprise, he did. But his hold tightened around her.

She was hoping he'd been right.

She was hoping if she'd let this happen, given into this bond, nothing else would matter. That's what he kept telling her, right? That once she gave into the bond, she wouldn't want anything else. Only this. Only him. That all her problems would go away. She could just exist without having to think or feel. She could just be and not care about anything.

Instead, a tear was tracking down her cheek as she felt his breathing become deep and steady. He may have been wrong about that, but he'd been right about so many other things he'd said to her tonight.

It's a little bit of hope you're too afraid to cling to, so you let yourself sink instead.

A lot of good hope did.

Not when all this had done was prove her fears right. Her power was valuable to him. Not her.

That's all she could think as she cautiously uncurled her fingers that were still clenched tightly around the blankets.

She slowly lifted a hand to find light glowing in her palm.

Never her.

Only what she could give.

When she blinked heavy eyes open the next morning, she had shifted in her sleep. Her head was on Theon's chest, her fingers resting atop the fine hair below his navel. Both were still naked from the night before. Thankfully, her power had waned. She wasn't sure how she would ever learn to control that.

His fingers were toying with her hair, and when she glanced up, he was awake, his phone in his other hand. He either hadn't realized she'd woken, or he was pretending he didn't know, trying to savor the moment of peace.

There was a soft knock on the door, and she tensed on instinct. He didn't acknowledge it, only called out, "Come in."

Pen came through the door, a tray of coffee, pastries, and fruit in her hands, and Tessa felt her cheeks heat as she buried her nose in Theon's chest.

"Thank you, Pen," he said quietly.

"Of course, Theon," she said. "Axel already left on his run."

"I'm aware. He sent me a message."

"Do you need anything else?"

"No. We're fine."

Tessa didn't peek out from his chest until she heard the door click shut.

"You should have warned me," Tessa said, her voice hoarse from sleep.

"Warned you about Pen?" Theon asked, his hand back in her hair.

"Yes. She doesn't need to see us like...this." When Theon didn't answer, she peeked up at him again. He was back to his phone, pointedly not looking at her. She sighed. "It's not the first time she's brought you breakfast with a female in your bed, is it?"

"No."

Something twisted in her stomach at his answer, and she had no idea why. But the bond stirred to life, also not liking the idea of someone else being in his bed.

Which was just great.

Not only had she not accepted this fucking bond after sex, but now she was godsdamn jealous of females she didn't even know.

The sound of Theon setting his phone aside had her looking up at him again as he gently extracted himself from her. She meant to ask where he was going, but the words caught in her suddenly dry mouth when she found her gaze fixed firmly on his perfect ass and, gods, those thighs.

She watched as he bent to grab two mugs of coffee, quickly turning away when he started to turn back towards her. His dark laugh skittered along her spine, and she pulled the covers over her head.

"Tessa," he chided, tugging on the comforter.

"Put some pants on," she grumbled.

"You're being ridiculous."

"You're being…stupidly naked."

Another tug of the blankets. "Tessa, come on. I brought you coffee."

She responded by sticking out a hand with a gimme gesture.

"Tessa."

"Theon," she parroted.

There was an exasperated sigh before the sound of footsteps, and she peeked out to find him gone. Wrapping the sheet tightly around her chest, she reached for one of the coffee mugs on the nightstand, moaning at the taste.

"I have to put on pants, but you get to make those sounds," Theon said dryly, reappearing from the closet clad in loose pants that hung low on his hips.

"The pants aren't exactly hiding much," she said with a pointed look.

"You're naked in my bed, Tessa. I'm going to be hard," he replied, swiping up the bowl of fruit and carrying it to the bed with him. He grabbed his own coffee, settling against the headboard, emerald eyes on her as he took a drink.

She cleared her throat. She may have been sleeping in this male's bed for weeks, but this was awkward. "Stop looking at me like that."

"I don't know any other way to look at you."

"Whatever," she grumbled, taking another sip of her coffee.

"I let Luka know you'd do training an hour later than normal," Theon said, bending a knee and resting his arm on it while he drank his coffee.

"Great," she muttered.

"You understand why this is important, right?"

She sighed. "Yes, Theon."

"We have a private dinner tonight with Dagian Jove."

Tessa choked on her coffee, and Theon arched a brow.

"Just us and Dagian?" she asked.

"Luka and Axel will be there. I'm sure Dagian will have another with him, as well as his Source."

"Why are you meeting with him?"

"He requested it," Theon answered.

"And you said yes?"

"Is there a reason I should have said no?"

She pulled her knees to her chest, resting her chin on top of them. "I guess not. It's probably a good idea to appear amicable while attempting to take over the realm." She could feel him studying her, and she glanced at him when she said, "What?"

"Why are you hesitant about this?"

"About you trying to take over Devram?"

He glared at her. "No. You appear apprehensive about Dagian."

"I'm not."

"You are. Did something happen that I need to be aware of?"

"No."

"Tessa…"

There was a warning in his tone that had her tensing. "Nothing happened, Theon."

"You're a terrible liar."

"Why does everyone keep telling me that? I'm an excellent liar," she admonished.

"You need to tell me why this bothers you, or I will have to force it," he said. "I cannot afford to be caught off guard with you tonight."

"What is that supposed to mean?" she demanded, straightening.

"It means I want to be prepared, and you appear leery of meeting with Dagian. I don't want any more surprises."

"Tristyn and Dagian are very different," she said, knowing exactly what type of surprises he was referring to.

"We will discuss Tristyn in a moment, but first Dagian. Last chance to tell me yourself before I force it."

Her eyes dropped to her coffee cup she was holding between her palms. "It's nothing, Theon. Truly. The Priestess put him in the visions at the assessment. He tortured me, and…"

It had felt real. So real, in fact, a part of her felt like he had truly been there somehow, and every time she saw him or had to be in the same room as him, it made her heart race at the memory of his power slamming into her.

"Tessa, you will not be left alone with him. All three of us will be there," Theon said, and she could hear the annoyance in his tone.

"I know."

A finger under her chin was lifting her face to his as he added, "I know that I have not done the best job of keeping you protected when you are not at my side, but I hope you know no one will ever harm you when I am with you."

She nodded mutely, Luka's sneered words coming back to her from that first day of training.

How have you not realized nearly everything Theon has done, including making you sit beneath a table, was to protect you?

The words had warred in her soul for days now, and as he reached to tuck her hair behind her ear, she said, "Can I ask you something?"

He seemed surprised, but quickly wiped the expression from his face as he nodded for her to go on.

"Last night I was speaking with the other Sources, and they implied that if you hadn't Selected me, I would have been assigned to serve in the Achaz Kingdom at the Sirana Villas." Theon said nothing, only held her stare, and it had her averting her gaze as she felt her cheeks flush for some unknown reason. Her words ran together as she rushed on, "And your father said I would have served in entertainment, and you've made comments that you saved me from worse fates and—"

"What are you asking me, Tessa?" Theon interrupted, his tone harsher than she expected.

"Is that true? What Maxson and Jasper were saying? That some are assigned to…repopulate the Fae?"

"Yes."

Startled by his bluntness, she lurched back, coffee sloshing from her mug, and the sheet slipped an inch down her chest. She caught the sheet as Theon swiped her mug from her hands.

Her fingers curled around the edge of the fabric as she felt the buzzing beneath her skin start up. That energy searching for a way out. She was starting to realize that it always preceded her power surfacing.

"And you—" She sucked in a shaky breath, forcing herself to look at Theon when she asked, "You believe that's where I would have been assigned?"

"My father is many things, but he knows the inner workings of the kingdoms well. He spoke the truth the day you met him," he answered. "Had you not been Selected, I am certain the plan would have been to send you to Achaz Kingdom. You're beautiful, Tessa, something the Legacy covet in their Fae, both for personal pleasure and for producing offspring."

Tessa swallowed down the bile that rose at the idea of that. How were the Fae on the Estates kept so oblivious to all of this? The blood? The basic breeding?

"However," Theon went on, "your emerging could very well have altered those plans. You could have still been assigned there with the hope of your children having the same power levels as you are antici-pated to emerge with. But the far more likely alternative is that the kingdoms would have fought over you."

"Fought over me?"

He nodded. "The most powerful Fae known to the realm? Tessa, blood will still be shed over you. We are preparing for it. Arius Kingdom will likely be accused of having known your gifts and power levels all along, that we somehow cheated the system."

"But that's not possible," she stammered. "Is it?"

Theon shrugged. "It doesn't matter, but like I said, we are preparing. *You* are preparing. It's part of the reason you're training."

"To protect myself," she said slowly.

"Yes," he confirmed. "When—not if—someone comes for you again, they will be smart about it. It won't be when you are with us. They'll wait for an opportunity, and when they take it, you need to be able to fight back until I can get to you."

"To fight for me," she said, and the words tasted weird on her tongue. No one had truly fought *for* her before. Not even Dex.

"Yes."

"Because I am your Source," she clarified, not liking the feeling stirring in her chest.

Darkness flitted across his eyes at her words. "Because you are mine to fight for."

She'd process those words later because all of this was becoming too much. All of this was pointing to Luka speaking the truth. That nearly everything Theon had done was to protect her.

"You need to get ready. I need to get you to Luka," Theon said after a moment. "Make sure you eat."

"Right," she murmured. "What do you do while I am with them?"

Theon's brow arched. "Are you missing me, beautiful?"

She scoffed. "No, but I prefer you over Luka's training."

"And Axel?"

"Oh, I'd rather run with him," she replied, reaching for the smaller blanket folded at the end of the bed.

Theon scowled. "And why is that?"

She strategically replaced the sheet with the blanket before she started to climb out of the bed. "I suppose because he's not you."

Fingers snagging around her wrist had her stilling and looking back over her shoulder. "You realize he will be in my position next Selection year."

"Yes, well, he won't be *my* Master, now will he?" she retorted. "And the Fae he Selects will likely want this life."

"Because you don't."

"Yes, because I *don't*."

"Tell me, Tessa. What kind of life would you like to live? What kind of life have you dreamed of?"

"What kind of life have *you* dreamed of?" she shot back. "Besides world domination, of course."

"If you think I desire Devram for the sake of ruling it, you truly do know nothing," he said, his voice going cold as he released her wrist. "Go get ready."

She pressed her lips together, slipping from the bed and going to the closet to put on her training clothes before going to the bathroom to brush her teeth and put her hair up.

Thirty minutes later, Theon was leaving her with Luka without a word, but she didn't miss the look exchanged between the two.

Luka sighed as the door shut behind Theon. Tessa was already in position, waiting for him to begin his torture.

"Tell me what happened last night," Luka said, crossing his arms where he stood before her.

Tessa blinked at him, unsure of what to say.

"I swear to Sargon, I will entrance you, Tessa. I don't have near the patience that Theon graces you with."

"Why don't you just ask Theon?"

"Because he has enough to deal with right now, which is why I am dealing with you."

"Dealing with me," she deadpanned.

Luka's lips curved into a mocking sneer. "Don't like that choice of words, little one?"

When she didn't answer, he moved before she could register what was happening. Her feet were swiped out from beneath her, and she was on her back with an audible "oomph."

Luka stood over her, a foot on each side of her hips, his hair hanging forward and brushing his jawline.

"Tell me what happened last night."

"You're not my Master," she sneered back.

"No. I would have never chosen you as my Source," Luka agreed. "But here I am. Forced to deal with your constant attitude. How is that fair?"

"*Fair?*" Tessa admonished, her hands clenching at her sides. "Do not speak to me about what is fair, Luka Mors."

"Tell me about last night."

"No."

Then she was hissing as the flames at her wrists bit into her skin.

"I can and will do this all day, Tessa. My loyalty is to Theon, not to you. I will do whatever I have to keep him protected."

"A slave to a bond, just like me," she mocked.

Luka dropped down, straddling her waist so he could bring his face closer to hers. "I *chose* my bond, little one."

"You were forced to choose it," she countered. "It was Theon or Valter."

"That's a fair statement, but do you see me bemoaning my situation day in and day out?"

"That's different."

"You just said it was a bond, just like yours. Which is it, Tessa? It's only the same thing when it fits your narrative?"

"What is your problem?" she snapped, her hands shoving against

Luka's chest. Not that he went anywhere. That was solid muscle beneath her palms, and dragon fire made his flesh so godsdamn hot all the time. But for the love of the gods, he'd been different since they'd arrived at the Acropolis too. So had Axel. Just like Theon. Any lightness they'd shown her in their time at Arius House was gone.

"You are not the only one forced into shitty situations, Tessa," Luka replied. "You have far more in common with me, with Theon, with Axel, than you realize. The difference is the three of us aren't lying down and letting it happen. We don't sit around and stare out windows all fucking day. You don't want this? Fight back."

"What do you think I have been doing for weeks?"

"Whining," he sneered, pushing off of her and getting to his feet.

"*Whining?*" she all but screeched, quickly getting to her own feet.

"Yes. Whining."

"And how do you propose I fight back?"

"First you need to figure out what you're fighting for. First you need to care about something," Luka said.

"Then what? Step on whoever gets in my way?" she demanded, blocking the hit Luka aimed at her side.

He smiled in approval. Barely, but it was there.

Then she was on her back again, completely having missed his follow-up attack.

Prick.

"No one can steal your thunder if you are the storm," he replied, stretching a hand toward her. "Be the fucking storm, Tessa."

"Why are you telling me this? Aren't you supposed to be protecting Theon?"

He yanked her to her feet as he said, "That's exactly what I'm doing."

39
THEON

"Right this way," the hostess said with a bow of her head.

Theon followed her through the lounge, his hand pressed to the small of Tessa's back. The dress she was wearing was such a dark shade of blue it appeared black in the lighting, and it was backless, leaving his palm pressed to bare skin.

Bare skin that had distracted him all godsdamn day as he'd remembered what it was like to have her beneath him. To feel that flesh pebbled with goosebumps. To feel her pulse beneath his fingertips.

But it wasn't happening again. Not until she finally admitted what he already knew, and he hated himself for drawing that line.

He knew she was tired. She'd been tired after training with Luka for nearly three hours. Luka refused to tell him about their training sessions, only reporting what they worked on and how she was improving. He never told Theon anything she said, and it made Theon agitated not knowing. But they were all getting anxious. The Source Bond was supposed to be firmly in place by this point. Tessa was supposed to be an asset by now, helping them form alliances and intimidate those who weren't.

She'd asked what he spent his time doing while she trained. He'd deflected because she would only ask more questions if she learned he was spending time in the Pantheon archives combing through ancient texts. He was trying to figure out so many things at this point, he didn't know which direction to go in. Her power. Their defective Source bond.

Who was trying to take her. But not only that, the texts at the Pantheon could shed light on the female in the mirror from a few years ago, or his theories on the Revelation Decree if he just knew where to look.

Which he didn't.

And when he was there, the bond only pulled at him to get back to her, somehow sensing her discomfort. The Legacy could control how much of the bond their Fae felt. For weeks, he'd simply let the bond bombard her, thinking that would push her into accepting it sooner, faster. Lately he'd gone in the complete opposite direction, hoping if she didn't feel him, didn't feel the bond, she'd crave it.

And maybe she had. She'd let him touch her twice in only a few days. Maybe he'd been playing this wrong the entire time. It shouldn't surprise him. Everything had been different with her from the start.

The hostess opened a large polished wood door to a private lounge, stepping aside to let them pass. Tessa was already sliding imperceptibly closer to him, and he paused when he found not only Dagian but Lealla as well. Wasn't this an interesting turn of events? The Achaz *and* Sera-fina heirs.

"Lealla," he greeted, not missing the way her Source sneered at Tessa. "What an unexpected pleasure."

Her lips tipped in a cold grin. "Theon, there's no one else here. No need for theatrics."

"What theatrics?" he asked, Luka and Axel taking seats before him and Tessa. He saw Lealla glance at them, momentarily startled at the lack of decorum.

With a cold smirk of his own, Theon pulled a chair out as he said, "Have a seat, beautiful."

Tessa didn't hesitate, playing her part perfectly, before Theon took a seat next to her. Luka had already ordered them glasses of whiskey, and Tessa passed him a glass before sipping from her own.

"I believe these are the theatrics Lealla was referencing," Dagian said. That fucker hadn't even bothered standing when they'd entered the room. His Source stood obediently at his side, waiting for instruction. She was a mirror of Eviana.

"Dagian," Theon said tightly. "Hope you haven't been waiting long."

"It's fine. I'm sure you're used to taking your time seeing as how Arius Kingdom is always last to be addressed. Besides, I know you prefer to make an entrance with your entourage. All those...theatrics," he said over the top of his liquor glass.

"I'd hardly call my brother and advisor an entourage," Theon said in a bored tone, settling back in his seat and ignoring the verbal jab at his kingdom.

Dagian only smiled back, and Theon was immediately on high alert. He was already suspicious of Dagian's insistence of this dinner after Theon had turned down two other requests for meetings in the last week.

Lealla took her seat to Dagian's right, motioning for her Source to sit as well. When they were all settled, Dagian said, "Are you ready for the Emerging Ceremony?"

Theon huffed a humorless laugh. "Getting right to the point then, are we?"

Dagian shrugged. "Unlike you, I don't enjoy theatrics. I prefer a more direct approach."

The male drummed his fingers on the table, light crackling from his fingertips as he did so, and Tessa winced.

Dagian noticed, the corner of his lips ticking up at the small mannerism, but Theon was too focused on his power because he'd seen that same power recently.

At his Source's fingertips.

"I don't think there is any need for power bragging," Axel drawled, downing his drink.

"You know how it is," Dagian replied. "Have to siphon off that extra power from time to time."

"Yes, gaining complete mastery over one's power so young is a feat, but I'm sure you'll get there in time," Theon said.

Dagian glared, that power in his palm instantly dying out. "Still an arrogant ass, I see."

"No need for name calling when I am simply expressing my confidence in your ability to eventually control your gifts enough to not need to siphon off that power."

"We've had the same intense training you have, Theon," Lealla cut in.

"Somehow I doubt that."

"Now, now, we aren't here to argue," Dagian cut in smoothly. "After all, we are to be working together for a successful Selection year, are we not?"

"Of course," Lealla said tightly, her Source refilling her already empty wine glass.

"And in the spirit of such things," Dagian continued, "I was merely making conversation about the upcoming festivities."

"I am sure we are all looking forward to the Emerging Ceremony," Theon said. "It is always an exciting time to see the new Fae who will be joining our kingdoms."

"And, of course, verifying that assessments were correct about our Sources," Dagian added, taking another sip of his drink.

"Of course," Theon agreed.

"It provides a means of further...building relations between the kingdoms."

"And what relations are you hoping to build?" Theon asked, unsure of where the male was going with this.

"We have all night to discuss such matters," Dagian said dismissively, opening the menu that his Source passed to him without so much as a look from her master. Completely in sync without their Marks. Exactly what he'd wanted to portray about him and Tessa.

Shit.

Act or not, the pair was certainly convincing.

A hand on his thigh nearly made him jump if not for the years of learning to never show surprise, and he glanced down to find Tessa's hand there. Without thinking, he was interlacing their fingers.

"You won't need a menu," she said. "I already checked on the drive here while the three of you were discussing the proposal from the Celeste Kingdom. They have your favorite."

"Thank you, beautiful," he murmured.

Her smile was soft, and again he was forced to keep his shock from showing. Because that smile? It was a real one.

When he looked back at the others, Lealla was already on her phone, no doubt reaching out to the Celeste heir, and he glanced back at Tessa, finding her smirking to herself as she tipped her glass at Lealla's Source.

Theon had no idea what that was, but he liked this side of her.

Maybe she wasn't as terrible at lying as he believed her to be.

It wasn't until after they'd taken the first bites of their meals that Dagian got to the point of this dinner. Honestly, Theon was surprised it had taken him this long. The Achaz Heir wasn't known for his tactfulness. The kingdom was blunt and demanding, always focused on the present, never the long-game, and it was no surprise the Serafina Kingdom went right along with them. After all, when Devram was created, the god and goddess were set to be Matched. It only made sense that such alliances still carried over in this world.

"About these relations you mentioned previously," Dagian said.

"I didn't mention any relations," Theon countered. "You were the one who brought up building relations."

Dagian hummed in contemplation, reaching for his glass and making a show of taking a sip. For someone who claimed not to enjoy theatrics, he was certainly dragging this out.

He was cutting into his meat, when Dagian finally continued. "I will admit, I thought relations with Arius Kingdom were a waste of time. You lot always appear to be so...obstinate."

"Being particular about who we do business with does not make us obstinate," Theon countered. "It simply means we evaluate our options before making the most lucrative choices."

Dagian hummed. "That much was made obvious last night."

Theon glanced at Axel, then at Luka. Their faces were impassive, but when neither of them spoke, it told Theon they didn't have any idea what Dagian was speaking about either.

"Arius Kingdom has never been one to share outside their own borders," Lealla chimed in.

"We are more than willing to share for the right price," Theon countered.

"Not to mention we take in all those deemed unworthy of your esteemed kingdoms," Axel said, signaling for another drink.

Theon had stopped counting Axel's drinks after he'd ordered his third before their food had arrived.

"I do find it interesting that you finally venture out of your borders, only to make alliances not with another kingdom ruling family, but with someone else entirely," Dagian continued. "My father was also intrigued by the news."

"I don't know where you're getting your information from, but there haven't been any alliances forged outside of our borders," Theon said.

"And when that information is what I witnessed with my own eyes?" Dagian asked. He'd abandoned his food, settling back in his chair. His golden hair reflected the low lighting of the room, and his features seemed even sharper as he smirked at Theon.

"All right, Dagian," Theon said, pushing aside his own meal. "You clearly have something you wish to lord over me, so let's hear it. I'm growing bored with your *theatrics.*"

"There is nothing I wish to lord over you. I only wish for you not to call me a liar when I witnessed such alliances myself."

"And what alliance is that?"

"The one with Tristyn Blackheart."

Blackheart.

The male's last name was *Blackheart?*

As in Tristyn Blackheart, the elusive silent founder of Lilura Inquest?

Theon recognized the male's name, but the male himself was rarely seen in public. He was more elusive than the Arius Kingdom, and while Theon knew who he was, many Legacy did not, let alone the Fae and mortals. He was the founder of the company that had single-handedly been responsible for numerous advancements in Devram, from healing compounds to untraceable glamours to studies of wards and Marks, even technological advancements. Lilura Inquest was the company that had created the technology that allowed phones inside the Pantheon. It was rumored that Blackheart himself had overseen many of the advancements, and with access to the company's glamours, he easily moved among the Legacy, Fae, and mortals without being noticed.

Until Tessa was Selected.

There was no way that was a coincidence.

Just another thing he needed to figure out.

"Why would you think I have an alliance with Tristyn Blackheart? Simply because he was dancing with my Source last night?" Theon asked, his face revealing nothing of the shock he was experiencing.

Dagian scoffed, any semblance of decorum melting from his demeanor. "Your Source appeared very intimate with him. The two even spoke of time spent together at a hotel."

He saw Tessa stiffen out of the corner of his eye, but he couldn't look at her right now.

"The other heirs and I, along with our families, find it odd that Arius Kingdom comes back onto the scene and not only chooses a Source none of us took a second look at, but one that also seems to get along quite well with a male who notoriously avoids everyone."

"What, exactly, are you asking me, Dagian?" Theon asked, picking up his drink and swirling the amber liquid.

"I am simply stating an observation that seems suspicious."

"The observation is noted, although I don't know what you would like me to do about it."

"Is she involved with Blackheart? Is that why you chose her?"

"No," Theon snarled. "She is mine and mine alone."

"The events of last night say otherwise," Lealla said.

"You can think what you want, but that Mark on her hand says she is mine," Theon said, letting his shadows out.

They coiled around his arms before reaching for Tessa, and she leaned into them, letting the darkness brush along her jaw, her throat. Then she lifted a hand, smiling pointedly at Lealla as she dragged her fingers through the shadows, letting them dance around her knuckles. Dagian and Lealla glanced at each other as they watched Tessa play with the shadows, as though she loved the darkness so much, she could command it.

As if she were his and his alone.

He could feel his magic. It was obsessed with her, nearly vibrating at having her interact with it. The shadows clung to her while she toyed with them, and he could feel her touch as if she were touching him herself. It almost made him forget what her actions last night had cost them.

"All things considered, it appears you have an in with Blackheart," Dagian said, having returned to eating his dinner.

"What are you getting at?"

"I would like an introduction."

Axel huffed a laugh that had Theon shooting him a glare.

"What?" Axel asked. "It's rather ridiculous if you think about it. He set up this big, elaborate dinner to ask us to introduce him to Tristyn Blackheart. The main headquarters of Lilura Inquest is *in* the Acropolis with the second largest location in Faven. Both are places he surely has unlimited access to."

"While I can certainly access the buildings, that does not grant me access to Blackheart himself," Dagian said tightly.

"Then ask Daddy to help," Axel replied flippantly.

Dagian glared at Axel, and Theon knew that look.

"Your father assigned you this task," Theon said, letting his darkness continue to linger. "What does he want with Blackheart?"

Dagian rolled his eyes. "You tell me Arius secrets, and I'll tell you Achaz ones."

Fair point.

"Well, I wish I could help, Dagian," Theon said, suddenly ready to leave. "But my arrangement with Tristyn is new. I can't jeopardize that. Surely you understand."

"Of course," Dagian said, rising from his seat before Theon could. "Arius secrets always come out in the end anyway." His gaze slid to Luka. "Isn't that right?"

"I have no idea what you are implying," Luka replied, sounding broody and bored with all of this.

"Here I thought a Sargon Legacy would be clever, but maybe you are just good for battles," Dagian sighed as if disappointed.

Lealla had followed his example, standing from the table as well. She was already standing near the door, a victorious smirk on her lips. "What ever will the other kingdoms say when they learn what Arius Kingdom has been hiding in their mountains?" she simpered.

"What the fuck are you talking about?" Axel demanded. "There are no Sargon Legacy left living. Your ancestors made sure of that centuries ago."

"Reports of a flying, fire-breathing creature say otherwise," Dagian replied, his Source falling into step behind him as she moved to the door. "Of course, how that information is received by the other kingdoms could be negotiated. If, for example, two kingdoms appeared to be thrilled by such a revelation, the other kingdoms would likely follow suit. If two particular kingdoms painted such news in an unsavory light, however... Well, that could be detrimental."

Theon didn't bother getting to his feet as he said, "Be very careful how you decide to play this, Dagian."

"I urge you to reconsider my request, Theon," he replied, and a moment later, he and Lealla were gone.

"Fuck," Axel muttered, sucking down the rest of his drink.

"For the love of Arius, stop drinking," Theon snapped, reaching over and snatching his now empty glass. "What the fuck is wrong with you drinking like that tonight?"

"I'm fine," he said, waving him off. "What we need to worry about is how the fuck they know about Luka."

"He said it was reported back to him," Luka said. "The only time I could have been spotted was the night at the river."

"But you said you got all four," Axel said.

"Unless there were more than four," Luka answered grimly.

They all fell silent. This was worse than Theon could have imagined. He'd spent the last two days cleaning up after that mess at the river to make sure this exact thing didn't happen. They'd hunted down the Night Children and destroyed all the evidence. They'd even taken care of the sentinels who had seen Tessa running, along with three Fae who swore they hadn't seen anything but had been along her path. He wasn't willing to take the risks. Nothing could jeopardize this.

Except she had.

She'd jeopardized *everything* with her wildness and her lack of control and her refusal to simply fucking submit.

He slowly stood and buttoned his suit jacket as he turned to look down at her. He could feel her nervousness, the fear bleeding from her. She'd once told him he didn't scare her. Another lie.

"Tessa," he said, far too calmly.

He saw her wince as his shadows thickened, stinging where they still touched her. Luka and Axel were standing, the half-finished meals forgotten on the table.

"I don't know anything about him," she stammered. She was gripping the arms of her chair, her face leeched of color.

The corner of his lips curled, and she shrank back at whatever she saw on his face.

"I swear. You know as much as I do. He—"

She was starting to ramble, but this couldn't be discussed here. Not where anyone could overhear.

Her eyes went wide when his shadows wound up her neck and down her throat. Not cutting off her air supply, but enough to gag her. Her hands were at her throat though, as if she couldn't breathe, panic filling her grey eyes.

Theon grabbed her hand, pulling her roughly to her feet, and she stumbled in her heels. Her fingers were squeezing his in a silent plea, but he didn't care.

It wasn't until they were in the vehicle and Luka was pulling into traffic that he pulled his shadows back. Tessa coughed and sputtered, glaring at him.

"Was that necessary?" she snarled, her hand on her chest as she dragged in big gulping breaths.

"Tell me about Blackheart," was all he said, cold and detached.

"I don't know anything about him."

"You've spent hours with the male, and you don't know anything about him? I find that hard to believe."

"Even you three didn't realize he was a Legacy in Rockmoor," she cried, a hand fisting into the fabric of her dress.

"Did you know his surname?" Axel asked from the front, not bothering to turn and look at her.

"Yes, but—"

"When? When did you learn it?" Theon interrupted.

"In Rockmoor, but I didn't—"

"So the night I found you with him, you already knew who he was?"

"No. I didn't recognize the name. I mean, he told me he founded a company, but I didn't know which one or what he did. Even when he gave me his card, I—"

"You have a way to contact him?" Theon demanded.

"I…" Her hand slowly fell from her chest, landing on the seat where her fingers curled into the leather. She swallowed audibly. "Yes."

"And have you contacted him? Is that why he was at the social last night?"

"How would I have contacted him?" she bit out. "You monitor my phone, tablet. Everything."

Theon smiled humorlessly. "You called your Fae without my knowledge. I wouldn't put this past you too. Have you had contact with him?"

"No," she insisted. "Only that night in Rockmoor and last night at the social. I didn't know he was going to be there. I swear, Theon. I didn't know. I didn't know who he was. I still don't understand why—"

"It is not your place to understand," Theon snarled. "Your place is to serve, Tessa, not to hide things from me. Do you have any idea what you have jeopardized?"

"I'm sorry—"

"I do not need your apologies," he snapped. "I need your obedience. I need your loyalty—"

"You've done nothing to earn it!"

He was across the backseat in his next breath, and she let out a yelp as he loomed over her. Snatching her hand, he held it up, twisting it so she could see the Mark. "This says I do not need to earn a godsdamn thing, Tessa."

"Th—"

But his name stalled on her tongue.

Luka had parked. Axel was already out of the vehicle, heading for the door off the garage. Luka had realized what Theon had though, and black flames flared in front of the door, blocking Axel's path.

"What the fuck?" Axel said, whirling to face them.

Tessa hadn't been able to say his name. He'd given her permission to use it in front of Pen, so that could only mean someone else was here.

"Did you feel anyone at the Wards?" Theon asked.

He was out of the vehicle. Luka was helping Tessa out.

Understanding flashed in Axel's eyes. "No," he ground out.

The three of them stood facing the door. Axel shoved his hands in his pockets. Tessa was wisely silent behind them.

"He's not coming until tomorrow, right?" Axel asked.

"Right," Theon answered.

He didn't know why he said it. He knew exactly who was waiting for them.

With a deep inhale, he stepped forward, pushing the door open and stepping into the foyer. Silently they made their way to the formal sitting room. The only sound was Tessa's heels on the wood floors.

They found him sitting in one of the wing-backed chairs, a glass of amber liquid in his hand.

Theon stopped a few feet from him. Luka was at his side, Axel hanging back with Tessa, as Theon said, "Hello, Father."

40
TESSA

She'd fucked up.

She'd fucked up so bad.

But her dread of Theon's wrath was momentarily forgotten at finding the Arius Lord here. He wasn't supposed to be here until tomorrow. He and Cressida were to arrive in the evening, right before the Emerging Ceremony. They were staying at the country estate, not here. He wasn't supposed to be *here*.

"Theon," Valter replied coldly to his son's greeting. The Lord didn't bother acknowledging Axel or Luka.

"This is unexpected. I thought you and Mother were arriving tomorrow evening," Theon said evenly.

"Your mother will arrive tomorrow evening as planned," Valter agreed.

"I see."

I see?

That was all Theon was going to say. Admittedly, she'd only seen him interact with his father a handful of times, and most of the times were when others were around. He'd tried to keep her from him as much as possible.

Yet another way he'd tried to protect her, she realized now.

She hadn't understood.

She hadn't tried to understand. Even if she'd tried, would she have cared?

It is not your place to understand. Your place is to serve.

She shoved the thoughts aside. This was not the place to spiral, to lose control. Despite what they all thought, she could control herself.

For the most part.

Thick tension filled the room, and where was Eviana? Tessa had never seen Valter without her. She forced herself to stand. No fidgeting. That's what Mother Cordelia had drilled into her, and gods, why was she feeling grateful for that right now? But she didn't understand what was happening. Theon and Valter seemed to be in some sort of stand-off. Axel was hovering close to her, and Luka was a foot from Theon, his muscles tight and his eyes already shifted to vertical pupils.

"I am waiting," Valter said after an entire minute of silence.

"I can see that," Theon replied. "I am unaware of what exactly you are waiting for, seeing as I did not know you were arriving tonight."

"Do not get smart," Valter sneered, setting his glass aside with a hard thunk. "Tell me why I have been receiving correspondence all godsdamn evening about a dragon being spotted outside the Acropolis."

Oh gods.

That's all Tessa could think as she watched this play out.

"My Source was attacked by Night Children," Theon answered. "Luka was taking care of them. We thought we had covered all our tracks, but just learned..." Tessa saw the muscle tick in his jaw before he finished, "Apparently we missed one."

"Night Children do not require a fucking dragon, Theon," Valter snarled, pushing to his feet. "If they were stupid enough to attack your Source in your presence, you should have been more than enough to handle them. Are you saying that is not the case? That you are not *strong enough* to protect what is yours? That you have failed at even that?"

"No," Theon answered. "There were several of them. Some ran. While I stayed back to protect my Source, Luka went after the others. It was dark. We stayed low—"

"*We?*" Valter interrupted. "What do you mean 'we?'"

Theon shifted his weight. Barely, but Tessa saw it.

Valter did too, and his eyes narrowed. "Do not even fucking think of lying to me, Theon."

"I thought it best to get my Source back here as quickly as possible, so I flew her back. But as I said, we stayed low," Theon answered.

"So this is your Guardian's fault?" Valter asked, his gaze shifting to Luka.

"No," Theon immediately interjected. "This is the fault of whoever was trying to abduct my Source."

"And who was that?"

"We do not know yet. Our efforts have been unfruitful so far."

"So what you are telling me is that instead of making alliances and doing what I have sent you here to do, you have spent your days trying to figure out who is trying to abduct your Source? And not only have you failed at that, but you have released secrets kept by our kingdom for *decades*?"

"Not that many people know—" Theon started.

"One person knowing is too many!" Valter roared. "Not only that, Rordan knows. Explain to me how the Achaz Lord knowing we have been harboring a Sargon descendant for decades is not a problem, Theon."

"We will take care of it," Theon answered immediately.

"Your recent failures say otherwise."

"I have not failed at anything," Theon retorted, and Axel tensed beside her. She glanced at him side-long. His features gave nothing away, but his eyes were nearly black, there was so much darkness swimming in them.

"You think I do not have eyes here? That I do not know exactly what the three of you have accomplished while here?" Valter demanded, and Tessa couldn't help the small flinch as his voice continued to rise. "Not only have you revealed some of our greatest secrets and jeopardized countless relations I have spent decades forging, you have also made us appear weak."

"How do you figure that?" Theon countered. "Being able to harbor a dragon shifter for decades seems anything but weak."

"No, but allowing another to publicly interact with your Source does," Valter said, a cruel smirk curving on his lips as his dark gaze settled on Tessa.

Any remaining blood drained from her face. She was certain she was paler than a spirit of the After right now.

"She was acting on my orders," Theon said quickly, drawing Valter's attention back to him. "She is trying to find out information for us."

Valter's brow arched. "So you can loan her out to a random Legacy but not your own kingdom?"

"I did not loan her out," Theon said from between clenched teeth.

"Then explain what was reported to me."

"I just did."

"Was I not clear on what was expected of you and your Source?" Valter demanded.

"Yes," Theon answered. "It is because of your demands this happened."

Valter scoffed. "She has caused nothing but problems since you brought her home. Perhaps a different choice needs to be made."

"Killing another's Source is punishable by death," Theon snarled, taking a step forward. Axel shifted so he partially shielded Tessa.

"And who hands out that judgment, Theon?" Valter asked with a cruel sneer, darkness beginning to pool around him.

"Killing her now would be foolish," Axel cut in. "Theon needing to begin a new bond with another Source would be a setback and impede upon our plans."

"Now you desire to have input?" Valter said, rounding on Axel. Axel reached back and shoved Tessa further behind him.

"I always have input, Father," he answered. "You simply rarely deign to ask for it."

A growl came from the Lord, but before he could answer, Theon spoke again. "I think the wise course of action here is to wait until we see what her gifts manifest as at the Emerging Ceremony. If they are not of value, then we can revisit this possible course of action."

What?

Without thinking, she opened her mouth to question that, but a hand slipped over it before she could.

"Tessalyn, *do not speak,*" came Luka's whispered voice in her ear, the entrancing slipping beneath her skin and holding her tongue. Where had he come from?

"From what I can tell, she is the source of every problem we are suddenly facing," Valter countered. "Perhaps it would be prudent to simply rid ourselves of her now."

"You know she will be an asset," Theon argued. "Her predicted power levels alone show that. If they are wrong after tomorrow's ceremony, then I agree with you."

Luka's hand was still over her mouth despite his entrancing, and an arm wrapped around her waist. "Be still, Tessa," he murmured.

But her entire body was trembling. She couldn't control it. Uncontrollable. That's what she'd always been, and now it was going to cost her life.

And she couldn't help the sudden rush of relief that went through her at the thought.

All these years of wishing for death, and now she was this close to finally having it. The idea of dying was terrifying, but the idea of truly not having to care anymore? That idea was freeing.

"I have no choice but to be agreeable to that," Valter agreed begrudgingly. "But I would suggest you observe the Fae closely tomorrow."

"I will make sure I have alternates in mind to discuss with you if necessary," Theon replied, the tension in his shoulders easing a fraction.

Valter was silent, giving a mute nod of his head, and Tessa thought they were done. That Valter would do nothing else until after the ceremony tomorrow. That she could prepare herself for everything to come, but then Valter spoke once more.

"Eviana, bring her."

Tessa had momentarily stopped trembling, but now her body vibrated so violently, her teeth clattered as Eviana came in from the other room with Pen. The female was bound in vines, and as they came closer, another thick rope of thorny vines appeared in Eviana's hand. There were no plants in this townhouse. Most Fae with the earth element needed some sort of nature around them. Only the strongest of the element could conjure it directly. It was unheard of for Fae. Only the Legacy of Silas were known to be able to do so.

"What is the meaning of this?" Theon demanded, taking a step towards Pen then stilling.

"There are still consequences for your multiple failures, Theon," Valter answered, casually swiping up his drink and taking a sip. He smacked his lips a few times, studying the liquid before he said, "A fate similar to your previous servant should do."

"No!" Axel and Theon yelled at the same time, and Luka's hold around her waist intensified to where Tessa was finding it hard to draw breath. She didn't understand what was happening. She knew their previous caretaker had been Caris and that she had died, but...

"I'll take it," Theon said. "The failures are mine. Whatever the punishment for that failure, I will accept."

Valter rolled his eyes, a scowl forming. "Still your greatest weakness. Always needing to be a godsdamn martyr." He strode towards Eviana and Pen, sliding his fingers along Eviana's torso as he moved. "But it certainly makes getting my point across easier."

"Father, please—"

"Enough, Theon!" he barked, and Theon fell silent.

Tessa couldn't see his face, but she could feel the dread rolling off of him. Surely he wasn't going to let this happen. This was *Pen*. They adored her. He would do something.

But he didn't.

He stood still, Axel beside him.

"What shall it be this time?" Valter mused.

There was a second of tense silence, and then Pen cried out, blood appearing around the binds at her wrists as thorns grew and dug into her flesh.

Neither Theon nor Axel moved.

"No additional begging or pleading this time, boys?" Valter asked with a mocking grin.

Neither one spoke. It didn't even look like either was breathing. Why didn't they do something? Surely Luka could do something. Why was no one doing anything?

But no one moved as Eviana produced a wooden stake and shoved it into Pen's side, blood dripping to the floor.

No one said anything as Valter berated them and told Theon this was his fault for failing.

No one *did* anything as a dagger was produced and dragged across the female's middle.

It wasn't until Eviana sent the vine in her hand snaking up Pen's body to her throat, wrapping tightly and thorns growing and digging in with every pass, that someone finally moved.

Axel *snapped.*

Or rather, his darkness did.

Whips of it appeared as he snarled, "For fuck's sake, that's enough."

Tessa's scream was muffled by Luka's hand when Axel's darkness took Pen's head and twisted, the crack echoing in the room before he stalked forward and snatched the dagger that had fallen to the floor and plunged it into Pen's heart.

And Valter was *smiling.*

Grinning from ear-to-ear as if he was proud of his son.

"Maybe you're not a complete waste after all," Valter said. Shadows rose up behind him, Eviana coming to his side, and he stepped backwards into the flowing darkness, disappearing.

"Fuck!" Axel bellowed, more darkness exploding from him. A shield of Luka's dragon fire surrounded her, protecting her as he shoved her down to the floor. Axel's darkness didn't just explode, it *destroyed*. The furniture went flying, the side tables splintering as they hit the walls. Mirrors and lamps shattered, shards of glass melting as they collided with Luka's shield. She had never seen Axel lose control. Never even thought he'd been on the edge of losing control. Even now, it had come out of nowhere. Theon had tells when he was riding that edge, but Axel?

That was terrifying.

From the floor, she found herself staring at Pen's lifeless body across from her, her features still twisted in pain and dull blue eyes staring at nothing. She had done nothing but serve the Arius House loyally for decades. First in the kitchens, and eventually becoming Theon and Axel's personal servant. And he had killed her. For nothing.

No.

Not for nothing.

Because of her.

"Burn the body and gather the ashes, Luka," Theon said, his voice strangely monotone. "We will take them to Sinvons Lake for a Farewell after the Emerging Ceremony. Scatter them where we buried Caris's ashes."

He didn't look at her. None of them did. Luka stood, his fire flaring out as he scooped up Pen's lifeless body. Tessa didn't know where he was going. Axel had already disappeared. She hadn't realized he'd left.

Theon turned and headed up the stairs, and she wasn't sure what she was supposed to do. For weeks now, her every move had been decided for her. Taking a deep breath, she followed.

When she reached the third floor, she found Theon had already changed. He had athletic shorts on and a long-sleeve top. The same clothes he wore when they went running. He was lacing up his sneakers when she entered, and he didn't pause, let alone look at her.

Wringing her hands together, she cleared her throat lightly before saying, "You are going for a run?"

"Yes."

"Do you...want me to go with you?"

"No."

And fuck, she didn't know what she was supposed to do.

"I'm sorry, Theon," she whispered. "I know Pen was...endeared to you."

"This was not the first time this has happened. It won't be the last," he answered shortly, pushing to his feet. He shoved his phone into his pocket before grabbing some earbuds. Two of his rings were gone, only the onyx one that matched Axel's remaining.

"Theon, I need you to tell me what to do," she said quietly.

"Why?" he sneered. Emerald eyes settled on her, the shadows so thick in them, they were more black than green. "Why do you need me to tell you what to do? You repeatedly choose to do the exact opposite of what I request of you."

"I…"

But she trailed off as he took slow steps towards her, and she was backing up with every step he took until her back hit the wall. She'd been wrong. Axel's unpredictable rage was terrifying, but Theon's cold, unyielding rage?

That was petrifying.

Theon's rage was calculating, just like his father's. When he let his anger out, it was with purpose. It would hurt where it mattered, just like forcing them to watch Pen be tortured had affected them.

Theon braced his hands on either side of her head, and his voice was low and far too calm. "I told you everything you did reflected on me, Tessa. This should not be a surprise."

She knew this was her fault, but to hear Theon speak it aloud…

"I'm sorry," she repeated.

"I told you before, I do not need your apologies nor do I want them. What is it I require of you, Tessa?"

"Obedience," she whispered.

"Did I not make it clear that the consequences for failure would be harsher now?"

"You did."

For several long moments, they only stared at each other, the shadows growing darker and darker in his eyes.

Until his darkness was wreathing his forearms and winding through his dark hair like an onyx halo.

"You were supposed to fix things," he said in a sharp hiss. "You were supposed to make things better. Help us stand against him. Instead, my world has been nothing but chaos since you stepped foot in it."

"I did not ask to be in your world!" she cried, the *thing* inside of her snapping to attention.

"You couldn't just do as you were told, could you?" he continued, ignoring her outburst. "I tell you to stay with us at all times; you leave and require Luka and I to save you. I tell you everything I do is to protect you; you fight me at every turn. I tell you not to let another touch you. Not only do you allow another to do just that, you do so in public where everyone can see, and now Pen is dead."

Tessa lurched back, pressing further into the wall. "I know that is my fault, but—"

"It is entirely your fault," he snarled, his words as sharp as the dagger used to take Pen's life. "Her death is directly correlated to your actions."

"I was trying to find out information for you! We already had this argument, Theon. You defended me to your father—"

"Of course I defended you, Tessa!" he shouted. "You are still mine to protect, even if it does require me to constantly deal with the messes you create."

The words hit their mark, whether intended or not, and she instantly shoved down every thought and insecurity.

She instantly became nothing.

So close to being *something*.

She nodded mutely as his words settled deep into her soul. He was still hurling verbal insults at her, but she couldn't hear them.

Too wild.

Too much to deal with.

Not worth the hassle.

Nothing.

A bruising grip on her elbow pulled her from her thoughts. She had removed her heels as she climbed the steps, but she still stumbled as she struggled to keep up with his long strides.

"Theon, where are we going?" she asked, stumbling yet again on the stairs.

"I am going for a run," he replied.

"I'm not in shoes for running."

"Funny, you ran all the way to the river without shoes. I didn't think such things mattered."

"Theon, I—"

But they'd reached the main floor, and he wasn't pulling her to the front door. He was pulling her to the kitchen, and she didn't understand what was happening.

"Luka and Axel are right. This isn't working," he muttered. "I try to be reasonable; you throw it back in my face. I try to give you space; you still refuse to give even a little bit. I push; you push back."

"Theon—"

"I'm done trying, Tessa," he snapped, his words growing more clipped the longer he spoke. "You have single-handedly ruined plans that I have spent years formulating."

"I didn't know—"

"It's not your place to know!" he shouted, yanking open the pantry door.

"Theon..."

But when he reached for the door that would lead down to the wine cellar, her heart rate picked up. "Theon, wait. Please. Just wait."

She dug in her heels, trying to find something to grab onto with her other hand as he pulled her down the steps into the cellar. It was a small, windowless space with stone walls and low lighting. There were two racks full of wine, with hardly enough room to move between them. The space was cool to keep the wine chilled, cold on her bare feet.

"Theon, why are we down here?" She could hardly speak, unable to keep her voice from wavering.

"I am going running. Luka is taking care of Pen, and Axel has left. You have repeatedly proven you cannot be trusted to be left alone."

"I won't go anywhere," she pleaded, clawing at his arm as he released his grip on her elbow. "Please don't, Theon!"

But his shadows were peeling her off of him, dragging her away from him, shoving her to the cold floor.

"Theon, don't." Tears were streaming down her face, and all she could do was say the same thing over and over. "Please don't. Please don't make me stay down here."

He slowly lowered to a crouch before her, his emerald eyes chips of hard stone as he brushed her hair back from her face. Hope bubbled up when he stared at her, and then it shattered when he said, "I told you there would be harsher consequences. If only I'd known this was all I had to do from the beginning."

Then he was taking the stairs two at a time, the door banging shut behind him. His darkness went with him, and she was scrambling up the stairs. But the door was locked, and she was screaming as she pounded on it. She was stuck, trapped within these walls. No windows. No way out. And she could hardly get down air. Just like when Mother Cordelia would withhold air.

There was no one to hear her cries.

Theon had left.

Axel had left.

Luka had left.

Alone.

Completely alone.

This was why hope was pointless.

This was why she didn't bother caring about anything.

This was why she wished for death.

She stumbled back down the stairs, dropping to her knees as she ran her hands along the floor. She wasn't made to be kept inside. She needed to be out. She needed to be able to see the sky, feel the wind.

There had to be a way out, out, out.

But there wasn't.

There were no cracks in the marble floor. Her fingernails cracked and bled as she clawed at the stone walls, trying to find some place that she could dig. That she could do *something*.

But there was nothing.

Nothing but the lightning crackling at her fingertips.

Nothing but the glowing of her palms.

Nothing but light floating around her like twinkling mist.

Nothing but her fury as she tipped her head back and screamed, streaks of light bursting from her palms. Wine bottles shattered as she broke, shards of glass slicing into her skin as they exploded.

She didn't feel them.

She didn't feel anything as she crumpled to the floor, curled into herself, and began going through song lyrics.

One more second.

One more minute.

One more song.

41
THEON

His feet slammed against the pavement as he ran along the roads outside the Acropolis. He had no idea how long he'd been running, but he hadn't slowed when the storm had rolled in. He hadn't stopped to catch his breath when the first drops fell. He hadn't faltered when thunder cracked and lightning streaked across the sky.

He ran and ran, trying to outrun hearing Pen's cries of pain. Trying to outrun seeing her crumpled body. Trying to outrun the failure of Axel ending her misery when it should have been him. He was the one who was supposed to protect them, and yet he'd failed once again.

Sweat mixed with the rain dripping down his face. His phone kept ringing, the callers announced in his earbuds as he ran.

Luka.

Luka.

His mother.

Unknown caller.

Luka.

He ignored them all.

There wasn't even music playing. It was just silence. Just him and his thoughts.

Him and his failures.

Him and Caris's tears as he was forced to watch her be tortured for

Him and Cienna's wide eyes when he'd told her to run.

Him and Pen's pained wails as Eviana drove a blade into her gut.

Him and Axel's snarls of helpless rage as he ended Pen's life.

Him and Tessa's cries as she'd begged him not to leave her in the wine cellar.

It wasn't terribly small. She'd be fine.

Another crack of thunder had him second-guessing that final thought.

He'd had no choice. He couldn't stand to look at her knowing her actions had caused all of this failure, and he couldn't leave her alone. On the off chance his father returned, he'd warded the cellar as well as drawn a Mark to soundproof it. Unless his father went looking in the wine cellar, he wouldn't find her. He also wouldn't look in the wine cellar. It was beneath him to do his own dirty work.

That's why Eviana had done the torturing.

That's why Axel had done the killing.

So many failures.

His shoes splashed in puddles, cold water soaking his socks and shins as the rain continued to pour down, but he didn't stop. Five calls came though, one right after another. All of them from Luka. Then came a message that played through his earbuds:

Luka: *Fucker, answer your phone.*

When a call rang through again, he ignored it, turning in the opposite direction of the townhouse as lightning flashed, illuminating the night sky.

It was after midnight when he stepped into the foyer, water dripping off of him and pooling on the floor. The storm was still raging outside. He could only assume the Fae he'd locked in the wine cellar was raging too.

He shook his head, water droplets spraying. He was exhausted and more than ready to shower, have a drink, and sleep. In the morning, he'd have a clearer head to deal with Tessa. He'd be back in control.

"Luka?" he called out.

"In here."

Theon followed his voice to the kitchen to find him sitting at the island, a bottle before him with an empty glass.

Peeling off his drenched shirt, he tossed it to the floor. Luka glanced at it before he refilled his glass. "We don't have someone to clean up after us right now, asshole."

Theon flinched, Pen's lifeless face flashing in his mind again.

"Did you…?"

Luka nodded. "I have the ashes in a glass case in my room."

"Good," he said, swiping the bottle and tipping it to his mouth as he sat beside Luka.

"Where is she?" Luka asked.

Theon didn't need to ask who he was talking about.

"In the wine cellar."

Luka's sapphire eyes cut to the pantry before fixing on his liquor glass once more. "How long are you leaving her down there?"

"I can't look at her tonight."

Luka only nodded, understanding all the reasons those words were true.

Neither of them said anything for a long time, the minutes bleeding into an hour, then two. They took turns drinking from the bottle, Luka having abandoned his glass.

He was sliding the bottle across the counter when he finally broke the silence. "This will break her. She'll never forgive you for this."

Theon brought the bottle to his lips, tipping the last of the *agaveheart* down his throat. "I know."

He stood in the pantry, a mug of coffee clutched in his hand. He'd removed the soundproofing Mark, but there was no noise coming from the other side of the door. The sun had been up for at least an hour, the sky clear for once, and he'd been standing here.

Staring at a door.

Trying to figure out what he was going to find when he opened it.

The sound of footsteps made him glance at the doorway to find Luka holding his own mug of coffee. He leaned against the doorjamb, staring at Theon, who had returned to staring at the door.

"Have we heard from Axel?" Theon asked without looking at him.

"No. How long have you been standing here?"

"Ten minutes."

Luka took a drink from his mug.

"I had to do it," Theon said.

"I know."

"I didn't have a choice."

"I know."

"We need to prepare for the Emerging Ceremony."

"I know."

"Stop saying 'I know,'" Theon snapped.

Luka just took another drink of his coffee, then took Theon's mug when he held it out to him.

"I don't feel guilty about this," Theon said, reaching for the door handle.

"We don't have the luxury of guilt."

"No matter what state I find her in, this was worth it. She'll understand the gravity of the situation. I'll never have to do this again."

Luka didn't say it, but Theon knew what he was thinking— That from the very beginning he had said Tessa wasn't the one for this.

Last night had proved just how right he'd been all along.

With a harsh breath, Theon pulled the door open, finding the wine cellar pitch black. He hit the switch, but no light turned on. He flicked it a few more times, but there was nothing.

Had the storm done something? That didn't seem possible. Storms didn't interfere with the magic that powered their homes and buildings.

"Here." Luka tossed orbs of black flames above them. It didn't really illuminate anything, but the faint glow allowed them to at least make out the stairs.

Slowly, Theon started down, sticking close to the wall. "Tessa?"

But there was no answer. Only the strong odor of wine. If she was drunk down here...

Well, he couldn't really blame her. He'd locked her in a wine cellar for fuck's sake, knowing exactly what kind of panic it would send her into.

"Tessa," he called a little louder. "Tessa, answer—"

But he was cut off by the sound of something crunching under his shoes when he stepped off the last stair.

"What the...?"

He blinked as Luka produced more dragon fire to illuminate the entirety of the cellar. There was glass everywhere. Broken wine bottles. Shattered lights. Wine covered the floor, red liquid staining the empty wine racks where the alcohol had dripped down to pool on the floor.

And in the center of it all was Tessa.

She was curled on her side, her knees clutched to her chest, and her face buried in them. Her golden hair was a mess of knots, as if she'd been pulling on it, and it was stained the same color as the wine racks.

"Tessa," Theon breathed, unable to move as he stared down at her.

He'd known this would break her, but he still hadn't expected...this.

She hadn't made any movement or shown any sign that she knew they were there. She couldn't be...dead. He'd have felt the Source connection break. Besides, Fae could only be killed in so many ways, and death by glass or wine was not one of them.

"It has to be you and the bond," Luka said, his voice quiet and tense from beside him.

Nodding, Theon slowly approached her. When he reached her side, he used his shoes to brush aside glass so he could lower beside her. There was nothing he could do about the wine though, and he felt it soak through the knee of his pants.

"Tessa?"

When there was still nothing, he reached for her, touching her shoulder, then he yanked his hand back.

"Fuck!"

"What?" Luka demanded, immediately dropping down beside him.

"I got a...shock when I touched her."

"A shock?"

"Yes," Theon gritted out, shaking his hand. His fingers were still tingling. In fact, his entire arm was tingling.

"Can your power protect you?" Luka asked.

Gods, he hoped so.

With shadows coating his hand, he reached for her again, sighing in relief when he didn't receive another jolt from his Source.

"Tessa," he said softly. "Tessa, I need you to look at me."

Reaching for her hands, he tugged them from where they were wound around her legs. Once he had her untangled from herself, he rolled her onto her back. Her eyes were swollen, puffy from crying. Tear trails tracked through the wine staining her cheeks. Her entire face was covered in cuts, smears of blood mixing with the wine. She didn't look at him. If anything, she seemed to stare through him.

"Fuck," Theon cursed again, low under his breath this time. He reached for her, moving to lift her from the ground as he murmured, "Come on, little storm," but she suddenly moved.

Fast.

Far faster than she'd ever moved before.

She scrambled back from him, hissing as her palms were sliced open on the shattered glass.

"Tessa," Theon said in shock. "Don't do this. We need to get you cleaned up. The Emerging Ceremony is tonight."

"Tonight," she repeated, her voice completely void of any emotion.

"Yes. Tonight."

"It's the next day."

Fuck me, Theon thought, swiping a hand down his face. What had he been thinking doing this the night before the Emerging Ceremony?

He hadn't been. That was the fucking problem. He'd lost control completely.

Another failure to add to the list with the consequences staring back at him.

"Yes, Tessa. It's the next morning."

"And the Emerging Ceremony is tonight?"

"Yes."

"Oh."

Theon looked at Luka, not knowing what else to do.

"Tessa, do you need one of us to carry you?" Luka asked, getting up and taking a tentative step forward.

"No," she answered.

"Do you need us to help you up?"

"No."

But she made no move to stand on her own.

Theon pushed to his feet, sliding his hands into his pockets. "Tessa, you either need to get to your feet, or I'm going to have to entrance you."

"Don't," she said. It was stoic and calm, but her mannerisms were anything but as she clawed at the wall she was pressed against, clamoring to her feet.

"Tessa, you don't have shoes on. At least let me carry you up the stairs," he tried.

"No."

"You'll cut your feet up with all this glass. Look at your hands."

She lifted them before her face, turning them over as she studied them in the faint light. "I'm bleeding."

"I know, beautiful."

She was quiet, continuing to study her hands in the low light of the dragon fire. "You made me bleed," she murmured.

"I'm going to carry you up the stairs. As soon as we reach the top, I'll put you down, all right?"

She didn't object again, so Theon cautiously slid his arms behind her knees and shoulders, trying to avoid the cuts on her back. His shadows kept him from direct contact with her skin. Any exposed flesh was cut, blood and wine dried to her skin. The dress she'd worn to dinner was covered in small rips and tears from the glass and was sticky and wet from the alcohol.

What had happened down here?

As soon as they reached the top of the stairs, he set her down as promised, but the bond snarled internally, reaching for her as she leaned against the wall. Or maybe that was his magic wanting to touch her again. Sometimes the bond and his gifts were so intertwined, he couldn't tell them apart anymore.

"We need to get the glass out, and then I can heal as much as I can before you bathe," Theon said.

"I can do it."

"You can...remove the glass from your feet and hands?"

"Yes."

"But it would be faster if we helped," Theon said.

Tessa shrugged, looking at something over his shoulder.

"We don't even need to go upstairs right now," Theon went on. "We can clean out the glass in the kitchen."

She pushed off the wall without a word, walking gingerly to the kitchen island where she pulled herself onto a stool.

"Get what we need," he murmured to Luka.

He could use his power to remove the glass, but having to heal all of those cuts would drain him even more. She needed to look perfect tonight, and he wasn't about to take any blood from her. Not after what he'd done to her last night.

"Do you want something to eat?" he asked her, leaning against the opposite counter.

"No."

"Something to drink?"

"No."

"Do I..." He swiped a hand down his face, sighing. "Do I need to heal a hangover?"

That had her dragging her eyes to him. It was the first time she'd looked directly at him, and he sucked in a breath. He could finally see her clearly in the light and that was violet ringing her grey eyes. Not around the pupils like it had before, but around the outer edges of her irises.

And it wasn't fading.

"I did not drink any wine," she replied in that same monotone voice. "I know I have my vices, but even I am above lapping wine off the floor like a hound."

"I didn't mean to imply that's what you did," he replied, his fingers clutching at the counter behind him, grateful she was speaking. "I'm just trying to figure out what happened."

"You locked me in the wine cellar."

"I—"

"You locked me in a wine cellar, despite knowing that's how I was handled at the Estate. Despite knowing I do not like enclosed spaces. Despite knowing that it would—" She stopped abruptly, those violet rings glowing brighter. Her voice had risen with every word, but when she spoke again, it was once again void of feeling. "You locked me in the wine cellar."

"How did the wine end up on the floor?"

"The bottles broke."

"You spent the entire time in the dark?"

"Was it dark?"

"The lights were shattered, Tessa."

"I didn't notice."

"You didn't...notice?" he repeated, perplexed.

"Shadows are cunning, don't you think? The light doesn't realize the shadows are circling until there's nowhere for them to go. It's either join the shadows, or drown in the darkness."

He didn't know what to say to that.

She'd fallen silent again, starting to pick at the cuts on her arm, and

Theon moved forward, closing his hand around her fingers. "I'll take care of it, Tessa."

"Once again, I need tending to because of you," she murmured.

And while it sounded more like she was speaking to herself than him, he still felt the words in the depths of his being. Another person he'd promised to protect, only to fail.

He looked down at where he held her hand. Her nails were broken, cracked and bleeding.

"What happened to your hands, Tessa?"

"I couldn't find a way out. There were no windows. No cracks. No where to dig..."

She trailed off as Theon realized she had tried to *claw* her way out of the cellar.

Luka reappeared, two forceps in one hand along with a few towels, but he also had a robe.

"You should get out of that dress, little one," he said.

Without a word, she slipped from the stool and began sliding the thin straps of the dress down her arms. Theon started to object, but Luka had already stepped from the room, leaving them alone once more.

"You were going to change in front of him?" he asked tightly, holding her steady when she stepped from the dress.

"He's seen me in every state imaginable. What difference does nudity make at this point?"

She turned, reaching for the robe where Luka had set it on the counter.

"Tessa, there's glass in your back. We'll need access to it."

"So I shouldn't put this on?"

"Yes, but—" He pushed out another harsh breath. "Maybe slip it on backwards?"

She did so without another word, pushing the sleeves up as she climbed back onto the stool. Theon called to Luka, and for the next hour, the two of them pulled shards of glass from her flesh. She didn't utter a word. She didn't whimper or cry out. She didn't flinch or wince.

She did nothing.

She *was* nothing.

When they finished, Theon stayed a step behind as she made her way up the stairs. Luka had found slippers for her so she didn't leave bloody footprints behind, and he stayed downstairs, attempting to get a hold of

Axel. If Axel didn't show up at the Emerging Ceremony, last night would look like a godsdamn party compared to what their father would do. His brother had to know that.

Tessa had taken a few steps into their room when she stopped so suddenly, Theon nearly ran into her.

"Tessa?"

"I have training. With Luka," she said, turning and heading to the closet.

"Training? No, Tessa," he replied, reaching out and gently gripping her elbow to stop her.

She *snarled* at him, wrenching her arm from his grip.

What the fuck?

He took a step back, blinking at her, but she was already back to staring at nothing.

"Tessa, there's no training today," he said carefully.

"But I need to learn to protect myself."

"Not today. You need to rest, to heal," he said, his mouth suddenly dry as he realized exactly what his actions had done last night.

"I can train," she insisted, the violet flaring brighter in her eyes.

"I know you can," he said quickly. "But Luka has to prepare for the Emerging Ceremony. We all do. There's no training on ceremony days."

"That's tradition?" she asked, her head tilting eerily to the side as he felt the weight of her penetrating stare.

"Yes, that's tradition. Everyone rests and prepares."

"Oh."

There was a tense silence before he said, "You need to bathe."

"Because you made me bleed."

"No, I..." He cleared his throat. "Yes, because I made you bleed."

She seemed to accept this answer as she moved to the bathroom, letting the robe slip from her body. He followed, mainly because he didn't trust her by herself. Definitely not now.

"Do you want help?" he asked, watching her adjust the shower temperature.

She only sent him a flat look over her bare shoulder.

Right.

So he stood in the doorway, watching as she unfeelingly wiped dried blood and wine from her skin. As she methodically washed her hair, letting the shampoo run down her skin when she rinsed it out. As she continued to stare at nothing with every movement.

As he let the reality of what he'd done sink in.

She had been trying.

These last weeks she had been trying to give in to the bond. She had been trying to obey his commands. She had been trying when she hung on to everything he said about the kingdoms, their history, and how they were run. He'd known all along she hadn't been prepared for this. She didn't understand the politics of the kingdoms. She didn't understand just how far things would go, how low others would sink to gain an upper hand. How far *he* would go to get what he wanted.

She'd been trying when she'd force herself to not fidget at the dining table, to follow his commands, to be what she wasn't prepared to be.

She'd been trying when she agreed to a Bargain, agreeing to pretend to be what he needed because she didn't know if she could actually *be* what he needed.

She'd been trying when she let herself try to enjoy time on a Chaosphere field, letting them see a side of her they hadn't experienced. When she'd let herself laugh and let him kiss her silly under the sun.

She'd been trying when she'd told them why she'd run to the river a few nights ago, hoping he wouldn't do the same thing to her. Hoping he'd understand. Trusting him not to be the same oppressive thing to her.

She'd been trying to care when no one had truly cared for her in so long, she'd stopped caring about anything.

She'd been trying to learn, trying to understand, trying to do what was expected of her. She'd been trying, and all he'd done was tell her it wasn't enough. That *she* wasn't enough. That he needed her to try harder. Needed her to be more. Needed her to give and give and give.

And now she was this.

She'd stopped trying.

She'd stopped trying to be anything but the unpredictable, wild thing she was.

It wasn't her fault. Everyone had demanded something of her she simply didn't know how to manifest. Instead of teaching her to harness her wildness, she'd learned to simply survive with it.

She'd repeatedly told them she had more self-control than they realized. He hadn't understood what she meant until now.

She was going to emerge stronger than any other Fae. She would be stronger than many of the Legacy in Devram.

And she'd stopped trying to control her chaos.

42
THEON

"Still no word from Axel?" Theon asked, pacing in the kitchen.

"He'll be there," Luka said, leaning against the counter. He glanced at the empty doorway. "Truthfully, I'm more worried about Tessa."

The lounge was in shambles from Axel last night, so Theon had left her sitting in the dining room. She'd slept all afternoon.

No. He couldn't say that. She'd lain in their bed, staring at nothing all afternoon.

When he'd told her it was time to get ready, she'd wordlessly done just that. Cosmetics. Hair. The other Fae would all be dressed in basic beige attire— loose linen pants and shirts for the males, simple dresses for the females. But not the Sources. They'd be dressed in the color of their kingdom, which is why Tessa was wearing a black dress. The straps tied at her shoulders, the neckline dipping low between her breasts while the remainder draped along her hips to the floor. She'd twisted her hair half up, securing it with a clip in the shape of a black flower.

"Has she said anything?" Luka asked when Theon remained silent.

"Yes, she's spoken words," he retorted, adjusting his sleeves despite the fact they were perfectly straight.

"But has she *said* anything?"

Yes. No. Too much and not enough.

"We're going to get through tonight, and then tomorrow we set about fixing the mess this has all become," Theon said.

"Is she prepared for tonight?"

"I was hoping Axel would be here before we told her everything."

Luka sent him an exasperated look. "Axel is going to meet us at the Pantheon. He's not coming back here. Not today."

Theon knew that, but he'd still held out hope.

"Fine," he sighed, rapping his knuckles on the countertop before exiting the kitchen. He found Tessa right where he'd left her, and her eyes tracked them warily when Luka followed him. Taking a seat in a chair beside her, he said, "We need to discuss tonight."

Her features remained impassive. Apathetic. Unsettling. "Of course. Expectations."

"Not…that," Theon replied, rubbing at his brow with his thumb and forefinger. "Tonight everyone will be focused on the Fae. Not the Lords and Ladies. Not the heirs and Sources. They will take notice of strength and power as the Fae receive their gifts. I will need your help."

"My help," she repeated, and Theon didn't know how to read her blank expression or the lack of emotion in her words.

"We have done our research, but you still know the Fae better than I do. If we see any that appear to be a good fit for Arius Kingdom, I am counting on you to provide me with additional information about them."

"A good fit," she repeated, her head tilting and golden hair slipping over her shoulder.

He itched to brush it back.

"Yes, so we can make informed decisions when the time comes," Theon replied.

"Why would you think I have insight into any of them?"

"Because you are Fae."

She blinked. "Despite what you apparently think, we are not all the same."

"I know that."

"I will have very little insight," she continued as though he hadn't spoken. "I was a social pariah. No one wanted to be around me as I— How did you put it? Only seem to create chaos wherever I go. Which was fine, I suppose. There's only room for one in small spaces. Otherwise it gets too crowded."

"Tessa, I know we have some things to talk about—"

"Do we?"

The violet flared in her eyes, and Theon glanced at Luka. Those violet rings appeared to be a permanent thing now, and he didn't know how to explain it. The only other being he'd encountered who had violet eyes was Cienna, and she definitely wasn't Fae.

Theon cleared his throat. One thing at a time. Tonight, they get through the Emerging Ceremony. Tomorrow, they could focus on other things.

"The newly Selected Sources will be last to have their power rituals performed," Theon said, choosing to ignore her question. "And since you are an Arius Source—"

"I will be last," she said in understanding.

"Yes, and we expect there to be some upheaval when your element is revealed."

"You said the other kingdoms would believe you planned this."

"Yes."

"And now they will believe you have kept me a secret like you have kept Luka's true bloodline a secret."

"Yes," he said again, relieved that she seemed to grasp the gravity of the situation.

Then her lips tipped up in a terrifying grin. "You've already made me bleed, Theon. What's wrong with a little more bloodshed?"

Luka coughed from where he was standing nearby, nearly choking on the drink he'd taken.

"Tessa," Theon said slowly, "we are trying to avoid bloodshed tonight."

"Oh."

She sounded disappointed in that statement and that was fucking unnerving.

Theon cleared his throat. "Yes, we want as little drama as possible tonight, but I expect there to be various reactions. Not only from the other kingdoms, but from my father as well."

"Will he draw blood again tonight?"

"Not in front of everyone," Theon answered, observing her closely.

She only hummed in response.

"I expect the brunt of his anger to be turned on me," he continued when she said nothing else. "Luka will stay with me, and Axel will retrieve you."

"Axel isn't here."

"He will be at the Pantheon. He will find you."

"Ah, the Tracking Mark," she said, pinning him with her violet-grey stare.

Theon shifted under it, wondering if she was intentionally making him nervous about how tonight would go. He couldn't have that. He couldn't risk yet another plan going to shit.

He couldn't handle another failure so soon.

Standing, he straightened to his full height so she was forced to tip her head back to look at him. Pushing past the wrongness he felt about it, he reached out and took her chin. She didn't react. Not even a flinch. "There is much at stake tonight, Tessa, but more than that, you are in more danger than usual. I have taken every precaution to protect you."

"How has that worked out in the past?" she asked, genuine curiosity in her tone.

"Tonight will be better."

She smiled, a coy and knowing thing, and he felt a sharp tingle at his fingertips.

A small spark of energy.

And then he felt the tug of the bond. He'd been keeping it muted all day, giving her space. Trying to let her...come out of whatever this was.

But it wasn't him who'd freed the bond at that moment.

It was her.

"This way, my Lord," the Fae male said, turning and guiding them to their private viewing box. It was up several flights of stairs, the ruling families all having private spaces that ringed the arena below.

Tessa was silent, following a step behind him and Luka. Axel was usually beside him so Luka could walk with her, but Axel still hadn't shown up. He'd tried calling him all day. Luka had only said it served him right for not answering his phone calls last night.

Dick.

When the Fae opened the door to their viewing deck, Theon was relieved to find they were the first to arrive. His father would be here soon, and if Axel wasn't here before him, Theon wasn't entirely sure how he was going to explain that absence yet.

"Your vials are atop the cabinet should you need them tonight," the Fae escort said. "Your private server will be along shortly, but in the meantime, can I get you anything else?"

"No. Leave us," Theon said shortly, already turning away from him.

"What are the vials for?" Tessa asked when the door had clicked shut behind them.

She seemed to glide to the balcony railing, peering down at the arena where the emergings would take place. Five separate stations would usher the Fae through until only the Sources remained. Then a center stage would be erected. She wore flat silver sandals with her dress, clearly more comfortable in them than she was in heels, and all Theon could think as she'd slipped them on earlier that night was how similar they were to fucking flip-flops. Fancier and detailed, sure, but the premise was the same.

Theon crossed the room to the cabinet in the corner, picking up one of five vials. Black shimmering liquid swirled inside.

"Each kingdom is given five vials," he explained. "We can use them at any time throughout the year to lay claim to a Fae before the official Selection night at the end of the Selection Year."

She glanced back over her shoulder. "How does that work?"

"If a kingdom wants to claim a Fae, we toss a vial."

"What if more than one kingdom wants them?"

"If multiple vials are thrown at the same time, there is a panel held to determine which kingdom gets them."

"Does that happen often?"

"There may be a few tonight if strong enough powers are manifested. But most of the time, we wait until later in the year, watching the various trainings and trials."

She didn't say anything else, turning back to look out over the arena. He glanced at Luka, who only shrugged, slipping off his suit coat and draping it over a chair. Neither of them had bothered with ties tonight.

"Do you want a drink, Tessa?" Theon asked, and that had her turning completely to face him. She leaned back on her elbows against the onyx railing, studying him.

Then she smirked. "Wine would be lovely."

Theon narrowed his eyes, but nodded. "One glass," he warned.

"I won't even lap it off the floor," she retorted.

"Get that out of your system before my father shows up," he replied, but internally he was sighing in relief. This was the most snark and emotion she'd shown all day.

"I know how to act, Master," she replied, moving to one of the plush chairs and sinking into it.

"If you wish to address me as something else in front of others, that can be arranged."

"Hmmm, like what?"

"My Lord, your Grace—"

She snorted a laugh. "No. You are neither of those things. Master is suitable for now."

"Tessa, I understand we are not on good terms at the moment, but you really cannot act this way tonight. Please tell me you understand that."

She pushed back to her feet, sauntering over to him. A hand landed on his abdomen before she smoothed it up his chest. "This beautiful thing happens," she mused.

Theon swallowed thickly as her fingers touched the skin at his throat, continuing to his jaw. "What thing?"

"When a person finally accepts they are nothing," she continued. "It's a freedom, really."

"You are not—"

"Shh," she hushed, placing a finger against his lips. "When you accept you are nothing, it frees you from caring."

"Tessa—"

"And when you're already nothing, you can really become anything."

The door was thrown open at that moment, Axel strolling in, a glass of alcohol already in hand.

"Where the fuck have you been?" Theon snarled.

"Out with the depraved," Axel replied darkly, his eyes stalling on Tessa. "What happened to you?"

"Theon made me bleed," she said simply.

"What the fuck?" Axel said, the accusation heavy in his tone.

"I didn't—" Theon sighed. "It's a long story, and one you would know if you would have been around at all today."

"I had things to tend to," he replied, moving to the railing and slipping a hand into his pocket.

"Like what? What could possibly have been more important than the ceremony today?"

Axel took a drink, smacking his lips as he pulled the mirror from his pocket. "Cienna made contact."

"Fuck," Luka cursed, stepping forward.

"Who is this Cienna you all keep cryptically mentioning?" Tessa asked, a Fae handing her a glass of wine. Luka had placed their order before Axel showed up. "Thank you," she said with a nod to the Fae, the server appearing startled at the address.

Theon waited until she was gone, and the door had shut again before he answered her question. Keeping her in the dark until she'd accepted this bond had clearly been a terrible idea. He'd thought it wouldn't matter. That she'd accept the bond, her place, and trust him enough not to care about his sins or the sins of the realm. He'd thought the bond would solve all his problems, not create bigger ones he didn't know how to fix.

So here he was, answering her questions as much as he could, hoping she'd gain a better understanding of the politics at play. Of his father. Of the inner workings of the kingdoms. Of all of it.

"Cienna is a Witch," Theon said. "She is the Witch who helped Luka and I with the Guardian Bond. She's in hiding in the Underground."

"In hiding?"

"As you can imagine, my father was unhappy when I stole his Guardian from him. Many lost their lives to his wrath, but he is determined to hunt down Cienna and make her pay for helping us."

Tessa took a sip of wine. "So you routinely fuck over others to get what you desire?"

Axel and Luka went still, but Theon smiled. The same dark smirk she'd given him earlier. "I do what needs to be done, and I show no remorse."

"Ah, but do you feel it?" she asked, a brow arching.

He stepped towards her, taking her chin in his hand. "If you're asking if I feel remorse about what I did last night, my answer is no."

"Because you do what needs to be done," she said, holding his gaze.

"Yes."

"To claim what is yours."

"Yes."

"So there is no remorse over Pen?"

Shadows appeared, swirling around his fingers where he gripped her chin. "Careful, Tessa."

"Or what? You'll lock me in a wine cellar? Or perhaps you'll go for something smaller this time? A cabinet without room to even sit properly, perhaps? That was Mother Cordelia's favorite."

Was she serious? The Estate Mother would keep her in a fucking cupboard? Cordelia had failed to mention that in their discussion. What else had she conveniently left out? But the challenging look in Tessa's eyes had him gritting out, "Please test that assumption, and take note of the results."

She smirked, lifting the wine glass back to her lips and draining the entire thing.

He wasn't sure how to react to this new attitude of hers, but the bond and his magic were both taking notice. Both bristling at the challenge in her eyes.

And for some fucked up reason, all he could think about was when he'd asked her if this was the way it would always be, if it would always be a constant battle with her, and her answer being yes.

Before he could respond, the door opened again, his parents striding in with Eviana. Tessa's entire demeanor instantly changed, and she stepped away from Theon. She set her empty wineglass to the side as she bowed her head to his father. Demure. Controlled.

In short, the perfect Source.

Maybe she'd been paying more attention than Theon had realized.

Theon said a tight greeting to his father before pressing a quick kiss to his mother's cheek, Axel doing the same. Drinks were ordered, and soon enough, the Emerging Ceremony was underway. His father paid little attention, constantly moving in and out of their box to visit others. He wouldn't care much until the Sources' emergings happened.

Which was fine. The space was less tense when he was gone. His mother had left an hour ago. Theon was certain he wouldn't see her again until the Sources were up as well.

"Do you know him?" Axel asked Tessa.

She stood between them, Luka to Theon's left. For the most part, she'd been quiet, not wanting to be caught acting inappropriately by his father. But Theon had watched her more than he'd watched the happenings below. He'd watched the small frown appear when a Fae she clearly knew emerged with a decent power level. He'd heard her small scoff when another one had displayed a strong earth element. And he'd felt her tense as the Fae below was escorted to a ring.

Theon recognized him from the phone call. He was one of the two that were involved together.

Tessa cleared her throat before she said, "Yes. That is Corbin."

"Which element is he predicted to have?"

"Water, but he is brilliant with technology," she murmured, engrossed in the ritual taking place.

Her hands were curled tightly around the railing, and Theon could see the slight tremor in them. He wanted to touch her, knowing the bond would ease that anxiety, but for all he knew, his touch would also send her over an edge.

The priestess stepped forward, and Corbin lifted his arm. Her scion pressed to his skin, tracing atop a Mark that was already there. A Mark the Fae couldn't see, not without the blood of a god in their veins. The moment she lifted the scion, a burst of water had the male's clothes soaked as he coughed and spluttered. Water element. Just as his assessments had predicted, according to Tessa.

He was escorted down and sent to receive the identifying marking on his wrist next to his estate marking. Tessa had relaxed next to him, a sigh of relief escaping her. What had she been so worried about?

The ceremonies continued, Theon noting a few Fae he wanted to keep an eye on. He watched as a few more of her friends went through the ritual. The female from the phone call produced water as well, while Lange emerged with air.

They were nearing the last few Fae when Axel straightened. "Do you know her?"

Tessa had started pacing back and forth, becoming increasingly fidgety as the night wore on. Theon couldn't decide if it was nerves or if it was the lack of windows in the arena. She paused now, glancing down to where a brown-skinned female was being led to a ring. Even from here, Theon could tell she was pretty with bright amber eyes and thick black hair that wound in tight curls.

"Her name is Kat," Tessa answered, resuming her pacing.

"Like the animal?" Axel asked, his head tilting as he watched the female below.

"No," Tessa said, her annoyance heavy. "Her full name is Katya. We call her Kat."

"Do you know what element she is predicted to emerge with?"

"No, but I'm sure we'll know any moment."

Axel sipped on his drink. "Just for clarity's sake, you still pissed at me, baby doll?"

"Furious," she replied, sounding anything but. The word was cheerful, and why did that only increase Theon's anxiety?

Axel hummed an acknowledgement, watching as the Fae below removed her sandals and stepped onto the platform. "We need to claim her," he said suddenly.

"Repeat that," Theon replied, completely dumbfounded.

"Claim her. Now," Axel said, his eyes fixed on the scene below.

"We can't claim her. We don't even know her element," Theon argued.

"I am telling you to claim her. Luka, grab a vial."

"Have you lost your godsdamn mind?" Theon asked. "Father will be livid."

"I'll deal with it," Axel replied, hands gripping the railing. "Hurry."

"No," Theon said in disbelief. "I know we are all dealing with the events of last night, but—"

"No!" Luka was growling, a hand stretched out as though to catch something.

But he was too late. There was nothing they could do as Axel's shadows threw a vial over the railing. It shattered in the air, black mist exploding from it as Axel pointed to the Fae to claim her.

"What did you just do?" Theon demanded.

"I would also like to know the answer to that question."

They all spun, finding his father in the doorway. Shadows were swirling around him, and Eviana's eyes were wide in shock.

"I..." Axel faltered, glancing back over his shoulder as if he just realized the magnitude of his actions.

Theon's heart was racing, his stomach dropping. If this Fae didn't show some measure of worth, the consequences for Axel would be dire. Even from here, he could hear the murmurings of the other Legacy at the random claiming of an ordinary Fae.

Until Luka said, "That's not possible."

They all turned back to the arena to find that her element had manifested.

And it was fire.

Flames of orange and red, blue and yellow danced at her fingertips. Her eyes were wide in shock as the female stood frozen, looking between the fire at her command and up at the balcony of the kingdom that had claimed her.

"A fire element?" his father breathed, the excitement heavy in his tone.

The confused murmurings from around the arena had shifted to outrage at Arius Kingdom having claimed a fire elemental. There would be no panel. No other kingdom had thrown their vial at the same moment Axel had. She had been claimed fairly under the Accords.

"How?" Theon asked in shock. "Anala Kingdom would never let one go to another."

"Doesn't matter," his father answered. "She is already ours. Axel, go make sure she stays that way."

Axel said nothing, disappearing out the door. His father moved to the railing, eyes sweeping over the expanse.

"This is a good thing for us," he said.

"It is," Theon agreed, still trying to process how such a thing had happened.

"This is a good thing for you," his father added.

"For our kingdom as a whole."

"But for you specifically. The Fae will be a suitable replacement if your current Source is found inadequate tonight."

Theon stiffened, but beside him, Tessa showed no reaction. In his spiral after Pen's death, he had completely forgotten about the agreement he'd made with his father. He wasn't concerned. Her power levels alone were going to be enough, let alone when her power fully manifested. But did she realize that? He should have reassured her. He should have explained why he'd even agreed to such a thing, but she didn't appear worried. No, she looked...impassive. About it all.

A knock on the door sounded before it was pushed open, a Pantheon sentinel on the other side.

"My Lords," he greeted with a bow of his head. "I am here to escort your Source down for her ritual."

Tessa straightened, glancing at Theon and waiting for permission to go with him.

"I will accompany you," Theon said.

The sentinel's brow furrowed. "I assure you that is not necessary. We go straight to the holding rooms outside the arena."

"She has already been attacked once since our arrival this week. I will accompany her, and it is not up for debate."

"Of course, my Lord," the sentinel capitulated, stepping to the side.

Theon's hand fell to the small of Tessa's back, and he didn't miss the small smirk that pulled at his father's lips.

They followed the sentinel down the stairs and along a passage until he stopped outside a glass door. "Each Source has their own warded holding area. She cannot leave and only a priestess or Pantheon sentinel can enter."

Theon almost huffed a laugh at the idea of wards keeping Tessa contained.

"I will be taking a private moment with her," Theon replied, ushering Tessa into the room. The door fell shut, and he sent a sheet of shadows to cover the glass.

She had moved to the center of the room, her hands clasped in front of her.

"Are you all right?" he asked.

Her head tilted to the side. "Why wouldn't I be?"

"I assumed you would be nervous, and this room is rather small."

She smiled humorlessly. "Bigger than some wine cellars."

He bit the inside of his cheek to keep from snapping back at her. Inhaling deeply, he said, "You know the agreement with my father was to try to deescalate the situation last night, right? That will not happen. Your power levels will be more than enough."

She shrugged. "I understand where my value lies, but even if that were not the case, I do not care if I live or if I face death."

Theon was fairly certain his heart stopped for the briefest of moments at her words, and he found himself directly in front of her, gripping her face in his hands. "You may not care right now, but *I* do."

"Of course you do," she replied calmly. "You're the one who gets to have all the power."

"That's not—"

"Do you remember the Chaosphere game on the way here?" she asked suddenly.

He blinked a few times before he said, "Of course."

"Do you remember kissing me there?"

"Every day."

"You were going to ask something of me."

"I was," he agreed, his thumb swiping along her cheek.

"What was it?"

He searched those hauntingly beautiful new eyes, memorizing the feel of her soft skin beneath his palms. "I was going to ask you to not let me kiss you again until you were ready to admit this is more than a bond. Because I knew..." He swallowed as she just stared back at him, no emotion filling her eyes. His voice held a thread of defeat when he said, "Because I knew the next time I kissed you, it wouldn't be enough. That I'd want more. That I'd want it all. Because you have become a *need*, little storm."

He waited. Waited for her to react. Waited for her to say something. Waited for her to acknowledge what he'd just said in some way.

He wasn't expecting her to push up onto her toes, but he didn't hesitate to bend to meet her lips. The kiss was intoxicating, her tongue swiping gently against his, and the bond shuttered in relief.

Or maybe that was his soul.

He pulled back first, looking into violet-grey eyes that were still dark with her secrets. Brushing his thumb along her bottom lip, he rasped out, "I will come for you. After."

She nodded, her features slightly flushed from the kiss.

"Does knowing that change anything?" he asked.

She stepped back from him, his hands slipping from her face. She intertwined her fingers in front of her once more as she answered, "No."

43
TESSA

The room wasn't small. In fact, it was probably comparable to her small room in Theon's suite back at Arius House. There weren't any windows, but the door was what made her feel trapped. No way out. Everything in here was smooth beige marble. Flat. Dull. Nothing to occupy her mind.

Nothing but her thoughts.

Theon had just left, and now she stood in the center of the room. Alone. Just like she'd been last night. Just like she'd been nearly her entire life. But maybe that was all right. Maybe alone was fine. When you were alone, there was no reason to trust anyone. No opportunity to let someone hurt you.

No room to allow someone in, only to be shoved into a cellar.

She slowly made her way to the wall and began dragging her fingers along the cool expanse, humming one of the stupid songs from Axel's playlist. She kicked off her sandals, wanting to feel the cold floor on her bare feet as she made pass after pass around the room.

Fingers dragging.

Throat humming.

Lips still buzzing from the kiss with Theon.

I was going to ask you not to let me kiss you again until you were ready to admit this is more than a bond.

He was right.

This was more than a bond; she just hadn't quite figured out what that meant yet.

She'd realized that as she'd lain on the floor of that wine cellar. They were more than Source and Master, Fae and Legacy. They were more than two people connected by a bargain and a bond. They were more than, but more than what?

The door opened, a sentinel saying gruffly, "They are ready for the Sources."

All the sentinels were Legacy. Gods forbid a Fae was tasked with guarding this sacred place. No, they were only good enough to breed and bleed.

Bleed.

Theon had made her bleed.

Her hand fell to her side, and she took a step towards the door, but the sentinel cleared his throat. "Your shoes."

Right.

Shoes.

She hated shoes.

She'd stopped humming, but she was still going through song lyrics in her head as she followed the sentinel down the hall. Not one of Axel's songs though.

Control the uncontrollable; Or to fury they both lose. Life must give; And Death must take. But Fate requires more.

She was jolted from her thoughts when they stepped through heavy wood doors and into the arena, the noise drowning out all other sounds. Excited Fae were one floor up, discussing their newly awakened power. Of course, they'd all been given black bands to wear on their wrists to keep that power muted until they learned to control it.

Uncontrolled power was dangerous.

Common Legacy filled the next levels, followed by the more elite. At the top, six private boxes ringed the arena. She glanced up, her gaze immediately connecting with Theon's. For all intents and purposes, he looked like the cold Heir of Endings he was destined to be.

He'd been the end of something all right.

But his hands were resting on the railing, and his posture was rigid, not the relaxed aloofness of indifference he usually flaunted. He nodded at her, Luka on one side of him, his father on the other. Cressida was there, and Axel had also returned.

Where was Kat? Hadn't Axel gone to make sure she was... Well, not all right because they didn't care about that, but to make sure she had been kept safe from the other kingdoms?

She didn't have time to contemplate it any longer. The dramatics of the Sources' powers emerging began with Sasha being led with fanfare to the center of the arena.

Tessa watched as she emerged with air. As Jasper revealed the same, and Maxson manifested water. Dade had sand and leaves swirling around him, confirming the expected earth element, and Gatlan, of course, produced fire, just like his Mistress. No one expected anything less.

Not until her.

The entire arena fell quiet when she was ushered to the center platform, slipping off her delicate sandals before she stepped up onto it. Her black dress swirled around her ankles, the material light and cool against her overheated skin. Stealing a quick glance up, she found Axel taking small steps to the exit. Because he was supposed to protect her. She found Valter leaning eagerly forward, his eyes narrowed. She found Luka in a defensive stance, the same one he'd been making her stand in for hours all week long.

And she found Theon, a mixture of anticipation and dread on his face. She felt the cord in her chest reaching for him, seeking comfort, but she felt the *thing* in her soul reaching for him too, wanting something much darker.

The priestess stepped forward, and Tessa started to lift her arm. But the sound of multiple gasps had both her and the priestess turning. The other priestesses who stood around the arena were all bowing their heads. The sentinels were standing at attention, and a hooded figure was making its way towards her. Two large wolves flanked them. One was a dark charcoal grey. The other was a shade of grey so light, it appeared almost silver. That one was the one she recognized as its bright eyes fell on her. It was the same wolf who had emerged from the trees right before the vampyres had attacked her.

"Your grace," the priestess said when the figure neared. "I was unaware you would be attending tonight's ceremonies."

The figure said nothing, only lifted an arm. Even their hand was hidden in the long sleeve of their cloak as the priestess held out the black scion. When the figure had taken it, she bowed once more before stepping down from the platform, retreating to the other priestesses and leaving Tessa alone with them.

They came closer, and she took a step back. Her eyes flitted to Theon, who was gripping the railing and staring in shock. Did he know who this figure was?

Then her gaze snagged on Dex on the level just above the arena floor. His expression was dark, his eyes narrowed as he watched the figure come to a stop in front of her.

The figure's hood was deep and pulled down so far, there was no way to see their face. It was completely concealed in the darkness of their hood. They reached out, a gloved hand appearing from the sleeve. It wasn't small and delicate, leading her to guess it was a male who gently grasped her forearm. He said nothing as he appeared to study her arm for a long moment before he twisted it slightly to look at the Mark on the back of her hand.

"So foolish," they murmured, and the voice was definitely male and somehow familiar.

He said nothing else as he brought the tip of the scion to her forearm, beginning to draw a Mark. She watched in fascination as he drew an inverted triangle.

And the *thing* inside her sat up in excitement.

Stretching.

Yawning.

Seeking.

Then he began drawing a star beneath the triangle, and her skin was buzzing with energy that needed out. She was hot and cold and her entire body was vibrating as she forced herself to remain still. Was it supposed to be like this? No one had told her. No one had prepared her. She was just expected to know so many godsdamn things, and she knew nothing.

The male didn't seem to notice when she started fidgeting, shifting from foot-to-foot. She was pretty sure none of the other Sources had taken this long.

He was marking a second star into her skin when he said, "Do you know why I like storms?"

The question was so random, it distracted her from whatever was happening in her soul. But she didn't know if she was supposed to speak. None of the other Fae had spoken during their ritual.

He didn't appear to care if she answered as he moved onto a third star. "Because it reminds us that even chaos needs to scream sometimes. That even with all the magic and power among the realms and between the stars, even with technology and all the tools we have at our disposal, some things are, in fact, uncontrollable."

Gods, his voice. Where had she heard it?

The wolves that were standing on either side of him began to whine, inching closer to her. Again, the male seemed unconcerned.

He was drawing the final line of the third star when he lifted his head. She could feel his stare from beneath the hood as he said, "A storm is coming."

And when he lifted the scion from her skin, light flared. Blindingly bright light emanated from her skin, glowing like sunlight. But that's not what had the entire arena in an uproar.

That would be the light crackling at her fingertips, flaring out and creating cracks in the platform she was standing on. Lightning striking the balconies and causing chunks of marble to crumble and fall.

That would be the water that was falling from above, a downpour of rain inside the Pantheon.

That would be the two wolves howling and circling around her as the hooded male disappeared into the crowd.

That would be her magic.

Impulsive as it struck out, another crack created in its wake.

Reckless as rain pelted against her skin.

Wild as air ripped through the arena like the winds of a tempest.

That would be the power that told the realm she wasn't Fae at all.

"Tessa!"

Her name was being yelled and carried away by the chaos of the storm. She could only stand there as her magic spiraled, devouring whatever it pleased, relishing in the freedom of being set free.

"Tessa!"

She blinked, rain drops clinging to her lashes, and Axel was standing before her. His black hair was plastered to his head, his suit clinging to his frame. Shadows also clung to him, clearly guarding and protecting him, but tendrils reached for her. She lifted her hand, light coiled at her fingertips, sparking with violet streaks of energy as it tentatively reached for Axel's magic.

But Axel was suddenly yanking his darkness back. "No, Tessa. This isn't the time to experiment." Her head tilted, and he swiped a hand down his face. "Fuck, Tessa. Stay with me, baby doll. I know your magic is calling. I know what it feels like to get lost to so much power, but we need to get you somewhere safe. Can you focus, Tessa? Just for a bit. Until Theon can come for you."

Theon.

His name made her blink, the bond in her chest seeming to gasp as if it'd been choking. Tessa shook her head, trying to clear her thoughts as she studied her hands.

"That's it, Tessa," Axel coaxed, a shadow-coated hand reaching for her. "Take my hand. Let's get out of here."

"Where are we going to go?" Her voice was that same dark thing it had been in the training room a few days ago.

"I know a place. Come on, baby doll."

"Where is Kat?" she asked suddenly.

"She's safe. Tessa, we need to—"

But he was cut off when four sentinels approached them, only to be thrown across the arena by a gust of air from her.

"Glad it was them this time," Axel muttered, but then his emerald gaze snapped back to hers. "Tessa, your magic trusts me. Don't you see? It's letting me near, but keeping others away. You can trust me, Tessa."

"I'm mad at you."

"I know, but we'll figure it out. We'll figure all this out."

He held out his hand again, and she slowly placed her fingers in his waiting palm. He immediately gripped her, tugging her behind him as shadows surrounded them like a dark screen, allowing them to see as they moved. Violet streaks of light flashed among them like lightning in a thunderstorm.

Light and dark.

And suddenly they were in the hall outside the arena, but there was just as much mayhem out here. People were running in various states of panic that only increased when Axel's darkness appeared. Screams echoed around her, and her magic seemed to *like* it.

It liked the idea of being feared.

She liked the idea of being feared.

"This way," Axel was saying, his wet shoes squeaking on the marble floor as they made their way down the passage.

"This is why I hate shoes," she said simply.

Axel glanced back at her. "What?"

She nodded at his soaked footwear. "Shoes are cumbersome. They interfere with escaping."

Understanding dawned, and he tugged on her hand, bringing her to his side rather than dragging her behind him. "Shoes slowed you down when you were sneaking in and out of undesirable situations at the estate."

"Shoes are an annoyance. And heels are impractical," she added as an afterthought.

If Axel found it strange they were having a seemingly normal conversation while navigating through the Pantheon, he didn't let it show.

"I can't say I have experience with wearing heels," he replied. "But they do make your ass look good, so I'm rather partial to them."

"You're not supposed to be looking at my ass," she replied. "I'm Theon's, remember?"

"Baby doll, with the dresses and pants you wear, I can't help but look at your ass."

"Theon picks out my clothes."

"He likes to show off his—"

"Things? He likes to show off his things?"

"No," Axel said quickly, shaking his head, but before he could say more, he was shoving her against the wall. "Don't move!"

Tessa watched with interest as shadows raced down the hall. Like a wave cresting, they crashed down on a group that had come rushing from the arena. These weren't just sentinels though, they were Fae guards from the various kingdoms. More and more people were pouring out of the arena, all of them with weapons with blades black as night. Weapons designed to kill Fae and Legacy alike. Power was flaring all around them, and it was only Axel standing between her and those who were hunting her.

He was backing towards her, his shadows continuing to take down Legacy and Fae. "Tessa!" he called out. "We need to keep moving!"

"But they will just follow us," she replied, panic bubbling up in her chest.

Her power flared, a cascade of pure light crashing into a group of Legacy and sending them crashing to the floor.

"You need to stay calm, Tessa."

"Sure, Axel. I'll do that," she retorted, peeling off the wall and pacing in a tight circle.

"Just keep moving, Tessa. Don't look back. Let me worry about those pursuing you."

"They keep coming," she argued. "You can't keep them all back. It's you against dozens."

"Then we best get to our destination," he said, another wave of darkness descending on five more. There were screams, and then there was nothing.

"What do you do to them?" she asked, his shadows slowly dissipating enough that she could see a male on the ground, his veins black.

"Not the time, Tessa," Axel growled, grabbing her wrist and once again dragging her along. "Do you not realize they will kill you if they catch you?"

"Will they?"

"That's a fair point, I guess," he replied, rounding a corner.

And then he wasn't gripping her wrist anymore. He was on the ground, his body jolting as a burst of light slammed into him.

"Axel!" Tessa screamed, her own magic scrambling, but it was as confused as she was. She spun back around to find herself face-to-face with Rordan Jove.

The Achaz Lord.

His shoulder-length golden hair was tied back, and he looked resplendent in a crisp suit of navy blue. His bright blue eyes were ringed with gold, a taste of his power. Light crackled at his fingertips, and it had Tessa looking down at her hands where violet and gold light was sparking at her own.

Slowly, she lifted her head, meeting the Achaz Lord's gaze.

"Tessa," Axel rasped, trying to push onto his hands and knees, but he collapsed when Rordan hit him again with more power.

She just stared at Rordan.

At the golden hair.

At the light he held in his palm.

At a descendant of Achaz, the god of light and beginnings.

"You've caused quite the stir, Tessalyn," Rordan said, a small knowing smile curling on his lips. "Not exactly the way I envisioned this meeting, but a little improvising was needed."

"I don't understand," she murmured.

"Not yet, but you will. Until then, I apologize."

Her head snapped up. "Apologize? For what?"

But a bolt of power slammed into her, and gods, it hurt. It was far stronger than Dagian's magic had been in her assessment vision, but it would be. Rordan could access his Source's power to make his own stronger.

Her magic howled inside her, thrashing against the power coiling around her so tightly she couldn't move. She was screaming, not because he was hurting her, but because she was trapped.

"Tessa," Axel rasped, and her eyes darted to him, finding him crawling toward her. There was blood dripping from his nose, and he was using his forearms to drag himself forward. "Fight, Tessa. He's coming for you."

She couldn't fight this.

He was the Achaz Lord. Stronger. More powerful.

And he seemed to know about her.

He knew the things Theon had kept from her.

That was her last thought before another burst of power hit her, and she slipped into the dark.

"You have repeatedly told me you had this under control. What part of tonight was under control?" Rordan Jove asked in a tight voice.

"We had everything planned. The priestess knew what to do. We didn't know the Keeper would appear to conduct her ritual," a male voice answered.

A male voice she knew.

Tessa tried to open her eyes, but her eyelids felt heavy, and her stomach was roiling. She couldn't decide if she was going to be sick or not.

"And what the fuck are we going to do now?" Rordan asked.

"I have this handled."

"Do you? Because when you came here twenty years ago and told me your plans, I was wary."

"I was sent here," the male snarled. "Are you questioning him?"

"No, but any time one is sent on a mission that promises a high reward, I grow wary. People are willing to sacrifice quite a bit when much is at stake," Rordan replied calmly. "Look at Valter and his ridiculous kingdom."

"Never compare me to a descendant of the death god," the male spat.

"And do not speak to me as though I am beneath you." Rordan's voice had gone low and deadly. "I know you stand to gain a seat in a world I do not care about, but you will not become a prince in that world by fucking me over."

"And I have not spent the last twenty years in this forgotten realm only to fail now. Failure is not an option."

Failure is not an option, Tessa.

Theon's voice rang in her head, pulling her closer to the surface. Again she tried to blink her eyes open, the room spinning around her. She was on a plush sofa, a pillow beneath her head.

"We have a common goal here," Rordan said now, sounding calmer and more casual. "Several common goals, in fact. We have agreed to help each other. I simply wish to confirm that is still the case, Dexter."

Dexter.

Dex was here. He would help her. He would fix this mess just like he always did.

Turning her head, her eyes started watering, two tears slipping free and dripping to her hairline. Her entire body ached, her muscles tense and sore. Her head throbbed, and sweat was damp on her neck and chest. And something was screaming inside her, trapped and dying.

Dex was standing there, and she blinked a few times because there was something curving around him. Soft. Feathery. An off-white color.

But that wasn't right. His hair was dark brown and shorter, not curving around him.

She squeezed her eyes shut, groaning softly as she tried to lift her hands.

"She wakes," Rordan said simply.

There was the sound of hurried footsteps, and then fingers were brushing hair back on her brow. "Tessie? Tessie, wake up."

She blinked again, Dex's dark eyes staring back at her. His hair was back to its normal color.

"Dex?" She tried to push up to a sitting position.

But his hands were at her shoulders, holding her down. "Stay still," he soothed. "Take it slow."

"I don't understand. What are you doing here?" she rasped.

Dex held up his arm, three symbols now marked on his inner wrist. One for the Celeste Estate, one to mark his newly revealed air element, and one to show he served the Achaz Kingdom.

"You were...chosen early?"

"Yes," he answered.

She brought her hands up again to rub at her face, but black glinted at her wrists. Two bands.

"To control your power," Dex explained when she continued to stare at them.

Right. Her uncontrollable power.

"That was quite the exciting Emerging Ceremony," he went on. "But you always seem to do that, don't you?"

"I'm sorry," she said with a wince, and she didn't know if she was reacting to the pain in her head or to his words.

"We'll figure it out, Tessie," he said. "We always do. I'll handle it."

He'll *handle* it.

I have this handled.

That's what he'd said.

This.

Her.

Her power stirred beneath her skin, roaring to be let out. It was so loud, she suddenly wanted to scream.

"Tessie?" Dex asked, cupping her cheek. "You're okay, Tessa."

"How am I okay when I am bound to an Arius Legacy yet I sit in the presence of the Achaz Lord?" It came out as a hiss, and Dex's eyes widened at her address.

"I believe I can shine some light on that matter," Rordan said, coming up behind Dex. He chuckled to himself as he lifted a palm, a ball of light floating above it. "No pun intended."

"I have that power," she rasped, her gaze fixed on the light he held in his hand.

"You do," he agreed.

"How?"

Rordan closed his fist, the light extinguishing. "It only stands to reason that you have some Achaz blood in your veins."

"But that's not possible."

"It certainly is possible."

"But I'm…" Her gaze darted to Dex, then back to Rordan. "I'm not Fae."

"You are not. Not even demi-Fae at that," Rordan agreed. "Would you like something to drink?"

"Would I like… What?" she asked in complete confusion.

"Water? Tea? I'd offer something stronger, but I'm afraid you may react poorly to such a thing given the power I had to use. Again, I apologize for that," he said, making his way across the room to a small beverage cart.

She shoved at Dex's hands before she pushed into a sitting position, taking in the space. This was a simple yet elegant lounge. It was a decent size, not overly large, and there were several windows with the curtains drawn. The walls were a soft white and so was the furniture. Everything was accented with gold and a light grey, giving the illusion of a soft glow when the light hit it just right.

"Where are we?" she asked, Dex having moved to sit beside her now that she was sitting up.

"My manor home in the Acropolis. If it were not well into the night, the view overlooking the Wynfell River would be stunning," Rordan answered, returning with a glass of water. "Is this all right?" he asked, extending the glass to her.

"Yes. Thank you," she said, taking the glass with a trembling hand. She took a sip before lowering it to her lap. "I'm sorry. Why am I here?"

The Achaz Lord took a seat on the sofa opposite her and Dex, crossing one leg over the other. He propped an elbow on the armrest, steepling a finger along his temple. "There are many ways to interpret that question, Tessalyn. You are in my home because I was forced to quell your magnificent power. It only seemed right that I look after you and make sure you recovered properly. But that is not the question I would like you to consider."

"It's not?"

He smiled, a gentle and patient thing. Not at all what she'd expected from the Lord that unofficially ruled Devram.

"No, child," he replied. "The question you should be asking is why are you in Devram at all?"

44
THEON

"What have you done?" his father snarled, darkness slamming into Theon and throwing him against the wall of their private viewing box. Theon slid to the floor, cursing under his breath at the unanticipated hit, sharp pain lancing up his side. "Do you have any idea what you have just compromised?"

Theon was climbing back to his feet as black flames sprang up around him, Luka grabbing his elbow and helping him up.

"Sorry," Luka said. "I was taking care of his plant bitch."

"So she's out of commission?" Theon asked, automatically tugging at his cuffs to straighten his sleeves.

"If she moves, she'll have fire up her twat."

"You are in a delightful mood today," Theon muttered, letting his shadows cover him for extra protection. It wouldn't stop his father's magic, but it would lessen the blows.

"Anytime I get to fuck with her, it puts me in a good mood," Luka replied.

Theon snickered. *A good mood.* But the mirth quickly fell as they prepared to face his father.

"Ready?" Luka asked.

He nodded, his body tensing as the black flames slowly receded.

"Still hiding behind fire instead of facing your problems," his father said, a sneer of disgust curling on his lips.

"My only problem at the moment is you standing in my way of retrieving my Source," Theon retorted.

"Your *Source*?" his father repeated. "She is not even Fae."

"She is still mine," Theon said, grateful to find Axel nowhere to be seen. He'd made it out to get to Tessa just like they'd planned.

"A Source must be Fae," his father spat.

"Says who?"

"It is how things are done."

"Maybe it's time for how things are done to change," Theon returned, repeating words his father would say when Theon was younger and would question his plans.

Until his father got tired of being questioned and found other ways to silence him.

His father's nostrils flared, shadows swirling in his hazel eyes. "You realize that any semblance of trust we have built with the other kingdoms is now gone. They were already upset about the fire Fae, and now they will accuse us of even more scandal. We should have killed the female when we had the chance."

"You will not lay a fucking finger on her," Theon growled.

His father scoffed, dragging a hand through his hair. It was a rare show of frustration from him, and the mannerism made Theon pause. He had expected his father to be angry. Furious. But this was...

This was trepidation.

This was dread.

"Cressida, leave," he suddenly spat, not bothering to look at his wife.

His mother did not question anything, sweeping from the room with her glass of wine in hand.

"Father," Theon started the moment the door shut behind her. "I fail to see how this is not a positive for us. Tessa is clearly a being of great power. I control her, therefore I control that power. This night has been lucrative for us."

"You think you can control *that*?" Valter murmured. "It is not some Fae elemental power. You cannot be this naïve. The godsdamn Keeper awakened her gifts. You know what that means."

He was pacing the length of the private box, continually dragging his hands through his hair. Theon glanced at Luka, completely at a loss. He felt like he was in a room with Tessa, unsure of how to handle the unpredictable male before him. His father was nothing but in control at all times, demanding the same perfection from everyone around him.

"Father, let me go get Tessa. We can go back to the townhouse or the country manor and figure out how to proceed from there."

"Yes," Valter muttered, suddenly stopping and straightening. He tugged on his shirt cuffs, straightening his sleeves. "That is a sound course of action. Luka, release Eviana."

The black flames keeping Eviana bound near the door went out, and she rushed to her Master's side. Theon was already striding for the door, but the moment he pulled it open, he stilled.

Standing on the other side were the Serafina and Celeste Ladies, along with their heirs.

"Did you honestly think we would let you get away with this?" demanded the Serafina Lady, shoving past Theon and entering the room. "Honestly, Valter, after all of our cooperation as of late, this is how you repay us?"

Cooperation? Theon didn't know what the Lady was talking about. And when the fuck had his father become on a first-name basis with the Serafina Kingdom?

The only thing that was becoming clear was that his father had way more secrets than Theon had realized.

"Maya, I have no idea what you are referring to," his father said.

"You have no idea?" the Serafina Lady scoffed. "Let's start with the *Source* your son randomly Selected. I'll leave the fire Fae to Kyra. She is livid."

"Kyra is always furious about something," his father muttered.

"True, but another kingdom claiming a fire Fae? She will be at your door next."

"Hopefully she will at least wait for a private meeting. This is too public, Maya. You know this."

The Serafina's silver stare shifted to Theon. "I suppose I should be speaking to your heir rather than you. It suddenly makes perfect sense why no one was able to gather her predicted element."

"My Source was predicted to emerge with air. You can view any of her assessment records," Theon said coldly.

"And yet she told *my* Source she was predicted to emerge with water and almost no power," Lealla piped in snidely.

Had she?

Theon had to work to keep the smirk from his lips at that. Instead, he shrugged, donning his mask of indifference. "Either way, clearly her assessments were inaccurate."

"How convenient," the Serafina Lady interjected.

"I don't know that I'd use the word convenient. She is rather wild at times," Theon said casually, scratching at his jaw. "But what's done is done, I suppose."

"That is your answer to this?" demanded the Celeste Lady. She swung around to face his father. "You know the division this will cause. Do you wish to go back to being the shunned kingdom you have been for centuries?"

Darkness appeared, pooling at his father's feet. "Do not threaten me, Luna," he said darkly, Eviana tensing beside him. The Ladies' Sources were stepping in front of their Mistresses, but before anyone could make another move, the door was being flung open.

Everyone spun to the sound, magic appearing at their fingertips and in the air, as Axel stumbled into the room. Blood was dripping from his nose and a gash along his temple, and Theon rushed forward to catch him before he collapsed to the floor.

"What happened? Where is Tessa?" Theon demanded in a low tone, trying to keep the others from hearing.

"Attacked," Axel managed to gasp out. "I got back as quickly as I could."

"You were attacked?" their father demanded. "By who?"

"Many. Legacy and Fae alike," Axel answered while Theon and Luka helped him to a chair. He lifted his head, meeting Theon's gaze. "But in the end, it wasn't them who took her."

"Who? Who has her?" Theon ground out, shadows filling his vision.

"Rordan. Rordan Jove attacked us both. The Achaz Lord has her."

And it killed him, absolutely destroyed him, but Theon turned to his father and said, "I need your help."

A Fae opened the door the moment his father knocked at the Jove country manor.

"My Lords," he said, bowing his head. "His grace is expecting you."

"I bet he is," Theon sneered, stepping into the foyer.

"Quiet, Theon," his father snapped, brushing past him and following the Fae who had started down a hallway to the left. Gone was the brief glimpse of uncertainty. The Arius Lord was back in control, shadows trailing each step.

Within a minute, they were being shown into a lounge. It was smaller and less grand than he'd expected. Nothing compared to the overcompensated displays his father insisted on.

He immediately found Tessa, who was seated on a sofa with a glass of water between her palms. She was paler than usual, but other than that, she did not appear to be hurt. Or if she was, her newly released power was already healing her.

His gaze dropped to her forearm where a new Mark stood out. It wasn't black like the Source Mark on the back of her hand, but it was a pale silver color. Identical to the Mark on his own forearm that he'd received at ten years to awaken his own gifts. A Witch had given him the Mark, his father having paid off one in the Underground so that word wouldn't get back to the other kingdoms which exact powers of Arius he had manifested, but the godsdamn *Keeper* had made an appearance for Tessa.

"Valter," Rordan greeted, not bothering to rise from his seat across from Tessa. "A pleasure to see you, as always."

It was only then that Theon realized who was sitting next to Tessa.

That Fae. The not-lover.

The one who told her she was constantly creating unnecessary chaos.

The same thing he had told her before shoving her into a small, windowless cellar.

"Rordan," his father said curtly. "I believe you have something that belongs to my kingdom."

Rordan smiled. "Would you like something to drink? Tessalyn has been sipping on water. We agreed that any alcohol may not do well with her body after I had to quell her impressive display of power."

"Is there a reason she is here rather than at the Pantheon?" Valter demanded.

"There is, in fact," Rordan replied. Then he turned to Dagian. Theon hadn't even realized the heir was in the room. "Do help Frederick with the drinks for our guests, Dagian."

Theon's jaw nearly dropped. His father would *never* ask another Legacy to wait on someone, let alone ask his son to do so. That was a Fae's job, far beneath a Legacy. Yet Dagian didn't question it, moving to the beverage cart where the Fae who had escorted them in was filling glasses. Two females, the Achaz Sources, were standing near an opposite wall, quiet and watchful.

"Please take a seat," Rordan said, gesturing to the surrounding vacant seating.

"This is not a social call," his father snapped. "We came to retrieve what is ours, and we will be on our way."

"Is she yours, though?" Rordan countered, his head tilting at the question.

"Of course she is," Theon interjected. "She bears my Mark. Tessa, come here."

Tessa was already tense, and now she stiffened at being addressed. But she had to obey him. It was in the oath to obey her Master above all others.

With a deep exhale, she slowly got to her feet, Dex standing to help her up and taking the water from her. She made her way to Theon, and the moment she was within arm's reach, he was pulling her into his side. She leaned against him, utterly exhausted.

"Are you all right?" Theon asked in a low voice, tilting her chin up to look at her.

She only nodded, her eyes darting to the side.

"We will be leaving now," his father said, turning on his heel.

But Rordan was pushing to his feet. "I am afraid we need to discuss these matters further."

Valter rounded on him. "What is there to discuss? She was Selected. It is done. Only death can undo it."

"Can a being who is not Fae truly be Selected as a Source?" Rordan mused, a hand slipping into his pocket while he brought his liquor glass to his lips.

"Evidently they can," Valter sneered.

"And yet she belongs here, with me."

"When, exactly, did you come to that conclusion?" Theon interjected.

"The moment she displayed the power of Achaz." Rordan's tone had gone low and dark, light flickering at the fingers gripping his glass. "Of course, not all of her gifts are like my own, and isn't that interesting?"

Theon tugged her closer, her breath hitching.

"What are you insinuating?" Valter asked, darkness drifting around him.

"I am proposing that she be housed at the Pantheon until it can be determined *what* exactly she is."

"No," Theon snarled. "She belongs with me."

Rordan smiled at him as though he were a child who couldn't comprehend what was being said. Then he returned his attention to Valter. "I am assuming you have already considered she may be the key to everything?"

"Of course I have," his father gritted out, and Theon didn't understand anything that was being referenced.

Rordan took another sip of his drink, seeming to savor the taste before he said, "Then you already know where she belongs."

"There is no proof," Valter argued.

"Not yet," Rordan agreed. "But when it surfaces, you understand what this will come to?"

"Do you?"

Rordan held out his glass, the Fae immediately appearing and taking the still half-full tumbler from him. "I look forward to further discussions on this matter."

Was he...dismissing them?

"This isn't over, Rordan," Valter seethed.

"No, it isn't," Rordan agreed. "But one does wonder: who will be left standing when Chaos comes to reign?"

He stood when Tessa emerged from the bathroom. Dressed in a pair of loose pants and a fitted tank top, she'd braided her wet hair over her shoulder. His father had strongly suggested they stay at the country manor tonight, so here they were. Theon would have much preferred to go back to the townhouse simply to be away from his father, but he'd already had to ask his father for help. Arguing against him tonight would not have been a wise idea.

This room was smaller than their room at the townhouse by at least half. Then again, their room at the townhouse was the entire third floor. He hated staying here though. It just felt like a smaller version of Arius House. Same dark decor. Same oppressive, stale air.

Axel and Luka were here as well, still seated on the sofa in the small sitting area. They each had rooms down the hall. Luka had gone with Axel to help him get cleaned up, and they'd only just settled down with drinks in hand. Axel looked like he'd seen better days and had admitted he had a pounding headache, which had made Theon wonder if Tessa was suffering from the same but wasn't admitting to it.

She paused mid-step when she saw them all, her arms wrapping around herself as she asked, "What?"

Theon closed the space between them, but faltered when he went to reach for her. He didn't know where they stood after everything.

"How are you feeling?"

"Tired," she answered, her eyes darting to the side. She unwound her arms, fiddling with the bands on her wrists. "These are uncomfortable."

When they'd arrived here, Theon had immediately replaced the ones Rordan had put on her with his own. Who knew what kind of enchantments were on the other ones. Luka had tried to incinerate them with dragon fire, but they'd withstood it. Another thing for Theon to research. For now, the bands were being stored in a pocket realm.

Luka was now drinking an extra ration of blood his father had suspiciously offered to all three of them. They'd had no choice but to take it, especially Axel with all the power he'd used protecting Tessa.

"I know they are uncomfortable, beautiful," Theon said, unable to stop himself from reaching out and playing with the end of her braid. "But you understand why you have to wear them for now, right? Your power is volatile until you learn to control it."

"And how will I learn to do that?"

"You will have lessons. It is part of the classes all Fae go through."

"Yes, but I am not Fae," she replied, an eerie ring to her voice that had been there after the cellar. It had disappeared, and Theon had been hoping it would stay that way, but apparently that wasn't the case.

He sighed heavily. "No, Tessa. You are not Fae."

"Do you think I am part Fae? Rordan does not believe so."

Rordan?

"What else does *Rordan* believe?" Theon asked, trying and failing to keep the bitterness from his voice.

"I have magic like his," she said. "Magic of Achaz."

"You do," Theon agreed.

"But also more."

"We do not know the extent of your power. It will take time to sort this all out."

"This?"

"You. Your power. How it will affect the Source bond."

"Right," she murmured, rocking on her toes as if she suddenly couldn't stay still.

"Are you hungry, Tessa?"

"Do you think I will need blood?"

"What?" Theon balked.

"Blood," she repeated. "Like you drink."

"No," Theon said immediately.

"It's a fair question," Luka said from the sofa. "If she's Legacy—"

"She's not Legacy," Theon interjected.

"Don't be stupid, Theon," Axel sighed. "She has Achaz power, which means she has *some* blood of Achaz. And based on the power displayed tonight? I'm going to go with a *lot*."

"Not to mention her Mark matches ours," Luka said, holding up his forearm to show the Mark identical to the one on Tessa's forearm.

Theon turned back to her. "Did the Keeper say anything to you?"

"Not really," she answered, rocking on her bare toes again. "Can we go outside?"

"It's the middle of the night."

"I like the dark. It makes the light shine brighter."

"Don't you think it would be better to rest? Or eat? Or..." he trailed off as she made her way to an armchair and plopped into it, apparently abandoning her efforts to go outside.

"You all have a lot of Marks. Why couldn't I see them earlier? You said they could be seen by those who have the blood of a god."

He had said that, and now that she mentioned it, she was right. She should have been able to see them all along. The only explanation he could come up with was that whoever had bound her power had somehow nullified all of her bloodline's magic. Bits and pieces of her power had broken through when her emotions had been in a heightened state, and to be honest, Theon was a little worried the same would happen even with the bands in place.

"Do they all mean something different?" she asked when Theon didn't answer.

"Yes."

"Will you tell me about them?"

His brow arched as he slid his hands into the pockets of his loose pants. "You want to learn about the Marks?"

"Yes, please."

The pleasantry made both his brows shoot up. "I can tell you about the Marks."

"And my lessons? When will those start?"

Theon glanced at Luka and Axel, who both just shrugged.

"The Fae begin lessons in three days. You will start them then as well."

"With you?"

"Some of them," he answered with a nod.

"And Mother Cordelia?"

"I think that is something we may need to reconsider, but not tonight."

"And training with my power?"

"Tessa," Theon sighed. "Can we discuss this tomorrow? After we've all had a chance to get some rest?"

"Of course," she murmured, her fingers repeatedly smoothing over the fabric of the armrest.

Silence fell, but it only took a few seconds for Axel to fill it.

"I'm going to bed," he said, getting unsteadily to his feet. "I swear I can still feel phantom shocks from that prick's power." He turned to Tessa. "You good, baby doll?"

She paused her finger movements, then held up her wrists. "I'd be better if you took these off."

He huffed a laugh. "Soon you won't need them," he replied, bending to press a kiss to her cheek. "Get some sleep."

"You too," she murmured, her hands falling back to her lap. When Luka stood, she looked up hopefully. "Do we train tomorrow?"

Luka studied her for a long moment, and Theon knew that look. He was trying to work something out. Finally he said, "Let's see how you feel in the morning, all right?"

They both knew she would not be training in the morning.

Tessa didn't answer, and when Luka and Axel left the room, the door closing softly behind them, Theon moved closer to her. He crouched down before the armchair, looking up into her violet-grey eyes. "Tell me the truth, Tessa. How are you feeling?"

Her head tilted to the side. "You told me to lie to you."

"But now I need the truth."

"Lie and truth. You can't have both. Just like you can't have light and dark, beginnings and endings."

Theon reached up, cupping her cheek. "Little storm, you're

exhausted. It is nearing dawn. Let's go to bed, and tomorrow we can discuss everything."

She hummed, beginning to run her fingers over the armrest again. He slowly lowered his hand from her cheek, folding it over her fingers. "Do you have a headache? Axel said he has a pounding headache. I can try to heal that for you."

"You cannot heal me, Theon."

"You are my Source. Of course I can."

Her lips tilted into a haunting smile. "You'd have to find all the pieces of my soul, and it's far too shattered to be put back together."

She wasn't making any sense, and she had to be overtired from the day.

He stood, taking her hand in his and tugging her to her feet before leading her to the bed. When he climbed in after her, he was momentarily shocked when she curled into him, resting her head on his chest. He quickly curled an arm around her though, breathing in the scent of her, relishing in the feel of her pressed against his bare torso.

With a finger, she began tracing along his Marks.

"I have this one now," she said, tracing the one on his arm that matched hers. Her breath danced along his suddenly overheated skin.

"You do," he agreed.

"And this one," she said, her finger moving over their Bargain Mark along his ribs.

"Yes," he said tightly at her touch.

One godsdamn finger and memories were flooding up of the nights she'd let him have pieces of her.

Her touch slid along his torso to the other side of his ribs. She traced the inverted triangle with three horizontal lines running through it that was opposite his Bargain Mark with her. "I don't have this one."

"You never will."

"What does it mean?"

He pressed a kiss to her brow, smoothing his hand along her hair. "Tomorrow, Tessa."

She didn't speak again, and he was grateful because he didn't know how to answer all of her sudden questions. He needed some time to sort this all out and research some theories. But even tomorrow he wouldn't tell her what that Mark was.

He wouldn't tell her about the Bargain he'd had to make with his father in exchange for his help.

45
TESSA

"Hold her in place," Theon said, spinning the black dagger in his hand.

"Theon, no! Please don't!" she sobbed.

"Shh, little one," Luka soothed. "It will all be over soon."

The dragon was near her head, pressing her shoulders to the ground. Axel was at her side, his shadows twining around her legs and keeping them still.

"We don't have a choice, beautiful," Theon said, still standing over her, his hair stirring in the breeze.

A light rain was falling, thunder rumbling in the distance.

"I still think there is another way to interpret this."

Tessa's head snapped to the side to find a tall male. He looked familiar somehow, but Tessa was sure she'd never met him. He had a sword strapped down his back, as did the female standing next to him. Her red-gold hair was braided over her shoulder, and flames flickered in her eyes.

"Life must give, and death must take," Theon said. "There is no other way to interpret that. Not if we wish to save our world."

For so long, Tessa had wished for death, and now, in this moment, she didn't want it. She'd finally found something to fight for, and she would be robbed of that too.

"Theon, don't!" she cried again. "It's more than a bond! I know that

Emerald eyes cut to her. "You're right, and now that I understand what that means, I'm the only one who can do this."

She was writhing on the ground, trying to free herself of Luka and Axel, but it was no use. They were too strong, and the ring on her finger was keeping her separated from her gifts.

"Theon, please!"

"This is wrong," the female with fire was saying to the other male. "This will alter everything."

"We cannot interfere," the male replied, reaching for her. "It will upset the—"

"Fuck the balance," the female seethed, shoving his hands away.

"Get on with it, Theon," Luka ordered, his pupils vertical and eyes glowing. Axel was refusing to look at either of them, but that was regret shining in his eyes when they connected with hers.

"I'm sorry, baby doll," he murmured before turning away from her.

"She can get here," the female was saying, panic in her voice. "She can stop this."

"Not even she will be fast enough," Theon answered.

He dropped to Tessa's side, smoothing hair off her brow. "You will forever be mine, Tessa. Whether in this life or in the After."

"Please don't send me to the dark alone," she whispered. She'd stopped fighting now, but her body was trembling.

The male and female were arguing, but Tessa couldn't hear them. Not as she got lost in dark emerald eyes and black hair. In a small dimple, and lips she'd kissed more times than she could count.

"I'm sorry I failed you, little storm," Theon said, sorrow flashing in his eyes.

"I'm sorry I loved you too late. But I'm yours. Every piece of me."

Theon didn't say another word.

Only lifted the dagger above her chest and sank it into her heart.

Tessa blinked her eyes open, the final vision of her last assessment still playing in her mind.

Those godsdamn priestesses.

Anything they could think of to try to force her gifts to manifest.

Trying to make her believe she could ever love the male wrapped around her.

Theon's breathing was deep, but his grip on her had not lessened. That was fine. The bond was comforting as it hummed away in her chest. She found it funny that she'd been fighting the thing for so gods-damn long when she could have been using it this entire time.

She shifted, needing to get up and move, but Theon murmured, "Where are you going?"

"To get a drink," she whispered, gently prying his arm from around her.

He huffed but didn't stir again, and she slipped from the bed, pulling on the thermal shirt he still left out for her. Making her way to the small sitting area, she was hoping to find a bottle of alcohol, but there was nothing and wasn't that disappointing.

Shrugging, she started across the room in the other direction towards a large window. She pulled the heavy curtain aside, and in the dim glow of dawn, she could just make out the darker lands of the Shade Plains starting to take over in the distance. She'd realized that each of the ruling families' country manors were actually in their own king-doms, just outside of the Acropolis boundaries.

Too restless to get back into bed, she dragged a chair out of the walk-in closet and took a seat near the window. She rested her chin in her hand, her elbow propped on the window ledge, wishing this room had a balcony. What kind of manor home didn't have rooms with balconies?

If she had to guess, the Achaz Lord's manor would have balconies for all the suites. They would overlook the Wynfell River, not barren shade lands.

Sighing, she finally let herself contemplate some of the things Rordan Jove had said to her.

Not Fae. Not even demi-Fae.

So what was she?

That's what she had asked the Lord. She clearly had Achaz gifts. She had assumed she was an Achaz Legacy, but Rordan hadn't seemed convinced. When she asked why, he'd said because the strength of her gifts not only suggested otherwise, but her gifts were not limited to Achaz.

Achaz couldn't call forth a storm indoors.

She'd asked more questions—some simple, some more complex—

and he'd answered every single one. Even the ones he couldn't fully answer, he'd told her his thoughts and why he had formed such theories.

No secrets.

Nothing withheld from her.

Honest and genuine answers.

Or so it had seemed.

Legacy were never honest and genuine. They always wanted something. Always looking at what she could give them.

She tugged the band from the end of her braid, unwinding the plait and letting the still damp hair fall over her shoulders. She didn't realize she'd started humming until she was folding her arms along the window ledge, resting her chin atop them. The lyrics of the song spun through her mind, matching the melody of her soft hum.

In all things, there must be balance. Beginnings and Endings. Light and Dark. Fire and Shadows. The sky, the sea, the realms.

Over and over she hummed the ballad as her thoughts shifted from one thing to the next. She didn't know who to trust anymore, so she would trust no one. Not until they'd proven themselves, given her a reason to believe there wasn't some ulterior motive behind every word and action.

But when the scales tip, and Chaos rains, who will fight? And who will fall?

Dex had been there, bound to Achaz Kingdom. His off-white hair curving up over his shoulders, soft and feathery. Wait, no. That hadn't been right. That part had been wrong, but he'd been there. That was still strange. Even if he'd been claimed early, what was he doing in the private manor of the Achaz Lord?

I have not spent the last twenty years in this forgotten realm only to fail now.

Forgotten.

The realm was forgotten.

She was forgotten.

For Dark must bow; And Light must rule. But Chaos does not choose. Control the uncontrollable; Or to fury they both lose.

The bond seemed to whimper inside her soul, seeking Theon's touch once more. This stupid, stupid bond. But they were more than that. That's what Theon kept saying. That's what she kept denying. More than Master and Source. What was it Luka had said? They were two forces that should repel each other. Instead, they were constantly drawn to each other. Opposites that only created chaos when they clashed.

Life must give, and Death must take. But Fate requires more.

More. Always wanting more. Never enough. Not for Mother Cordelia. Not for Dex. Not for Axel or Luka or Theon. Always pushing her, telling her to try harder, to give more and more and more. That if she could just control herself, not be so wild, everything in her life would be easier.

They were all liars.

Sitting up suddenly, she tugged at one of the bands on her wrists, slipping it over her hand. She left the other. She'd been relieved when Theon had removed the bands Rordan had put on her. Then she'd panicked when he'd produced a new set of bands. But these? These were not like Rordan's. The bands the Achaz Lord had bound her in had seemed to slowly bleed her magic from her. These... Well, these just seemed to trap her power inside her, and they seemed to think she could not remove them at will.

So she'd let them think that until she figured out why. She'd need them to keep her magic controlled until she learned how to do so herself, but she was used to figuring things out as she went.

Making up plans in the moment.

After all, she was an exceptional liar.

Destiny beckons, and sacrifice demands. Who will be left standing when Chaos comes to reign?

Over and over she hummed that ballad.

Over and over she contemplated all the secrets being withheld from her.

She'd find them. She'd figure out every last one. And not just about her. About Theon. Luka. Axel.

About the Achaz Lord and the Arius Lord.

About every kingdom.

About all of Devram.

She'd learn all their secrets and then decide what to do with them. Then she would decide if the things the Achaz Lord said were true.

That she'd been forgotten here for a purpose.

In all things, there must be balance. Beginnings and Endings. Light and Dark. Fire and Shadows. The sky, the sea, the realms.

She glanced over at Theon's sleeping form, a small smile curling on her lips.

He'd succeeded. He'd broken her, made her bleed. Shattered her soul so completely, there was no way to ever put it back together.

So she'd build herself a new one. One no one could touch, no one could break. One who did what needed to be done without remorse. Isn't that what he'd said to her?

She'd get back up.

She'd be the fucking storm.

Because the thing about light?

When strong enough, it could obliterate darkness.

THE WILD AND UNTAMED

The god strode quickly through the castle built along the cliffs in the forest. His long black hair was tied back at the nape of his neck, pine green eyes narrowed and focused on his destination. Twin swords were at his waist, a crown of gilded leaves and feathers on his brow.

His feet were silent as he ascended a set of stairs, a black eagle perched on his shoulder. He could see the thick trees beyond in each window he passed, could feel her flitting among her ashes and smoke. Nestled in the depths of this forest, they were protected. Hidden. This place was a secret as much as his existence had been for so long. A river wound through the forest, cutting through the castle. Waterfalls raining over various cliffs, animals roaming freely, birds calling among the trees. The entire place was enchanted, full of wild adventure. An oasis he had spent centuries cultivating and creating.

A place he had once thought he'd share with another.

He passed through a sitting room and flung open doors to a balcony, finding a female stretched out on a chaise. A black panther lifted its head at the sound of the doors, silver eyes honing in on him, tail switching back and forth. The female's silver hair flowed down around her shoulders, silver eyes that matched the feline's meeting his.

"I need to get someone into Devram," the male said.

The female blinked once. Twice. Then she slowly closed her book.

"We cannot go to Devram, Brother. No god can enter Devram," she said slowly, watching him carefully. "More than that, that realm does not know we even exist."

"I did not say *I* needed to go there," he retorted. "I said I need to get someone into Devram."

Her brows rose as she set her book aside. The crown atop her head was stars, shadows drifting around them as if they were in the night sky itself.

His sister.

The goddess of night and shadows, while he was the god of the wild and untamed.

The hidden children of Arius and Serafina.

"You intend to send another into Devram? What business could you possibly have there?" Saylah asked.

"No business that is yours."

"Then you will not have my aid."

"I am not asking, Saylah," he snarled.

"If you desire the aid of my children, Temural, you will tell me your business in Devram." He opened his mouth to argue, but she held up her hand, silencing him. "If you do not agree to such terms, consider your request denied."

Temural glared at his sister. "I need to send in Auryon."

The goddess slowly got to her feet. "You have only sent out a Huntress two other times."

"That you know of."

"Tell me your purpose."

"I need her to train someone."

"If Auryon is training someone, then you are training her to hunt for and to feed death," his sister countered.

"I am training her so she can protect herself and survive," Temural sneered.

"*Her?* A lover?"

"No," he bit out through gritted teeth. "You know there will never be another. Only Akira."

His sister nodded. "This is for her then?"

"Yes and no."

"I will need more than that, Temural. My children have already fought a war that was not theirs. If you want me to ask them to step into another, you will need to be more convincing."

"I am not asking them to fight in a war," he countered. "I just need a way into Devram."

"She will not do so without just cause, and I would not ask yet another thing of her without the same."

"Saylah," Temural sighed, the eagle on his shoulder rustling his feathers. He held his sister's gaze, but she would not back down from this. She would protect her children at all costs, placing them before even him. Placing them before oaths sworn to their parents.

But he would do the same for his child.

"This is for my daughter."

Saylah gasped. "A daughter?"

He nodded.

Saylah opened and closed her mouth several times before she finally sputtered, "What in the realms is she doing in Devram? We were not even in existence when Devram was created and left to its own prosperity or destruction."

"Akira sent her there."

"Why?" Saylah said in shock.

"A tale for another time, Saylah. She sent aid before her. Taika helped her. After I learned where she was, I sent more protection at a great cost, but it is proving not to be enough."

Realization flashed in his sister's eyes. "That is where Xan is. You sent your Guardian to Devram."

"I sent him there to take his son to my daughter, but I have not heard from him since he left here."

"Xan has another child?"

"Yes, and he was to be my daughter's Guardian, but I fear things have not gone according to my will. The realms are restless."

"I feel it too," Saylah murmured, toying with shadows at her fingertips.

There was a flurry of ashes, a female stepping from them. She wasn't wearing her usual leathers, but her vambraces still adorned her arms and her bow was still looped across her back. Midnight hair was braided over her shoulder, blending in with her black pants and tunic, her eyes swirling as she looked Saylah over with a hard stare.

Temural gestured at the Huntress. "Auryon has seen her. It is how I know she needs help."

"How?"

"With the aid of Serafina."

A hand flew to her chest. "You have brought our *mother* into this?"

"She helped me get Auryon into a dream plane. She was being attacked by an Achaz Legacy."

Saylah's lips thinned. She knew Achaz's vendetta to hunt down every descendant of Arius and Serafina. To see every bit of life that came from them extinguished from existence. She'd just finished a dangerous battle of her own and nearly lost everything.

"I need to get Auryon into Devram. Can you help me or not?" Temural finally said.

He didn't have time to waste on this. If Saylah wouldn't help, he'd find another way with the help of his Huntresses.

Saylah straightened, her palms running down the sides of her black gown. Shirina, the panther, leapt from the chaise, stretching and yawning wide. She went to Saylah's side, his sister winding her fingers through her silky fur.

"It is not my aid you need, Temural," she finally replied.

"Will she do it?"

"She will want to go there."

"She will barter with a god?" he scoffed.

A flicker of amusement entered Saylah's silver eyes. "She will not care in the slightest that you are a god because she is more than one. That aside, the choice is hers, but I doubt she will decline your request." She looked down at the panther, stroking the feline's fur once more. "A world walker will not be enough." Then she looked up, meeting Temural's gaze once more. "You need the High Queen of the World Walkers."

BONUS CHAPTER

Wondering what was going through Axel's mind when he claimed Katya at the Emerging Ceremony? Don't miss out on a special bonus chapter from Axel!

You can find it on my website at https://www.melissakroehrich.com under Book Extras.

A NOTE FROM MELISSA

I wrote the first half of this book in between *Lady of Shadows* and *Lady of Ashes*. Then it sat. For over a year, this series sat and brewed. The world grew. Theon and Tessa grew. We got to know each other a little more. The story changed some. Then changed again. And again. Until it became what it is now. To be honest, it was something that I never intended to release. It was a story written just for me, that I needed to get out.

Until it became something so much more.

If you've read the Darkness series, you know mental health is so important to me. My characters aren't perfect, and while they may be descended from magical beings, their reactions to trauma are so incredibly human. Everyone reacts to trauma differently. Grief and trauma, processing and healing is a journey unique to each and every one of us. These characters are no exception. So while I'm sure you are wondering how you can possibly forgive some actions or move on from particular motivations, as always, trust the process. I promise there are stars to fight for, even if they look very different from stars of the past.

We'll be back in Devram before you know it. Until then, remember salvation or destruction, the choice is yours. Just make sure you get back up.

XO- Melissa

ACKNOWLEDGMENTS

To those of you who found me with Darkness and have been anxiously awaiting this new series like feral little wraiths, thank you from the bottom of my soul. You make the writing process so fun, and you lift me up on the hard days when it feels like giving up would be easier. None of this is possible without you being willing to pick up a book and read the words that have made it to the page. It sounds so simple, but the ripple effect of you reading is one you can never truly understand. You help me provide for my family. You help me show my boys that their dreams are worth chasing. You remind me the stars are always worth fighting for, even when hope feels pointless. Thank you.

My Book Slut Besties… We did it. The start of another series. This one was…rough. My anxiety got the best of me more than once, and you repeatedly talked me off the ledge. Thank you for always being there. For putting up with my ADHD and for keeping me on track. Thank you for the laughs and letting me dump tasks on you. Thank you for being you.

To my beta readers and editing team: Megan Visger, Ashley Nolan, Rachel Betancourt, and Dana Schmit Curren, thank you for making this book better. I appreciate you beyond words. To Covers by Jules, I will forever be obsessed with your covers. To my audiobook narrators Laura Horowitz and Christian Leatherman, I adore you both and absolutely love how you bring characters to life.

To my ARC/Street Team, you guys are simply amazing. Thank you for cheering me on, for shouting from the rooftops, and for loving on these books so dang hard.

To my boys— Thank you for understanding when mom needs to write and edit. Thank you for your patience when I need to be in front of a computer screen extra hours. I hope you see that dreams take work, and that the payoff of hard work is worth every late night and tear shed.

To my husband— I'm yours. Every piece of me.

Made in the USA
Monee, IL
05 November 2023

45839087R00386